Caret

ADAM MARS-JONES

Caret

{ *novel* }

faber

First published in 2023
by Faber and Faber Limited
The Bindery, 51 Hatton Garden
London EC1N 8HN

Typeset by Ian Bahrami
Printed and bound in the UK by CPI Group (UK) Ltd, Croydon CRO 4YY

A CIP record for this book
is available from the British Library

ISBN 978-0-571-28006-3

MIX
Paper | Supporting
responsible forestry
FSC® C171272

Printed and bound in the UK on FSC® certified paper in line with our continuing
commitment to ethical business practices, sustainability and the environment.
For further information see faber.co.uk/environmental-policy

2 4 6 8 10 9 7 5 3 1

Dedicated with love to
K the keen-thinking

I was shocked by the confidence with which this unknown hand had inserted the missing letter — in a library book of all holy places! — with a caret. The act uneasily combined correction and desecration, disfigurement and repair. Was this a vandal or a proofreading vigilante riding the range of print in the name of maintaining order? It made a difference that the mark was in ink, and green ink at that. Indelibility bespeaks courage and commitment — it's not for nothing that Mephistopheles declines to give sellers of their souls the option of a pencil, however nicely they ask. 'Caret' means only 'it is missing' or 'there is a lack'. Its symbol resembles a lambda pointing the wrong way. It's a sturdy little jemmy, able to prise open a sentence for as long as it takes for missing elements to be restored to the body of the text.

Knife, fork and spoon, the basic equipment. 'Eating irons' as some people call them – as my dad called them. In terms of acquiring cutlery I didn't do badly out of my three undergraduate years, from 1970 to 1973, at Downing College, Cambridge. If that was the point of the exercise then I did better than most. I ended up with a useful haul. It wasn't that I was greedy, I don't think. I didn't want a six-piece place serving, let alone twelve-piece. I wasn't planning dinner parties or dainty lunches in punts. Everything was for my own personal use, to borrow the formula that defendants of the period fell back on when they were caught helping themselves from a smörgåsbord piled high with illegal drugs. In my case, though, it was true. I wanted a single knife, single fork, single spoon, nothing else. One of each item, but they had to be the right ones.

Everyone needs to eat. This informative sentence pushes together two separate propositions, according to what is meant by 'eat'. In one sense, 'to eat' means to take part in the economic structure of society and thereby to have food on your plate. More narrowly it addresses the next stage of the process, the conveying of food from plate to mouth. I won't pretend the first stage has always been smooth sailing, but the second one has never been anything but tricky.

Right knife, right fork, right spoon. These had to be tools I could use, and the requirements were strict. My left elbow had (and has) no movement, and the right elbow isn't exactly spry though there's a little play in it. My wrists don't rotate, so there aren't many utensils that can serve my turn in the first place. When I find them I don't let them go. I stay loyal, I hang on like grim death. It so happened that my ownership of these items was illegal, knife-fork-spoon, and I'd like to point out that I would have acquired them respectably if that had been an option. I don't break rules for the fun of it, or only when the assured dividend of fun is considerable. I'd rather be in the clear when I can manage it. It's just that sometimes honesty is a luxury beyond my means.

I

Peter Gladwell, the domestic bursar at Downing, in charge of the kitchens, was always complaining about how much money the college lost through pilferation of cutlery. Thousands of pounds were lost to the college over the years, and pilferation was something he was always preaching against. I never thought I'd be one of the bad boys, the light-fingered ones, but I have to put my hand up just a few token degrees of elevation and admit that I snaffled some myself. I scrumped a few plump apples from the laden branches of Downing's catering department, branches so weighed down with fruit as to be within my reach.

I wouldn't have had the dexterity or the cheek to take anything away with me from a communal meal in Hall, but towards the end of my time in A6 Kenny Court it must have been obvious that I was at a low ebb. A meal tray would sometimes be sent over for my benefit, a spontaneous kindness but also an invitation to wrongdoing. Sometimes filching went on and the tray made its way back to the college kitchens a cutlery item short. On the occasion of the first crime I stage-managed a tableau of innocence, in case a steward returned to ask what had happened to the College fork which had been entrusted to me, by dropping it onto the floor. No one came to ask, and I wasn't required to go through an I-must-have-dropped-it routine, inherently hollow since though I'm always dropping things (the notion of dropping should be expanded to mean any loss of mastery over an object's whereabouts) it's rare that I don't notice. After that I realised that the reason Peter Gladwell laid so much emphasis on the seriousness of pilfering was that everyone but him thought of it as trivial.

At the time, stealing from shops was routinely referred to as 'liberating' things, a usage that must have started as irony but soon lost any sort of edge. I certainly wouldn't say that I had liberated my Downing knife-fork-spoon set, when they had liberated me, or at least liberated my mealtimes for an indefinite period.

It's true that if you bend backwards the spoon part of a standard spoon (the language insists on this redundancy) it can be made much more serviceable, but it isn't something I can accomplish without help. You'd be surprised how reluctant restaurant staff are to modify the cutlery for the benefit of their diners. So much for the customer always being right!

The Downing cutlery wasn't exactly luxurious though it was smart enough, the design vaguely Scandinavian-modern in a way that has come to seem sixties-retro in its own right. The style is neither here nor there, it's just that nothing else feels right in my hands. I take those eating irons with me wherever I go. I never use anything else. I eat left-handed, reversing the implements to cut food up if that's required, slicing with the left by pushing with the shoulder. It's the only way cutting of any sort will get done, though of course not all food needs to be cut up. Vegetarianism offers an unfair advantage in that respect, with food more likely to be bite-sized already. Then the fork in the right hand makes the deliveries.

It has sometimes happened on æroplanes that the stewardess has brought me 'proper cutlery' from First Class, a lovely piece of good manners though not actually a functional improvement on my own tools. A starched napkin sometimes comes along for the ride, and this does serve a purpose, lending the Vegetarian Option a little reflected glamour.

The Downing knife has its point of balance just where it should be, halfway along its length, not thrown out of equipoise by a weighty handle. The tines of the Downing-issue fork have quite a pronounced curve – I think that's part of the secret. I hold a fork in my right hand, since my right shoulder has the more movement of the two, though I still can't manage to reach my mouth with the fork horizontal. The technique I've learned involves accelerating on the upstroke to keep the food in place. It's like dive-bombing, only in the opposite direction, bombing upward. It works with most foods. The Downing cutlery is lightweight, which is certainly an advantage. It's easy to manœuvre. Crucially it's not too long. Since my forearms are short, a long fork requires a more finicky angling effort towards the mouth, and that's just the sort of movement my arms don't run to.

The Downing spoon isn't quite so uniquely designed to suit me – most dessert spoons can be modified appropriately, if someone is good enough to increase the kink at the neck so as to improve the angle of incidence of the bowl. But it makes sense to have the full set, the integral place setting. Each item bore the engraved letters D C C – for Downing College Cambridge – at the larcenous moment, though the incriminating markings wore off after only a few years.

If knives and forks and spoons can't be too long or they stop being suitable (being Johnable, as I call it) then teaspoons are impossibly short. To suit my needs a teaspoon would have to be so long-handled that it would no longer fit the technical description of a teaspoon. In fact it would be a sundæ spoon, and that's what I had brought with me from home when I arrived at Downing and used ever after. Again, it suits me perfectly, and perhaps my hand has conformed to its handle over the years as much as the other way around. There's always a molecular exchange between tool and user, and it goes on in its marginal fashion even when the tool-user is as calcified and recalcitrant as I am.

I know the use of the ligature 'æ' in sundæ spoon is somewhere on the continuum between optional, wayward and plain wrong, but my feeling is that so much typographical variety is being lost from year to year that it becomes an act of solidarity with the alphabet in its fullest form to keep ligatures and diacriticals alive. In some languages 'æ' has the status of a separate letter – why should we let the Faroese get all the credit for alphabetical hospitality? Let's open the doors of orthography a crack, so that 'æ' and 'œ' can softly slip in.

It looks so unassuming as an object, the sundæ spoon, that people think of it as interchangeable, a standard item. They hold it up and examine the trade name stamped on the stem – EYE WITNESS. Then it's Oh I'm sure I've heard of that make. I'll pick you up some spares, they say, shall I? Next time I'm in John Lewis (or Selfridges as the case may be). How many would you like? I'll get you a handful. My pleasure. They never mention it again, not because they've forgotten, I don't think, but because they've underestimated the task and feel embarrassed now that their breezy confidence has been shown up. They come back empty-handed, not having noticed the subtle cant to the bowl. A sundæ spoon with a six-inch stem, in stainless steel. It doesn't sound like the Holy Grail, exactly, does it? Though it would be just the job if you happened to have the Holy Grail tucked away in a kitchen cupboard and wanted to serve a Knickerbocker Glory from it. Is it irreplaceable, my sundæ spoon? Let's hope I never need to find out. It's getting worn thin at a couple of edges. Lovingly eroded away, licked by the years and the abrasion of my tongue.

At least the sundæ spoon isn't stolen goods, unlike the rest of my eating implements. Perhaps my loyalty to these dishonestly acquired utensils softens the original crime, and at least when people ask what I got from my fancy education I know what to say. Downing knife, Downing fork and spoon. In that limited sense Cambridge equipped me for life.

Cambridge also provided intellectual cutlery, of the sort you are actively encouraged to take away with you – that being the main idea behind those years of study. Furnish your mind with tools: confidently impaling fork, butterknife that lays on the charm, fish slice adept at lifting the flesh of an argument away from its bones. I suppose I use them too.

The most primitive education would have given me adequate tools for a future of sitting around, sometimes in a wheelchair and sometimes not, supported by a half-resentful State. I was likely to be at least half-resentful myself unless I was able to meditate my way to serenity on a daily basis, to throw myself off the cliff of ego and plunge into the waters of not-I. Unfortunately my basic spiritual technique had broken down and my mantra had failed me. For three years I had been unable to meditate, when a five-week visit to India somehow drained the battery it was meant to recharge. My guru Ramana Maharshi often used mechanical analogies in discussing spiritual states. He wouldn't have minded me saying that a devotee without a mantra is like a refrigerator with a broken thermostat. I had no confidence that my inner life was under warranty. Cool detachment from problems, uncompromised awareness of their illusory status, all this was a long shot in my present state.

I still get begging communications from Downing, appealing to my generosity to endow this and that. I'm not tempted to reach for my cheque book. If I'm not in the bottom percentile in terms of income of any Downing product then I'd like to know what has become of my academic generation. Something has gone badly wrong! Then again perhaps I should take a broader view, change my will and set up a small fund, a Cromer Trust. Its aims would be highly specific: to provide appropriately modified cutlery for disabled students, not as loan items but as gifts outright. Why should they be beholden? Let them exercise proprietary rights in perpetuity. The design would be based on the Downing set in my possession, but the engraving on the handles (even on the sundæ spoons) would be C D rather than D C. Not Downing College but Cromer Donation. It's an appealing idea, but I'll only take the necessary steps if the guilt of my early-seventies thieving becomes too much for me. For the time being it's no great weight.

I don't mean to suggest that our domestic bursar had no other subject of conversation, but I do remember Peter Gladwell playing another variation on the theme of cutlery one evening in Hall, addressing a little group of us who had perhaps shown polite interest. I doubt if it was more than that. 'Believe it or not, gentlemen . . .' he said – and 'gentlemen' always seemed to have a satirical tinge, as a recognition of mutations in the student species, in the years after the riot at the Garden House Hotel – 'a college in the Other Place spent a fortune on knives and forks – the domestic bursar there must have let the architect walk all over him. Academics don't live in the real world, that's what domestic bursars are for.' We pretended not to know what was meant by 'the Other Place'.

Sledges pulled by scandalised huskies

According to the traditional Cambridge understanding of the universe Oxford was a blank space on the map. There was nothing there. It was the non-existent county town of Blankshire, itself scratched out on any map available locally, on the shelves of Heffers, Bowes & Bowes and even W. H. Smith. University study is meant to expand the mind's horizons, but there are always areas of darkness opened up at the same time. Oxford? The place simply didn't exist. When indirect reference was made to the university it was as a byword for folly of some sort. I'm sure that an equivalent distortion applied in the other direction, with dons at Oxford murmuring 'Cambridge?' over their madeira. 'Where might that be? Doesn't ring a bell. In Massachusetts perhaps?' The two rich little cities had something about them of mortified identical twins trying to forget their mother had once dressed them alike. They were obsessed with denying a resemblance that would never entirely go away.

'This architect, Danish chap,' Peter Gladwell told us, 'made all the decisions about fixtures and fittings. All of them special. So every time a light bulb blows, they have to send off to Denmark for replacements.' There was definitely some exaggeration going on here. Bespoke items or not, they could be kept in a cupboard until they were needed. He made it sound as if they had to be specially delivered (to St Catherine's was it? I think St Cat's) from the far North, on sledges perhaps. Sledges pulled by scandalised huskies, howling at the moon in protest against the folly of architects.

'That's enough madness to be getting on with, or so you might think, gentlemen. But when it came to designing the fittings for High Table the architect surpassed himself. It was the cutlery of bedlam. The knives and forks were one thing, but the soup spoons . . . they weren't even symmetrical! The bowl was over to one side.'

At this point I entered the conversation, or rather I politely registered my exclusion from it. 'I say, Peter, would you mind taking a seat somewhere I can see you? Otherwise I'll just be lobbing words in the general direction of your voice.' I've put in years of that sort of lobbing in my time, dropping words into the post with no real idea of whether or not they will be delivered. I was taking only a slight risk by using his first name – this was cheeky but acceptable. The real risk lay in my claiming the right to take part in the steering of the conversation, not just following and laughing at the appropriate places. Assertive behaviour even of this mild kind always makes things awkward and the gambit has been known to misfire. In general I'm supposed to fit in with the standard ways of doing things, and I do my best, but when I can't and I point this out people can get huffy. It's normal for me to be at a disadvantage, apparently, doesn't call for comment. And of course if you make too much of a fuss about being included actual conversation, real live human interchange, dies the death anyway.

In the land of asymmetrical spoons

Everybody budged up and fair play, Peter sat down opposite me without showing any irritation at being ambushed, though I imagine he felt some regret at having opened his mouth on a subject that turned out to interest me. Specialised cutlery isn't a topic that usually sets conversation on fire. 'Let me see if I've got this straight,' I asked, 'this architect designed soup spoons that went round a corner. So that the bowl, I think you called it, faced the eater?'

'It's more that the spoons bulged on one side, John. They ended up looking like musical notes, crotchets or whatnot.'

'How very sensible. Did he do the same thing with the forks?'

'No, he left the forks alone, more or less. Though they were a bit narrow and odd-looking.'

'Then, with respect, you're wrong to say he was mad – he didn't go far enough. A fork that went round corners would make all the difference to me. What was it Blake said? If the foolish designer would persist in his folly, he would . . . design a better folly.' Repartee is always a hit-and-miss affair, even in the dining halls of second-tier colleges in world-famous universities. You just hope people remember the bullseyes and forget the clangers. 'Something along those lines.'

'But you can't expect everything to revolve around you, John!'

'And I don't. Not even my place setting. I'm glad to know someone somewhere has given it some thought, that's all. Oxford's better than nowhere at all, I suppose. Or don't you agree?'

'There was one snag with the chap's spoons, though. You'll never guess—'

'I suppose left-handers couldn't use them. If they tried to bring them to their mouths, soup just splashed onto the tablecloth, is that it?' Classic Cromer own goal – I just couldn't resist the opportunity to score points. I couldn't seem to stop myself from trundling on, guessing away when I'd been told I would never guess, meaning that I shouldn't try. I trundle on, life likewise trundles on. We trundle as one. In the land of asymmetrical spoons, the ambidextrous man is king – at least I stopped myself from saying that.

'I'm warning you, John, my wife is the only person who's allowed to spoil my stories. And even so . . . that's just on her birthday.' All perfectly jovial, but I could see he wasn't pleased, first held hostage at an undergraduate table and then pre-empted anecdotally. He wasn't an academic but had picked up some of the mannerisms of high table, the rankling politeness. Prickliness is highly infectious in academic circles – it should be considered for listing as a notifiable disease.

'Yes, you're right, of course. Left-handers needed special spoons. More pointless expense.'

'Well, Peter, it would certainly be cheaper to weed out left-handers at the interview stage, eliminate them from the shortlist, or else provide a compulsory salad starter for the southpaws.'

I had taxed him too far. 'No doubt. And now, gentlemen, I must leave you. I have a college to run.' He levered himself away from my line of sight, striking suavely off towards the real world, natural habitat of domestic bursars, and away from my dim little aquarium of drifting weed, where I lurked inside a plastic castle and waggled my fins uncertainly in the half-light.

'Blimey, John, what was that about? I thought you liked Gladwell!' And all I could say was 'So did I.' The general verdict was that I'd excelled myself. 'Trust you to take that line, John! That's you all over!' As if it was my ambition to intersect so very rarely with other people's ways of thinking. I was always being told I was a fully paid-up member of the awkward squad, which was conceivably a compliment. I tried to turn it into a joke anyway by saying, 'Not so. They waived the entrance fee.' Such a shame that meetings are held on the top floor of a building without lifts, but that's in the constitution so there's nothing we can do about it.

What was it about, that little cutlery skirmish in Hall? It was a fair question. I had struggled for three years as an undergraduate, determined to make the best of what was offered to me, as I assumed, in good faith. I was accepted as a student before the Chronically Sick and Disabled Persons Act became law in 1970, so that Downing was under no legal obligation to take me. Legislation takes a long time to percolate by capillary action through the social fabric, and I certainly wasn't expecting a red-carpet welcome. I don't have much use for carpets at the best of times, and a red one wouldn't have done much to disguise the unwelcoming approach to the room allotted me. My particular needs were only approximately met by A6 Kenny Court, access to which was blocked by two steps – not a full flight, but more than enough to make entering and leaving the premises difficult. Never mind! I would manage. I managed. And at least I had the privilege of not being shunted around like my contemporaries but staying there for three full years.

My trust in Downing even survived the discovery that Dad had been billed for the ceiling support system which allowed me to take a bath. Eventually charitable funding was found for this expense, in a way that offended me almost more than the original injustice. Why should a charity (one set up to help servicemen in need, and I suppose Dad was in need of help after being dunned) have to stump up for expenses that my college had knowingly incurred by taking me on? I was fully visible during the interview, and my difficulties must have leapt to the eyes. Being accepted to the university wouldn't be enough in itself to reverse my medical history, and the equipment wasn't for my exclusive use anyway. Any able-bodied student could treat himself to a joyride in that bathroom. It wasn't as if I would be taking the rail away with me when I left, though I can't deny I was tempted to contrive some subtle sabotage. A small explosive charge, detonated by remote control, at a time of my choosing in consultation with the I Ching.

Ripe for the snaffling

It was more that I had seen the indifference, or the hostility, of the institution as essentially faceless, and now I could put a face on it. I had chatted perfectly amicably with Peter Gladwell, without quite putting two and two together and understanding that if I was being denied certain basic rights then he was the one who determined that it should be so. The administrative decision that allowed me to stay in A6 Kenny for all three of my undergraduate years also allowed for some forward planning, and at the end of the third year there was still no sign of a ramp on those steps, front or back. Presumably such modification was deemed a pointless expense. It followed that I myself was a pointless expense. My well-being didn't warrant an entry on a balance sheet. It's true that a ramp wouldn't have enabled me to manage on my own in my non-electric wheelchair, but it would have made it very much easier for my fellow students to lend a hand, and that would have been worth something, if only to me.

In the tussle over the rail over the bath the college's representative had been the Dean, and it was only now, very late in my life as an undergraduate, that I realised he wasn't the real adversary. It was

Peter Gladwell who had spoken against my comfort, and though it would be exaggerating things to say I had seen him as a friend, there seemed to be an element of betrayal in his cordiality just the same. Domestic bursars lived in the real world, apparently – as if I didn't, when I inhabited the consequences of their decisions.

At this point the whole debate concerning the nature of reality needs to be put to one side, philosophically and spiritually riveting but not useful just now. I particularly resented the fact that the course of my life was being dictated by my physical needs, when my whole practice was to deny the designation of 'mind' and 'body' as separate and opposed. Binary oppositions are essentially fictions. It can never be that simple. Binary stars pool their light and even binary code is a subtly shifting form of expression, its noughts just longing to merge into oneness while the ones are constantly tempted to be noughty. Take it from me, it's exhausting to maintain a non-dualist worldview while you're forcing yourself, in the full knowledge that you're part of everything that imagines it excludes you, to argue for your rights as an individual and a special case.

The conversation about Danish cutlery revealed an unwelcome truth, though no one else seemed to notice it. A shocking revelation, even: over the course of my undergraduate career I'd learned to say things for effect. Reconfiguring the design of Downing forks, or spoons for that matter, would be no improvement from my point of view – in fact they suited me just fine as they were, making them in due course ripe for the snaffling. I was just showing off in conversation, building castles in the air out of bricks without straw.

Of course this character trait was part of what the University had been established to instil, and many of my contemporaries would find themselves well served by it in their working lives – it might even see them smoothly through to retirement. Those, though, were not the circles in which I would be moving. If a certain amount of posing had always been part of my character then it had become more pronounced, an aspect of the survival technique of any undergraduate. I exempt the sciences from these strictures. It was only in the humanities that learning to love the sound of your own voice was an unacknowledged part of the curriculum, printed in invisible ink on every prospectus.

Even so, it was true that I found something perversely admirable in the architect's elaborate and expensive way of solving a problem he had himself created. For the benefit of High Table at Crazy College there must be left-handed soup spoons commissioned to cater to the needs of the oppressed minority, a minority that had never previously been disadvantaged during the soup course. There's something so very Mayan about that procedure, and by 'Mayan' I intend no reference to an extinct South American civilisation but to Maya, the Hindu word for the domain of illusion, also known as the 'real' world, past or present (and consequently including Mayans, Aztecs, Inca and Norte Chico along with everyone else). I couldn't leave it at that, though. I had to take a line and make a case, exaggerating and distorting mild opinions and fatally drawn towards absurdity. If the wise man would persist in his wisdom he will become foolish, as Blake didn't say but Hinduism slyly suggests.

My tendency to preen and pontificate did nothing to set me apart from my fellows, it was absolutely part of the air we all breathed, but my future was going to be different from my contemporaries'. To be brutal – I was going to be living in a backwater on state benefits, while they would go on to greater things, to the Civil Service, to industry, to advertising, to Unilever. Empty poses would do them no harm, empty poses might even become their stock in trade, but my condition was different. The corridors of power were not wheelchair accessible any more than my old college room had been. I couldn't expect much more from the cluttered passageways of self-sufficiency.

The flavour of a gypsy encampment

If as a rule I don't join groups, it's partly that I'm not asked very often. Sometimes I join a group because I have no choice, can't help it, kicking and screaming making no odds. That's what happened in the summer of 1973, when I became a graduate from an ancient university. In a fairground arcade game I loved as a boy, coins are mechanically nudged ever so slowly to a mirrored edge, until it seems from second to second that they must tip over, and still they don't, however much you urge them to the drop. It felt rather different when I was one of the coins concerned, particularly as I personally don't do well with changes of level. I balanced on my polished ledge as long as I could, but eventually there was no flooring left underneath me and I must fall.

Between my college room in Kenny Court and the flat in Mayflower House that I had been assigned by Cambridge Council there was nothing, three days and nights of unbroken nothing to be got through. The college could no longer house me, and the flat reluctantly made available to me by Social Services wasn't yet ready. The only possible bridge across the yawning gulf of disaccommodation was my faithful red Mini, registration number OHM 962F. Though this car had made my education possible in its later, independent stages, it wasn't in itself very accommodating. It did a poor impersonation of a bedroom.

On the morning after Downing College had washed its institutional hands of me, sending me out into the wider world, I woke up early in the Mini, sore, shivering, tired, hungry, homeless, and as I discovered after a racking series of sneezes, afflicted with a summer cold. Perfectly cheerful, though, within the limits set. In the night Maya had sent out little disembodied whines, to dramatise for my benefit the futility of feeling sorry for yourself.

The night had been uneventful, since discomfort and desperation, hanging on for dear life, aren't actually events. There were two little incidents, or a single incident that happened twice. I was woken during my first sleep by a knock on the car window. I squirmed round to see who it was, and laboriously wound down the glass to make possible a conversation I couldn't really avoid. It was a man wearing a hat, taking his dog for a walk, and wanting to know if I was all right. While the master looked down at me with an expression of slightly brusque concern the dog, a chocolate Labrador, looked up with the most sympathetic gaze I had been treated to for some time.

It can't have been more than an hour afterwards that dog and owner paid me another call. Another tap on my window. The dog's tenderness was unchanged, and the man wanted to know if I was *really* all right, though his benevolent aura was very threadbare by now, and his underlying question showed through the charade of neighbourliness: why are you still here? What exactly are you up to?

I understood that my status was becoming precarious. If I didn't make some sort of appeal for help fairly soon I would become actively unwelcome in that neighbourhood. Unless I fitted a recognised category of innocent distress before too long, the Mini would take on some of the flavour of a gypsy encampment. I felt sure that the chocolate Lab would have shared his last bone with me, but unfortunately a dog lead is not an osmotic medium allowing for the interchange of emotions across a karmic membrane. Putting it more simply, the owner didn't have a clue. He had a lot to learn from the being he led around.

I broke the surface of consciousness before it was light, and dozed between cramps, twinges and episodes of sneezing. I expelled air from my lungs through nose and mouth in a semi-autonomous, convulsive explosion that did nothing to relieve the irritation of my nasal mucosa. With a wriggle I could find a position in which one nostril cleared itself, with another I could persuade the second one to follow suit, but the first one promptly closed up. I stayed poised for a time (while time reconstituted itself) on the frontier of awareness, not having much of an incentive to present my papers. The day was inherently unpromising, and my cold was one more obstacle added to it. If you are a person so constructed that he can't reach his nose without an instrument, a cold is a humiliating thing, or to put it another way, highly beneficial to the ego-diminishment project. If need be I can construct a little flower of tissue paper, lodge it in a cleft stick, and use it as a sort of remote-control handkerchief, the way window cleaners tackle panes on the upper floors with a series of connecting rods. But if I'm going to all that trouble then I'd rather wipe my bum than my nose.

Micturition syncope is real

Eventually the wisps of sleep became too scanty to be meaningfully gathered round me, and I shrugged them away, accepting that I had been dealt a new day and must play my hand accordingly. Thursday. And on Saturday I would enter into a home of my own.

I suspected the delay was artificial. Rents traditionally run from Saturday to Saturday, and it seemed highly likely that a flat that was fully prepared, gleaming with welcome, was being held back for reasons of administrative tidiness. And as a consequence I, who experience

14

even smooth conditions as bumpy, was expected to rough it. Though in *Roughing It* – the book – I don't remember Mark Twain having to sleep on any bed more uncomfortable than a pile of mailbags.

It's not easy to assess that night's sleep, non-sleep and semi-sleep. Was it really such an ordeal? Objectivity requires measurements, so let's imagine a hundred recent graduates spending the night in Minis . . . but no, the mental experiment, the scenario as people were beginning to say, breaks down immediately. It's not just that the others would have an easier time of it, with the benefit of being fully articulated rather than merely articulate, but that they would have alternatives available in the first place. Why would anyone heading to an interview or a job on the *Telegraph* or with Unilever, wearing a tie that his mother picked out for him, sleep in a Mini except as part of some perversely delayed Rag Week exploit? So a perverse logic was in force, according to which I was faced with this episode not despite my particular difficulties but because of them.

Don't get me wrong – some of those hundred graduates would have a perfectly horrible summer. One of them might, for instance, pitch forward while taking a leak out of a full-length window in the course of a drunken party, suffering the combined consequences of bad manners and the sudden drop in blood pressure known as micturition syncope. It's a real thing – look it up. And don't risk it again.

My joints loosen up to an extent with activity and warmth, as everyone's do, even if the process is much less pronounced in my case. My neck is more or less exempt. It's not that I get a crick in my neck. My neck is a crick, the crick is my neck.

It was marginally more practical to drive somewhere while my body warmed up than to venture out of the car just yet. I had filled my pee bottle during the night, but with any luck I wouldn't be driving fast enough, or turning corners wildly enough, to upset it. In general I had planned poorly for my Mini residence, not really being willing to contemplate it in advance. I had no supplies of water, and though I can swallow pills dry if I really must, I'd rather not, and first thing in the morning isn't the best time to explore that particular talent.

I hardly knew what I was looking for, unless it was a café that opened early, one that was neither empty nor full to overflowing. At the corner of Regent Street and Lensfield Road there seemed to be such a place. Modest prices were written directly on its windows in large red and green letters, which meant that I could strike a mental bargain between thrift and appetite before I even went in. I had £1.54 in liquid currency, and I was anxious not to splash it about. I could do the sums in the safety of the Mini, and then undertake the project of entering the premises in a state of approximate arithmetical calm.

A woman was putting a display board out on the street, to alert passers-by to the immediate possibility of tea, coffee and sandwiches, just as I opened the Mini's door. So much for the option of somehow emptying the pee bottle discreetly in the gutter. Discretion is a tall order in my case, since it normally calls for speed and inconspicuous-ness, two things that go against the grain. Taking my own sweet time is my normal pattern, and I've got used to being taken notice of several times during even the simplest procedures.

The woman from the café went back in to fetch a broom and started sweeping the pavement. This seemed a slightly old-fashioned activity, a *Coronation Street* move, and it seemed more likely that she wanted an excuse to keep monitoring my progress. She had wildly frizzy hair, the sort that you imagine needs a lot of attention to keep it unruly, and was wearing platform-soled shoes, which I wouldn't have thought ideal wear for waitressing work. She shielded her eyes with her hand as if the sun was in her eyes, or as if I was a distant and mysterious object, a boat far out to sea flying unfamiliar colours. In fact we were well within hailing distance, even if she seemed startled when I sang out 'Good morning!' True, it wasn't one of my more con-vincing performances. Dryness of throat, blockage of nasal passages, these things between them robbed the greeting of its intended suav-ity. I would have needed hours of honey-gargling to smooth over the cracks in my vocal cords.

She said 'Good morning' back, and I tried again with 'Are you open for business?' Nothing could be more obvious than that they were, but I've found it's no bad thing to keep small talk undemand-ing while people weigh up what subtle threat it is, exactly, that I represent.

'We're serving breakfast.'

I beamed at her. 'I'd like some.' Still keeping scrupulously to the reading-primer level. If the experiment was any sort of success I could introduce complex sentences later on, fancier grammatical ventures suited to more advanced projects than getting myself fed.

'I'll set up a table for you.' She turned to go indoors, stumbling on the step in the process. Perhaps her platform soles were newly bought, and she hadn't adjusted to the added height when changing levels. I wondered if she would still be wearing them by lunchtime, or if she had been sensible enough to bring an emergency pair of pumps in her bag.

The rigours of perching

I think there must be a particularly intense flash of mortification that people feel when they make a mess of simple locomotion in my presence, and I was glad I couldn't see her face.

How much does it take to prepare a table for my needs? My constitution may be eccentric but my demands are drearily orthodox. It would be more useful for me to have help, confronted with a step that was clearly treacherous even for the able-bodied. Waitresses are often psychic (it's a useful skill when you want to avoid someone's eyes) so I wasn't particularly surprised when this one returned to help, after all.

I kept up a reassuring stream of comments during the manœuvre. I know people are particularly vulnerable at this juncture, when they've nerved themselves to be helpful however inadequate they feel, and I do try to make sure they're supported all the way through their little ordeal.

'That's the ticket . . . really I don't need support so much as . . . hands ready to catch me. You could hold my stick for a moment . . . or else – no, that's fine, put your hand against the small of my back. Or, yes, against my bum. Why not? – if that's easier . . .' I was very tired, and I dare say it wasn't my most inspiriting performance. I hope I didn't let her down. People like to be told they're doing a good job. I like it myself.

When we got inside I realised she hadn't been preparing the table but a chair, piling it high with cushions. The gesture was kind but not helpful. Most upright chairs defeat me though it's hardly their fault, having more to do with the lack of give in my midsection. Cushions can't remedy the underlying geometrical mismatch. I was actually more likely to cope on a stool, once I was installed there, though on this particular day I wouldn't have been up to the rigours of perching. I didn't feel that I was in a position to dictate terms just then, either. The management has the right to refuse admission without being obliged to provide a reason, and this ominous restriction placed on hospitality is something I never forget. Under my coaxing she got rid of all the cushions but one, and I wedged myself in as best I could.

I wasn't quite the only customer, but the clientèle amounted to four young men in tee shirts, donkey jackets on the backs of their chairs. To my rudimentary trade-spotting eye, they seemed likely to be council workers. They were obviously a group, but oddly distributed, with one sitting at a different table and keeping his back turned to the other three. When a packet of cigarettes was passed around, he wasn't offered one, though he seemed to be as much sulking as rejected. The mood of the group was not sunny. The three took turns to read out football scores jeeringly from a paper, while the outsider banged his tea mug fiercely against the tabletop with every result. He spilled a fair bit of it without seeming to care or feeling the need to mop up. I was exhilarated. This was just the sort of non-academic tableau that I had gone short of for the last three years. If one of them had had a hand-rolled cigarette tucked behind his ear, almost hidden by a lock of greasy hair – better yet a half-smoked one – I would have been in heaven.

I'd grown up with a mother who despised anything suburban and longed for the sense of superiority that her own mother didn't need to simulate. The effect of so much suppression of impulse was to give me the idea that the lower classes were in touch with life, as almost anyone was likely to be when set beside Mum. Dad's life in the RAF (we always said Raff) gave him a different sense of hierarchy, which extended into the world of civil aviation. He saw the world in terms of ranked competence rather than stations fixed at birth, but he was always more hidden in his judgements anyway. His assumptions were so different from hers that he no longer thought of contradicting her, if he ever had.

When as a child I lived in a hospital I learned to disown the poshness that others smelled on me, training myself for instance to pronounce nougat as *nugget* rather than *noogah*. Then in rural India before I went up to Cambridge I encountered a different set of distinctions, more rigorously patrolled but mysteriously flexible, so that a woman of a farmer caste could voluntarily undertake the hygienic tasks barred to all but untouchables and devote herself to my needs. Yet the downward pull of desire drew me if anything to the caste below the farmers, the ones described by my hostess in India as 'colony', the lowest of the low. It's mysterious that I should be attracted to outsiders. Didn't I have enough untouchability in my own right?

There was a welcome feeling of activity in the café, not just of working-class people expressing primary emotions but of food being prepared for later in the day. I wasn't made to feel like a startling distraction.

More than anything I needed a pee, but I know better than to ask for the facilities right away on unfamiliar premises. It runs deep, the suspicion among café staff that you want to take advantage of their plumbed porcelain without using their crockery. I can't tell you why. I can only say that I thought it best to undertake the ridiculous business of sitting laboriously down and then standing up again to prove my good faith, though I'm an unlikely candidate for the old slash-and-run. The moment I had sat down I said, 'Come to think of it, I need to use your toilet first. Would you mind helping me off with my shoulder bag?' Surely nobody could have doubts about my trustworthiness if I was leaving it behind as a guarantee? – my dismal brown Greek tapestry bag on which a couple of badges still clung, of the many that had once been lodged there. SAPPHO WAS A RIGHT-ON WOMAN. TO THE ENGLISH LIBERTY MEANS A SHOP ON REGENT STREET. Cheap pressed-metal rallying cries of radical intent. Perhaps it was time to get rid of these activist stragglers, now that I had diverged from my generation and its rites of passage. I was no longer part of the student body. The expectation had been that I would be nourished and developed by Cambridge, but now a different model suggested itself. I had been moved on through the alimentary tract of higher education. Over three years in the university system I had been stripped of my nutrients and evacuated.

The badge on my bag wasn't referring to the Regent Street in Cambridge, where I was now, but the one in London. I don't think it had subliminally steered me towards breakfast.

The waitress graciously escorted me, the preposterous soles of her built-up shoes making a strange and stately clatter. In the rudimentary loo, though below mirror level, I wondered uncomfortably if my grooming was below par, making me vulnerable. If you're going to throw yourself on the mercy of the public, it's a good idea to be clean and fresh. Bad breath, overtones of urine, a whiff from the pit, all these are strong suppressants of Samaritan impulse. Perhaps the original altruist, the one in the parable, had no sense of smell.

When I was back in place, uncomfortably reinstalled barely ten minutes after leaving my post, she offered me a menu.

'No need,' I cried. I knew what I wanted. Tea and two pieces of toast. That was my ticket, my return ticket. That was what my metabolism needed to regain equilibrium, and that was also what my pocket could afford. I thought about splurging on an egg, and decided against it. If appetite and budget were at odds, I would not be siding with appetite.

A voice overruled me, coming from behind the direction of the counter. It was female and deep. 'Hettie, darling,' it said. 'Give this young man the works. Bacon, two eggs, sausage, mushroom, tomato, beans. Forget about toast, what he needs is fried bread. I can see his ribs from here. I didn't think they made starving orphans any more, but he's the real thing. If he makes trouble, just keep frying eggs and serving them up.'

Maddeningly the owner of this voice, who was either freeing me from hunger or saddling me with debt, remained invisible behind me. I felt a large damp hand on my shoulder, but that was all. On the home territory of this manageress or proprietrix I didn't feel able to try the approach of simply saying 'Why don't you come round to the front where I can see you?' It sometimes works.

It may have been the case that I was visibly underweight. Looking in the mirror doesn't count as self-enquiry and even when I was a young man it wasn't an activity that took up a significant amount of my time. I had certainly been going light on meals. Of course we who spend our time below the shoulder level of the general population (we adults I mean, since children clamber on chairs) live largely unmirrored lives. Domestic interiors by and large keep us innocent of our reflections. Modern architecture is less tactful, its silvered surfaces so often stretching down to the ground, ready to ambush us with our illusory selves.

The young woman called Hettie brought a little posy vase with a rosebud in it and placed it in front of my place setting. I asked if it was scented, and she picked it up and held it in front of my nose. Clever girl – very trainable, responsive without being servile, a promising mixture. I go through life explaining my limitations and my needs, but even when people are quick on the uptake we're usually birds of passage relative to each other and the process must start again. My ideal is elusive though not altogether impracticable – to be surrounded by people who have developed a casual expertise, not an advanced degree but a modest diploma in John Studies. Then the machinery of personal interaction can mesh with such perfectly lubricated smoothness that no one feels the need to mention its existence. But naturally people move on and then it's back to teaching strangers the alphabet, or at least *The Cat Sat on the Mat*. Though of course that's part of the point. Mat-sitting isn't for everyone.

I was a vegetarian, even a mildly self-righteous one, but my empty stomach had forgotten all about that, and my sausage-piqued nostrils and shamelessly responding salivary glands were no better. It was a truism of the Russian labour camps that the stomach has no memory. It also has no conscience. I had been outmanœuvred and outvoted by a quorum of amoral organs. Once more I was in the minority. I would have to lecture my guts on the need for solidarity later on.

Even so I had a qualm of sorts, a twinge of nausea when I thought of the overloaded plate being prepared for me. I'd rather be given a small portion and then ask for seconds. I don't know whether this is a psychological recoil or just how a small stomach reacts. If I had my way, every restaurant would be buffet service.

Me and food – I don't usually know if I'm hungry or just going through the motions until I've had five or six little bites. To start with I masticate more or less mechanically, giving the salivary glands their cue to build up ptyalin for the digestive task ahead. Sometimes a snack is more than enough, and sometimes when the snack is gone I've really only got started. That's why buffets suit me so well – they're elasticated, gusseted even, opening up or pulling tight to accommodate my very variable appetite.

Hunger is a mysterious and biologically complex state. We let children believe that taking food into the body is as simple a process as filling the fuel tank of a car, when in fact a substantial proportion of the energy contained in food must be devoted to converting the rest of it into a form that can be absorbed. There's a sophisticated set of interlocking mechanisms in place to make sure that, even so, energy can be made available the moment our mouths are full. The metabolism makes an advance before the cheque has cleared, an emergency payout or bridging loan, to head off the risk of bankruptcy while the necessary funds are on the premises but not yet safely stored in the vaults. In this analogy is my body the bank or the customer? They can hardly have the same interests. I realise that I've gone straight back to explanations on the level of a nursery school, with money entering a bank as simply as petrol being pumped into the tank of a car.

The joys of the buffet are multiple. There's no dancing of attendance, no pestering of the customer in the interests of inflating the bill. Would Sir care to be informed of Chef's special recommendations? No indeed. Sir has doubts about Chef's motives. Sir suspects that Chef is only a step ahead of the food inspectors and is trying to get rid of anything that's brewing horrors in a hurry.

A menu places itself between appetite and satisfaction, when hunger is best addressed directly. Let the food arrive on the warming dishes without fanfare, and let eyes and nose decide. The buffet is a little theatre of independence and liberty. If you want mint sauce on your coleslaw no eyebrow will be raised even a fraction of an inch to impugn your preference.

Naturally I have to send out scouts to gather information about what is available, waves of scouts in fact, the second wave to answer supplementary questions, asking staff if necessary. The principle of self-service cannot be a capitulation to ignorance, and if food service personnel are reluctant to divulge, for instance, what type of oil has been used in frying (and in what quantities) then they could consider alternative careers.

Any number of nutritious skirmishes

The All-You-Can-Eat buffet is the best possible approach to eating in public, despite the foolish name appealing to greed and the chimæra of the bargain. As if it would be a budgetary triumph to eat exactly one mouthful less than would make you throw it all up again! In my mind the All-You-Can-Eat buffet goes by a more tempting name. Secretly it's called the Take-As-Little-As-You-Like buffet. When I've cleared my lightly loaded saucer I may want a few mouthfuls more. I'm better suited to grazing than to any sort of frontal assault on an overcrowded plate. At a buffet I can enjoy a series of nutritious skirmishes without being exposed to the panorama of the battlefield, which is all too likely to make my appetite close down with a shudder. Give me a big plate and I'll leave most of it. Put a little ramekin in front of me and the chances are I'll be purring for a second helping.

I know what you're thinking – what about the waiters? The waiters whose unchoreographed dances give you such reliable joy as they pass between one world and another, the crudeness of the kitchen and the decorum of the dining room, negotiating the gross and subtle sheaths that separate the orders of being? And of course you're right. The only thing I would miss at a lifelong Take-As-Little-As-You-Like buffet, when set beside the hotel meals I enjoyed or endured with my grandmother, would be the tight black-trousered bums of the waiters, always bending over, for a reason or no reason at all, in my line of sight. But that's a different appetite.

At the café this Thursday morning there had been no particular fuss over ordering. It was all very free and easy. I had stated my modest wishes and been overruled.

I now knew the waitress's name but wasn't sure I should use it. On balance I thought that laying claim to familiarity was likely to backfire. It was a better idea in the short term to appeal to neutral professionalism. 'Excuse me. Excuse me? Oh hello. I've brought my own cutlery. I hope you don't mind.'

23

'That's a new one. Don't suppose we mind too much. Any particular reason? Maybe it's to do with religion?'

I was tired, I'd hardly slept. I take a childlike pleasure in mystifying people. There's no excuse for what I told her. I should have said 'Not at all. It's purely a question of practicality.' That's even what I meant to say. What I said instead was 'Indeed it is. I'm a Brahmin. A sort of Untouchable in reverse. Our cutlery is sacred. Anytime you want a crash course in Hindu table manners just say the word.' Hettie made a neutral noise and left me to stew in my own stupid cleverness.

Really, I'd rather not have a psychology at all than one that worked like that. Which was how Hinduism came to attract me in the first place, I suppose. My guru Ramana Maharshi started life as a Brahmin, but that all changed in the most casually propitious way when he arrived at the holy mountain Arunachala, having run away from home. He had his topknot cut off before he entered the temple, and this act, known as the puberal tonsure, though not ritual in itself, nevertheless marks a rite of passage. He ignored the ritual bath that was obligatory for his caste but it so happened that a shower of rain made up the lack as he approached the holy precincts, so that everything necessary was accomplished without effort. He didn't renounce Brahmin status any more than a snake 'renounces' its skin when the time comes to shed it. His caste simply dropped off, like a scab when the flesh underneath is healed and whole.

I envied Ramana Maharshi the clarity of his decisions, though 'decisions' is entirely the wrong word, just as envy is an inappropriate emotion for a devotee to feel. He could shed possessions so simply. A man might walk away from the ashram with a tiger skin rolled up and carried over his shoulder, and when stopped by the acolytes he might claim that the guru said it was all right for him to take it. Disbelieving, they did at least check with the guru, who said simply, 'Somebody comes in and says sit on the tiger skin. I do so. Somebody else comes in and asks to keep it. I say yes.' His desires not being involved at any point. He hadn't consented to the fantasy of possession and could hardly be surprised when an object wandered away from him.

Then Hettie was back, sitting opposite me with no better excuse for her visit – she wasn't bearing actual food – than bringing salt

24

and pepper. 'They're very anti left-handers in India, aren't they? Very unfriendly.'

'I don't really know.' I didn't really know. It wasn't a subject that had come up in the five weeks I'd spent in Tamil Nadu, following the footsteps of the guru in exactly the way he'd indicated was self-indulgent mimicry rather than self-realisation.

'I went there last summer,' she said, not specifying which 'there' she meant of the swarming number of 'there's that are there, 'and you should have seen the dirty looks I got when I reached for the serving spoon with the wrong hand. It was horrible.'

'Um . . .' This was the stylised sort of Um, registering polite dissent. Not everybody twigs, but credit to her, she did.

'Go on. What's bothering you?'

'Well . . . were you eating with your left hand?'

'I've told you I'm left-handed so of course I was eating with my left hand. That's what left-handers do!'

'And you were eating with your hands.'

'Yes. Yes! This wasn't in a city — we didn't want to go anywhere touristy. There were no tools provided so of course I was eating with my hands. What about it?'

'It's just that Indian eating habits involve a hygienic element . . .'

'And left-handers are unclean, is that it?'

'Well, that may be what they thought. I really don't know.' I really didn't know. 'But what is certainly unclean, and I don't mean in religious terms but scientifically, is using the same hand for the food and the spoon that sits in the serving dish.'

'I don't follow.'

I've not had the rhino virus

'Well, suppose your saliva contains some harmful organism, such as rhinovirus or flu or glandular fever, the people who eat with you are safe from it as long as the hand that goes to your mouth doesn't touch the serving spoon that everybody uses. I mean, it's not like the sort of infection barrier you'd aim for in a hospital, and if you have an airborne infection then it won't help. It's rough and ready but it works, as a first line of defence, at least.'

25

'I've not had the rhino virus – I've had the others.'

'Really? That would be surprising – that's just a cold. The common cold in all its forms.'

'Oh. Why didn't you say so? And why don't they explain the reason for the hand routine in India?'

'They may not know it themselves – you don't have to know how it works to get the benefit. Maybe it's folk wisdom, like people in the olden days putting cobwebs on a wound. Mind you, the "hand routine" was explained to me by a highly sophisticated Indian businessman in Bombay.' That was dreamy Raghu.

At Raghu's table on my first night in India in the summer of 1970 I had been given a demonstration of Indian eating habits but had been exempted from trying something that was out of the question for me physically. I admired what I could not imitate. Use of the hand is traditional and regarded as showing the proper respect for food. There's not much in a grain-based diet that can't conveniently be eaten using the hand. Metal cutlery bespeaks cutting, impaling, mashing and scooping, operations stained with violence and destructive of the reverence that looks on every meal as a gift from divinity. Cutlery whether edged, tined or bowled disrupts the sacred transaction, while any gift received humbly into one's hands has been received into the heart also. Unfortunately my hands aren't up to the job, and I can't believe that I'm supposed to express my reverence for food by starving.

India was an infinite door that had been opened to me then firmly closed in my face. There was no slamming, no indication of cosmic pique, but it was clear that if I ever went back I would need to leave behind any sense of spiritual urgency. If Hettie didn't know the first thing about India then I didn't know the second, and ought to be ashamed of passing myself off as some sort of expert. I was just a tourist, barely a rung above those who used the subcontinent as a backdrop for egotistical little excursions, to get a tan and smoke a joint on the beach.

I asked her if she went to an ashram.

'Oh yes.'

'Which one?'

'I don't remember. It started with a Sri, I think.'

'So many of them do! And was there a charge to go in?'

'I think so. They may have called it a donation but you weren't going to get in if you didn't pay up. Yes, definitely.' Oh, there always is, except at the ashram Ramana Maharshi allowed to be installed around him, where free access was one of the conditions he imposed for staying there. The spiritual life doesn't always come cheap.

Enough brooding about India! 'Actually, Hettie, I've got my own cutlery in my shoulder bag.' Until I get to know someone, deciding how sharp a hint is needed to produce action can only be guesswork. 'If you don't mind getting them out for me.'

'Of course, sorry.' Hettie picked up the standard set of tools and slipped them into the wide front pocket of her apron. She gave my ones a thorough polish with a tea towel before laying them in front of me. My property, my stolen property, the Downing cutlery about to get its first criminal outing. It was as if she was a nurse assisting at an operation.

My nostrils had been sending delighted alarms for some minutes as the smells of cooking reached them. Now the laden plate itself arrived, laden beyond the possibility of appetite. I wasn't in two minds about this feast, more like two bodies, one convinced that salvation had been served up in front of it, the other already fighting against disgust. 'Have you got everything you need?' Hettie asked.

'Well . . .' I said. I did and I didn't. I had all too much on my plate, but perhaps there was something missing even so. 'Perhaps you'll show me how that works.' I indicated a playful part of the table setting, an outsized plastic tomato whose capped stalk was actually a nozzle for the dispensing of ketchup.

She flipped the cap open and passed it towards me, saying, 'Just give it a good squeeze.' I went on looking puzzled, hoping she would work out for herself that I had an intellectual grasp of the principle behind the device, but lacked the manual flexibility to do the squeezing she specified, however much I longed to improve the composition of my fry-up by directing a decorative squirt of acrid (but lycopene-rich) ketchup onto the nutritional canvas. A brutally explicit flavour that would make my palate ring, even in the addled state brought on by the cold I had.

The lycopene is present in cooked tomatoes only, not in the raw fruit. This peculiarity, even before it was generally known, gave tomato ketchup a bumptious eminence on the kitchen shelf and the school menu, as if it had knowledge somehow of its own super-condimentary status. The bottle squares its non-existent shoulders and looks down on its neighbour, brown sauce harbouring no nutritional secret weapon.

'Oh for heaven's sake!' came the same rich voice that had overruled my thrifty breakfast order, but this time its owner swept into view (the owner I suppose of the business also) and grabbed the dispenser. She was plump, though well-shaped, and wore a polka-dot dress. She uncapped the nozzle and held the masquerading fruit in the palm of her hand, bouncing it up and down as if getting ready for the shot-put. 'Stripes or swirls?' she asked.

'Free expression,' I said. 'Free choice.' I was interested to see what shapes she would produce with the viscous fluid in its lurid container. Thixotropic isn't a word I use lightly, and may not even be the most accurate way of characterising the behaviour of extruded ketchup, but it's still true that anyone who has a grasp of the processes at work in that nozzle is well on the way to understanding the physical world. She narrowed her eyes and then delivered an even spiral of red starting on the outside of the plate and working in. The final flourish, accompanied by a rather unfortunate farting noise, was a jet aimed directly at the yellow of one of the fried eggs, forceful enough to rupture the yolk. 'Sorry, no money back,' she said, 'but then breakfast is my treat. Oh, Hettie? Take that mug away. It's no use to him. Bring him tea in one of my cups.'

She sat down opposite me and lit a cigarette. Smokers took their rights for granted in those days, and even faculty libraries at the University had tables designated for the free exercise of self-destructive vice. 'I'm not making you cough, am I?' she asked breezily. 'Not at all,' I said, 'I was coughing anyway.' She would have to do a lot worse before I scolded a benefactor. I have a soft spot for buxom, bosomy ladies, I'd say motherly types except that there's so little overlap with actual Mum, who was, as she said (without regret), 'straight up and down'.

The teacup steaming in front of me was an improvement on the vast mug it replaced, but not by much. The ideal vessel is actually a small mug, since I control the tilting action with a couple of fingers wedged through the handle but balance the mug itself on the back of my knuckles. With an unfamiliar cup or mug, particularly when it's full, there can be an uncertain moment as it travels towards my mouth. Then I must prehensilise my lips, thrusting them forward in an attempt to create an effective seal rather than let liquid spill. It's hard to give an impression of any great intelligence while executing this chimps'-tea-party manœuvre. I can feel as if I'm wearing a nappy and being fed from a bottle for the amusement of jaded zoo visitors with no actual interest in wildlife.

I squared up to the teacup relatively successfully, then with a little embarrassment started to ply my imported cutlery. The lady's eyes were slightly screwed up against the drift of her own smoke, but she managed to raise an eyebrow and called out, for the benefit of staff or anyone else in earshot, 'Fair play to him, this one isn't a stealer. He might even leave us a teaspoon as a tip. My name's Whyvonne, by the way.'

'Whyvonne with a W?'

'Whyvonne with a Why.'

'John.' John with a baffled look.

'Pleasta meetcha.' Definitely invoking some sort of Hollywood musical I hadn't seen. My cinematic range of reference was not wide. Yes, I'd seen a few musicals over the years, but the films that had made most impact on me during my time as an undergraduate were *Wild Strawberries* and *El Topo*.

Yvonne, Y-vonne, or even Whyvonne, smoked while I ate and kept an eye on me, as if she wanted to make sure every scrap was hitting the metabolic bullseye. She matched me mouthful for mouthful, making the smoke she swallowed keep pace with the fry-up on my plate. The alternative possible spellings of her name flickered unstably in the peripheral vision of my mind's eye like the beginnings of a proofreader's migraine. I was grateful that she didn't make conversation, having too much respect perhaps for the mysterious processes that unlock the energy in food and make it available. It's hard enough to co-ordinate the rhythms of breathing and eating without complicating the equation with talking. There's only one mammal that can choke on its food, and that's us, the reason being the evolutionary changes in the layout of our throats that conspire to make speech possible. To talk while eating is to play Russian roulette at table, with your œsophagus as the gun.

She wanted to see me fully fed now, in the present tense, while she watched me and talked in my direction. There was to be no tucking of bacon into pockets for later. She had obviously enjoyed establishing an ascendancy over her underling by anticipating my dilemmas with the giant tomato and the giant mug. Such little breakthroughs often send people crashing into my orbit.

She leaned forward to inspect my face, in a friendly way though the effect was still disconcerting. She said, 'I think you've been bitten, darling.'

'Bitten?'

'You're coming up in red bumps.' She produced a powder compact with a stylised black daisy embossed on it and used the mirror inside to show me what she meant. I was really more interested in the design, which used five overlapping discs to represent petals, though a daisy with five petals would be a poor thing, with a thin white ring vaguely hinting at a carpel. We complain about Chinese written characters not resembling the things they are supposed to illustrate, don't we – *that's never a horse!* – but we ourselves are capable of a thousand acts of oblique decipherment a day. This shape on a plastic compact certainly said 'daisy' to young female shoppers, though not in the language of flowers, hardly that.

'You see what I mean, darling?'

'I see what you mean. Coming up in red bumps.' The little disembodied whines Maya had sent out in the night weren't as disembodied as all that. They had borrowed the bodies of mosquitoes. I shouldn't have been surprised, since the stagnant water of Hobson's Conduit lay just the other side of the railings from where the Mini was parked. By leaving the window on the driver's side slightly open I had advertised my deliciousness, sending out appetising John smells to lure members of the family Culicidæ over the glass threshold for their feast. And I know the ligature on Culicidæ is wrong in this Linnæan context but I can't help myself. To my way of thinking vowels are balls of ice cream in a bowl and will always half melt into each other if given the chance.

Somewhere Nietzsche says a clever thing about mosquitoes and their consciousness, but as usual I can't remember if it was wise or only got as far as clever and stopped short.

'When you've finished your breakfast, darling, I'll see if I can find some TCP.' I'd never really liked TCP, partly because of the smell and partly because they changed the formula sometime in my childhood, and I'm a bit of a traditionalist in such matters. Meanwhile Whyvonne bent down and picked up a large black cat with white markings, holding it on its back in her lap. It was certainly long-suffering. She swung it about as if it was no more than a scarf or a shawl. Perhaps she cultivated the habit of disconcerting her customers, though Mum had always done the same sort of thing, with cats and even with birds, wearing them as accessories in a way that compensated for her lack of interest in clothes.

The cat under the woman's stroking, searching, manipulating hands, their nails thickly coated with red polish, seemed absent in some definite way, though cats of course rather specialise in abstention from the attention they have demanded. He let himself be dandled rather fatalistically, and I wondered whether this unusual cat would even have the energy to make a landing, if she happened to drop him.

'He's not been well,' she said, in a tone of voice that would have been suitable in a bulletin about a member of the royal family. 'You'll never guess what brought him down.'

I was well stuck in on the second egg, the one with its yellow membrane intact. 'A bad batch of catnip?' I coughed, not surprisingly, since I was now, against my preferences, requiring my mouth to handle breathing, eating and talking duties simultaneously. The apparatus was overwhelmed.

She made a face. 'I'm serious.'

'Don't know.'

'Antifreeze.'

Antifreeze?

'Antifreeze. It must taste good, or at least it must taste sweet. He came back from a prowl and could hardly stand. When I phoned the vet and described the symptoms, he diagnosed antifreeze poisoning.

Apparently it's rather common. He said it sounded like a severe case, and he asked if I had any alcohol in the house – clear spirit at least 40-proof . . . I told him I know how to choose spirits. I don't need help. Then he explained it was to stabilise the cat! If you've ever tried to give a cat a pill, you can imagine what it might be like feeding vodka to a sick cat. Luckily he was too ill to put up much of a fight.'

It doesn't take much to arouse my medical brain, even when I'm exhausted. Curiosity overrode my dislike of mealtime conversation, inadvisable at the best of times, the brain's way of taking in nourishment being inherently at odds with the body's. 'I wonder,' I said. 'Perhaps it's a way of reducing the strain on the kidneys, if only temporarily – everyone knows the kidneys are a cat's Achilles heel – by administering something that will be processed preferentially by the endocrine system, making the antifreeze wait its turn, and so buying time for more specialised intervention from the vet. Could that be it?'

She seemed irritated rather than pleased that I had shown so much technical interest. 'I have no idea. I expect it was something like that, some mad bit of veterinary cleverness . . . Did I miss you on *University Challenge*, darling? He pulled through, though he's been rather floppy ever since. I quite like him this way. He was a bit of a horror with birds and mice in his time. Once he left a rat's head under my bed. Charming! Particularly if you don't find it right away. I'm glad that's all over and done with. I haven't asked you where you're from, have I, darling? I mean, whether you're local or just passing through. I've not seen you around and about.'

Keep those insoluble polysaccharides coming

When Whyvonne crossed her legs I could see she was wearing strappy silver shoes, rather smart, suitable for dancing. Perhaps if I'd known more about Hollywood musicals I would have been able to place her in the genre. Was she the aspiring ingénue who gets a shot at stardom when the established lead breaks her leg? More likely a sturdy hard-working hoofer who would never miss a rehearsal, nor ever rise through the ranks however many of her fellow chorines were carted away in ambulances.

I said I was local in the sense that I had slept within a mile of Great St Mary's for the last few years. It turned out that I didn't need to explain that this was the residence requirement for undergraduates.

'So are you what they call a braingrader, darling?'

'What's that?'

'It just means a student, I think – someone who is here to get his brain graded.' Logically that should be a gradee rather than a grader, but tortuous are the ways of the vernacular, and 'gradee' also looks like a printing error, missing the middle letter that would produce 'grandee'. A few students in my time had seemed ensnared in that very confusion. There was even a name for them – 'members of the Pitt Club'.

'Who uses that word, I wonder?' It could be hostile or self-mocking, it seemed to me, depending on the context.

'Someone was using it down the pub. He tried to sell me a magazine.'

'Which magazine?'

'A rather scruffy one. I believe it was called . . . it's on the tip of my tongue. Oh, yes . . . I rather think it was called *Braingrader*.'

'Well then, to answer your question, I suppose I'm a braingrader. Or I was until very recently.'

'And what are you now, darling? – not that it's any of my business.' This was a question with a sharp point. Any more pointed and it would have punctured, once and for all, both appetite and ego.

When Whyvonne said she hadn't seen me 'around and about' it was a way of saying that I'm intrinsically memorable – she would remember me if our paths had crossed – and this of course is a tribute to the accoutrements of wheelchair, crutch and stick rather than the sociable creature needing these things to get around and about if he is to have the opportunity to sparkle. Never mind. I take it kindly, on the whole. And the same proposition worked the other way round. Even without silver shoes she would have made an impression, just as in a university context there were little celebrities in whose presence people would take a step backwards and mouth to each other the magic word 'Footlights'. Members of the famous amateur dramatic society who might go on to greater things, neither playing by the rules of straight society nor quite throwing in their hands with the counterculture. They might end up in a West End revue and make their parents embarrassed or proud, depending on the parents and of course the reviews.

Even without conversational obligations I don't enjoy eating in front of strangers, however friendly they are. There's no point in pretending. It makes me feel like a circus act. I have my own streak of showmanship, I can hardly deny it, a streak a mile wide, but the conditions have to be right. In those days I was much more likely to perform if helped to perch on a stool in a pub, encouraging people to bet against my being able to throw peanuts into my mouth, using the winnings to maintain the level of Abbot Ale in my glass, one with a stem not a handle. It made matters worse that I had a cold. My eating took on an animal quality by force of my having to breathe through my mouth while also shovelling nutrition into it. For once my appetite arrived in full at the same time as the food. The ptyalin in my saliva was raring to go. Keep those insoluble polysaccharides coming, waitress — we have extra staff on hand to deal with them. We know all about breaking the glycosidic bonds.

I could feel where a blob of egg-yolk which hadn't reached my mouth was congealing in the short whiskers at the edge of my lip. Facial hair can be a trial, though shaving it is an unending series of trials. I wasn't going to try to reach out for the blob with my tongue under the eyes of a rather exhausting café owner and her inert cat. I had to remind myself it was still morning. My university career had tailed away in silence, solitude, undernourishment and sombre contemplation of a narrow future. If this first day was anything to go by, my graduate life would be all snot, gorging, endearments and non-stop chat.

I was having trouble keeping my eyes open. Luckily the aches in my joints kept watch over me and warded off sleep.

Or so I thought, while in fact I dozed off. I was dimly aware of the manageress taking my plate away. She must have cleared my place with exaggerated discretion, and the sharp clicking sound I was hearing was her attempt to walk on tiptoe in shoes that didn't permit it. Perhaps they were actual tap shoes and had metal plates at the front. My eyelids snapped open and I said, 'Don't take my cutlery away!' in tones of high paranoia. I wasn't going to be tricked so easily out of the only tangible benefit from my student days. She leaned over me and murmured, 'Mind if I wash them for you, darling? I hate to be a bother, but it's all part of the service. Close your eyes – blow – and when you open them again all your lovely things will be right there in front of you.' As she spoke the word 'blow' she held a paper napkin against my nose with a gentle squeezing motion. I was too startled to speak, for once, and surprised myself by doing exactly as I was told. I could imagine the sharp tang of her nail polish without being able, in my current state, to smell it.

I had been working for years to eradicate every scrap of my mother's claims on me, and now as Whyvonne's fingers softly clenched my nostrils to increase the volume of mucus being expelled into the tissue I realised that this too was an area where Mum could be replaced. I was learning not to confuse access with intimacy, and not to be disproportionately grateful when my independence needed bolstering with a little outside help, in this case a brief constriction of the wings of the nose to guarantee an efficient discharge of the nasal mucosa. This person had a life of her own that wasn't derailed by a little obligingness. Look! She was going off to supervise the sandwich-making. She was putting dishes in the sink and giving Hettie grief about leaving her handbag where anyone could fall over it. She wasn't summoning all her friends to make sure they knew what a cruel trick fate had played on her.

I can honestly say that I haven't picked my nose since the mid-1950s. Do I win a prize? I can reach a nostril with my handy table knife but frankly I don't see the appeal. It must be an addictive pattern of behaviour, though, one that yields a great deal of pleasure to the initiated, to judge by the number of people I see either surreptitiously or blatantly sliding digit into orificial socket, the nostril that seems to have co-evolved to accommodate it.

As it turned out, there were quite a few things going on that I would rather not have had happen. I had made the choice not to eat meat. I would rather not have an overfilled plate in front of me, death-riddled or otherwise, I would rather not have conversation while I am eating, I would rather not have my nose blown without permission, without negotiation of any kind. But I could hardly say I was being treated badly at this address.

I was conscious even so that I was merely floating on an unstable layer of welcome, like a flightless insect on its leaf boat, while maliciously innocent boys chuck stones from the edge of the pond. No direct hit was required to unseat me. Any near miss would do the job. As a child I was alarmed by the passage of scripture concerning wheat and chaff and their respective fates (garnered into the barn of glory or brusquely burnt), certain without needing to be told that I was chaff. This had nothing to do with any sense of sin, either particular or general. It was simply a fact that I was the useless husk that surrounds the good grain. Yet at the same time that I was despairing, and awaiting my destruction, I was also thinking, since God is not wasteful, that there must be a use, however humble, to which chaff might be put. Chaff must be good for something.

In time I outgrew the God I had been brought up to worship. I found a much bigger God than the manic-depressive bigot of the Old Testament. God was unbelievably great, so great that he didn't live in some far-off corner. He was so great that you couldn't even limit him to being inscribed within a name. Yet this bigger God was closer than we can imagine, closer to you than your jugular vein, to borrow a lovely phrase from the Qu'rân (it's at 50:16). I wanted to do away with unproductive distinctions, to let the goats back in among the sheep just to see how they get on, even-toed ungulates together. It seemed an odd separation to make in the first place. Were the goats making use of their harsher voices to tell the bleating sheep that there were alternatives to blind obedience? I wanted to mix up the scriptures into a nourishing broth with all the doctrine boiled away, and I wanted the chaff to rejoin the wheat in hearty wholegrain goodness. Now, though, it really seemed that I was being winnowed out from the graduate harvest, and incineration seemed almost preferable to the half-existence that was in store for me. At that time only seven per cent of people in the relevant age group went on to tertiary education, and seven per cent of that seven per cent − to pluck a figure from thin air − needn't have bothered.

Breakfast had stunned my system but also anchored me to the world. I opened my eyes, and the next time Hettie was passing I asked her for a glass of water, two-thirds filled. When she brought it I had her search through the tapestry bag for one of the paper sachets stowed away there. Acting on my instructions she shook the sachet to settle the contents, then tore the top across and tipped them into the glass. I did some stirring with the sundæ spoon then drank the thick elixir down.

I had clamoured for Fybogel from the moment I heard of its existence in the *Monthly Index of Medical Specialities*. The surgery with which I was registered on Trinity Street took an enlightened approach when it came to the supplying of reading matter for patients waiting their turn – or perhaps it was my doctor specifically, Dr C. T. M. Wilson, who authorised the provision of out-of-date issues for my particular use. Any publication addressed to Doctors Only was bound to be of the first interest to me, who had no intention of being only a patient.

You would expect advertising material circulating within the profession to be technical and free of gimmicks, and much of it was, but there were also dreamier ones. The campaign for a sedative might show a middle-aged lady, palms folded, leaning against a mystic cloud as she drifted into sleep. Another advert showed a drawing of a fat little face, the nose replaced with a dripping tap, with the caption *Dimotapp turns off runny noses*. I don't remember the caption for Fybogel, but the picture showed a substantial orangey-looking bolus passing through a man's gut like a Hoover, mopping up recalcitrant bits and pieces as it went, leaving everything fresh and clean in its wake. I wanted that! I had to try it.

Delivered of an obese torpedo

This wasn't really a medical necessity since my digestion gave no particular cause for concern but it was a sensible precaution just the same. The chief motor of digestion is physical activity. More than anything it is movement that winds the clock of the bowels. Compromised mobility makes the processing of food sluggish. It struck me that this was a good basis for testing a product, free of the distorting influence of immediate fears about health. I had greatly enjoyed amateur experimental science at school, and in the absence of any other available project or piece of apparatus I would experiment on myself. My bowels would be my chemistry set. Dr Wilson made no difficulties about prescribing a supply of sachets.

Twelve hours after the first dose I was comfortably delivered, in the communal toilets of staircase A, Kenny Court, of an obese torpedo. It was clear that Downing food left any amount of detritus behind, to be tidied away by this subtle internal sponge. I examined it visually, prodding it with my bum snorkel, the curved Perspex rod that was part of my personal equipment, not a standard medical item but a one-off design devised as an aid to self-wiping for the manually compromised. The imposing object spun lazily on its axis. Rigour would call for closer scrutiny, some sort of dissection procedure, but although my bedder Jean Beddoes was by our third year of intimate dealings highly devoted and even batty about me, she was nowhere near batty enough to go bowl-fishing on my behalf. I activated the flushing mechanism and watched it dive towards its leisurely oblivion.

I've never proselytised for Hinduism or homosexuality but I must admit I've put my weight behind Fybogel. Little travelling salesman with his sample sachets. Drummer with a very restricted manor. From that point on I took to preaching the gospel according to Fybogel, tireless in my huckstering. Medical students were well represented at Downing and overrepresented in my social circle. I enjoyed picking their brains, sometimes unpicking them also, when they seemed less than fully informed about what they had been taught. Personal testimony can only go so far, and conversion experiences aren't infectious. I got into the habit of distributing sachets of Fybogel to my medic friends as if I was a benign version of the pusher, that bogeyman of the day. 'Good stuff,' I'd mutter with a wink. 'Medical grade. Not a laxative, mind – no nasty surprises – merely a bulking agent.' Handing out free samples until a need was created. 'Tell me how it works for you. Plenty more where that came from.' I pointed out the preponderance of natural ingredients, the inherent advantages over chemical-stimulant alternatives.

Reports were favourable. My guinea pigs benefited from improved regularity, enhanced digestive efficiency. They promised to prescribe Fybogel to their bunged-up patients as a matter of course when they were practitioners themselves, and this is how change comes about. If in the years since then a serene peristaltic murmur has spread out from Cambridge to the world, in gently pulsating waves, then I can claim to have played a part in that. Fybogel is a mantra that can be taken internally, taming the disorder of gastric thoughts.

When John the Baptist spoke of the one mightier than he that was coming after, whose fan was in his hand, who would thoroughly purge his floor and burn up the chaff with unquenchable fire (Matthew 3:11–12), he was speaking from a different perspective from my own, not just in religious terms but also digestively. Being a prophet in old Judea was anything but a sedentary occupation. John, and after him the disciples, spreading the word in an era when the primary form of mass communication was coinage, will have gone to great efforts themselves to circulate, going almost everywhere on foot. It may be an exaggeration to say that peristalsis is nine parts walking, but ordinary activity certainly makes a major contribution to the digestive process. Ambulation winds up the guts and keeps them chiming. Constipation is not a problem those holy men are likely to have encountered. My super-sedentary style of life, on the other hand, needs all the help it can get to keep the system moving. I have to tickle things along by other means.

That's where Fybogel comes in. And what is Fybogel? Pulverised ispaghula husk, that's what, and just about as chaffy as it's possible to get. Quintessence of chaff, a disgraced substance nevertheless performing a salutary function. In fact there are plenty of uses for chaff, once it has been relieved of the burden of symbolising worthlessness. It makes a fine insulating material. Compress it into bricks and you have a viable fuel.

I've always been more attuned to the subtle hint than to the explicit statement, to the footnote in tiny type rather than to the blaring headline. I responded to the suggestiveness of homœopathy as an idea before I found it to be effective as a practice. Even so I would have to have been in an unusually sensitive state to notice the tickling of a gossamer thread, a little filament of meaning drifting across the breakfast table this Thursday morning. It might have soothed my feelings of somehow being doubly exiled, from a Britain where I didn't belong and an India that had welcomed me only to reject me, perhaps offended that I had so presumptuously pronounced it my spiritual home. I might feel there was nothing to connect me any more with either my guru or the sacred mountain Arunachala, those identical twins who were always dressed alike, being manifestations of each other, however little the human eye could detect it – yet here I was in a café in Cambridge innocently drinking an agglutinated preparation of psyllium husks whose base plant, *Plantago ovata*, is native to India. Packaging in those days was remarkably reticent about its contents. Consumers weren't expected to take any interest in the source or composition of what they bought, but India is the major exporter of these unglamorous but undeniably hygroscopic seed-fragments and with every dose of Fybogel I was ingesting a homœopathic dose of India, a subtle eupeptic whisper of reassurance taken internally. *Quant. suff*, meaning 'as much as is needed', words that used to appear on medicine bottles. Nobody ever thinks Latin is being used to mask vagueness! It's as indefinite an instruction as Alice's *Drink Me*. Medicine bottles kept just as quiet about their contents, for fear of diluting the authority of the doctor whose name appeared on the label. Failure couldn't diminish the standing of a GP, even if people (by which I mean men, who were often secret hypochondriacs) tended to label such people 'quacks'. As a word, 'quack' was disparaging but still carried a charge of superstitious respect. As for consultants, they were little divinities whose word was not to be questioned.

I could write FRESH in letters a yard high

I didn't need to have my eyes open to realise that the café was beginning to get busier. I heard a man's posh voice ask if the sandwiches were fresh, and Whyvonne letting some acid show in her reply without overriding its fruity quality. 'Well, my dear, that's an interesting question. You'll have seen the blackboard outside on the street, as well as the signs on the windows, and it's true that they say Sandwiches without going into the business of freshness at all. There's a reason for that. I could write FRESH in letters a yard high and it still wouldn't mean anything. Are you following? It's a word and not a fact. But if I ask you, "What filling would you like?", and you tell me, then you can see me taking the bread out of its wrapper, just here, and dip my knife in the butter just here, and you can see that it's fresh because you were here even before there was a sandwich. So, dear, what filling would you like? And if you're wondering about the coleslaw I'd give it a miss. It's almost half an hour old, well past its prime. Don't take the risk.'

It was a very suave and hostile performance. Of course there's nothing like dealing with the public, and the repetitive questions thrown out every day, to put an edge on the dullest tongue, but I wonder if there wasn't more to it than that. In a university town you can never rule out the cropping-up in an unexpected place of a disaffected philosophy student, dialectical blades angled to shred any opposition, intellectual or otherwise. It's also possible that the concentration of mental mass in the student group boosts levels of quibbling in the general population by social osmosis, but this wasn't something I had noticed in the past.

Whyvonne's 'dear' and 'my dear' to the seeker after freshness were obviously insincere, but her 'darling's to me seemed warm even when slightly barbed. It's strange that I should respond to motherliness in almost every form it takes except the one that I was allotted by the illusion of birth. As I imagined it 'Laura Cromer', or 'Mum' to use her other Mayan name, was as stranded in her home surroundings of Bourne End, Bucks, as I was in my current unhoused state, but without the scalding grace of knowing it. She hadn't made a step towards anything that could be called her own life, since it was probably the last thing that she wanted. She seemed unable to move without the crutch of my dependence. As her firstborn I was a special case, which may have been part of the reason for her frozen state. My brother Peter had been allowed to grow away from her without reprisal, though she was holding tight to little sister Audrey, not yet free in law to go her own way. And when that day came at last, there were always cats to keep and to breed. She prized independence in cats but penalised it in her children.

Behind closed eyes at Whyvonne's café I made a mental list of the things that I absolutely had to do that day, without fail. It didn't take long – there was only the one item on it. Everything else was optional, but it was incumbent on me to devise a proper stack of priorities. With a little effort I knocked up a few flimsy plans for making the time pass until I resumed my poor approximation of a sleeping posture in the Mini. A nap in the long hours of daylight was a treat I didn't dare allow myself.

41

The blank hours must be given a contour, however arbitrary. I would have to blast cavities in the day, for the sole purpose of filling them in again with whatever amalgam I could scrape together and tamp down.

I thought of visiting the Fitzwilliam Museum, which had seemed pretty much impregnable on the one occasion I had sidled by. Museum visiting is a traditional way of passing the time, but I didn't feel up to it. With my batteries charged I could usually galvanise a small group, a little gang to smooth the road for me, and I could probably manage to have myself conveyed to the galleries without too much indignity, but the problems of such excursions don't begin and end with the brute question of access. To meet the needs of this particular art lover the Fitzwilliam staff would have to try a little harder, lowering everything eighteen inches or so from where it was normally, bringing the treasures on offer into my actual line of sight. As things stand, what I mainly get to see is the glare from the lights, bouncing off the glass in the picture frames.

I realised such radical obligingness was unlikely on the part of the Fitzwilliam. A museum is pretty much by definition an arthritic organism, and it doesn't even take one to know one. Perhaps I could sidestep the proper channels with the coöperation of those who had helped me up the stairs. We might be able to arrange a piecemeal rehang, alarms permitting, with one painting at a time brought into proper focus. If necessary a female of the party could stage a faint to distract any small-minded curators.

It takes enormous effort to gather a modest team for a basic task, such as entering a theoretically public building, to get some momentum behind me, and it has always seemed a waste to disperse the group before *esprit de corps* has a chance to root itself at all deeply.

Elven financial instrument

It's not that I want a standing army, but levying troops even for very limited manœuvres is always an exhausting business, and I have better uses for my energy than press-ganging strangers for short campaigns. With no king's shilling beyond a smile. Some sort of Territorial Army system would be ideal, obviously, some agreed dispensation from professional commitments to allow for indenture of the able-bodied. No more than two weeks a year.

No Fitzwilliam, then. But there were other institutions, familiar and unfamiliar, at which I could throw myself, to see what would happen. Even so, it's the way of some institutions not actively to debar me but instead to admit me to a sort of vestibule or side porch, nominally indoors but with none of the attendant privileges. You could say the University had followed that sly pattern, since I had arrived to read Modern Languages but found out over time that the element of the course involving residence abroad was being scrapped in my case, without my being consulted. The authorities threw up their hands. My 'alma mater' had never really planned to suckle me and withdrew the breast sharpish. I hardly got a glimpse of it before it was tucked decorously away.

The fixed element of my day was an expedition to my bank to withdraw money. I had £1.54 on me, in the form of three fifty-pence coins and a brace of two-pence pieces. I would need more of it. More rhino. More spondulicks. More bread. This was hollow-seeming money, the decimalised currency that made calculations easier but had no roots in deep memory. Its copper coins were neither big nor small, neither a substantial disc like the old penny nor diminutive like the farthing, that elven financial instrument, Queen Mab's preference when she must pay the final demand for her gas bill or be cut off altogether. The lumpen seven-sided fifty-pence coin seemed a poor substitute for the ten-shilling note, printed in the reddy-brown of dried blood. I remembered when breaking into a ten-bob note seemed to open a crack in the cosmos at large. It sounds as if I'm being nostalgic, which I'm not, since both sets of objects, both forms of cash, are equally bloody inconvenient from my point of view. Those weren't better times, it's just that we didn't know how bad they were, and that helps.

I wasn't confident that the manageress would make good on her promise of a free meal, but she did so in some style, sending Hettie to place a saucer in front of me. On it lay a numbered sheet of paper torn from a pad with nothing on it but the imprint of a lipstick kiss. This charming flourish would have made a good ending for a scene in a film. Cut and print! Unfortunately I had to make my exit, which was necessarily as ungainly as my entry, accompanied by embarrassed scraping of chairs and calls from Hettie and Whyvonne of 'Goodbye! Come again!' that needed to be repeated as my departure prolonged itself, apparently forever. I wish people would just go about their business. There's no need to stand and stare. Surely it's obvious that I've left rooms before? If not to the satisfaction of others then at least to my own. Look away. Get back to your own lives. That's all I'm trying to do myself.

I storm the vestibule

Hettie, having said goodbye, had to catch up with me and help me with the door and the step. By the time I reached the car I had the impression that there were people waving hankies and wishing me *Bon Voyage* from every window in Lensfield Road.

I wanted to be noticed until I suddenly didn't, and this peculiarity makes me, well, just like everyone else, really. It's an inexhaustible source of ordinariness. My devotion to my guru, though I was having a bit of a rocky time of it in the early 1970s, is very much an attraction of opposites. Ramana Maharshi, who must have believed less than anyone in the reality of what was in front of him, nevertheless submitted to every rule, somehow turning it inside out in the process. At the time of his last illness he went on giving audiences to anyone who turned up, and when his disciples (though they sound like a meddling bunch and should perhaps be called something more like 'indisciples') tried to clear the chamber so that he could rest he followed the crowd out, saying that if the room was to be emptied he obviously couldn't stay there. In his quiet way he out-Jesused Jesus, rendering unto Cæsar the things that were Cæsar's so relentlessly that Cæsar was left looking like a proper twit. Compliance with a trace of irony must be the best way of responding to whatever Maya throws at you, though I can't claim to manage it often.

My bank, like my doctors' surgery, was in Trinity Street. 'My bank' is one of those formulas, 'my death' being another, where the possessive adjective loses all force. Funds held in my name were administered, and small cash sums watchfully issued, at the Trinity Street branch of Williams & Glyn's Bank, near the heart of the ancient university, where the great treasure-barges of learning were moored side by side.

44

The gangplanks and walkways that connected these floating palaces with dry land were precarious as a matter of principle. Cobbles were a favourite material, higgledy-piggledy stumps of snapped-off battlement that were effective deterrents in their own right to any dreams I might harbour of boarding. Sometimes the massive wooden door of one of these flagship colleges would have a smaller door set into it, for the admission of favoured individuals rather than whole processions of the entitled, but even then the suggestion of welcome was ambiguous. The smaller door seemed to invite a smaller visitor – but the inset door never went down all the way to the ground. Blocking any possible entry on my part there was always a low wall, only the height of a skirting board, a six-inch hurdle that might as well have been made of barbed wire with a high voltage passing through it.

St John's, Trinity, (Gonville &) Caius and King's all basked in their own impregnability. My own college was less scrupulously defended, so that with a concerted effort I had been able to storm the vestibule.

I didn't get a special kick out of banking so centrally, though my dealings with William & Glyn's were fraught with dark intentions, on both sides as I have to admit. In those days bank managers were not approachable figures. They had real authority, and took a fierce joy in saying No. It was understood, even by less distinguished concerns than Williams & Glyn's, that opening a bank account was a privilege and not a right. Cheque books weren't simply thrown into the baying mob. Applicants had to give proofs of their substance and responsibility before the magic booklet of watermarked promises-to-pay was handed reverently across. Williams & Glyn's Bank was definitely a top-people's bank in my estimation, a sort of subaltern Coutts, and I had taken it for granted they were out of my league.

Then at the Societies Fair in my first undergraduate year there was a representative of the bank offering accounts to new students, to general scepticism. Why would a bank be so rash? Pete from my college staircase, who pushed me, rather erratically, round the Societies Fair, said he had heard you needed a hundred thousand pounds to play with before they would let you get so much as a sniff of an account.

We had no idea about money, children of privilege who didn't even know it. We thought we were being thrown a lifeline by the hated forces of capitalism, not noticing the lifeline took the shape of a hook.

It didn't occur to us that from a bank's perspective we were larval herring highly likely to grow into plump adult fish saturated with fiscal oil, major future earners amply justifying the tiny risk taken by those who offered to stand surety for us – who could in any case apply pressure on our colleges or our parents if there was trouble. Since people don't change banks except for pressing reasons, a fair proportion of these tiddlers snapped up by Williams & Glyn's would stay in the revenue tank, fattening up steadily till retirement and beyond.

I dare say we were all fooled by the impression of solidity that no bank can dispense with, whether it is upright or crooked as an institution. Could any institution sound more soporifically trustworthy than one called Williams & Glyn's? After 'Williams & Glyn's' any fair-minded person would expect 'male voice choir' or 'Methodist funerals' as readily as 'Bank'. It could hardly have sounded more Welsh if it was playing the harp with a leek. In fact Williams & Glyn's was itself freshly minted in the year it solicited our custom, product of a merger between two subsidiaries of the Royal Bank of Scotland. That's not how you build trust! Or perhaps that's exactly how you build trust, by lying early and often.

My career prospects weren't in the same category as my fellows', as the bank must have known rather better than I did at the time. I was small fry and would never get any bigger, but then again, it wasn't a necessary precaution for me to be plucked thrashing out of the bank's net. It isn't always worth the bother of throwing the little ones back.

As for my own base motives: I was pitifully keen to show I was different from Mum and Dad. To show who(m)? Myself, I suppose. I would have opened an account with Beelzebub himself rather than follow their example. Better the Lord of the Flies, better the Father of Lies, than dreary, suburban old Lloyd's. Never mind that Lloyd's also sounded Welsh! It's true that Williams & Glyn's waved an additional temptation in front of me. There's no getting away from the glamour of an ampersand, and every cheque book I was issued, every cheque I laboriously made out and signed, announced in faint microscopic repetitions of the bank's name the distinction of my financial arrangements. I suppose those magical markings were also a way of making forgers work for their money.

Perhaps in the end we were exploiting each other quite satisfactorily, the bank and I. I got my private snobbish pleasure from our association, with a little typographical cherry on top, while the bank, without making anything much from me in the way of profit, could still leave a favourable impression with the world in general by making sure that junior employees knew my name and helped me to gain access to the premises. Perhaps there was some sort of Identikit portrait of me behind the counter, alongside the various villains, the conmen and the outright robbers, with a caption encouraging them to greet me as if I was the sprightly uncle they never knew they had.

I'm not sure exactly when Williams & Glyn's introduced cash machines. If they had come in when I was a freshman then I took no notice, though there was certainly one outside the Trinity Street branch in 1973. In the beginning it wasn't something that was likely to attract my interest, this highly technological opportunity to practise in combination three things that don't come easily to me even separately: standing up, typing and fighting a passer-by for possession of a banknote, all in the teeth of an embittered Cambridge wind.

Safe passage of baked goods

The area in front of Trinity College was crowded, and a guide was pointing upwards to something on its façade above the gate. I didn't need to follow the finger to know that he was indicating the chair-leg installed in place of his missing sceptre in the grip of a stone figure of Henry VIII, a high-spirited prank carried out while he was an undergraduate by the heir to that very throne, clambering up with a smile of confident mischief while the porters politely looked the other way. The crowd of tourists being given this history lesson tittered with the same politeness, while the lesson I learned, one more time, was that mobility is wasted on the able-bodied.

It wasn't simply the crowdedness of the pavement that made progress difficult but the sense of multiple tempos at odds with each other. There was a stream of the city's residents more or less trotting on their errands, with more than one matron dangling a white cardboard box by its cradle of ribbon, a box with *Fitzbillies* written diagonally across it in a typeset version of flowing script. Such ladies

47

will take extreme measures to protect their cakes against impact, glaring at any presumptuous wheelchair-user who might threaten the safe passage of baked goods. Tourists by contrast are either being herded at high speed through the glories of the town by their guides or making sudden stops to consult maps or entreat passers-by for directions. Every now and then one of them would notice me. Sometimes people beam at me so fiercely it's almost frightening. Beyond a certain level of intensity goodwill from a stranger takes on a demoniac tinge.

There were always people who smiled, stood aside and made a gracious sweeping gesture to indicate that I had right of way and was at liberty to proceed. It was as if they anticipated a sudden burst of speed from me or wildly flailing movements. The real worry, the frown that lurked behind the smile, was perhaps that a spark of misfortune would leap the gap unless they stood well clear. Sometimes too, after a moment, there would be a faint double twitch of the curled fingers to beckon me forward, perhaps not even a conscious movement but still sending a second message to undermine the first. *Get a move on. I don't have all day.*

Most of the time the eyes of tourists are raised and fixed on the middle distance, which is fine unless I happen to be straight in front of them just then, selfishly hogging their collective blind spot. Then I'm under the hooves when the herd moves on.

The atmosphere inside the bank was quite a contrast, relaxed and almost village-like in the absence of undergraduates. To judge by the conversations I could hear, everyone in the bank, on either side of the counter, was just back from a holiday or about to leave on one. The holiday mood was inaccessible to me that Thursday morning, and I tried to feel businesslike as I took out ten pounds. This was in reality a *dies non*, a day on which no business could be transacted, and the first of a series of such non-days to be got through before I could find safe harbour. I wasn't going about my business but going about a lack of business. Just filling in time – it's a revealing phrase, that, one that imagines the hours as so many potholes to be made good.

I asked for a fiver and five single notes. Large denominations perform differently from small ones, it's a fact. Large sums are viscous and conserve their energy, small ones tend to dribble away through the cracks, the classic text on the subject being *The Million-Pound Note*. On the small scale of my financial dealings, of course, the difference was submicroscopic, or to put it in homœopathic terms, highly significant. True, there was little chance of people rubbing their eyes when granted a glimpse of my fiver, rushing to offer me unlimited credit while dazzled by the glare of its aura, but those single fingers of specie would make their way through the world differently from the consolidated fist of a fiver.

It was eleven thirty, too early to think of seeing a film, though I was relying on the Arts Cinema to mop up a couple of hours in the afternoon. My digestion was dealing incredulously with the biggest breakfast it had encountered for years. My guts expressed both resentment and exhilaration, along the lines of an understaffed fire station called on to tackle a major blaze. This is what they signed up for! Enzymes that knew meat only by rumour were learning from scratch how to crack its codes.

Metabolism is a strange old economy. You eat, you drink, and expended nutrients are replenished, simple as that – except it's nowhere near as simple as that. Satiety is preabsorptive, which is a curious state of affairs when you think about it. Our bodies tell us we are full and can afford to stop eating long before the nourishment has been processed. There are mechanoreceptors in the stomach that register pressure and the fact of fullness. There are chemoreceptors in the small intestine alive to the presence of sugars and amino acids. Neither of these fully accounts for the phenomenon. The mouth seems to play a crucial part, passing on to the brain the good news that eating is in progress. The brain triggers a temporary rise in the levels of blood glucose, accompanied by a sharp reduction in the sensation of hunger. Experiments have shown this happens even when what is in the mouth, for instance a solution of saccharine, has no nutritional value at all. It doesn't matter – emergency funds of energy are dispensed from the vaults just the same, long before the incoming cheque can be cleared. As I say, it's a strange old economy.

And what should I do while my digestion purred and sputtered? At the moment it was a toss-up between a visit to the Botanical Gardens, much loved, completely familiar, or to the Catholic church, which I only really knew from the defective sound of its clock-chime, something that had infused my sleep (and occasionally dissolved it) during every night I had spent in Downing. A little light œcumenical prayer in spiritually nourishing surroundings, leading by stages to an afternoon nap without loss of pious pretence. This was clearly a suitable programme for the middle parts of a day that gave no sign of being finite. Either institution would be able to provide the facilities when I felt the need of what was surely in the works, the excretion-event of a lifetime.

The church got my vote since the Bot would wait. Its welcome would never wear out. Perhaps it's the Bot that is entitled to the status of *alma mater* in my case, if any institution actually wants to claim me as a suckling.

A boom preceded by its echo

I have to hand it to the Catholic Church in general, or perhaps The Church of Our Lady and the English Martyrs in particular. I was made welcome. The wheelchair was hauled indoors without complaint and I was given a guided tour. Pamphlets were made available. Anecdotes were passed on. I learned for instance that the building of the church was funded by a single person, at first sight an unlikely benefactor. She had been a ballet dancer in Paris and at Drury Lane before marrying a grandee, whose wealth she went on to inherit. A happy ending, though no one funds the building of an entire church because there's nothing keeping them awake at night, now do they?

It was accepted at Our Lady and the English Martyrs that I was simply sightseeing. I was simply a 'young man' who was 'taking an interest' in a landmark of the city he knew only from a blinkered University standpoint. I was beetled up the steps by a collective of friendly ladies, and then left tactfully alone – just the sort of solitude I like, in fact, where someone comes to check on you every three minutes.

There was no service in progress, but I was disappointed by the absence of any lingering smell of incense. Shouldn't there be spectral curtains of scented fumes hanging in the transept, Mass or no Mass? In my ignorance I assumed that holy smoke was constantly being puffed out on church premises, but in my unwashed state I was probably making the only aromatic contribution to the atmosphere of the building.

Since then I've learned that it's Anglo-Catholics who are the real bells-and-smells merchants. Any that actually convert are likely to feel let down by the bareness of Catholic ceremonial. It's like a flamboyant transvestite winning the right to live as a woman, and then finding that the wardrobe has been emptied of everything but tweedy suits and twinsets.

Cambridge is full of ample spaces, but they weren't my natural habitat. The Hall in Downing had been relatively intimate, and filled up with the clattering roar of a student body feeding itself without stopping talking. Otherwise I had been in the Senate House twice, once for matriculation and once for the dutiful expression of student unrest, and that was about it. I experienced the quiet of Our Lady and the English Martyrs as anything but soothing. The calm seemed deceptive, as in the opening sequences of a horror film.

When I closed my eyes, the sense of space collapsed immediately. It was as if I was listening to a radio play set in a church, with sound-effects men winking and grinning at each other in a cramped studio as they produced the noise of a chair-leg scraping against a stone, a hassock thudding to the floor, the organist during his practice negotiating the hairpin bends of something that aspired to the ideal of melody but kept falling away. I pondered the curious acoustic that accompanies the closing of a church door, a boom preceded by its echo. When I opened my eyes the church materialised very promptly – everything 'came back' – but I wasn't deceived. This was partly a consequence of sleep deprivation but mainly an insight into the workings of Maya. There's no point in talking about the special-effects department of Maya, because that's the only department there is. It's the whole show.

I had been confirmed in 1962, while at the Vulcan School (A Boarding School for the Education and Rehabilitation of Severely Disabled but Intelligent Boys), by the Bishop of Reading. There was a certain amount of pressure at school to sign up for the sacrament, presumably because piety piled on top of disability multiplied our magnetism when it came to raising funds. I can't speak for anyone else, but I certainly didn't plump for the sacrament of confirmation because of the present it was hinted we would get if went through with it. The present turned out to be a copy of the Book of Common Prayer, signed *Eric Reading*, which wasn't a disappointment to me anyway. I hadn't realised that according to protocol bishops take the names of their dioceses cognominally. I just thought it rather wonderful that someone with the surname of Reading had fulfilled what must have been a lifelong ambition in the church, by presiding over the diocese that happened to share his name.

As worn by Father Brown

My upbringing was Christian, and I dare say my head is still full of pious remnants. In an emergency there's no guarantee that what pops into my head is a mantra rather than the Lord's Prayer. But from the moment I started using my thoughts to make a little headway in the world it seemed to me very unsatisfactory, full of murky and contradictory doctrine. 'Who Art in Heaven'? So you're not here then. 'Hallowed Be Thy Name'? So you have a name. Funny, I'm trying to shed mine. 'Thy Kingdom Come'? So it doesn't exist yet. 'Thy Will Be Done'? So you have a will, do you? Funny, I'm trying to shed that too. The rhythms are soothing because familiar, but the whole thing is a minefield of untenable assumptions about divinity. I don't deny it has a certain sedative power, but it won't do for grown-up worship. It's a teddy bear of a prayer, and although there are people who go through adult life dragging their soft toys along I was doing my best not to be one of them.

At one point, eyes closed, I thought I heard steps approaching the wheelchair and marking a graceful pause before moving on. There was a sound of fabric in motion, and somehow I knew that the whispering skirt in question was male in character. I didn't come near enough to the surface of consciousness to open my eyes, and so I missed the chance to see for myself an item that I'd only come across in the pages of *A Portrait of the Artist as a Young Man* and perhaps in G. K. Chesterton, as worn by Father Brown. A soutane. Unless Maya was positively in overdrive and crashing her gears, the priest of Our Lady and the English Martyrs was paying a polite house call on this pilgrim sojourning, if not stalled, on his premises.

When I opened my eyes, there was a cup of tea and a biscuit within reach (more or less), laid out on a little portable folding table which had been erected in tactful silence. Who put that there? Thanks very much.

Elevenses was as much refreshment as I could hope for there and then, though my spiritual batteries were becoming dangerously depleted after so long disconnected from the trickle-charger of meditation. My next port of call was the Bot, which had become a sort of second home for me during my student years. It was open to the public and (more important) free, and full of offstage places where Minis could be parked and fuss made of their drivers. One particular worker had made me her particular pet. I don't mind being made a pet of, every now and then, as long as I get to decide who does it and don't altogether give up the right to bare my teeth. I don't exactly set out to enlist people as helpers, but though the Old Testament isn't much of a guide to behaviour I've found the idea of casting your bread upon the waters and having it return to you tenfold rather appealing (though Lord knows where 'tenfold' crept in from – it's not in Ecclesiastes). I'm not in the least systematic about it, but I've learned to give the bread a good old buttering first, and then it sometimes comes back with jam.

Celia was Australian and always wore shorts, long and sturdy shorts, possibly hiker's shorts if such garments exist, very different in ethos from the hot pants that were enjoying a furious vogue in 1973, and looking alluring on barely one pair of legs in ten. I'm hardly a connoisseur of women's clothes, but my low standing in the world has made me a captive audience of skirts and shorts, of waistbands and the nervous smoothing-down of cardigans. I find it fascinating that so many women with knock knees wear outfits that advertise them when fashion dictates, and if I'd hung on to my old Box Brownie I would have had quite a rogues' gallery of them by 1973. The great glory of the Box Brownie was that I could hold it some way from my eye, as I must, and still see the prospective photo nicely framed in the viewfinder. The moment it was considered an advance to have the user's eye glued up against the body of the device then technology kicked me out of the camera club – and I'd left my Box Brownie behind at 'home' in Bourne End before the family ructions that made it impossible to ask for it back.

During the winter months Celia's calves, any tan long since leached away, took on a blueish tinge. Gooseflesh seemed to be her skin's natural state, but I understood that it was existentially impossible for her to change her style of dress. Celia in long trousers and Celia in skirts were equally unthinkable, definitely different creatures from her despite the superficial resemblance. I don't think there was an ambiguity about gender at the root of her stubborn loyalty to shorts. More likely she was afraid of going native, returning to Alice Springs wan and tentative, addicted to crosswords and dark beer without fizz, her vocal cords turned plummy with exposure to cold and genteel ways. Some people assimilate to their surroundings on their travels but others positively condense their national identity. Celia was one of those. She didn't need to fear being swallowed up by plummy Pommy affectations.

She was instinctively caring towards other forms of life, something that is routinely called motherliness but is more of a gardener's reflex to my way of thinking, even when its beneficiaries are fauna rather than flora. She had seen a fox at the Bot, for instance, in a very bad state, and had ground up mange pills and hidden them in honey sandwiches so that it shouldn't suspect her good intentions. After that it sought her out. She had tamed it, or (to look through the other end of the telescope) it had tamed her. She had trained it to trot right up to her, or to put it another way it had trained her to keep the honey sandwiches coming. Of course if you bring honey sandwiches for foxes for too long (she did try to be discreet) you end up resembling a lunatic rather than St Francis of Assisi.

An organism that differs from itself

Sometimes it happens that gardeners who are used to extreme conditions are a little bit patronising about the demure flora of our temperate zone, but Celia wasn't like that. She didn't feel that an organism which had flourished against the odds was more valuable than one that had been cosseted by its environment, and I had seen tears in her eyes when she described a bearded iris which had flowered in surprising localised hues of brown and cream. That's what in botany is called a 'sport'. Peel away the outside leaves of that word, its associations with being a good loser, its matey meaning in Australian slang, and you have a fascinating idea at its heart. An organism that thanks to a chance mutation generates a variation in one area. Is it putting the matter too strongly to say that this is an organism that differs from itself? Evolution, so amply theorised in animals, seems to work differently in plants, perhaps because their genetic material is so exposed, easily accessible to mutagenic sunlight, while we animals keep ours hidden darkly away. Evolutionary theory in all its ramifications is a disenchanting spell that brings its own mysteries with it. We bipeds find it shocking to imagine that rooted beings might have their own changeability, wily ways of moving without moving.

Celia never greeted the Mini with yelps of delight in the Dalmatian or red-setter style (though her colouring tended towards red setter), but she would reliably turn up soon after I arrived. Dalmatians are silly and red setters are flighty, and Celia was neither of those things. Still, there was the hint of a subtle lolloping in her welcome, as if I boosted her energy level as she reliably boosted mine. If I didn't see her at the Bot when I visited then it meant that she wasn't working that particular day. It was as if she was attuned to the engine note, as dogs learn to be, but didn't want me to feel under siege. In practice I can take quite a lot of affectionate welcome before I feel the slightest bit intruded on, though it has to be said that dogs are no respecters of wheelchairs. They need to have their goodwill kept within bounds. Only the very small ones are polite, rendered so not by temperament but by the shortness of their legs and the consequent impossibility of overstepping.

There's nothing gardeners like more than a good old chat about pests and parasites. In the past Celia and I had discussed our worries about *Pythium* and possible strategies for use against it. People are always talking about animal attraction, and I don't dispute that such a thing exists, but most relationships make more sense as a matter of vegetable attraction and the progressive intertwining between soundlessly rustling tendrils of affinity.

Celia provided my first experience of that curious phenomenon HRT, though it wasn't called that then. It hadn't even been identified by sociophonetics, for the very good reason that the relevant subdiscipline hadn't come into existence, and I wonder if Celia wasn't an early case, possibly even a carrier. It seems quite wrong to stigmatise someone who was so consistently kind to me as a sort of Typhoid Mary of the High Rising Terminal, but her case may have some historical interest. This might be the first recorded instance of an invasive species of intonation, the equivalent of the first *Sciurus carolinensis* setting its beady little eyes on the habitat of *Sciurus vulgaris*. The original grey squirrel jinking with ominous intent towards the doomed dreys of the red. When Celia made what was meant to be a statement of fact, even a defiant assertion such as 'Australian wine is good already? And it's going to be great?', it reeked of uncertainty. When she asked an actual question, on the other hand, it was stripped of the customary upward cadence. I suppose she needed somehow to distinguish the two very different types of speech act. She resorted – 'How are *you*' – to a strange downward curl of the voice. I'm sure there's a way of notating such things in print. There must be. A struck-through question mark? No, that's hopeless. In bold? No better. Though for her actual questions, which didn't sound like questions, would it not be legitimate to borrow the upside-down question mark from Spanish¿, though using it for a different purpose?

Flexing its nonseptate filaments

Some entities seem actively amused by efforts to eradicate them, and I'm no longer referring to the recalcitrance of High Rising Terminal. *Pythium* is one of those stubborn ones, flexing its nonseptate filaments, mustering its motile zoospores to induce damping-off and root disease. It lurks for years in soil and plant refuse. When you're up against *Pythium* it isn't a gunfight but a game of chess whose most likely end is stalemate. The struggle is endless, with seedlings subtly undone by this relentless fungoid, eaten away from the very beginnings of their lives, reduced to sludge under the surface of the soil or else doomed to topple over in rot mere days after their emergence.

Celia preached a gospel of calm, stressed the value of composted tree bark and the importance of avoiding the overcrowding of seedlings. She warned against the 'legginess' caused by insufficient light, open invitation to pathogenic fungi. I tried to match her expertise, passing on one tip that Dad had found useful: use pre-warmed water and make sure your drainage is up to snuff. A waterlogged seedling is a dead duck.

We exchanged this hard-earned knowledge with the cheerful fatalism that is the hallmark of the horticultural personality. I doubt if Celia, as a professional, needed any reminder about attending to proper drainage and avoiding unnecessary lowering of the temperature of seeds and seedlings by cold watering, but that wasn't important. Better that gardening lore be duplicated needlessly than not be passed on at all. We gardeners recognise each other not by a green thumb but by a brown one. Not everyone has the instinct to take the pulse of the soil, checking humidity as a matter of crucial importance.

Celia was only at the Bot on a temporary basis. She had travelled from Australia by sea, as many people still did, on some sort of cargo ship. She was the only passenger on it (and the only woman). They had stopped off at an out-of-the-way place called Whyalla, New South Wales, to take on some iron ore, where the local paper had seized the chance to interview her, plucky Aussie girl going to France to study viticulture and winemaking. Local papers are always pressing the same exhausted vintage, and in terms of local journalism Celia was a plump grape with some real juice in her.

The Suez Canal was in mothballs, of course, after the Six Day War, and so the journey took three months. They went round South Africa and broke down while battling terrific winds in the Roaring Forties. All this adventure made me feel that the only card I could play to match it, my trip to India before I arrived in Cambridge, was of low face value.

Celia insisted that I abandon all snobbery about Australian wine. It had a real future? It would be a world-beater? I probably thought Australian wine was all old-fashioned and sweet, like muscatel and frontignac, when it wasn't German-style riesling? I should forget all about the Aussie wine served in Earls Court from boxes on the bar – Bondi Bleach they called it, the white, and the red was Kangarouge. In fact I didn't need to have my mind wiped clean. It was aseptic. I was so ignorant that I lacked even the basic prejudices. I was a hopeless case.

Celia had chosen a bad time to learn the secrets of French winemaking on its home ground. Diplomatic relations between Australia and France were close to breakdown. Mail delivery was unreliable even when not formally suspended. These administrative problems had played havoc with Celia's paperwork, and paperwork turned out to be something on which the French authorities were extremely keen. She had to postpone her course, and since she didn't have the right to work in France she found a temporary job in the U.K. This job. So looking at it from the broadest possible perspective, if France hadn't persisted in testing nuclear weapons in the Pacific, and if Australia hadn't mounted a case at the International Court of Justice, and if France hadn't ignored the verdict of the court . . . then I'd have had one less friendly presence to count on while I was living in my car. It was a nuclear-age version of the old saw about it being an ill wind that blows no one any good, in this case a tropical breeze laden with fallout. If an oppressive colonial power hadn't exploded warheads on Mururoa Atoll in French Polynesia then Celia would be learning about grape varieties in Bordeaux rather than discussing the menace of *Pythium*, before escorting me back to the Mini.

Celia had been very concerned when she realised I would be without a home of my own between Downing College and Mayflower House, but couldn't offer me a place to stay. 'I live up two flights of stairs?' she explained. By this time the difference between indicative and interrogative had been washed clean away, and I no longer knew whether my own voice should rise or fall at any given point in a sentence. The pitch and roll of her intonation had cost me my sea legs.

In my determination not to be a charity case I had given Celia the impression that I would have a roof over my head, and this could be defended as truthful. Cars have roofs, of course they do. How else could they have roof racks? Now to give more detailed reassurance I said I was staying round the corner from the Hobson Monument, which was also true since I parked the Mini off Lensfield Road. The monument was mere feet from the parking spot where I had spent the previous night, harassed by an unwelcoming neighbour though consoled by the love in the eyes of his dog.

Thomas Hobson was a Cambridge worthy of the sixteenth and seventeenth centuries, whose improvements to the city's water supply are commemorated by the Hobson monument, though his name has become proverbial in a different context. I explained Hobson's Choice to Celia – 'Hobson's Choice' being that you take what you're given. Hobson in his livery stable didn't let his customers have their choice of horses, though he had plenty of them. You had to have the one from the stall by the door, and so Hobson's Choice had come to mean any choice that wasn't really a choice.

Then Celia explained Hobson's Choice right back at me. 'I went on a guided tour? A walking tour?' All the way to Great Shelford, near the spring where the water rises. She took an interest since the Conduit itself passed along one edge of the Bot as it flowed along Trumpington Street. From the walking tour she learned that the reason Hobson didn't allow his customers to choose a mount wasn't just to be difficult. If he did, his customers would always pick the animal known to be the fastest, which rapidly became exhausted. Accepting Hobson's choice meant that you might not get a fast horse but you were guaranteed a rested one.

When I had parked the Mini off Lensfield Road that first night I had no conscious knowledge of the closeness of the Conduit, mere feet away, nor of Hobson's Memorial being round the corner. Any awareness of them would be framed according to the wryly pessimistic principle I thought I knew, so that I was choosing a place whose associations made a mockery of choice. Now the same place had shifted in its overtones, and so had the principle, so as to suggest the benevolent withholding of short-sighted options. I was learning that there is more than one way of having no choice. Much apparent fixity permits a wobble.

I don't think we need go so far as to imagine that the guru was speaking through Celia, though it's never quite a matter of ventriloquism. The words of the guru float on the breath of the mundane speaker. They emerge from him (or from her) without being imposed from outside. It is a consensual visitation.

It made sense of a sort that Celia, a relatively recent arrival in Cambridge, should be better informed about the city than I was. I too was an incomer, but my relative seniority meant I could make a more authoritative approximation to the native's entitlement of ignorance – like those born-and-bred Londoners (and proud of it) who have never stepped inside St Paul's (and are also proud of that). There comes a time when not having paid a world-famous building a visit is almost a mark of distinction. Had I set foot inside King's College Chapel, for instance? I kept meaning to. I keep meaning to. It'll wait.

When we got back to the Mini I could smell something new, and with my sense of smell blunted by my cold it could only be a strong odour. Disinfectant. I had managed to empty my pee bottle when I left the café that morning, but its lingering aroma had been bothering me all day. Now it had been rinsed and made fresh. The debris that had accumulated in the Mini during its and my student years, when it became some sort of undersized communal taxi, had been disposed of. I doubt if I had heard of the word 'valeting' at that point, applied to a car or anything else, but it has the right associations of Jeeves-like suavity and self-effacement. Bless you, Celia! I cringed with the embarrassment of being in need of such a favour, but it made a difference that it had been done with supreme tact, something approaching legerdemain.

My waste had been conjured away. If only the trick could be repeated indefinitely . . . Abracadabra. Pee gone! Alacazam. Poo gone! Sign me up to apprentice membership of the Magic Circle – I enclose my stamped, self-addressed envelope, not risking a first-class stamp because I'm not getting my hopes up.

Dragging their C-value down

After I had started the engine she came round to the window and started talking into my blind spot. Not my deaf spot, obviously, and I could hear her perfectly well, but it's bad manners to stare straight ahead of you just because it's what your body demands, so I wriggled round as best I could. 'I have a riddle for you, John?' she was saying. 'Something for you to think about? Why should *Rhizanthella gardneri* be the national flower of Australia¿ That's *Rhizanthella gardneri* – I've written the name down for you?' She waved a slip of paper in front of my eyes and then tucked it into the breast pocket of my shirt. Just where I can't reach it. Then she banged on the roof of the Mini, as if I was a rally driver and she had just changed my tyres. She often had that effect on me anyway, giving me fresh traction on the day, and I liked having her riddle to ponder. It's good for the brain circuitry to be shorted out from time to time, not to get too used to the illusion of knowing answers. All I knew about the given subject area was that the official national flower of Australia was in fact the Golden Wattle, *Acacia pycnantha*.

I decided to inspect this Hobson's Monument that had perhaps exercised a magnetic effect on my decisions. Normally I think it's good manners for cars to restrict themselves to the road surface, but the pavement was wide, not an easy expanse for me to cross unaided and by the same token able to accommodate the Mini without inconvenience to pedestrians, so I mounted it and drew up by the railings. I felt safe enough from criticism – people don't exactly fall over themselves to say Yes to me, but they think twice before saying No. The monument looked like an enormous white chess piece, most closely resembling a rook thanks to the effect of crenellation produced by the alternating coats of arms, cherubs and heraldic beasts (lion and unicorn) mounted at the top. In the English temperament – I know I've read this somewhere – the lion of common sense is matched by the unicorn of fancy.

At least one of the cherubs had a visible willy and was carrying some sort of vessel, perhaps an ewer, which would make sense (the ewer not the willy) in a monument honouring an improvement in water supply. There was a rounded object installed as a finial that I eventually identified as a pineapple. Isn't that the symbol of hospitality? It seemed to me that the case was made and well made. If ley lines, the invisible alignments that either marked ancient sacred sites or brought them into being, could imprint themselves on human awareness over the millennia, dry conduits through which the chthonic energies flowed, then this thumping great monument, with a pineapple throbbing on its top like a landing signal, had certainly affected my choice of a parking and sleeping place on the previous night.

In mid-afternoon, refreshed by Celia's talk and kind attentions, I went to the Arts Cinema. I didn't much care what was showing, in fact it was their toilets I mostly had need of. A breakfast bigger than any meal I was used to had first stunned and then accelerated the digestive rhythms, and I hadn't gone short on liquids either.

'I'm afraid Granddad's been caught short.' Is that what has happened, or has the sanitary porcelain that would meet his needs migrated out of his reach? If so I feel for Granddad, and I'm quietly confident he would feel for me. Continence isn't purely a physical matter. There are other variables.

A little part of the brain is permanently thinking, 'Where can I go, when I need to?' but if your body conveys you smoothly to wherever it is you want to be then the urinary cortex (I've just made that up) can shrink almost to nothing. If on the other hand there is an obstacle course placed between you and any socially acceptable receptacle, then bladder preoccupation can come to dominate your mental activity. My bladder was in its pomp, a remarkably elastic organ taking quiet pride in its distensibility – these at least were muscles I could rely on – but even so there were limits.

Equations don't explain everything, and I have no special fondness for them, but in this area formulating things algebraically is a real help. C (continence) equals M multiplied by PF, where M represents Mobility and PF the proximity of facilities. So C would have a similar value for an able-bodied person wandering the streets of a strange town as it would for a disabled person in his home equipped with the proper amenities – unless the able-bodied person simply had a piss against a wall, which in algebraic terms would be, I don't really know, but in human terms would be cheating. On the other hand an able-bodied person like the ones who undertook the King Street Run (eight pints in an hour at eight different pubs, with a ban on urinating) were dead set on dragging their C-value all the way down to zero.

If those days of homelessness seem stubbornly unreal to me now, it's only because they were unreal then. Maya was showing her hand, and I should have taken the opportunity of seeing right through her once and for all, but I went on trying frantically to keep up on a treadmill that I had built in the first place. One more opportunity to grasp the nettle of the unreal, and I was too busy thinking about the best environment for a bowel movement to take advantage of it.

I punted myself along Arts Cinema passage to the box office, though Dad preferred the word 'guichet' for such retail outlets, not so much because he was cosmopolitan as because he liked to baffle the world, and particularly Mum. I disliked the affectation but loved the word, as perhaps he knew I would. The glass of the box office counter started at waist level, but that's not where my waist is, even when it isn't artificially lowered by being in a wheelchair. The young man behind the glass (in term time the guichet was mainly staffed by students, and maybe this was one such creature, oversummering) peered forward and blushed when he saw me. There's a remarkably small variety of expression available to the human facial muscles, and perhaps my angle of vision, looking upwards, militates against the perception of nuance. Even so it's surprising that the proud and eager look meaning 'At last my chance to make a real difference to the life of a fellow-citizen!' should in its lineaments so much resemble the one that means Here Comes Trouble.

Then the young man's face changed and he beamed at me. 'Hold on, I think I've got a note about you.' He rummaged briefly and produced in triumph a slip of paper. 'We have to build you up in your seat with cushions, don't we?'

Only if you want me to see the screen.

People certainly seem to enjoy having written instructions and the comfort of knowing they have a dispensation from making decisions of their own.

'And does your piece of paper say anything about helping me downstairs to the loo?'

He turned the paper over and sang out 'Yup' very cheerfully. 'When do you want to go?'

'No time like the present.'

This was all going remarkably smoothly. The phone next to him rang, and he dealt with the caller's needs by the ruthless expedient of picking up the receiver and putting it right down again. 'Clare!' he shouted.

'What is it?' came a voice from a distant point behind him.

'I'm taking my break. Mind the wicket, will you?'

'All right,' the voice answered in a faintly resentful sing-song.

'She'll be fine,' the young man explained, though I wasn't worried. 'We're quiet today.'

Then he swooped on me and swept me up out of the wheelchair. I didn't have time to give him instructions – oral rather than written – about putting the brakes on first, and the chair trundled backwards at a fair pace to bump, without any great force admittedly, against the wall. If I had a pound for every time that has happened . . . actually

I'd still have to watch the pennies, so let's not let things get out of proportion.

When it comes to giving me a carry, people (by which I usually mean young or youngish men) take one of two approaches: human forklift or ambulant hug. The human forklift, in which one arm supports my back and the other goes under my legs, gives me a view of my porter and a slice of the world through which I'm travelling. It looks a bit melodramatic, as if I'd just been dug out of the rubble somewhere and was being rushed to get medical treatment, but it gets the job done, and though I can never relax when I'm being carried up or down a flight of stairs (it's funny, being dropped even once can bring on a state of tension that never quite goes away) at least this position means that the person doing the carrying has an unobstructed view. The ambulant hug is much more intimate, with the intermingling of breath it brings, and I certainly prefer it for short journeys on the flat. Over greater distances it can become claustrophobic, and changes of level are very unrelaxing indeed, especially if I can feel tremors of uncertainty or tiredness in the body whose choices are currently overriding mine.

The rapidly spreading bloodstain

The young man from the guichet chose the ambulant hug and we set off down the stairs. I'm very aware that any person carrying me has both hands full, so that from the immediate perspective of our transit between floors the architect need not have bothered with installing a handrail or banister. As things stand there is nothing to impede or cushion a fall. My life was in his hands and my heart in my mouth.

There was definitely the sensation of a melting between us, something that I've often noticed when the masculine defences have been sidestepped. It's touch that does it, touch sustained enough to exceed the duration of handshakes and even conventional hugs, touch able to establish a shared boundary. Heat is more easily conserved by the amalgamated organism, as the mirage of separateness dissipates. Either method of 'giving me a carry' is likely to achieve this welcome state. The ambulant hug raises temperatures faster than the human forklift, but in both cases physical closeness readily takes on a tinge of the sensual.

My porter and I were both lightly elated when he put me down at the bottom of the stairs, congratulating ourselves on our safe passage between levels before we progressed to the toilet itself.

I glanced at a dark mark on his shirt, and he looked down too, with the sort of dismay gunslingers show in films, raising a disbelieving hand to the rapidly spreading bloodstain on a shirtfront that lets them know they've been shot. This stain was different, being brown and not red, since it was chocolate rather than blood showing in a little patch through the loose weave of his summer shirt. There wasn't a full bar of chocolate in his breast pocket, just a group of four squares roughly wrapped in foil and being hoarded, I imagine, for a slack afternoon moment, antidote to the energy dip that afflicts so many at that time of day. These sweet squares (we call them squares though their rectangularity leaps to the eye) had surrendered their solidity to a three-pronged attack, from the warmth of the day, from the thermal output of two bodies combined and from the pressure of the contact between them.

There were other processes at work. He glowed with the relief of not having dropped me, just as I glowed with the relief of not being dropped. The melting point of a young man is less predictable than the melting point of chocolate but this too had been reached. My escort's energy, far from dipping, was rising to a peak. Those aroused rectangles in his breast pocket were trembling on the edge of liquefaction, and I could detect a tingle of interest below his waist. Gingerly he pulled the misshapen chocolate out of the pocket that had failed to protect it and did his best to peel off the foil, which was partly embedded in it. It would be wrong to say that he broke the chocolate in two, since the notion of breaking belongs to a world of solids that this confection had left. He separated the chocolate into two parts and posted one of them into my astonished mouth. As he did so, and before he ate his own two Dalí quadrilaterals, he murmured the words 'Old Jamaica'. Normally I'm not a fan of being told what I'm eating or am going to eat. If anything it's one of my pet hates – let the taste buds find their own way, make their own discoveries. But this had the status of a special occasion, when the sensual impact of the chocolate with its (let's be frank) slightly rancid tang of rum and raisin coincided so precisely with the arrival of the words in my brain, perhaps in the immediately adjacent neural ganglion, as they delivered their message of soothing piratical nostalgia.

I didn't have any appetite as such, not after the monstrous transgression of breakfast, but then chocolate's secret is that it bypasses appetite, addressing greed directly. And greed I had.

It makes perfect sense that anyone who has acted as my porter should have a certain amount of power over me, even after I'm back on my own two feet (with crutch and stick helping out) or four wheels. It's much less obvious that I should have a residue of power over them. All I can say is that I have found it to be the case. The results are consistent. I wasn't shocked that this box office worker at the Arts Cinema (not founded by John Maynard Keynes as the Arts Theatre was, in case you're interested – the great man didn't have much time for the flicks) should waggle his chocolate-smeared fingers in my field of vision, and yes, I was slightly disappointed that he didn't in the end offer those clibby digits to me to be licked clean but did the job himself. There was perhaps a last-minute loss of nerve on his part. 'Clibby' is a lovely word I picked up from *Call My Bluff* on television, and I'm reasonably confident that 'sticky' was the real meaning of the word rather than one of the false definitions. It's not an adjective that has ever cropped up in conversation, but I'd hate to be committing a solecism even in the privacy of my own head.

That fleeting moment of affinity with its rum and raisin flavour was the high point of the adventure. Then we had to get me into a toilet cubicle before I burst. Even when I was established he understood that he would need to mount guard duty, since I couldn't lock myself in, though I encouraged him to wait a little way off. 'Do you have a match?' I called after him, and he called back, 'Sorry, I don't smoke,' as if I had only wanted to come down to the basement to sneak a ciggy. That wasn't at all what I meant. He and I might both feel the benefit of a lit match, with its eerie though nevertheless empirically provable ability to cover up shit smells, in such proximity to an imminent fæcal event. Perhaps it isn't a matter of covering the bad smells up so much as making them change key, shifting them towards a more appealing set of associations. I suspect the reason for this olfactory rhyme is an underlying correspondence. Digestion is a slow form of combustion, the ignition of a match-head a rapid one.

At CRX in Taplow, the hospital-cum-school where I spent the years after my belated diagnosis, my nickname had been Dropper, quite an accolade in an institution where few of use had better than rudimentary control over our bodies. Objects disobey me, always have. I couldn't pretend to be surprised, therefore, when I dropped the bum snorkel in that toilet cubicle at the Arts Cinema. I hadn't finished using it, so there was a little clump of loo paper held in its Perspex cleft, clean rather than soiled though these are nuances of indignity not easily calibrated. There was no room to manœuvre in the cubicle, and even in a less restricted space I wouldn't fancy my chances at retrieving the thing. I called out to my assistant in the corridor. 'Oh, Mr Porter!'

I couldn't help myself. *Oh, Mr Porter!* had been shown more than once at CRX, and I think I speak for my generation when I say that it's a film I could happily watch once a week. I needed to attract attention in the basement of a cinema – do I need apologise for resorting to a film reference? By the 1970s Will Hay's name was not exactly one to conjure with, and I realise that not every temporary guichet worker at the Arts is saturated in film knowledge, but pandering to ignorance is hardly a virtue.

He didn't hear me anyway. I had to resort to crooning, and then bellowing, 'I say! You there.' I tried to imagine my imperious Granny saying those words, which would have had the world come running if she spoke them, but her intonation was inimitable. Eventually he opened the door a crack and asked if I was ready for the return journey. I had to explain that I'd dropped something necessary for completion of the sit-down session. 'Oh dear – what is it?' There seemed no need to spell out the precise design and function of the bum snorkel. 'It's a device . . . and this is rather an awkward situation,' I said, meaning that I didn't want him to see me with the Velcro strip installed by Mum to secure my waistband (to say nothing of anything else) flapping in the summer breeze. Few people look their best with knickers at half-mast. 'Do you mind . . . if we pretend this is a party game?'

'I suppose not. What sort of game?'

What I had in mind was halfway between Hide and Seek and Blind Man's Buff. 'The sort where you close your eyes. If you keep your eyes closed and reach towards me at ground level, and I'll say Left A Bit, Right A Bit and so on until you find it.' In my childhood Dad had suggested that I might have a future on stage, as the unmoving character to whose tune everyone danced, but that was mainly a dig at his mother-in-law. In practice it isn't easy to exercise authority without physical power to back it up. 'I could say Warmer and Colder if you'd rather.'

'Can I ask you a question?'

'Of course.'

'Is going to the loo always such a carry-on for you?'

'Only when I drop my – device.' Under normal circumstances the script for *Carry On Snorkelling* was fairly uneventful, but then under normal circumstances I was on home ground, not evacuating solid waste extempore, as and when I could locate the necessary plumbing. I was beginning to think I had been unwise in not specifying the object I had dropped. What must he be thinking it was used for? 'I should explain about the device. It's just something I use for—'

'No need. I'm closing my eyes now. At least tell me it's not dirty.'

'It's not dirty, though I suppose you should wash your hands when we've found it, considering where it's been.' More possibility for dismay and confusion, as I realised too late. 'I mean the floor!'

'If you'd told me this morning that I'd be crawling around the toilet floor of the Arts with my eyes shut looking for a mystery object – am I getting close, by the way? – I'd have said you were mad.'

And if you'd told me I'd be sharing a melting rectanguloid of Old Jamaica with a stranger I'd have said the same thing. 'Left a bit, I mean your left. There it is!' A happy ending, or at least a happier one than if I'd had to retrieve the snorkel unaided, but I could hear the forced good cheer in my voice, as compared to the rapturous mood of such a short time before.

When chocolate cools down from the molten state it doesn't return to its previous shape but moulds to what surrounds it. The actual chocolate that had passed between us had of course been consumed, but the corresponding flow of mood followed similar laws. The rectangles, each with its inscription, in a machine-stamped version of a cursive hand – *Cadburys* or *Carnal Appetite* as the case might be – surrendered their identity. I had to resign myself to a sort of retrospective annihilation of the moment. Even with the benefit of aromatic smoke the bathroom visit would have compromised the earlier intimacy. There was no going back. The best I could do was to suggest the human forklift as the best technique to use for the return journey upstairs, not really for any inherent advantage but because I imagined this poor man feeling soiled by any repetition of full-body contact. At close quarters intensity of experience is more or less guaranteed, but the polarity can change in a moment from attraction to repulsion. The moment he had forklifted me back up to the top of the stairs I was convinced he couldn't wait to put me down, and yes, I understand the extra effort involved in going up rather than down, but my feeling was that something beyond physical tiredness was manifesting itself, a flinching deep inside the contact.

By the time I was set down again by the guichet I had almost forgotten that the admission fee of 30 pence entitled me to watch a film as well as to use the loo and have a tumultuous affair with a member of staff, its intoxication and disillusion telescoped into a small handful of minutes. A tiny fling whose epitaph could only be *Here Lies One Whose Name Is Writ In Chocolate.* Not quite the legend on Keats' tomb though I seem to remember he had something of a sweet tooth.

The first film I had seen as an undergraduate had been *Wild Strawberries*, and perhaps it was a piece of mischief on the part of the cinema programmers to schedule sombre and existentially troubled works to coincide with undergraduates at their most insecure. The film I saw that summer Thursday was also Swedish, but could hardly have been more different. You don't pull in the summer punters with films that set their face against escapism.

It seemed to be about two nice-looking people who ran away together. There was some pretty music playing, a piano and an orchestra carrying on civilised conversation in the forest. I was nicely built up on a firm cushion (I had trained the staff well) and there was no one of inordinate height in front of me. Really, nothing could be more conducive to dozing. I suspect the same was true even for cinemagoers with full tanks of vitality, no lack of sleep to make good. Sometimes the subtitles were too low on the screen for me to read, but there wasn't a great deal of dialogue and I was confident that I got the gist of the thing, which was that life is sad but beautiful.

The man of the couple started off with a trim and handsome beard, then shaved to reveal a handsome moustache and handsome cheeks. Later still he shaved to reveal a handsome upper lip. The woman ate some forest food that didn't agree with her – berries, mushrooms, who knows? She was sick. I don't mean that she ailed prettily but that she regurgitated the contents of her stomach, and I have to say that if there was an Oscar for the photogenic vomit then as far as I was concerned it was hers. It was in the bag. Watching a film is one of Ramana Maharshi's most eloquent analogies for life as a whole. Everyone in the audience is beguiled by the projected images, when for true self-understanding they should be mindful of the screen instead. I did my best to follow this guidance and reached not enlightenment but sleep. What is the place of the projector in this analogy? I wish I could ask him, or the diffusion of understanding from which he emanated. Perhaps for a moment I became at least one with the screen as time abolished itself and moments ceased to exist. A gunshot remade the world by waking me up. I believe there was another while I was still getting my bearings in the story. I'm afraid the two of them must have put an end to themselves, but I'm confident that there was no disruption to the lovely texture of the film.

The presence of metaphysical toxins

I shouldn't be flippant on this subject, since it's something I feel strongly about, and in fact converge in the starkness of my disapproval, to my surprise, on the prohibition of the mediæval Church. Not that suicide is a crime against the Holy Ghost, obviously. I feel about suicide the way old-fashioned parents used to feel about their children pulling faces – when the wind changes it'll stay that way. Those who take their own lives carry a grimace with them into the next existence. Suicide is a crime against your future lives, forcing you (by your own act) to dive away from your reunion with the white light of achieved nothingness and begin again in self-imposed ignorance of the way ahead. Suicide sends you not to Hell but to the back of the queue.

As the lights came up I noticed that an audience member in the next row was scraping the back of his hand across his face almost angrily. Men hate to cry. I can't say I mind it, as long as there is someone handy with a hanky, but on this occasion I didn't feel the slightest urge. My ducts were unvisited by tingling.

It was early evening, with darkness still hours away. I rejoined the Mini with the usual exhausting help and made my way over to Lensfield Road, stopping only to procure a meal. I sounded the horn outside a Chinese takeaway restaurant until a member of staff timidly approached. I sent him back for a menu and gave him my order. Egg Fu Yung, please, with fried rice and mixed vegetables. Thank you. I'm sorry, I can't tell you to keep the change, but I would if I could. The price of survival is vigilant budgeting.

The food was all rather sticky. Distinctly on the glutinous side. Snow peas should be left in the snow as far as I'm concerned, and bamboo shoots held back for the exclusive use of pandas. As I returned to my arbitrarily chosen sleeping-space I could hardly control the Mini. Any alert policeman would have tested my sobriety, and any properly calibrated breathalyser would have registered the presence of metaphysical toxins (exhaustion, self-disgust) in every breath I exhaled. Laboriously I squirmed the shoes from my feet and passed out in an atmosphere of disheartenment and monosodium glutamate.

At this distance it seems obvious that there were people who would have taken me in if appealed to. There was George, for instance, my closest acquaintance in the town's gay group, CHAPs (the Cambridge Homosexual Activism Project), almost as much of a misfit in that company as I was, marking time by his own account until he found his soulmate, not a term he would dare to have used in that company, with its well-developed and often-repeated critique of monogamy. CHAPs itself would not meet again till the beginning of the autumn term, despite its stated opposition to an academic bias, but I could have located George even without the benefit of a phone number. All I needed to do was track him down in the China and Glass department of Eaden Lilley (assuming he wasn't on holiday) and throw myself on his mercy. But though my resourceless state was a psychological rather than a physical fact, a fact is what it was.

There might have been others to contact in an emergency, but I had persuaded myself that there was nothing out of the ordinary about having to sleep in the Mini. It wasn't quite that there was nobody to play the part of Rilke's angels ('Who, if I called, would hear me among the angelic orders?'), more that I was unaccountably opposed to making a fuss. Anyone who counted as an acquaintance would have been concerned to solve the problem without thinking me in any way self-dramatising for mentioning it. I hadn't consciously taken on my father's stiff-upper-lip, take-it-on-the-chin attitude, any more than I'd consciously rejected my mother's, her yearning to be anointed the queen of misfortune.

I could strangle a Mandie

I had been rationing my medication, mainly so that I could feel in control of at least one aspect of my daily life. Warm weather takes the edge off pain anyway. My basic medication at the time was co-codamol. I know it's not a mild drug, certainly at the strength I was prescribed it, and I try not to be blasé about such things, but I certainly experienced it as mild. It produced the mood music of analgesia rather than effective pain relief. It masked pain the way an air freshener masks bathroom pongs. The faint euphoria co-codamol brought with it was a distraction rather than a pleasure, and mixed oddly with the after-effects of monosodium glutamate, which doesn't agree with me. What I would really have liked was a nice comforting Mandrax. To be exact, the words in my head were 'I could *strangle* a Mandie.'

In reserve I had a prescription for Drinamyl (dexamphetamine 5mg + amylobarbitone 32mg) which I could get made up at Peck's chemist on the corner of Trumpington Street. Peck's, opposite the Fitzwilliam (the museum not the college), well known as the junkie's chemist. Peck's dispensed for all the registered drug addicts. Still, I was trying to go easy on the pharmacopœia, and didn't want to be tempted by possession of the actual drug as opposed to the mere prescription. There's no doubt that it would have got me going the next morning, the Friday, even if I didn't have the proper accompaniment to hand – everyone agreed that it was most effective in combination with a cup (say 200 millilitres) of Nestlé Gold Blend.

It was summer, and the night was warm. I was not. I felt the cold particularly in my legs, not so much the thigh as the calf. A muscle between two ankylosed joints is like a furled sail, stirred by the loco-motive winds but never in a position to catch them. It would be silly to say that joints are there to warm the muscles that connect them, but it's an aspect of their functioning, and my calf muscle, slung between unmoving knee and no less stubborn ankle, felt no benefit. The result doesn't have to be atrophy, but it's likely, isn't it? Tissue disaffected, labour force redundant and in a sulk. My muscles had survived the years of bed rest almost by chance, thanks to some encouragement given me by my childhood GP, a beloved figure for whom I would perform any number of exercises whether I understood their purpose or not. Dr Duckett had persuaded me to flex my muscles (particu-larly the quadriceps) and shown me how. Isotonic exercise, though the word wasn't in common usage then and even a doctor may not have known it. So although I was supposed to stay still I had my own secret way of moving without moving, with the bonus that I could be disobedient and a good boy at the same time.

When I say my life has been sedentary, I don't mean what people tend to mean when they say that – that they shouldn't have taken the bus so much for short journeys. I should really use the ugly word 'non-ambulatory'. I mean that certain muscles have hardly been used. A working muscle expands, it acquires a tendency to bulge. Unemployed muscle lies low. And above all, a working muscle warms up, as any other motor does. That's the cardinal difference between the two dispositions of tissue. A muscle that is more passenger than engine, like the muscle between two ankylosed joints, stays cool. Thanks to my bilateral arthroplasties, my hips had a little movement, but the knees and ankles were fixed. The muscle of my thigh was any-thing but warm, and the muscle of my calf, further from my heart, was actively chilled. I felt its chill as an active force. I flexed like mad, hoping to strike a spark among those underused fibres, a spark that might then urge my heart to a higher level of activity. That's the way of it. The firing heart oxygenates the muscle, and takes up oxygen itself. I'm old enough to remember car-owning neighbours in Bourne End who would start up the engine every few days in cold weather, just to turn it over, not to move off, as a way of helping their cars overwinter. I was trying something similar, though it's also a good way to run your battery down.

Of course body temperature involves many variables, morale among them, and there's no denying that my sense of my own value was barely ticking over.

There was very little preparation I could do for my sojourn in the Mini, but I had experimented with the idea of extra pairs of underpants. I have to admit that over the course of my time as an undergraduate I had stopped bothering with such things, nor socks either. When I was in my twenties my feet tended to overheat unpredictably, for some strange glandular, chakric or indeed karmic reason. When I was planning for my Mini residency it seemed reasonable that an extra pair of underpants, perhaps multiple layers of socks, would materially assist in the conservation of body heat. Logically I should have worn a hat, for that matter, but though I don't actively avoid ridiculousness courting it is a different matter. The multiple-underpant idea was a non-starter anyway. Once I had struggled into an extra pair it became clear that taking a pee would be next to impossible. Even with a single pair it wasn't easy to align the openings of underpant and overpant – one of the reasons for abandoning such things in the first place. So I gave up on the idea of building up the layers. There were plenty of obstacle courses to be negotiated in life without my installing an extra one inside my clothing. I would shiver rather than wet myself, hanging on to the dignity that, I dare say, nobody noticed but me. My dignity was something that could be named without needing to go to the added trouble of existing. This is a well-known category in Hindu thought, the classic teaching examples being the horns of the hare and the children of a barren woman. There must be similar examples in a more familiar context. I suppose 'the man who's a better driver drunk than sober' will do until I can think of something more definite.

I was woken up by a rocking motion of the car, so I must have gone to sleep, though this statement isn't logically defensible, assuming as it does a common-sense notion of waking and sleeping as mutually exclusive, to say nothing of the manifest existence of other states. A philosopher would laugh at such simplicities, though even a philosopher would have had trouble sleeping through the rocking of the Mini. My first thought was that the dog-walker, who had already shown a certain muted territorial aggression, was now trying to make my chosen parking place even less welcoming. It was full summer dark, and though my previous encounters with him, with them, had been in the early morning, dogs need a little outing last thing at night also. I couldn't rule it out though my instinct told me that he had some more self-righteousness in him to express verbally before it spilled over into action.

The Mini let out a low shuddering cry

I didn't have many options. I thought of taking off the brake, to see what would happen. Those famous last words. To do something rather than nothing and to bring on a change of state willy-nilly, just to confirm that I existed. What is it Pascal says – that every human trouble arises from an inability to stay quietly parked in one's Mini? Something along those lines.

Even so it soon became clear that I must find out what was happening. The impulses agitating the Mini were speeding up and becoming more extreme. My angle of vision was far from ideal but in the mirror I could make out that the rear window was blocked by something. By someone, by two someones, one of them with blonde hair. An additional sound set in, plausibly of a head softly knocking against the Mini's roof as a result of repeated thrusts from . . . thrusting and knocking. Oh dear. Thrusts from a gentleman friend.

Harsh sodium lighting was being installed little by little on the major roads of Cambridge, but here on Brookside the illumination was softer and warmer. That had been one of the reasons for me choosing this quiet stretch of road, where the crude beams from Trumpington Street were filtered by intervening leafage and the street lights on the protected little stretch of roadway I'd chosen shone more kindly. Of course by the same token it was the nearest spot to the Royal Cambridge Hotel that could qualify as a Lovers' Lane. It was easy to imagine that there were little signposts displayed in the hotel bar,

75

for the convenience of patrons who were not residents. I happened to know that there was an arch under Fen Causeway where a footpath went under the road, an ideal place for the consummation of intimacy, but perhaps in high season it was overbooked.

There was a perfectly convenient telephone box a little further along, by Pemberton Terrace – why couldn't they have used that? It would stand up to much more rough use than my poor Mini. Phone boxes are built to survive any amount of rough treatment – impatience, desecration, violent assault. My poor car had led a sheltered life and I would much rather it had been left with its illusions.

The Mini let out a low shuddering cry of mortification at its public shaming as the thrusts subsided. This was not what its inventor had designed it for. Bad enough for Alec Issigonis's brainchild to be used as an emergency bedroom without its rump doing duty as a leaning-board for an al fresco knocking shop.

Only minutes had gone by since I had decided against a provocative move, releasing the brake, which it was clear, now that I had fuller information, would have been a mistake and possibly a consequential one. Now all I had to do was stay quiet and wait for this couple to leave. How likely was it that they would make small talk to any great extent after the event? The imp of the perverse, however, is not to be bottled, and I watched in fascination as my hand approached the Mini's horn control. What mischief exactly was this hand setting in motion? I waited, the hand waited, the horn waited, until the young man entered my line of vision. He was carrying something gingerly in his fingers.

A car's horn is not an expressive instrument, or at least the Mini's wasn't. If I'd been able to inflect it, I would have aspired to a tone of dry worldliness with a slight sardonic edge. 'No one can blame you for acting on impulse, old man, and your lady friend looks charming—' not that I could see her '—but next time you might think of knocking on the windows before you start? Just so that I can get my earplugs in, you understand. Nothing unwholesome!' The sound of the horn was a great deal more abrupt than that – it startled even me. There was a little scream from behind the car, where the girl was, and the boy (young man, I suppose) jumped, but recovered remarkably quickly. He may have been drunk enough to be irrationally confident, though he certainly hadn't been too drunk to perform. Of course in young and healthy people the middle ground is extensive. He grinned broadly and then gave me a thumbs-up with his free hand.

Little bundle of thwarted instructions

He waggled the object he was holding and I was able to confirm my working hypothesis that it was a full condom. A faintly disgusting, a faintly baleful, strongly fascinating thing. He had been making his way, as I now realised, to a council bin, a metal tub inside an old-fashioned ornamental basket, by the kerb a little way off, and now he finished the errand and disposed of his milky trophy, that little bundle of thwarted instructions.

I was fully awake now, and took the trouble to wind down the window a little way. What my restricted angle of vision denies me attentive listening can often supply. On his way back from the bin this lad gave me a grin, a wink and a double thumbs-up – a whole barrage of man-to-man signals. He didn't have real winking skills, not of the sort I remember from the men in my childhood. Winking was an important part of men's dealings with each other. There was an art to that lizard-flicker of connivance, man to man, or actually – now I think of it – man to boy. I expect women can wink as a matter of anatomical fact, it's not an accident of gender like ownership of a prostate, but they don't rely on it, perhaps because they have other ways of expressing themselves. A wink happens quickly, in a moment that practically exists outside time, but long enough to point out some shared information or attitude. This lad, admittedly, screwed up the whole of one side of his face to act out our secret sharing. I could see that his shirt was fully unbuttoned although his tie was still round his neck. Without a tie he wouldn't have been served in the bar of a respectable hotel, but since then it had been loosened and yanked to one side, by one or the other of the let's call them lovers. He went back to his lady.

'What was that noise?' she asked in a harsh whisper.

'There's someone in the car. He used his horn.' He too lowered his voice, presumably to humour her. The time for discretion had been and gone.

'What did he do that for?'

What did *I* do that for? What did *you* do that for? I mean, I understand the general principles of lust and impatience, but shouldn't you check that there isn't someone sleeping in a car before you start having a poke against it?

I suppose not. If I think about it, definitely not. It would be like looking underneath the bed in the honeymoon suite.

In fact I didn't much like 'poke' at the time, even if it was less brutal than 'fuck', and 'screw' was no better. I was really waiting for the word 'bonk' to come into usage. It was waiting in the wings of time. It would fill a need by sweetening the parlance.

A new thought struck the lady. 'You mean there was someone in the car . . . all this time?' The only alternative was that I'd somehow inserted myself into the car while they were – please can we say bonking? Anachronisms are annoying, but there are other priorities.

'Was he watching us? *Was he watching us the whole time?*'

'Not likely, Susie. We woke him up, that's all.' Not only did he use a condom, he knew the lady's name. One of nature's gentlemen!

'But why was he sleeping in his car? Doesn't he have anywhere to go?' A question that could just as fairly be asked of the lady and her squire. 'I don't like it here. I'm going. You can stay if you want.'

A shrug on a grand scale

I can only assume she mooched off without waiting for him. I was facing the other direction, after all. But the boy had better manners, and went to the trouble of taking his leave in some marginally formal way. He came round the front of the car. I wasn't entirely convinced by his earlier amiability, so I turned the headlights on, irrationally thinking this would warn him off. It was as close as the Mini could come to arching its back and bristling up its tail. Beyond that there was only the horn, which would have lost the element of surprise, though I suppose I could have gone on sounding it until I woke someone up in the houses opposite, though at this moment they looked rather far away. My door was locked but the window was open, though not fully. He was standing too close to the beams for them to show his face, but I needn't have worried.

He made one last gesture, inherently theatrical and made more so by the bright lights illuminating his lower body. It was a shrug, but not one that involved the shoulders only. A super-shrug, in fact, a shrug on a grand scale. He threw out his hands, palm upwards, and if I'd been able to make out his face properly I'm sure his eyebrows would have been raised. The performance considered as a *Gestalt* conveyed the message – this is guesswork and I won't pretend otherwise – 'Women, eh?' Then he too sloped off.

This animal was not *post coitum triste*. Not by a long chalk. At that moment he may have been the most contented man in all Cambridge. He had succeeded in transferring all his tensity and woe into the condom, that disgusting, baleful, fascinating thing. It was already clear that I had missed my vocation as a cell biologist. Why else would I feel the need to examine such a thing, this strangled bulb of protein? I had been cheated of my proper course of study, mistakenly thinking that dexterity was indispensable, as if there was no such thing as a lab assistant. I should have been quicker to understand my advantage. Glib hands and confident arms barge in without thinking, they wash up the dish on which the crucial enlightening spores are quietly growing and nullify the research they imagine they're helping along. The able-bodied need to be saved from themselves.

He had pumped the little balloon full of negative energies, and it was only right that he should dispose of it responsibly. His lady had been spared not only the disaster known as the creation of a human life but the more diffuse misfortune of being injected with all that dissatisfaction, a karmic burden that would have long outlasted her spasms of pleasure, if spasms on her part indeed there had been.

I was oddly attached to my little parking place, but the tryst I had witnessed made me see its disadvantages. Cambridge had an underbelly that I didn't normally see – and this was only a Thursday night. If this was a taste of the sort of thing that went on mid-week then what saturnalia would the weekend have in store? The pineapple landing-signal on top of the Hobson Monument was burning altogether too brightly. They'd be queuing up to use the Mini as a baseboard for their knee-tremblers. I could only think that its angle must be especially well suited to the activity, a happy accident rather than a concern of the designers. The car was strongly associated with the 1960s and a modern attitude, but not I think actively aphrodisiac. It was more like the jaunty four-wheeled embodiment of a straight-up-and-down fashion model of the '60s, Twiggy for example, than anything more fleshly. It was as much an innocent bystander as I was myself, happening to be in the wrong place at the wrong time, minding its own business, not flaunting the swell of its nates like an Austin Maxi. Shameless hussy of a vehicle! Everyone knew you could get a double mattress in the back of one of those if you folded the seats down. Salesmen in showrooms must have struggled to suppress their impulse to leer.

On Friday night they'd surely be piling in from all sides, rapping on the windows to make sure I was keeping score. Would the Mini's brakes even hold? On Saturday night the carnival would no doubt be even more frenetic, but with any luck I would have a proper home by then.

The student and the incontinent tramp

At first light the man with the dog was back, knocking softly at the window. There's no point in doing it softly when the goal is to rob me of sleep. Hammer away, why don't you? Crack the glass. I squirmed round to see him better. He was holding out towards me an empty pint glass with a crisp packet stuffed into it, and he seemed to be wanting me to roll down the window fully and take these trophies in.

'What's that got to do with me?'

'It was on your roof. The roof of your car.'

That was as might be, but didn't mean I could hold the thing. Or rather, I could manage to hold a pint glass between my hands, but not do anything with it afterwards, certainly not drink from it, nor even put it down. The best I could have managed would be to drop it, and eventually my visitor understood this, though the noise he made – an aggrieved 'h'm' – showed no sign of a softening attitude.

'Perhaps you'd be kind enough to put it on the pavement,' I said, 'somewhere where people won't trip over it.' This got a grunt.

In a few moments he was back with a new item, this time something that dangled from a stick he was holding. It was a discarded pair of knickers. These I could have handled reasonably adroitly, and

I almost volunteered to take custody of them on no better basis than that. Pert though I can be on occasion, I wouldn't quite have dared to say, 'I was wondering where those had got to.' Flippancy is a real temptation in absurd circumstances, but its effects are unpredictable and often inflammatory.

He gave me a baleful look, the equivalent in body language of a final warning. He seemed to regard me as the catalyst or precipitant of a decline in social amenity. In my small person I was the equivalent of a boarded-up building. I should be encouraged to move on while there were still windows unbroken in the street. I suppose the waft of stale takeaway and stale pee emerging gently from my wound-down window suggested my affinity with at least two classes of undesirable, the student and the incontinent tramp. The man took my number – not only that, he let me see him taking my number. It's easy to do things out of my line of sight. An immobile neck conspires against omniscience. So he wanted me to know that OHM 962F had been added to a register of suspect vehicles. I was being given notice that I was only a short distance away, perhaps only another night away, from a citizen's arrest.

Just as hamsters chose their wheels in a previous life, so I seemed to have set a pattern in terms of how to spend an empty day. I returned to Whyvonne's café but negotiated the terms of entry before I would consent to leave the car. I bargained down the hospitality of the house, indicating that I would accept a single scrambled egg and a half-slice of toast, and that I would insist on paying for it. This message from the kerb was delivered inside by Hettie, my terms put to an invisible Whyvonne and her acceptance of them duly relayed to me. Then I graciously agreed to enter the premises for the second time, borne across its threshold on a wave of assistance, even if Hettie was still oddly approximate in her handling of a body not so very far from the norms of humanity. Still, I'll choose slow learning over no learning at all.

Hettie's style of lifting wasn't frontal but involved a curious cocked stance, so that I seemed to make a lot of contact with one hip. She seemed a person largely composed of softness but she offered a surprisingly sharp edge when assisting me into or out of Whyvonne's café. There was an element of lurching that wasn't comfortable for me, and presumably no better for her. Finally I asked her about it, saying, 'I've been told I'm heavier than I look – is lifting me very tricky?' She looked embarrassed and relieved at the same time, if that's a possible combination, and said, 'It's not that, exactly. I don't know how to hold you. Believe me, I'm not shy, but it doesn't seem right to hold you against . . . against my boobs.'

'I understand. But I can't honestly think of a better way to do it. At least we wouldn't bash into each other. Let's try it. I promise you won't suffocate me. And I promise not to get ideas. How's that?' After that all the difficulty went out of the situation and we got on like brother and sister, bony brother and buxom sister, when we needed to collaborate on John-moving. My skinny Mum would have called her 'pneumatic', her standard description of any woman curvier than her. The word seems rather disparaging and I don't have a use for it outside discussions properly focussing on tyres or, I suppose, at a pinch, drills.

I don't think I was being entirely dishonest with her. I had no axe to grind or furtive arousal to nurse, but I was mildly fascinated by the difference of sensation offered by women who had abandoned the bra. Statistically it was overwhelmingly men rather than women who had helped me, but I had some sort of indirect access to the changes going on.

If I wasn't given a carry by women all that often then that only made it a treat and I paid extra attention. The bits of bra wiring that had occasionally dug into me, though more often into the tender flesh of the wearer, melted gradually away, replaced by softer bindings and then, sometimes, nothing at all. Whether the new arrangement was entirely for female convenience or for the delectation of men I couldn't say. I personally benefited from the release of elasticated tension and a freer flow of warmth across the upper body.

Women of older generations somehow both envied and disapproved of these changes. My formidable Granny regarded herself as having lived through the Dark Ages of underwear, by which she meant life before something called the Kestos, the first properly shaped brassière. Before the Kestos, she said that what you had to wear was no more than a hammock for the chest. 'Not even a pair of hammocks, if you follow me. The Kestos was the first brassière with – forgive me, John,

82

but clarity is important – separated cups. They were like gold dust, the originals, not the imitations. The factory couldn't make them fast enough. You had to wait your turn.' I couldn't quite see Granny queuing outside a shop, even a shop in Mayfair, but she stopped short of claiming that feat of endurance.

Whyvonne offered a welcome but seemed to warn Hettie off any real engagement with me. She might say to me, 'One of these days we're going to have a real talk, you and I – there's so much I'm dying to know,' but in practice she never had the time. If Hettie tried to ask me questions about India, a subject on which she had decided I was an expert, Whyvonne would break in with something tart like 'For God's sake let the little swami eat his breakfast in peace!' It was as if she was claiming the conversational equivalent of *droit du seigneur* without actually exercising it. She even said to Hettie once, 'Don't forget you're only the wench' – a word I don't think I'd ever heard used in conversation before. Perhaps it was more important to her than anything else to assert authority over an underling, not even by cultivating me herself but by declaring me off limits. There are people like that, and although this is a less than attractive characteristic it doesn't necessarily correlate with blackness of heart. A fly on the wall of a beehive (however unlikely an event in terms of insect behaviour) would hear the queen bee treating her workers with a similar lack of respect.

Wheelchair manhandle with cup-of-tea-and-biscuit finish

At my next port of call I have to say I was impressed by the rapidly improving coördination of the ladies who manned Our Lady and the English Martyrs (OLEM, as I was beginning to call it in my mind). Perhaps they had been practising with a stand-in. Their teamwork was flawless. I'd experienced nothing like it since my long-ago visit to the Royal Tournament, where my favourite stunt, outranking even the motorcycle figure-of-eight, was a race between two teams of artillerymen to disassemble a cannon, convey the constituent parts over a twelve-foot wall, then put the weapon back together to fire a round. The beefy ladies of OLEM could have held their own against the Royal Artillery in this, their chosen event, the wheelchair manhandle with cup-of-tea-and-biscuit finish. In time I wouldn't put it past them to get me over a wall, either disassembled into handy sections or in my integrity.

I had stayed so long the previous day and had returned so promptly that I must have seemed to have an ulterior motive, perhaps a conversion coming on. The soutane whose swish had reached so deeply into my innermost ear may have just been biding its time before swooping to catch my soul. I'd done all I could to indicate an interest that was merely historico-architectural, concerned chiefly with the Gothic Revival. I had been offered pamphlets detailing the architects (Dunn and Hansom of Newcastle) and the builders (Rattee and Kett, a local firm), not to mention the polygonal apse and the various types of stone used in the church's construction — Combe Down, Casterton and Ancaster. I had also been offered any amount of information about the English Martyrs commemorated in the name of the church, including the Blessed Margaret Pole, S. John Fisher, the persecuted Carthusians, S. Thomas Cobbleigh and all.

I was beginning to feel like an English Martyr myself. Was I incompetently finished off with eleven blows of the act by a novice headsman, like the Blessed Margaret Pole? No. Had my severed head been stuck on a stave on London Bridge, like S. John Fisher's? No indeed. Had I been hung in chains from the battlements of York, like Dom John Rochester and Dom James Walworth, or chained to posts in Newgate and starved to death, like a number of their unfortunate fellow Carthusians in 1537? Absolutely not. But there was another side to things. Had any of the Martyrs spent a night in a Mini, whether or not it attracted fornicating visitors as lamps attract moths? Hardly. Honours were equal. I could hold my head up, at the usual fixed angle.

Whyvonne's café, Catholic church, the Bot — the only element I dropped was the cinema. Seeing *Elvira Madigan* just the once (mainly through closed eyelids, those subtle perceptual filters) was enough, and more than enough. We've all of us died too many times to be fooled by the idea that the actual experience is pretty. Death is a shock to the system, like any drastic change of state, and it's always something that the ego resists and resents, however often it happens.

Suicide casts a longer shadow than the other deaths. Even if there's a pause of a thousand years till the next incarnation, the gunshot will still be echoing in the ears of the newborn. For the rôle the Arts Cinema had played the previous day I substituted the central public library, on Wheeler Street, more or less part of the Guildhall. If I'd been able to wait a year or two, I could have been an early patron of the library's promised premises in Lion Yard, for which fantastic sums had been reserved – a million pounds was talked of. A world-beating collection of incunabula? Solid gold panels? Better than that – lifts! Proper access.

Lion Yard had been an ancient warren of pubs, boutiques and tatty bookshops, a recent civic memory when I arrived as an undergraduate. It was already a building site when I first saw it. Now it was taking shape as a shopping centre and in due course would play host to a public library. Everyone agreed it looked absolutely horrible, and no one but me was mollified by the information that new buildings were beginning to take into account the needs of the disabled. The pioneering Day of Action to which I had lent support in my second year, designed to call attention to the problems faced by my kind of person, was surely bearing fruit.

My early experience of libraries had been of the one near home in Bourne End, Bucks, whose librarian Mrs Pavey was a bristling gatekeeper turned tireless helper, a Cerberus who licked my hand with a tongue surprisingly silky. She would track down any printed work for me and slip it into Mum's gloved hands. To some psychologies it will always primarily be germs rather than books that circulate in libraries.

The UL, Cambridge's University Library, was heavily defended by its architecture against the tiny band of students like me, but even so I managed to make use of it, having books smuggled out by arrangement (much more practical than having myself smuggled in). Now I found on Wheeler Street the last atmosphere I expected, an armed neutrality. Getting in was a challenge, though not on the scale of the UL. I needed to recruit someone to go in and request assistance on my behalf, and it took a little time to find a suitable someone, a city employee with time to help someone who had no higher status than citizen.

Finally I was chairlifted onto the premises. I chaffed them as we crossed their resistant threshold – 'I bet you're looking forward to your new building, eh?' – but it didn't seem that they were in any great hurry for change. It was only me who was looking forward to the transfer to the Lion Yard complex, an eyesore by unanimous acclamation but an eyesore with ramps and lifts.

My rather tepid helpers left me in a sort of twilight zone. In a fair-sized town like Cambridge, public libraries inevitably become the place of last resort for those who have no other roof to huddle under. It wasn't just me. In a digestive system the Central Library would have been the appendix, in a washing machine the fluff-trap. The point is that I attracted no special notice by using the premises as a specialised type of time machine, one that slowed down the passing moments very effectively but lacked the final power to stop them dead. There was quiet, there were newspapers. Sleep wasn't actively encouraged but only snoring was penalised, though without direct reproach. All that happened was that a librarian, innocently passing by on the way to the stacks, or on the way back, would just happen to drop a book of medium size near the offender.

The stacks themselves weren't particularly accessible to me, except in their lower-middle zone, but staff were fairly willing to extract a book I wanted from between the shoulders of its fellows. I say 'fairly willing' because there was an element of reluctance built in, a definite refusal to be at the general beck and call. Not every appeal was immediately acknowledged, and this was policy rather than chance. Otherwise, I can see, the facility could turn by degrees into nothing more than a day centre unusually well stocked with books.

I did a little research on Celia's botanical riddle. First I had to extract the slip of paper she had tucked into my breast pocket on the mistaken assumption that it was accessible to me. It was Mum who had made all my shirts for me, with Velcro tabs for fastening, and she knew perfectly well that a breast pocket wasn't functional, but clothing has a formal aspect too and it smartened the look of her boy. Clothes last me a long time, which has aspects both positive and negative. I didn't need to worry about locating and being able to afford another tailor, but I risked being reminded of her at the beginning and end of every day.

My trousers also had Velcro fastenings, proof that Mum and I had once been a team, though they were losing their ability to grip. I could sometimes get workable adhesion by introducing the panels to each other at a slight angle, so that new matings of loop and hook could take place, but the miniature hooks and loops had become furred over, overfamiliar with each other, so that everything blurred into a matted texture with only phantom powers of attachment. I'm not trying to sneak in a sketch here of the way things deteriorated between Mum and me, by the way, under cover of evoking my difficulties with trousers. That sort of slow detachment, parting of the ways, would be much closer to the normal course of events between a mother and son – the hooks becoming less hooky, the loops losing their loopiness. Happens all the time. What went on the year before between Laura Cromer and her son John had been more like a zip breaking or a seam being torn apart, an abrupt event despite so many years of warning signs.

The tapestry bag had been so useful to me over the years because it was a big untethered pocket that could be winched up and groped into. I needed to ask a librarian for assistance in retrieving Celia's note from its hiding place six inches away from my chin, just as if I was after a volume in Reserve Stock. The distance was greater but the inaccessibility was the same. He was young, he was junior – he didn't have the status required to ignore me with confidence. His shirt collar was too big for him, and though men's fashion at the time favoured the oversized and floppy I fancied he wanted to keep his Adam's apple out of sight. It kept popping up just the same. It was like a busybody spying on the neighbours over a fence.

When he understood what was wanted of him, he reached two fingers very gingerly into the breast pocket of my shirt. He might have preferred to use tweezers. Perhaps he was expecting to bring to light some treasure or horror, either a brittle shard of papyrus bearing an epigraph in need of decipherment or a venomous caterpillar.

He unfolded Celia's slip of paper in front of me. *Rhizanthella gardneri*. Since I now apparently had a research assistant I asked for a book on the flora of Australia, but this was too specialised a request. On a hunch that *Rhizanthella gardneri* might be an orchid I asked for a book on those instead, but the only book available didn't list it.

I could have tried asking for Arthur Osborne's *Ramana Maharshi and the Path of Self-Knowledge*, though I had my own copy (even if it was currently being kept in storage by the porters at Downing). I hadn't opened it for some time. Since my visit to India in the summer before my first Cambridge year, when I had visited places of supreme holiness and not been improved by them, my devotion to my guru had been patchy. The bond between us hadn't broken, but the line had somehow gone slack. Of course a guru is a cunning fisherman, knowing exactly how to play a snagged soul until its own wilfulness exhausts it and delivers it up. If there was anything I felt I knew about Ramana Maharshi, it was that he wasn't a coarse fisherman. There was no danger of him throwing me back, though the image he used himself was more dramatic, of the devotee held safe in the tiger jaws of enlightenment.

I felt his eye upon me often, and it was almost worse than the eye of Sauron in *The Lord of the Rings*. I could have withstood the scalding glare of an enemy, I felt, but not Ramana Maharshi's intimate twinkle, the sense he gave that he was indulging me almost humorously in the despair that I was so determined to lapse into, while he himself was the secure bedrock beneath me. Why wouldn't he come when I called? His expression suggested that I knew quite well why that was. I wouldn't come when he called.

My mistake in mounting an unaccompanied expedition to India had been to think that Ramana Maharshi's spiritual signal had a geographical source and an amplified local resonance. As if his natural setting could be restricted to Tamil Nadu rather than the whole world! I felt that I had been punished for failing an elementary test, an especially galling conclusion to come to, given that my chosen religious framework denied any place to either punishment or trial. I didn't choose Hinduism on intellectual grounds, but I certainly responded to its emphasis on dissolving character rather than building it. My family was littered with the wreckage that character-building creates: stiff heedless father, mother unable to let go, brother pretending nothing was wrong, sister too young to escape the toxic karma of the home. I was better off without them, getting by on the illusion of solitude rather than relying on the illusion of help.

For a while after India, I told myself a comforting story about what had happened there, and why my loss of spiritual self-possession was perhaps not as ominous as I sometimes felt. I was hoping to be recharged with religious fuel by visiting the place where my guru had lived and which he'd never left. And perhaps the experiment had worked.

After all, what happens to the heat output of a fire when you put fresh coal on? That's right, it goes down. The room cools, though you may not notice it. People who haven't lived with a real fire may never have known this, but it's not like turning a knob or flicking a switch. The new coals disrupt the thermal flow. They need to be heated up themselves before they can contribute any energy of their own. They suck heat from the coals that are already burning, and in the short term – in the short term – the room gets less benefit from the fire. So I told myself I didn't need to worry if the short-term effect of visiting India was a cooling. As the months went by, though, it became more likely that my little flame had been snuffed out by an avalanche of coals.

So instead of anything Hindu I asked for Brother Lawrence's *The Practice of the Presence of God*. Even the title had always pleased me, with its combination of directness and mystery. Why should we need to practise for the presence of God? But we obviously do.

A rat can survive a long time on the moisture content of a single grain of rice. Ask any exterminator. A mouse can eat frozen food just as it is, if nothing else is available. So too with the spiritual thirst, the metaphysical appetite. I would get by.

I couldn't stop myself from currying favour by asking for a book that would show me in a good light, although I did genuinely want to read it. Brother Lawrence is a fascinating figure, and I'd been very taken with his style of spiritual thought since my later schooldays. Back then it was always allowed to ask about Christianity, and you could get away with reading Greek mythology as long as you didn't pay too much attention to gods and goddesses going to bed together. With *A Thousand and One Nights* you were on shakier ground, and the *Bhagavad Gita* was out of the question. I never understood why.

I've been fairly strongly repelled by most aspects of Christianity, particularly those that are dangled in front of people as if they were tempting. I reacted violently against the *Screwtape Letters* when they were pushed on me by a teacher at the age of twelve or thirteen, though there may have been a mistake in tactics involved, as well as C. S. Lewis being a bad choice of fish hook. I'm strongly counter-suggestible. It may sound silly coming from someone who has spent so much time being pushed around in a small wheeled vehicle, but there it is. I hate to be steered, even towards a man (this is C. S. Lewis) who said you could never find a cup of tea big enough or a book long enough for him.

To chew an Energen roll for God

Religious faith requires both the presence and the absence of divinity. Continuous presence makes the saint (no one else could withstand the flame), continuous absence makes the addicted suicide, self-sentencing, trapped in a punitive repetition that has no outside agent. Perhaps practice can help to get the rhythm right, the alternating current of faith and doubt.

When the book arrived my mind floated into it without friction while my fingers busied themselves with mischief. Library books in those days, swathed in plastic, had an agreeably sticky feel to them, slight on the front covers but more pronounced if you scratched at the inside flaps and could manage to get one to yield an edge and peel off a little. My fingers lack flexibility but can prove themselves quite effective little levers in the right circumstances. Touching that hidden stickiness was a great perverse pleasure and comfort, particularly for good boys like me with few avenues of delinquency open to them. I seem to remember that the trade name of the product responsible for this fine sensation was Librafilm. And perhaps my quietly scrabbling fingers were being taught a spiritual lesson of their own, since a persistently sticky surface both invites attachment and shows it up as illusion.

I've always relied on books to lay their threads across my own actual experience, transversely, back and forth, running now over and now under. Life needs books as warp needs weft to make up cloth.

'Brother Lawrence', born around 1614, started life in Lorraine as Nicolas Herman. He fought in the Thirty Years' War, essentially for economic reasons. As a soldier he would have food in his belly and a few coins in his pocket. During this period he had a spiritual experience, though not a vision as such. He explained it as a moment of supernatural clarity transfiguring a common sight. Looking at a bare tree in winter, he felt a rush of conviction that its flowers and fruit would be restored to it. He too felt dead, but also knew somehow that new life was waiting for him.

He found work as a valet, though he was clumsy and tended to break things, before acting on his vocation in his mid-twenties by entering the Priory of the Discalced Carmelites in Paris. That was where he took a new name, Brother Lawrence 'of the Resurrection', and spent almost all the rest of his life inside the priory walls.

Many religious figures have a privileged background – people forget that the Buddha was brought up in a palace, and my own beloved Ramana Maharshi, though not raised in luxury, was no less a Brahmin for that. If I have a sneaking sense of kinship with the spiritual underdog then it finds a perfect companion in Brother Lawrence. Since he didn't have the education necessary to become a cleric, he couldn't be anything more than a lay brother. For many years he worked in the kitchen, and this too was a plus for me. At Downing I had often felt on more of a wavelength with porters and the waiters in Hall than with its academic side, and I don't necessarily mean I flirted with them, though of course the possibility can't be ruled out.

Later Brother Lawrence repaired sandals. Even so he attracted followers, and visitors came to seek him out for advice. His spiritual thought, always remarkably down to earth, expressed in conversation and in letters, became the basis of *The Practice of the Presence of God*, compiled after he died. In Brother Lawrence I particularly loved the idea of 'common business' being an opportunity for worship. This was an idea which Ramana Maharshi developed magnificently, but it was in Brother Lawrence that I had met it first. I think for once the school library at Burnham Grammar School must get the credit, rather than the public institution in Bourne End.

The idea of common business is that we can do little things for God. 'I turn the cake that is frying on the pan for love of him . . . It is enough for me to pick up but a straw from the ground for the love of God.' This humility made a powerful appeal to me, perhaps enhanced by the odd added ingredient of megalomania – 'I began to live as if there were no one save God and me in the world.' In terms of my own spiritual development it seemed to be an asset that all my future business was likely to be common. I wouldn't be devising brutally coercive advertising campaigns, though I had got as far as an interview with J. Walter Thompson, an interview that was recorded on videotape but will be archived somewhere in the Akashic Records along with every other thought and event in the cosmos. I wouldn't be pondering half-lives for the United Kingdom Atomic Energy Authority, the other line of work suggested for me by the careers-advisory service of the university I had just left. I wouldn't be frying cakes or scrubbing pots in a priory kitchen, nor buying wine in Burgundy for my brothers or mending their sandals in my cell. I would be keeping body and soul together in Mayflower House, making no contribution to the existence of anyone else. Could I really hope to turn the kettle on for God? To chew an Energen roll for God, conversing with Him bite by airy bite? I would have to try it and see.

This was a Christian version of the Buddhist doctrine of mindfulness that had impressed me so much in my teens. The last thing I respond to in religious matters is doctrinal purity. I treat doctrines, parables, dogmas and commandments as if they were so many bins of sweeties at a pick 'n' mix counter.

People are always pointing out the cost of religious intolerance, prejudice, dissent. Pogrom, jihad – thanks! I had noticed. The reason for all this disastrous history is strongly paradoxical, the inbuilt tendency of religions to flow together, overlap, coalesce. The blobs of mercury refuse to be kept apart, they long to abandon their separateness. It's only the believers that need to stand apart. The faiths know more than the people who live by them. Religious flux seems to be what religious people abhor, but it's just what I like, and drowning in undifferentiation seems to me the entire point.

As a syncretist I get real joy from the history of Josaphat, who was accidentally venerated as a saint for about a thousand years, without anyone realising that he wasn't really a Christian at all but actually a version of the Buddha, whose story had snaked its way from Sanskrit through Sogdian (Middle Iranian to you) and then into Arabic. There's a Hebrew version also, containing important variants. Josaphat, like Siddhartha, was kept confined in a palace, shielded from knowledge of imperfection and suffering, until one day he did some exploring, witnessed a funeral, met a leper, and then the jig was up with an unworldliness based on ignorance.

A printing mistake in a Bombay Arabic version makes its own contribution to the elaboration of the legend, making Kashmir rather than Kashinagar the place where the Buddha died. The name Josaphat is actually a corruption of 'Boddhisattva', but it almost seems to be yearning to undergo one more mutation, from Josaphat to Jesus himself. This final step was taken on his behalf by Mirzā Ghulām Ahmad, who set up his own particular brand of Islam in the late nineteenth century. Perhaps influenced by the local Kashmiri cult inspired by the printing mistake, he proposed that Jesus hadn't died on the cross but had come to India after his supposed death. This notion started its own stubborn heretical little tradition. From Buddhism to Christianity by way of Hebrew and Islam – quite a Cook's tour of religions. Josaphat gets his saint's day in various calendars: August 26 as Greek Orthodoxy reckons things, November 27 by the Roman martyrology. A place is laid for him at the saints' table, but he shares his feast with Barlaam, Barlaam the hermit who helped him to enlightenment, as is only polite.

A holy sandal-mender with sciatica

Isn't that absolutely wonderful? As far as I'm concerned, 'venerated by mistake for a thousand years' competes in beauty of cadence with 'a green thought in a green shade' and 'the buzzing of innumerable bees'.

One of the appealing things about Brother Lawrence's practice was that it was so direct. I hope I'm not looking for shortcuts, but I do love a frontal assault on a spiritual objective. Access to divinity should be accessible to anyone at any time, not of course as a right but as a possibility.

On the other hand, few of my daily tasks could really be classified as 'common business' because they required so much effort. Picking a straw from the floor would require careful planning, perhaps a special tool. The goal of this spiritual exercise seemed to be to turn patterns of thought against themselves, to locate a mindfulness within the mindlessness of routine tasks, but I found mindlessness itself hard to come by. Perhaps this meant I had an unfair advantage and was verging on prayer most of the time.

If I'm allowed to have preferences when it comes to choosing spiritual guides then I like them to have experienced a certain amount of physical difficulty. In Ramana Maharshi I have a guru who had arthritis, and in Brother Lawrence, even before that, I had chosen a holy sandal-mender with sciatica. He is regularly described as 'crippled' but perhaps nothing more than lameness is meant.

Intelligence is the great misleader. Both Brother Lawrence and Ramana Maharshi were shrewd rather than intellectually gifted, though for that very reason able to run rings round those with a reputation for cleverness. All that is necessary is the desire to go forward. Any spoke will lead a questing ant to the hub of the wheel.

In Cambridge's Central Library it happened that a few sentences of Brother Lawrence struck me with sudden impact. Diving into a book, whether it's a new one or an old one, should never be mistaken for escapism or regression. You never step into the same river twice, and for 'river' read 'book'. I thought I knew Brother Lawrence like the back of my hand, as people say to express profound familiarity, and I have less excuse for ignorance than anyone, since I can't rotate my wrists to see anything other than the backs of my hands. It's the palms that are the mystery to me. It often happens that lightning strikes out of a clear blue sky to electrify the reading brain, when a passage that seemed bland and characterless suddenly shouts your name. The sentences were only these: 'He could never regulate his devotion by certain methods as some do. At first, he had practised meditation but, after some time, that went off in a manner of which he could give no account.' Nothing very dramatic there, except that it seemed to correspond exactly with my own case. Meditation, which had been the natural form my inner life had taken when I was a teenager, had melted away while I was in India, and never really resumed its normal working. I realise that 'meditation' will have meant something different to a seventeenth-century lay brother in Paris than it had meant to

94

me, but I was still struck by the observation. I hadn't stopped longing for a mantra which would help restore the balance of my dealings with myself.

A working mantra is a snake of syllables that eats its own tail. In theory it evanesces quite cleanly, leaving no residue, and the classical Hindu analogy is with camphor, camphor that is crystalline, aromatic and volatile. It may be the analogy is in need of an overhaul, since as a terpenoid ketone camphor, derived from the tree *Cinnamomum camphora*, of the laurel family, would certainly leave traces detectable by science. Better perhaps to say that a mantra is the smile left behind by the Cheshire Cat as it disappears. Except that in my case the smile too had vanished, leaving me with no proof that I had ever had the benefit of my guru's *darshan* – the presence-in-absence of his grace.

Somewhere in the distance I could hear a funny honking sound, which made me think of clowns at the circus and their coercive jollity. It was repeated in raucous patterns, relentlessly, but my mind shifted and perceived with a sense of welcome a lulling hooligan rhythm. Perhaps it was my longed-for mantra arriving at last, swimming up through drowsy layers to meet me on my way down. It's pitiful how keen I was to be back on the track towards enlightenment, though praying for a mantra is like whistling for a cat. Of course I was very tired. I didn't struggle to free myself from the grip that held me stupefied. I found myself being nibbled at and then swallowed whole by unconsciousness, but I went on listening while my ego drowned. Sleep in a library is a soft mantrap, and in this case the mechanism had sprung shut in perfect silence.

Nah Nah Nah-Nah. Nah Nah Nah . . . these were the sacred non-referential syllables that would lead me along the path of Self-Enquiry. *Shhh! Nah Nah Nah-Nah, Nah-Nah-Nah-Nah-Nah Nah.* I tried to tune in to this wisp of enlightenment without fully surfacing, and my non-effort in my mystical state on the border between sleep and the illusion of wakefulness was richly rewarded. I could now make out an Ouroboros phoneme in the middle of the mantra, a recurring Alpha-Omega. The mantra went *Nah Om Nah-Nah* . . . *Nah Om Om.* Then there was a strange concluding sound, like a blown raspberry, which would be hard for a devotee to inhabit spiritually, slow to lose its apparent meaning of jeering dismissal even if it became part of

95

daily devotional practice. Still, the mantra is not there to be analysed in worldly terms but humbly dissolved into.

My doze didn't last long. A hoarse voice began to reach me, not in the approved library murmur but with a jarring urgency. 'Mate? Mate?' I had no mates, otherwise they would be helping me out in all matiness, and so I tried to stay unconscious, but that's a hard trick to bring off, like the knack of remembering to forget something. Then I felt a sharp pain in my ankle and I started forgetting to forget, remembering to remember. Maya dealt me in on her exhausting game once again. She tricked me into playing another hand. I opened my eyes.

My ankle had been jabbed by a foot in a tatty gym shoe. In fact I was looking at three feet, and two of them were mine. Instead of another foot the stranger had a knot at the bottom of the cut-off leg of his dirty jeans. I was also looking at another wheelchair. Its occupant, ratty and wild-eyed, was poised to give my ankle another jab. He was carrying a horn with a rubber bulb, the sort of thing I associated with vintage cars or Harpo Marx. It explained how he had attracted attention from out in the street, getting the job done much more quickly than I had managed with politeness and charm. 'Mate? Oi mate?' he was saying.

When people take charge of the wheelchair, they often leave me wedged in place at a desk or a table, which may look neater but leaves me more or less trapped, so I always make sure I'm left at something of an angle. Then I can adjust my position quite straightforwardly by punting myself along with my stick.

I can't imagine I used the word 'punt' before I arrived in Cambridge to describe the way I would jolly the wheelchair along with little strokes of the cane, helped out with nudges of my more workable foot. The word has a lazy-summer-afternoon feeling that will strike anyone who has seen me in actual motion as laughable, but I'm attached to it just the same. It's my little link to the earthly-paradise aura that clings to old university towns, despite the suicides and nervous breakdowns that go hand in hand with the birdsong, the madrigals and the riverside pubs in any self-consciously intellectual atmosphere.

At about this point something clicked in my mind and I realised what it had been that I heard in my semi-conscious state. It wasn't a mantra, alas. It was nothing like a mantra. It was a football chant that

96

had been turned into a pop song, and the words went *Nice One Cyril /
Nice One Son . . . / Nice One Cyril / Let's Have Another One.*

This profane wastrel had been singing his ditty in the sacred spaces
of the Central Library, and my brain had made it welcome! I was mortified that in my hunger for guidance I should have latched on to a
novelty single, even at the lowest level of consciousness. A mantra is
the polar opposite of a novelty single. I gave my answer to this stranger as frostily as I could, but I felt very vulnerable, and would have
done almost anything to make him go away. 'What is it?'

'Where you staying tonight, mate? You got a place? You got a
cushty billet? Bet you have.'

'I wouldn't say that.' Ever since I became aware of class I had felt a
strong romantic interest in those on the wrong side of the tracks, the
sort of people I had heard described in India as 'colony'. I didn't enjoy
it quite so much when the colony claimed me as one of its own.

'Who's letting you stay? They got a big place?'

The lips of this pestering ferret

'Not big at all. Tiny. There isn't room to swing a cat. That's not a
joke. Now do you mind if I get back to my book? I have an essay to
write.' It was cowardly for me to attempt to claim student privileges,
and it was also unlikely to work in this company.

'No call to get sniffy, mate. We're all in the same boat, so how's
about you help me out?'

'I can't. There's no spare room.' I was flustered, and that wasn't
what I had meant to say. I had meant to say there was no room to
spare.

'Doesn't need to be, mate. I don't need a whole room. I can kip
down in any old corner. I'm good at that.' Hearing the word 'mate' on
the lips of this pestering ferret was rapidly estranging me from one of
my most cherished words. The rankness of his breath was a blowtorch
that scorched the edge of every word he spoke. It seemed to cure my
cold, or at least shock it into an asymptomatic state.

'I can't help you. This is a library, and I'm reading.'

'No need to get shirty with me, mate. I've been friendly, haven't I?
And aren't we mates?' He produced a fairly horrible smile. 'We even

drive the same make of car . . .' For a paranoid instant I thought he had spotted the Mini outside as belonging to me, before I realised he meant the humbler vehicles in which we both sat.

I said, 'I really have to be getting back to my book,' hoping that I sounded serenely snooty rather than panicked.

'*Tosser*,' he growled, which suggested I had achieved my goal.

Then he disappeared. When my rather alarming new mate had started talking to me he had placed his wheelchair more or less facing mine, but now he changed position. If his vehicle was similar to mine then our driving styles were very different. He was Stirling Moss and I was a typical Sunday driver. His arms were functional, they were even wiry, and when he worked his big rear wheels in opposite directions he managed something close to a wheelchair pirouette. Then he backed himself deep into my blind spot. My blind spot is extensive. I don't have much movement in my neck to the right, and my blind spot swallows quite a lot of the landscape. It's not normally too much of a problem. I can hear people perfectly well even when I can't see them – so if you're over on the right side from me, try not to be the strong silent type.

There was silence to my right, but I didn't find it reassuring. A hand grasped the side piece of my wheelchair and gave it a fierce tug. Both machines rocked as he pulled mine up against his. My tyres squeaked on the floor when they were dragged sideways, and I felt my stomach go tight. I had been frightened by people once or twice in the past, but I had never before been frightened by someone in a wheelchair, by one of my own kind, except that we were such different kinds.

The voice in my right ear forced itself down into a more seductive register. 'Shouldn't we be sharing? We should share. I've got ciggies and I've got bikkies, and you can have as many as you like. I've got Cup-a-Soup – is there a kettle where you're staying? Never mind. It's just as good cold.' There was a strange swallowing moment in the middle of this sentence, as if his throat had clenched somehow, his œsophagus making its own involuntary protest against what was being said. 'Just tell me where you're staying. I won't be any trouble. Promise. We can be mates.'

I'd never had a Cup-a-Soup. I didn't want to try one. I wanted nei-ther ciggy nor bikky. I wanted a mate, any number of mates, just not this one. I wanted to be left alone, and for the library staff to chuck Mate out, gently if possible, kicking and screaming if necessary. 'Can I have some help here please?' I croaked.

I didn't think it would be hard to get attention by making noise in such a quiet and supervised space. It must have been obvious that this wasn't a narrow issue of librarianship – difficulty with the card index or some such. In general terms the getting of attention has rarely been a problem for me, though it's true I've had to learn to be wary of its quality.

The greedy pulsing berry

Mate manœuvred his wheelchair more or less back to its original position facing me, and looked at me with great intensity. 'You don't need help, mate,' he said. 'I do.' He started to move his wheelchair back and forward in savage little swerves and lunges, so that his surviving foot, the right one, made painful impacts on mine. He alternated his kicks between my feet, which I could do nothing to draw out of harm's way. My legs don't retract and my arms didn't reach my wheelchair's little wheels, and couldn't have turned them if they did. All I could do was try to block the vicious little kicks with my stick, but my skill at parrying low blows is very limited and Mate had every advantage. My shoes were sturdy enough to protect me from normal wear and tear, but this was not that.

I kept shouting for help and nothing kept happening. I looked at Mate and suddenly had the thought that he was possessed. His chest under the stained denim jacket was actively heaving, as if swarming with some infestation whether verminous or demonic. Then through a gap between buttons I caught a glimpse of something alive and non-human. The greedy pulsing berry of a small dog's nose.

Now I could be sure of getting the attention I needed. Instead of crying out for help as the victim of an assault all I needed to do was assert in a voice of low outrage that there was an animal on the premises. 'Someone's brought *a dog* into the library!' A shock wave crashed across the premises and bounced back off the rear wall. Suddenly social currents were made manifest beneath the enforced calm of the library, and high emotion sloshed unstably back and forth.

99

I wondered why the mere assault attracted so little notice, even when there was someone calling for help, and decided it was the fault of the wheelchairs. People look away from one wheelchair, and perhaps two wheelchairs count not as a wheelchair doubled but a wheelchair squared, actively repelling the visual sense. Or perhaps any encounter between wheelchairs short of a high-speed impact qualifies as some sort of family reunion. Whatever the reason, it was only the providential appearance of a puppy that brought me back into the world of shared things. Yet when the librarians came at last to intervene, it was with a sort of heavy disgust, as if they were tavernkeepers in the Wild West breaking up a fight between habitual offenders, sozzled desperadoes. I dare say it was Mate who sparked this response, but I felt the stain of a general disgrace.

Of course once the little dog's presence was revealed ejection was the only possible response. This was accompanied by foul language, insistent toots on the clown-horn, and eventually frantic barks. The dog really only gave tongue once they crossed the threshold into Wheeler Street, an unnaturally high standard of respect for the premises which made me wonder if it hadn't actually been a librarian in a previous life.

I tried to re-immerse myself in the thought of Brother Lawrence, but just as there is a perfect temperature for a cup of tea there's an ideal state of mutual preparedness between a book and its reader, and the thought of Brother Lawrence had gone cold on me. The molecules of book and brain were no longer moving at the compatible relative speeds that encourage exchange, in cycles of resonance. My molecules had speeded up with the excitement of being assaulted, while the book's had slowed down in preparation for its sleep in the Religion section.

One thing which bothered me about the scene just past, as I forced myself to take unrefreshing little sips of the tepid book, was the idea that the dog had done me a favour beyond giving me an improved claim on the righteous indignation of the world, held back when I was only being relentlessly battered at ankle level. If the dog hadn't put in an appearance, the chances were good that the person to be ejected would have been me and not Mate. Not because I was the guilty party but because I was easier to expel. I would have provided less opposition to the saloon staff. I could be wrangled into the street without difficulty.

Free from the immediate grip of a paranoiac mood, I can see that I am slandering the good people of Cambridge's library staff. No such outcome was ever likely. It's just that I am susceptible to a recurring sense of grievance when my resistance is low (and this was clearly a time of low resistance), in the way that some people are prone to recurrences of styes or cold sores.

The problem was the wheelchair, a satisfactory piece of equipment in its own way but fatally flawed by the fact that any hand could lay hold of its handles. The wheelchair wasn't my enemy, but not everyone who took control of it was my friend. In the future as I grandiosely planned it (fatigue promotes unrealistic states of mind) I would find a pair of hands to steer it that would do exactly what I asked, neither more nor less, hands belonging to a warm-blooded robot. A robot whose body heat would help me to maintain a healthy temperature when he wasn't working, plugged into the mains to recharge his battery.

I waited in the library as long as I could, convinced that Mate would lurk outside and treat me to a proper ambush. For my protection I would have liked to be transferred out of the building and to the door of the Mini in a single operation, but that would have seemed to presume on the good will of a single agent or team of agents. It's important to leave helpers with a reserve of strength and human feeling, or your next approach will send them scurrying away on other errands. Consequently I was left on the pavement for an unrelaxing interval. I thought I was familiar with the experience of vulnerability in a public space, but obviously it hadn't been the real thing. My eyes must have been rolling about with little simulation of sanity, since my neck and shoulders don't do a lot to help me when it comes to watching out for the eruption, from my outsized blind spot, of one-legged ruffians using their wheelchairs as dodgems or guided missiles.

I no longer looked like someone who deserved help. Mate had demoted me to his level merely by coming near. Without even touching my hand he had passed on the Black Spot of his outcast status. I was fully exposed to the existential elements. Only when I heard an outburst of yapping and the toot of a handheld horn at some distance, expressing who knows what combination of bullying, begging and mockery, did I relax enough to stop frightening off potential helpers with the wildness of my manner. I needed to keep on terms with that fragile constituency, the human pool of help never to be taken for granted – unless and until I could find someone to take control of the wheelchair full-time and steer me through the social oceans in both their calm and tempestuous states, either a warm-blooded robot as outlined above or a congenial companion. It was hard to judge which possibility was less likely.

I was on the last lap of my little homelessness marathon, my three-day slog, and despite everything that had just happened I began to cheer up. I was on the home stretch and would take possession of a home in the morning. Only one more takeaway to go before I had a permanent address – perhaps even a rent book, though I was trying not to get too excited about that intoxicating possibility. To Mum and Dad a rent book was a badge of shame, since they had struggled to achieve home ownership, but to me it would be documentary proof that I belonged in the world somewhere, safely embedded in an oppressed and impoverished underclass.

After that evening's takeaway I would even have a bed of sorts to look forward to. I could look forward to a decent approximation to the horizontal. On Friday morning Whyvonne had wormed the outline of my predicament out of me and offered me what she referred to as a 'shakedown' on the café premises that evening after it had closed. The doors shut at six and cleaning up took an hour or so. At seven o'clock I could put in an appearance there and take my chances with accommodation that was highly likely (unless they balanced me on the cash till) to be an improvement on the nights before.

I couldn't help noticing, just the same, that even when Whyvonne was making this generous offer she couldn't stop herself from blowing her cigarette smoke in my face. The habit of revenging herself on her customers, irritating as a class even when she had a fondness for the odd individual member, was just too strong. I was reminded of the female lead ('heroine' puts it too high) of Roald Dahl's story 'William and Mary', who reacts with quiet delight when her bossy husband is kept alive as a brain in a bowl, saying she can't wait to get him home, and breathes smoke into his single floating eye. Of course in my imagination it wasn't William's eye wincing in the bowl but Mum's. Let her have everything done for her for a change. See how she liked it.

Whyvonne was proof that people don't have to be angels to do you favours. The converse proposition is that people don't have to be monsters to do you bad turns, but the ego finds that a much harder principle to absorb. Part of me didn't want to accept help at all at this point, however desperately I needed it, but I decided this was the residual, incorrigibly Christian part of my thinking, which saw suffering as having a value. Even if Celia from the Bot had lived on the ground floor, with every amenity laid on for me (ramps, hoists, automatic back scratcher), I would have found a reason to say No. The help she gave me was by existing.

Focussed ignorance is a precious yeast

Celia even had a house-warming present for me that day, which proved how imaginative she was – she could imagine me living in a house! It was a possibility I had almost stopped believing in myself.

She had already loaded her gift into the boot of the Mini. She showed me what it was, a tray of pots covered in foil – a garden-warming present, then, even a window-box-warming present. Then she sat in the car with me to give me more information. 'Let me explain? These have been sterilised and allowed to sit long enough to detoxify? Don't take the foil off till you're ready to sow your seed? Never forget how invasive and persistent *Pythium* is! It's actually called *Pythium insidiosum*, and there's a reason for that? Those pathogens will kill your young plants if you give them half a chance?' Good advice, and such a lovely gesture. Pure generosity. No charge for the pots of earth, no charge for the sterilising spell she had put on them with the help of that magic wand the autoclave.

I had hoped that she wouldn't provide the answer to the riddle she had set me just yet. Focussed ignorance in the brain is a precious yeast that should be allowed to multiply and not be sterilised into the small beer of informed opinion before it's had a chance to develop any real flavour. But Celia couldn't help herself. She had to tell me, and however reluctantly I have to admit it, she passed on something worth knowing.

In those days I was rather attuned to the outlandish aspects of the natural world, since those were the parts with which I felt the greatest affinity. Immaturity on my part, of course. Orchids, on the other hand, had always seemed to me rather obvious in their exotic appeal, and no doubt the fact that they were one of Dad's great loves played a part in this. *Rhizanthella gardneri*, though, also known as the Western Underground Orchid, has come up with a fairly remarkable way of being alive. Brace yourself. It's a myco-heterotroph!

Rhizanthella gardneri is white, having no leaves and no chlorophyll. It's not much more than a fleshy rhizomatous tuber half an inch wide but is able to produce a tightly packed cluster of tiny flowers in a terminal capitulum – over a hundred of them. It was discovered in the wheat belt of Western Australia in 1928, after a farmer started to investigate a crack in the soil of his garden and noticed that a sweet smell was wafting up from it. *Rhizanthella gardneri* spends its entire life underground. No sunlight (and no chlorophyll), so no photosynthesis. And what do you do when you run out of food? You borrow a cup of sugar. If you've never had any food in the first place then you have to borrow any amount of sugar. Cup after cup of the stuff, sack after sack.

Rhizanthella gardneri's kitchen cupboard is a shrub, the broom honey myrtle. That's *Melaleuca uncinata*, dangling its nutritious root system nearby. The only problem is that the cupboard is locked and bolted.

Dylan Thomas was still in vogue when I was an undergraduate, both the life and the work, and everyone's favourite story about him seemed to be the time he was locked in his dressing room during a reading tour by a manager who wanted to make sure he stayed sober. So he bellowed through the keyhole until a stagehand came running, and sent out for whisky. For whisky and a straw, so that he could drink through the keyhole as well as shout through it. I enjoyed this anecdote more after I understood that it involved not a pitiful chemical dependence – silly me! – but resourcefulness coupled with an unbridled appetite for life. Dylan Thomas found his own way of securing what he needed to survive. He too was a sort of heterotroph, call him an alco-heterotroph. The point is that *Rhizanthella gardneri* has contrived something very similar, the rôle of the straw in the keyhole being played by a mycorrhizal fungus named *Thanatephorus gardneri*. If '*thanatephorus*' doesn't mean 'death-bringing' or something similar then I don't see why not, unless the system of botanical nomenclature is letting us all down. Perhaps a misprint has crept in along the way ('*thanatephorus*' for '*thanatophorus*'), a defective fingerstroke eternised in Linnæan taxonomy. But what the fungus brings to *Rhizanthella* is life. *Thanatephorus gardneri* extracts photosynthesized carbohydrates from *Melaleuca uncinata* and *Rhizanthella gardneri* crashes the party. What's that you've got there? Second-hand sunlight turned to starch? I'll have some of that. As for what *Melaleuca uncinata* gets out of the bargain, that seems to be a secret of the boudoir. In complex relationships, and in simple ones come to that, it's not always easy to tell who gets what.

There's a lot of debate about how this complex interlocking arrangement could possibly have arisen in stages. In effect, how is it possible to be alive and yet never to have eaten? Starving and long dead yet able to poke a straw through the keyhole of a dressing-room door and to inhale the whisky you need to live? There are other mysteries also. The plant reproduces vegetatively and also sexually. Since the flowers die without leaving the mother plant, it's unclear how they can be dispersed. Small marsupials may be the vectors, but no evidence of their contribution has been identified. Those who dislike evolution love *Rhizanthella gardneri* as proof positive of their case, but I'm not of their party. It's the reality of matter I resist, and once I've accepted that (just for argument's sake) evolution doesn't trouble me. Having swallowed the camel I can accommodate and digest any number of gnats.

So the full version of Celia's botanical riddle should go:

Q: 'Why should *Rhizanthella gardneri* be by rights the national flower of Australia¿'

A: 'Because it lives down under . . . Down Under?'

As someone who had long understood that the ordinary arrangements of living were unlikely to suit me, I was very struck by this extraordinary set-up of an orchid, a shrub and a mushroom . . . a subterranean *ménage à trois* of perverse and asymmetrical needs, living in a blissful harmony disturbed only by the occasional small marsupial until a farmer's spade broke into its privacy, dragged it into the light and made the whole arrangement look freakish.

Qwok's Quease, the Chinese restaurant on Regent Street which had benefited from my custom for three nights running, could hardly suspect that my patronage was about to be whisked away as abruptly as it had materialised. A fortune cookie had never been offered as part of my takeaway even on the first night, which was a bit galling. Breaking open a fortune cookie is an activity that sits squarely in the middle of my physical capabilities. I could open fortune cookies all day. Perhaps the management was preparing a uniquely personal cookie for Saturday night, which would never be picked up and read, at least by me, bearing a suitably cryptic and mystical motto such as *Any fool can turn a blind eye, but who knows what the ostrich sees in the sand?*

Don't let the *Pythium*s bite

I have to admit the place wasn't actually called Qwok's Quease. Kwok's Quease is a nickname for 'Chinese restaurant syndrome', an allergic reaction people are supposed to have to monosodium glutamate. Medical students at Downing were always warning against it between spicy belches . . . and the saying about the ostrich is actually one of Samuel Beckett's. The imp of the perverse seems to be working overtime today.

I had a shakedown at Whyvonne's. I don't know the dictionary definition of a 'shakedown', if it's always an airbed as it was in this case, a lilo whose parallel inflated tubes were contrasted in colour, alternately yellow and red, laid down in a space where tables had been cleared away and made up with a blanket. It carried a phantom smell of sun cream. Whyvonne had delegated the administration of her kindness to Hettie. Perhaps she wanted an alibi in case she was accused of virtuous behaviour. Hettie had kept some cheese sandwiches for me, either on instructions or off her own bat, in case I was hungry. I felt it was only right to give them a nibble, though it was no secret that I had already eaten – in fact she had washed the tinfoil container of my takeaway and returned it to me. She even included the cardboard top, which was rather a quixotic decision. By the time it had been soaked long enough to let go of its impregnation with grease it had more or less turned to glue.

Hettie didn't want to leave, though I told her she didn't need to worry. I was much safer where I was than I had been on the previous nights. It was still early and I wasn't ready for sleep, but it seemed polite to let her discalce me, for the last time that this operation would need to be performed before I had a home of my own, a bed to sleep in and with any luck a chair to leave my shoes beside. She handled my shoes as if they were the relics of an unlikely religion. She may not have realised that their built-up soles were functional, unlike her own.

'I've been meaning to talk to you about India,' she said as she helped me settle. 'And I've been thinking about what you said – you know, hygiene at meals. Did I tell you I got sick while I was there? I've never been so sick in my life. So perhaps that was my fault, do you think? I was too busy thinking they didn't like left-handers to see that it was me taking silly risks.'

Well, perhaps. I realised I hadn't said it aloud. 'Well, perhaps. You might have . . .' You might have got sick anyway. My conversational style was breaking down. I was starting sentences and then turning off the loudspeaker halfway through, to conserve energy, without even noticing I was doing it. Speech was a stream that kept losing its way and disappearing underground, though my eyes stayed open and I expected, out of habit, to be understood.

'If I go again, I'll try to learn the language.'

Which one?

Oh, sorry. Have to speak aloud. 'Which one?'

'Hindu?'

An error of fact was always likely to rouse me just a little, nudging me over the border into consciousness. 'Hindi. Not spoken so much in the south. There are so many. Tamil . . .' Punjabi. Telugu. Malayalam. 'I love palindromes, don't you?'

'What's a palindrome?'

'. . . like Malayalam.'

I wasn't making sense, but I wanted to be on my own and I certainly didn't want to be fussed over. I mustered all my concentration and told her I'd be fine. She should go. When she hesitated I tried a different approach. Didn't a pretty girl like her have better things to do on a Friday night? It worked like a charm – I think it came out with quite an unwholesome quality. The sinister-avuncular tone acted like a dose of salts, and Hettie left in a matter of seconds. Her last words were, 'Good night, sleep tight, don't let the *Pythium*s bite,' but I must have made up the last bit, mustn't I? I've never worried too much about bedbugs. On her way out she arranged a standard lamp so that it was within my reach, or what she must have assumed was my reach. By the time I got up the nerve to tell her I might not be able to turn it off she had left the premises in search of the pleasures of the young. What do pretty girls do on a Friday night? I have no idea.

I remember thinking that I would probably be able to reach the switch with my stick eventually, even if my first attempt wasn't a success, but then I fell asleep before I had a chance to try. Consciousness shut down abruptly. The effort of creating a world and keeping it spinning, making myself plausibly separate from everyone and everything else, was suddenly too much.

Of course being a person was only my day job, though this was a bit of moonlighting that didn't make me special in any way. Far from marking me out, it gave me common ground with everyone else in the world. Nobody can be a person twenty-four hours a day – it just can't be done. At night the sets dissolve and the performance falls away. Then a very different set of protocols holds sway, just as convincing while it happens though like everyone else I'm not allowed to take notes. We're off the books. Separation of realms is what you might call it. The border guards of sleep take their job very seriously, they're sticklers, and they make you turn out your pockets every time you cross. It's not often you can sneak anything past them. Just the occasional liquorice allsort, or a gold coin with the profile smudged and the inscription effaced – it could be anybody.

I slept sound. I was pretty far gone in exhaustion. Brass bands could have used the room for night practice and I would have known nothing about it. Rats could have walked on my face.

I was woken with a crash, several crashes in fact, the noise of milk crates being delivered outside, enough milk to supply a thriving café on a summer Saturday. By the time I had reconstructed time and space and oriented myself within them I had missed my chance to listen for the milkman's whistle, though it's general knowledge that milkmen are incorrigible whistlers. With my early-rising cheerfulness and love of a catchy melody I'm something of a milkman *manqué* myself.

Whatever my underlying mood, my future was a wilderness of *manqués* – yes, I was an English graduate and could play games with Shakespearean tags, but that didn't lead to anything. Every now and again I would think of my consultation with the Appointments Board (invariably known as the Disappointments Board), itself a mark of failure since the people with real prospects had no need of it. My verbal skills might have made me into a reasonably accomplished setter of crossword puzzles, but deep down that isn't the way my mind works. I like putting words through their paces but have no interest in making letters jump through hoops. One job that had never been suggested was suddenly staring me in the face, as it had been staring me in the face only weeks ago. Disappointments officer! Looking sorrowful behind a desk. I could stretch to that.

I hadn't woken in the night to use my pee bottle, a rare dispensation from inconvenience since my bladder has a nagging temperament, and a fact worth recording. My need for it now was correspondingly urgent, and I was lucky to manage without splashing or spilling. A stained lilo is a poor return for hospitality freely offered and spilling over. Bladders are tricky things. If there's one thing more troublesome than a youthful bladder raring to go, deafening fellow-widdlers beyond the partition as its profuse jet crashes against porcelain, then it must be an ageing one forever losing the thread, dithering in midsentence and only remembering too late what it was trying to say. Where was I?

On another day I might have enjoyed a little dozing, letting the newly built sandcastle of the day be washed away for the pleasure of starting to rebuild it from scratch, but I was suddenly rigid with tension. In housing terms this was judgement day, the day of being taken in or turned away for ever. Wheat and chaff with a vengeance. The birds in the dawn chorus discussed my fate, some voting for Yes and some No. I had the idea that if I arrived after ten o'clock at Mayflower House, if I was even a minute late, then I would be cast into outer darkness, condemned to sleep in the Mini until the doors rusted shut, graduate hamster of the Cambridge side streets lacking even the basic amenities of exercise wheel and clean scattered straw. I was supposed to meet Maureen from Social Services at ten o'clock and it wasn't yet seven, but I was anxious to be on my way.

As a child I had felt the days came in distinct colours, with Saturday's aura the most vivid of all, a saturated red. I don't know whether this was true synæsthesia or just self-hypnosis, but the effect had worn off somewhat by the time I was in my twenties. The idea of Saturday had taken on a grey tinge from the dulling experience of Saturdays on which nothing particularly wonderful had happened. This Saturday just beginning loomed almost purple.

The milk bottles had hardly stopped reverberating in their crates before Hettie arrived in her clumpy Saturday finery to lug them in. Then she swooped on the pee bottle, emptied it and rinsed it. She put the kettle on, and while it was coming to a boil she came over and blew my nose for me. I didn't enjoy this, partly because my cold was reaching the almost enjoyable crusting stage and I was hoping the abraded skin around my nostrils would get its chance to recover soon. She had obviously seen Whyvonne obliging me in this way without a scolding and assumed it was open season on John Snotnose. I tried to think of a way of conveying to her that emptying a pee bottle without being asked is a tactful act – wiping a nose without permission is downright cavalier. Disposal of a pee bottle counts as a communal responsibility. My nose is my own. Hands off!

'Hettie, darling,' I said, as she brought me a cup of tea, 'for future reference . . .' Then I realised there was no future to be referred to in which she threatened my peace of mind with more presumptuous hanky work. I managed to turn the remark in the direction of simpering. '. . . your tea is terrific.' Simpering doesn't come naturally to me – this may have been the first time I've called anyone 'darling' in my life. In general I've had more success with hypnotic dominance than knowing my place. Most of the time Napoleon outranks Tiny Tim Cratchit in my book, though of course they want different things from life.

I told her I didn't want breakfast, and she seemed a little shocked. Perhaps there really are people who think breakfast is the most important meal of the day, and it makes sense that they should gravitate towards the places where it is prepared and offered for sale, or perhaps she had already become used to our routine, however new it was by most measuring.

'Are you sure?' I was sure. On the other hand I wished that I had taken the conversation in a different direction, while I was still able to use the phrase 'Hettie, darling' without awkwardness. If she was eager to wipe my nose perhaps she could have been persuaded to give my armpits a going-over with a flannel. My thinking on this issue had evolved. Apparently I had forgiven the original trespass and was now pining for further indignities.

There had been nothing to stop me having some spare shirts in the car. Even a single clean one would have made the looming meeting with Maureen less awkward. Psychologically it would have done me good, since from the folds of any such shirt would be released the fragrance of my Downing bedder's attentiveness. Jean Beddoes and her disinterested motherliness, devotion without a gravitational claim, would be much missed – though I hoped she wouldn't come to see me in my new 'digs' as she had promised.

I feel I can detect in my decision to do without a spare shirt a residual Christian impulse of mortification, to earn redemption by the choice of suffering. Mortification is a subtle tempter of the unwary ego, appealing so strongly to the exhibitionist impulse. The drama of renunciation only produces more preening, when the point is to give things up without noticing they've gone.

Usually I try to drown out the voice of common sense. Common sense is an infinite litter of kittens, mewing to be heard, and all too often I end up giving one of them a good home instead of sensibly thrusting it into the fatal sack with its fellows. And common sense tells me that there's no need for me to seek out mortification anyway. There's plenty available if I want it, there's mortification in spades never far off.

Perhaps doing without breakfast was just another mortification, though my desire to present myself at Mayflower House at the proper time ate up all my energy and would have left nothing remaining for the work of digestion. If I was neglecting myself, which is only another way of putting yourself first, then perhaps it was play-acting, but not play-acting undertaken for my own benefit. In the long crusade to avoid taking me in, Cambridge Social Services had seemed to characterise me as an importunate beggar outside its gates. I would live up to that billing. You want the lowest of the low? You want a stinking beggar? I'll see what I can do. This, in its needling abasement, would be closer to a defensible attitude, and so I'll lay claim to it retrospectively.

With a little chivvying Hettie was persuaded to help me get on my way, with a reasonable approximation of the haste I craved. Nothing is ever instantaneous in this life, unless the term is very indulgent, the instants allowed to roll lazily on their backs, presenting their bellies to be stroked. From the driving seat of the Mini I called out, 'Thanks for everything – tell Whyvonne I'll be in touch!', and I wasn't being actively insincere. In fact I did run into her years later when she had started a new enterprise in the Grafton Centre called Eleven's Nest. I didn't become a regular, not wanting to scrounge but not having spare cash to spend on snacks, and I never summoned up the courage to ask her why her new place was called that.

Like any other son of an Air Force father (never mind that Dad now worked for an airline) I had done a recce before the mission itself. Time spent on reconnaissance is always a good investment. I had flown by Mayflower House and had hovered near my target for a few minutes. I didn't turn the engine off. The full address was Mayflower House, Manhattan Drive, as if those responsible for the name had set out to combine the pristine-Puritan with the metropolitan-bustling, without hitting either of those targets. I chose to ignore the warning of the double meaning latent in the name. Buds may flower, or they may not. They may be blighted and wither on the branch, after all. It looked a dull place even in sunlight, being a tower block in a cul-de-sac off the Elizabeth Bridge. How far up did it tower? Not easy to say, for someone whose neck is even more lacking in movement in the vertical plane than it is from side to side.

Granted, 'reality' is no more than a series of those Potemkin villages hurriedly built to reassure Catherine the Great on her travels that the empire was thriving, façades like theatre flats propped up in front of squalor or emptiness. Even so I was disappointed by the shoddiness of the enterprise. So little trouble had been taken. Shouldn't 'reality' try a little harder for realism? But perhaps Maya was saving her budget for more important projects, with special effects that weren't as downright ordinary as they were in my case. A cul-de-sac? An actual cul-de-sac? It all seemed a bit crassly symbolic to the sensibility of a Cambridge graduate in English, even one who hadn't exactly distinguished himself on his way to a degree. I had bagged one of those coveted things, a 'gentleman's Third', the reward of those who have diverted themselves in all aspects of student life, without narrow-minded attempts to make study its be-all and end-all. I'd had a narrow escape, though – with a few more marks I would have ended up in the no-man's-land of a lower Second, not raffish in the slightest but a fully accredited dullard.

My proposed home seemed to scream 'backwater', to someone who had spent three years reasonably near the alleged heart of Cambridge. It was some kind of halfway house, defined by the things it was not, perhaps not a punishment but certainly not a reward. Whether this particular offender against the social order had a hope of rehabilitation or was going to slide back all the way down to the barely imaginable bottom wasn't yet clear. A one-legged man in a wheelchair might be waiting for me down there in the depths, grudgingly prepared to share his tins of shoplifted dog food.

I may have missed out an ancillary Pedley

After a few minutes a woman came out, frowning, to investigate my presence, and the Mini's. She wore a matching skirt and cardigan in dark green, a twinset as I believe it's called. That was as I would have wished it, not the costume as such but the vigilance. There should certainly be some sort of genteel Cerberus of a concierge on the premises to bark at any sort of riff-raff invasion, hawkers, pedlars and suchlike, even if it was in fact my private project to introduce a fair cross-section of riff-raff into my quarters. I drove off satisfied.

In one important respect I already fell below the standards of the premises. The rent for my flat was £12, and Social Services wouldn't stump up any more than £8. It was expected that I would make up the difference, which would leave me very little from my Supplementary Benefit. I didn't exactly go begging to my maternal grandmother, who had already taken up some of the slack in my finances after the family bust-up the previous year, but she made no difficulties. Granny had no objection to arming either side in a civil war, or both at once, but there was always a certain risk involved in appealing to her. She was a reliable fairy godmother with a reliable sting in her tail, the scorpion as benefactor or benefactor as scorpion. Granny could well afford it, with properties in Fleet Street and elsewhere. Her solicitors, Pedley, Pedley & May (I may have missed out an ancillary Pedley), had no need of other clients, her family's estate and the interlocking trusts it entailed providing more than enough work for a medium-sized firm. That's what she told me, anyway, though this may have been what various Pedleys led her to believe rather than the strict truth. Then the Council relented and shouldered the full weight of the rent, on the understanding that I would move to cheaper premises without making a fuss as soon as any such became available.

I would be introducing anomalous elements onto the premises every day, whether I wanted to or not, in the form of a home help and a district nurse. Between them they would provide the services that had mainly been performed, during my university years, by the college kitchen and by my bedder Jean. She and I had started off very guarded and ended by making tremendous pets of each other, and perhaps some similar trick might be worked on this new territory.

Mayflower House, CB4 1JT, was the back of beyond, or so it seemed to my Downing sensibility, but it took only a few minutes to drive there. I parked outside, this time positively eager to be challenged by porter and concierge, which meant (I knew) that I would be perfectly safe from molestation. I flicked a couple of Polo mints into my mouth. My electric toothbrush, far from new, had run out of charge since I had left the protection of A6 Kenny, and I knew just how it felt. I drifted off to sleep, and woke in panic from a dream in which I was living at the bottom of a well, having to catch boulders in my mouth whenever passers-by were moved to chuck them down at me. This dark imagery was a very modest transformation of the 'outside world', explained by the fact that only a few 'seconds' had passed. My mouth was still full of minty shards. I crunched them to nothingness, or perhaps only to a weak sugar solution, likely to disintegrate my teeth in the long term but perhaps giving me in the short some approximation to freshness of breath.

I must cut back on the inverted commas – it's not that they're not accurate but they become very annoying, and once you've started there's no logically convincing place to stop.

I was woken by someone tapping on the car window. When I opened my eyes I could see not just a single person but a vista of activity. A big scene had started with no expense spared and I had almost slept through my cue. The person tapping on the window was presumably Maureen, but there was more going on behind her. A van from Downing was being unloaded, and the resulting piles were being valiantly carried indoors by a slim girl wearing a primrose smock dress and the statutory raised and clumpy footwear. This was Maya at her most insidiously seductive, one of those disorienting moments when the plumber turns up on time and has the relevant spare part in his pocket, so that you almost find yourself believing that the world is real and workable.

Maureen was wearing a trouser suit of jaunty gingham, lilac check on a white background. The fabric had a vividness that was almost hallucinatory, putting the person wearing it into the shade. Might it have been seersucker? If so the ridged and puckered character of the weave might have been partly responsible for the unreal intensity of the garment's presence, it might have been an enchanted tablecloth from a folk tale, one moment doing duty in the family taverna or trattoria, the next (after a wave of the wizard's wand) helping disadvantaged people settle in to social housing. I explained that the wheelchair was in the boot, and how to get it out. The rigmarole about the importance of putting the brakes on makes me feel like some veteran airline steward, in for the long haul, explaining safety procedures for the ten-thousandth time. And the exits are . . . everywhere and nowhere. While she was helping me sit down the Downing porters finished unloading – at least, one of them made a salute in my direction, looked lingeringly at the girl as she bent over my things, and then they drove off. It was a bittersweet pleasure to be reunited with my companion in so many naps and trances, the Parker-Knoll recliner. There's nothing like moving house to make you realise that you don't in fact live an austere life but have every sort of unnecessary thing stowed away or even frankly displayed, invisible only because you've decided not to notice it. Julian of Norwich herself might have been surprised, if called upon to change anchoritic cells, to see how many shopping lists she'd hung on to, not all of them scribbled with fragmentary drafts of her *Revelations of Divine Love*.

I wish I could say that I had made an inventory of my possessions, so as to tick off objects arriving against a cyclostyled list, but my retreat from university life had not been particularly orderly. For instance I didn't discover for quite a while that my copy of *Kiss Kiss* had gone missing, leaving a hole in my Roald Dahl library, but even if I'd known about it at the time I like to think that I would have wished the porters Godspeed. Let Downing staff reap the benefit. It was only a paperback but one with a nice supple spine – I hate Venus-flytrap books that snap shut at a moment's notice. I have no difficulty understanding the irrelevance of the body to the life inside it, but I don't always manage to convince myself that it's the same book no matter what the cover, and I was fond of the design Penguin had devised for *Kiss Kiss*. The flightless bird of British publishing soared pretty high in those days. The cover showed a pair of stylised lips in lurid colours against a black background, though the moment I've said so I wonder if I haven't given my vanished copy a retrospective promotion, when actually it was a woodcut of pheasants flying out of a pram.

Before we entered the flats we had to wait for the girl who was carrying another load. 'That's Paula,' said Maureen. 'Your home help.' I had a home help! It was no odder than having a bedder, in fact considerably less odd, but I felt an inrush of feeling just the same. Perhaps Bertie Wooster felt the same way when he learned he had a gentleman's gentleman, someone who would shimmy into rooms and get him out of scrapes.

Paula's primrose smock had a pocket, and this smock pocket was just the right size to accommodate a little radio, one that happened to be tuned to Radio 1.

Just now, as she clumped back and forward with awkward arm-fuls of my things, the song emerging in all tinniness from the little speaker, filtered through bright yellow cloth, was a chart single by George Harrison, a religious statement lightly disguised (as was often his way) as an artless pop song suitable for teenagers to sing along to. If Paula was out of her teens it wasn't by much. 'Give me love' went the chorus. But who among the millions that tapped their toes to it understood that it was godhead itself being addressed in those ama-tive terms? Years had passed since I had last watched *Top of the Pops*, but there was no reason to think that the current crop of girls bopped any less stiffly to the new songs than the old ones. Last Thursday and the Thursday to come they would be shaking their heads and swing-ing their hips from side to side, moving their lips in time to lyrics they pretended to understand. The absence of understanding was rea-sonable enough in the case of this particular song since they would be asking not only for love but to be kept 'free from birth'. A handful of the less innocent girls might suspect a reference to contraception. Their parents might do the same. Would anyone of either generation recognise what was being invoked here as *samadhi*, the blissful dis-mounting from the treadmill of life and death? It's a lot to ask of the pop-picking public.

Perhaps I'm just hard to please, but George Harrison's voice seems to be badly in need of exactly the lesson his song was trying to teach. There's a self-pitying catch to it despite his claims to enlightenment, and what business does he have referring to his 'heavy load'? That's slapdash Hinduism, that is. The 'load' of suffering has only the weight you give it – it's like the strongman's barbell weights in the old circus routine, the ones that he lifts with so much straining and bulging of eyes, to general applause, but are then tucked under the arm of the scrawniest stagehand and carried blithely off.

Paula held the door open and Maureen pushed me over the thresh-old. In the entrance hall we were greeted by the lady who had sniffed the air round the Mini when I had made my recce. She too seemed to interpret the weekend as a signal for a general loosening of clothing protocols, and was wearing pale pink slacks. She had far more reason to sniff the air than she had before, since I was now frankly stinky, but she maintained decorum, saying she was Mrs Baine the manageress (or did she say receptionist?) and would bring me a *Cambridge Evening News* later on, when my 'company' had left. This was a kindly gesture, though not actively exciting as an offer. If anything had happened in the supposed world while I was between addresses I would wait for it to impose its relevance on me. I had no plans to meet the headlined trivialities halfway.

The common parts of the building were fairly spacious but the flat was tiny, a bedsitting room plus a corridorette leading to a mini-kitchen and a dwarf bathroom. Only the addition of that dwarf bathroom made the premises larger than what I had been used to in Downing. It didn't help the impression of pokiness that Paula was valiantly dragging in the Parker-Knoll behind us singlehanded – the contingent of Downing porters seeming to think their help unnecessary. It was hard to think where the mighty recliner could go without dominating the space. I should have been celebrating my safe arrival in serviceable accommodation, grateful for the amenities of walls and roof, but instead I was agreeing with the Council (for my own reasons) that this was a makeshift arrangement. Not because £12 was too much to be spent on an unnecessary person's rent but because it was a flatlet, and despite appearances I am not a personlet. I was a person and I needed a flat.

Perching as best she could, Maureen made conversation. I assume she was trying to draw me out, as a good hostess must, but shouldn't I have been the host on this occasion? If I was leading the conversation, getting her to talk about herself, I seemed to be doing a fine job. Maureen had a nephew who had just moved to Islington and was planning a *Great Gatsby* party, with cocktails called 'sidecars' and a jazz band. Nodding is hard work. I wish there was another way of conveying assent without use of words. Was I supposed to be taking notes for a housewarming of my own? The space in which we were sitting was crowded as it was. We were already a housewarming party of a rather awkward institutional sort.

I realise it's a mistake to put small talk under a microscope but I can't help that, the microscope being my most reliable piece of equipment. On a weekday Maureen would probably be more businesslike.

Since it was Saturday morning I got the benefit of her gingham trouser suit and the social lives of her family.

Maureen admitted that though she had got used to decimal currency she couldn't abide people who said 'twenty pee' instead of 'twenty new pence', the way everyone did nowadays. She was going to stick to her guns and hold out against vulgarism. I shared her feeling, but I knew my resistance was finite. I could feel my willpower stretching beyond its limits and it wouldn't be long now before I too swallowed the bitter solecistic pill and started pee-ing all over the place. You can't be a rebel all your life.

'This is quite a swanky building, I must say, John,' she said. 'I almost envy you.' I already knew that the flat had originally been assessed as being beyond the Council's means, and would certainly have been beyond mine if it hadn't been for Granny's promise of help. Then eventually the authorities relented and decided they could just about afford me if they did without biscuits with their tea. 'There must be a hundred flats in the building.'

'A hundred? There can't be!'

'John, it's a big place and there are seven floors.'

I managed with an effort not to say 'Seven floors? There can't be!', as if I'd lived in a hamlet all my life and never seen a city. How was I to know how far up the building went? It's not just a matter of having eyes to see, you need a neck to crane if you're going to be able to judge the heights of objects from close to.

'Oh yes, there are views of the Cam.'

'Not from the ground floor there aren't. Not unless there's a lift. Is there a lift?'

'No,' Maureen. 'There doesn't seem to be a lift.' Usually when there doesn't seem to be a lift it's because there isn't one. Maya is always changing her tune, but it's more her style to break a promise than to offer an arbitrary amenity, a convenience where there was none a moment ago.

'Why don't we go up there now?' I said. 'You can give me a carry and we can both see what the Council is getting for its money, even if it's just the once.'

Poor Maureen didn't know what to say. I counted down in my head – ten, nine, eight, seven, six. If you make someone squirm for more than ten seconds, you've lost their goodwill in perpetuity. You can kiss it goodbye – in fact you already have kissed it goodbye. Five, four, three – time to pull back from the brink.

'Actually, I'm very tired. Do you mind if we do it another time?'

Paula squeezed past us carrying my stereo system, a Hacker I had picked up from the factory gates in Maidenhead. 'Stereo system' may be too hopeful a description, since one speaker was integral to the deck and the other was attached to it by a wire of modest length. To get a stereo picture you needed to line up your ears fairly precisely – it was stereo minus or else mono plus, but it delivered good sound just the same. If it had been protectively packaged in some way while Downing had responsibility for it then the wrappings had been removed, and Paula was balancing the speaker on the lid. Then she laid both items on the floor without bending her knees, though also, I have to admit, without endangering either deck or speaker.

Maureen told me that the Council would happily have looked after my things while the flat was being prepared for me, so I hadn't needed to throw myself on the mercy of my college. Asking the local authority for their help wasn't something that had occurred to me. I wasn't well briefed on my rights, and had experienced the Council as wily opponents rather than allies. People in authority are always saying you should know your rights, though I've noticed they don't much enjoy it when you do.

For me to ask about my possessions would have meant considering the possibility that the Council might take more trouble over my things than my person, and really it was healthier not to entertain that thought. At one point Maureen raised her eyebrows and indicated the toiling girl. Some message was being sent. I was singled out for an intimate communication, even if I couldn't immediately decide what it was. I tried to work out what she was trying to say with her raised eyebrows, and how it might apply to the young woman working away in front of us, who was now labouring to put my books on the table and to arrange them in piles (though no 'pile' can ever really be tidy). She might perhaps be asking, 'Aren't people bendy?' – something that I've often thought myself. But no, somehow there was an element of disapproval involved. The young woman was being criticised, or (I felt I was getting warmer as the game went on) regarded as somehow being an inadequate performer in the tasks she was discharging. Pauline repeated the eyebrow raise and the indicative move of her head, but added in a faint incredulous shake this time, to make her meaning clear. I got it at last.

Where do they get these girls? She hasn't a clue . . . If I hadn't been so tired I might have cottoned on more quickly. I hadn't expected my first day of somewhat-independent life to contain this element of charades, party games making up for the lack of a party.

Just ask for BURLIES

Maureen had a clipboard with her, and at this point she began to write something down on a notepad. I wasn't well placed to see what she was writing, and in my insecurity I imagined she might have been commenting on my lack of personal hygiene – 'Client Mr Cromer self-neglecting, positively humming with B.O., mental illness very much on the cards' or something of the sort. It seemed to be quite a lengthy summary of the situation she found this Saturday morning. Then she slid the pad slyly across to me. She had written: *This silly girl is doing it all wrong. She'll do her back a mischief. She's not meant to move anything for you anyway. Not allowed to touch furniture.*

She took back the pad and started a fresh sheet. *Still, I don't think we need tell her just yet, do you? Not while she's making herself useful. She can lift YOU, that's all right. For anything else that needs moving you're going to have to get 'burlies'. They're the beefy chaps who do the heavy lifting. Just ask – not too often, mind – for BURLIES.* I wriggled myself round so that I could see her expression properly. She was holding her lips in a firm straight line, leaving me to guess that she was fighting the curve of a smile.

While Paula was making one last trip Maureen said aloud, 'She's a good girl really. Doesn't have to work today, but seemed to want to see you settled in . . .' So having encouraged me to join a mocking conspiracy against the poor girl she was now making me feel guilty about being party to it. When Paula had finished, I thanked her with a fair amount of embarrassment while Maureen asked her briskly to make tea and bring biscuits.

I didn't know much about how my new life would work. I learned that my home help would come for a couple of hours on Mondays,

Wednesdays and Fridays, and apparently the district nurse would call once weekly. The safety net was largely holes but the same is true of every net that ever was.

After our tea and biscuits I tried a pretend yawn that rapidly turned out to be the real thing and was followed by a string of entirely authentic repetitions. This was perhaps a lesson in the dangers of fakery. It wasn't exactly that I looked forward to being on my own, but I didn't know how long I'd be able to keep all these plates of consciousness spinning, spinning on poles that my hands couldn't control, particularly as the plate that was me seemed to be so deeply cracked. After Paula had washed up the few things we had used for our tea and biscuits she said she'd see me on Monday, and Maureen said I knew how to reach her, which was technically true. She had written down her work telephone number and unlike many people I had not only a postal address but a telephone number. Then I was alone again, but reconnected with society after a bruising interruption. I had experienced my three days on the common mercy as being the equivalent of three years with the Foreign Legion for anyone else, but how can I justify an exaggerated comparison like that? It seemed hard, that's all. It seemed adequately hard, even if I didn't get sunstroke or even sand in my mouth.

Was it the Spartans who made their young people live without help, with every man's hand against them, to prove that they could live without a community before being admitted to one? It doesn't seem to be a sensible way of carrying on, but the mood of the experiment felt familiar. One pin-up boy of Spartan culture was the legendary youth who stole a fox (presumably with the idea of killing it and eating it) and hid it under his cloak when intercepted by a citizen asking questions. The boy remained composed while the fox ate his heart, then keeled over dead without making a sound. Admirable! – not just stiff upper lip but stiff upper ventricle. Even before the boy had a chance to discover whether fox meat agreed with him or not, the fox ate a human heart and found it good. Perhaps it's a parable whose true meaning is that we should leave the eating of meat to creatures with no other option. I had already forgotten Wednesday's bacon and sausage. They had been metabolised into oblivion, though not erased from the Akashic Records.

Of course not every man's hand was against me, and certainly not every woman's. I might have had a crash course in non-attachment, but I had stayed stubbornly stuck to those who stuck by me. I had been helped by, among others, a capricious café owner and a sturdy Australian in mud-streaked shorts, bringing pots of earth fresh from the autoclave, baked clean and made safe for new growth.

The thing I liked most about the flat was the windowsill, which got a lot of sun. If windowsills could talk, this one would be chirping, 'Isn't this the perfect spot to grow the Portuguese sundew you're always talking about?' Too right. They're perfectly happy in pots, and I had sterile soil just waiting, thanks to Celia. I would keep the foil in place until the moment I had the seed in my hand and was ready to grow.

As gardeners know, repotting is a traumatic event in the life of a plant, however successful in the long run. There was no reason to think it would be any different for me. Even when the operation is smoothly managed it sends a pulse of panic through every cell of the organism, the terror of organic life separated from its sources of nourishment. Transplant surgery is always a risky enterprise, as many a herbaceous border can testify.

The Canadian Red Cross Memorial Hospital at Taplow arose among the outbuildings of a stately home, the Vulcan School was in a castle, Downing College though not glamorous by Cambridge standards was modestly distinguished architecturally. Now I was going to be living in a building without aspirations or memories.

When I was alone I approached my new telephone in a state of tension bordering on arousal. Had it been accomplished, the unlikely thing that had been promised? And there it was, on the paper disc behind the plastic lamination on the dial: CAMbridge 65628.

It wasn't just the presence of a phone, though such things couldn't be taken for granted. I had fought long and hard enough to have one installed in my college room. It was the fact that this new apparatus had the same number, magically transferred from over half a mile away. The things they could do these days! And I knew that where my phone had been in A6 Kenny there would be smoke and ash. The telephone had been deeply rooted in the wall, and ripping out both the device and its number must have produced an electronic mandrake scream that anyone susceptible could hear for miles around. The apparition of the phone number at Mayflower House would have to be balanced by something like exorcism on my Downing staircase, performed by a telephone engineer of high ceremonial accomplishment or perhaps a ring of chanting Druids.

My successor in that college room couldn't be allowed to inherit my privileged connection. That was out of the question. After the ritual of excommunication I'm convinced they used a red-hot poker to heat-seal the wire where it went into the wall. It's not too much to suppose they pumped in poison just to be safe, as is the practice with tree stumps, to prevent any regeneration of the communicative root. There must be no possibility of a pale tendril sprouting, the next spring or in any other season, from the cauterised nub in the skirting board of A6 Kenny.

I had finally managed to convince the college authorities that a phone was a necessity in my case, but it was also a pleasure and a resource. As an immobilised child I had been allowed to read out the weekly order to the greengrocer. To my way of thinking no instrument can rival the telephone in delivering the elusive dream of action at a distance. Since then Telephone John has been able to stake a claim on amazing tracts of territory, which flesh-and-blood John has struggled to consolidate and often finds himself sternly marched away from.

At Downing I had encouraged my neighbours (who encouraged their neighbours) to treat the phone as being in some way community property. Yes, I'd complained about being used as a message service, but it was inevitable when my ownership of a telephone was such a distinction. My unofficial position as receptionist for the staircase, intelligence officer in charge of my own little GHQ, was one of the mainstays of my undergraduate happiness. I could for instance tell the girlfriend of some dirty stop-out what she wanted and needed to hear ('Yes, I saw him up and about bright and early – I think he'd been for a run. Probably still in the shower . . .'). I was in my element. There's no better way of building a little power base than doing favours for everyone. Make yourself indispensable. Now the switchboard was dark.

There had always been limits to my obligingness. I wouldn't countenance my number being given to people's parents. It had been hard enough to disentangle myself from my own self-proclaimed creators, if that job had even been done. I wasn't going to let other people's parents, still further removed from any possible claim, get their hooks into me.

The numbering of rooms at Mayflower House started at 00, and I'd have moved heaven and earth to be transferred to 007 if there had been any possibility of taking up residence there, but it was a broom cupboard and I had to put up with what I had been allotted, with 005.

Still, I was on the books at last, and specifically a rent book. It was based on a 48-week year, with Xs printed across four weeks, corresponding to Christmas, Easter and two weeks of summer holiday. These exempted weeks were described as 'rent holidays', which was obvious nonsense. The figure of 48 was purely for administrative convenience, and the yearly rent was divided by that number – there was no reduction and therefore no holiday. I was incensed. Don't underestimate the working class! We're not idiots. You patronise us at your peril.

I had become rather abruptly proletarian, fulfilling a long-held dream, at the moment that I took possession of that rent book. It might just as easily have been Mao's little volume, the one that sold so well in those days, sending a surge of world-historical underclass power through this little Red Guard's locked fingers every time he touched it. I had always wanted to belong to the lower depths, and if poverty and dependence on handouts were qualifications for membership I was well on my way to achieving my dream.

Encashment must always have the edge

Meanwhile Supplementary Benefit came in the form of a little book of weekly vouchers, like raffle tickets, two to the page, date-stamped and provided with a counterfoil. Printed on each ticket was 'This voucher must be encashed within three months of the above date, or we may have difficulty keeping your benefits up to date.' Encashing is so much nicer than cashing, the very word is encased in cashmere. That 'en' is like an honorific ennobling a word, as 'enrobing' makes being coated in chocolate seem like something to do with the Queen's birthday honours, a distinguished walnut being enrobed in a simple ceremony at Windsor Castle. Even so encashment must always have the edge over enrobification.

With the phone transferred as had been promised me, I could feel residually connected with the outside world without needing to take any active steps to communicate. The telephone might ring at any moment, or it might hold its tongue for three months. It wasn't up to me. I installed myself on the bed and wondered if I would be able to sleep. I was a bit puritanical about naps in those days. Why abolish time and space when I'd only have to start devising them from scratch later on?

If anyone rang it was most likely to be Granny, freely offering favours that would not by a long stretch be free. There would be a whole cat's cradle of strings attached. She wrapped cheques around her fingers to make knuckledusters. Consequently her largesse left bruises.

Mum and Dad weren't likely to make overtures, though even in their non-communication they pulled in different directions. Mum's was a hot silence and Dad's a cool one, aspiring to indifference or perhaps merely pretending. Only Jodrell Bank's most powerful radio telescope, probing the remotest lightless zones of Dad's character, might be able to detect a twinkle there where no star was mapped.

The chances of my siblings making contact weren't much greater. Peter was travelling, very sensibly, and when last heard of was in the Southern Hemisphere, working with heavy machinery in Queensland. I imagined him wearing ear protectors that would filter out even the faintest reverberations of family. He might find a way to mark my birthday on the 27th of December but was otherwise out of radio contact. Never mind that a birthday is less than nothing according to Hindu thought, and marking it perverse to the point of necrophilia. The standard comparison is with adorning a corpse. Why celebrate a birth when what is born can only die? I wasn't sure that Peter had broken the mind-forged manacles of family, but he had certainly run as far away as he could. Elasticated manacles, though, that's the secret that accounts for the durability of these attachments.

The person with the sincerest need to stay in touch, and the least ability to do so, was my little sister Audrey, much more of a casualty of the previous year's epic family bust-up than I was. In some families a girl born ten years after the first child (me) and eight after the second (Peter) would qualify as an afterthought, but in the Cromer household it was clear that we boys were failed attempts at the daughter Mum had always wanted, however much of a headache the mother–daughter relationship was as it developed. Audrey was born with adult willpower as some babies are born with hair and teeth. She was tightly curled around a No that Mum couldn't override. She consented to be lulled to sleep by the hundreds and thousands that I sorted by colour and prescribed to her, but perhaps that was less of a yielding to me than a way of demonstrating that Mum had no power over her. Certainly Mum felt threatened by my 'magic beans' and wanted me to stop prescribing. She went to the doctor and got something whose workings she could understand.

As for what Dad wanted, that was always a little mysterious. His most characteristic posture was a drily mocking acceptance of things he hadn't chosen, or wouldn't admit to having chosen, a strange abstention from the very principle of choice. In many respects he came close to an accidental enlightenment, though of course a miss is as good as a mile.

I had gone on writing letters to her, and when no answers came assumed they had been intercepted. After that I tried sending them care of Dad, who sometimes took a different line from Mum's in family matters, without ever quite saying so. He could keep quite a warm little truce going in the heart of a feud, but still I heard nothing back. In fact I had no news of Audrey except through a tender Bourne End neighbour, Joy Payne, who would brief me without giving away much detail. This wasn't a stripped-down communiqué in the military style, more of a tactfully blurred sketch, since Joy's loyalties were divided and she didn't want to take sides any more than she had to. As she put it, 'I'm not spying for you, John, if that's what you mean. Not even for you. Not for anyone.' Her reports usually amounted to *All quiet on the domestic front*. Not necessarily a reassuring bulletin when attached to a household where chronic seething tension was the resting state. Dad's habit of pretending not to notice amplified the eruptions when they came, and perhaps in some obscure way he fed off the leakage of its radiation before any detonations arrived.

127

If I describe the family explosion of summer 1972 as epic I'm hardly thinking of the Mahabharata. A better comparison would be with the marathon late-night showings of horror films that they used to have at the old Kinema on Mill Road, films that were gruelling rather than frightening. The only title I can bring to mind is *Revenge of the Blood Beast*. Was there a *Return of the Blood Beast* shown after it? I think so. It was no odder that there would be a sequel than that there should be such a film in the first place. In Hindu cosmology Brahma is the god of creation, but he occupies a relatively lowly place in the pantheon, perhaps because he just doesn't know when to stop. Consistently in Hinduism creation takes second place to transformation. Annihilation itself lies closer to the sources of bliss than creation does. Annihilation holds hands with rapture but with creation comes only maintenance. No offence to Vishnu the preserver, but it's Śiva who brings the house down with his dance.

Audrey had rescued me from the house the previous summer, in a way that I attributed to the direct intervention of my guru partly because she was so matter-of-fact about it, not going in for any sort of drama. It was the opposite of a confrontation. In fact she removed me from a grinding confrontation that had been going on for some days at that point, simply picking me up and carrying me to the Mini. She drew on a strength and a decisive calm that lay outside herself.

I don't know in general how entertaining an aspect of divinity affects the psyche, but I was confident that Ramana Maharshi would be a considerate visitor, while a barnstorming showman like Sai Baba would throw his weight about and very likely wreck the place. There was no reason to anticipate after-effects, though of course given the rupture in communication I couldn't be sure that I would learn about them even if they happened.

To fluster an opal

I could easily imagine Audrey sneaking up to Mum's handbag while she was in another room. I summoned that mental image and tried to induce her to open the clasp and ferret inside for Mum's little address book but I couldn't make it happen. What was Audrey doing that Saturday morning? I had even less idea of what thirteen-year-old girls do over their summer holidays than what young waitresses do on Friday nights, and that's as it should be considering the arbitrary nature of blood relationship. Brahma had visited the marital bedroom of Trees in Bourne End on two occasions a decade apart and had breathed out new life, as if there wasn't enough of that already. It's hardly a link, is it? 'Blood is thinner than water' isn't an explicit principle of Hinduism, but the whole tendency of the religion is anti-coagulant. Still, I couldn't help wondering.

I knew that Granny would phone me sooner or later, and if the phone ever rang at 11.30 or so it was highly likely to be her. 22.5p for a three-minute peak call over 35 miles! Granny's favourite time for phoning me was about half an hour before the cheap rate began. It was as if she couldn't wait to hurl money at Her Majesty's Minister of Posts and Telecommunications.

I felt the need to contact her first, giving formal notice that I had moved, having a nebulous sense of indebtedness towards her. After all, she had agreed to make up the difference between the rent at Mayflower House and what Cambridge Social Services thought I was worth, though she didn't need to make good on the offer in the end. It wasn't explained to me what had changed, my value as a person or the funds available, and I was hardly going to make difficulties.

'Good afternoon, Granny.'

'John.' The ball was in my court. The ball would always be in my court. Granny made a point of treating me the same as she would treat anyone else, as if to compensate for all the punches being pulled elsewhere. Possibly she was overrating the general pulling of punches.

Granny wasn't a relaxed presence on the phone, but then it was the last thing she would have wanted to be. A phone conversation for her was a form of single combat, even when she happened to be on your side. She withheld the neutrally encouraging noises that most people supply as a matter of course. It's true that her generation wasn't generally chatty on the phone, inculcated with the feeling that this was an instrument suited only to making or breaking arrangements urgently, but she took the rationing of speech further than most. Her silence was a taut and steely thing, not to be confused with the absence of communication, but sooner or later I would find myself saying, however much I had told myself not to, 'Granny . . . are you still there?'

Then I would hear an acidulated little sigh. 'How am I to answer that, John? I can hardly say "No". No doubt you are accustomed to your dear mother's tender manner on the telephone. She chatters positively like a lovebird. If one was as attached to Hindoo ideas as you are, one would say she had perhaps been a lovebird in another existence.' There's no difference in pronunciation or meaning as between *Hindoo* and *Hindu*, but I doubt if I'm mistaken about the way Granny wrote the word in her head. My 'dear mother' – that word 'dear' lay between us trembling, in the manner of a traumatised puppy at the dogs' home waiting to be claimed. 'But lovebirds, like any other type of creature, are seeking food and safety merely. Or a mate! John, I have had an idea that may help. The next time you worry that I may have died or slipped away on some errand more pressing than speaking with my grandson, perhaps you will be more logical and simply ask me to make a noise. "Noise, please" – that will express your meaning well enough. But you will hear no noise from me for a few seconds, since I'm about to fetch a pencil. I'll be needing to make a note of your new telephone number.' She had put down the phone before I could explain that it wasn't necessary. 'All ready,' she said a little later. 'Fire away. Or should I say, "Noise, please, John"?'

'There's no need, Granny. It's still the same number. I took it with me.'

'How extraördinary.' She gave the word six full syllables in the manner of her class and generation, where younger and more slapdash speakers would have abridged it – *extrordinry!* – to a shrunken four. 'You took it with you? However did you manage that?'

I realised that I had given her a mental image of her unlimber grandson moving house in the manner of a Russian pedlar, with the phone and all his other belongings lashed onto his back. 'I took the number with me, Granny, not the phone. It took a bit of organising, but it all worked out in the end.'

'I can't pretend to understand what you're telling me, John. I am defeated. Would it not have been more sensible to take the address with you?' She stopped for a moment, as if unsure whether she'd made a joke. She wasn't entirely comfortable with the practice of humour, perhaps because its effects were unpredictable. A joke for her was like the silver threepenny bit ceremonially added to the Christmas pudding mix. All part of life's rich pudding, but if you lost track of it you might end up breaking a tooth.

'I believe I've lost my thread, John,' she said, as if she'd heard of such a thing but never previously experienced it. 'I'm positively woolgathering. What was it we were talking about?'

'We were talking about my new phone number being the same as the old one, Granny.'

'Then why, pray, am I standing here with a pencil in my hand?'

'Perhaps you're going to write down my new address.'

'I'm waiting to hear it.' The reflex of asserting dominance was too strong for her to own up to her moment of confusion, though she rang off soon afterwards, leaving me to wonder if perhaps I'd interrupted a nap that she would deny to her dying day having succumbed to. Though denying something to your dying day is the surest way of booking a return flight, which is the last thing you should want. Don't risk the cancellation of your exit visa!

There were two flies in my new flat the day I moved in, tenants without a rent book, who alternated positions between the ceiling and somewhere on the bedside table. My father, being ex-RAF, would have approved of such manœuvres, which he called 'circuits and bumps', the creatures lightly touching down (or up, in the case of the ceiling) before taking off again, testing their reflexes and the functionality of their landing gear. I lay on the bed watching the flies alternately landing on the ceiling in their impossible way, and I day-dreamed about having a ray gun or some such needle of destructive light at my disposal. Would it constitute a great sin to vaporise them with it if I did? Perhaps some sort of maser or laser beam. I'd watched *Tomorrow's World* on the telly, so I knew that a laser beam was the result of exciting a ruby in exactly the right way. There are times when science seems the dreamiest form of knowledge, much more so than religion. Who first got the idea of exciting a ruby? It seems no more plausible a project than trying to fluster an opal or intimidate an amethyst. Perhaps the angels dancing on a pinhead in that famous formula, countable only by God, are really particles of excited ruby, in which case they may be countable by man and his instruments after all.

Flies were much more stupid in those days. They hadn't learned the advanced techniques of evasion they use now – just as blue tits in my childhood were only just beginning to learn how to peck through the foil tops of milk bottles left on the step. At Mayflower House I managed to catch flies quite a few times. 'Catch' is a misleading word in this context, just as it is when someone 'borrows' a cigarette. What is caught cannot be released, what is borrowed cannot be returned – the transaction in each case is final. I would regularly catch flies (sluggish, end-of-season flies, but never mind that) under the blade of a knife, after waiting patiently for them to position themselves in readiness for the swift squash of self-transcendence. Do better next time, while hoping there's not a next time. Perhaps I hypnotised them. I don't always know when I'm doing that.

There have been plenty of times when insects have touched my heart, and I'm not generally repelled by them. Mum was the one who couldn't abide spiders, to the point where I had sometimes overridden her will, talking low and reassuringly until she was able, almost in a trance, to place a glass over a sturdy specimen in the bath, sliding a piece of card to shut it in and then shaking it out of the window, after which she would start shaking in her own right. I couldn't do it for her, but I could talk her through it, and she would have been more traumatised by the squashing of such a creature than she was from helping it escape.

My introduction to scientific method came when Dad studied a water bug under the microscope, and let me take a look. Of course the bulb that enabled us to see what was under the microscope was not a neutral part of the endeavour. The heat started to evaporate the water surrounding the bug, and I was waiting for Dad to top it up, but he just said, 'Let's see what happens when he dries out, shall we?' I thought he was being cruel, but he told me to look carefully and let me monopolise the eyepiece. I could actually see the last drops of water disappearing under the glare of enquiry. But then I saw a sort of fizzing shell forming round the bug. It was building itself a cyst at short notice, locking in moisture so as to survive the hard times and get through somehow to the next rain. Dad was playing God in an almost literal way, laying on a drought to see how a creature would cope with it. His interest was great and contained no component of sympathy. I've never been able to read the Book of Job without that picture in my mind, of the creator who doesn't care, but that's just my Christian upbringing speaking.

And now I've forgotten the name of the bug, which Dad would find it hard to forgive me for. Really I'm hopeless. The other day I got confused between the ichneumon fly and the dytiscus larva, though they hardly overlap in taxonomy or habitat. How long before I forget my own name? And not by dint of self-realisation.

After watching those two flies for some time I became bored with their routine, something that showed my limitations rather than theirs, exposing my morbid need for variety. I remembered that in my scanty medical kit – certainly scanty compared to what it is now – I had some syringes, which I used on occasion to inject pentazocine (under the trade name of Fortral) intramuscularly, and some alcohol to sterilise them. It wasn't much work to fill a syringe with some alcohol, and then I had a fly-extinguisher ready to hand. It took me a while to get my eye in, but after I'd snuffed out the first two there was a steady supply of replacements. I was resuming the war games I had played with my little brother after a lapse of almost two decades. That must be my excuse for the fact that I had escalated hostilities. It wasn't much of a game for the flies I sprayed with annihilating liquid. I was taking lives as real and imaginary as my own.

Foreknowledge of the brouhaha

Hindus, mind you, are not Jains. It is legitimate to consider some living organisms as pests and to encompass their destruction. Saying it straight out: to kill them. Did my guru ever explicitly pronounce on the sacredness of insect lives? I'd have to do some research to be sure, but there's indirect evidence pointing to an acceptance of the category of vermin, entities outside the operations of karma, and a willingness to eliminate such uncreaturely creatures. When his devotee Lakshmi was badly troubled by lice, Ramana Maharshi suggested that her stall be dusted with a new insecticidal powder.

Lakshmi was both a spiritual disciple of my guru and a cow with a particular fondness for mountain banana. As a calf she would lay her head at his feet. Her tenderness was reciprocated: Ramana Maharshi held her head in his hands while she died, or rather achieved enlight-enment, which she did on June the 18th 1948.

For quite a time I was uneasy about this particular piece of animal husbandry on the part of my guru. I wasn't troubled by the fate of Lakshmi's lice, which clearly deserved no better, but on account of dichloro-diphenyl-trichloroethane, the preparation he had chosen to eliminate them.

I remember the reverberations in the Sunday papers of the shock wave produced when *Silent Spring* was published. We had underesti-mated the ubiquity of the destructive forces, and Kali had not only occupied the missile silos but infiltrated the fields and streams in the baleful many-armed shape of DDT. I must have been twelve. Even Dad was shaken by the coverage. He went to the shed after break-fast to make sure that his hands were clean, his watering can above reproach.

I've lost count of the times when I've assumed that Ramana Maharshi was wrong about something, and then found out that I was the benighted one. Easy to imagine him having foreknowledge of the brouhaha, ignoring it in advance, understanding perfectly well, as we do now, that DDT is an effective pesticide, dangerous only when improperly used.

My guru was much on my mind, though it would be going too far to claim that these were spiritual thoughts. I was more like a disap-pointed lover getting maudlin over a photo of the beloved taken in happier times. I did in fact have a photograph of Ramana Maharshi, unpacked by Paula, though I hardly needed to look at it to refresh my memory. It was an image of him in old age, with white beard and creased neck, but he had put on no authority to go with them. His face suggested an unusual version of enlightenment, expressing fond amusement as much as joy, faint secret hilarity available to anyone disposed to claim it. The colours of the photograph seemed slightly unreal since it had originally been black and white, a period artefact tinted by hand.

I described him as my guru and myself as his disciple, his devotee, but what did this actually mean? A disciple has no rights over the guru, and devotion is not an identity but a shedding of it, a hopelessly defective shedding in my case. Only the dimmest sort of introspection was needed to understand that what had first attracted me to Hinduism was beginning to dissatisfy me: its lack of structure. Raised a Christian, I hadn't enjoyed my experience of organised religion but now I seemed impatient with the disorganised variety. In Hinduism there were loosely constellated beliefs but no one to keep the faithful in line or to persuade them that they belonged. No Hindu vicar, padre or chaplain would be making house calls at Mayflower House.

In India I had met Hindus, but here in Britain I knew none. Most people turn to religion for the company it brings with it, but I had made a less sociable choice. I had turned to something unknown, though it had seemed instantly familiar.

Hinduism had nothing to compare with Christianity's confident list of sacraments. Its spiritual mechanisms were ramshackle by comparison. A *puja* is a personal ritual that may involve the lighting of a flame or the making of an offering but can be purely internal. There's no prescribed form of words. *Darshan* is a sort of manifestation of holiness, but it's no more (and no less) than the gift of presence. Ramana Maharshi gave *darshan* to a devotee lower down the sacred mountain Aranachula by choosing to brush his teeth where he knew he could be seen by her. It's hardly the Sermon on the Mount, is it? All spectacularly informal. *Prasad* is in a sense consecrated food (though flowers also count), so there should by rights be useful analogies with communion, but the operations of divinity are fluid and not to be pinned down. *Prasad* is offered to godhead, but then freely shared. The whole batch of sweets or snacks, whatever it may be, is equally holy. There's no quibbling over transubstantiation, and the food remains real food capable of satisfying real appetite. I feel another bout of inverted commas coming on, wanting to settle on that word 'real' like crows on goalposts, but will hold back. The only technicality seems to be that the food shouldn't be tasted during the process of cooking, in defiance of accepted chef protocol, since the deity (or swami, or guru) must be the first to eat. You don't presume to anticipate Krishna's palate. If he wants to add salt it is not beyond his powers to do so.

You could interpret the feeding of the Five Thousand in terms of *prasad*, but in that particular case the catering aspect seems to be an afterthought rather than the whole point. The blessing came before the food instead of the food being the blessing.

Thoughts about the guru are always (for a devotee) thoughts from the guru, sent by him to nourish and inform. They have a high ontological status. By these incoming thoughts I was being reminded with typical and relentless gentleness that my task was no different from Lakshmi's. No Cambridge degree was required, though of course that's half the problem – education narrows the vision more often than not. All I had to do was lay my heart in the guru's lap, my head in his hands. If possession of a B.A. stopped me from recognising the basic nature of my own needs then it was an infestation rather than an accomplishment. I'd be better off with a simple case of lice.

I clung to Ramana Maharshi as my guru, and could at least claim to have been constant in my adherence to him (there's a lot of guru-hopping that goes on, I'm afraid). But what could I point to as evidence of a connection with him? Only numerological correspondences, individually embarrassing but overwhelming in aggregate.

Our lives overlapped by one hundred and eight days. For that period we breathed the same air. I've checked and re-checked, and it's a fact. A hundred and eight! Infinitely propitious number, buttressed by no end of favourable associations. Not just anyone who is remotely devout or Advaitic, but anyone with any sensitivity to the arithmetical mysteries would recognise the special properties of the number, its flagrant, even shameless divisibility, falling like a ripe fruit into equal segments, whether halves, thirds, quarters, sixths or ninths.

Pessimism, garrulity, sarcasm

There are 108 Upanishads. Krishna has 108 Gopis, or consorts. There are 108 beads on the *Japa maalaa*, equivalent to the Catholic rosary, and even those who don't use a rosary are encouraged to repeat a mantra 108 times for maximum effect. Take 1 to the power 1 (that's 1), 2 to the power 2 (4) and 3 to the power 3 (27). Multiply them together and what do you get? That's right. Carry the process one step further and you end up with 27,648, a number spilling over with mighty power, no doubt, but a rosary on that scale could rope off the Albert Hall.

There are 54 letters in the Sanskrit alphabet, each having an aspect of *Śiva* or *shakti*, the masculine or feminine principle. Vaishnavite

Hindus, devoted primarily to Vishnu, recognise 108 holy places. And as if that wasn't enough evidence, it's also the number of verses in Ramana Maharshi's *Marital Garland*.

It's not just Hinduism, either. There are 108 virtues in the Jain religion (them again!), or rather attributes of the five supreme beings – they're a little recherché, such as 'visibility of Tirthankar's face from all directions while delivering sermons' and 'thorns face downwards while Arihant is walking'. There are 108 Auspicious Illustrations in Buddha's left footprint and a corresponding number of Buddhist Defilements (not so recherché, and including 'pessimism', 'garrulity' and 'sarcasm').

Some Buddhists do their calculations differently, multiplying the number of the senses (six by their count, since 'thought' is included) by the three aspects of time – past, present, future – the two conditions of the heart, pure and impure, and the three possible sentiments of liking, dislike and indifference, and still they arrive at the same resonant number.

108 is also the number of missing episodes of *Doctor Who*, I believe, though I'm not sure that's strictly relevant. And part of my relief over the safe arrival of my phone and its number was itself numerological. Cambridge 65628. If you add the digits up and successively resolve them, they yield first 27 and then 9 – as does 108. I'd rather be given £108 than £200 for the symbology of it, but if you're in that territory already why not round it up to 216? Then everybody's happy.

I've never mastered my guru's sublime ability to make those who gave him things feel that they had been granted a privilege. The word 'make' is all wrong in that last sentence, I can see that. He didn't make them or even let them feel anything, being genuinely indifferent and undistracted by emotion. In my case raw need keeps breaking through. Ramana Maharshi spent years in a cave without moving and would have starved if disciples hadn't pushed food into his unresponsive mouth. I had spent years in bed unmoving as a child, but I was allowed to read for half an hour a day and Mum was never far away, devising treats to tempt my appetite. She'd probably be coming in any moment with a tray of Scrambled Egg Boats. I had it made! I should say in my defence that I was clinging to life because Mum needed me to, not on my own account. If I'd been thinking only of myself then there was no better opportunity to melt back into bliss. Did she feel more important, and love me more, when I seemed to be in immediate danger? I doubt if it was as clear-cut as that, and it was only when I was living in a hospital that I learned at first hand how stranglingly the tendrils of care and control can twine round each other.

When Mrs Baine called with the *Cambridge Evening News* as promised I was, of course, asleep, but not deeply committed to the process of unravelling the world. I was able to shrug myself back into consciousness, and even to cobble together my surroundings without too much fuss. Mrs Baine knocked, waited a few seconds and then let herself in.

It happens fairly often that people seek to relieve me of the burden of privacy, and there are times when no resistance is possible, but at this point I felt the need to protest, however indirectly. I didn't want independent living to be over before it had begun. 'Good timing, Mrs Baine!' I sang out. 'If you'd been five minutes earlier you'd have got rather an eyeful. Something to tell your grandchildren, I suppose, as long as they're broad-minded. It's not easy for me to close the lavvy door behind me, you see.' 'Lavvy' was a piece of conscious crudity that I hoped would repel her. It was still a time when you could rely on the odd inhibition here and there – I don't know what I'd have done if she'd come over all earthy and said she'd seen worse. Luckily she flinched a bit, had a think and then suggested that in future she would wait for me to ask her in. I agreed with a sort of wonder, as if I would never have thought of this arrangement by myself. We agreed that it was perfectly convenient for her to leave the *Cambridge Evening News* outside the door. I would pick it up at my leisure.

She wasn't a busybody, or she wasn't just a busybody – and of course if I ever met people without an element of nosiness in their makeup I'd consider them less than fully equipped. She gave me a fair amount of useful information. She opened the little fridge to show me that it contained the basics: a sliced loaf, six eggs, a bottle of milk and some slices of ham sharing a plate with a halved tomato. She said she could keep me supplied with milk, at four-and-a-half pence a pint. We agreed that the cost of living was creeping up day by day, inexorably, and we didn't know where it would all end.

That little tabletop fridge was my favourite aspect of my new living arrangements, the only thing that might have been installed with a disabled person's needs in mind, though presumably thriftiness and space considerations had converged on it as the appliance of choice. 'How much do I owe you?' I asked, grateful that I had cash handy and wouldn't be starting my period as a resident with an unsettled debt.

'Oh no, dear, none of this is from me. I just mentioned milk because that's something I do for everyone in the flats, but I can't be providing special services, I'm afraid. It's your daffodil girl who's got you started.' I must have looked blank because she went on to explain who she meant. 'Your girl got up in the bright yellow that makes her look all washed out.'

Of course I could work out who she meant after that, but I didn't at all agree that Paula had looked washed out, though Mrs Baine certainly would have if she had made the mistake of wearing the same colour. This unsympathetic assessment of dress and self-presentation reminded me of Mum's sewing circle, the little world of self-important Bourne End to which her dressmaking skills had given her the entrée. The whole conversation gave off an estranging whiff of home.

Seedy Maigret overtones

I felt bad about young Paula, though, who had carried my things into the flat and been derided for her poor lifting technique, who had done my shopping unasked and not pressed for payment. I would give her a proper welcome on Monday, the next time I saw her. It was a shame that I hadn't announced my vegetarian preferences in advance, and it would feel equally wrong to eat what she had laid on (though I was by now rather hungry) and to spurn her thoughtfulness, catering for me outside the working week. Flesh-food was in my system already, and it felt as if I had lost my appetite for purity. I could already feel myself deciding not to tell her my preferences, and eating in docile disgrace any horrors she served up.

My vegetarianism seemed to have changed, shifting ground unobtrusively. Even in its original state it wasn't entirely a physical revulsion, just an inability to understand why a thinking being would deprive another of life and cut it, suitably prepared, into mouth-sized pieces. Now what I felt was an intellectualised nausea, surprisingly easy to set aside when I was hungry.

I'd square things with Paula somehow. In the meantime I made myself butter up Mrs Baine, despite fatigue and a certain reluctance. I was paying rent like everyone else, wasn't I? Why did I have to make myself especially agreeable? In fact the answer to the first question was no, not really. My rent was being paid by a caring authority, and this was not a standard arrangement at Mayflower House. But even if I had fitted in as far as the ultimate source of my rent was concerned, I would still need to make an extra effort to be liked. There's no point in questioning the world's need to be buttered up. Just get on with it.

How long had she been the – I managed to suppress the word 'concierge', with its seedy Maigret overtones – receptionist at Mayflower House? Four years. Was it a friendly place? She should say so, people in and out at all hours. There was a definite hint of disapproval involved here, though it turned out that she didn't live on the premises and so was not necessarily a witness to whatever depravity was endemic.

According to Mrs Baine it was common knowledge what went on, particularly on the upper floors. There had been a Chinese couple who . . . it didn't bear thinking about. And both of them doctors! The mattress had to be got rid of when they left, not just thrown out but burned. She hadn't wanted to come in that day, what with particles floating in the air for anyone to breathe in. People did the most horrible things, particularly when they were far from home. She looked at me quite hard, as if she was trying to determine my exact origins and distance from native habitat.

The Major had almost been sick when he had opened their door, and he'd seen some things in his time. He was a manager for the whole building, was the Major, and had a flat on the premises as well as an office, and a very nice one too, nice flat, nice office – lucky for some – but I shouldn't think of going to him about matters arising, any more than I should expect her services outside the stated hours. Her phone number was for emergencies only.

I didn't have her number and hadn't asked for it! – though I had the sense not to point this out. I could only too easily enter a suspect category to her way of thinking, either asking for special treatment or indulging in behaviour typical of the upper floors. She left the *Cambridge Evening News* for me, promising to keep me regularly supplied with the paper. I had little enough interest in the national press, let alone a local paper, but this was one more thing I kept myself from saying.

While I had no home but the Mini I had struggled to fill my days, but here at Mayflower House I had appointments to negotiate. Paula the home help would come for two hours three days a week (Monday, Wednesday, Friday) while the district nurse would come just once a week, on . . . I'd been told which day it would be but had already forgotten.

When eventually I cast my eyes over the *Cambridge Evening News* that Mrs Baine had left I found it was a week and a half old. I know time passes slowly in county towns, and of course time properly considered doesn't pass at all, but this indifference to topicality struck me as a bit rich. It was partly a quibble over language. I had cut my teeth on literary texts, but anything would do to satisfy the compulsion to split hairs. Had she not promised to bring me 'the' *Cambridge Evening News*? Had I entirely misunderstood the respective implications of definite and indefinite article? Someone who offers you 'the' *Cambridge Evening News* is tempting you (or not) with a particular edition that can be expected to meet your need for up-to-date information, however misguided you may be to hanker after such a thing. By rights Mrs B should have promised me 'a' *Cambridge Evening News*. Then I would have grasped that she was proposing to bring me any old discarded issue of the many thousands that had been published in the paper's long history. If I had felt no great urge to read the paper when I thought it was fresh then my appetite could hardly be sharpened by staleness.

'How much do I owe you for the newspaper, Mrs Baine?' I asked, just the same, the next time I saw her. There was nothing to be lost by buttering up the old girl.

'Don't be silly, Mr Cromer. It's from last week!'

'Ah, but don't you think, dear lady, that old newspapers should be more expensive than today's edition?'

'How ever do you mean?'

'Just that they're so much harder to find.'

For the moment it took her to take in this wise paradox she looked as if she had walked into a door, and then she gave an uncertain smile. I realised that I had struck the wrong note. If I went on in this vein I would soon get a reputation as an eccentric or a graduate. There aren't many places where I fit in, but I have some leeway in terms of deciding in what way, precisely, to jut out and I needed to improve my performance of protrusion in Mayflower House.

It seemed to me that time was taking on a friable quality. It had a tendency to crumble that I hadn't noticed before, when I was used to a viscous, even a glutinous texture. You'd think there was no easier question to answer than whether you have spent one or two nights in a new home, yet I found myself forced back into reasoning deductively, working backwards from the eggs and bread remaining. I couldn't have eaten two eggs in a single day, surely? Not when I didn't have the machinery of Whyvonne's café to drive me onwards across a loaded plate beyond my habits and instincts. Then it must be Monday already.

Time for the first official visit from my home help. Paula was a sweet kid and very willing. I didn't know what she was supposed to do or not do, and I dare say I made stupid mistakes. She was new enough to the job herself to be unsure of the boundary lines. Some things we could agree on. She would be doing my laundry, for instance, or else it wasn't going to get done, and between us we located the laundry room down the corridor, converted from a flat rather bigger than mine. It was downright spacious. It seemed logical that she would shop for me, too, but I didn't immediately grasp how the system was supposed to work.

There had been a cleaning lady or what was then called a 'mother's help' back home in Bourne End called Ring (no one ever called her 'Mrs' Ring), but though in theory she was an underling, and lived in a council house whose rent was fourteen shillings a week, she was anything but deferent and gave the impression of doing exactly as she pleased. Paula by contrast was keen to help in a way that I found almost disorienting.

All she needed was a little gentle training in Johnability. Not a demanding curriculum – I just stood there and moved my arms to their fullest extent, as a way of demonstrating the limitations of my reach and the implications for the process of tidying up. The information could have been conveyed by means of a multiple-choice questionnaire: *Is John's reach a) 8 inches, b) 8 feet, c) 8 yards?* The answer is straightforward, yet people need help to get to it. There are obvious things that aren't Johnable – stairs, slopes. But there are plenty of others. There could be no question of tucking things away in the name of neatness. In my case the gap between easily available and why-not-just-throw-it-away? is a stark one. This line here on the countertop – in front of that I can reach it easily. A little further back, and I can likely hook it out with a knife. Any further away and you might as well post it to Tasmania. The catering-sized drum of Gold Blend, not yet opened, was self-evidently a special case. It could safely be pushed out of my reach since opening it would be a special occasion by definition, with guests attending who would pass the jar to me for the ritual breaking of the laminated membrane over the freeze-dried coffee granules.

On top of restricted mobility comes restricted flexibility, and on a day-to-day basis it's my limited reaching power that feels most frustrating. I don't fantasise about getting out of the wheelchair and walking, but I do daydream about fetching a book from its place on the shelf without getting up, just twizzling a hand above my head. Twizzle is necessarily the reference point, to my generation, for magical reaching. Twizzle on television, a toy or doll (boy or girl? Nominally a boy, I think) but also a superhero in a small way, whose special power was limb extension, arms and legs growing in length to the accompaniment of a painful-sounding ratcheting noise.

Paula was wearing a less revealing outfit than she had on Saturday. Perhaps she had realised a little too late on the Saturday that she was giving the Downing porters a chance to ogle. Her defective lifting technique must have shown off her knickers every now and then, while the effort darkened her yellow dress under the armpits. Now she was wearing a floral pinafore dress, round which she tied an actual pinafore, or at least an apron.

She always wore one when she was working, whether or not there was a real risk of mess, and I admired the brisk grace with which she put the garment on, catching the long strings behind her, swapping them over between hands so that they crossed, then bringing them smoothly in front of her to tie a brisk little bow, before squaring her shoulders and getting to work. It was as if there were little subsidiary eyes in her hands that meant they needed no supervision, no thought of any kind while they saw to what needed to be done.

The business of crossing the strings behind the back seemed to be accomplished simultaneously, with the right hand passing the right apron-string to the left just as the left one passed across its own string to the right. I never saw it happening clearly enough to be sure of what was going on, but the smooth changeover was like something from a relay race, or two relay races run at once in opposite directions, the batons being transferred back and forth without a fumble by runners so fully alive that their decisions took place almost without them. Was there a little memory-stab of Mum in this? Perhaps there was. Mum's character was at its most harmonious in the kitchen, despite an occasional resentment of the workload she insisted on.

I found it difficult to ask Paula outright to do specific things, but the roundabout way I made my wishes clear wasn't necessarily any improvement on being peremptory. It's funny that as long as someone is a free agent I can boss them around. It's only those who actually have responsibility for me that make me tentative. So I didn't like to say, 'Do you mind getting the last of the peanut butter out of the jar? It's the shouldery bits that are so awkward. You can just leave it in the spoon and I'll use it later.' Even though this would hardly lead to staff unrest and rebellion. Instead I would arrange myself in a tableau before Paula arrived (luckily her timekeeping was good), so that she could surprise me working away at the shouldery bits of the jar with a knife held at a ridiculous angle. I can't think of a better way of putting it than 'shouldery bits' – the curved inner surface of a jar just below the neck, only presenting a challenge in terms of retrieval when the substance in the jar has clinging qualities. Not everything viscous is delicious, but many delicious things are viscous. It can't be helped that the adjective 'viscous' lacks glamour, that shouldn't be relevant. Then of course she had called out, 'Let me do that for you!' And I simpered, 'Would you really? Thanks awfully. You're a tremendous pet.' Sounding posh and unnatural, even to myself. Still, for some reason I considered this laborious piece of stage management a better way of getting things done for me than making a direct request to someone who was being paid, though not by me, to meet my needs.

Unacknowledged subordinate agents lurk in the simplest statements of fact. Say 'Napoleon won the battle of Austerlitz' or 'Beau Brummell liked to air his laundry on Hampstead Heath to be sure it smelled fresh' or 'I moved house' – and nobody will turn a hair. Why should I be denied the same benefit? 'I climbed the stairs'; 'I picked up some cut-price tinned tomatoes from the Co-Op – oh, and a bumper pack of bog roll.' These are not cryptic formulations even if they don't mean exactly what they seem to say. Everyone has help, and that's the point.

No doubt there's a language with a special tense to express actions performed without assistance. My money's on Papua New Guinea. It's always Papua New Guinea when it comes to quirks of language. So when you say 'I moved house' in Papua New Guinea, and use that tense, everyone round the dinner table gasps in amazement that you didn't have help. 'Dinner table' sounds wrong in this context, but I'm not sure 'cooking pot' is any better, and they may or may not have actual movers in Papua New Guinea but I'm sure there are cousins who will turn up on the day and make themselves useful. Do they perhaps not move house in Papua New Guinea, being born and dying in the same long-house? H'm – you may have got me there.

I made a shopping list for Paula, on which there was one item that puzzled her. What were 'coasters'? Special biscuits? No, *coasters*. You know – the circular mats that go under mugs and glasses, preventing heat damage, absorbing condensation. I'd had enough of sticky rings at Downing to last me all my lifetimes. I had done my best to educate my generation at Downing, smiling at them when they brought along beer mats from the bar and laid them reverently down, frowning without rancour when they put down their mugs onto the unprotected surface immediately adjacent. She couldn't find them in a supermarket anyway, and I had to ferret them out myself, making a special trip to Robert Sayles.

Paula seemed surprised that I should want coasters before I had any guests, but that's the logical way of doing it, to establish a clear and stringent coaster protocol. No mugs or glasses on the surfaces, please. If there hadn't been coasters ready before my first guest then a fatal element of leeway would have been introduced. Lax enforcement becomes creeping amnesty, and then where are you? I would be put in the position of someone who has once allowed a dog up on the furniture and must battle ever after to keep it down at floor level.

Robert Sayles in Cambridge was always really John Lewis, even if the name didn't appear on the frontage, just as Heelas in Reading, where Mum had used to go for special shopping, was a far-flung tentacle of the same benign cephalopod Partnership, genteelly writhing through the Home Counties and beyond. Heelas was always just Heelas to us. Would Peter have enjoyed his tenth birthday present as much if it had been from John Lewis and not John Heelas & Sons? It's hard to say. Names have their importance.

One of us will have ginger twins

In general we got on very well, Paula and I. Some parts of our relationship were almost like a game. I trained Paula to leave bread in the slots of the toaster before she left. I could conveniently press down the timer knob with my stick, and a snack was never more than two or three minutes away. If I described a thermal mattress, both disposable and organic, with the property of keeping cooked food warm without drying it out you might not immediately recognise the specifications of a piece of toast.

She kept an eye out for things that might be suitable additions to the flat, always claiming to have picked them up on Market Hill for a few pence. First there was a dinky little hot water bottle, much less than standard size, then a miniature kettle which can't have held much more than half a pint. Finally there was a diminutive teapot, suitable for one. She said it wasn't really tea if it was made in a cup. She had a slightly odd notion of my physical capabilities, given that she was employed to make good their shortcomings. A teacup I could manage, a teapot was essentially a millstone with a spout. But she wouldn't have it any other way, would young Paula, on top of which she insisted on turning the pot round three times before pouring out. 'Otherwise,' she said, 'one of us will have ginger twins.'

That was what her grandmother said, anyway. It wasn't quite the broadening of cultural horizons I had hoped for from my life in

Cambridge, but it would have to do until something more broadly suggestive came along. If I lived long enough, and remained in a state of dependency, I could compile some sort of concordance to the superstitions of council home helps. Not comprehensive but in its small way authoritative. I just hoped she had more substantial knowledge of reproductive biology than what she was currently showing me.

I was becoming more at ease with the idea of having a home help, which made sense. To survive on my own I would need all the assistance I could get, from home help and district nurse and anyone else I could recruit. I would need a whole little team if I was to take responsibility for myself. I reminded myself that all lives are mutually connected. No existence bathes in its own solitary meaning. Everyone needs help to be 'alone', though it's not a term I really respect. Robinson Crusoe had Friday, not necessarily to do the donkey work but at the least to discuss breadfruit recipes with, and new ways of cooking the catch of the day. I had Paula not just on Friday but Monday and Wednesday too, even if I had to share her with my fellows among the marooned of Cambridge.

She strongly believed in scalding the pot. I asked her to explain why, feigning innocence, something I should do well by now considering all the practice I've had, and she explained that it was crucial for the tea to be piping hot at the moment of infusion. And the cosy? Is that there to make sure the tea is piping hot at the moment of pouring? Exactly. I seemed to understand. She seemed pleased with the way I was catching on. And how about the cup? Shouldn't you scald the cup too, to maximise thermal retention? So I added another ritual stage to her tea ceremony, and enjoyed her tea very much.

The cup-warming idea was originally a way of teasing her for being so precious, but I've never stopped doing it. I've come to understand that it really makes a difference. There's many a true word spoken in the process of winding someone up. As for turning the teapot round three times before pouring out, all it does is introduce into the liquid a faint vortical vector, friction from the walls of the pot acting on the inertia of its contents, a diffuse churning effect very little different from what people traditionally produce with a firmly stirring teaspoon. The result produced is the same in either case, the more uniform perfusion of hot water through the leaves.

A few weeks later she turned up with a knitted cosy that perfectly fitted the teapot. I strongly suspected that she was carrying on a campaign of unbridled benevolence. It seemed likely that these objects cost her more than the pennies she claimed, though of course it was the thoughtfulness that was so striking, almost disorienting in a relationship that could never be balanced as between equals. It bothered me a bit, and I did a little snooping around the market stalls. The square where the market is held is properly called Market Hill, which is something I very much appreciate. I prefer hills with no discernible gradient, and a tennis ball dropped on Market Hill would hardly know which way to roll – but there's no surface less Johnable than your cobbles, even in a wheelchair. I made myself cover the ground fairly thoroughly just the same and I couldn't see any bric-à-brac stall of the sort Paula described. It seemed fair to ask around before I dismissed her claims entirely, and it turned out that on Mondays there was indeed a stall selling treasures of a miscellaneous sort for charity. The charity was for the benefit of dogs, and the stallholder was a Miss Barbara Duff, though I was told she was generally known as Dogs Duff. Alliteration has a lot to answer for. 'And is she friendly?' I asked. The answer that came was 'Very friendly. Couldn't be nicer, as long as you're a dog.'

Her stall was only there one day a week, on a Monday. Miss Duff was a well-turned-out woman in middle life, wearing her tweed suit even in summer. Her steel-grey hair seemed to have no connection with the ageing process but to be a conscious decision, as if she had willed those fibres to take on the colour that evoked firmness of purpose. That pewter helmet, tolerant of hairspray but strongly opposed to dye, marked her out as a senior Valkyrie, one who had made more than one dragon crash-land, if that's what Valkyries do. I'm not sure. Her posture suggested not a welcome to prospective customers but the fierceness of a ship's captain preparing to repel boarders. I cast my eye over her wares with an attempt at casualness. The stall over which she presided was thickly populated with china animals, and my divided soul was wrung with contradictory responses to these atrocious objects and/or authentic expressions of popular taste.

Then I saw something utterly beautiful, an object the size of an ostrich egg, rough on the outside but cleft open to disclose an interior of glassy cerulean honeycomb. A geode! I adored the contrast between the craggy outside and the spangled interior, made up of crystals that had formed over thousands of years, aggregating in the dark until the ripe mineral fruit was cut open. If it had been able to give an account of itself it would have said, 'I am an ancient bubble that gas formed in melted stone. Once the gas had leaked away from me the void was filled and refilled with water then gradually, over the ages, with crystallising minerals left precipitated by the water as it drained away.' And that blue! I had lost most of my sense that the days of the week were of different colours. If I had seen this object as a child, when my synæsthesia was at its most vibrant, I would have recognised it as a gorgeously calcified Friday. By 1973 the blue of a Friday was solid rather than piercing. Dust clogged its lapis lazuli vibrancy.

When I had heard about Chinese hundred-year-old eggs during the bed-rest years I was thrilled. I pestered Mum to bury an egg in the garden, just one, to undergo the necessary changes. She was adamant in her refusal, partly because of her generation's unwillingness to treat even a single egg as expendable, rationing having formed her as surely as bed rest was forming me, and I dare say also because she suspected it was just another dodge on my part, one more way of refusing food. I might well have wasted away by the time the egg was ready, even if she had bargained the time of its burial down to a month. If it was hard enough to persuade me to eat even a mouthful of egg when it was fresh and scrambled, she didn't fancy her chances of success when the stinking treasure was finally disinterred and laid before me on a plate.

But of course I had been thinking too small. A hundred years is far too short a period for the proper alchemical making-over. Many thousands are required for the proper ripening. I stood gazing in wonder at this mineral egg laid for me by geological time, both fossilised and strongly alive. I had to have it.

My original idea was to feign interest in something so as to ascertain her attitude to pricing, in particular her susceptibility to haggling, but now my interest was real.

'How much is the pretty paperweight?' I asked. 'I can't make out the price tag from here.' Not true, since Miss Duff's handwriting, done with a fountain pen, was admirably clear. Was I feigning not to be able to read it in the hope that the price would soften all by itself thanks to the tableau of pathos I was presenting, saving me the trouble of haggling? Possibly. I won't pretend such things haven't happened. And I was being sly by not admitting I knew what a geode was, in the hope that ignorance would further shape the discount.

'The price is two pounds and forty pence.' Not a fortune, but more than I wanted to pay.

'Ouch.' I mimed dismay. 'That's quite a sum for someone whose rent is twelve pounds a week.' Which I didn't myself pay. Really I was sinking pretty low in my search for a bargain. 'Could you come down a bit?'

'The price is two pounds forty. And always will be.'

'My friend Paula says you were kind enough to reduce the marked price on some items for her.'

I wouldn't have thought that Miss Duff could have stood any more squarely, but she braced herself at this hint of opposition, as if she was Gandalf confronted with an onslaught of Orcs. 'Your friend Paula doesn't know what she's talking about. I'm not here to truckle to my customers. I'm here to earn money for the dogs.'

I love 'truckle'! Let's all truckle! How is it done?

'Young man, have you ever been locked in a shed for a week to lie in your own filth, deprived of light and exercise? With a loop of barbed wire instead of a collar? These things happen all around us, all the time, and no one will speak up for victims who can't speak up for themselves.

'A boxer, barely a year old, is nailed to a tree in Six Mile Bottom. Will you look after him? Will you pay the vet's bills and try to find a home for an animal that has been treated in that fashion? No. I will. And these things happen all around us, all the time. Don't tell me there are other problems in the world – I know that, but this is mine to tackle. Yes, there are charities, and I'm sure they know what they're doing. So do I.

'I dislike accepting donations but I will do it. I will swallow my pride for the sake of creatures that have no pride to swallow.

'People think me funny, I don't understand why. I let out a couple of rooms of my house, all for the dogs, in Eltisley Avenue, students mainly. And one day I was sorting the post and something caught my eye. There was a letter for one of my lodgers, and on the envelope was written, after the name but before the address, "Editor, *The Batsford Book of the Poodle*". Which I well knew he was not. What a hoot. Mock the old girl, why not. So I raised his rent. Never said a word about it, just raised his rent. Let him ask me the reason if he wants to. He can have a joke at my expense, but it won't be at the dogs' expense, I can tell you that.'

The annoying thing about this, apart from the obvious fact that I would be paying a fair whack for the lovely geode, was that I couldn't fault the argument she made, as a dog lover turning her reproachful light on the human world. Compared to a boxer nailed to a tree I was sitting pretty, there was no doubt about that. In the scorching glare of her cynophilia I was being invited to wonder about my own style of going about things, and whether my daily refusal to be given special treatment wasn't just another way of asking for favours. Hadn't I disparaged George Harrison's claims to be carrying a 'heavy load' in just the same way? I could sniff out the egotism lurking beneath the garb of radiant humility as long as the garb wasn't mine.

I don't mean to say that Miss Duff had been visited by the guru so as to offer me a spiritual lesson ventriloquially. She struck me as pretty much guru-proof, comprehensive in her immunity to outside influence – not that it's up to me to make such determinations of agency.

The geode and the cauliflower

'Miss Duff, would you be so good as to keep the paperweight for me while I go to the bank?' One last bluff, though by now I should have realised I had come up against a supreme exponent of the hard sell, the sell as hard as stone. I had the cash on me but wanted to play for time and to show that I knew her name. Why I thought that would make a difference I don't know.

'No, dear, I won't be doing that. What happens if you don't come back and someone turns up a minute from now and wants to buy it? The dogs will suffer, that's what, and I'm not having that.'

All I managed to squeeze out of the granitic Miss Duff was that 'dear', not in my experience a reliable mark of fondness, and I had paid dearly for it. To give substance to my claim of needing to go to the bank I had to disappear for a quarter of an hour or so, and now I began to worry that the possibility she had so casually invoked, of fierce competition for acquisition of the geode, a bidding war or at least bidding skirmish, would materialise in my absence. Did I still want the geode? I certainly did. Would I get back in time? Anybody's guess.

I wasn't making fast enough progress on my way back to Miss Duff's stall, with no one offering to give me a push though I dare say I looked desperate enough. The general public of Cambridge were either respecting my independence or not giving a toss. I became a little irrational and bought a cauliflower for 6p on condition the stallholder pushed me the last twenty yards. I have to say that the cauliflower was below par as a specimen, displaying those telltale black flecks in the curd that indicate its decline into decrepitude. Clearly it had been languishing without a buyer. Miss Duff watched my assisted arrival with no sign of interest and reacted only when the £2.40 was handed across. Then she wrapped up the heavenly geode not very tenderly in a page of an old *Cambridge Evening News*. I have to say that I admired her very much. She lived up to her reputation. There was only a short list of things that I would need to win Miss Duff over: an extra pair of legs and a tail to wag. Otherwise the Valkyrie armour offered full protection. She was certainly immune to my mutely pleading looks, horribly reminiscent I dare say of the winsome expressions on the china animals arrayed in front of her. In a life of more or less continuous wheedling I had never come across as unflustered a refusal as Miss Duff's. Her No was absolute, needing no expenditure of nervous energy to maintain it. She was adamantine – in fact she was something of a geode herself.

The geode and the cauliflower were of course exactly as miraculous as each other, even if I had forgotten this important fact in the thrill of the chase.

I had established at some personal cost that my home help had been unjustifiably generous towards me, but I managed not to hold it against her. I hoped at least that Paula liked dogs herself, after contributing to their welfare so substantially. I don't remember the subject ever coming up.

During my first week at Mayflower House I wasn't particularly organised. I knew that a district nurse would be coming at some point, and I hoped I remembered aright that it was to be on Thursday. That left Tuesday a free day, with no visitors. I was certainly looking forward to having a bath and being clean again, but it wasn't the only priority.

It turned out that I had remembered not aright but awrong. The district nurse came early on Tuesday afternoon. This was bad timing since I was in the middle of an experiment. There was a knock at the door and politeness demanded a response, though I can't say I was happy to be disturbed. I could only offer a welcome so qualified as to be bristling with reservation. First encounters are perilous. Doors can either refuse admittance or permit it. The choices seem so open-and-shut but what a range of implications is called into play when someone passes through them!

I'd managed to keep Mrs Baine at bay, discouraging her from entering the flat, but that's not a possible course of action when it comes to district nurses. You can't be given a bath from out in the corridor.

The district nurse knocked on my door. That's the recommended procedure, and in theory the sequence of events unrolls quite smoothly. I see it happen in films all the time. There's a knock at the door. The resident opens up, acknowledges the visitor with a few words, then says, 'Do you mind waiting here just a minute?' Controlling the disposition of bodies in space without fuss or the risk of giving offence. The visitor is unfazed and murmurs assent – but not in my world as it was then. Everything seemed to happen in extreme slow motion, though of course that's not an accurate account of how things unfold. It's space that slows down, while time opens itself up for inspection.

I couldn't get to the door in a suitably short time, and if I'd managed it I would only have created more awkwardness, owing to the difficulty of my getting out of the way sufficiently to let someone pass. So I called out 'Come in'. The nurse entered and came to lean over me. A slowly dawning delight spread across his face, as if he was very taken by what he saw. In the whole of my life he may have been the only person to be favourably impressed with my stature. He must have been told I was two foot tall.

I was expecting a woman rather than a man. He reached down a hand, saying, 'I'm Tony Gerling – call me Tony.' I said, 'And I'm John Cromer – please don't call me John.' Perhaps I shouldn't have owned up to having a first name at all, except that it was to feature in his paperwork.

If you had told me in advance that the district nurse assigned to me was male I would have been thrilled at the prospect. Yet from the first breath it was obvious that we weren't going to get along together, Tony Gerling and I, which is quite a depressing discovery to make when intimate unreciprocal sponging and scrubbing are going to be the key elements of your dealings with someone. There's a word in the Tamil language that means 'instinctive antipathy such as prevails between cats and dogs'.

Lavatory, Laboratory, Lavoratory

Winslow's *Comprehensive Tamil Dictionary* is a marvel, and Tamil itself a worker of wonders. It seduces, it converts. The Reverend Winslow arrived in Madras as a missionary, and needed to learn the language in order to evangelise the heathen, but clearly it was Tamil that converted him, not to Hinduism, merely to itself and the beauty of its way of looking at the world.

Instinctive antipathy was the state of affairs between me and Tony Gerling, though it took him a little while to catch on, and which of us was cat and which dog I wouldn't like to say.

Having opened the door to this man I had to override any implied welcome almost immediately to avoid being swept along by someone else's decisions. I didn't want this stranger to feel he had the run of the place. I wanted him to stay near the door while I made certain necessary adjustments in the little bathroom. My 'Do you mind waiting there just a minute?' can only have sounded odd to him, but I couldn't help that. He was employed to help me and had been despatched for that purpose, but within seconds I was asserting a perverse independence and showing a desire to restrict his movements.

Never mind. I had to reach the bathroom before he did. By sheer good luck I was in the wheelchair, so it didn't take me too long to turn around and start punting my way towards the bathroom, using my right foot to move me along. I'm sure Mr Gerling's fingers were twitching with the desire to grab the handles of the chair and push me along at decent speed, but he didn't quite dare to do that. He was even polite enough to call out, 'Take your time.'

I had to conceal some embarrassing evidence. For all its limitations, the Mayflower House flat had one amenity that I had never enjoyed before. I had exclusive access to the lavatory, and I was taking full advantage of that kingdom now that I didn't have to share its throne. At home Mum was all eyes, at Downing the facilities were shared. If I'd been able to stipulate a lavatory-pan layout to my ideal specifications, I'd have plumped for the German style, with a little platform raised above the water level so that stools could be examined properly before the flush was summoned to sluice them away. I remember Klaus Eckstein, my German teacher at Slough Grammar School, telling me that this willingness to confront the unglamorous aspects of physical existence was one of the defining features of German culture, despite its underlying strain of purity-madness. When reading a page of Mann, a page of Brecht, we should be aware that these were men who scrutinised their bowel movements on a daily basis. He didn't exactly tell us that the unexamined stool was not worth leaving, but I doubt if he would have minded the paraphrase, and his teaching methods certainly engaged the schoolboy mind, if I was any guide to its workings.

Lavatory. Laboratory. Lavoratory. The words blended together without any urging. Obviously I'm not the first to have noticed that they have a secret affinity, one that is perhaps not so secret. On the train that took me from Bath to Taplow all those years ago, when bed rest had been replaced by hospital incarceration, I had been too terrified to use the lavatory. Then Mum suggested that I should inspect it as a scientist might, with a view to improving the system that disposed of waste. Should raw sewage really be flushed onto the tracks? She sowed the seed, and as we know seeds kept in conditions that don't favour sprouting can germinate many years after the event. Now with unshared access to a lavatory I could conduct at least the basic research. It may be relevant to point out that I'd had very little chance at the proper time, my teens, to be quietly, routinely disgusting, and this was an opportunity to make up for lost time.

Observation is far more the keynote of scientific endeavour than active experimentation, which is often driven by the ego without real openness to adventure. It's no easier to describe a stool than a cloud, though the range of colour is more impressive. Texture words don't gain much purchase on these daily sculptures, formed as they are from the intimate digestive clay by a moody nozzle. All that separates such artefacts from the coproliths proudly displayed in museums is a few million years of petrification.

I had no baseline readings for normal fæcal behaviour, and my own bowel movements, thanks to Fybogel, tended to be shapeless spongiform clusters of excreted matter, pale in hue, even beige – beige turds! – but I could still establish a potentially useful set of data. One aspect that I could document was specific gravity and behaviour in water over time, not just an instant assessment of flotation versus sinkage but a tracking of changes of level as they occurred from hour to hour. Fascinating things could happen when a stool was just under or just over a specific gravity of 1. It might bob very slowly up and down over the course of a day, and it seemed unscientific not to make some sort of methodical note of such behaviour. The objects in the bowl that day were grey and amorphous, less like 'loose motions' in the hallowed hospital phrase than children of chaos and old night. Over the hours since their extrusion from this body they had floated, sunk and floated once again, and I had tracked this behaviour, with the associated changes in colour, on a home-made chart. Naturally I had also itemised my consumption of food, already able to correlate the high protein intake of my car-bound period with recent episodes of ferric compaction lying well outside my normal range.

It's hard to say which is the bottom-most layer in my attitude to solid waste. Is it fascination or disgust? Both are involved, certainly. I think it's fair to say that I was experimenting on myself as much as on the objects that lurked in the bowl. In my view of the world bodies were (and are) irrelevant and unreal. Shit raises recurring objections to this truth, particularly for someone whose encounters with plumbing are generally awkward. I've tried to turn excretion itself into an act of worship, contesting the instinct of revulsion. Feelings about the body's solid waste go back so far in time and so deep into the personality that it can be difficult to decide which emotion is at the bottom.

A boy child can see his wee leave the body, can take pride in the accuracy of its trajectory and the extent of its reach. I certainly did. It is distinctly mercurial as a substance, isn't it? A playful jet in total contrast to poo, poo so sombre and saturnine, emerging disgraced from somewhere out of sight and making no attempt in the course of its fatalistic fall to resist the pull of gravity.

Am I allowed to claim that the relatively short, even absolutely short distance between backside and nose in my case predisposes to loathing in one organ for the stench of the other? I don't have a visceral sense of the other side of the relationship, but I can easily imagine bafflement and hurt on the part of the blameless anus, this processing plant that has simply done its job. Why the constant carping from head office?

It was a great day for me when I discovered the stench-suppressing power of a lit match. The one smell doesn't seek to smother the other, as any perfumed product does, but blends with it and takes away the offensiveness. It's almost an osmic pun, a play on smells. It stands to reason that digestion itself is a sort of slow-motion burning, a combustion without flame whereby the heat energy is released from food. The two odours rhyme, like the phrases 'shit batch' and 'lit match'.

Mr Gerling called out again, 'Take your time.' This is a formula that collapses after a single usage. Even on first appearance it gives a restricted permission, strongly implying that the speaker is being inconvenienced and may come to resent it. On repetition its sheen of politeness is gone for good.

I needed to dismantle the research facility in short order. It wasn't just a matter of flushing the lavatory but of tipping away the pee bottle I had been filling so as not to interfere with the chemical balance of the experiment as it developed. These awkward actions took some time, and I could hear Mr Gerling moving in the other room, exploring my surroundings and possessions in a way I didn't positively enjoy but could hardly prevent. To have attendants is to forfeit privacy, and though I've been told I have an exhibitionist streak that's a different matter. Even before their differences of character emerged I felt more vulnerable to Mr Gerling than to Paula. I was necessarily more at the mercy of the district nurse than the home help.

I tried to tuck the plastic pee bottle away discreetly but it tipped over out of my reach with a bouncy clatter and I hadn't been able to rinse it anyway. Alas! Alas and never mind. I was as ready as I'd ever be. I punted my way out of the bathroom – give the man room. He could hardly be expected to work around the wheelchair in a confined space.

If I hankered after the touch of a stranger it wasn't this stranger. My first view of him in the doorway had already revealed a certain plumpness, a chunkiness of thigh and something odd about his hair, which somehow didn't seem to belong where it sat. It wasn't quite right, though I would need a closer view to work out exactly how. I hadn't seen anything of his back view but foresaw with complete certainty a squashy bottom. I'm afraid that's not a feature I've got a lot of time for. Nothing good can come of such a thing.

Mr Gerling waited for me to vacate the bathroom with a patience that was, I felt, on the ostentatious side. I heard him say something just as he started running the bath, something not meant for my ears – but then my ears have learned to extend their reach, to be my scouts in the next room. I've also developed a certain expertise as a sidler. If sidling is your mode of locomotion you'd better find a way to make it pay. In my prime I was quite good at sneaking up on people, and I was nearer Mr Gerling than he thought, and well within earshot before the taps were fully, deafeningly on.

It was 'down you go' that he had said in the moment before he turned the taps on. It seemed unlikely that he was talking to the plug, which left only one alternative. He was addressing a creature before he washed it down the plughole. He was communicating with a spider that he then rinsed away to its death.

I had to face the possibility that the person who had been assigned to tend to me was more naturally a killer than a carer. The fact that he was about to give me a bath didn't alter his basic preference for sluicing creatures into oblivion. It was perhaps even a distortion of his nature. Over time his resentment at being expected to abstain from annihilation in his working life would inevitably build up. How could it not? It was only a matter of time before he was muttering

'You're next, John' under his breath. I couldn't even count on his having the professionalism to say 'You're next, Mr Cromer'. The presumptuous use of my first name led by queasy degrees to the likelihood of murder. Each unconsensual intimacy ratchets closer a worse one. Having no power to resist enemies who have come close, my only safety is to deter their earliest approaches. Addressing someone, or certainly addressing me, by a first name without permission strips the subtle sheaths of protective formality from the naked organism. It's plain wrong.

There's a part of me, naturally, that wants to be overwhelmed, just as there is in everyone, my defences sent crashing to the ground, but there needs to be a rigorous screening process in place to ensure that only the right undesirables gain access.

I was inwardly certain that the bathroom was now a murder scene but there was no harm in a little interrogation. 'Do you like spiders, Mr Gerling?'

'They're all right in their place, John.'

'And what's their place?' He didn't bother to answer, having the handy excuse of bustling about to familiarise himself with a new working environment. I've always loved spiders, and sided with the one in *The Incredible Shrinking Man* even when it had a size advantage for once as the hero dwindled. It was the same with Shelob in *The Lord of the Rings*, clearly more interesting than she was meant to be, a heroine worthy of her own saga. Tremble, bipeds! You're outnumbered four to one.

I'd rather be a spider on the ceiling than a fly on the wall. Such dramas – nature in the raw, wildlife documentary round the clock. Can I even make the claim that I think like a spider? I can't be the first human being to notice that the standard English plughole, or rather the rudimentary lattice that stops people's wedding rings and old plasters from going down the drain, has a six-fold symmetry and a central circle. Surely there's a connection here with the marked tendency of spiders to end up in the bath? If research hasn't been done into the relative frequency of spiders falling into bathtubs in countries where plughole design is different then it should certainly be undertaken now. Yes, I know spiders have eight legs not six, that's what I'm getting at. It's flies that have six legs, and *spiders eat flies*.

159

As the bath empties an acoustic pattern corresponding to this stylised fly-shape is bounced upwards by the reverberations of the water. Spiders respond to this disturbance — think of the Bat-Signal being projected onto the night sky of Gotham City. You can't blame spiders for mistaking this accident of bath design for an announcement that grub's up. Come and eat hearty. And then they slide down the enamel into a vast white trap, one that might have been designed to detain them. People assume that spiders are incapable of tuning in to such a message, but the arachnid sensorium contains no end of mysteries. Let's just wait till the research results are in, shall we?

'Hot enough for you?' Mr Gerling asked, presumably an enquiry about the weather since I wasn't yet in the bath. 'Well,' I said, 'Maya always knows how to keep us comfortable, to stop us asking too many questions.' He was blithe and chatty in his tunic, more or less blocking the light with his tallness and plumpness. There was an attempt at banter yet a complete absence of conversation.

'You make a nice change from my normal round of old dears,' said Mr Gerling, and I could feel the effort he was making to convince himself that this was true. I wish I could say that my hackles rose at this patronising notion, patronising to me and the old dears alike. In fact my hackles were already up, formidably erect, however unwise it was for me to bristle at someone who was one of the chief manifestations of the welfare state's commitment of tenderness towards me.

I didn't mind that Mr Gerling processed me rather briskly from an unclean state to a clean one — this was his job and he was entitled to do it according to his professionalism. I didn't mind him saying 'Upsy daisy!' as he lifted me into the bath. I didn't even mind him saying 'In-a-getty' as he settled me there. He was perhaps used to reassuring insecure and disoriented elderly people by treating them as children (if that's reassuring). It was almost touching that he should remove his steamed-up glasses, fold the stems together and rest them on the side of the bath. He was exhibiting some incidental nakedness of his own. In this game of strip poker I was no longer the only player.

He asked me if the water temperature was all right, and when I said I wouldn't mind it warmed up a bit he obligingly turned on the hot tap. The particles of his aftershave flavoured the heated air rising from the bath. If he kept it running a little longer than I would have liked then I don't make too much of that – he was unfamiliar with the ways of the boiler, as was I. It's important to keep a sense of proportion. Even a single near-drowning in childhood at the hands of a sadistic nurse can overshadow all subsequent dealings with bodies of water. In the same way, being dangled helpless over banisters or accidentally dropped while being carried between floors (I can lay claim to both these experiences) takes all the fun out of a staircase. Those of my dreams that have starring roles for pools and flights of steps are not among the tranquil ones, though any fearfulness is deeply buried and doesn't usually put in an appearance by daylight.

As I lay in the water I tried to concentrate on the sensations rather than the company, the warmth of the water and the smell of the shampoo. Then a thought came to me unbidden, if thoughts are ever really unbidden, and I felt the approach of a giggling fit. I had suddenly thought, as Mr Gerling's flannelled hand dispassionately fumbled my privates, of the ninth chapter in the *Kama Sutra*, the one that speaks so disparagingly of 'those who live by shampooing'. Obviously 'living by shampooing' wasn't the only way of describing Tony Gerling's professional existence, but it was accurate as far as it went.

'What's so funny?' he asked.

All I could think of to say was 'Sorry, private joke,' which was also accurate. As far as it went.

My toes were curling frantically upwards

Chapter nine of the *Sutra* is devoted to *Auparishtaka* or 'mouth congress'. Oral sex, that's correct. It lists eight possible subdivisions of the act: 'nominal congress', biting the sides, pressing outside, pressing inside, kissing, rubbing, 'sucking a mangoe fruit' and 'swallowing up'. Who performs it? Eunuchs apparently, 'disguised as males' and keeping their desires secret. Such people lead the lives of shampooers and indeed use the intimacy that shampooing requires to make their overtures, viz. touching the joints of the thighs and the *jaghana* of the man being shampooed to investigate the stiffness or otherwise of the *lingam* before daring to go any further.

I can't say I'm impressed. It's disappointing that Indian lore, as displayed by its most famously sexual work, should be almost as benighted as the Western tradition. When you consider that the Indian medical practice, as exemplified by the *Sushruta Samhita*, with origins going back to the first millennium before Christ, considers wounds dealt by the teeth to the *glans penis* as a possible cause of infection, then the barely concealed disgust of the *Kama Sutra* is a real let-down. There are ignoble quibbles about purity, the *Auparishtaka* being the preserve of unchaste and wanton women, apparently, when it's not a matter of eunuchs arousing men on the sly and getting them into a lather. There must be more recent editions than the Burton one I cut my teeth on. Perhaps he was encrusting the *Sutra* with his own assumptions. There's a particularly distasteful argument making a distinction between the natural uncleanness of women and their acceptability for sexual purposes, relying on the analogy of a dog being clean when he brings down a deer on a hunt, though dogs are bywords for uncleanliness in other circumstances. A cow's udder, like-wise, ritually clean only when it is being milked.

I was grateful that Mr Gerling showed no interest in my *jaghana*, let alone my *lingam*. I have to say that his shampooing technique, narrowly considered, would have gained him no great reputation in the time of the *Sutra*, since he gave my hair only the most cursory rinse, perhaps because of that giggle, the private joke that he must have understood was somehow at his expense. I was anything but a satisfied customer of his professional services – hair that hasn't been properly rinsed is almost worse than hair that hasn't been washed at all. He hardly bothered with my beard at all, though I imagine it wasn't free of stains from food. The fried egg and tomato ketchup of two breakfasts could hardly have failed to make their mark. I suppose my giggle was sixty per cent snigger, and any body of water, however small, bounces sound upwards to humans as well as to spiders, even when it's a bathtub barely on the right side of the Elizabeth Bridge, and Mr Gerling was not deaf to the overtone.

Admittedly mine would never be a famous or admired beard, full and lustrous like the sailor's on the classic packet of Player's Navy Cut cigarettes, not much of a show of virile pomp. Plucked from my face and inserted in tufts onto the smooth surface of a waxwork figure's cheeks and chin it would have furnished perhaps ten per cent of a Rasputin at Madame Tussaud's, hardly even a hundredth of an Edward the Seventh. Still, the follicles were recovering from the damage I'd done to them by the frenzied use of depilatory cream in my teens. At the time I thought my mother would reject me if I showed signs of adulthood – before I realised that if I was ever going to become an adult on the inside I would need to shake her off. I'd overdone the Immac on one side more than the other, and had become an object lesson illustrating the maxim 'depilate in haste, repent at leisure'. Even so my beard was no poorer a specimen than many to be seen on the streets at the time, though the hippy vogue for such things was fading. Christ shaggy in his beard and sandals, benignly stoned in the normal course of things, was less and less seen on the streets of university towns. My facial hair might not be entitled to elaborate rituals of grooming, perfuming with rose water, oiling with spikenard, but it should have had some claim on a basic wash.

Even so I experienced a moment of great contentment when I was lifted from the water and embraced in warm towels. Mr Gerling was strong, he had the basic competence, I didn't need to like his cologne. This wasn't a breakthrough in my relationship with Tony Gerling, just the same. It was the ordinary ecstasy of hygiene coming to envelop someone who couldn't take such a thing for granted.

I nerved myself to let him take the clippers to my fingernails, and had more or less reached the end of my endurance when diligence overwhelmed him and he decided to do the same job on my toenails. I closed my eyes and had the sensation, no less strong for being impossible, that my toes were curling frantically upwards, away from the nibbling grin of his predatory clippers. I know that can't happen even with toes of standard flexibility. When I opened my eyes my toes were back in their accustomed knot, not that they had ever left it, and the sheet of newspaper underneath my feet was speckled with dainty curls, keratin rinds like pale brackets fallen from a moulting page of print.

The printed paper on which those rinds rested was my unsought second-hand copy of the *Cambridge Evening News*, and I might have disposed of it unread if I hadn't taken pity on it after seeing the treatment being meted out to it. I feel a pang at the dishonouring of anything written, finding it hard to accept that such a thing could be entirely worthless. I asked Mr Gerling not to throw it away or even crease it unduly. I'm confident that this love of marks on paper has been a constant of past lives, though I'm not necessarily claiming any particular history of accomplishment or even literacy. No one loves the look of a word as much as those who can't read, its power untainted by intelligibility.

When Mr Gerling left for the day he called out rather feebly, 'See you next week.' There was no rising intonation to denote a question. It had the sound of a stoical acceptance, but wasn't I the put-upon one in this partnership? My every chakra throbbed with the reply 'Is that a threat or a promise?' What a strange phrase it is in English, the cadence taking priority over common sense. No one ever says, 'Is that a promise or a threat?' though it makes a better job of the tone intended, producing a sting in the tail not a nip on the nose – but the rhythm is inferior, as everyone must feel, and the formula that makes less forceful sense prevails as a consequence. Rhythm is a tyrant and no mistake.

All the way through that first meeting I had made efforts to get a proper look at Mr Gerling's head. It's not easy to make a steady inspection of that sort when the intended object of your scrutiny is methodically lifting you, helping you off with your clothes, lowering you into a bath and generally attending to a district nurse's duties (apart from rinsing the shampoo out of your hair properly). The best I could do was to put together a sort of composite portrait of my target, like an artist's impression of the suspect *sought by police*. The reason for my curiosity was that there was something subtly strange about Mr Gerling's hair. It seemed out of keeping, not in the way of a wig but quietly and absolutely wrong on him. The mismatch registered almost subliminally, as when a tennis ball has been left provokingly in the fruit bowl among green apples. It wasn't bizarre enough to cause scandal but quietly bothered the memory. His hair was styled to look both sleek and fluffy, but the same could be said of a fair number of trendy young men at the time. Trendy-ish, young-ish men. Mr Gerling must have been in his thirties. The hair itself seemed somehow both wet and dry, but don't ask me for technical terms. That whole caravan passed me by.

It must have seemed to him that I hated his being gay. In fact I hated the way he was gay, but the nuanced character of my aversion will hardly have been obvious to him. More than anything I wanted a gay mentor, a more experienced man who would guide me, not towards the local cottages and cruising grounds (which I knew reasonably well), but towards a greater wholeness of self, to fill in the only area of life knowledge where Ramana Maharshi would understandably fall short. I wouldn't have refused the role of mentor myself, if Mr Gerling had wanted tips on comportment at Four Lamps, Cambridge's premier cottage, where I could navigate quite handily.

If he had been mentor material, or had asked for guidance himself, I would have forgiven him his chunky thighs and the residue of shampoo he left – they would have become badges of honour, consecrated quirks – but how could I forgive him for flinching when I asked any remotely personal question? He was desperately in hiding, and nothing sticks out more starkly than a secret frantically concealed. I'm not a great fan of Confucius, all that stuff about the 'superior man' rather sticks in my craw – the superior man is a bit of a pill – but he was on the money when he said that nothing is more obvious than what a man seeks to hide. If he said it – we non-sinologues are pretty much held hostage by our ignorance.

Mr Gerling would have done a better job of hiding his closetry if he had stuck his fingers in his ears and chanted, '*La-la-la – Not gay! Not gay!*' Did we say 'closetry' in those days? I don't think we did. The word would have suggested woodwork rather than a pattern of psychological cringing. Perhaps I'm being unjust – perhaps there was a cadre of radical furniture-makers marching in early Gay Pride Marches (I've never been and don't imagine it will happen now) under the banner *Better Marquetry Than Closetry*. When Mr Gerling was cagey about his household arrangements it didn't make me think he cohabited with another man in the way that raised so many eyebrows in those days. I thought he lived with his mother and twenty cats, something that raises eyebrows even now. As it ruddy well should.

By the time he left on that first day I had solved the mystery of his hair and where I had seen it before. It wasn't that he had stolen it, exactly. The follicles were his all right, and the hair that sprouted from them (technically a stratified, squamous and keratinised epithelium) belonged to no one else. But it was the hairstyle you got in 1973 when you walked into a hairdresser's anywhere in the Western world and produced from your pocket, whether shyly or defiantly, a photograph of teen singing sensation David Cassidy.

On his way out he handed me my second-hand *Cambridge Evening News*, passably neatly folded and with most of the toenail clippings shaken from it. The local newspaper had waited patiently for my attention, and now it must have its reward.

I made a resolution, once he had left, that if I ever had evidence of Mr Gerling opening a drawer without being asked to then he would have to go. I might not be able to make a convincing formal case against him, but as far as I was concerned he was already perched on the cusp between helper and unwarranted intruder. It was a toss-up.

On subsequent visits I learned to close my eyes and dream up a more congenial context for my physical sensations, imagining that I was being attended to by a machine, some sort of Heath Robinson contraption whose whirring pulleys and drive belts ran in mysterious silence. What will they think of next? They've already devised a strange *vox humana* stop that simulates someone breathing through his nose. Oddly convincing. How long before they add a little tape recorder and a loudspeaker to ask what I'm doing for my holidays?

By this time I was an experienced navigator of print. I'd read the *Gita*, Goethe, Lorca. I'd read Paul Gallico's *Snowflake* and *Gardening for Adventure* by R. H. Menage. Nothing prepared me for the *Cambridge Evening News* in its Zen emptiness. The absence of any possible stimulus from those pages was an extraordinary achievement. The paper was a few days old, but that wasn't the problem. It wasn't out of date, it had bypassed the present altogether. It hadn't had time to ripen. These news items would have to be buried for a long period then dug up again, like, yes, the hundred-year eggs of Chinese banquets, to take on any sort of flavour, let alone any pungency.

It was only a few years since *The Times* had allowed actual news to push the small ads off its front page, an innovation that Dad (a *Telegraph* man himself) had deplored on general principle. I'd never been able to work out, and may not have succeeded even now, whether he was a man of strong opinions or weak ones since he seemed to care most about the things that were least important.

The Times's front page before 1966 would inform its readers, for instance, that any relatives of the late A. J. Summerson, of Ashby-de-la-Zouch, should contact Madison and Humble on the high street of that town, from whom they would learn something to their advantage, before reluctantly notifying them of declarations of war and election results. Yet such a front page, with its fusty advertisements for lady's companions and notices of lost property sales, was a carnival of lurid immediacy compared with the *Cambridge Evening News* of 1973. The *Cambridge Evening News* had gone *The Times* one better by removing urgency from every page impartially. I read it several times over in wonderment, item by item, making sure there wasn't some tiny spark of interest that I had missed, but a report on a demonstration of traction engines in Babraham was the closest thing to a contender. If homœopathy is a true doctrine, as of course it is, and relentless dilution unleashes the most fantastic curative powers, then the *Cambridge Evening News* was an astonishing pharmacopœia, a mighty cabinet of topical medicine richly stocked with preparations for every symptom under the sun.

The forest is full of ears

How can I single out an item from the range that the *Cambridge Evening News* laid out for its readers six times a week, page after page, the nugatory treats that I acquired such a perverse taste for? Ærated nugget of news nougat that melted into nothingness on the tongue, being nothingness already. I'll do my best. How does this rate, printed as it was under the headline 'Waiting for *Nethergate*'?

Norah Lofts' novel Nethergate *remains the most sought after book on the fiction shelves of the Cambridge libraries. It has remained top of the pops for three months according to the City Librarian, Mr Eric Cave.*

This took place on the far side of any scale of triviality hitherto imagined by the yardsticks of science. It subjected the phrase 'news item' to a withering philosophical scrutiny. If this was an event worth reporting what would constitute a non-event? If a pine needle falls from a tree in the forest does it make a sound? Yes, it does, but it doesn't make a news item.

I've always thought the original form of the question, with a tree falling rather than a single pine needle, was remarkably stupid. The forest is full of ears. Presumably the beavers whose gnawing caused the tree to fall in the first place hear the crash with some satisfaction. Yes, I know it's only a thought experiment . . . and it needs more thought.

Even if you were a library user who had your name down on the waiting list for *Nethergate* it could hardly affect your heart rate. The waiting list is where people wait, and it's something on which the British have traditionally prided themselves, the talent for sacrificing the present to the future, in queues and doctors' surgeries, waiting outside lavatories with no one inside them because our manners are too good to allow us to knock on the door. The power of our waiting is immense. We wait things out. We wear them down with the superfine sandpaper of not-in-a-rush. We've all the time in the world. If you've put your name down for a library copy of *Nethergate* it's not so much that you want to read it as that you want to wait. Have you delved deeply into the Lofts *œuvre*? Are you confident that *Nethergate* will be streets ahead of *Uneasy Paradise* and *Lovers All Untrue* as a reading experience? To be brutally frank, did you put your name down for *Nethergate* because you thought the day would never come when you'd have to plough your way through the bloody thing?

In fact from the moment the postcard lands on the doormat with the news that the book is waiting for you, your leisure will be very limited, since you'll have to rush through it at top speed if you're going to return it to base on schedule for the next patient customer. The time that lay around you in still pools when you were safely waiting for *Nethergate* is first of all ruffled with a chill wind, the appalling prospect of getting what you said you wanted, and then drained away with hardly a gurgle. Much less stressful to return the book immediately and then put in another request for it, so as to draw out indefinitely the pleasure of waiting for *Nethergate*. Godot? The latest Norah Lofts? It makes no odds. The waiting is the important bit.

I began to understand that the *Cambridge Evening News* was conducting an enquiry, one possessed of an eerie purity, into the infinitely small. At what point did a minute fraction dwindle to nothingness? In my boyhood there had been rumours of a race between scientists of supposedly allied nations to build the smallest possible tube, no doubt for the improved development of weapons and rockets. Proudly the Yank researchers had sent British Intelligence the smallest tube in the world, and our lab boffins had returned it with a thank-you note they had engraved onto an even smaller one and tucked inside the original. Take that, Uncle Sam! It was the fantasised national style at the time to win without seeming to care, and to triumph without gloating (while invisibly gloating). The news item about *Nethergate* was an immaculate hollow cylinder that could have fitted inside that rumoured micro-tube a thousand times over. But what could it contain in its turn? It was already full to bursting with emptiness. I knew, though the knowledge brought with it a sense of ecstatic vertigo, that there were transfinite numbers somehow parallel with infinity though not identical to it, and now I was learning – not from a scientific journal but from the pages of an evening paper! – that alongside the infinitesimal seethed the transfinitesimal.

Over time I realised that Mr Eric Cave, the city librarian, was a Zen master of this sort of coverage, though again the word 'coverage' shrivels to nothing in this context. What is being covered? What, to approach the question from the other end, is being left uncovered? The language crumbles to dust.

She was all over mousetraps

In the absence of guru, mentor or circle of friends, it was Paula who took up the slack. Getting along with someone on a daily basis has more to do with rhythm than temperament, I think, if that distinction even holds. Paula rarely seemed to hurry and she never hurried me. One day, though, she was moving away from the kitchenette to clean the bathroom and I thought of something that would interest her, so I started to speak. She kept moving, and for a moment I felt embarrassed, as if I was trespassing on her time by chatting when she was really only there to clean. But then I thought, if I'm not a person in the first place why does it matter whether the non-entity's bathroom is clean? If I was treated as less important than the bathroom floor by the person sent to make my life viable then it was the end of me. If she was only there to clean then I only existed to be cleaned for.

So I went on chatting implacably until I winched her back into the kitchen, slightly resistant to the relentless flow of syntax I dare say but at least acknowledging my existence. I couldn't follow her, after all. Since then I've made it my policy to go on talking when people decide without consultation that our conversation is over. I can't vote with my feet, but I have learned to override their veto with an unstoppable flow of chat.

It took me a while to accept or adjust the other ground rules of our relationship. I'd sent her off to buy canned goods at the Marcade on East Road, and she returned flustered and unhappy. It was a lot to carry, and she was on the clock, with another client waiting after me. I was mortified to have taken liberties – somehow I was both an oppressed party and something of an exploiter myself. I have to admit that my thrifty side had been inflamed by the Marcade's advertisements in the *Cambridge Evening News*. I was forgetting that she had the legs and the strength, but I was the one with the car. After that we made the trip together when the lure of the bargain overcame my resistance, whether I'm to be pictured as a crew member equipped with waxen earplugs or Odysseus himself tied to a mast while the sirens warbled, 'Eggs a penny apiece, can you Adam-and-Eve it? Peas, baked beans and prunes all a penny a tin – hurry before we come to our senses.' A trip to the Marcade was ever so much nicer as an expedition rather than a chore. Paula showed bargaining skills that you wouldn't expect to have a chance of working, here at the rock bottom of the market, getting dented tins at half price. A ha'penny each! When she slid her eyes towards me during the negotiation I tried to look as disadvantaged as humanly possible.

One turning point between us was the day I asked her to add four Crunchie bars to the shopping list. I said they were for a scientific experiment, and she rolled her eyes, asking, 'Is it an experiment to see how many Crunchies you can eat before exploding?'

'No, it's a serious study, an enquiry into truth. Do you not want to be my lab assistant?'

'Well . . . I didn't say that.' So it was agreed.

She duly bought the bars of cinder toffee covered in chocolate – I prefer the description 'cinder toffee' to 'honeycomb' since there's no overlap with the structures bees build out of wax, the wax that

Mæterlinck describes so beautifully as 'a strange sweat' that seems to be the 'soul of the honey', while honey in its turn is the spirit of flowers.

The equipment we required was all available: a fridge, a pair of scissors and a pair of hands – capable hands, which ruled my ones out. In the end I had abandoned the attempt to maintain, even in my mind, the apostrophes required by correct usage at both ends of the word 'fridge', doubly abbreviated from *refrigerator* (and also by 'flu', doubly abbreviated from *influenza*). All my pedantry and tiny zeitgeist-resisting power was invested in the more important struggle to go on saying 'new pence' and not 'new p' or just plain 'p'.

I asked Paula if by any chance she had such a thing as a pair of nail scissors in her handbag? Ladies often do. She did, and this was convenient in practical terms but also propitious for the spell I was trying to cast. I was exploiting the stage magician's knowledge that an audience member who contributes a personally charged object to the trick potentiates its magic.

'Now,' I explained, 'you must break one of these Crunchies into three or four pieces *without opening the wrapper or damaging it in any way.*' I made sure she understood this stipulation, getting her to repeat them back to me before giving her the signal to start. She did a good job, looking up at me anxiously between awkward snapping motions to make sure I approved.

There was an element of theatre about all these preparations, but I didn't mind that. Take away explosions and bad smells and chemistry lessons lose much of their appeal.

Then I directed her to take up the scissors and explained the next experimental stage in the protocol. We would be turning our attention to the second bar. Scissors are just not Johnable, and I can't say I'm too up in arms about that. Any device that was able to harness my minimal skill at bringing my fingers together wouldn't bear much resemblance to a pair of scissors. Any such device would be of little use to me, none whatever to anyone else. And no, homœopathic principles don't apply on what we might call the 'macro' scale. It's only at the profounder levels of existence that weakness and strength unpredictably change places.

Paula needed to make small incisions in the wrapper but not in the smooth chocolate skin of the bar itself.

'How many?'

'Twelve.' The precise number was less important than the confidence with which I announced it.

'And now what do we do?'

'We put them in the fridge.' The fridge was tiny, but a couple of Crunchies could be accommodated.

'Now what?'

I gave her one of my favourite answers. 'We wait.' While you wait for something you are both inside and outside the time it takes to happen, the time it takes to happen or not happen. I'd say simultaneously inside and outside, except that 'simultaneously' is so exactly the wrong word.

'How long do we wait?'

'When do you come here next?' It was a Friday, and I knew the answer.

'Monday.'

'Then we wait till Monday.'

'Hold on,' she said. 'I must be missing something. Didn't you ask me to buy *four* Crunchies?'

'I did.'

'Then what happens to the other two?'

'You're going to cut one of them into twelfths. How are you with a knife? Do you have a steady hand?'

She hesitated. 'Fair, I'd say. Do I unwrap the Crunchie first?'

'That's the idea. Then I suggest you cut it in half, then each half into half, then each quarter into thirds.'

She thought for a moment. 'Making twelve pieces.'

'Affirmative. Aim for a single decisive stroke with the knife each time.'

I have to say she did a good job. There were crumbs, of course. There will always be crumbs.

'And now what?'

'And now we eat them. Eight-twelfths for you, four-twelfths for me.'

'And this is part of our experiment?'

'Not at all. This is part of our elevenses. Though you could say we're establishing a baseline reading for the flavour of Crunchie. I say . . .' – a thought occurred to me – '. . . you do like Crunchies, don't you?'

But her mouth was already full of Crunchie chunks. When she had finished her allotted portion she licked her thumb and used it daintily to pick up the crumbs. It would have taken another experiment to establish whether the increased viscosity of her saliva, emulsified as it was with suspended chocolate particles, made the process more efficient than it would otherwise have been.

Finally, sated, her shoulders noticeably more relaxed than they had been pre-elevenses, she asked about the fourth and final bar. 'I'm going to ask you to tuck it away in a drawer. We need to protect it from scavengers over the weekend.'

'You mean it wasn't needed today?' I don't think she was looking at it with greed, necessarily. 'I could always bring another on Monday.'

'Oh no.' I shook my head homœopathically. 'We need to be sure it's from the same batch. Tiny variations can have large effects on results. There are no half measures in methodology. I dare say the scientific approach takes some getting used to.'

'Well,' she said. 'I'm learning. I'm certainly learning *something*.' But the sugared surge those Crunchie chunks had given her metabolism made it impossible for her to find the right note of mock exasperation.

Was there a subtle tingle acting on Paula's weekend? I know there was on mine, though it was a secondary tingle based on imagining her anticipation – and not to be sneezed at on that basis.

On the Monday I let Paula do her chores without mentioning our experiment. I behaved as if I had forgotten, as if it had only been a caprice soon driven out of my head by another, though I would have been deeply pained if she herself had failed to remember. Luckily she was dying to know what it was all about. She was hooked.

An experiment is always an experiment on yourself as well as on the little slice of Maya you are setting out to investigate. Paula used the nail scissors to cut the Crunchies out of their foil-lined shrouds. If I had owned a set of scales I would have weighed them – establishing a baseline is always a good idea. A blind tasting would have been experimentally desirable, but we managed without. Paula cut the intact bar into chunks, the one that had been marginally exposed to the air. Time had added a gooey complication to its crunch, darkening the flavour in the process, but it had also changed us as we waited. The other bar, broken in pieces but not exposed to the atmosphere, seemed not to have changed – a disappointing result, narrowly considered, but satisfactory in every other way since Crunchies are delicious. We ate both bars with an enhanced attentiveness and enjoyment. The marginally transformed Crunchies had been emancipated from their subservient status as snack by the timescale allotted by the experiment in our little game of planning. A snack isn't planned, it's what you put in your mouth when there's no plan. This was both less and more than a meal, lightly dusted as it was with the powder of ritual.

By posing as a teacher I could pretend to be passing on an experience, when in fact I was receiving it as a gift. I would never have had an interest in chilling two slightly different Crunchies if I didn't have a pupil to instruct or pretend to instruct. I wouldn't have bought a Crunchie in the first place, not one, let alone two, without the pleasure afforded me by the fiction of knowing more than Paula. That's the secret power of the pupil–teacher relationship, that no actual knowledge is required to make it work. Each of us basked in a warmth that neither of us was capable of generating unaided. The educative current passes through different personalities rather than different bodies of knowledge. It's a matter of electrolytic activity, not hydraulics. An alignment of electrons lays down a coating of new particles, transforming the current as it travels. It's not a case of information in liquid form gurgling from one container to another. The sound of education in action – do you hear that? – is a subtle crackling, not any sort of slosh.

There was a Zen of everything in those days, a Zen of tea, and even a Tao of Pooh. Even so, I'm not sure anyone attempted the Zen of Crunchie before me. This may make me a pioneer of do-it-yourself mystical practice using confectionery.

The only serious disagreement I had with Paula was about mice. In that first week she discovered a tiny dun cylinder under a kitchenette counterette which was, yes, a mouse turd, yes, a compressed Euclidean solid of excreted matter but really minding its own business when viewed from any enlightened karmic perspective. I would be much more reconciled to the business of defæcation if I myself could produce so neat an excretion, clipped off by a sphincter whose action was as dainty and definitive as the click of a camera shutter.

When I say that Paula discovered it, I mean that I pointed it out to her. I wanted to inspect it, and a mouse turd on the floor does not feature on the very short list of things I can pick up, so naturally I asked her – the home help – for this little bit of help around the home.

The limitations on my ability to pick things up are relatively straightforward. I can pick up something reasonably small on a surface reasonably near me. You shouldn't bet against me when it comes to retrieving, say, a sugar cube from a tabletop. Under the right circumstances I flirt almost with dextrousness. I can retrieve with some suavity an After Eight mint from its envelope of darkest brown. I could almost appear in an advertisement for those seductive sweetmeats – I long to use the Shakespearean word 'comfits' to describe them but the definition is strict and won't stretch. Then of course I must wait for a helping hand to slip the rippled delicious tile of chocolate into my mouth or at least pass me the ceremonial mint tongs, modified to suit my fingers' rudimentary gripping abilities. Getting it out of its envelope is the easy part. I can flick a peanut into my mouth more or less reliably but an after-dinner mint is a long shot, and a failed party trick is a fiasco in the making, not to be lived down in a hurry.

Picking things up from the floor is pretty much beyond me, though I can manage to hook up a sock or a pair of pants with the crutch or the cane. The biggest thing I can pick up from the floor is . . . well, the crutch or the cane. I can hook up the crutch with the cane or the cane with the crutch if I happen to drop one or the other. It's not an easy operation but I can do it. I can, or I could in those days. 'Can' or 'could'? The past tense keeps pushing itself forward, strange old soldier forever grumbling but volunteering for another mission, but I'll stick to using the present for clarity's sake. It's easier to use the stick to get purchase on the crutch, but the crutch is heavier and harder to keep in balance so the level of inconvenience is roughly equal. If I happened to drop both crutch and cane, and it wasn't for nothing that I was nicknamed Dropper at the Canadian Red Cross Memorial Hospital, then I was pretty much dished. As long as I was in reach of the telephone I could summon reinforcements, but Mrs Baine made it clear early on that this was not how she saw herself.

Mrs Baine came to pick up the crutch and was very stiff indeed about it, very I'm-not-your-servant. She'd be good at charades. After that I stopped buying milk from her and got Paula to spend my money on sterilised instead, which with a little effort I came to prefer.

Paula refused to pick up the mouse dropping for me to inspect. Instead she swept it up into her dustpan, brisk disgust powering every bristle of the brush, and the next time she came she was all over mousetraps. As far as she was concerned she had a licence to kill every rodent on the premises of 005 Mayflower House.

I tried to defend my dependent fellow tenants, shapers of cylindrical turds, the mammalians no more parasitic than I was myself, clinging to their living space without even the support I was granted. I did my best to persuade her that having mice was a good thing.

'How do you work that out?'

'Well . . . if you've got mice then it means you don't have rats. Mice clear out at the first sniff of a rat.' Is that true? I think it's true. At the word 'rat' she gave a convulsive movement almost from the pelvis, arising from some deep well of disgust, negative programming that most likely had nothing to do with experience. Human beings aren't born with a fear of rats, though I dare say I should make an honourable exception for those who have died while rats ate their faces, trapped under rubble for instance, in the aftermath of an earthquake, but even so . . . dying comes with a pretty intensive cleaning process. The Karma Laundry does good work. Plenty of time-outside-time for any amount of soak, rinse and spin. It takes real stubbornness to hang on to your skid marks.

'Have you ever seen a rat?'

The same shudder from the depths of her. 'No, and I don't plan to.'

'Then how do you know they're so horrible?'

'You're not going to talk me round, you know, John.' My arguments had misfired, as is bound to happen sometimes. Now the absence of mice she so much desired would rob her of sleep with its implications.

What happened next wasn't really a game though it had the look of one. She laid the mousetraps down in out-of-the-way places. The moment she had left I would spring them with my stick, leaving her to wonder on her next visit at the resilience of the local vermin, shrugging off the brutal snap of the device. There shouldn't have been any need for me to hurry as I set about disabling Paula's rodent artillery after she had left, but there seemed to be a real rush among the mice to get themselves reborn, something of a reincarnation stampede. Once she had hardly closed the door behind her before a mouse hurled itself onto the cheese between those cruel jaws, ignoring my lectures on the folly of making such decisions unilaterally. Reincarnation is such a mug's game. You can end up absolutely anywhere, looking out of any eyes whatever, if eyes are even supplied. You can cross your fingers and hope to escape the whole cycle but there are no guarantees, and rebirth entails redeath. That's the way of it – no rebirth without redeath.

In this particular case the mouse's spine was crushed by the metal bar but it wasn't killed outright, managing instead to drag itself several inches, leaving a smear of suffering on the cosmos and indeed the floor, so none of us was happy – not mouse, not home help when she reappeared and certainly not client. I talked to it soothingly, reproachfully, while it died. 'Why did you have to go and do that?' was roughly the message I was sending. I understand the urge to disappear, but it isn't practical. At best you end up where you started, at worst you set yourself back quite a way. The new life can only be conditioned by the pain which was the final impression left on the last. We don't get out of the trap so easily. There's a death canal that corresponds to the birth canal – and how can your rebirths be few if you get wedged there screaming in your final agonies?

We had quite a sordid dispute about disposal. I insisted that Paula take the little body home with her. Why should she be entitled to leave behind the outcome of her cruelty? She said it was a mouse caught on my premises and belonged in my bin. I said it was a corpse created by her actions that was linked to her forever, and then she cried, which gave me pain but didn't change my mind though I cried a little too. I've put in the hours, over the years, to turn myself into someone it's hard to say no to. She left with the mouse in a plastic bag though I doubt if she took it all the way home, and we weren't exactly friends for a little while after that.

After that shared ordeal I tried to be quicker off the mark in rendering the reincarnation-bringers safe. Paula pretended not to notice me as I sidled about triggering the traps, and I pretended not to notice that she reset as many of them as she could before she left. Perhaps the experience of causing that first terrible mouse death had seared off all her qualms and turned her into a hardened killer.

Mr Gerling's second visit didn't mitigate the disappointment of the first. Again he took off his glasses when they steamed up in the bathroom, though I didn't feel quite as tender a second time towards this revelation of his vulnerability. I inhaled deeply, hoping to detect some animal signal behind the pulsing wall of cologne. As he leaned over me for the all-too-perfunctory hair-rinsing part of the operation some sort of locket fell down from the neck of his T-shirt and dangled there on its chain. He went very red and tucked it fiercely back in place, as if some great secret had been revealed, but I had no interest in what it was. A tuft of ginger cat-fur, I dare say, to remind him of home.

I have nothing against cats, mind you, nor against the people who keep them, though here inverted commas aren't optional: the people who 'keep' them. Cats make the choice. They're exemplary creatures. You could sum up a great deal of spiritual endeavour as the attempt to turn an anthropoid dog into an anthropoid cat. Dogs' attention, much as I love them, is all over the place. Cats were born with a mantra, an internal tuning fork. Something effanineffable – even T. S. Eliot could see it, or hear it.

The smallest fart

My antipathy to Mr Gerling had been instant and irrational, but I didn't seem able to leave it at that, to allow myself to have a *bête noire* and to leave it at that. No, I had to give myself reasons. And the best reason I could possibly give was that he was a mean trick played on me by the usual illusory forces, a gay man I saw on a regular basis and with whom I had nothing in common. The hand behind the flannel that soaped my privates was utterly uninvolved and thereby unwelcome. I tried to tolerate the hygienic intrusion but it was a hand that would never be invited to take the next step and provide a warm pedestal for my balls.

Mr Gerling would always say, before he left, that he had time for a cup of tea if I wanted one. I never rose to the bait. I couldn't stop him being the council employee designated to meet my needs, needs shallowly defined, but he would never be my guest. It lay in my power to make sure of that. How rarely in those days could I formulate a sentence in that regal style – 'It lay in my power'! So little did lie in that small spotlit circle of effective action. I would waste no opportunity for magnificent flaunting of my independence in the face of those who made it possible.

Mr Gerling, for his part, didn't work on his welcome. He merely relied on the fact that I would be dirty without him, as if that would be enough to secure his place in my bosom. My bosom is not an address without standards, however, and I observed his behaviour to see how it measured up, to wit, whether he was entitled to the intimacy he claimed. He wasn't. On his second visit, once I was installed in the bath, he mentioned that he was thirsty. Would I mind if he got himself a glass of water? A hard request to refuse, even if I was mildly suspicious of it. Of course he was taking a good look round while I was guaranteed to stay where I was, though with me, in the short term, it's usually a good bet. Even in the bathroom itself he was on the shameless side, picking up the item I called the bum snorkel, the utensil, vaguely French-curved, that made it possible for me to wipe myself after defæcation with the help of toilet paper craftily inserted into a cleft designed for the purpose. On the bum snorkel Mr Gerling cast an admiring and even an appraising eye. It might have been something he had spotted in a jumble sale. Though it would look a bit odd on a mantlepiece.

'You don't need toileting, do you?' he had asked on that first visit. I'd not met that particularly rancid gerund before, and we hated each other at first sight. If it makes me a snob to loathe the word then so be it. I wear my disgrace as a tiara.

'I'm not completely helplessing,' I said.

'Beg pardon?'

'I'm not completely helplessing.'

'I suppose so.' He seemed unsure of himself. 'And do you need toileting?' He separated the syllables helpfully in case I was having trouble – *toi-let-ing*. If I'd thought the word had achieved its full potential for ugliness he was showing me just how wrong I was.

If I had needed help with excretion, of course, I'd have exploded long before he arrived. I imagine he must have been given some paperwork about me, so he either hadn't been bothered to read it or was just making conversation. Making conversation! Along with the home help he was my prescribed dose of social life – these were the people who would come into my flat and talk to me without being invited. Them and only them. So far the conversational prospects with Mr Gerling were not good. In Downing I had something that could almost be called a *salon*, if you half closed your eyes and boosted your wishful thinking until it turned into a headache. At least I had people dropping in on a regular basis, putting their mugs and glasses right next to the coasters provided to receive them and idly putting the lid on the coffee jar so tight that I would never be able to unscrew it. I reminded myself that my new address only seemed different from the last. Wherever I am, great events come through my door. I can't stop them. They have to stoop, they enter in a crouch to avoid bumping their heads, but enter they do.

One time after Mr Gerling had left I found that he had surreptitiously moved the African violets I had been bringing on with so much singleness of purpose from the top of the lavatory cistern to the windowsill. How dare he! That's no way to behave. What sort of monster intervenes in the private life of the bathroom-nursery? And he can't have been much of a gardener to think my African violet would benefit from its new position. A fart even muffled by underpants is a plume of nutrients for an African violet. Plants aren't fools. They've learned some tricks along the evolutionary way. The closer a plant lives to the lavatory the richer its life. If you (or, less happily, your visitors) can smell a fart then it has released in small but sufficient doses at least some of what a plant requires to live – nitrogen, hydrogen, oxygen and, yes, the sulphur that makes the nasty smell. Why deny your plants the incidental benefits of your diet?

Mr Gerling had already taken an interest in the autoclaved pots of earth and offered his help on any little botanical projects I had in mind. Not so fast! I explained that I couldn't afford a gardener and would just have to struggle along somehow, but he was slow to take the hint. 'I'm happy to help,' he said, and seemed quite put out when I said, 'But I don't want you to.' Tact has its uses, in an ideal world every transaction would be fully oiled and free of friction, but sometimes you have to accept that it isn't going to bloody work and just say what you mean.

Sometimes I could hear him rolling his eyes. I have persuaded myself that my hearing can detect it when someone outside my range of vision rolls his (or her) eyes, not entirely from the sound of extra-ocular rectus and oblique muscles working in relay, which must be the tiniest of signals, but perhaps with additional help from changes in breathing. There's an exasperated nasal exhalation, half suppressed, which accompanies the movement of the eyes.

Mr Gerling, never to be called Tony, at least by me, had a suggestion to make on one of his early visits. 'John, I'm very impressed with the contraption you use to wipe your bottom – what do you call it, the bum snorkel? It's fab.' How had I come to let slip the private name of a device I used every day? I didn't enjoy hearing what was a pet name, almost an endearment, on those uncongenial lips. Every bit of information acquired by someone you don't like gives them power over you, or so it seems, though I dare say that's an unhealthy way of thinking about it, not to mention a primitive one.

'But John, you must realise there are limits to what it can do. It can't make you what the Americans call *squeaky clean*.' I winced at this description, though I couldn't quarrel with its accuracy. Would I even want my back passage to be so clean it squeaked? Actually, on mature reflection, I think I would.

'John, do you ever strain at stool? I realise these are normally private matters, but there's really no need to be shy, not with me . . .' Apparently I wasn't entitled to privacy. If I wanted to discuss defæcation in depth wouldn't I raise the subject myself? I'm capable of it. Of course by giving him a maximum dose of the silent treatment I may have given the impression, for once in my life, of being, yes, shy. 'You see, it's important to avoid hæmorrhoids – piles – if at all possible, particularly as you're someone who spends so much of his time sitting down. I could put some Savlon on your back passage when I visit, if you like. Not really a job for the bum snorkel. Better to use it every day, but once a week is better than nothing, isn't it?' I was very anxious in my dealings with Mr Gerling to keep every possible barrier in place – and if a sphincter doesn't represent a barrier then I don't know what does. His finger, even anointed with soothing cream and covered with the sheath known as a fingerstall to guarantee that this was a professional visit, would not have right of access. I told him I would manage on my own. I would manage somehow.

I could hardly mention, since I was restricting the flow of information to the best of my ability, that my home help Paula was already on Savlon duty, patrolling my southern perimeter. This was something that had arisen and been smoothly arranged with only the most transient embarrassment for either party. There was even a little merry giggling involved.

For three years, in a competitive environment, I had tried to show my fellow students, my supervisors, my tutor and all the college staff, down to the smallest bursar and catering manager, that I was clever, funny, original and above all interesting. There could be no less effective method of finding out what you might actually be like. Now, in the absence of the people who had (under pressure) found me interesting, I found it hard to be interested in myself.

Naturally I reacted by repeating the pattern of behaviour that had just been seen to fail. I tried to convince everyone from Mrs Baine and the Major to dear Paula that I was in every way an exceptional being. This second round of charm offensives wasn't necessarily any more successful than the first. The only person whom I had made no effort to impress was Mr Gerling. I had probably managed to impress him just the same, impressed him as being unappreciative, rude and generally unbearable.

Paula was always rubbing Nivea into her hands. She offered to anoint me in the same way, having perhaps an exaggerated idea of its softening properties, as if the grease she swore by (I hope free of tallow, though no ingredients were listed on the little flat pot) might penetrate down to my bones and soften them. I enjoyed the contact, and she had the makings of a talented masseuse, but it would have been more enjoyable without the skin cream, which took forever to be absorbed and had me leaving sticky smears on everything I touched. We could neither of us say out loud that the experiment had been a failure, in terms of reversing long-standing arthritic damage by the topical application of fat, so we carried on with the routine quite a few times.

Mr Gerling was a lost cause, as far as I was concerned, and no doubt he had the same feeling about me. Over time my relationship with

Mrs Baine showed a distinct improvement, though we never became close. She was careful not to abuse the privilege of her pass key but would knock on my door and wait for a greeting. I think it helped that I was careful from my side also, calling her Mrs Baine without the final *s* tacked onto it by the other residents, for no better reason than that this is the commoner form of the name. Showing respect for her name was a small courtesy, but that's just what you need to maintain a respectful acquaintanceship. Stiffness and excess of intimacy each has its danger. Rituals have a part to play. Most afternoons she came in with the *Cambridge Evening News*, saying, 'You do love your newspaper, don't you, Mr Cromer?' and before long I found it was true. I came to rely on the *Cambridge Evening News*, not as a source of information but as an aid to self-enquiry, as if the publication which so many people worked to produce was really only a vast collective mantra intended to help empty the mind. Certainly the paper was powerless to fill it.

Paula sometimes listened to her pocket radio as she worked, though there was also my own little set. It was Russian-made, something that seemed pleasingly naughty at a time when international tensions were taken for granted. The company's slogan was 'Another gold for Russia'. The set was cheap and worked well. I didn't have a television and didn't want one. In that restricted space I wouldn't have known where to put it.

I loved William Hardcastle's voice on *The World at One*, its English timbre left intact by the Soviet transistors and speaker, perhaps even enhanced by them. One day Hardcastle told us to make sure we were sitting down. 'If you're not sitting down, at least hold on to something solid. This is an extraordinary moment.' He sounded very grave. 'The price of petrol will soon reach . . .' (he was enough of a journalist to stretch out the timing of the revelation) '. . . *fifty pence a gallon*. How many of us will be able to afford to keep our cars on the road?' It was certainly a facer. I filled up the Mini once a week, and I was rationing my use of it already. It was hard to see how I could cut down any further. The needle of the fuel gauge hovered just above half-full for ages, and I could never quite catch the sneaky moment when it slipped down to a quarter.

The price of petrol was subject to any number of worldly pressures. I followed politics very little, which is one of the things that is likely to happen if you have a strongly mystical bent and a glut of super-annuated editions of a local paper. I took pleasure in *The World at One* because of the latent double meaning in the title of the programme. I wanted the world to be at one, but whether that fusion was con-summated at one o'clock or any other hour of day was a matter of indifference to me. If *The World at One* had been broadcast at one in the morning I would have set my alarm clock uncomplainingly. In some ways I would have preferred it. There has always been a ten-dency in my character towards austerity, a hankering for difficulty over ease and subsistence over plenty. Just as well, really. Even so (it's a lesson I must go on teaching myself, however little I want to hear it) the value of something bears no relation to the ease or difficulty with which it is obtained. The law of supply and demand has no spiritual application. This is one of the aspects of Ramana Maharshi's thought that I've struggled the hardest with, the dismissal of struggle itself. To be consistent, of course, I can't claim the effort expended as a gauge of merit. That's exactly the problem – I go on wanting points for the hard work I've put in, instantly showing that I haven't, in fact, understood.

I seem to remember William Hardcastle dying quite soon after that, though I expect memory has done its usual dusting and tidying up. Still, perhaps he really did feel the full force of the shock he passed on to his listeners that day. It hit us all hard.

One of the first trips I made in the Mini, as soon as it was practi-cal, was to the University Library. My privileges had not lapsed at the point of graduation, and there was no real danger of my rights being revoked, but I thought it was a good idea to reinforce my presence there, while there were still so few students about.

When anyone I met in those days said, 'Oh, did you use to be a student?', or even before, I would say with great firmness, 'I am a graduate member of the University.' My relationship with the institu-tion might have become more abstract, but it still held. A Cambridge graduate is not a finished article but a work in progress.

I was a graduate pebble hurled from the academic catapult, like thousands of others that summer, and since the university firing me into the future was Cambridge my status would have momentum for some time to come. Six years from the end of my first term of residence, without any effort on my part beyond putting a cheque in the post at the proper time, I would become an M.A. (Cantab.). There was a countdown going on, however inaudibly. After that, admittedly, any momentum I might develop would need to be of my own making.

The B.A. (Cantab.) matures into an M.A. (Cantab.) without any effort or visible change. It's either a subtle ripening or a hoax of privilege. Perhaps I shouldn't be endangering the mystique of this advanced degree by dispelling the ignorance on which it depends. That's too bad – it's done now.

I think it was already true that a graduate is a member of the University, whether engaged in active study or not, but it became truer every time I said so or even thought it. Even silent assertion substantiates a truth though it can do nothing for a falsehood. I needed to remind the University that I was part of it. I needed to circulate regularly through the vessels of the Library, if nowhere else, so that I would never be mistaken for a foreign body. The University must be made to understand that I am a corpuscle of its own blood.

I'm not sure when I encountered Rupert Sheldrake's idea of 'morphic resonance', his theory that there is a hidden layer of communication that surrounds and connects individuals. Morphic resonance neatly explains the developing skills of the blue tits in my childhood when confronted with foil-topped milk bottles, and also the increased evasive skills of flies, though I have to say the flies were much slower on the uptake. It can't have been as early as 1973, since at the time he was a fellow of Clare College and was just beginning to hypothesise the existence of telepathic interconnections between organisms and collective memories within species. In other words we were living in the same small city, and might well have interacted in some indirect way. He might have arrived at Miss Duff's stall on the Market Hill just too late to buy the geode that would have been the star of his collection. Or when I had the sudden definite sensation of being stared at in Arts Cinema Passage before seeing *Elvira Madigan* it might have been Rupert Sheldrake himself conducting empirical research into scopæsthesia, though I have to own up to being a poor experimental subject. It's much easier to tell that someone has felt the weight of your gaze if they can turn without difficulty and meet your eyes.

Cats are so clearly scopæsthetic that it's hardly worth while running the tests that would prove it. In any case cats are highly resistant to projects involving coöperation with human beings. Their vibrissæ baulk at participation, sensing the narrow passage ahead, and they don't necessarily want human beings to know too much. They'd keep morphic resonance a secret if they could.

Cats seem to know when they're being experimented on, which must count as a sophisticated form of scopæsthesia in its own right. Cats are not simple creatures nor do they pretend to be.

1973 was the year that Sheldrake left Britain and moved to India, working on the physiology of tropical crops at a research institute in Hyderabad, though it's pretty obvious that he was already attuned to Indian spirituality in general and Hinduism specifically. When he needed time off to refine his ideas on morphic resonance he stayed for a year and a half in an ashram in Tamil Nadu, run by a Christian yogi, Swami Dayananda, who was born Alan Richard Griffiths and wrote a book called *Christ in India*. Yes, it all connects up! You don't have to tell me that.

The ashram in question, Saccidananda in Tannirpalli, was founded by two Frenchmen, a priest and a monk, to reconcile the two mystical traditions of Hinduism and Christianity. There was tension, though, with the priest wanting to Christianise other religions while the monk suspected that non-Christian religions could have a transformative effect on Christianity itself. Conversion is a two-way street. It's generally understood that the drop merges with the ocean, often forgotten that the ocean also merges with the drop. And when a sledgehammer is used to crack a nut, the nut too has a subtle impact on the sledgehammer, though this side of the event tends to be neglected by researchers with crude models of the way the world works.

The second approach certainly seems the more promising of the two, with the colonising power mysteriously saturated by the forces it set out to tame, just as the Tamil language made amorous advances towards the missionaries who to start with had only wanted to learn it as a means of instructing the heathen. That's the idea that makes the hairs on the back of my neck horripilate so promisingly. It brings on the scopæsthesia hot and strong.

If there is receptiveness among sentient beings to signals below the threshold of consciousness, who's to say it taps into the cerebrum, cerebellum or rhioecephalon? My vote would go to the last one in the list, developmentally the most primitive. And where there is receptiveness there is also a duty to broadcast. I constantly murmured little spells or introduced them into casual conversation, seeking to fecundate the noösphere around me. 'Is it Johnable?' I would say, hoping that the phrase would bed down in the minds I encountered, a little scurry of syllables suggesting itself whenever an expedition to a new place was proposed. 'Shall we have a pint in the Baron of Beef?' 'I dunno . . . the Mitre is more Johnable.'

I seemed to have succeeded with the declaration 'I am a graduate member of the University.' It no longer met with scepticism. As for whether it was true before I started bruiting it about, that is the mootest of moot points. If it became true because I believed it then that is evidence of the effectiveness of the process, but science demands that the result of an experiment be confirmed by a repetition, and I didn't quite see how I could manage that.

Morphic resonance is a fruiting body whose spores are carried on the universal wind, ineradicable because self-seeding.

Haven't I always felt that there was a continuous osmotic exchange between supposedly distinct entities? For consistency's sake Dr Sheldrake could hardly maintain that he was the only one in that place, at that time, to visualise a shared consciousness lapping at the edges of our being. It's against the spirit of the enterprise to claim sole credit for the discovery that nothing happens to a single individual only. To give himself a pat on the back he would need to shoot his theory in the foot.

Hang on a sec. Going back to my own affinity for fieldwork, the difference between a poor experimental subject and a good one need only be a shift in emphasis. Suppose I was rigged up with a walkie-talkie, or even some sort of electrical clicker, so that I could indicate when I felt I was being stared at, without being able to discover for myself whether or not the sensation was truthful, while Dr Sheldrake, hovering in the middle distance, scrutinised my surroundings to establish who was doing the staring. Surely that would excite interest at the Society for Psychical Research? Except . . . how to be sure it wasn't Dr Sheldrake's eyes that were burning a hole in my pineal gland? The experimental protocol involved needs a certain amount of work, clearly, but I refuse to be discouraged. There is valuable work to be done here.

Tins of intellectual caviar

The system in place for my benefit at the University Library (and one reason why the telephone was such an asset) allowed me to phone ahead, persuading staff to consult the catalogue on my behalf. During vacations in particular it was wonderful what I could get away with. I would turn up in the Mini at an agreed time, sound the horn in a sprightly rhythm, and my choices would be brought down to me, so many jars of intellectual caviar (on account) being loaded into a taxi outside Fortnum & Mason.

I wasn't exactly having withdrawal symptoms from the essay régime that constitutes undergraduate life, but I certainly wanted a task that would be mentally stimulating. I had decided to do some homework about a pioneer of gay rights who was often mentioned at meetings of the group I was loosely attached to, the Cambridge Homosexual Activism Project, or CHAPs. Magnus Hirschfeld had set up his own activism project, an Institute for Sexual Research (motto 'Per Scientiam ad Justitiam') that was then destroyed by the Nazis, following their own ideas about science and justice. In fact he had learned about the destruction of his life's work from a newsreel that gloated over the event. He went into exile and died in Nice in 1935, even more clearly the casualty of a cultural shock wave than William Hardcastle. We bandied Hirschfeld's name about freely enough at meetings, where the air was thick with counter-patriarchal ideology and the smell of cooking.

Hirschfeld was mentioned at CHAPs meetings as a martyr for the cause, which wasn't quite right anyway since he died peacefully enough, however troubled in his social and political mind. It was the books from his Institute for Sexual Research who were the real martyrs, the witnesses to truth who had been tortured and put to death. They were burned alive. There was a sort of pride expressed at meetings that books from the Institut für Sexualwissenschaft had been such early victims of the infamous book-pogrom. The Nazis had waited barely three months from the time they came to power before attacking the Institut – that's how important a target we were! A back-handed compliment, it's true, but that's the sort of compliment minorities tend to get. It was all oddly exciting, though the Institut was housed in a villa just round the corner from the Reichstag, which can't have helped its chances. An institute can't run and this one couldn't hide either.

I was puzzled by the way Magnus Hirschfeld seemed to have value to the radical cause of CHAPs only because he had been persecuted, because his Institut was shut down and its work destroyed. No one seemed interested in what he might have thought, felt, even discovered about sexuality, so of course I had to be different.

The hosts of our meetings were a couple, both called Tony, who might just as well have been married for all the dismantling of the heterosexual template they had buckled down to, though their cooking skills did a certain amount to mitigate their benighted monogamy. One year they made a special cake in celebration of Hirschfeld's birthday, May the 14th, a Black Forest gâteau iced with pink triangles if I remember aright, in a rare convergence of radical politics and baking. In fact Magnus Hirschfeld died on his birthday, a piece of calendrical tidiness that had the consequence of making it impossible to celebrate his birth without also commemorating his death. I'm against the marking of birthdays in general, but this was a complicated case, since the end of Hirschfeld's life was so obviously a defeat rather than a triumph. '*Per Scientiam ad Justitiam*' may have been inscribed on his gravestone, but he knew all too well that in the city of his greatest success injustice had allied itself with ignorance while cruelty had made common cause with purity-madness.

I didn't remember any actual reference to the man's books being made at CHAPs meetings, so I set out to inform myself. If Hirschfeld was a pioneer then so could I be, in my own small way. I looked forward to having the drop for once on the group's intellectual avant-garde (name of Ken).

As usual I phoned in advance, hoping to hear a familiar voice. More importantly, a voice that warmed up at the sound of mine. I was lucky. 'Is that Mr Cromer? I was wondering what had happened to you. What's it to be this time, sir? Oceanography? Linear B?' I was absurdly flattered, as well as relieved, to get such a welcome, though it meant very little. Any number of undergraduates were reading more widely than me, they just weren't getting so well known to library staff.

'Oh . . . Mark, is it?' I was embarrassed to be unsure about the name of someone who remembered me so well.

'Mike, sir.'

'I was thinking it was time for some sex, Mike.'

'A bit early in the morning for me, sir, but don't let me stop you. What name am I looking for?'

'Magnus Hirschfeld, I think. H-I-R-S-C-H-F-E-L-D.'

'Understood, sir, I've got that. And the book title?'

'I'm broadminded, Mike. You choose. Spicy as you like.' For all the world as if I was ordering an Indian takeaway.

'Usual drill, sir? I'll consult the catalogue and phone you back. Forgive me, sir, I've not made a note of your number.' What fantastically good manners! Really I was being spoiled, on that particular day. I would have hated the idea of losing my special status, since for once my deficits had been royally made up, the playing field not levelled but slanted in my favour. Ordinary undergraduates were the underprivileged ones in this case, only being allowed to consult the books, not take them away. They could only gaze at the burnished ingots of learning, while I was the gold-fingered one who could brazenly take the treasure out of Fort Knox.

Mike the perky librarian was soon trotting across the car park of the UL and reaching in through the window of the Mini to show me a copy of Magnus Hirschfeld's *Sexual Anomalies and Perversions*. The spiciest item in the catalogue, he said, though that is to perpetuate the confusion between serious sexology and mere erotica. He had put the book inside a giant envelope and murmured, 'Plain brown wrapper, sir, I thought that would be best,' before laying the package onto the passenger seat.

I had imagined that any UL holdings of Magnus Hirschfeld material would be in German, and I was half looking forward to resuming my generally pleasurable dealings with the language. I would content myself with an Englishing of the great man. It spared me the awkwardness of showing off without an audience, impressing no one but myself.

The Scarlet Pimpernel of flagellant ambushers

It was a hefty tome, not at all like the miniature books I so loved as a child. The restricted compass that doesn't limit but amplifies. Why do people persist in producing such absurdly bulky publications? Anything bigger than Beatrix Potter format should be heavily taxed. I had to get help from Paula to prop the Hirschfeld up and even arrange kitchen utensils to hold its pages open, but even so old Magnus won my heart.

The book turned out not to be a book by Hirschfeld himself but a volume compiled as a 'humble memorial' to the great man by his pupils. The only names given were the publisher's and the printer's. Copyright was owned by the publisher, Francis Aldor, Ltd., London, but with no date given. How is that possible, copyright without a date? The printer was S. Sidders & Son Ltd. of 115 Salusbury Road, London NW6 – I think that must be Kilburn. The whole enterprise testified to bravery, yes, but also to extreme anxiety, with no editor or translator being named. It was easy to imagine that Hirschfeld's pupils might also have been forced into exile, and would not necessarily have confidence in the safety of their new haven. Even the book's year of publication seemed to have hidden away for fear of reprisals.

The book was presented as 'A Textbook for Students, Psychologists, Criminologists, Probation Officers, Judges and Educationists'. That's a real period touch, the appeal to a respectable readership. Aroint thee, smut hounds! They certainly seemed an unshockable bunch, so I was in good company, though perhaps a trifle stodgy. And then the book gave me a shock after all, a highly beneficial and enlightening shock.

The book was hundreds of pages long, but I read right through it. It was actually not spicy like a curry but refreshing like a cucumber *raita.* I have to say I didn't enjoy the way that, in what was supposed to be open-minded exposition of sexuality, a solo orgasm in a waking or sleeping subject alike was referred to as 'pollution'. And I'd have liked a little evidence to support the idea that every country had a national perversion: male homosexuality in Germany, lesbianism and '*cunnilinctio*' in France, flagellation in England.

The contents page had an incongruous *Pickwick Papers* jauntiness thanks to its style of presenting subject matter within the chapters, the topics separated by dashes. The passage that made such an impression wasn't in the section on 'Masturbation and Self-Love' (Dancing Narcissism – Self-Torment – Lace Skirt before the Mirror) nor 'Forms of Homosexuality' (Choice of Object – Young or Old? – Predilection for Soldiers – Complicated Cases). I breezed through 'Genuine Sadism' (Sale of Virgins in England – Sticking Pins into Sexual Partner – The Tickler), though I was arrested by the case history of 'Whipping Tom' from the late seventeenth century (English of course), a flagellant ambusher so elusive as to seem possessed of supernatural powers. He haunted the alleys and courts around Fleet Street, seizing upon 'such as he can conveniently light on, and turning them up as nimble as an Eel, makes their butt end cry Spanko'. After that he would vanish. He was the Scarlet Pimpernel of flagellant ambushers.

I had no real trouble with 'Physical Masochism', though *Picazism* was a new one on me, and I've always had something approaching a fetish for technical terms. I love to bury my nose in them, to snuff them up till my lungs are full of their aroma. This one turns out to mean 'the sexual urge to lick and sniff'.

There's a politer word for fetishism – paraphilia – but I'm not sure I like it any better. The 'para-' means that the instinct has gone astray, so that the side dish is prized above the main meal. I don't agree with that account of things. All philia is paraphilia. There's no legitimate or illegitimate target for desire. Desire itself is the overshooting of another impulse.

Was Goethe a Shoe Fetishist?

It seems unlikely that *Sexual Anomalies and Perversions* was modelled in any conscious way on the *Divine Comedy*, yet here too the reader was guided through levels of guilt and punishment, inferno and purgatory, to a sort of paradise.

I learned about 'hair snippers' like S., a student from Hamburg, prudish enough about sex as such to have joined the Ethos Society of Public Morality but unable to resist the urge to cut off the pigtails of strangers. After one of his arrests thirty-one severed pigtails were discovered in his quarters, trimmed with coloured ribbon and labelled with the date and the hour when he had cut them off. Burying his face in the hair that excited him was enough to 'bring about a discharge'.

Equally specialised was a civil servant whose pleasure lay in standing behind a man, preferably a young and timid one who had sleek dark hair brushed back, then applying hair oil to it and combing the hair towards him. He would ejaculate at the moment when the comb reached the top of the head. What a performance!

Another of Hirschfeld's patients was fixated exclusively on 'the seventh key of the collarbone' – the topmost of the seven cervical vertebræ, I suppose, where it joins the clavicle. Presumably he would have been disgusted by someone who idolised the sixth cervical vertebra rather than the seventh, just as Mr Hair Oil was horrified by the idea of anyone cutting off hair as Mr Pigtail did. Here were hells below hells, here was ditch within ditch of a Malebolge that severed sufferers from each other. In separate trenches of misery lay the breast-phobic doctor, unable to bear even the words for the body part he so hated, able to examine the female chest only from the back (until he sensibly switched to pædiatrics), and the schoolteacher suffering from a confusion about orifices dating back to his childhood and searching for the woman of his dreams, one with nostrils wide enough to admit his penis.

None of this had anything to do with my own feelings about sexuality, though my mild specialism of dark-trousered-waiter's-tight-bottom seemed to condemn me to this company. I have waiter on the brain – but how to explain that this object-choice felt somehow radiant, shot through with immanent intimations, rather than doomed to the dark? Then the book's bombshell exploded in front of me in the section on 'Inanimate Objects as Fetishes', after 'Fetishist Opens Shoe Shop' and 'Was Goethe a Shoe Fetishist?'. It was a great burst of white light with no attendant shrapnel.

Starting on page 593 was a ravishing case history, its subject a woman about whom no details are given beyond the bare fact of gender. 'Since my earliest childhood,' she begins, 'I have surrendered myself to the joys of crystal. How and by what means this love of crystal was first aroused in me I cannot say. Before I transferred it on the crystal objects in our home, I had already had sweet dreams of crystal palaces which I thought must exist somewhere on earth. Later I used to sit for hours over pictures I found in books, representing ice grottos and fantastic structures, and lost myself in fancies of the play of light on the crystal formations.

Gold dust seeping through my blood

'For some time the cruet was to me the nicest thing on the table. Throughout dinner I looked forward to the compote because it was served on crystal plates and when at last it was in front of me I was too excited to eat, for the refraction of the light on the crystal round the rim of the juice was something divine.

'The fact that it was served in crystal has contributed a great deal to the enjoyableness of many foods and drinks, and there are some things that I could only eat out of crystal. On one occasion I found on the field near our house the prism of a candelabra, wrapped in a piece of paper. As I unrolled the paper and the sun fell twinkling and shimmering on the crystal, I became intensely excited and masturbated.

'I used to watch a candelabra with crystal prisms very often with deep absorption, intoxicated with the play of lights and colours. I studied the candelabra in the various phases of daylight. I always knew when the sun would strike it and I never omitted to go to the candelabra at that hour. The light radiating in all directions gave me enormous pleasure. I felt as though gold dust were seeping through my blood. I felt ripples of heat vibrating through my whole body, until I was exhausted with it.

'I often went to a shop and asked the price of all sorts of crystal plates, glasses, jugs, etc., merely in order to be able to handle these objects, touch them, feel the way they were cut, and, above all, feel their weight. The weight of precious crystal gives me particular pleasure.'

Her testimony, in terms of the household described, makes it possible to assign her to the middle class at the lowest. Paupers don't eat compote off crystal. She can't have been born any later than 1910, and more likely considerably earlier. This is where I get a little vexed with the humble memorial volume for not including dates and references. Is it going too far to suggest that her preoccupation with ornamental glass takes to extremes a taste that seems very *Belle Epoque*? *Belle Époque*, even. I know the typographical rules about French accents on capital letters have changed since my day and I must do my best to move with the times.

'On one occasion,' she goes on, 'when I was 20, I caught sight in a shop window of a crystal saucer of extraordinary beauty. It appeared to be mysteriously veiled, so that the refracted light was vague, and the object was all the more fascinating to me. Every day thereafter I felt I had to go to that shop window again in order to see the miracle; I dreamed about the sort of rooms in which it ought to stand, about queer little tables with a precious stone tray for the saucer, about coloured silks on which it ought to stand, reflecting their delicate colours. But my favourite fancy was the crystal saucer on a tray of tarnished silver, cool and simple, without any reflection of other colours. Then I imagined it in the middle of a room on some slim, tall stand. The room was dimly lit; there were only a few candles on the walls.

'I then poured oil into the saucer, an oil that was clear as water, but thick and heavy, so that the crystal should reflect strange colours and its base should twinkle like stars. Then I would throw a ruby into the oil. There was no end to my dreams of the wonders that would be revealed to me. I went into the shop and asked what the crystal saucer cost, although I knew in advance that I could not afford it, but it gave me a chance to handle the thing and feel its weight. Afterwards I turned it over in my mind whether I could not after all obtain possession of it. Then one day I found that it had disappeared from the window and I was certain that it had been sold. I went in and asked about it, and when my fears were confirmed I was broken-hearted.'

She had a rival for the affections of the saucer. It had slipped away from her, bought by someone who would never appreciate it at its true value, turning it bathetically into nothing more than a display surface for plums or bonbons. It would be dragged down into the world of utility or mere ostentation. There was an element of comedy here, but only because there always is when what's under discussion is a desire you don't share. My *Belle Époque* idea made the 'crystal fetish-ist', to use the inadequate phrase from the Hirschfeld book, seem very French, but perhaps I was being swayed by an old prejudice, a silly spasm of chauvinist feeling against the country where Chauvin was born. It may be that I have a slight induced inferiority complex about French literature.

I had read Modern Languages for Part One of my degree, and would happily have carried on, but as it turned out my physical limitations debarred me from the immersion in a foreign culture that would put the final gloss on my fluency. Pause here to reflect on the implication that there are no disabled people abroad, and no flexibility in the system anywhere. So the *A La Carte,* let's say *À La Carte,* choices of German and Spanish were off the menu, and I was forced back onto the academic set lunch of my native tongue. But while I was still a student of modern languages I had felt a certain amount of competi-tiveness with my fellows who studied French, a language I'd always disliked for the lack of a clear correspondence between spoken forms (which always seemed to rhyme with *hay*) and the way they were writ-ten down. In conversation with the Francophiles I would bang the drum for Kafka and Lorca, Mann and Unamuno, but would always be beaten back, apparently, by Proust. Nothing in my heroes' novels, or so I was told, could approach the depth of psychology in Proust's portrayal of the worldly Monsieur Swann's passion for a woman who wasn't even his type, and suspected by him in his jealous agony of affairs with both men and women.

Cromer's Law

Ha! Now I wondered if Magnus Hirschfeld's grateful pupils hadn't handed me the key to the mystery, serving it up on an iridescent dish. What if crystal fetishism was the explanation for her enigmatic behaviour all along, her withholding of herself? Perhaps his loved one wasn't seeing other men or women at all but diddling herself for pure joy at the way the sunlight struck the glassware the moment his back was turned. Let him follow the maddening *cocotte* as she prowled along the boulevards in her carriage, let him intercept her post if he must. He would never guess that she had eyes only for her precious Lalique, hidden in plain sight on the sideboard. He was being cuckolded by a condiment stand, given horns by a mere epergne.

That's enough mockery, enough and more than enough. In fact I felt there was something magnificent about the nameless woman's obsession, a ruling passion which drove out any possible attachment to a person. I thought of her as Madame X, as if she was giving evidence, perhaps wearing a domino cloak and an elegant mask of black velvet, in a scandalous trial, though what was on trial was our prevailing notion about what people should want, and where our wanting comes from. In the witness box was someone who was sexually aroused by something altogether discarnate – light, as it fell on a particular type of glass ornament. She was able to elevate as banal an object as a cruet (in Hirschfeld's original case study perhaps the word was *Gewürzständer*) into a sort of monstrance, though a monstrance is intended to exhibit an object deserving veneration and the cruet was such an object in its own right. This lady was interested in a secondary way by the touch of its surface, and by the weight of it, but it was her visual sense first and last that was thrilled and engrossed by particular objects of crystal.

I could follow her some of the way along that path, even if my equivalent of the crystal saucer, and the refraction of the light on the crystal round the rim of the juice, might be something as routine and as invisible to other eyes as a hotel waiter in smart black trousers flexing his buttocks, consciously or unconsciously, as he lays down a tripartite metal dish whose central ridge divides zones of creamed spinach from potato croquettes from boiled carrots, its edges likewise catching the light. In both cases there is an element of mysticism, of immanence, the shining through of pure value from another order of being. Isn't desire prismatic? I think it's prismatic. William Blake, bless him, could see everything as holy, but most of us simply aren't made like that. The nameless woman who made her confession to Magnus Hirschfeld in his study was more blinkered in her outlook, as was I. Ours was a narrow church, ours were different narrow churches. Still, something from elsewhere can be refracted through a longed-for person or a longed-for object, and when this happens standard theories of sexuality fall hopelessly short. They don't even begin to account for what is going on. Sooner or later the throb of worship must be acknowledged.

Confusion of appetites had gone so far, in the world as it was when I entered it, that sex was entirely bound up with couples (gentleman and lady), with marriage and the manufacture of babies. Yet there was still evidence that other ways of connecting the dots of desire existed. Madame X, for instance. What possible area of overlap was there between baby manufacture and a woman who was sensually attuned to a mineral item manufactured out of sand, soda and lead oxide? The gay liberation movement to which I paid more than lip service had a different agenda (even an analysis, when it happened that our leader Ken had the floor), according to which we were overthrowing oppressive stereotypes with every act of revolutionary love – every time we took someone to bed we were also somehow manning the barricades. I was regarded as a non-combatant, and had the sense not to mention my own little skirmishes, which were sometimes rather satisfying.

We all toed the line, more or less. Never mind that a fair few of the group just wanted to find someone nice to settle down with, though at meetings they went along uneasily with the idea that a gay couple was a fatal piece of heterosexual mimicry. I would enjoy the private knowledge that I had actually read something of Hirschfeld's work, but I had an inkling that I wouldn't be presenting a corrective opinion of my own if I could help it. I would be only as brave as my cowardice would allow. Crystal fetishism was just as much of an insult to the CHAPs-approved notion of sexuality as it was to the go-forth-and-multiply crowd, perhaps more so. Not perverse so much as frivolous. The patriarchy would not be dismantled by getting the hots for bonbon dishes.

The unnamed lady who made such a striking cameo appearance in *Sexual Anomalies and Perversions* was lucky to find, in Magnus Hirschfeld, one of the few people in Europe who might hear her mystical testimony without outrage or mockery. In 1973 I was part of a politically radical and socially inclusive discussion group devoted to examining issues of heterodox sexuality under patriarchal oppression, and I wouldn't have dreamed of mentioning my conviction that a tidy bum in black trousers was an aspect of godhead, as was the drifting smoke from a hospital incinerator when I was a child. Not to mention a revelation of crystalline erotics in a book borrowed from the UL almost by chance. It was out of the question, not to be thought of.

A ray of light, bounced off the crystal saucer, brimming with its divine juice, had transfixed me on the rebound. If Hirschfeld wasn't a martyr he might perhaps be a saint to have worked this miracle. *St Magnus, pray for us now and at the hour of our death*. Catholicism isn't at all to my taste, but the excellence of its cadences isn't to be doubted. Now I'm sure Hirschfeld had feet of clay, knees of clay, hips of clay. I dare say that he too had only as much bravery as his cowardice would allow, but that's not a reason to forget him.

Those pages of *Sexual Anomalies and Perversions* were and are precious to me. They confirmed my idea that all this longing that we weigh down with the name of sex had only condensed around bodies rather arbitrarily in the first place. There was no necessary connection. The instinct to worship and give thanks had got mixed up with the urge to reproduce although the two drives have nothing in common. The lesson I drew from this lady, pierced as she was with melting shards if she so much as looked at crystal tableware, like some St Theresa of Avila ambushed by ecstasy in the homeware department, was not that she represented a bizarre departure from the path but something much more inspiring as an idea, the lesson that the path is not where we think it is. It's in the extreme cases that the general principles are most clearly illustrated. Call it Cromer's Law, though like any other scientific law it makes no claim to prescribe events. It amounts to nothing more than a humble description, though perhaps a useful one, to be judged on the basis of how closely it conforms to the patterns of reality. We make lazy assumptions about the centre of things and its location. Who's to say that the centre of things isn't in a corner, way over there?

There was one more thing about *Sexual Anomalies and Perversions* that made a particular impression on me. On page 233, the opening page of Chapter XIV, there was a mark added by a reader, of the sort used to mean that something has fallen out of the text and must be reinstated, the symbol known as a caret. The mark indicated where in the text the lacuna missed by the professional readers was lurking. It was in green ink. In the margin, level with the line, was another caret, supplying the missing letter – a 't'.

I was shocked by the confidence with which this unknown hand had inserted the missing letter – in a library book of all holy places!

– with a caret. The act uneasily combined correction and desecration, disfigurement and repair. Was this a vandal or a proofreading vigilante riding the range of print to maintain order? It made a difference that the mark was in ink, and green ink at that. Indelibility bespeaks courage and commitment – it's not for nothing that Mephistopheles declines to give sellers of their souls the option of a pencil, however nicely they ask. 'Caret' means only 'it is missing' or 'there is a lack'. Its symbol resembles a lambda pointing the wrong way. It's a sturdy little jemmy, able to prise open a sentence for as long as it takes for missing elements to be restored to the body of the text.

The sentence as printed concerned Krafft-Ebing's original belief that homosexuality is attributable to excessive masturbation, and his subsequent acceptance of Hirschfeld's view 'that homosexuality is congenial'.

Was it wishful thinking at the typesetters' that made Hirschfeld not merely accepting but enthusiastic about orientational difference? Just under the mark that put the 't' back in 'congenital' was another addition in green ink. An exclamation mark, though I have a fondness for the more old-fashioned term 'point of admiration'. The invisible annotator had marked the teasing misprint with a reined-in dry humour that might not only be donnish but actually a don's.

I had started off horrified at his gall, and barely a minute later I was disappointed that he had been so stingy with his comments. There were no other marks, though there were places in the text that begged for them. Take a look at page 437, for heaven's sake: 'Stimulation craving, submissive impulse, and infantile regression, are only the various aspects of the same condition, individual accords in the polophony of perversion.' How can your nib doze in its cap when 'polophony' is making eyes – making 'o's – at you? It can't be a matter of doubt whether it was 'polyphony' or 'polo pony' that the writers intended.

It took a while to notice another oddity. A caret mark is like a letter 'y' rotated through 180°. Its tail now points to the right, though tail is exactly the wrong word for the shape in its new position. What would be the right word? It can only be plume. The plume of this caret points the other way. It's a left-handed caret, or a gay one. Everyone at the time knew that the Greek letter lambda was the international symbol of gay liberation, and by 'everyone' I mean well over a hundred people in Cambridge alone. How could this be a coincidence, given the subject matter of its only intervention? Can you fill the reservoir of a fountain pen with an attar of green carnations, come to that? I'm rarely an inattentive reader, but I pored over that book obsessively at a level well below its textual surface, there where the glyphs seethe, and found no trace of any other mark, let alone a phone number. This was a single breadcrumb in the fairytale forest, not a trail of them. It had neither plume nor tail and led precisely, perversely, anomalously, nowhere.

Maya has a ladder in her stocking

One day, feeling peckish at some point after Paula had left, I used my stick to press down in the usual fashion on the lever of the toaster. The top edges of the bread slices with which she had loaded it sank obediently out of sight. For a moment all that happened was that the heat rising from the element of the toaster warped the air above it, creating a disturbance of my visual field, but the illusory fabric of time and space was actually being torn open. Maya had a ladder in her stocking.

As I reconstructed the event, once the elementary particles had knitted themselves back together again: I wasn't the only one to find the pre-loaded toaster a convenient arrangement. A mouse had slipped down into the slot to feast in the protected space so considerately provided. The noise made by mice is conventionally represented by the word 'squeak', and under normal circumstances the term serves. This one, though, when the current surged through the coil, found a note of outrage. It squawked. The sharp smell that my nose picked up, though at the time I had no idea of its origin, must have been urine landing on that same coil, from a bladder shocked out of the habit of retention, if mice even have that habit. I'd need to conduct a rather cruel experiment to confirm the hypothesis. The mouse swam upwards through air to escape from what was now part bakery and part crematorium, with the balance shifting decisively towards crematorium. For a moment the aggregated heartbeat in the room must have gone above a thousand. Who knows what other hearts were palpitating in the skirting board? With what was presumably its last breath the scorched mouse scrabbled from the kitchen counter to the table, and disappeared from sight on the far side of *Sexual Anomalies and Perversions*.

Shock, horror and regret. When my heartbeat returned to normal from its painfully excited state, and I had sat down for a few minutes, I had to think how to dispose of my victim. 'Victim' seemed the right word for this unfortunate creature. All the time I had been disabling mousetraps where they lay in ambush for innocent rodentry on the floor of 005 Mayflower House I had failed to notice the *de luxe* model sitting disguised on my countertop, not wafting around anything as banal as the smell of cheese but luring potential victims with the myriad browning reactions that do so much to give our food its appetising taste and smell, not just to human sensibility but the mammal palate in general. This diabolical machine even had a crematorium facility built in to it, and I had noticed nothing, while the device sent out its savoury signals day after day, turning mice into lemmings induced to plunge off a cliff of electrical flame. I exaggerate. Only one mouse made that atrocious pilgrimage.

I had preserved it from Paula's traps only to offer a more Satanic one of my own, harnessing the destructive power and showmanship of electricity rather than the honest crushing release of a spring. I had thrown the switch on the electric chair before the condemned prisoner had done more than set a tooth in the prescribed and even sacred last meal. I was the worst sort of sadist, one who wears a mask of kindness over his cruelty. If there was such a thing as a tribunal capable of trying charges against murinity I would be Public Enemy Number One. The least I could do was dispose of the body with honour. What does mouse culture perceive as honour?

Obviously I didn't want to risk endangering relations with Paula by calling on her for help. Our last tussle over a mouse corpse had severely tested our friendship, and besides, I wouldn't be seeing her for a couple of days. I had Mrs Baine's phone number, and vermin disposal seemed to lie within a concierge's duties, broadly defined, yet I couldn't really see her taking it in her stride.

I decided to place the call and then play it by ear. I would be spontaneous for once. There's so little in life that I can make up as I go along that logically I should exploit every opportunity for improvisation that comes my way. When Mrs Baine answered I started to explain, and lo and behold the words formed themselves as required. I'd got as far as saying, 'I hate to trouble you, Mrs Baine, but there's a dead mouse in the kitchen – it's had rather a shock, to be honest we've both had rather a shock – and I was wondering what to do with the remains.' There was a dreadful agonised silence on the other end till the right words somehow bubbled up my throat. I went on to say, 'It seemed to me this might be a job for a man . . .' Something like a sob of relief reached the receiver and I knew I'd said the right thing. 'I wonder if you could possibly have a word with the Major . . .? I don't have his number, you see, and I wouldn't normally bother him but I thought in the circumstances . . .' I couldn't resist pressing the advantage now that I was in the rare position of enjoying one. 'Of course if you'd rather not trouble him I quite understand . . . I know his time is valuable.' Pure mischief madness, or else reflexive manipulation descending on me from my mother's side, having only too obviously skipped a generation.

Mrs Baine reassured me that I had done exactly the right thing by making the suggestion. The mouse would be taken care of by the Major and I had apparently lost no status by asking for this to be done. Mrs Baine was positively grateful to me for making it easy for her to pass the distasteful task along to her commanding officer. Briefly I was flooded with the joy of pulling levers, controlling events. I could see the great addictive power of manipulative behaviour. It was almost a pity that I would never lay my hands on sufficient supplies to get hooked on the drug.

The Major turned up in my flat ten minutes later, wearing a tweed jacket, not most people's idea of summer wear. There was a knitted tie at the collar of his checked Viyella shirt, in fact the tie overlay the collar in a way that suggested he had put it on in a hurry. This was flattering – the idea that I counted as a respectable element of the Major's working life, so that he should be properly turned out even if called out at short notice. Of course in those days styles of clothes were in general more formal, and it may simply have been that he didn't feel dressed without a tie. Even so he didn't look well, with a grey complexion that might suggest secret (or not so secret) drinking or anæmia or both. With someone I knew better I would have proposed taking a homœopathic case history. I drew back from such an approach, potentially disruptive of our institutional relationship. There are pitfalls to any outcome. In a strange way the stunning relief of symptoms can be harder to accept, when an unfamiliar set of ideas is being implemented, than a total therapeutic flop.

He leaned over me and said grimly, 'So where was this little bugger last sighted, Mr Cromer?' I saw that he had dried blood on his earlobes, crusting over. Not just on one earlobe but both of them. I suppose there are people who shave their earlobes, there must be, but don't they get enough practice to pick up some expertise? I'd have given a lot to know the story of those fierce little wounds, but we had business to attend to.

'It disappeared behind that big red book, Major.' Magnus Hirschfeld's *Sexual Anomalies and Perversions*, but let's not worry about that.

'And will the little bugger fit in here, do you think?' With modest pride he produced a cardboard box that could almost have been designed for the job of giving a toasted mouse a tolerably respectful send-off, not far off full military honours. There's a progression of appropriate funerary containers, isn't there, starting with the matchbox suited to a pet beetle or bee. When I was a schoolboy I had enjoyed mourning my beetle more than I had ever enjoyed its company while it was alive. Then there's the shoebox, traditional for pet rabbit or cat. What the Major brought was somewhere in between, and if it resembled a miniature cereal box there was a reason for that. It seemed that the Major kept a Kellogg's Variety Pack handy, perhaps in his office desk. Whether, like a five-year-old, he had headed straight for the little box of Coco Pops when he first opened his package of delights, the eight-chambered treasure chest, I couldn't say, but that was the one he brought along.

He turned the box upside down and moved rather stealthily over to the area I had indicated. I suppose the idea was to drop the box down onto the mouse and then manœuvre it inside without the need to touch it, using it as a clumsy sort of scoop, but the stealth of movement seemed unnecessary when approaching a corpse.

Except that the mouse was no longer dead. There was a flurry of movement and the Major jumped back with a hoarse shout of 'Christ alive!'. If he had been given the leisure to refine his choice of phrase he might have settled on 'Leaping Lazarus!' instead. It was a miracle, a grievous one. I caught a glimpse of the mouse skittering past the toaster and then it was gone. Sudden movement from a corpse is always disconcerting, and I wasn't shocked that the Major's hands were shaking. He had dropped his little box.

He bent down to retrieve it, and the momentary absence from visibility gave him a chance to compose himself a little. He crumpled it up and threw it in the bin. Both actions took place out of my line of sight, but my ear picked up a little charge of aggression in both the crumpling and the throwing. Still invisible to me, he said firmly, 'I do think, John, that you might have briefed me more fully.'

Campaign for Real Apologies

And how was I supposed to have done that? By producing a death certificate signed by a vet? It wasn't my fault if a singed mouse had stepped back from reincarnation at the last possible moment. The Major's use of my first name, an exceptional move in a man who wore Viyella shirts, might be counted as conciliatory, even pleading, but he clearly wanted me to say I was sorry, and this was something I was bound to resist.

The Campaign for Real Ale – CAMRA – had started having an impact on the availability of draught beer in Cambridge, but though I appreciated the organisation's efforts I had never joined it. If there had been a Campaign for Real Apologies I would have signed up on the spot. A rival CAMRA, though I'm not going to be perverse enough as to apologise for that. People are always apologising for things that aren't their fault, which sounds a small enough failing until you realise that there's a sort of Gresham's Law in force, which makes bad apologies drive out the good ones. Soon you realise that people are apologising for absolutely everything except the things they have actually done wrong, and then it's too late to do anything about the degradation of manners and language. But I had decided long ago to stand firm, even without the benefit of an association of like-minded refuseniks, and I was not now going to apologise to the Major for disturbing him, since helping me was at least part of his job, nor for a rodent's miraculous resuscitation, which was none of my doing. The mouse had its share of blame – I believe this is known

205

in law as contributory negligence. Dissuade the mouse from entering the fatal chamber and the whole sorry chain of consequences can be averted, multiple-species tachycardia, crumpled miniature cereal box and all. I had to applaud the creature for stepping back from the brink of immolation but deplored the lack of consideration for human wear and tear. If I want this to be my last life, and I do, I need to pace myself.

Nevertheless some act of goodwill was called for, and a hospitable gesture outranks any number of words. I was willing to offer the Major a cup of coffee. In fact I would do better than that. I was willing to yield him the privilege of being the one to break the seal on the big drum of Gold Blend. His could be the spoon to break the plasticised protective film my Downing brethren, mainly medics or engineers and unsentimental about membranes, grandiosely called its hymen. The Major could exercise *droit de seigneur* over a vast granulated territory, thousands of freeze-dried particles submitting to his sovereign will. Not that I put it quite like that — I said, 'I'm about to start a new jar of Gold Blend . . . perhaps you'd like to do the honours? The great big one back there.' If that didn't count as meeting him halfway then it was just too bad. We would remain in our current mild state of estrangement.

He turned down the offer, perhaps without realising the honour that was being done him, but came into my field of vision long enough to say goodbye with reasonable warmth. Then he spoiled it by saying, 'I hope you're not going to make a habit of this, Mr Cromer.' Make a habit of what? Exercising my right to make toast without fear of persecution?

I couldn't help noticing that by the time he left the Major's complexion had taken a marked turn for the better. Gone was the grey facial tint of a few minutes ago. Now there was plenty of colour in his cheeks. It was clear that his visit and the whole mouse drama had done him the power of good, though of course I couldn't say so.

After that he wasn't exactly hostile when our paths happened to cross, nor even especially distant for a man of his generation. I didn't mind him keeping a certain distance, understanding that he had his reasons. He wouldn't be in a hurry to be reminded that he had trembled with fright when a mouse had second thoughts about reincarnation. And after all I knew that he bought cereal marketed to children.

Eventually it became a question of opening the giant jar of Gold Blend or giving up coffee indefinitely. The innovation of the freeze-dried coffee granule had taken its time to percolate through the social world, but by now its victory was complete. In my home town of Bourne End there were those who set themselves against anything 'instant' on principle, others who thought that powdered coffee was quite pricey enough without looking for new ways to spend money. Muriel Foot of Mum's sewing circle had cast what was in many ways a decisive vote thanks to her friendship with the wife of a wholesale grocer, made through a different social network, this one based on mah-jongg. She could buy tins of Gold Blend the size of dustbins by the back door, perhaps not contraband in any legal sense but having some of the flavour of booty. The large discount more or less made up for the palaver that was required to decant the contents of the tin into manageable containers.

The catering jar that I had been keeping back wasn't quite so formidable, and in some way I had been relieved that the Major had turned down my rash suggestion that he be the one to start it off. There are plenty of jobs I'm not qualified to do, but when one comes along that is practicable for me, and symbolically rich, I'll undertake it with pleasure. I'll cut the ribbon to open the village fête as long as it's on my level and there are only a few fibres remaining to be severed. I'll switch on the Blackpool illuminations provided the switch is within handy reach and I don't have to make a speech. Even so there's no getting round the sense of anticlimax when I broke the seal on that coffee jar with no one there but Paula. It was like the launch of an ocean liner in a deserted shipyard, the vast bulk sliding down the slipway in total silence, the bottle of fizz smashed against its bow a total fizzle.

Under these circumstances there could be no ritual celebration, only a residual protocol to be observed. The metallic membrane to be punctured with a decisive stroke, to amplify the pop, but avoiding a slashing motion so as to leave only a small opening. This was a luxury product of sorts, and it made sense to open only a little flap in the aromatic armour, to keep the fragrance inside intact. Later Paula and I got a bit blasé and would just tear off the remaining shreds of foil, letting the essential oils (if any survived at that late stage of the processing) look after themselves.

For weeks it seemed that Mrs Baine's assessment of Mayflower House as a place where there was constant traffic between flats was no more than her lurid dream of what people in general got up to. Then a tiny seed of companionability found its cranny and started to sprout. Mid-morning one day there was a knock on the door. 'Come in,' I called out, assuming it was Mrs Baine, who had the key. When the knock came again I shouted, 'Come in, Mrs Baine!', and an unfamiliar voice on the other side of the door said, 'Be careful what you wish for.'

I said, 'Come in anyway,' but there was no answer. Consequently I had to hurry, and I hate to hurry. Even if I had started moving with the first knock on the door, it would have taken me a long time to open it, long enough to count as rude, and I had lost many seconds dawdling. Even in that tiny flat it would take me half a minute to reach the door from a standing start, and when do I ever get a standing start?

This body does not hurry, but here it was doing what it doesn't do. If when I had opened the door at last my visitor had stabbed me in the heart I doubt if it would have stopped me apologising for being so slow. I'd have told him with my last breath that I was sorry to have kept him waiting so long, betraying my principles and forfeiting membership of the Campaign for Real Apologies along with my life. In those days I tried to meet standard expectations using substandard or let's say non-standard equipment. I've learned that lesson since.

The vast human unity offstage

The person waiting for me was a furry creature grinning at me with big snaggled teeth out of a round face. He had exactly the Jesus-, or perhaps only disciple-, style beard that was steadily going out of fashion, and shoulder-length hair held untidily by a rubber band. Long hair had started so well, spelling out a loving defiance and freedom, before it fell into bad company, becoming associated with the smell of patchouli, stubborn greasiness and a tendency to loaf about.

He introduced himself as Marco, 'Marco from upstairs'. I asked him in, which gave him the awkward alternatives of pushing past me or hanging back while I undertook the return journey, so I made things easier for him by suggesting that he made us tea.

'Why is your kettle so small?' he asked.

'So I can lift it. It's what's called a travelling kettle.'

'Why, where is it going?'

Banter is a pump that must be primed. The first few scraping pulls of the handle produce the barest drips, but it's necessary to keep at it and hope that somehow the dribble will build to a gush.

'To the tap and back, I hope.'

I could hear him rummaging in just the way I wouldn't have forgiven Mr Gerling, but found I didn't mind.

'Why do you buy funny jam?'

'I don't. I buy tasty jam.'

'It looks funny.'

I bought Polish jam, the Krakus brand, especially the plum, which was a wonderful dark blue. I learned about it from a Doris Lessing novel – I wish fiction always offered such useful tips. Polish jam in those days was an everyday marvel. The layout on the labels was poor and the crude illustrations of the relevant fruit against a white background were barely recognisable, but the jam had a fullness of flavour that made English products seem like wan impostors. Even Tiptree jams, strongly represented in Mum's larder, were made to seem like wartime leftovers. They might have been made up from turnip pectin, sugar and wooden pips, with a little colourant added to waken memories that the mere experience of taste would leave dozing.

Marco asked me how I was getting on. I'd have preferred to settle in before getting stuck in to any sort of personal history, but that's a lot of holding back for a stranger to do, so I did my best to answer the question. I told him about the Major and the mouse, and somehow it became a set piece, The Major and the Mouse That Died Then Changed Its Mind, even though out of some odd qualm I suppressed the detail about the little box of Coco Pops, probably the only thing that might have made it funny. He laughed just the same and said I should tell his girlfriend the story. She'd love it. It was right up her street. Oh, and I'd like her.

Sometimes strange men (I mean strangers, men who are strange to you rather than strange in some objective way) are making a point when they tell you about their girlfriends, but it seemed a bit early in the conversation for that bit of clearing the air. The question I always ask myself is, why does the air need clearing? What is the fogging factor? If anything the air seemed to me a little less breathable after this manœuvre. Once he had brewed our tea Marco stretched out on the bed (I should say in fairness the restricted space didn't offer a wide range of options) and had fallen asleep before either of us had taken the first sip.

I was not just surprised but impressed. Imagine being able to let your personality slide to the floor, to join the vast human unity offstage, during your first encounter with a stranger! I also had a sense of being set to watch over him, not something I often get to feel. I imagined my protective instincts as courting atrophy from the long intervals between times they could be exercised, but here they were, sharp and strong as ever. After I had drunk my tea I made my way over to the bed and watched over him fairly intently. He opened his eyes and said, 'Getting an eyeful, eh?', but he didn't seem displeased or put out in the least. It was more that he took it as his due. He was grinning, and when he gave a stretch the languorous movement went down as far as the hips, which aren't as I understand it anatomically integral to the stretching process. Mentally I did my own sort of stretching exercise, reaching luxuriously for the exact word that describes cats' movements on waking. Panda . . . pandemic . . . *pandiculation*. I'm told that in Kundalini yoga the spiritual serpent sleeping at the base of the spine is encouraged to uncoil so as to strike open the pineal gland, the brain's third eye, but in the case of this visitor it seemed to have turned over and gone back to sleep.

He sat up, running his hands over his face luxuriously. If he had been a blind man reading Braille I would have assumed it was a good book, and an engrossing page. He seemed to catch sight of the pile of books and made an exaggerated sniffing sound, saying, 'Fee fi fo fum, I smell the blood of a graduate man . . .' I admitted it, and asked if he had the same smell.

He laughed and said, 'Not quite.' Before he told me his history he asked if he could put a record on. His beady eye had fallen on my Hacker 'sound system'. There were people I knew who had fancier set-ups, but plenty were less well equipped. In the country of the monophonic the stereo owner was king, and my rather rudimentary set-up, with its supplementary speaker at the end of a wire, nevertheless qualified me as something like landed gentry. It didn't take him long to choose a record from my collection – the selection process was never going to take long, given my small haul of LPs. But he pulled out Supertramp's *Indelibly Stamped* without the slightest hesitation, flipped it over in his hands as if to remind himself which side he preferred, and put it on.

He explained that he was from Cumberland and had come up to Cambridge in 1970, the same year as me, to study History at Sidney Sussex. To my ear he didn't seem to me to have a regional accent, more a neutral educated diction, but when I said so he told me it was simple. When people take the living piss out of your accent you change the way you speak, and you change it in a hurry.

It's true that in those days there weren't regional accents to be heard on the BBC. Did the voices on the radio sound like mine, or did mine sound like the voices on the radio? Either way, I experienced a lack of disharmony that was almost shocking.

I had learned to say 'toilet' and not 'lavatory' to meet the demands of an environment in which I felt vulnerable (the Canadian Red Cross Memorial Hospital), and I had learned at the same address to pronounce a certain confection as 'nugget' rather than 'noo-gah'. But I had been allowed to make minor sacrifices of diction, not wholesale remodelling of the speaking apparatus.

It's amazing how quickly people can strip off an accent that gets them mocked or disliked, but the secret cost must be huge. A South African, to take an obvious example, who got off the train at Cambridge during those years and walked into town would have shed the first few molecules from his despised accent by the time he had turned right from Station Road onto Regent Street. No one enjoys being disliked. At Marco's college he was routinely treated as if he wasn't a student there but just someone who worked in the college bar. This was all the more humiliating for someone who, to make ends meet, sometimes worked in the college bar.

As Marco explained, he wasn't really Marco. He was a Mark who had coincided with another Mark at school, so he had been called

MarkO because his surname began with O, to avoid confusion. It's the sort of nickname, circumstantially dictated, that you'd think people would be happy to get rid of as soon as they could. Perhaps the name becomes a sort of old schoolfriend in its own right, not to be abandoned however life wears it down, and whether or not you actually like it is beside the point. So he wasn't Marco, promisingly Italian, nor Marko, promisingly Slavic, but MarkO, promising nothing in particular and logically therefore incapable of disappointing.

Tweeters with delusions of grandeur

MarkO (I was getting the hang of it, with some topics I catch on fast) said that if I wanted to hear some authentic Cumbrian speech I had only to say so. This was ancient British speech whose roots went back to the Vikings, and those roots well watered with blood. Naturally I jumped at the chance of getting so chthonic a blast of language. North of *Coronation Street* my dialectal map was more or less a blank, though I knew Newcastle was home to strange beguiling sounds, until even further north, where things turned reassuringly tartan at the border. To oblige me MarkO produced a series of dense vocalisations, as compressed as cattle-cake, in which I could just about make out the words 'laal' and 'gadger'. When I asked him what he had said he replied, 'Don't be such a patronising berk,' but this was free-standing commentary rather than translation.

By the time we had reached the third track on Side One of Supertramp's *Indelibly Stamped* it was clear that MarkO and I were on some sort of wavelength. You know those people who 'light up a room'? MarkO wasn't like that. He did gradually warm the room up, though, and that's not nothing. He praised the quality of the Hacker's reproduction. My woofers were really only tweeters with delusions of grandeur, but it was true that they put up a decent noise. Track 3, 'Rosie Had Everything Planned', was my favourite on the album, and it seemed to be his too by the way he joined in with the lyrics right from the start, the bit where, acting upon information received, Rosie had everything planned, standing in the garden, shotgun in hand. '*What a woman!*' we sang together, then had an enjoyable wrangle about whether this wistful, well-harmonised song was about a murder-suicide or just plain old murder. There was evidence to support either interpretation.

I mentioned that I had an itch on my ankle and asked him to scratch it. It may even have been true, but it's never a bad idea to test the permeability of physical boundaries. If there's a significant degree of recoil to be mastered on your part I'm not sure we should even be talking.

MarkO did my ankle the honours, chatting all the time about his foreshortened university career, halted by a bout of glandular fever towards the end of his second year. It had knocked the stuffing out of him, he said – 'I was very *debilitated*' – and he hadn't been well enough to resume his studies after the long vacation. By then he'd met the girlfriend he was living with on the second floor of Mayflower House, Bernardette – I'd like Bernardette, he told me again – and they managed pretty well. Bernardette was a knockout, he said. He had no idea why she chose him. She worked at a tobacconist's, which didn't sound exactly glamorous.

I don't remember MarkO ever coming out with a historical fact or reference in all the time we knew each other, but that doesn't cast doubt on his account of himself. He warned me not to expect him to remember too much about the history he studied, speaking about the intellect-erasing powers of Tolly Cobbold ale very much as old soldiers used to talk about the bromide that they claimed was put in their tea to kill the sex drive. It's not as if I was always quoting Brecht myself, and I had learned from experience to keep more offbeat interests such as homœopathy and Hinduism under wraps with people I didn't know well.

MarkO asked if he could come again, at about the same time of day perhaps, and offered to play me his own favourite record sometime. Naturally I said yes. I wouldn't be in and out of his flat because of the physical obstacles, but I had no objection to him being in and out of mine. I'd leave the door on the latch.

It always was anyway. Mrs Baine's promises of constant hurly-burly had been entirely misleading, and I felt no great need to protect myself against intrusion. Doors are too binary – surely everyone has felt this? A locked door is too shut and an unlocked one too open. If the door of 005 had been locked then I would feel trapped inside; if it wasn't I was at anyone's mercy. There are so many more intermediate states, or there should be. For instance a person can be both in and out, and this isn't just avant-garde physics but Victorian social etiquette. (Scottish jurisprudence has something similar, with its blessèd verdict of Not Proven.) You can be in but not At Home, physically present but not 'receiving'. Of course when you're your own butler it's hard to convey the message satisfactorily to visitors, but that's only an administrative problem.

After MarkO's first visit I left the door on the snib. I was At Home. I was receiving. It rapidly became a routine. I who inveighed against *vasanas*, those inherited set patterns in Hindu teaching that must be shed for the Self to be realised, couldn't wait to scratch myself out a new rut. Most weekdays he would come for a cup of tea, to listen to records and to offer himself up to me in sleep. Was he perhaps suffering from narcolepsy? No, he had a temporary job as a milkman. He was certainly suffering from that.

The phrase he used to describe his employment, mind you, was 'dairy roundsman', and I'm sure that was how the job was advertised, but it didn't fool me for long.

Of course he fell asleep! He never acquired the habit of going to bed early but stuck to his usual routine of pubs and cinemas. Every morning was a fresh shock to his system, and by the time he had finished his round he was knackered. Bernardette seemed to have a gift for sleeping through his alarm, but he knew there would be trouble if he didn't reset it for her later waking, and he placed a cup of tea on the bedside table before he left for work. It was very likely that she didn't wake before it was cold and never drank it, but the gesture was required even if it had only the function of ritual homage. MarkO wouldn't have known the word *puja* used in Hinduism to denote a sort of physical prayer, the enacted invocation of a deity, but the practice itself was perfectly familiar to him.

I call it wankerage

The favourite record he had promised to play me was a far cry from Supertramp. It turned out that MarkO was a great fan of classical music, recently converted, and was keen to share some of his discoveries with me. It was partly that he wanted to hear how they sounded on the Hacker, which from the way he talked about it was an Aston Martin of audio technology, though of course I don't know what he had himself. Possibly the second-floor flat was an Aladdin's Cave of gadgetry, including the large reel-to-reel tape recorders everyone wanted in those days, just like the nine Sony TC-800B machines used to record conversations in Nixon's White House.

The Watergate scandal was unspooling more or less day by day, and couldn't altogether be kept from percolating into the *Cambridge Evening News*, caffeinating those becalmed columns with a brutal stimulant kick. Whatever its competition, the Hacker was good enough for me, and it was certainly good enough for MarkO.

He told me he had a particular interest in baroque music, and had placed an order at Miller's on King Street to extend the range of his holdings. I was on the point of making a reference to baroque-and-roll, thinking it fresh and amusing, but a sudden fierce frown on his face made me pull back in time. We did quite often seem to be on a wavelength.

MarkO's status as a milkman with esoteric musical tastes tickled me, and there's no doubt that it tickled him too. University towns are full of people with wayward enthusiasms, and I enjoyed being under the same roof as one. The reason for MarkO's interest in classical music being so recent was that he hadn't heard it in childhood, for the simple reason that there wasn't a medium-wave transmitter near Maryport. He would have needed a VHF radio to pick up the Third Programme, as it was before Radio 3, and in those days this was an expensive and bulky piece of equipment. At home he listened mainly to pop on pirate stations. Then when he moved to Cambridge he was in range of a suitable transmitter and his MW/LW radio picked it up loud and clear. A whole new world opened up to his dazzled ears.

MarkO's girlfriend paid a visit with him one Saturday. There had been little titbits about her family background. 'She's posh, John, but you won't mind that, will you? Being a little posh around the edges yourself.' A little posh around the edges – hard to argue with that assessment. The equations governing the interaction of social status, solvency and family history are immensely complex, writhing with variables, but MarkO had seen in me genteel poverty unpredictably alleviated by donations from a grandmother too posh to need the endorsement of the word. That was enough to go on.

'Her Pa, yes, her *Pa*, is in wankerage.'

'What's that?'

'I call it wankerage. It's really "bunkerage".'

'And what's that?'

'I almost dozed off when Bernardette explained it to me, but I think I got the gist.' It occurred to me that having a three-syllable first name that your lover didn't abbreviate was a distinction in itself, some sort of badge of character. 'It's to do with making sure oil supplies are laid on in far-off places for rich people's boats, so when Mr Onassis rolls up in his yacht he doesn't have to ask the locals for a cup of paraffin.' I didn't exactly have my finger on the pulse of the world's economy, but I could see that there were worse businesses to be in, at a time when the Suez Canal was closed and the cost of oil rocketing up.

I hadn't formed a visual image of Bernardette the supposed 'knock-out', so there was no tinkling collapse of mistaken ideas, but meeting her was still something of a shock. She was built on a large scale, and extremely beautiful. The flat was cramped at the best of times, but now it strongly resembled the White Rabbit's house with the expanded Alice bursting out of it, windows and chimneys at risk, though Bernardette had dark hair and Alice is fair in the illustrations. What was this masterpiece of flesh doing working in a tobacconist's? MarkO looked undersized next to her, though I hadn't thought of him in those terms previously. I have to admit that my assessment of size is unreliable. There are days when I feel tall myself, though this isn't an impression that the world goes along with.

It wasn't just that she was tall but that she seemed to enjoy it. The confidence with which Bernardette carried herself was unusual at the time. Women weren't supposed to be taller than their men, and if they couldn't necessarily avoid this unfortunate state of affairs they weren't supposed to behave as if they got a kick out of it.

1973, after all, was the year that Princess Anne paid an official visit to Ethiopia. In every one of the photographs that document the event she is committing the rudeness of remaining seated while Haile Selassie stands, to avoid the greater rudeness of a female person towering over the Lion of Judah. An odd bit of knowledge for me to have, since of course this item was several orders of magnitude too interesting to feature in the columns of the *Cambridge Evening News*. Perhaps it was mentioned on the radio.

I must have passed on my amazement to MarkO, because the next time Bernardette came round with him she said, 'I gather you think I should be a model, John.' She turned to MarkO for the go-ahead. 'Shall I give him The Look? Do you think he's ready for The Look?' It was as if a weapon was being tested, a biological weapon like the ones at Porton Down, being kept in secure flasks, let's hope, in freezers, which I suppose is one way of looking at it. Sex appeal is a biological weapon, and if you have it in spades then you win every trick. 'Shall I give you my model-girl look? You can tell me if I've got what it takes.'

'If you like.' I could hardly stop her. She leaned over me so that her long hair swung forward and hung around me, and then she did something remarkable with her eyes. She uncoupled them, somehow, so as to look beyond me, and the effect of being both gazed at and ignored was very powerful, though Maya knows I should be used to it. Her breath was sweet. She filled my field of vision, but a lot of people do that. This was different. A blast of abstract glamour passed through me. It was as if the wall at my back had been set on fire. I felt as Walter Tell must have done after the firing of the arrow – no, not William Tell, his son Walter. Unsure for a moment as the two halves of the apple fell from his head whether he had survived at all. This might be the falling apart of his own bisected skull. She looked beyond me, establishing either a double focus or no focus at all. This was a horizontal whirlpool into which passers-by might helplessly disappear.

For a moment I couldn't speak, though she can't have known me well enough to understand what strong testimony this was to the effectiveness of her gaze. 'So, John,' she said. 'Will that do? Do I get the job?' She added in a whisper, 'It's very easy, you know.' I'm sure that's true, but not everyone can do it, just the same. It was admirable, though, that she should prefer to keep her beauty as a hobby. Bernardette moved away from me and kissed MarkO on the top of his head.

Of course I'd underestimated Bernardette. She didn't just work at 'a tobacconist's', she worked at Bacon's on Market Hill, with a frontage extending round onto Rose Crescent. Bacon's was the Cambridge equivalent of the premises in St James's where Edward VII might have gone to pick up an enormous cigar, before enormous cigars changed their name in honour of Churchill. Bacon's was a solemn palace, a Masonic temple pledged to the destruction of the lung. It didn't seem the right workplace for a goddess, though of course Bernardette's wages were no higher than a mortal's. Didn't dons pick up their ready-rubbed shag, bank managers their coronas, a few superannuated scholars their snuff, without needing to get an eyeful, and such an eyeful? How much cleavage, flaunted, hinted at, or provocatively withheld, would make a tweedy smoker seeking to replace a pipe carelessly nudged from the mantlepiece splash out on a meerschaum worthy of display in the Fitzwilliam at the other end of King's Parade, not half a mile away?

Perhaps randy schoolboys queued up to buy pipecleaners just so they could pay their homage to Bernardette. The moment I had formulated this thought I realised it was likely to be true. The queues must go all the way into Trinity Street, unless they were marshalled round the corner into Rose Crescent to avoid obstructing traffic, and whoever it is that makes pipecleaners must have been thrilled that a business apparently caught in indefinite doldrums had itself turned the corner at last.

She liked the job, saying the people were nice, even the customers, except for a little group of Newnham students who wanted her to break up a box of Sobranie Cocktails, the cigarettes with the gold tips and the range of bright papers, so that they could pick out colours to match their outfits. She told them this was Bacon's, not Woolworths. What she actually said was, 'This isn't Woolworths, girls . . . *We don't do pick 'n' mix.*'

Once or twice MarkO called Bernardette at work, using my phone. There wasn't one in their flat. The first time I thought it was a bit of a lark – he got me to ask for her, saying I was a customer wanting to discuss 'your special shag'. I enjoyed the idea of Old Man Bacon (not that I knew there was such a person) raising his silver eyebrows as he summoned Bernardette to the phone. I imagined him complaining to the rest of the staff 'that young madam doesn't know cake from ribbon cut', until Young Mr Bacon, also someone I made up, showed him the transformed sales figures across the board, from the humblest packet of spills to solid-silver lighters, while at home Young Mr Bacon's wife looked at herself unhappily in the mirror. I can only apologise. These dim wraiths seems to have strayed in from an Arnold Bennett novel, not one of the good ones.

On her first visit to my flat she left behind, as if casually, a box of extra-long matches from her workplace, the sort designed to make cigar- and pipe-smokers' lives easier. She wasn't a smoker of any description, and this was an act of quietly imaginative kindness intended to make my life easier too. She may not have known that for me the lighting of joss sticks was a daily part of both religious practice and shit-smell exorcism ritual, but she guessed that ordinary-sized matches in their little box, despite my love of small things, presented practical difficulties, in terms of first lighting the match and then lighting something else with it.

It would have taken a further leap of intuition on Bernardette's part to understand that large matches bring problems of their own. Yes, a faint panic attended my use of standard matches, since they gave me only a few seconds to pass on the flame to its destination. It sometimes happened that the match burned down, endangering the fingers that gripped it as best they could, so that I would have to blow it out and hope that I had enough puff in my small-body-habitus lungs to work the magic of extinguishment at a little distance. Using long matches I had to change my grip once the thing was alight, not an easy thing for someone whose wrists don't rotate, which brought an increased risk of droppage. Even so, Bernardette's gift of those specialist smokers' matches made me feel like a proper grown-up arsonist, though my fire-raising was confined for the time being to the reverent pyromania of *puja*.

Nietzsche says, doesn't he, that the urge to destroy is also a creative impulse. By that logic the urge to burn things down would coexist with the desire to build things up, which seems a bit far-fetched. In Hinduism the two impulses are assigned to different aspects of godhead.

Bernardette was clever but seemed to disapprove of women who made a public show of their brains. It wasn't that they posed a threat – if anything she felt sorry for them. They had sacrificed the rich benefits she derived from encouraging men (in particular) to under-estimate her. Female solidarity was a new thing, from what I could see, and Bernardette was in no great hurry to enlist in sisterhood.

It's an ill wind that blow job any good

MarkO was a smoker, and smokers whose girlfriends work in tobac-conists' shops aren't likely to go short on its vices. I tried to protect the air in my little flat, since it was in such short supply. Obviously joints were all right, as long as they were made with herbal tobacco, but I didn't want the hard stuff being smoked on the premises, the demon nicotine. I couldn't have been clearer on this point, saying time and time again, 'I have no objection to dope, but I draw the line at tobacco.'

MarkO asked me to repeat myself, but still he seemed unable to take in the inversion of the expected meaning. What we hear is affected by what we expect to hear to such an extent that a surpris-ing message can be corrected into supposed normality as it reaches our understanding, and that was what was happening here. It's like a version, self-imposed and non-surgical, of those brutal experiments performed on cats, in which their optic nerves have been rewired to show them the world upside down. In a surprisingly short time they adapt, their brains reversing the reversal that had been imposed on them. MarkO, hearing a permission to smoke dope as long as he abstained from tobacco, received only the message that he was used to hearing in other settings, that cigarettes were fine but joints out of the question.

It's an experiment to be tried at home. Say 'broccoli' when people expect to hear 'probably' and 'probably' is definitely – definitely – what they will hear.

I used to exploit this peculiarity of human understanding by smug-gling suggestive or sexual words into innocent sentences, and not just with MarkO. I do it even now, sometimes, out of habit or maybe on principle. Remarks that are too wayward simply don't register on people's consciousnesses. It's not that they don't hear but they hear without knowing they're doing it. It's surprising how often you can say 'It's an ill wind that blow job any good' without anyone noticing the difference, and if someone says, 'What did you just say??', you have only to frown and say, 'It's an ill wind that blows nobody any good. What did you think I said?' Then the ball is firmly back in their court. Some people have dirty minds, it's a fact. As for the reason behind this game, apart from an inveterate need to create mischief, my theory is that every little sexually charged particle helps to transmit a subtle throb to the whole. Many such subliminal excitements can lead to the change of state we call arousal. The information bypasses the surface and goes in deep, which I like to think imparts a subtle perfusion of shamelessness to the whole conversation, making possible things that weren't so before. There's nothing quite as wearing as a constant undercurrent of innuendo, I understand that, but just the same it's what has made me the man I am today.

Finally it was as if MarkO played back in his head the tapes of what I'd been saying week after week, and he said uncertainly, 'You know that thing you're always saying, about not minding dope but drawing the line at nicotine, the demon nicotine? Is that what you mean or have you got it back to front?'

'No, that's what I mean.'

'Then why am I smoking ciggies in your flat?' Which really wasn't a question I could answer.

So the garbled message was partially restored to its original form, and MarkO started smoking joints in 005. The part of the message that stipulated the use of herbal tobacco somehow formed no part of either version, the thoroughly garbled or the partially restored. It seemed probable that Bacon's would have no truck with nicotine-avoiding products, but I happened to know that a wide variety of herbal mixtures could be bought at the health food shop on Rose Crescent, just round the corner.

I imagined MarkO's cilia working in the night, slowly recovering from the knockout blow of nicotine inhalation, beginning to reweave the seamless garment of his lungs' protective mucosa, wafting impurities upwards without him knowing anything about this rescue operation though he knew all about the smoker's cough that started nagging at him when morning came. It would have been perfectly in character for him to wake up in the early hours expressly to light up a Player's No. 3 and keep the cilia under control. Show them who was boss.

You could buy Krakus brand Polish jam, of which MarkO was now an addict, at the same health food shop. I had to watch him or he would help himself to it straight from the jar, especially when stoned – I suppose I should have been grateful he used a spoon rather than fingers. He referred to it as 'your Auntie Doris's jam'. I had told him more than once that I had seen it praised in a Doris Lessing novel, but he preferred to think it was made up in batches by a non-existent Doris Cromer. As so often happened with him, the message had got through only some of the way.

MarkO was not one of those whom marijuana rendered eloquent. He tended to loll there, saying, 'The thing is . . . the thing is . . .' I didn't mind at all. We spent a lot of time in those days trying to remember, or perhaps to discover for the first time, what the thing was.

Mrs Baine had some of the gifts of nature's busybodies, but not, thank heaven, the full complement. Eventually I trained her not to use the arrival of letters for me as an excuse to play postman, knocking on my door in her eagerness to oblige me and making sure she had a good look at whatever might be going on. One day before I got the message across she advanced into a room so thick with dope smoke you could have sliced it and sold it in the cafés of Amsterdam as pie. She sniffed the air and frowned. 'I don't like to mention it, Mr Cromer,' she said, 'and you know I'm not one to pry . . . but have you been cooking with garlic?' She had a snooper's nature. It was the detecting equipment that let her down, the nose itself. I had been cooking up a facial expression meant to convey bewildered innocence (Funny smell? What can you possibly mean, Mrs Baine?). At short notice I managed to substitute one of rueful guilt, to suggest that I was mad for foreign cuisine. Just can't help myself.

I wish people didn't always say 'I'm not one to pry', and so on. Either reform or own up! Personally, I'm absolutely one to pry. I pry whenever I get the ghost of a chance. It's only shortage of opportunity that keeps me so horribly virtuous and nowhere near as well informed as I'd like.

We had our serious conversations, did MarkO and I, though perhaps they didn't quite live up to that billing. They were closer to silly discussions of serious subjects. Pain, for instance. MarkO wanted to know if I was In Pain? Pain that was audibly capitalised, a special territory inaccessible to those who merely stub their toes or do themselves a mischief opening a tin of corned beef. It shouldn't be a trick question, whether asked by doctor or layman, but it often turns out to be. If you admit to being in pain then there's a tendency for you to be considerately excluded from any but the least stimulating activities, while if you say you're not people think you're playing the hero and want applause. The moment it has been decided that you're brave then you might as well be tucked up for ever in the Tomb of the Unknown Cripple in Westminster Abbey (though King's College Chapel is nearer and just as nice, I hear). You'll get all the minutes of silence anyone could possibly want, but you'll never get within groping distance of a plumpy crotch ever again.

As this was a period in which I was being included by virtually no one, it seemed important not to whittle away my desirability as a companion. I learned to say things like 'It hurts but it's not painful' or (for variety) 'It's painful but it doesn't hurt.' Thanks to the inherently paradoxical nature of pain, statements along those lines are as defensible as any.

I stayed vague about the details of my medication *régime*, which was less *régime* than carnival. I had a dolly-mixture approach to medication at the time. Mix it all up, why not? Surprise your system, as long as you know the basic characteristics of what you're dealing with. I had a few ampoules of Palfium, some Omnopon, some pethidine. Palfium was a trade name for dextromoramide tartrate, which packed quite a punch. If you told people it was three times as potent as morphine they were always impressed, but that wasn't really the point. Its effects are much more short-lived – with me its half-life was only about three hours or so. It would be even shorter with standard subjects, but small body habitus means I take longer to metabolise medication. Palfium doesn't bung you up as most of its rivals do, which was a definite plus. Constipation would be the bane of my life if I let it.

Pain, but also God. MarkO was a great believer in the 'transmission of the culture pattern', and the way people take on ideas without examining them. Under that heading he included religious faith. 'I don't believe in God. Do you? It's just something people are brought

223

up with and haven't shaken off.' This was his opening gambit, spoken with a manly briskness, as if we could settle this religion business once and for all, something that has preoccupied our species for almost its entire history, just to clear the ground, and then move smartly on to more interesting topics. I don't know what he expected me to say!

'Well, first of all, why don't you tell me about this God of yours.'

'What God? I just told you I don't believe in God.'

'That's just it – tell me about this God you don't believe in. If you said you believed in God I'd ask you about the God you believe in. It's only natural that I should ask you the same question.' I'm often drawn into, or saddled with, conversations of this sort. If you don't know what it is you don't believe in, how does that constitute unbelief? That's just the sort of sloppy mental process that gives atheism a bad name. Atheism shouldn't be an excuse not to consider the issues. 'So tell me about this God you don't believe in.'

Then of course MarkO come up with the usual list of Aunt Sally gods, and seemed surprised that I agreed with him in dismissing them. Man in the clouds with white beard? Don't believe it for a moment. Special providence in the fall of a sparrow? Don't make me laugh. Pie in the sky when you die? More like non-pie in the un-sky if you're lucky enough to dismount the treadmill of reincarnation, to turn off the stroboscope flicker of life–death–life–death–life and the migraines it triggers . . . though I may not have said so in those exact words.

'Any other ideas, MarkO?'

'I don't meditate – I bet you meditate.'

'I seem to have lost the knack.'

'I didn't know it was a knack.'

'Nor did I, till I didn't have it any more.'

'I bet you pray anyway. I don't pray.'

'What do you mean by prayer?'

'Oh God, here we go again. No, that's not my example of a prayer! Why is arguing with you such hard work?'

'I don't know, particularly since I'm not arguing. I'm just asking a question. Still, I'd be interested to know – if you were caught up in an earthquake or an avalanche or something, wouldn't you pray?'

'I suppose so. Wouldn't anyone? – when their number's up, or it looks that way.'

'So wouldn't it be better to practise before it happens? Test your parachute, make yourself familiar with the ripcord? Practice makes perfect.'

'There's such a thing as beginner's luck, you know. I'm relying on that. Beginner's luck will see me right when the walls cave in.'

By this time the conversation, if it had started serious (and I can't say I'm sure about that), had become pleasingly frivolous and even frolicsome. This was a tendency of all our exchanges, not to mention one of the reasons I looked forward to his visits. Spending relatively little of your day with someone to talk to can make your conversational style heavy-going, and MarkO wasn't going to let that happen. A sort of mutual metaphysical tickling took place when we talked together, and tickling can only thrive in the presence of consent, whether on the astral plane or in what is so very approximately called the flesh.

He didn't ask me about my own experience of the Divine, which was no reason not to tell him about it. 'My divinity is bliss, and I constantly feel the hands of the Divine sliding all over my being. Isn't that something you might enjoy yourself, you soulful hedonist, if you just relaxed and let it happen?'

'I'm perfectly relaxed, ta very much.' Or stoned, not quite the same thing. 'And why are you always confusing religion with sex?'

'Why can't you see they're the same thing?'

By now these were practised and satisfactory roles for us. We were very comfortable with this sort of wrangling, though since we were usually in some sort of physical proximity and even innocently intertwining we were probably coming closer to my philosophical position than his.

He stuck to his guns just the same. People are always telling me how relentless I am when I want to prove a point. Apparently I won't take no for an answer. I just don't get it – if they knew this all along what on earth was preventing them from giving in right away? Concede. Save your breath to cool your porridge, and then we can choose a subject with a bit more flavour to it.

I've learned you have to tread a bit carefully so that you don't offend people's unbeliefs. If the atheist will persist in his unbelief he will find God, don't you agree? Isn't that so? Chisel away indefinitely at the stone block of faith, acquired or inherited, and when all the whittling is done . . . you may not be left with nothing after all.

I try to avoid technical terms. It's not everyone who takes kindly to being told that they aren't atheists at all but apophatic theologians. It's a real distinction though perhaps one that's best approached indirectly, through poetry. As a recent English graduate my mind was full of the stuff. It was an Artesian well that bubbled with remembered lines and stanzas. I found it almost as easy to remember poetry than forget it, I was a walking anthology, but of course as time goes by the aquifer doesn't spurt so freely. The singing source sinks back into the rock as a burbling trickle.

Cataphatic and apophatic – two ways of describing the indescribable, equally doomed to failure but indispensable just the same. Cataphatic theology approaches God through his attributes. God is good, God is love, Jesus wants me for a sunbeam. When George Herbert piles up the analogies in a poem, describing prayer as 'God's breath in man returning to his birth', 'the soul in paraphrase', 'heart in pilgrimage' and so on, he's providing a set of comparisons that collectively lead the mind towards something ineffable. That's cataphatic theology, folks! And that's one way, but it's not the only one. There's more than one way to skin the ineffable cat. Apophatic thinking goes entirely the other way and proceeds by paring away everything that God is not. You eliminate characteristics one by one so as to approach God's essence asymptotically, making closer and closer approximations without the possibility of getting there. The yearning curve proves, under magnification, never to reach its goal. So when Auden asks to be told the truth about love, he comes up with a series of comparisons that are obviously wrong and jarring. 'Does its odour remind one of llamas?' 'Are its stories vulgar but funny?' That's apophatic. He takes the mickey out of the idea that love can be 'like' anything. 'Love' is an easy word to rhyme, but he shuns 'dove' and 'above' and the rest of them, even eye-rhymes like 'move' and 'prove', in favour of clanging misses like 'stuff', 'enough' and 'rough'. Why does he do that? Maybe just to point up his theme, that love has no overlap with anything else, by avoiding words that mimic it at all closely. Or maybe he's simply saying, in a phrase that resounds through Hinduism and Buddhism . . . *neti-neti*. The Sanskrit that means 'not this, not that'. That's the *via negativa*, the mystical path I'm drawn to, made visible as it is by shafts of darkness.

Where had this richness of ideas, this readiness of expression been when I was in need of both those things, with an essay deadline bearing down on me? I think I was at my mental peak at this point in my life, living in Mayflower House, my academic training fully absorbed but still fresh, though it coincided with a time when I had no intellectual company. Perhaps that isn't such an unusual state of affairs.

Mine was what botanists call an oligotrophic environment, the social equivalent of leached soil or an anoxic bog, lacking in mental and emotional nutrients. Still, intellectual loneliness is the lightest of the solitudes and the easiest to remedy. Books are as well suited to keeping an unbalanced life on the level as they are to propping up a wonky table.

I was uncomfortably aware that my guru Ramana Maharshi had spent many months unmoving in the oligotrophic environment of a sacred cave, his indifferent mouth filled with physical food by devotees. His being, though, had no need for spiritual nourishment but achieved the successive phases of mystic ascent without help of any kind. He was sealed in his selfhood as it evolved, basted by his own spiritual juices.

My yearning for the cabbalistic and arcane wasn't intellectual but instinctive. From the egg I've ranked the Cloud of Unknowing above the blue skies of certainty in my spiritual meteorology. As a teenager I had flirted with Rosicrucianism, essentially because I liked the name, unless we say I was responding to signals being emitted on a high hermetic frequency. It wasn't the cosmology that attracted me, just the veils of mystery, or maybe the cosmology reached me on the esoteric plane so that I noticed without noticing. I didn't begrudge the Stamped Self-Addressed Envelope I sent to receive a pamphlet, but I didn't have the resources to fund actual membership. There was an informal tithe system in operation, requiring you to send the equivalent of a week's wages, and I could have saved up my pocket money if I'd really been committed, but something about tithing doesn't sit well with me. It's a tax on something beyond the reach of taxation. The sense of connection is not to be harnessed for any purpose.

But then it turns out – blow me down! – Rosicrucianism was aligned with the *via negativa* all along. According to the Rosicrucian sense of things Creation is less an emanation of divinity than a limitation of it. In the act of Creation God confines and negates himself. According to this cosmology the universe is no more and no less than an embodiment of the death of God, but I'm sure you could argue – lovely dark quibble – that even the death of God constitutes an aspect of the divine. So perhaps I should have stumped up the tithe without grumbling to the Ancient and Mystical Order Rosæ Crucis and have taken things beyond the stamped-self-addressed-envelope stage of our relationship.

The Return of the Culotte

There were some tiny compensations for the unilateral suspension of my no-nicotine rule. MarkO was in a privileged position as regards supply. He smoked fancy brands that sometimes produced distinctive flavours. I remember him brandishing a packet of Gold Flake, with a gorgeous red and yellow packet influenced by Art Deco, and another of Player's No. 3, whose austerely simple design made use of an attractive font of the same period. Turkish tobaccos have more to offer the nose than their Virginia counterparts, and I particularly relished the aroma of Balkan Sobranie No. 5, which came in boxes of fifty.

At some stage MarkO brought down a little ashtray of cheap metal, hardly more substantial than tinfoil, for use when he smoked in the flat. What I really liked was when we'd curl up together on the bed at weekends while Bernardette sat in the Parker-Knoll reading a magazine. It would be a fashion magazine, though it was impossible to imagine her needing beauty tips or hints on style. She shone through whatever clothes she wore, and a lighthouse takes no interest in net curtains. In fact every now and then she would make a disgusted noise and turn the magazine round, without comment, so that we could see some particularly ridiculous fashion spread. I never knew what to say, but MarkO had apparently learned from experience that the right response was to shake his head and make a *kh-h-h-h* noise deep in his throat, whether the title of the feature was 'Going for Gold' or 'The Return of the Culotte'. Those magazines were expressly designed to make young women insecure about their looks, so that they bought clothes and accessories they didn't need in order to meet standards they would never reach, but no one had told Bernardette.

MarkO might rest the little ashtray on my leg or my lap, so that I could feel the residual heat of the ash through the thin metal, distinct from the heat of his body and pleasurable in its own right. I kept thinking he would leave his cigarette burning there, and kept myself in readiness to protest before I got a proper scorching, but somehow he seemed to know what he was doing. It didn't quite seem to count as playing with fire.

I couldn't help noticing that MarkO was more intimate with me physically when Bernardette was around. In one way that was easily explained, a matter of distributing an increased number of bodies over an unchanged quantity of furniture. It would have been odd for a visiting couple to occupy my bed, and silly for the two of them to occupy the lounger and the only other chair when there was a vacancy next to me. The first thing anyone entering the flat would need to do, to create a little space, was fold up the wheelchair and tuck it away somewhere. That was my visitors' job. My job was to remind them to unfold it again before they left.

One weekday MarkO went to the trouble of going upstairs after his shift at the Dairy and brought down the jewel of baroque music he had been promising to play me. I wasn't altogether looking forward to it. By and large other people's enthusiasms aren't infectious. From the build-up he had given them I had expected the records MarkO brought downstairs to have been pressed by fanatics in the Black Forest, their labels written by hand. In fact they were issued by the Deutsche Grammophon Gesellschaft, its label a splash of vivid yellow in the centre of each disc. MarkO seemed to enjoy the suspense of cueing up the record, making me wait for the moment the stylus stooped to kiss the shimmering vinyl.

The music wasn't outlandish, as I could hear immediately. No museum-piece instrument had been resurrected after centuries of well-deserved neglect, the Flemish clacket or the minikin, though I don't know why those names are faintly familiar. This was just . . . music. In fact after a while it even seemed to be familiar music. It wasn't 'God-Save-the-Queen' familiar, it wasn't 'All-You-Need-Is-Love' familiar, but it was certainly in some way known to me.

MarkO was tapping his feet possessively, grinning and nodding. 'Isn't it amazing?' It was certainly very nice, but I wasn't entirely sure it was the esoteric item he seemed to think it was.

I followed the rules laid down for people self-consciously listening to music, smiling dreamily, rocking infinitesimally from side to side. Then I made the mistake of asking a question. It was a tentative question, since I was unsure of knowing anything about what had been announced as a cultural corner thick with cobwebs, but it still has to qualify as a mistake. 'Is this – by any chance – the Brandenburg Concerto?'

For a moment MarkO looked very crestfallen, but he recovered quickly enough, asking, 'Which one?' I had already come very close to treading on the toes of MarkO's baroque expertise by identifying what we were listening to. I could still step back from the brink. It was time for a deliberate mistake. How many Brandenburg Concertos were there likely to be? I needed to choose a suitable number. At this point it was vital to be wrong. 'Number Ten?'

He relaxed at once and gave me one of his best smiles. 'You're a bit out of your depth here, aren't you, John? If you'd said Number Three you'd have won a small cash prize.' Exactly what I had just managed to avoid, the booby prize so often earned by the rage to know better and to show it. In Hindu terminology a *vasana*, and in my case the *vasana* of *vasanas*, the arch-rut that swallows all the other ruts whole.

I made the most of the rôle I had been allotted, meek ignoramus. 'And the conductor? Might I have heard of him?'

'You might have. There's really only one man who can produce that quality of sound. He's unique. Herr Bert.'

'I don't think I know him. Is that all of his name?'

'No, but that's what I call him. Herr Bert. Herbert von Karajan.'

Him I had heard of. 'And the orchestra?'

'The Berlin Philharmonic. Who could it be but the Berlin Phil? No one else sounds remotely like that.'

Quibbling is not a habit that makes friends or binds them close. There was no mileage in me pointing out that he had given first the conductor and then the musicians one hundred per cent credit for the performance, first Herr Bert and then the Phil. Would Karajan get that same quality of sound out of the student orchestras that were so common in Cambridge? Would the Berlin Philharmonic make the same impact if MarkO was waving the magic wand in front of them? Or if I was?

'And how does Bernardette feel about Herr Bert and the Phil?' I asked. 'Does she share your taste for the baroque?'

'She likes the Brandenburgs, though she asked me if Bach was the same guy who wrote *Jonathan Livingston Seagull*. I'm joking! She's better educated than I am. She's a tease, though. What we'd call a stroppy yow where I'm from.'

'A stroppy what?'

'A stroppy yow.'

'What's that? What's a yow?'

'It's what we call a lady sheep where I'm from.'

Yow. *Ewe!* Got it.

'She's only dug out a pop version – it's even called *Brandenburger* – and she puts it on when she thinks I'm getting carried away, the stroppy . . . The stroppy what, John?'

'The stroppy . . . yow.' I felt uneasy to be maligning someone I hardly knew, but MarkO had at least learned the first trick of language learning: to reinforce new vocabulary by repetition.

'Honestly, John, how am I supposed to help myself? Good old Johnny Bach is like a sewing machine, isn't he? When his music is played right it's like God's sewing machine, don't you think?'

Mum anxiously seated at the Bernina, treadling away for dear life on a tricky seam, didn't remind me much of the serenely bustling music coming from the record as it revolved round its yellow hub, but everyone sounds silly when they talk about music and that isn't going to change any time soon. If Bach is a sewing machine then Beethoven is . . . a traction engine, I wouldn't wonder. MarkO closed his eyes and drifted off.

Krishna would have managed

When he woke up he told me about the sorrows and consolations of his working routine, until I felt I knew his route backwards and forwards. I was driving it in my dreams. He had every excuse for being tired, since he worked six weeks solid before he got a week off. Mind you, he got £25 a week, paid in cash in a little brown envelope, which wasn't a bad amount to take home in those days.

He worked for the Co-Op Dairy off Sleaford Street, on a site shared with an industrial bakery. The 'Dairy' itself was no more than a milk transfer facility, where tankers came to discharge their loads into reservoirs that fed the bottling machinery. If Krishna, protector of cows and sacred utterances, had dropped by Sleaford Street in search of milkmaids to disport with he would have had to make do with a rough-and-ready crew, though I have to say Hindu deities are remarkably adaptable and I feel sure he would have managed. The filled bottles were capped with aluminium foil and loaded into plastic crates. The crates were barrowed to a loading bay to wait for the milkmen to load their floats up. The whole place smelled of stale milk. What else would it smell of?

MarkO's 'interview' was no more than a driving test, not conducted on one of the seductive electric floats but in a substantial van instead. He had driven dumper trucks and tractors on holiday jobs so was reasonably sure of himself, but the gear lever wobbled like a loose tooth and the synchromesh on first gear was non-existent. He revved the engine, stamped down on the clutch and managed to bang the lever into gear. The manœuvres required of him were very limited – no three-point turns or emergency stops, just some parking drills and a little light reversing. Highway Code questions? Don't make me laugh. They drove back to the Dairy, where the man told MarkO his driving stank to high heaven but since he hadn't stalled once despite having been in second gear the whole time he had scraped through. He had to come back to the depot the next Monday at five-thirty sharp (the less popular of the two five-thirties the day contains) for his week of induction.

He didn't know whether to feel proud about his mastery of the gears or embarrassed that he hadn't noticed he wasn't in first.

A lot of my experience is vicarious, but still it's rarely as concentrated as this was. I was reeling. There was only so much excitement a starved organism like mine could absorb without damage, and I asked him to save the rest till later. There's no record of the Sultan who listened to Scheherezade's stories begging her to break off long before dawn to spare him narrative indigestion. *Have a care, dear girl!*

Leave something for tomorrow. Likewise no indication that he was ever so viscerally agitated by her storytelling that he left his customary sachet of Fybogel unopened next to his beaker of rosewater sherbet, but that doesn't mean it didn't happen.

Bernardette was indulgent in her judgement when it came to Herr Bert and the Berlin Phil, but at other times her verdicts on music could be downright cutting. As MarkO said more than once, she was a lady who knew her own mind. One day after leaving my flat to return to his own he came right down again. I won't say he was shaking but he was certainly pale. He had an album in his hands that showed a lurid screaming face, mostly purple, on the cover, but what was inside was worse. He pulled the disc out of its cellophane-and-paper sheath and showed me jagged marks on the playing surface. 'Did she scratch them, do you think?' he asked me. 'With her nails?'

Not very likely. Bernardette kept her nails cut short, in defiance of fashion, just as she wore her hair long and uncurled, ignoring the imperatives of the magazines, issued weekly if not daily, that undermined women then told them what to do to recover their self-esteem. 'Not with her nails, I don't think.' My money was on scissors or a nail file.

'I told her it took some getting into. You have to listen to it a few times to get into the groove of it. Give it a fair hearing. It's a classic, it's literally a classic. Virgin Records include it in their list of Classics, on permanent discount. It's not just me. It's up there with *Astral Weeks*, up there with *Wee Tam and the Big Huge*.' I'd had a strange first encounter with *Astral Weeks* and wasn't in a hurry for a second. As for *Wee Tam and the Big Huge*, I wasn't falling over myself to get an earful.

On the other hand, King Crimson's debut album *In the Court of the Crimson King* was intended by its makers to mount a comprehensive assault on the senses. You could argue that Bernardette had done no more than retaliate in kind. 'I told her she would need a few more listens before she got into it and she said she'd heard it enough. That's normal, is it? To scratch a record to fuck because you don't want to hear it again? You can't say that's normal behaviour.'

I really couldn't say one way or the other. I've walked so little along the paths of normality that I can't pretend to know where that trail ends up. He was still miserably flipping the record over between his hands, as if the damage might miraculously disappear, when he noticed something else. 'Well, well,' he said. 'Who'd have thunk it?' He held the playing surface up close so that I could verify his observations, and now there was a little smile on his face. Both tracks on Side Two had been comprehensively vandalised, and the same was true of Track 1 and Track 3 of Side One. But however closely we looked we could see no scratch on Side One, Track Two. It took a little while for the truth to dawn on MarkO. 'Do you know what this means? I can hardly believe it!' I wish I could say that he widened his eyes, but I'm not convinced that he really displayed maximal dilation of the optical apertures, the pupils approaching 7mm across. I waited for him to share his conclusions.

'It means she likes "I Talk to the Wind"! She likes it!'

Only one track out of the five had been spared the sabotage. Fully eighty per cent of the record had been rendered unplayable (more if you go by running time, since I could tell by eye that 'I Talk to the Wind' was comparatively short) but MarkO decided that this episode represented a triumph for his powers of persuasion. If it was the first time he had succeeded in changing her mind about anything, however trivial, then yes, it must count as a breakthrough, but it seemed unlikely that the compromise and conciliation would carry all before them in the immediate future.

The next day he reported back that Bernardette did indeed like 'I Talk to the Wind', or at least didn't hate it. She said it had a nice mood. Was he allowed to play it again? Yes. She didn't see why not. Just not too soon.

That King Crimson song, sole survivor of a mutilated album, in which the singer laments that the wind does not hear, the wind cannot hear, so that his words are carried away, had somehow been proved both right and wrong. Bernardette had consented to listen to it a little more, so perhaps MarkO's words hadn't altogether been carried away by the wind.

Easier to explain with dogs

If I hadn't seen those lacerations with my own eyes I would have thought MarkO was unduly sensitive to Bernardette's opinions about his musical taste. His state of mind couldn't really be blamed on the paranoia that was so much the rage in the early 1970s; it was more a case of once bitten, twice shy – or once scratched, twice shy, to be perfectly accurate. If her verdict came down against a particular record then its safety couldn't be guaranteed. It made sense for him to bring such vulnerable items down to me. I would take them into protective custody. The Cromer embassy would grant asylum to the persecuted. Bring me your huddled masses yearning to revolve freely at 33.3 revolutions per minute without fear of reprisals!

MarkO was curious about my physical limitations, which I didn't mind. There's something oppressive about excessive tact about something that would certainly engage my interest from a distance if I had been squinting down the eyepiece of a microscope instead of being laid out on a specimen slide.

As a boy I loved the word 'chronic', ubiquitous in that period and applied to anything that disappointed or didn't work, anything unsatisfactory or defective, any excessive reaction – *He took on something chronic!* – and it was only much later that I understood that the word referred much more precisely to my physical difficulties. I was a chronic case. The damage to my 'body', to borrow a technical term from materialism, had been intense and I lived among the aftershocks. The level of 'pain' was variable, but other things were not. My bones were not variable – they were invariant. They took their duties all too seriously, declining to bend in the proper places. Martinets! My knees were fixed, though I had a little hip motion thanks to bilateral arthroplasties and one elbow was more tractable – less immobile – than the other. It would stretch to a point.

I enjoyed showing off little pockets of ability. Could I turn the tap on? Yes I could, assuming that some conscientious person hadn't closed it very tightly, imagining that the possibility of a drip was a more serious disadvantage for the occupant of 005 Mayflower House than not being able to turn the bloody thing on. If it was reasonably loose I could turn it on with a knife. Even Cambridge Council hadn't seen fit to install me in a flat whose kitchenette had those idiotic round or nearly-round taps that pride themselves on providing no purchase to a poking lever in a disadvantaged hand, offering no surface more Johnable than ridges or dimples.

Could I strike a match? Yes I could, as long as the matchbox was wedged or propped against something so that it didn't need to be held. The striking action itself came from my arthroplasties, I imagine, rather than the arms, the replacement hips giving me some slight degree of spring higher up the body habitus.

I like the term 'body habitus', which was used by a tactful locum doctor long ago – 'small body habitus', she murmured, skimming the opening chapter of the triple-decker Victorian novel that my medical notes amount to, and I wasn't slow to adopt the phrase. I don't feel it reduces me to a set of restrictions and dimensions. It's just my way of being. It's as neutrally informative as saying that I drove a Mini rather than, say, a Bentley. I see the world with eyes that are at a certain height from the ground, I hear things with ears attached to a neck that can't easily be rotated to confirm the direction and distance of a sound. The very modest elevation of my nostrils makes me more likely under standard conditions to detect crotch smells than armpits.

Lighting a joss stick was my basic everyday *puja*, a corrective to bathroom smells that also functions as a tiny act of reverent attention, a sliver of worship. A lit match can also do double duty in this way, but I don't think a preference for the smells of the East convicts me of spiritual frivolousness.

I was tempted to mention to MarkO my ability to give myself injections with a hypodermic, but it was highly likely that he would want a demonstration. Such things as syringes exercise an unhealthy fascination on the young.

MarkO tried to come up with another challenge. 'Cutting your toenails?' That was the point when I lost patience with the game and the man. I said as lightly as I could, 'Oh, I do those the same way I cut my fingernails . . .'

'Really?'

'Yes. I use a handy, remarkably flexible device called a *home help*.' Not strictly among Paula's duties but I wasn't going to give Mr Gerling any sort of visiting rights with the clippers. 'Idiot! How do you suppose I could do that?' At this point I realised that it would be a mistake to give MarkO any sort of serious scolding. Much better to keep things between us playful. 'One thing that may surprise you, MarkO . . . I have one body part, just the one, that's bigger than yours.'

236

'Is this conversation getting dirty, John? Because I'm really not ready for that . . .'

'Is my acnestis dirty? That's a very good question. In a way that's the whole point. There's a real risk of an acnestis getting dirty. It's not easy to clean – that's almost the definition of an acnestis. You probably need help with yours, but I'm sure that's all laid on.'

'*My* . . . acnestis? I have an acnestis too?'

'I expect you do, though it's probably a small one. Mine is enormous. There must be a few people around who have a bigger acreage of acnestis than I do, but there can't be many. Mine is one in a thousand . . . but don't worry, if you don't want me to tell you what an acnestis is and where you could expect to find it, I'm not going to insist.'

'John, you bastard, now I have to know. You're really winding me up!' Those who have keys sticking out of their backs will always get a good winding-up if I have anything to do with it. 'Am I going to regret asking?'

'I don't think so. It's easier to explain with dogs.'

'. . . now I know I'm going to regret it.'

'The acnestis is the part of an animal that it can't reach to scratch itself, usually most of the back, up to the area between the shoulder blades. That's the bit that dogs particularly appreciate being scratched by humans, that and the bit between their ears. Failing that, they lie on their backs on the ground and writhe like mad.'

'So your acnestis is outsized because . . .'

'Because reaching isn't my strong suit. And nor is writhing on the floor.' I didn't mention that my face forms part of my acnestis, though of course I can reach it with an implement.

I had been so enjoying the game that I didn't quite see where it was heading, very much into undesired territory. 'Well, John – if you absolutely need a tickle . . . you can always talk to my secretary.' I was grateful that MarkO had found his own way out of the pity trap I hadn't meant to set.

In point of fact what my back wanted wasn't a tickle but a good old scratch. The nerves that detect an itch have their own wonderful name. They're the pruriceptors. They send in their messages of muted distress – not a subcutaneous emergency call, but definitely a signal that can't be ignored. Do something! *Do something!* My skin became itchy when I came down with measles when I was thirteen, and the itching never wholly went away. My brother Peter was appointed honorary head-scratcher, and he took the job seriously. Scratching the affected area produces an innocuous stimulation interpreted as pain by the brain, tricked into pouring out its most soothing balms of serotonin. Dad caught the measles from me and was in really quite a bad way, though I don't know if itching was ever a part of it. And who could he have asked to afford him the exquisite relief of finger-nails scouring an itch? I could have directed operations, but I'd have needed to bring Peter along to be executive scratcher.

A little later MarkO consolidated himself even further in my favour, despite the cheek of asking me how I managed when I needed a pee in the night. I hesitated, not wanting to own up to the opaque plastic pee-bottle, an object of little glamour, so I was glad when he suggested I take a leaf out of his Granny's book. 'You could always do what she did – she always used a gazunder.'

'A gazunder?'

'Yes. You Southern berks might call it a chamber pot. Nan always called it a gazunder.' Not a word I'd ever heard.

'And it's called that because . . .?' But then I heard myself answering the question at the same time that MarkO did, either because we had an eerie rapport or because the penny has to drop sooner or later. '. . . because it gazunder the bed.'

It may be that MarkO was paying me back with gazunder for acnestis. If so it was a nice little vocabulary joust. No broken lances, still both in the saddle, let's shake gauntlets and seal our comradeship with a nice sup of small beer.

A bulb of scrotum

Over time MarkO became bolder in my presence, you could even say friskier, though never as tactile as he was when Bernardette was there to play her part of strangely inflammatory chaperone. He started doing exercises in my flat, first of all saying he had forgotten to do them at the beginning of the day and then dropping all pretence. It was hard to imagine him undertaking any unnecessary activity at the crack of dawn, or as he put it, sparrowfart. He would step out of his jeans and start bending and stretching. Meanwhile I would sniff the air discreetly, hoping for some male whiff, not perhaps sufficient to nourish an African violet but more than capable of feeding my little fantasies. I wasn't disappointed. MarkO smelled like a pet shop, and I think we can agree there is no higher form of praise.

Bernardette, though, was on the fastidious side and I once asked her how she squared that particular circle. It turned out that she would insist on MarkO taking a bath before he approached her intimately. If need be she would run the bath and clap her hands to summon him when it was ready. I thought of the outsized wooden tongs Mum used when she was boiling clothes and imagined Bernardette holding him under the surface with a pair of her own, until every trace of nicotine and pastry was washed out of his whiskers.

There was one particular exercise of MarkO's, I suppose you'd have to call it a deep knee bend. As a measure of his flexibility he wanted me to tell him how close his balls came to touching the floor. I was poorly placed to make this assessment, since it's as impracticable for me to position my eyes below the level of three feet as above five. Litheness is not my middle name, which doesn't rule me out as a judge of such matters but makes it difficult to find a suitable angle. I took my task as observer seriously nonetheless. MarkO's Y-fronts were made of nylon and had suffered considerable erosion over time, though with the declining performance of the Velcro whose foreshortened hooks and eyes kept my trousers together I was in no position to pass judgement. Sometimes, as I watched and tried to estimate the distance of his ball-sack from the floor, a bulb of scrotum would pop softly through a rent in the synthetic fabric. Benign protrusion! Pimply, and trailing golden hairs. If this was an eccentric form of herniation it appealed more strongly to the visual sense than most such things do. I could have popped it back in place with a finger if I possessed that kind of finger, as we know I don't. It seems unlikely that MarkO was unaware of these cross-currents, though the harmony between exhibitionist and voyeur is a subtle accord, not something that needs to be jangled into language.

I can testify to MarkO's having owned a pair of string pants, which must have been part of a set along with a string vest. He wore them once. They weren't all that revealing, since the genital area in front and the corresponding panel in the rear were rendered discreet with a zone of ærtex, replacing the wide-set mesh in the area where a trimmed-down nappy would lie, but even he must have realised he was being a bit obvious. The underpants of his I remember best were Y-fronts in pale blue nylon, with tapes of a darker blue along the seams, and so worn that they had little ladders in them like a lady's stocking. I also remember a pair of boxer shorts that he wandered around in, with the tip of his cock just peeping through the fly, 'taking the air' as he put it. As if this was the family dog leaning out of the car window, letting the wind ruffle its ears.

Once he asked me, 'Why does Tarzan change his loincloth every day?'

I knew the routine to follow. 'I don't know, MarkO, why does Tarzan change his loincloth every day?'

'To keep his nuts jungle fresh!' Which was an advertising slogan, for Golden Wonder peanuts if I remember correctly, safely sealed in their savoury pouch. I mimed the state of helpless laughter, access to speech suspended by hilarity, known at the time as 'falling about'. There are worse ways of inching your way towards popularity than pretending that the jokes people tell are new to you. In any case MarkO would want to say, 'John fell about when I told him that joke,' and I didn't want to let him down. I'm sure his own struggle for popularity seemed arduous enough. Perhaps the burden being pushed endlessly uphill by Sisyphus in the myth should be understood as the rock of popularity, always so likely to roll back down and crush the person who 'likes to be liked'. MarkO, however, did not change his loincloth every day.

Sometimes after his callisthenics MarkO felt the need to work off some calories with cerebral exercise. One day he nipped upstairs and returned with a chess set. The board was the type that folds in the middle, though its cloth hinge was beginning to come apart. The pieces, living in a lightweight wooden box with a sliding lid, were a motley crew, the survivors of a number of original sets, as if the game really did involve the capture of soldiers, dragged off from one army to serve in another. It was the sort of chess set that you sometimes see in pubs, battered and unloved, or loved by altogether too many people in passing. I didn't ask how he had acquired it.

'Do you play?' he asked.

'Has been known.'

'Fancy a game?'

'If you like.'

He started to lay out the pieces. I let him get on with it, and then intervened myself, to turn one of my rooks upside down. MarkO was baffled. 'What are you doing that for?'

'How do you mean?'

'Why are you turning that piece upside down?' From the mis-matched pair I'd chosen the rook with the intact castellations, and it stood upside down perfectly happily.

'I always do that. Don't you?'

'Of course not. Is this some freaky John variation? Some special set of rules?'

'Not at all. Standard rules. This is how I've always played. You should do the same.'

He humoured me. 'There. Does that make you happy?'

I looked down at the four rows of squares between the battle ranks, thirty-two squares in all, and for a few moments I had an impression that they were flickering. Of course regular patterns in black and white are particularly conducive to the stroboscopic illusion – with-out such effects Op Art could hardly exist. The after-image left by a grid, black on white, white on black, produces interference patterns that destabilise each fresh cycle of perception, and the result is the subjective impression of restless motion, of a swarming. It seemed to me, though, that I was responding to a different set of clashing cur-rents, thanks to my deep though partial attunement to MarkO. I was becoming aware of a repressed competitiveness on his part, in fact a desire to win that was positively feverish. In preparation for our game MarkO was rousing his aggression from its customary doze. It stirred a little and gave a gibbering bark in its dreams. Soon it might snarl. As a person he wished me well. As a player of the game he wanted my graduate scalp, and the chessboard seemed to buckle with the intensity of his need to lay waste my troops, to massacre the rank and file.

My pieces were white. I was owed the first move. I looked down at the board, made a disapproving noise and changed over the positions of my king and queen. MarkO raised his eyebrows and gave a sigh.

'Do you have to do that?'

'I think so, yes. I want everything to be right before we start. Does it give me a very big advantage?'

'I don't mind. If it makes you happy. Have it your way.'

I narrowed my eyes and surveyed the board with as much intellectual menace as I could muster. There has always been a fascination for me in the idea of action at a distance, and in this context it would have been perfectly legitimate to tell MarkO my opening move and leave him to perform it, but at this moment, this dramatic though also silly moment, it seemed important that I move the fatal piece myself.

Instant reaction. 'What are you doing, John?'

'Making my first move.'

'That's not a move! You're joking. I thought you said you knew how to play?'

'I'm doing my best, except that my opponent is doing such a good job of distracting me. Not very sportsmanlike – are you going to get on with it? Play!'

'John, I keep trying to tell you. That's not a legal move. That's not a square that a pawn can reach, just like that. Ordinarily pawns can move one square straight ahead, but from their starting position they can move two squares as a special treat.'

'Yes, I see. Both legal moves from where I'm standing, but not the only ones.'

'The only other legal starting move is for a knight to move onto the third rank like this.' He demonstrated. 'I'd be able to call them king's knight and queen's knight, by the way, except that you've messed with the board for your own amusement. The rules have been around for about a thousand years, you know. It's not hard to pick them up.'

'*A thousand years?* Are you sure? I thought it was quite a newly invented thing.'

'Then you don't know what you're talking about.'

'I hear that a lot. But what was the name of the piece you were just demonstrating?'

'It's a knight, for God's sake.'

'I have to admit I've never heard it called that.'

By now MarkO was exasperated and I was having enormous fun. 'What the hell do you call it then, John?'

'I call it a Long-leaper.'

'And that's because?'

'Because it captures by jumping over a piece – more than one if the state of play on the board permits a compound manœuvre.'

'I see,' said MarkO, very much in the spirit of someone soothing a deluded nursing-home resident. I've been called a little Napoleon often enough in my time, though why anyone would want to be Napoleon with Alexander the Great on offer I can't imagine. He touched my king. 'And what's the name of this piece?'

'He's the king. Crucially important yet somehow powerless. Moves a single square in any direction. The game ends when he's threatened with capture and can't escape.'

'That's a relief. There's hope for you yet. Maybe. And how about this chap?' His finger was on my upside-down rook.

'Immobiliser.'

I'd had a relapse.

'And why is it upside down?'

'So you don't get it mixed up with the Coördinator.'

His finger went from the reversed rook to the one that was still upright, at the other side of the board, and he raised his eyebrows. I nodded.

'And this game is called . . . chess?'

'Oh no. At least I've never called it that.'

'I see.' I saw he was seething, and I wondered for a moment if I had gone too far. Leading him on was an irresistible treat. 'So this game is called . . .?'

'Ultima. If you'd wanted a game of chess you should have said so.' It was technically true that he hadn't specified a game, simply asking if I 'played'. I played all right. I played him for all he was worth, exploiting his eagerness to trounce me on the black-and-white killing field, though this quibble wouldn't have saved me from being pelted with rooks both reversed and right-way-up if he took it the wrong way. It took a moment for the deception to sink in, and for a further moment I wasn't sure how he was going to take it. Then he said, 'Do you know what you are, John? You're a taker of the piss and a wind-up merchant, that's what.' Taker of the piss and wind-up merchant. In that time and that place each of these phrases in isolation was high praise, and to be called both at once almost made my heart burst with joy.

Perhaps it was a factor in our rapport that I was tempted to call his bluff but also to indulge him, just to see how far things would go. He may have had the same complicated attitude to me. And in fact he recovered his good temper very quickly. Annoyance was rapidly displaced by fascination with the new game. I explained that in Ultima only the king moves as it does in the traditional version, and the pawns have unlimited orthogonal movement – that is, they can't move diagonally. They move like rooks. All the other pieces have a chess queen's powers of movement. It's when it comes to capture that things get a bit complicated. The piece that does the moving determines the method of capture, and only the king takes by the primitive strategy of replacement, dislodging a piece from its square. The other pieces . . . well, like King John in the poem I loved so much as a child, they have their little ways.

Pawns take by pincer movement – when a pawn moves into a square adjacent (horizontally or vertically but not diagonally) to an enemy piece with a friendly piece immediately on the other side, the enemy piece is captured. Strong-armed and taken into custody. I explained to MarkO that this actually harks back to an earlier style of capture, historically, even if Ultima was only invented in the 1960s. A pleasing piece of archaism. MarkO was so intrigued he forgot to roll his eyes. Any player of the Roman game Latrunculi relaxing between orgies, any Saxon who enjoyed a game of Hnefatafl with his evening mead, would understand at once what was going on.

I explained to MarkO the distinctive attacking technique of the Coördinator, which can potentially eliminate two enemy pieces, if they happen to be on the square where its file intersects with the king's rank, or where its rank intersects with the king's file. This sounds complicated, but all it involves is drawing an imaginary rectangle, with two of its corners marked by the king and the Coördinator, and vaporising enemy pieces positioned at the other two corners. The uninverted rook, meanwhile, the Immobiliser, has a different tactic, freezing all enemy pieces on squares adjacent to it for as long as it's next to them.

Perhaps some anti-clerical impulse in the game's inventor turns the bishops into Chameleons, who capture any piece by behaving as that piece would do – co-ordinating to attack a Coördinator, leaping over a Long-leaper, freezing an Immobiliser and so on. Naturally a Chameleon can't take another Chameleon. Like a vampire, a chameleon sees nothing in the mirror.

Most attractive to me was the destructive power of the queen, given an ominous new name and character as the Withdrawer. She annihilated a piece by occupying an adjacent square and then moving away. It was as if the enemy piece had been invited to a royal garden party and then ostracised. Publicly ignored, it expired of sheer social shame. It was snubbed to death.

Introducing MarkO to Ultima started off as a tease but turned into something rather different. That first day I enjoyed the swerves in his assessments of my IQ as he first revised it down to about ten, then up into three figures before it stabilised grudgingly at around a hundred.

A Chameleon on the rampage

I hadn't played a lot of Ultima, though it would have been silly to say so – I had picked up the rules by being at the edges of a chess-minded set at Downing, with one counter-faction touting the superior fluidity of Go and another singing the praises of this new game played with the same pieces, so fiendish in its ramifications that it made chess look like noughts and crosses. Downing had a reputation as a relatively down-to-earth college, what with its strong constituencies of engineers and medics. If that was true what must the atmosphere have been like at a place like Peterhouse? How did anyone get any sleep, with every last molecule of intellectual oxygen fiercely fought over? Ultima exercised only a faint abstract fascination for me then – chess itself seemed unmanageably intricate. Still, my love of simplicity would be a shallow thing if I had never felt the lure of the overelaborate. And now that I seemed to be reduced to the basics in Mayflower House what better time could there be to plunge headlong into complication?

We had a recurring wrangle about how a Chameleon would take the king, producing the Ultima equivalent of check or potentially checkmate. I said that the Chameleon had to start from a square adjacent to the king, and then move to replace it – but MarkO said from that position the king would already have taken the Chameleon, and didn't 'I'm about to take your king' mean the equivalent of 'check' anyway? Which would require the king to take evasive action or else to capture the Chameleon, either personally or by delegating the task to another piece. I thought this was the whole point, that you had to plan a Chameleon regicide well in advance, making sure that you had guards in place before you took out your sword.

We spent many happy hours disagreeing about this, the disagreement being an abstract one since the position didn't develop on the board. In chess questions of strategy arise almost immediately, while in Ultima it takes quite an apprenticeship to master the elements and to stop arguing about the legitimacy and implications of every possible move. All of this made Ultima much the better accompaniment to our friendship. The competitiveness in evidence the first day he brought the board downstairs was swallowed up for a considerable period by fascination with the technicalities of the game.

Bernardette came in once when we were wrangling about the rules of Ultima and finally lost patience. 'Honestly, you two,' she said, 'you're just like kids sometimes. You boys need to change the record. If you keep on talking about Chameleon strategy and bloody Immobilisers I'm going to scream.' When her lovely back was turned, MarkO made a face with puffed cheeks, releasing air as if relieved to have got off so lightly. As for me, I enjoyed being included in a group, even a delinquent one. I'd been singled out for torture a few times during my education (I hope that doesn't sound vain) but I'd rarely felt the glow of a shared scolding. What the little scene meant also, once I'd thought of it, was that Bernardette, who had put on a consistent display of shrugging off the attention that came her way, was feeling just a little neglected. Otherwise she wouldn't have issued her ultimatum – her 'Ultima'-tum. She'd already shown what could happen when she wanted a record changed and wasn't listened to.

MarkO was keen enough on Ultima to locate a book on the game in the Central Library. It was actually called *Abbott's New Card Games*, and Ultima featured only as a sort of appendix, though that was the invention that had the most impact, or I wouldn't have been able to come across it almost a decade after the book was published. Does anyone play Leopard these days? Care for a game of Eleusis, anybody? It's the fun game where the dealer chooses the principle that governs play, and you have to work out what it is if you're to win. The blurb on the book, under its thick protective sheet of transparent plastic, seemed to throw its weight behind Babel – 'In Babel, it's always your turn! Babel is the game that's sweeping the country!' But perhaps people play Switch behind suburban curtains, as a refreshing change from Cluedo or wife-swapping.

MarkO was wildly excited by Ultima's alternative name. 'John, why didn't you tell me? Why keep shtum?' Because I'd forgotten it, that's why, or had never learned it. 'Were you biding your time? Waiting to deliver the knockout punch? *It's only called – wait for it – Baroque Chess!*' Baroque Chess. Perhaps I'd sensibly suppressed that piece of knowledge, just for my own peace of mind. It's always a bit ominous to have things dovetail too neatly. When Maya gets up to her tricks there will always be trouble.

The book was of some use to MarkO. It resolved the *Alice-in-Wonderland* question of Chameleons and kings. I was right. But then MarkO said he was right, that what it said in the book was what he had been saying all along, which wasn't at all the way I remembered it. Still, if you go through life being perpetually right what chance do you have of learning anything? When I tried to protest he cut me down to size, as people always do from time to time. 'You're very full of yourself, you know, John,' he said, and I said cheerfully, to cover the fact that I felt put out, 'Of course I am. Who else would I be full of?' Just a little hurt. A little got-at.

Sometimes while playing Ultima with MarkO I found the constant voice-weaving of Bach on the Hacker, with Herr Bert's substantial foot on the treadle of the loom, too distracting. Baroque music and Baroque Chess seemed to set up interference patterns, so that I wasn't able either to make intelligent moves or to enjoy the music. I knew how attached MarkO was to those discs, and I wanted to find a form of words as different as possible from 'Please turn off that racket!'

One day I had a brainwave. 'MarkO, do you mind if we listen to *musica callada* for a change?' He was good-natured about it, reverently removing the Deutsche Grammophon disc from the turntable and replacing it in its swaddling bands, the paper inner sleeve lined with the smoothest possible pouch of transparent polythene. Then, understanding that I was not well suited to the rôle of DJ, he went over to my own little stack of LPs. 'What was it called again?'

'*Musica callada.*'

'Can't see it. How about this – *Neu!* Looks interesting.'

'I'm not in the mood. It's rather murky.' I was rarely in the mood for *Neu!*, which I had inherited when someone left Downing.

'Well, I can't find your bloody record!'

'What record?'

'*Musica* something.'

'Oh, it's not a record. Didn't I mention that? It's from a poem by St John of the Cross.'

MarkO expelled air from his nose in his own variant of yogic breathing, the left nostril expressing exasperated impatience, the right one resignation. 'If this is one of your little tricks, John, it's not going to work. I'm in control on the chessboard, and I still will be when we start to play again. I haven't forgotten it's my move. Now tell me about this bloody poem.'

'It's rather a lovely thing, now that you mention it,' I said. If there had been no gamesmanship in play when the conversation began it was certainly a factor now. 'The *musica callada* of the great Spanish mystic St John of the Cross is the music that holds its tongue while solitude and silence make themselves heard. He compares spiritual receptiveness to a solitary sparrow perched on the highest branch, its beak towards the wind of God, hearing the solitary music of resounding silence.'

'What a fantastic wind-up you are, you great fucking Spanish mystic! If you're planning to write poetry, John, you'll need a better pen name than "John on the Cross". Talk about ego trips! Everybody's got problems, you know. So next time you're baroqued out, just say, "Turn off that bloody racket!" Herr Bert and me, we're not sensitive. We can take a hint.' The guru can speak through anyone at any time, but normally MarkO would be an unlikely choice for that subtle ventriloquism. He was too wayward. You wouldn't choose MarkO to voice a hidden truth any more than you'd choose a pogo stick as a getaway vehicle, but just the same there may have been some inspired truth in a piece of scolding I found tonic rather than crushing.

Thanks to *Abbott's New Card Games*, MarkO enjoyed a closer relation with the technicalities of Ultima than I had managed to secure from observing play, and he got the drop on me in one game by committing 'suicide'. This turns out to be a legitimate manœuvre according to the rules, actually labelled 'The Suicide Move' in bald print. A player may forfeit a move as a way of taking an immobilised piece off the board and thus opening up fresh avenues of attack. The willingness of troops to kill themselves in the interest of their king brought an unnerving touch of extremism to proceedings on the board, but once you've accepted that this is metaphorical combat you should probably just gird your loins and get on with it. Suicide leads all too directly to rebirth and look! MarkO was already setting up the pieces for another game.

Robert Abbott's motive in devising a new game to be played with a chess set, apart from the morbid desire for novelty (which can never be discounted), was his conviction that chess itself was losing vitality and becoming exhausted. Why else would so many games at the highest level end in a draw? It's a sign of depletion when strategy is more and more like a science and wars of attrition become the norm. Games of pure skill are under the disadvantage that they can never be ripped open by the operations of chance. Nothing fertilises the possibilities of game play like the throwing of dice.

Ultima too is a game of pure skill, but luckily its rules are so complicated that the formation of gambits and suchlike, patterns of play, is, or was, a distant prospect. Abbott himself estimates 350 years (corresponding to the time chess has taken to develop) for that point to be reached. In the meantime MarkO and I goggled at the diagram on page 134 that showed the havoc that can be wrought in the game by a Chameleon on the rampage – in the example shown it captures a Long-leaper, a Withdrawer, a Coördinator and three pawns in a single move, and gives check to the king into the bargain. Beat that, Mr Bobby Fischer!

It goes without saying that MarkO had some talent of his own as taker of the piss and wind-up merchant. I can't imagine he developed these skills purely as a way of getting one up on me, though it's a possibility. MarkO said 'literally' when he meant 'figuratively', or 'tropically', to use an old-fashioned word I remember from preparing for my Latin O-level, in a desperate academic scramble that became smooth sailing at the last moment. Literally and tropically, 'lit. and trop.' in the dictionaries.

'I literally jumped out of my skin,' he might say.

'And what did you do with it?'

'With what? What did I do with what?'

'With your skin. Did you just leave it there on the floor, or were you able to squeeze back inside somehow?'

I got into the habit of pulling him up on such occasions, and he got into the habit of anticipating me. It wasn't long before he was setting little traps of his own, countering corrective tease with sly double bluff, saying for instance, 'When the gaffer said that to me, I literally . . . John, I literally had a cuppa tea.'

His way with cupsa tea and also cupsa coffee was quite a spectacle – a couple of noisy gulps and the brew was gone. When I say I found it endearing I'm only indicating that I was predisposed to be charmed by MarkO's habits. They might not have appealed to me in another context. All I'm doing is owning up to a personal susceptibility or lack of immunity. I'm not trying to paint a nuanced portrait of any sort of rogue or non-rogue, loveable or otherwise.

He was good, though, at that sort of recovery, getting himself back from the brink, bluffing more outrageously when his bluff was called. Once he said, 'The cockcunt and the brain are opposite ends of the same organ. Blake said that. The cockcunt – that's good, isn't it? That's clever.'

'Blake said that? William Blake the poet? Born 1757, died 1827?'

'That's the man.' MarkO seemed just a little less confident.

'Where did he say that?'

'Hold on, let me think. I remember . . . yes, that's right, it was at the top of a left-hand page.' MarkO claimed to have a photographic memory, though it was probably just a way of having the last word in arguments. In my experience it usually is. I've made the same claim myself in a tight spot. I offer the extra refinement of the top-of-a-left-hand-page dodge, which I learned from MarkO, for the benefit of anyone in trouble, anyone who needs to be airlifted at short notice from a sticky wicket. If you've got the nerve, specify page 122. It costs you nothing and it buys you time. There will always be a fractional hesitation as people try to work out, without seeming to pause in mounting their own argument, whether page 122 is in reality a left-hand page, and in that tiny interval you consolidate your advantage.

The nail file of Damocles

Meanwhile he went on buying records, sometimes on his way back from his shift, playing them anxiously while Bernardette was at work. Often he bought second-hand, though £25 a week was a good whack. He would try to guess whether they fitted in with her musical tastes, knowing that the sword of Damocles, the scissors or perhaps the nail file, was hanging over the vinyl until it got the all-clear. The refugees who came to me over the weeks needing to be taken in often became firm favourites with me. I got a certain amount of pleasure from the knowledge that we were more on a wavelength in certain areas than he was with Bernardette. We had an affinity.

One Sunday, up in the flat they shared, he put on a record that he had been listening to on his own. He liked it, he thought the songs were strong and the performances did them justice (he prepared himself for confrontation by imagining he was writing a review for the *Melody Maker*). He was ready to test the waters, to see if it would pass muster with Bernardette. He made tea and brought it in but couldn't settle himself. It was worse than a job interview, with him striding up and down, hardly daring to look at her face. When he nerved himself to do it her face was very closed off, as if they were strangers to each other. Even then she made him wait for it. 'The only thing worse than jazz . . .' He would have gone down on his knees in front of her if that would speed up the arrival of the rest of the sentence, the train stalled outside the station.

'She's not moody. Is she moody? She doesn't get upset about most things. Some chicks, some ladies, they make a fuss about any little thing. She's not like that. For instance . . . we both had a little problem soon after we met – crab lice if you really have to know . . .' I didn't have to know, didn't want to know, wanted to know – the standard permutations. 'And John, the lotions aren't much fun. They're smelly, in fact they stink, and they sting. She likes to be clean, you know – she might have freaked out. But we got through it without shouting at each other, and it was even nice when we made up, so I knew this worse-than-jazz thing must be pretty terrible, whatever it was. Honestly, do you understand women? No reason why you should. No reason why anyone should, when they don't understand themselves . . .' This didn't seem the most accurate assessment of someone whom he had previously described as knowing her own mind. Knowing it to an almost frightening extent.

I decided to be tactful, saying, 'I am more familiar with the sons of Adam than the daughters of Eve.' This was horribly true though phrasing it *à la* Blake made the revelation seem mystical rather than sheerly embarrassing. Invoking Blake or even sounding like him was still a licence to talk bilge in those days. 'If the doors of perception were cleansed . . .' MarkO might murmur in his stonedness, and I would think but not say, then we'd see just how shabby the furniture is. Boasting that your quiver was full to bursting with the arrows of desire worked better than just saying you were randy.

When Bernardette's ominous sentence finally concluded, and the last bogey of information had trundled into the station of meaning, brakes grinding, shooting out sparks, it brought with it the information that the only thing worse than jazz was . . . jazz-rock. Unfortunately this was the category, or circle of hell, to which Bernardette had consigned MarkO's newly bought LP, so of course he brought it down to 005. MarkO's ego was still in a state of mild hæmorrhage from the narcissistic wound dealt it by this dissident opinion, coming as it did from an intimate companion, someone he thought he could trust. Little disagreements were one thing, but when you couldn't see eye to eye on the basics it really made you wonder.

From that point on, thanks to Bernardette's intransigence, MarkO and I had another piece of forbidden music to enjoy. The record's cover was slightly baffling in its lack of information – not in the mischievous style of the Beatles' *White Album*, where those words appeared precisely nowhere on the double-album sleeve, and the words 'The Beatles' were merely embossed on the bottom edge without any use of colour. That was the whole point, that the Beatles could afford to hide because everybody was looking for them, could afford to withhold information because the world would demand it. Their status was so high they could get away with advertising their humility and submit themselves to a guru without real loss of ego, though if you ask me they could have done better. If you want mango chutney, fine, but shop around, don't go straight to Sharwood's Green Label. Frankly, their chosen Maharishi was a little bit wishi-washi, so very much the West's idea of the holy man, not someone who might bite you with a teasing severity or overwhelm you with radiance like my own Ramana Maharshi. Did the Maharishi tell them to ignore the pendulum swings from psychedelic colour to blank whiteness, to think of the pivot from which the pendulum swung, or did he slide down to join them on the pendulum?

This album was different. The cover showed a woman seen from a fair distance, a lady even, sitting side-on to the camera by a stone wall and a body of water, only her hair visible against a parasol not entirely innocent of frills, her body fully covered. I knew, without ever having paid conscious attention to women's legs, though they were often in my line of sight, that they were beginning to be tucked away, made mysterious again after an exposure that had often been merciless.

The colours in the photograph had been altered somehow, drained rather than boosted, another sign that the brightness of the 1960s had lost its grip on the collective imagination. What colours were left? Some cream and a little red – call them ruby and ivory – while the stone had somehow turned greenish, and some foliage near the front of the picture had become dark pink. A slightly sinister image of things that are in no way sinister, leisure and repose. There was a single word to be seen on the album cover: 'Affinity'. Was this the name of the album or the group? Might it be both? There was no way of telling. It was possible that MarkO and I not only had an affinity but *Affinity* by Affinity. The back cover gave some indication that the music inside had not been made by a robot or a committee by grudgingly listing a handful of musicians' names. Then there were the track titles, and that was your lot. If the counterculture had been more scrupulous about documentation I'd have enjoyed it more. Am I missing the point? Of course I'm missing the point.

When MarkO took the record out of its sleeve to place it on the revolving altar of the Hacker's turntable there was more withholding of information. The Vertigo label itself was a sort of celebrity, claiming top billing. The trademark design took up the whole of the label on Side A, a black-and-white 'logo' made up of eccentrically nested circles that refused to remain two-dimensional. The pattern played tricks on the eye as it rotated, seeming to erect a gyrating cone whose apex coincided with the centre hole and the Hacker's spindle. MarkO seemed almost entranced, as if the label was enough to hold his attention without the need for actual music.

He started nodding the moment the music started, but despite what might seem to be the special pleading of his enthusiasm, a nudge directed at my own responses, there was undoubtedly a contagious sense of rhythm, a relaxed urgency. The song was called 'I Am and So Are You', and actually I preferred the title to the lyrics that elaborated on it. The song supplied complements galore for the self-sufficient verb, explaining that I am various things (singer of songs, righter of wrongs, hater of lies *und so weiter*), and so are you, but it's always better to stick with the basics. I am and so are you. Isn't that enough?

There are two men in my life

I really didn't like the fact that the songs weren't credited to their writers, or even to their publishers, either on the sleeve or on the label. It's true that the nature of Vertigo's design meant that there was only room for information on one side of the record, but surely there was room for the basics! I was unpleasantly reminded of Practical Criticism seminars, where you were required to assess a poem or a passage from a novel without having any information regarding its authorship or date. In theory this was supposed to develop your analytical skills without the crutch of external information, but some of us need our crutches thank you very much. Now that I was a graduate I felt I was entitled to leave behind me any such academic exercises in pinning tails on donkeys. I wanted record labels to label things as their name promised they would, and to let me know which of the songs on *Affinity* were original compositions, if any, and which cover versions. I knew that at least one song had to be a cover version. Though MarkO sometimes told me I lived in a cave, it was a cave on whose walls 'All Along the Watchtower' had been beaten out and sung along to more than once. Perhaps all the songs were cover versions. It seemed to matter to me though I couldn't have said why.

We sang along with the lyrics as best we could make them out. They weren't printed on the sleeve, but then that degree of critical apparatus was a bit of a gala event. When the Beatles did it with *Sergeant Pepper's Lonely Hearts Club Band*, in fact, it seemed just a little bit smug to me, as if they were wanting a big tick from teacher for the neatness of their homework. Somehow we managed without benefit of a transcript. The ear can give its assent to words the eye would boggle at. Did we really believe, as we sang along to 'I Am and So Are You', that the line the vocalist was delivering with such conviction was 'Mess up your head in my lawn machine'? We knew no better. Perhaps there was no better to know.

We sang out the version we heard, though we shrugged wildly at each other according to our shrugging capacity. We were on much surer ground with the next line: 'You know what I mean.' That must be Lesson One in the songwriters' teach-yourself book. When you've written something nonsensical don't bother to work on it, just throw yourself on the listener's mercy. Pretend there's nothing wrong.

MarkO told me, mysteriously excited, that Linda Hoyle, the vocalist of the group, had another musical credit. *'There are two men in my life . . .'* he crooned, while I looked blank. He sang the silly line again, not the best way to dispel blankness. *'There are two men in my life . . .* Don't you recognise it, John?' No, I didn't, and at least this time he went on with the ditty. *'To one I am a mother, to the other I'm a wife . . .* you must know it! Everyone knows it!'

'Is it something that's on television?'

'Of course it is.'

I could have tried explaining the subtle distinction between stupid people and people who don't watch television, but I couldn't resist asking if it was on the Light Programme instead. I said I never watched the Light Programme. More winding up of MarkO, since this was how Mum referred to the commercial television channel – to ITV. The phrase had become second nature to me even when I knew

I should really explain what I meant. The Light Programme on the radio wasn't called that any more but had now become Radio 2, so that the joke, not strong to start with, was receding in time. The solar wind was carrying it out into space.

MarkO didn't seem to notice but carried on with his singing, finding a register of throaty sweetness worthy of Linda Hoyle herself. '. . . *and I give them both the best, with natural Shredded Wheat.*' What a change of tack in the ditty! It started suggestive (two men! you hussy!) then turned abruptly wholesome, with the singer ringing the changes from siren to *Hausfrau* in ten seconds flat.

'The singer from Affinity is the voice on the Shredded Wheat advert?' An advert I hadn't seen and didn't care about. 'Do you really think so?'

'I know so. There's no mistaking that voice.' Later, really quite a lot later, he admitted that he'd read about it in the *Melody Maker*. MarkO seemed inexplicably thrilled that a singer he liked should have been chosen to warble about breakfast cereal. So much for the hippy dream!

MarkO did a different version of his Linda Hoyle voice when he sang along to the song 'Mr Joy'. 'My Mr Joy – Joy – Joy,' she crooned, the melody rising in breathy intervals. She was clearly getting very carried away, and he wasn't far behind. Then he would ask me, 'What do you think she's talking about, John? This person that she winds up, apparently, who comes to her bed when she's lonely?' And I would give it some thought, and say, 'I wonder, do you think perhaps it's not a person? Any ideas, MarkO? Over to you.' And of course – *of course* – a part of me wanted to burst out with, 'Oh for heaven's sake, it's not a metronome! She's obviously talking about a vibrator. How dim do you think I am, exactly?' No doubt I'd get a snort of approval. But it's taking a bit of a chance, and on the whole people prefer me to play the innocent.

In the time of our intimacy there was one other album brought to me for safekeeping, after Bernardette had added it to the roster of undesirables. 'Is it jazz-rock?' I asked sympathetically as I took charge of the endangered album being escorted to a place of safety, a new life free from persecution.

'No,' he said. He looked grave. Apparently it was more serious than that. 'She called them *a comedy folk act*. Her exact words. Gas

Works a comedy act, can you believe it? Those are proper songs! Take a listen and see what you think. She's hitting below the belt if you ask me, and we're not far off the point where there's not a lot we can both listen to. Can't be healthy.'

I listened to the record and liked it very much but I had to be a little bit tactful, since 'comedy folk act' wasn't impossibly wide of the mark. When MarkO said they were a great band I politely agreed. People had started saying 'band' rather than 'group' by this time, but my tongue resisted the fashion. To me, the word 'band' more naturally followed 'brass' or 'Salvation Army' than 'rock' or 'pop'. Gas Works were MarkO's tip for future fame, and he wanted me to remember I'd heard about them from him first, when they exploded. I could absolutely hear their merits – just enough of a beat, just enough melodic sense, funny lyrics. It's just that I wouldn't know the Next Big Thing if it knocked on the window of the Mini and asked for directions.

We had our habits. We listened to Herr Bert, watching the Deutsche Grammophon Gesellschaft label rotate in its yellow splendour, edged with blue patterning that harboured mild stroboscopic designs on our eyes; we listened to Affinity and were spellbound by the Vertigo 'logo', which refused to remain two-dimensional as it revolved, until it came to resemble the dazzle-camouflaged nose cone of an alien craft poking its way into our dimension. We listened to *Gas Works*, about whose label I don't remember much. I must be losing my touch, though perhaps it's a historical failure of neck movement rather than a lapse of memory. It's possible that I was never pointing in the right direction at the relevant moment. As soon as I've said that, though, I have a sense impression of a rather retro design, something dating from the 1940s perhaps. The 1970s seemed a bit early for the 1940s to be returning, but there were signs that it was happening.

I had asked MarkO to ration his accounts of life as a temporary employee of the Cambridge Co-Op Dairy, to spare me the brutal impact of so much roughage in my conversational diet. Finally I asked about his week of 'induction' as a temporary milkman. I wouldn't have thought there was an enormous amount to learn about the business of delivering milk, and I dare say MarkO thought the same when he turned up for his week of training. A week seemed far too long an apprenticeship – surely a day would be plenty? He was young, he was strong, he could keep a lorry's engine turning over even in the wrong gear.

The foreman took him over to meet Ron. Here was his teacher, the guru of his working life, the one who knew how everything should be done. In fact Ron sounded less like a milkman than an extra in a spaghetti western. He was tall and lean, and smoked cigarillos even in the early morning, the time of day that MarkO referred to without fondness as sparrowfart. Sometimes MarkO rhapsodised about the beauty of Cambridge early on a summer morning, the fresh air, the light on a golden slant, the sense of something like ownership but without any contamination by possessiveness (I don't think he put it quite so smoothly). The smell of Ron's cigarillos displaced his appreciation of the summer splendour of Cambridge with the dew still on it, vulnerable in any case to the exhaust fumes of cars and the general disheartenment of being taken for granted.

Ron was a man of so few words he made Clint Eastwood look like a chatterbox, while MarkO was soon close to bursting with pent-up talk. MarkO had no intention of dawdling, but he had anticipated a brisk amble compatible with a certain amount of chitchat and daydreaming, while Ron was always looking at his watch and parked the float according to an obscure calculus that minimised the number of steps he would need to take. When Ron wasn't driving the float he took everything at a jog-trot, not an easy thing to manage with a full bottle carrier. The foreman had indicated that there was no particular hurry, though they should have finished well before eleven. Ron, though, considered his round a failure if it wasn't done by eight-thirty. It was as if he was in training for some sort of championship, if not actually taking part in some silly television tournament like *It's a Knockout!*. MarkO kept an eye out for cameras mounted on walls or cloaked by shrubbery. He wondered if Ron needed to take everything at such a lick because he had another job to get to. It seemed likely, but as Ron didn't volunteer information and ignored questions there was no way of knowing. There are people who are unable to dawdle under any circumstances, people who will arrive at their own funerals with plenty of time in hand.

Ron's round was bounded by Mill Road between Devonshire Road and Mawson Road as far down as Harvey Road, then Hills Road on both sides up to the railway bridge. It included part of Brooklands Avenue, Clarendon Road and the Botanic Gardens. Many of these streets were familiar to me after three years in Cambridge, and I was particularly delighted that MarkO should be delivering the pinta that might find its trickling way into Celia's tea mug, if she was still working there.

(I imagined, though, that she had moved on, most likely not to France, to undertake the œnological studies that had been her original reason for travelling to Europe, nor back to Australia whether daunted or undaunted.

Late in the summer I had noticed a delicious smell wafting through the Bot. I kept catching it out of the corner of my nostrils, and I'd ask what it was. No one knew what I was talking about, I suppose because the olfactory system is attuned to defence as much as anything else and tends to screen out familiar fragrances. A new smell is the one to be wary of, when there's predation in the air. Eventually I had the idea of asking Celia to meet me at the entrance of the Bot, at the beginning of her working week, when she'd had a day or two off to reset the detecting mechanism, and then it was easy. 'There!' I said. 'What's that fantastic fragrance?' And this time she could smell it, and between us we tracked the deliciousness down to the spot where its splendour lurked, nestled among mossy branches. *Lycastes aromatica*.

She told me then that she had made an excursion to visit the University Botanic Garden in Oxford. Perhaps she expected me to be shocked, overestimating the hostility between the universities, or perhaps it is I who am underestimating it. Not only is Oxford older than Cambridge as a university, the Oxford Botanic Garden has two centuries' worth of seniority over the Cambridge Bot. Older siblings can be dismissive, younger ones resentful.

'I've heard good things about the Tropical Lily House,' I said, in a peacemaker's tone.

'The thing is?' she said. 'I met someone there?' For once the artificial tentativeness of her vocal delivery seemed to convey real shyness and uncertainty. It's even possible that she was blushing – the complexions of those who work outdoors tend to mute such signals.

She had gone back to the Botanic in Oxford a number of times. Travelling between Oxford and Cambridge on public transport has been anything but easy since the closure of the Varsity railway line. The axes wielded by Dr Beeching and others cut deeply into the national rail network, but perhaps it's not fanciful to see a special intention in this piece of hewing, the deterrence of just such fraternisation across enemy lines. Best not to have too clear a path swept between the establishments of the Montagues and the Capulets. 'And there may be? A job there too?' I wished her good luck in every possible form that luck can take. Being poached by the opposition couldn't have happened to a nicer person, and I knew that in the shared struggle against *Pythium insidiosum* she would never put down her spray can.)

Admire the extra-strength parenthesis, capable of binding multiple paragraphs without bracket fatigue.

The Hills Road stretch of MarkO's round included the blocks of flats between Coronation Street and Union Road, and also Highsett on the other side of Hills Road. Highsett was a modern development of executive flats and townhouses surrounded by lawns and shrubbery, socially distinct though its postcode gave nothing away. The final leg was Station Road all the way to the Station Hotel opposite the station itself.

MarkO's narrative of his working life had the same sort of riveting nullity as the *Cambridge Evening News*, though he would have been displeased by the comparison. He had once picked up a copy of the paper in my flat, hoping to find out what was on at the ABC that evening, and was perversely vexed to find that its advertisements were long out of date. He took the old-fashioned view that newspapers were there to provide information, something that I had left far behind as I dived deeper and deeper into the paper's bottomless reservoir, its cool nirvana tank of the lovingly archived non-event. He didn't share my fascination with the way the *Cambridge Evening News* mirrored the emptiness of Maya, calling the bluff of illusion by reproducing it so perfectly.

I started setting my alarm early in the morning to match MarkO's, until eventually I too was nudged brusquely into the day at sparrowfart sharp. Five o'clock. I can't say I derived my own independent ecstasy from the beauty I drank in then, though if I really forced myself to notice I could sense that the air coming through the window was alive in a way that was gone later in the day, long gone by the coarsened hour that sleepers-in call breakfast time. Though I might wake at sparrowfart I didn't get up any earlier than I had before, and the drowsy extra hours that added themselves to my day contributed little more than sensual daydreaming.

As the week wore on MarkO began to feel he knew his round and its quirks, and was even accepting cigarillo smoke along with stale milk as part of the complex bouquet of his working life. He had swallowed the bitter pill of discovering that the lifts at the block of flats off Union Road, though an amenity to residents, were no help to milkmen. It would have been lovely not to rush up and down stairs carrying heavy milk crates, but the business of waiting for the lift to come slowed everything down far too much. Under its Maya disguise as an accelerator, the lift was a brake. Then there was a complication he hadn't anticipated. At the end of the week people had to pay for their milk – as many as would answer the door on the Friday, the rest on the Saturday. Even Ron couldn't apply his ergonomic agenda on human encounters with any stringency.

There was a lot of waiting outside doors, listening for movement inside that might or might not build to a surly encounter. The hatefulness of the halfpenny coin was one of the few subjects that could tempt Ron from his silence. There were times when MarkO expected him to toss one of these hated coins in the air in slow motion and drill a hole in it with a gun, either a real one produced from his satchel or simply his cocked finger and thumb, triggering the release of accumulated vexation.

A small minority of customers were organised enough to calculate the amount owing the night before and to leave exact change in an envelope. Such people had earned the right to a lie-in, and MarkO and even Ron would try to muffle the clink of the bottles they put down and the empties they picked up. Normally, of course, it's considered good form to make the maximum of noise, so as to dramatise the eternal antagonism between early risers and slugabeds.

Customers hated the halfpenny too, though if the price of milk had gone up from three-and-a-half to four pence a pint they would have discovered a fondness for it. Meanwhile MarkO, having learned the hard way how heavy a loaded milk crate is, was getting an equivalent lesson in the weight of a money satchel towards the end of a Saturday round. One of the effects of the job was to teach him a new respect for volume, for mass and weight, for time and motion.

Outsiders might think of milkmen as libertines of the underclass, ready to take advantage of any décolletage, innuendo or fluttered eyelash that was offered by the ladies on their route. That was the assumption behind Benny Hill's novelty single 'Ernie', after all, that milkmen delivered more than milk. Ron seemed to take the idea rather literally, seeming to set his sights on being the fastest milkman in the West, or in East Anglia anyway. MarkO wondered if there was any truth in the stereotype, and was oddly excited when Ron told him, on the last day they did deliveries together, when they were in Tenison Road, to watch out for Brenda at Number 16. 'Believe me,' Ron said, 'I've been shown things at that address I'll never forget.' When it comes to the territory of taboo there is no real difference between deterrent and incitement. They melt into one another.

Finally Ron handed over the logbook and the keys to the float. The keys to his kingdom. The schedule was for MarkO to take over Ron's round for six weeks. After taking a fortnight's holiday, Ron would cover other milkmen's rounds while they took their own breaks. This suggested that Ron's round was relatively easy, even a cushy number, though MarkO didn't find it so. Ron was some sort of marathon runner, if not a pentathlete, his events being running, climbing, route-planning, mental arithmetic and customer intimidation.

MarkO felt confident when he arrived for his first morning of flying solo. He wouldn't miss cigarillo-fug and Ron's negative charisma. The confidence had gone by the time he had finished loading the float. He got into a terrible muddle with the various kinds of milk, as indicated by their foil bottle-tops. There was whole milk with its silver cap, red for homogenised, even red-and-silver for semi-skimmed, and green for unpasteurised. A few people wanted sterilised milk which looked altogether different, the bottle a different shape and the closure too important to be trusted to a piece of aluminium foil. Sterilised milk bottles had crown caps, like beer bottles.

Ron had a real head for figures, not a trained calculating mind but an absolute grasp of quantity, the sort that darts players develop. MarkO only realised the importance of this when he had waited his turn and was parked up at the loading bay. Had he imagined that he would inherit Ron's expertise along with the keys and the logbook, or that he had somehow acquired it during his apprenticeship? There in the logbook were the figures for what was required, in Ron's not immediately decipherable handwriting, all loops. Overconfident and dopey from his early start, he had failed to realise that he would need to master the list in advance, not add columns of figures in his head at the collection point, his flusterment inflamed by the grumbling of the milkmen queuing behind him. The understudy can't expect to step into the spotlight without having slept with the script by his bed, even under his pillow. He had been driving the milk float for most of his training week, but his foot was unsteady on the pedal as he moved off at last, knowing that everyone in the depot was thinking the same thing. He wasn't filling Ron's shoes. Those were big shoes and no mistake. Size twelves, implacable on the control pedal of a milk float, impossible to dislodge once he'd got one inside a late-paying customer's door, when delivery boy must turn bailiff. Ron's resemblance to a dour Clint Eastwood minus poncho gave him an advantage when the projection of doorstep menace became a priority.

MarkO had done an imperfect job of remembering the round's hallowed stopping-places. He began to wish he had made chalk marks on the road at the appropriate spots, like Hansel and Gretel trying to remember their way through the forest. Ron's mental skills, as it turned out, extended beyond calculation to a sort of instinctive trigonometry. These were not just vaguely suitable areas but precise sets of coördinates. Just as some druidic mystics dowsing with hazel twigs could tap into the ley lines immemorially connecting sacred sites, so Ron could detect with great exactness the optimal placement of the float to give access to as many as three, four or five (five!) clusters of delivery points. If MarkO parked the float even a few yards away from this throbbing node of beatitude he would add minutes to the round. He was already behind schedule.

So much so that when he reached the Hills Road section of the route he found that the morning rush hour was in full swing. Then he really began to panic, got stuck in the traffic and couldn't find anywhere remotely convenient to park.

If he had originally thought of Ron as a displaced contestant from *It's a Knockout!*, with his loping laden run and his fierce focus on the pointless task in hand, now he was thinking of a different televised contest. He himself was like a bewildered and incompetent player on *The Generation Game*, trying to throw a pot or perform a can-can after a professional potter or dancer has made it all look easy. He had a mental image of Ron watching him with folded arms and a cold glint in his eyes, while behind him Bruce Forsyth simpered, grinned and waggled his chin.

I hardly knew who Bruce Forsyth was, but the picture was clear. MarkO was in despair while Maya withheld her favours and froze him out. He hadn't made a great job of being a student, and now he seemed to be failing at being a milkman. Cambridge was grinding him down, Cambridge was grinding him to powder. He told himself that Ron was always absurdly ahead of time, and that eleven o'clock wasn't too bad a time to finish up on his first day, but it was gone twelve when he limped back to the depot, and he knew that he was the last one in by miles. He parked the float at the charging station and hoped he'd be able to slip off with the minimum of fuss.

Unfortunately the foreman was waiting for him, looking anything but pleased. There had been a number of phone calls complaining of late delivery. The epicentre of customer dissatisfaction seemed to be Highsett, lovely Highsett with its lawns and landscaping. Executives had been deprived of milk on their cornflakes, had eaten them dry or gone without. They had gone to work by the time he had made his delivery, which was likely to mean, assuming that there was no one on the premises to take it in, that their milk would sit on the doorstep all day and be off, if it was still there at all, by the time they got back and wanted a nice restoring cup of tea. MarkO was given a bit of a lecture by the foreman. He would have to do better, starting immediately.

'And that's where you came in, John.' I didn't know what he meant until he explained. This was the day he first knocked on my door, at his last gasp, chatted a bit and went into a deep sleep, establishing our durable routine of shared chat and unilateral unconsciousness. I had cheered him up without really trying, with some help from Supertramp.

'You could see for yourself I was worn out. I'd always thought I was reasonably tough, but that day I had to admit I was no Joss Naylor. Cumberland born and bred, but no Joss Naylor.'

'Joss Naylor. Who's that?'

'Oh come on, John! Joss Naylor of Wasdale, that's who.'

'Beg pardon. Joss Naylor of Wasdale. Who's that?'

'You really do live in a cave, John. Everybody's heard of Joss Naylor.'

Everybody from Cumberland, perhaps. Apparently I should be familiar with this legendary figure, a shepherd from MarkO's native region who runs up and down hills and never tires. 'Joss of Wasdale', I imagine, to echo 'Robin of Sherwood'. Easy to imagine such a miraculous being in the world of Virgil's *Georgics*, which fought my understanding so fiercely as I prepared for my Latin O-level, or in Hindu scripture for that matter. If Krishna dallies with milkmaids then there seems no reason why a minor Cumbrian deity shouldn't join in a foot race just because he was in the mood. When a group of runners passed by his farm Joss of Wasdale suddenly felt the urge to join them – never mind that he had no experience. Off he went like the wind, leaving his sheep to fend for themselves. And then, of course, following fairy-story archetype, he led the pack of runners mile after mile. It was only the blisters caused by his clodhopping work boots that made him drop out. After that, having acquired suitable shoes or perhaps running barefoot, he became a sort of Lake District demigod, a local Hercules with a rather narrow repertoire of Labours. Run up and down this fell . . . now the next one . . . and the next one. See how many you can do in twenty-four hours. Do without sleep. He never seemed to do anything else. There's a similar figure in American folk-lore, I think, heroic but not exactly three-dimensional – Paul Bunyan, though wasn't he a lumberjack rather than a shepherd?

Part of my fascination with MarkO's milk round derived from the fact that before him nobody had told me in detail how they spent their days. After Dad stopped actually flying planes I only had the dimmest idea of what he got up to, as a personnel officer for BOAC. Normally it was sheer guesswork on my part as to how people filled the time. It was all unknown territory, but MarkO mapped it out. I was grateful to him for that. Work was far more of a mystery to me than sex. In the matter of sex I had made a little progress. Work was *terra incognita*, but in sex I had made inroads, past the signs saying *Here Be Monsters*. I hadn't met anything particularly monstrous yet.

I'd heard about the public lavatory on the roundabout known as Four Lamps back in my student days from Frank, who had taken me into the flat he shared with his girlfriend one Christmas. As we were driving past, he'd said, 'That's where the queers go, John.' It wasn't said viciously but on a cautionary note. 'They hang around like flies. You need to think twice about taking a Jimmy Riddle there if you're caught short anywhere in the area. You may get more than you bargained for.'

I was grateful for the information and stored it away for future use. If it was good enough for the queers it was good enough for me. As for getting more than I bargained for, this was a highly unlikely outcome since there was no upper limit to the bargaining I was willing to engage in.

MarkO sounded a similar note. It was as if all the straight men in town had collaborated on the wording of a cautionary bulletin. Don't take a leak in the Amazon or tiny carnivorous fish will swarm up your urethra, don't take a leak at Four Lamps or . . . what will happen exactly? Will queers swarm up my urethra? Chance would be a fine thing.

'I don't know if your bladder is strong, John, or if you sometimes feel the need of a wee when you're out and about, but I wouldn't advise you to answer the call of nature on that roundabout by Jesus Lane. It's got a bad reputation.' In fact the only bad reputation that Four Lamps had was of being a bit hectic at weekends.

My early explorations as a teenager had mainly been conducted in public conveniences, and I never quite understood the cloud of disapproval that hung over such premises, not just in straight people's conversations but gay people's too. Personally I felt grateful that such facilities existed, widely distributed and maintained by council funds, catering to more than a single set of needs.

I must have looked impossibly innocent, because he went on to explain, 'That's where the queers go, so don't be surprised if the stalls are chock-a-block and you can't do what you came to do.' That would depend, again, on what I went there to do, but I managed to bite my lip in deference to MarkO's illusions. I quite liked having secrets from him. If my life had dark corners then it couldn't be as uniformly grey as it sometimes seemed. If there were secret compartments then it stood to reason there couldn't be absolute emptiness. Absolute emptiness was the religious ideal I aspired to but I knew not to confuse it with mere twittish vacancy.

Since the day I had left the Vulcan School and thrown in my lot with mainstream education I had lost track of my peers. I was not one of those integrated souls who can say, hand on heart, that some of their best friends are disabled. I had no real sense of what life was like for anyone but myself, and it would obviously be rash to generalise from a sample so tiny that no one but me even knew it existed. And yet, thin data is better than no data at all, as long as you don't push it too hard towards a conclusion. In terms of education, Cambridge (in the form of Downing College) had treated me both badly and well, well to admit me at all when there was as yet no obligation, badly by not making life easier for me when the relevant statute took effect. Royal Assent had been given to the Chronically Sick and Disabled Persons Act on May the 29th of 1970, some little while before I arrived for my first year of study, and you might think three months or so would be enough to make a start on unambitious modifications such as ramps for wheelchairs, but the metabolism of institutions is sluggish. As is well known, an Act has to bed down over a period of time. It's a sort of denture which has got to settle into place for quite a while before it's truly at home in the mouth of the body politic.

At some point in September I paid a return visit to Downing, taking MarkO and Bernardette with me. For the first time I noticed the college's motto. *Quaerere verum* – to seek what is true. I had been so far off course in my time as an undergraduate that truth-seeking wasn't

267

on my radar. In fact I was so incurious that I hadn't even sought to know the motto of my own college. We slipped in by the back gate and did a recce of A staircase Kenny Court . . . and there it was. A ramp. I just stared at it, not so much at the thing itself as at the Zen beauty of Maya's patterning. First a wheelchair and no ramp, now a ramp and no resident wheelchair to benefit from its installation.

I suppose it's possible that the new occupant of one of the ground-floor rooms was a wheelchair user, perhaps a paraplegic who thanks to the modification would be able to enter and leave the premises unaided. But I doubt it. As to whether this represented delayed implementation of the Chronically Sick and Disabled Persons Act 1970 or simply the workings of Sod's Law I couldn't say. Sod's Law, which is always on the statute book.

Bernardette seemed a little intimidated on our Downing visit, and she and MarkO stuck close to each other when not pushing the wheelchair, as if they might be asked to explain their business there. They even held hands. It may be that they had wondered, before the visit, if I was telling the truth about my history. Nobody challenged my right to be there, but that's something that can go either way. I'm so obviously out of place in many contexts that people hesitate to call my bluff. It wasn't likely that I would be positively recognised as a Downing product unless someone actually pushed up a sash window and called out, 'I wondered where you had got to, John. Fancy a game of Ultima? I'll put out the pieces. Sorry I missed the grand opening of the Gold Blend drum. I bet it made quite a pop!' For maximum *Brideshead* impact the noise of the sash scraping upwards would startle a mother duck and her ducklings as they inspected an oarsman passed out in the Paddock, cradling an empty champagne bottle and wearing a blazer but nothing below the waist, but you can't have everything.

Now I thought it was my turn to lead MarkO down memory lane. 'Why don't we go on to Selwyn, MarkO?' I said. 'We could look up your old haunts. I can leave the car pretty much anywhere. That's the joy of disability.'

MarkO looked stricken, and Bernardette gave him a couple of consoling pats on the bottom. 'I'm not sure I could face it, John, to tell you the truth. It wasn't a good time for me.'

'Of course,' I said. 'I understand.'

An access ramp on that staircase would have made life easier for me, not directly but by dint of lightening the effort required of friends and passers-by to get me in and out. For more direct benefit I would have needed a wheelchair with motive power, something I hadn't had since I went to Burnham Grammar School. Either that or be able to spin myself along in an unpowered one like the sportiest of paraplegics.

You could make a case for Downing itself as being born out of a tangle of broken promises and refused obligations. The provisions for its foundation were laid out in the will of Sir George Downing, the 3rd Baronet, who died in 1749. Sir George was legally separated from his wife and had no children. In those days I think divorce required a private Act of Parliament, and you'd imagine that Sir George as MP for Dunwich, a famously rotten borough that was already largely underwater, would be in a good position to help such a thing along, but perhaps there was a reluctance to wash dirty linen in public, particularly if it was heavily monogrammed. Was legal separation a different way of dissolving the contract of marriage in those days? I'll do some research on the subject when I have nothing better to do. First of all the estate passed to George's cousin Sir Jacob, who became the 4th Baronet, and then by the terms of the will to three other cousins in succession. The baronetcy was extinguished with the death of Sir Jacob, but the other three cousins could have kept the flickering flame of their inheritance alive by the simple expedient of having children. They all very sensibly decided against the solecism of procreation and died 'without issue'.

If a *vasana* is the empty repetition of a pattern then the arch-*vasana* must be reproducing yourself, for no better reason than that your parents did the same. There could hardly be a shallower response to the mysteries on offer. Anyone who fills a cradle fills a grave. Reverence towards procreation is highly insidious, it's a very *Pythium* among sentimental attitudes. The emotional terrain needs to be thoroughly autoclaved if we're to have any prospect of eradicating it. Still, those five cousins of the Downing tribe immeasurably improved their chances of not being reborn by abstaining from fatherhood. At this point, which was reached in the year 1764, Sir George's will stipulated the setting up of a new college in Cambridge to bear his name. If it had really been a project close to his heart wouldn't he have given it a higher priority? He seems to have put 'endow a Cambridge college' in his will where someone else might have put 'donate to a donkey sanctuary'. Perhaps – who's to say? – with a higher karmic dividend.

There was a lot of money to play with, a fortune established by the first baronet, who had been first a republican and supporter of Charles I's execution, then a diplomat and spymaster under Cromwell who encouraged the Lord Protector to adopt the royal title. He continued in high office after the Restoration, receiving from the new king both a knighthood and a plot of land next to St James's Park. He hunted down the regicides whose cause he had supported. As for the suitability of the Prime Minister and Chancellor of the Exchequer operating from premises developed by a multiple turncoat and named after him, well . . . we can't say we weren't warned.

The 4th Baronet's widow indulged in some bad faith of her own by refusing to relax her grip on the estate. Her lawyers fought a rearguard action on her behalf, one that continued after her death in defence of the imagined rights of her second husband and her niece. The Downing fortune slipped from branch to branch of the family tree before finally tumbling to the ground in 1800, when at last it was permitted to enrich the general academic soil.

If my college had to wait thirty-six years for its foundation, then it would be churlish on my part to resent a delay of three years in the installation of an access ramp. It seems I have found a way to come to terms with my experience of Downing as ungiving. In those thirty-six years the estate had been much depleted by the pretenders to it and the lawyers they employed. William Wilkins drew up plans that were ambitious if not positively cheeky, since the proposed courtyard of the college would be larger than Trinity Great Court, but the grand plans had to be scaled back for lack of funds and a large slice of the site was sold off to the University. For some reason, as this story of dispossession came down the years it became simplified, so that my generation of students thought it was a renegade bursar who had run off with the funds. Either way the college was a starveling itself, it would never wholeheartedly nourish others. Institutions can have *vasanas*, engrained administrative reflexes; in fact institutions are best thought of as clumps of *vasanas*. Self-realisation, alas, is not an option for institutions, and that is where we have the edge.

I can't measure Downing's performance against any other college, but in the area of my post-graduation housing, another area of institutional non-coöperation, I could enter into evidence more than a single sample, since I had approached the authorities in two counties, Buckinghamshire and Cambridgeshire. As far as I could see, High Wycombe had Johnable accommodation only on paper. The relevant disabled units fell into the category of things that can be named without actually existing, such as (the hallowed Hindu examples one more time) the child of a barren woman or the horns of the hare. Cambridge's performance was hardly better, as I knew to my cost. I had been offered somewhere to live in the same way a stunt motorcycle rider is offered a landing area on the far side of a row of buses. In my case those buses would be represented by the three nights I had to fend for myself, and admittedly the analogy is wildly overdramatic. If I was Evel Knievel I wouldn't be in need of that sort of accommodation, unless of course I crashed on landing and severed my spinal cord – but here we're caught in a tangle of logical loops and must chew our way free.

Riding the tide of synovial fluid

Complaint after complaint, but perhaps room can be found for celebration. Whatever the shortcomings of my adopted city, its University and its Council, in the areas of access provision and adapted accommodation the cottaging facilities for the disabled had been laid on with great style.

I would pull the red Mini into the wide lay-by near the lavatory complex. Wonderful really because Midsummer Common was so pretty anyway and you could sit there watching the traffic, the people coming and going – that's the sort of traffic I mean, the men coming in and out of the toilet. I would take note of who went in and how long they spent inside before coming out. Which direction they came from when they arrived, what direction they took when they left. If they disappeared, how long it was before they reappeared and whether they went into the bog again or came and leaned against the green-painted railings to smoke a cigarette before the time was ripe, by whatever mysterious set of calculations, for another inspection of the facilities. They would gaze out, at likely prospects, at likely police cars, as if they were on the deck of a ship. A cruise ship. 'Cruise' was the new word for 'looking for sex', though some of the senior members of CHAPs still said 'troll'. I can't pretend I adopted the new term at all swiftly, though I hadn't liked the old one. In my mind the activity had a different name, simply because so little activity was involved, at least in my case. I thought of it as 'lurking'. Lurking with intent, any amount of intent.

If you'd wanted to devise a lurking area fit for the disabled, you couldn't have done better than this. Excellent lines of sight, hygiene no worse than expected. I became a fixture of sorts, a reference point for the regulars. Sometimes I would go in, to be sure, sometimes even to use the facilities for their intended purpose, though I didn't trust the slipperiness of the floor on rainy days. Occasionally a passer-by would unload the wheelchair from the boot of the Mini and push me onto the premises, though it wasn't always easy to explain that I was in no particular hurry to make the return journey and could safely be left to my own devices.

On rainy days there was the compensation that visitors who didn't want either to become conspicuous by spending too much time in the lavatory or to get wet while waiting outside found a compromise solution. They would simply join me in the Mini, installing themselves in the passenger seat and grumbling about the weather. This wasn't a sensually charged situation in itself and I didn't get my hopes up, but companionability without secrets is not something to be sniffed at. It's not a commodity in guaranteed supply.

Logically there were only two categories of people who hung around those premises for reasons other than brute excretion: legitimate devotees and *agents provocateurs*, the 'pretty police' dispatched to lure citizens into transgression, and if I was disqualified on a number of counts from belonging to the second group then my place must be with the first.

At times I would go into the toilet, but that was the riskier aspect as you had to check the floor for slipperiness, and it was only practicable on dry days, but there was plenty you could do by staying right there in the driving seat.

One evening a guy in his early twenties or perhaps late 'teens leaned casually against the railings in my line of sight, looking around and occasionally adjusting his crotch with a fond motion of the hand, drawing attention to the lie of his well-fitting brown trousers. I say well-fitting rather than tight-fitting because they aren't the same thing at all. There's all the difference in the world.

His idea of a good fit in the matter of trousers fitted neatly with my prejudices. His soft brown flannels weren't so loose that you couldn't see anything at all, and not so tight as to force the outline of his bits and pieces down your ocular throat. It occurs to me that I like tight trousers on waiters but not on other sectors of society, though I have no idea why. And to my mind there's no fabric less mysterious than denim. I couldn't wait for its vogue to pass. I still can't.

This young man had the knack of emphasising or playing down his parts with nothing more than a slight shift of posture. Weight wasn't thrown harshly from one hip to the other but followed its own sweet flow, free to ride smoothly on the tide of synovial fluid lubricating his superbly functioning joints, femoral head engaging perfectly with acetabulum. His face was open, as I thought, kind and friendly, wholesome rather than knowing. I felt he was far too pretty to want anything to do with someone like me, so my heart leaped when he turned in my direction and gave me a friendly smile. I smiled back, reining in my joy so that I didn't send signals of active idiocy. Meanwhile I thanked the multiform Lord that I'd remembered to get the passenger window wound down a bit before I started my journey, a move that made communication a real prospect. Nothing kills the rich potential of such moments like the struggle with a recalcitrant crank. This flirtatious stranger bent down slightly to fit his face in the gap of the window and tapped his unwatched wrist with a finger, a sufficient mime even before he asked if I happened to have the time.

The old jokes are the best ones, there's no doubt in my mind about that. What did the Tower of Pisa say to Big Ben? If you've got the time I've got the inclination.

'As a matter of fact I do,' I said. 'It's just coming up to a quarter to seven.' He nodded and asked if he could sit in the car for a while. I said, 'Help yourself.'

Once he was installed he was polite enough to go through a few opening gambits.

'Do you come here often?'

'Oh, not that much really. Just every so often. You?'

'Oh, 'bout the same really. Depends.' Did he say, 'I've not seen you here before' or 'I've seen you around now and then'? Despite appearances, these statements are not opposite in meaning. They are purely phatic, as vital to the performance as it unfolds, though free of content, as the tuning-up that precedes an orchestral concert.

'I'm Malcolm, by the way.'

'John.'

(A pause.)

It was considered good form to maintain the tone of artificial diffidence even when a little heat was implied by the topic under discussion. Perhaps there were those who rushed into things, but I can only describe the set steps of the pre-foreplay quadrille with which I became familiar. There was a protocol to be observed. At this juncture the question 'What do you do?' was not a chance to reveal that you were a trainee solicitor or the Master of Pembroke.

We knew better and stuck to the formula. 'What do you like?' →
'Don't know really. You?'

'Oh, oral mostly.' → 'Seems a fair enough place to start.'

These exchanges serve their function irrespective of the assignment of speakers. If I was the one who first mentioned oral sex, then Malcolm wouldn't necessarily take this as the expression of a real desire, let alone a pressing one.

'Things got pretty heated at Fenners last night,' I said.

'I'm sure they did, John, but you weren't there any more than I was . . .' It turned out that Fenners was the name of the University sports facility. How was I supposed to know that? I was only repeating something I had heard said within the walls of Four Lamps, and perhaps it was unwise to rely on the exchange value of a nugget of information when I didn't know what was meant by it. Still, as far as I can see a great deal of what goes on between people is Chinese

Whispers by another name at the best of times, a more or less creative garbling. In any case my little blunder hadn't lost me any ground with Malcolm. He wasn't disapproving but simply amused.

'I've not got into Fenners myself but I still have hopes. There's a rumour that one of the guys who uses the weights room, he's a rugger Blue, has done so much work on his thighs that he can't cross his legs. Don't you think that's the sexiest thing ever, a guy who can't cross his legs?'

'I'll take that as a compliment.'

He didn't react, which was probably for the best.

'Oh well, to each his own. But it doesn't do to be too fussy. Take it from one who knows.'

It was time for a little escalation. I released the slide lock that freed up the runners on the driver's seat, easing it back a few inches.

'You can get a bit stiff,' I said, 'sitting like this for too long. I'll just shift position a bit.'

Golden age of civic delinquency

I shuffled slightly, opening my legs as much as I could, and thanking my lucky stars that I too had picked up the art of drawing attention to parts of myself, though by producing much smaller shifts in body posture than Malcolm had at his disposal. My neck has more movement to the left than the right, which was handy, as I could make out an appreciative expression on his face, which was accompanied by a little cooing noise. I couldn't meet his eyes, but that's a bit of a luxury, and anyway though there's a sexiness in gazing into someone's eyes it's not the only sexiness there is. On the other hand if I was supposed to be keeping watch, then there had better not be a policeman, pretty or not so pretty, sneaking up from the right.

In the next moment Malcolm had dropped his right hand down – without a by-your-leave, how shocking – half curled, so that its concavity fitted pat over the convex contour of my crotch. The fit was remarkably snug, and a shiver of exhilaration zipped up and down my spine. Malcolm gave me a gentle squeeze and the chakras in my groin responded, not in the brisk way of the Mini's gearbox engaging with the help of the clutch but as smoothly as the hydraulic suspension of

a Citroën DS might do, if maintained in accordance with the manu-
facturer's instructions. As it turned out, I had the inclination as well
as the time.

He warmed me up, making me feel as a ladleful of brandy must feel
around Christmastime when it is held over a low flame and tickled
on the molecular level, until it trickles over the pudding and without
even noticing bursts softly into flames.

One overlooked advantage to having your joints locked and your
bone growth restricted is that when the circumstances are propitious soft tissue looms large. Not every part of a small body habitus
is necessarily small, and this discovery has brightened any number of
encounters. 'John,' Malcolm said, 'I'm almost impressed.' I take flattery well. This boost to my confidence helped the excitement along
a little bit further, something he remarked on. 'I'm now officially
impressed, John. You're quite the Hunker Munker. Another time we
should certainly take this further. We could have a lot of fun. In the
meantime I'll get the word out. I have friends in low places.'

He pulled a little notebook out of his shirt pocket, almost as a
policeman might, and I gave him my full name, address and telephone
number. Why my full name? I wanted to project back at him the self-
confidence that he ascribed to me. In return he gave me a quick kiss
on the cheek. As he moved to open the door I had a moment to decide
whether to risk spoiling the moment by asking him to return my seat
to its forward position before he left the car. I could make the little
journey backwards but not forwards. Luckily, Malcolm understood
without needing to be asked.

On the way out he gave me a tremendous grin, as if we'd somehow
put one over the whole world, which I suppose in a way was the truth
of it. That was certainly how it felt. As I drove off out of the lay-by I
could see him in my rear-view mirror. He waved at me before I turned
left at the roundabout towards Mayflower House.

The talk of 'getting the word out' about my sexual serviceability
was obviously absurd, but heartening. Malcolm was an accomplished
flirt, but flirting needn't involve insincerity. I certainly didn't think
he was taking pity on me. His crotch had visibly plumpened to
match mine, and altruistic impulses cut the supply of blood to the
groin, as everyone knows. There had been no sign of such a thing.

I just hoped that he hadn't taken too much notice of my jauntily expressed preference for oral acts. The obstacles were not slight. My jaw doesn't have a great deal of movement and my neck is very set in its ways. T'other way about there are possibilities, to be sure, but even with the play afforded by their lovely McKee pins (still under warranty then) my hips weren't in a position to offer visitors much of a welcome.

Hunker Munker he had called me. What a lovely phrase. At CHAPs we'd had a little lecture from Our Leader about the word 'hunk' and its hidden freight of racial and class consciousness. A 'hunky' was what Americans called Hungarian labourers, so when we said someone was a hunky, or just plain hunky, we were characterising him as lower-class and foreign in origin, a typical ploy for dehumanising a person and turning him into a sexual object and nothing more. Ken was not going to tell us how to think, how to feel (like hell he wasn't!), but he also knew we wouldn't want the language of desire to be muddied and distorted by imagery that was not only objectifying but nationalistic. Desirous bodies were so much more than hunks of meat.

We all listened but carried on with our unliberated practice. It was all very well to be told of our ideological errors, but no better formula was being proposed, and as a formula of sexual admiration 'dishy' was showing its age. Was 'dishy' even any better? Perhaps it suggested that someone was a plate of food to be consumed rather than a human being to be experienced in full selfhood. Our Leader would have been able to find a sinister overtone in the most innocent formula of approval – 'a bit of all right', 'easy on the eye'.

Then in the middle of my glow about the compliment a new thought came along and spoiled everything. Not Hunker Munker but Hunca Munca, who was from Beatrix Potter, being one of the title characters in *The Tale of Two Bad Mice*. There wasn't a lot of juice left in the compliment once I'd realised I was being compared to a delinquent mouse from a children's book. I could only hope that Hunca Munca was at least a male delinquent mouse.

Despite this setback within a triumph, I became rather cocky at Four Lamps after that. I would sound the horn in peremptory style – poop poop! look alive! – and sooner or later someone would come to my rescue, lift the wheelchair out of the boot and push me into the toilets. This was the style of horn call that had earned me the nickname of Mr Toad among the staff of the University Library, when I used it to indicate that I was ready to receive a consignment of books. If it was a passer-by he might be surprised, after the urgency of my appeal, that I seemed to be in no particular hurry to use the facilities, but was unlikely to loiter on his own account. If it was a denizen of the toilets who emerged to help he might be a little put out, checking that his flies were properly done up as he emerged into daylight, but all things considered a lot less grumpy than the Porter in *Macbeth*.

Once inside, empowered by the relative mobility of the wheelchair, I could get a good look at what went on. I learned not to punt myself too close to the wide urinal, a single ground-level trough (though with porcelain partitions) rather than the other traditional pattern of raised fixtures, individually plumbed, often three of them in a row with a fourth installed at a lower level for the presumed convenience of a lad in short trousers, keen to show Dad he can hold his own with the big boys. Neither configuration was particularly suitable for my personal use, but I took an interest in what was played out on this stage, where white cakes of disinfectant took the place of footlights. I needed to approach warily so as not to freeze events from some distance away, since this was a grown-up if not potentially criminal game of Grandmother's Footsteps. Glances would transgress the theoretical barrier established by the porcelain protrusions, with stares following if the glances seemed to be welcomed. A hand might slide across and make contact – once I saw the man in the middle reach a hand out on either side – though it seemed customary at this point to look straight ahead again, as if a technical innocence could be maintained just as long as the separate parts of the action, the looking and the touching, weren't fully joined up.

I kept expecting to run into CHAPs members at Four Lamps, not particularly anxious about the prospect since I felt that the standard French-farce impasse – 'What are you doing here?' 'Never mind that. What are *you* doing here?' – would give me some sly advantage despite the apparent symmetry of the situation. I could simply say, 'Oh, I keep turning up like a bad penny,' and no one would contradict me. Of course, Lurking with Intent and the acts that it led to weren't exactly approved of in the context of a gay liberation discussion group like ours. If we had internalised our shame to such an extent then . . . we should be thoroughly ashamed of ourselves. And then what? Where did the revolutionary dialectic go from there? I did idly wonder, though, if everyone in the group except me knew about a public lavatory complex that made Four Lamps look like a hole in the ground, like one of those French provincial lavatories that tourists remembered with a shudder. Was there a cottage somewhere else that was positively palatial? It didn't seem likely. We were well catered for. It was a golden age of civic delinquency.

The derogatory word for places of brusque sexual exchange was 'meat market', but Four Lamps seemed to me more like a fruit-and-veg market, though one that didn't give two hoots for the injunction that was so prominently displayed on the stalls in Market Hill when plums and peaches were offered to the public gaze.

Dont squeeze me 'til Im yours.

There were times when my presence as a witness was barely tolerated, others when it seemed that I was somehow crucial to the proceedings though not socially acknowledged, like the photographer at a wedding.

Naturally anyone misbehaving at the urinal would freeze when a newcomer entered Four Lamps, even though such a person might turn out to be an initiate seeking to join the party. I learned to burnish my welcome by giving a stage cough as a way of announcing a new arrival. Sometimes the men at the urinals seemed stage-bound in their own right, their illicit activities being instantly arrested, though they were unable to simulate the splash of innocence. Male biology is primitive in this regard, and it's not easy once aroused to resume a tranquil flow. The gearbox in the groin is not to be crashed or hurried. I learned in these circumstances to play my part, saying, 'These gentlemen seem to be occupied – would you be kind enough to assist me to a cubicle?' The newcomer might give a disgusted snort, but he was unlikely to refuse such a request, and by the time we had finished our little expedition there was no one to be seen in the public spaces of the civic amenity known as Four Lamps.

A low-cut gown beneath the plumber's overalls

Were these acts unhallowed? Not necessarily. It all depends on your choice of statutory authority. Græco-Roman deities are less profligate in their functions than Hindu ones, to be sure, but they can have a wider portfolio than is often assumed, a whole cluster of part-time duties. One of the aspects of Venus, for instance, is Venus Cloacina, she who presides over sewers and public sanitation, necessarily the tutelary goddess of Four Lamps. In Rome as it was in classical times her shrine overlooked the stream that became the main outlet for the city's sewer system, the Cloaca Maxima. But just because she's conferring her blessing on the pipework doesn't mean that she has stopped being the Goddess of Love. She's still wearing a low-cut gown beneath the plumber's overalls, and sexual arousal on premises dedicated to the disposal of waste (in theory, anyway) is hardly likely to offend her.

Major episodes of my life have been conducted under her auspices, even before I was so ardently her devotee and made pilgrimage to her temples. Once her protection had failed me, when a drunken undergraduate dropped me onto the floor of a pub urinal on King Street, but perhaps pub premises fall under the tutelage of a less vigilant god. It's plausibly part of Silenus' portfolio. Isn't it Silenus who leers woozily over the grain, and Bacchus over the grape? – randy godheads the pair of them, even with a skinful. I can imagine a pratfall in the lavvy being right up Silenus' street, so perhaps he got a laugh out of my misadventure, and even a hard-on. That's par for the course for an arch-satyr, or whatever Silenus is exactly.

Men on a warm night choosing to embrace on Midsummer Common itself may be leaving Venus Cloacina's immediate zone of influence but are hardly abandoned wholesale by the pantheon. Priapus, being the god of both genitals and gardens, watches over them there, though with ambiguous benevolence. If ejaculation doesn't always crown the lovers' efforts then that may be due to Priapus' influence, rather than in spite of it. He had a rather melancholy history on Olympus before (like Vulcan) he was cast down to earth. Hera cursed him with impotence, and not a general inadequacy but a particularly humiliating style of failure in performance, not difficulty getting started but an abrupt wilting on the home stretch. I'm tempted to add 'Or so I'm told', but that style of bragging by implication really won't wash. There's no denying that old Priapus can be a snake in the grass, though perhaps he's only the Græco-Roman equivalent of Ganesh in Hinduism, he who removes obstacles but sometimes goes to the trouble of installing them first. Likewise Priapus may open wide the path to pleasure and then capriciously seal it off.

The privacy of the cubicle was prized, but it brought with it a greater risk of exposure. It was hard for two men to come up with a convincing excuse for sharing so snug a space if discovered.

Obviously by 'two men' I mean able-bodied ones. Suddenly my market value had gone up and my deficits became assets. Naturally I would need assistance. Sometimes I had the feeling of being a piece in someone else's game, though not perhaps a pawn, more like the king in Ultima (or chess, if you insist), having a restricted power of movement yet somehow being indispensable to the playing of the game. What would happen if I resigned? Presumably the game would have to be changed.

Once there was an attempt by two men to hustle me out of the wheelchair and – I assume – into a cubicle with them, but I cried out, 'Unhand me sirs!', which turned out to be much more effective a protest when uttered in a gentlemen's toilet than it is in its home territory of Victorian melodrama, where it merely accelerates the arrival of a fate worse than death. And once I was propped up against the wall of the cubicle my companion stood on the lavatory seat to spy over the partition on what was going on in the next stall, which struck me as very unsportsmanlike. If you're going to do that at least recognise the obligation to provide a running commentary of some sort.

I gather there's an argument that the satisfaction of carnal desires runs counter to the project of self-realisation. I don't hold with that. True asceticism is not abstention from the act but from the appetite. Celibacy should never be a refusal but a shedding. To experience desire but refuse it only embeds it more deeply in a suspension of shame, guaranteeing its longevity. So if I was susceptible to the urge, it was hypocritical nonsense to shy away from satisfying it. Western thinking is very muddled about such matters.

A public lavatory with a reputation for depravity is almost as melancholy a prospect when empty as the deserted village in Goldsmith's poem, but once on a mid-morning visit I profited from the absence of traffic. A man was standing at the urinal but nary a splash nor trickle reached my ears, cocked and attuned though they were. Some men get inhibited in mid-stream, but he hardly seemed anxious. He had his hands on his hips, a posture that doesn't prevent urine flow, as far as I know, but it's an odd choice of stance in the circumstances, ostentatious in its relaxation. Habitués of cottages tend to be strongly scopæsthetic. Did he know I was there, and watching? I began to think so. He didn't do anything vulgar like peeking over his shoulder, so with any luck he wasn't an *agent provocateur* or pretty policeman, who were reputed to be unsubtle in their approaches, rather too obviously a dream coming true.

I remember there was a lot of noise in the background, from workmen erecting a marquee on Midsummer Common for some sort of trade fair, so that I worried I might not be able to hear the approach of a passer-by perverse enough to use a public toilet for the purpose of urination.

He was wearing a denim jacket and bell-bottomed jeans, and desert boots. Now I come to think of it, this was exactly the sort of outfit a pretty policeman might choose, but I had no doubts on that score. I'm not a fan of jeans, never have been, so if anything I felt I was doing him a favour by taking an interest in what the material covered with such smug snugness. If he had been tall, properly tall, I wouldn't have had a chance of reaching this target area. He was something below medium height, I think. I find such things hard to judge.

If you spend a lot of your time at wheelchair level you become familiar with bottoms in the way that other people learn to read faces. You come to understand their expressions, the stern and the placid. A wallet bulking out a back pocket produces the effect of someone chewing gum or suffering from a painful abscess. There's a whole empirical science based on the expressiveness of the *gluteus maximus* that is at least as useful as Victorian phrenology was in inferring character and level of intelligence from bumps on the skull. This face was definitely winking and bespoke a disposition of genial mischief. Mind you, without an appetite for mischief we would neither of us have been there.

I had been delivered to Four Lamps in the wheelchair by a helpful passer-by who didn't linger. There was no one else in sight. Now I made my none too stealthy approach to the waiting figure at the urinal. Stealth implies slowness and I could certainly muster that. The other aspects, the silence, the discretion, those were beyond me. A few times I've been able to sneak up on someone, and very delicious it has been too, but this was not one of those times. To punt the wheelchair forward, judging the maximum placement before I put on the brakes, to brace myself with crutch and cane to reach the approximate vertical, none of this could be managed in silence. Then to let the cane fall back against the wheelchair so that the crutch was supporting my elbow and my hands were free . . . if this stranger wasn't confidently expecting a surprise, and not the surprise of me toppling against him and knocking him over like a ninepin, then he would be bound to wonder what on earth was going on behind him. Was it a pedlar with a wide range of pans? A one-man band? In fact he seemed remarkably unbothered. He swung his admirable hips slightly from side to side, by implication swinging a considerable apparatus as counterweight on the other side from me, while also showing anticipation for the creeping approach of my hands on his bum.

My hands, though not my palms. Without the benefit of working wrists, and with my elbows not much better at their job, the palms of my hands face downwards. A message written on my palms will never reach me. There are plenty of things I can do with my fingers, all in a limited quadrant below my waist, and fiddly things rather than feats of strength. You don't need the ability to chuck a typewriter across the room to peck out a stinging letter of complaint. I reached carefully upwards with the backs of my hands, anchoring myself on the crutch and trusting that the balance of forces would permit more than a grazing contact. It was a long shot. If the odds had been equally poor as regards the effort to put man on the moon no funding would have been allotted it. It was the slimmest possibility, but those are the ones I have spent my time exploring.

A Parisian *garsong* of the most lubricious stripe

My knowledge of the Parisian *demi-monde* has never been extensive, and my source for it is still primarily the extraordinary Jimmy Kettle, my spastic friend at Vulcan (spastic but not quite athetoid, and his arms worse affected than his legs), an American who had washed up at that special boarding school for the education and rehabilitation of severely disabled but intelligent boys. If I was precocious, and a case can be made for that, then Jimmy inhabited some remote realm of premature sophistication far beyond me. This teenager had a favourite cocotte in Paris called Minouche, whose face he described as 'scrunched-up' in the cutest possible way. He offered me her services at his expense, 'on my dollar' I think he said, the next time I was in Paris, an offer that I wouldn't have thought sincere if it came from anyone but Jimmy. He also told me the perverse tricks of Parisian waiters.

It was part of the professional life of these debased creatures smoothly to help ladies take off their coats. If they had been shameless enough to caress the bottoms of their customers in the process there would certainly be protests made – but that applies only to a caress of the conventional sort, performed with the palm and the fingers. In most people the palmar aspect of the hand is far more sensitive to stimuli than the dorsal aspect. So French waiters would cultivate their dorsal sensitivity, nerve ends tingling with appetite, until they were able to derive as full a thrill from gliding past a lady's bottom with the back of the hand as they would from full momentary sliding contact with palm and fingers.

This hint, whatever Jimmy's reason for passing it on, was not wasted on me. I have tried over the years to absorb as much sensory and indeed sensual information from the backs of my hands as possible, modelling myself on a Parisian *garsong* of the most lubricious stripe, depraved skimmer of unsuspecting *derrières*, so as to compensate for the relative starvation of stimulus I experience from the palms. In this context I like *garsong* even more than *garçon* – the gain in xenophobic coarseness more than makes up for the loss of a cedilla. Is it possible to rewire the brain in this way? At this point I'm confident that it is. It doesn't take much to get the backs of my hands going.

In Four Lamps that day, unseen spinnerets shot jets of liquid silk towards the target area. There were filaments and fibres of anticipation growing between the waiting bedenimed buttocks and my hands, restricted in their range of movement, able to make limited journeys in one plane only, but charged with their own stubborn

284

will-to-fondle. Not so much *der Wille zur Macht* as (at a guess, I'd have to check) *der Wille zur Liebkosen*. Under my eyes they covered half the distance and then half again, arrows chasing their target and re-enacting Zeno's Paradox in Venus Cloacina's temple of dripping cisterns. Half again. Nearly there. One more half should do it.

It's a Persian proverb, isn't it? Or Afghan or Pathan? *There's a boy on the other side of the river with a bottom like a peach, and alas I cannot swim.* I know I came across it in a John Masters book, and there were certainly some of those on Dad's shelves. Might he have shown me the passage? It hardly seems likely. Perhaps I sniffed it out by myself, though I'm easily caught red-handed and tend not to take that sort of chance. My experimentations with taboo literature were normally conducted under the ægis of Bourne End library. Safer that way.

But that's not the point. No one ever seems to have called across the waters to ask the boy whether *he* can swim. Perhaps he's in the mood for a little expedition. Why not? And that's the approach I've taken overall. Oi! Over here! I'm neither waving nor drowning, I'm just a beacon washed up on dry land but still sending out pulses of appeal. Is it an emergency? Not necessarily. Come within earshot and I'll tell you all about it. Then you can decide.

Abruptly the texture of the fabric in front of me changed. It lost tension. For a moment I failed to understand what this meant. It was as if I was witnessing some natural phenomenon, mudslide or sand-storm. Then I realised that the man in front of me had undone the top button of his jeans and was letting the waistband gape open so as to give access. He was no doubt anticipating delicious ambush from above, but unless my bones melted in the next couple of minutes he wasn't going to get it from me. Even if it did happen I wasn't guaran-teed to deliver what was wanted. I might have other priorities.

My fear about not being able to hear approaching footsteps was justified, though the outcome was not to be expected. Suddenly I could smell tobacco smoke, which could only mean that someone new had entered the premises. Every few weeks some kind soul, or a prissy one, would splash eau de cologne liberally round the premises, tem-porarily masking ambient odours and prompting strange murmurs of 'nothing beats the great smell of piss'. Sometimes the word 'piss' was replaced by the word 'Brut', but the intonation stayed the same.

If there was forbidden fruit being consumed in those premises it must be one that combines lusciousness with a back-note of the disgusting, the Malaysian durian perhaps, whose taste has been described very much in those terms, as reminiscent of the finest custard in the world, but eaten in a public lavatory.

But now it was the smell of smoke that dominated. I was just at the point of successfully laying my hands on the bum in front of me, or to be exact the backs of my hands on the backs of the thighs in front of me, just there at the top, at the bum frontier.

I froze, though considering the slowness of my approach the cessation of motion can hardly have registered on my partner in crime. Certainly my balance was too precarious, braced as I was by the crutch supporting my elbow, for me to take the risk of reversing my slow-motion pounce. Nor could I turn to assess the physical risk I was in.

The jig was up. How could the jig be other than up? And the voice behind me, when it came, was full of righteous indignation, but it wasn't directed at me. 'Aren't you going to help the little chap? Aren't you going to give him a hand?' Those were the words, well meant though gruffly spoken. The accent was local. 'Have you no goodness in you?' I could hardly explain that he was helping me already.

Apparently what the newcomer saw was an unfortunate making an appeal for help with the limited physical means at his disposal, while the party being appealed to turned his back – the turned back being a staple of stage melodrama, representing stark rejection all the way to the back of the theatre. He failed or refused to see that the posture of supplication was actually my bespoke version of a grope.

The man in front of me performed a strange manœuvre, one that was both calm and panicky – it was as if he gulped with his whole body while he tucked away an excitement that I had never laid eyes on, then gingerly pulled up the zip to hide it and fastened the top button. He turned round and made a very good imitation of being surprised to see me – not in itself surprising in its convincingness since he hadn't actually laid eyes on me, though of course he had known that I (let's just say 'someone') was there.

In fact he gave a bit of a lurch when he saw me, and I gave one too. There was nothing wrong with him, though he was, I don't know, perhaps a bit rabbity. Certainly his rear face had the greater power to charm. It was more that until I saw his face he stood in for every man in the entire world, while afterwards he was, for better or worse, just a single specimen of the breed.

'Sorry, mate,' he said, 'I was miles away.' Again this was accurate as well as misleading, and if you subscribe to the theory that successful lying depends on the incorporation of some element of truthfulness it was highly likely to compel belief in any fair-minded passer-by.

Awkwardly he hoisted me up to his level at the urinal. Is it possible to hold someone upright while also keeping them at arm's length? He was doing his best. By accident he pushed the crutch out of my grip and it fell to the floor with a clatter. He gave a sigh eloquent of my loss of status. Clearly I had made a big mistake by becoming visible. I wasn't exactly thrilled by his beauty either, but I had the good manners not to show it.

Meanwhile the newcomer betook himself to one of the cubicles and locked himself in, though it was clear from the sounds he made that he could just as easily have joined the two of us in our awkward posture at the urinals. With my skewed view of working-class life I was surprised that a scaffolder, as I imagined him to be, would urinate indoors at all when trees were so widely available. There's an off-colour joke, isn't there, in the title of Joyce's rather pallid book of poems, *Chamber Music*, hinting at the tinkle of a lady's urine landing in a chamber pot . . . really, Joyce should have taken the time to speak to Magnus Hirschfeld, not for help since none was needed but to enlarge the good *Doktor*'s understanding of what he or his translator persists in calling urolagnia. In the case of the young man in the cubicle at Four Lamps there was no question of chamber music but of a full orchestra. These were torrents of sounds symphonic in length. He was certainly setting an example of C-value to the nations.

Meanwhile I was doing my best to construct an image of this interloper from the tiny amount of information available. It seemed impossible that he had interpreted the tableau in front of him in such respectable terms. After all the trouble I had taken to infringe the norms and lay the backs of my hands on, or close to, a stranger's complicit nates. On some level I was disappointed rather than relieved. Did I have a poisonous wholesomeness about me capable of scrubbing clean even the most depraved endeavours? Did he not have eyes? Call me old-fashioned, but I don't see the point of exhibitionism without witnesses.

First possibility – not eyelessness as such but a limiting condition of some sort, whether amblyopia or optical trauma. The stranger might suffer from defective depth perception, so that he imagined a greater distance between the laboriously reaching hands and the buttocks in their feigned indifference than actually existed. Or rather that he registered the scene accurately but dismissed its troubling implications as being illusory, caused by a long-standing anomaly of vision.

Also on the cards: innocence of worldview, slowness to think the worst even when it is happening in slow motion right in front of you. Historically there has been a strong presence of Baptists in the villages around Cambridge, and sophistication of outlook is not something to be assumed *a priori*. Didn't the unembarrassed invocation of goodness in itself suggest a religious perspective? A conservative background and inculcated bodily shyness were perhaps subtly indicated by the choice of cubicle over urinal.

Smoking, though, the strong smell of cigarettes that had announced his presence – how did that fit in? Stern morals and a tobacco habit didn't harmonise.

Of course innocence is one of things that doesn't exist in a pure state. You must always expect a healthy dose of adulteration. In fact it may be one of those atomic elements whose existence is hypothesised without being observed, and of which only a few fleeting particles have ever been conjured from the back of the void, under the most stringent laboratory conditions.

By now the two of us who had once been partners in a victimless crime, or an attempt at one, were preoccupied not with each other but with the fellow who had disrupted our pleasures, and this was not shallow behaviour but supremely sensible. We had exhausted each other's mystery without succeeding in converting it into anything else. The newcomer had it in spades.

Neither of us, conjoined at the trough, had produced so much as a drop. Eventually my companion said, 'Nothing seems to be going on here. We might as well go home.' No response was required. He picked me up and carried me to the wheelchair, then reluctantly went back to retrieve the crutch, which he laid sternly across my lap, as if it was a sword on a crusader's tomb.

It's possible that I disliked being treated as an inconvenience, and reacted by insisting on being more of one. 'Do you mind doing up my flies?' I asked him. I hadn't made an actual decision to open them, but that's the way it is with elderly Velcro. It joins fabric by consensus, and holds things together out of habit rather than mechanical necessity. Even when Velcro is new (perhaps I should get out of the habit of according it a capital letter?) there's not much likelihood of every little hook marrying with every little loop, and over time more and more of them abstain from closure. A working majority becomes an unstable coalition. I dare say there were days when I went about with my groin ajar, even agape, without anyone liking to mention it. To do so would mean admitting to inspecting me at that base level.

Every now and then Paula would use a comb in an attempt to clear the little loops of the residue of clogging fluff and other debris, but I can't say it made much difference. I hinted that she might replace them altogether but she disclaimed any sewing skills. Mum still had the monopoly and the whip hand in that regard.

By having this rabbity stranger lift up the crutch from where he had put it and do up my flies I suppose I was insisting on the present lack of symmetry in dealings that had begun with such a delicious charged equilibrium. Afterwards, perhaps understandably, he pushed the chair back to the Mini at quite a lick. As we moved away from the premises I could hear the crash of the flush in the occupied cubicle, not much quieter than the lush splashing that had preceded it. I imagine he could hear it too.

Then when I was roughly installed in the driver's seat he said, without meeting my eyes, 'On second thoughts I think I'll hang around a bit longer. You never know, do you?' I supposed he had noticed that the interloper had not yet emerged from the building and took this for a good omen. And off he toddled, again at some speed. It would serve him right if he found he was dealing with a sermonising Baptist after all. Some pretty pastors want to make converts as devoutly as pretty policeman want convictions.

I was being bundled off from interfering in a possible encounter. That's right, go ahead! Don't mind me. Put out the voyeur the way people put out the cat at night.

Altogether it was a slightly frustrating half-hour for the versatile erotic epiphyte I felt myself to be. For an exhibitionist-cum-voyeur to be confronted with an observer who notices nothing, and shortly afterwards to be bilked of the chance to get an eyeful himself, was hard lines indeed. I began to feel that the patterns of play at Four Lamps were so complex they made Ultima look like noughts and crosses.

'Epiphyte' is more accurate as well as kinder than 'parasite', since the parasite feeds on another organism while an epiphyte merely takes advantage of a habitat – ivy is parasitic but orchids are epiphytes.

As I was moving off in the Mini I saw two men enter Four Lamps from opposite directions in a way I thought was a little ominous. None of my business, of course. My presence was not required at the rites of Venus Cloacina, so much had been made very clear by the celebrants. But I found myself reluctant to abandon them. I sounded the horn three times, not my usual rhythm though they might not know that. That was all I could be expected to do. The rest was up to them. There might come a time when they wished I had stayed, since I seemed to be an innocence grenade whose pin anyone could pull at a moment's notice, producing an instantaneous blast of amnesty and alibi that gave loiterers with intent an almost infinite excuse for louchely lingering.

Just the same I kept an eye out for an item in the *Cambridge Evening News* about men being assaulted in a public toilet off the roundabout at the bottom of Jesus Lane. The worst of it was, as Ken kept telling us, that the victims of such violence rarely reported it, having no liking for publicity if not positively ashamed and the police being unsympathetic if not downright hostile in attitude. Ken was in love with his opinion but that didn't make him wrong. If I had come across such a newspaper report I would have felt obliged to come forward myself to say . . . what, exactly? I had only had a glance of those I imagined to be potential assailants, and I could only describe those I imagined to be their victims in the most general terms. Jeans and desert boots – everyone had those. Even Dad had a pair of desert boots, though he regretted it the one time he wore them to church (there were still such things as standards) and always drew the line at jeans. The other man I had never set eyes on, and my photofit of a Baptist scaffolder with defective depth perception might seem less than persuasive to the police.

It was only some time after the event that a simpler explanation for the interloper's inability to see what was in front of him occurred to me. My unusually upright position made it impossible to see what was going on. I was used to having my view obstructed on a daily basis, but now the built-up shoe was on the other foot. In my little way I too could block the light.

All told there was satisfaction in my recollection of the scene, as well as frustration and a little niggling worry about my (so to speak) companions, impertinent since after all they had abandoned me and had no great claim on my loyalty. I had certainly played my part in the drama at Four Lamps, even if it had only been in the overture, more than rising to the occasion. I don't mind admitting that the little foothill of foreplay that had been involved was a Himalaya to me. There was no obvious next move. I had done all I could in that line. If I had some ritual presence at this Saturnalia then it was after the fashion of the mayor declaring a garden fête open. The difficulty was that although, given time, I could get within snipping distance of the ribbon I couldn't lift the ceremonial scissors, let alone ply them adequately.

The next time I consulted Magnus Hirschfeld's fat volume of sexual anomalies and perversions, I was disappointed to find that the dorsal *frotteurs* of Paris were not listed among the miscellaneous paraphiliacs, but the book doesn't claim to be exhaustive, and despite the welcome prominence given to the crystal fetishist I admired so much its focus is possibly a little parochial, rather too closely bound to the German-speaking peoples.

I can't remember exactly when the original stall doors at Four Lamps were replaced by ones that didn't go all the way down to the floor. I couldn't tell you the month or even the year. There was general consternation at this development, in which I did my best to join. I would be exaggerating if I said that a queue formed outside the Mini, with regulars wanting someone to talk them through their dismay, but not by much. A shock wave ran through the clientèle of Four Lamps, though clientèle doesn't seem quite the right word since we were essentially clients of each other, in an exchange economy that involved no recourse to money as such. In the mobile confession booth that the Mini had become I heard complaints about the Big Brother society, about the restriction of our outlaw freedom, and I dutifully deplored the anti-social or anti-subcultural action that had been taken, even agreeing that this was the end of an era not to mention the shape of things to come, while also thinking that my prospects of fun hadn't in fact been dented. If anything the odds of having a good time on those premises had shifted even more outrageously in my favour.

I was already in a privileged minority, able to spend any amount of time in a public lavatory without suspicion of impurity. One taboo serves so beautifully to mask another. Now it was as if I had been given a master key. A law-enforcing eye glancing along the cubicles would not be shocked to see four ankles under the newly abbreviated door, as long as two of them were mine. Such an eye might even register concern if I didn't have company, worried that I might not be able to manage on my own.

If I had arrived in the wheelchair then I would find a cubicle with good sight lines and base myself there, with the door open and . . . well, I won't say I would conduct interviews to see who might be interested in joining me there, but I certainly had the sensation, unusual for me, that market forces were conspiring to my advantage. If the atmosphere of a gents' toilet with a louche reputation can sometimes resemble a pressure cooker of sexual tension then I was uniquely well placed to offer assistance in the letting-off of steam. If someone wanted to join me in privacy he had only to help me out of the wheelchair.

Altogether it was a lovely little heyday of iniquity, with just enough risk to add spice to the dish, not enough to burn the tongue. The cubicles were reasonably generous in their proportions, testament to a period that invested in the public realm without self-righteous penny-pinching. My cloak of invisibility has a certain amount of give to it, but isn't infinitely extensible. Physical disability easily provided indemnity for two. Indemnity for three, though I tried it once or twice, was pushing our collective luck. It had the disadvantage of restricting the movements of my able-bodied companions, those spoiled creatures, in a way they found intolerably frustrating. The element of control, which I admit I found mildly intoxicating, could evaporate very suddenly if they decided, after profiting from the amenity I had provided, to carry on their explorations elsewhere. I can't say I enjoyed it when the moment of pleasure, which sounds like a scientific term and certainly should be one, accelerated away from me.

Reluctantly I had to impose a quota on visitors – one at a time, please, and form an orderly queue. But within its limits the system worked remarkably smoothly. If there's a more effective way of saying DO NOT DISTURB than leaving a wheelchair parked outside a lavatory door I haven't discovered it.

In a way my various needs were being separately met in this period, so that I reached a sort of atomised equilibrium. There was the social and voyeuristic nourishment provided by Four Lamps, sometimes spilling over into physical release, and there was the comprehensive analysis of patriarchal oppression that I could look forward to when CHAPs (the Cambridge Homosexual Activism Project) resumed its meetings. At CHAPs I could hope to be given a warmer welcome now that I was no longer a student. As an unemployed person I had slid down the social scale and could hope to boost the group's underclass representation. CHAPs was always keen to stress, rightly or wrongly, that it wasn't a university organisation, though it looked so much like one.

Then too there was the strange duelling dialogue with MarkO, our affinity palpable though not physically expressed, and renewed almost on a daily basis, with mid-morning accounts of his early mornings. When MarkO started his solo career as a milkman, his own man, master of the round, he tried to dawdle a bit, to establish his own tempo. But the training went too deep. It was as if Ron had left little pockets of adrenaline on stairwells, at street corners, and MarkO found himself picking up the pace despite himself, his heart thudding. It was all he could do to stroll round the Botanic Garden for a few leisurely paces, or spend a moment or two inhaling the honeysuckle at Highsett. The fragrance was so strong that it seemed to be puffed out of giant aerosols rather than mere plants, as if piped perfume was being diffused for the joy of the nose, puffing out of tiny tweeters tucked into the decorative trumpets of the shrub. But then the drive to finish the round in a hurry would return irresistibly. The cereal bowls of Highsett would not be left dry a second time while he was responsible for their milk supply.

MarkO now realised that there had been advantages to Ron's edge of aggressiveness. Customers were highly likely to pay up. MarkO could aspire to competence in the delivery aspect of the job, but the implied-bailiff part would always be beyond him. With payment expected at the end of the week, milk was being sold in effect on credit, and it seemed to be up to the individual roundsman when to call in the debt without further postponement. It was strongly implied, though not spelled out, that he would be personally responsible for any defaulters. He was told that student households needed watching, since they tended to build up substantial arrears and then decamp without paying – but the idea of adding a third component to the job, playing private detective and anticipating when a particular nest of undergraduates was about to do a flit, so as to nip the bad debt in the bud, wasn't something he could imagine attempting. He had enough on his plate.

Some households had a regular order, so that each week's bill was the same. Others had a milk-bottle holder with a dial and a pointer, so that they could indicate their needs day by day, from one bottle all the way up to six. They were entitled to be changeable, but MarkO was inexperienced and lacked the professional reflex to make a record of these variations. Ron was in complete control of the arithmetical element of the round, and would enter the quantities into his logbook when he moved the float to the next sacred site. In fact, MarkO now realised, this eerie piece of efficiency, his ability to fill in the logbook at the same moment that he stood on the accelerator and started to move off, made a major contribution to the dazzling speed of Ron's round when the man himself was in charge.

MarkO couldn't hope to match that. He tried taking the logbook with him, so as to make entries as he went along, and he tried to improve his memory skills, muttering 'four at Number 7, three at Number 8' to himself, but nothing solved the problem. Even when he was confident that he had got his sums right the householder might differ, having forgotten perhaps an extra pint or the surplus that had required that the pointer be set at 'No Milk Today'. There were doorstep disagreements, which could turn surprisingly nasty. With no higher authority to consult, no court of dairy appeals, it came down to who was able to make the case most forcefully. Under stress MarkO could feel his accent reverting to Cumberland, making him feel even more out of his element and allowing stroppy customers to make out that they couldn't understand what was being said. There were doors that MarkO could hardly bring himself to knock on, come Saturday morning.

If it was his word against theirs, it was also their time against his. On a Saturday the residents of Cambridge might enjoy a stand-off on the threshold and wouldn't mind drawing it out, but MarkO had other places to go, other accounts to settle. He had to keep an eye on the clock, and sooner or later he would have to cut his losses. One Saturday a householder voiced the thought that others had held back from articulating: 'I'll settle up with Ron when he gets back, if it's all the same to you, sonny. He'll know what's right.' It hadn't previously been apparent that being a milkman was a calling for which much testosterone was required, but here was proof of it, in this summer-morning emasculation. He was cast as a deputy quaking in his boots while the sheriff was away on important business, in Benidorm or Dodge, Lanzarote or Tombstone, wherever it was Ron had taken Mrs Ron and any little Ron-sprogs. 'If it's all the same to you, sonny?' He was being invited to collude in the removal of his testicles.

Another time-related question was an entirely theoretical one. How much time would he be able to afford for some deputy-milkman leg-over with Brenda at Number 16, Tenison Road, if the occasion presented itself? He didn't want to jeopardise the timely completion of his round. MarkO could never hope to match Ron's 8.30 finish, but he was now reliably back in the depot at 10 o'clock, sometimes even 9.30, and could justifiably claim that he had earned a little slack in the schedule. Not that he was seriously interested in the legendary

Brenda, being (as he put it) a happily unmarried man. There wasn't even the faintest possibility.

Curiosity is another drive altogether. It took MarkO quite a while to realise that Ron's suggestive remarks about Brenda were part of some hoary old hoax, one that must have gone back many years. Standing outside Number 16, Tenison Road on several consecutive Saturdays – collection day – he made an effort to look over the shoulder of a scrawny old boy in winceyette pyjamas counting out his change, in search of a sultry temptress flaunting herself in a black negligée before her kitchen cabinets.

Perhaps it was his sense of being a defective stand-in, outgunned on the Saturday doorsteps of Cambridge, that made him drive his float a little recklessly. In the same way, a young cowpoke who had emptied his six-gun at the row of cans ritually placed on a fence without hitting even one of them might try to cut a better figure by making a particularly athletic leap onto his horse. The floats in use by the Co-Op Dairy at this time were made by a firm called Morrison. Their top speed was very modest, not much over fifteen miles an hour, but they could certainly move off at a good lick, and acceleration up to cruising speed was pretty nippy. MarkO had greatly admired Ron's pose at the wheel of the milk float, standing up, with his logbook in one hand and a pencil held between his teeth, but should perhaps have realised by this time that Ron was inimitable. Since the floats had a windscreen and a roof but were open at the sides, Ron could just jump on board and he was off.

A carnival of torques and stresses

The controls were basic: no gear lever of course, and no clutch, just a switch for forward and reverse and an accelerator. Braking was done by the other pedal though there was also a handbrake. One day MarkO was parked at the top of Station Road and pointing towards the station. He had just delivered to the Station Hotel on the other side of the road, and now climbed on board without sitting down. He aimed the float at the mini-roundabout in front of the station and moved off. In the standing position his pressure on the accelerator was unduly heavy, not fully under control. The pencil was in his mouth but not quite *à la* Ron, who would hold it sideways, like a dog in a cartoon with a bone. MarkO held the pencil as if he was smoking a cigarillo, and was clearly feeling his way into Ron's skin.

He wasn't quite there yet, and might never be. Relatively late in the manœuvre he realised that he was expecting quite a lot of coöperation on the part of the laws of physics, in seeking to accomplish a tight 360-degree turn at considerable speed. The forces at play threw him briefly off balance, which increased the pressure of his foot on the accelerator. If he'd been sitting down it would have been easy to take his foot off one pedal and apply it to the other, but he wasn't. As he entered the vortex of instability he had created, factors more often associated with sailing seemed to come into play – pitch, roll, even yaw. Time seemed to slow down and then stop inside the mælstrøm of forces. He was in the heart of the storm, and the float was doomed, unless . . . There was one faint hope. The sheer weight of its batteries gave the vehicle a low centre of gravity. He prayed this would be enough to counteract the disorder he had summoned up and enable them, the float and he, not a compound being like Ron-and-float but two tragically separable units, to escape overturning.

It was enough, though not by much, and there was a moment of uncertainty, of rippling cosmic doubt, before the float emerged from the turn. Time consented to return to something more like its accustomed pace, with the result that a crate that had been balancing on one edge toppled slowly off the back of the float then dashed itself with full force against the road surface. If Ron had been in charge the float wouldn't have been exposed to such a carnival of torques and stresses in the first place, but even if it had the crates would have been spared damage of this sort. Ron was meticulous in his stacking, while MarkO tended to be slapdash, not making sure that they nested properly. He had also bitten off the end of the pencil and cut his gum on a splinter from it.

Naturally enough the fallen crate had been one of the uppermost ones, and consequently loaded largely with empties. MarkO stopped the float and went to inspect the damage. He gathered up as much broken glass as he could without lacerating his hands, and kicked most of the rest into the gutter. Then he set off again down Station Road at a very moderate rate, trying to put together an expression of lofty indifference sufficient to arm him against the stares of commuters heading for their early trains.

The incident was still fresh in his mind when he called on me after work that day. He worried about the consequences. Complaints about his driving would have had to move pretty fast to reach the depot before he did, but the next day was a different matter. He would get a bollocking. It was a racing certainty.

I thought he was being paranoid, and though it was hard to get through a day of the 1970s without accusations of paranoia flying about I was confident I could convince him he needn't worry. It seemed unlikely that there had been many witnesses to the kerfuffle on the mini-roundabout. Suppose there were three. Safe to assume that two of them couldn't care less – was it really likely that the third would have the number of the depot on Sleaford Street handy or else be willing to go to the trouble of looking it up?

I sensed that this statistical approach to reassurance was falling short of its objective and tried another tack. Surely there were other drivers 'in the frame'? The moment I had said this I realised that Station Road was essentially a cul-de-sac, not useful for reaching other destinations. Finally I hit on a winning argument. Wasn't it safer, in terms of potential repercussions, to smash a whole milk crate on largely non-residential Station Road than a single bottle on a doorstep at Highsett? MarkO grudgingly agreed. Even so he was still residually tense, and he played Herr Bert's Brandenburgs several times over, skipping the slow movements so as to have a strong pulse to beat time to. In fact he always preferred his Bach up-tempo, in a way that made me wonder how deep his attachment to 'baroque music' really was. He liked the chugging-along aspect of Bach, sewing-machine music as he called it, better than the slower-moving parts, where it seemed more as if the tune was being embroidered freehand.

In an early conversation MarkO had talked about expanding his collection of baroque music, and there was one name he kept bringing up. He was going to be laying his hands on a hard-to-obtain recording of music by a composer I had to admit I'd never heard of, ordering it from Miller's on King Street. If the disc was so very obscure then Miller's might well have difficulty obtaining it for him, but as the weeks passed and it continued not to arrive I began to wonder if he'd ever ordered it. More likely it was the ribald connotations of the name that gave him pleasure, since the composer in question was Samuel Scheidt, 1587–1654. He was really looking forward to listening to some Scheidt. As far as he was concerned, it could be any old Scheidt. Any old Scheidt would do.

Sooner or later the associations of the name must declare themselves to anyone, but certainly MarkO seemed more suited to the belly laugh of the pub drinker than the thin smile of the purist. In other words MarkO was showing something of his form as a taker of the piss. I was wonderfully slow to catch on to the joke, and honoured its spirit by never laughing or showing by any other sign that I'd caught on.

There were no repercussions from the Great Milk-Float Disaster of 1973. I doubt if he even told Bernardette what had happened. Perhaps I had a little marginal status as his confessor. He always told me about his day, but he could hardly ask about mine, since the major event of my day was hearing about his. I don't know whether he rehashed those mainly uneventful shifts with Bernardette, revisiting the splendours and miseries of his working life, or whether he pinned his ears back to listen to hers instead, having reached some sort of equilibrium by talking to me.

The last thing I expected was that Bernardette would come to consult me without MarkO, as she did one Saturday afternoon. She came alone for two good reasons: because she had a question for me that was (as she judged) outside MarkO's competence, and because he was asleep.

I hoped she wasn't going to tell me any secrets. People confide in me more often than you might think, and it makes me wonder what makes them imagine I can be trusted. No offence, but I'd rather find out the secrets you don't want me to know than be given a guided tour of trifling intimacies. They can't be much cop as secrets, can they? Not if you don't mind me being in on them.

Voicing the implied solidus

I needn't have worried, not this time. She had brought something to show me, a piece of card that she had removed from its place in the

window display at Bacon's. Normally it sat next to the bowl containing a sample of the Calverley Mixture of pipe tobacco. It was from a
poem of Calverley's to tobacco – called in fact 'To Tobacco'. The question she needed to ask me was, 'Is this really poetry?'

My academic history was being called into play, my English degree
and everything that had led up to it. I was in a position to set her mind
at rest. 'Yes,' I said. 'It's certainly poetry. Very bad poetry indeed.'

The lines on the card went:

> *Sweet when the morn is gray,*
> *Sweet when they've cleared away*
> *Lunch; and at close of day*
> *Possibly sweetest . . .*

Bernardette wanted to know if this was likely to make people buy
the Calverley Mixture. I told her I thought the odds were a thousand
to one against. 'Couldn't we do better?' she wanted to know. 'Me and
MarkO . . . and you with your brain.'

Me with my brain, working to galvanise a team. The offer was
irresistible. By the end of Sunday the three of us had hammered
out something we were satisfied with. It had taken much hysterical
laughter and a joint or two to come up with it. When herbal tobacco
is not available I have learned to extract cannabinoids directly from
the air, a technique distinct from the well-known phenomenon of
'contact high', not in itself a thing to be despised.

There were also chocolate bars consumed. MarkO and Bernardette
clashed fiercely about the relative ability of Mars and Aztec bars to
satisfy marijuana-induced esurience, a condition informally known
as 'the munchies'. MarkO insisted that the Aztec bar had been
developed by Cadbury's not just to cut into the market share of the
all-conquering Mars bar but specifically to meet the late-night needs
of our generation. Confusingly there was a confection actually going
by the name of Munchies, widely available but powerless against the
condition whose name they shared.

We started with

> *Sweet when the day lacks point . . .*

Already I felt we were improving on the original. We were showing the author of *Fly Leaves* and *Literary Remains* a clean pair of heels. To sharpen the satire I thought our second line should mimic the awkward, broken-backed way the sense in Calverley's poem carried over the line break. What I actually said was, 'We should reproduce that shoddy enjambment,' a remark not actively intended as comic, though we had reached a stage of collective giddiness where giggles were self-sustaining. In an atmosphere saturated with mischief and cannabinoids any flint will set the spark.

I suggested we go on with

Sweet when fierce rains anoint

'Anoint what?' asked MarkO.

'You have to wait and see – that's the whole idea. Formally the line comes to an end but the meaning carries on.' He still looked baffled so I said, 'The street. *Fierce rains anoint / the street!*' There being no agreed way of voicing the implied solidus, I left a strangulated pause between the words on either side of it. Even with so much explanation and acting-out MarkO still looked uncertain, though Bernardette seemed to have caught on.

It was in our third line that we set our countercultural seal on the subversion of Calverley's insipid little ode.

. . . fierce rains anoint
The streets; in a big fat joint

Then of course our travesty rejoined the original in the simpering flow of

Possibly sweetest . . .

For parody to be effective the seams should be inconspicuous.

Credit where credit is due, and I don't mean to share it unduly, I made the greatest contribution to our spoof poem. I shaped the tone. It's as close as I came in this period to showing off the mental prowess born of advanced study. More importantly, I was exercising one of the prerogatives traditionally reserved for Cambridge graduates in their subsequent careers – I was steering a committee, give or take. I hope I managed to thank my helpers convincingly for the trifling amount of work they had put in.

And I still had work to do. The hardest part of the whole spoof was trying to match the handwriting on the card so that our mocked-up card didn't immediately announce its status as a fake. Logically either MarkO or Bernardette would have been better placed to execute the lettering, but their efforts at penmanship were very inconsistent. I ended up doing it, for the slightly perverse reason that writing was always so laborious for me that it took relatively little extra effort to copy someone else's. Only at this stage of the proceedings did it occur to me that Calverley's poem might have been written with tongue in cheek all along. Victorian cheeks were so plumped out as a matter of course behind the Dundreary whiskers that the lurking pressure of a tongue is not an easy thing to detect.

Bernardette took the forged card with her when she went to work on Monday morning and slipped it into the window display next to the little bowl of the Calverley Mixture. MarkO and I waited a day or two and then made a special trip in the Mini to marvel at it, convinced that there would be assembled crowds wheezing with laughter, helplessly convulsed outside the windows of Bacon's. There was nobody there, and though the day was drizzly we thought this strange. We made a great show of pointing at our hoax quatrain and laughing very loudly, in a way that was unpleasantly familiar, to me if not to the others. Forced jollity is a regular feature of university towns, manifested in the grim rictus of Rag Week. Citizens acquired the knack of ignoring any number of hospital beds pushed or occupied by stubbled nurses.

Although the three of us got some odd looks ourselves none of them strayed beyond us towards the tobacconist's window display, however extravagantly MarkO and Bernardette pointed and guffawed. Wild laughter from a wheelchair was not something that was bargained for, socially, and people made more than their usual detour. I hadn't noticed before our visit that Calverley's poem was reproduced in full on a bronze plaque outside Bacon's. This would certainly enable passers-by to compare the texts and marvel at our cleverness, but I have to admit to feeling a little let down, as if we'd taken aim at a very broad target.

I told MarkO very firmly, 'We have flung our signal to the furthest edges of the cosmos, there where the surf of stars grows thin. We have lodged it in the Akashic Records. It has been countersigned and is in triplicate. We have done our bit – the rest is up to Maya.' We went home deflated, just the same, and Bernardette later confirmed an absolute absence of impact. Sales of the Calverley Mixture remained stable, and minimal. Still, we told each other, we'd had fun and that was the main thing. For all I know, our lampoon was still in the window, wagging its youthful finger at pomposity and fustiness, when Bacon's closed its doors and all those gentlemen's-club fitments were finally cleared out.

MarkO and Bernardette seemed to accept me without needing to think about it, not exactly uninterested but certainly incurious, and this seemed healthy enough. Often at weekends when Bernardette was in the chair and I was leaning against MarkO I could detect an erection, but I didn't make too much of that. An erection needn't be a personal thing. A fair number of the erections I've taken advantage of in my time have had someone else's name on them, if there was a name on them at all. In young men an erection means as little – or I suppose as much – as a dog wagging its tail. Besides, Bernardette was in his field of vision on those days. I was naïve in those days, green for my years, and assumed that young lovers would be in a constant state of arousal.

I can smell the sauerkraut

To go with the increase in physical contact when Bernardette was around there was a certain amount of raillery about the antics of homosexuals. I assessed its tone as amused and dismissive but not hateful. MarkO's position about 'queers', 'poofters' or 'chutney ferrets' – an esoteric phrase he had to explain to me, and even then I had difficulty understanding it – was, roughly, *Let them get on with it. Good luck to them, I say*. Even the word 'poofter' had a warm association on his lips, with no more poison to it than, say, 'duffer' or 'codger'. I noticed, though, that when Bernardette left the room to fetch a fresh magazine or to use the bathroom in their flat upstairs – my facilities offered hardly any physical and absolutely no acoustic privacy – MarkO tended to retreat from physical contact. He might disengage from me on the bed and change the record on the Hacker for no real reason, though always saluting the high quality of its sound reproduction. 'That's a great system you have here,' he would say. 'I can't get over it. Everything sounds very real, very 3D.' He would tap on the single auxiliary speaker and call into it. 'Come out, Herr Bert, I know you're in there.' He sniffed the air. 'I can smell the sauerkraut.'

Sometimes the three of us went on little outings. Bernardette even took her turn at pushing the wheelchair, though when she did I noticed that she tended to follow directly in MarkO's wake. It was as if she wanted me to pay the proper attention to his bum, and I was happy to play along. In fact MarkO's buttocks went in for a certain amount of seductive sideways action on their own account. I scrutinised the centre seam of his jeans, which as it seemed to me moved a considerable distance to either side of the median line. That seam travelled from left to right to some purpose, it shifted to the side and back again in front of my eyes with an effect in mind. It might have been the hypnotist's watch being swung in front of the eyes of the subject to be 'fluenced, but there was no prospect of making me feel s-l-e-e-p-y. I was wide awake.

When the rôles were reversed, with him pushing and her in my line of sight, there was rather less displacement of weight from side to side. Bernardette would no more have swung her hips than batted her eyelids. She left cheap haunch theatrics of that sort to her less fortunate sisters.

I didn't understand how our threesome worked, or even if it worked at all, having nothing to compare it with. I had been involved in a complex friendship with a pair of twins in my schooldays, but that mildly wounding experience offered no guidance now.

We'd have been a stranger threesome if they hadn't been a strange couple in their own right. Passers-by seemed to be mesmerised by the height and beauty differential between MarkO and Bernardette, and the mobility differential between the pair of them and me was relegated to a lesser importance for once. The occupant of the wheelchair got a lot less attention than the occupant of a pram would have, if they had happened to be pushing one of those. Strangers would have been craning down under the hood to see how the high-stakes genetic gamble had worked out in the end.

MarkO's stories about life as a milkman were somehow fascinating and boring at the same time. Get that mixture right, pipe it into every old folks' home in the country and you'd soon clear those places out. The poor old dears in the day room would waste away, alternately too absorbed to eat what was in front of them and too catatonic to feel the pangs. The idea gave me a fair bit of heartless satisfaction, though I knew that in the long term I myself was a strong candidate for institutional living and could be faced with it at short notice. I need await no additional infirmity to qualify. I qualified already under every heading but consent. Which is why it was so important, quite apart from the question of social amenity, to bed myself down in Mayflower House, to make a convincing show of belonging, here where I had been so arbitrarily plonked. The day room was a permanent possibility, and every other possibility must be explored in full to make sure it didn't come to that.

You'd have burned a hole in my forehead

Despite everything I felt a degree of mental convergence with MarkO, and he seemed to feel the same. It's possible that my telepathic powers had flowered since the summer. Certainly I had more success controlling daddy-long-legs in their brief September season than I ever did with spiders or flies, who seemed very stuck in their pseudo-autonomous ways. Perhaps it was because the daddy-long-legs is an imago with only a few days to live, impelled towards the dismal business of reproduction, eating little if anything. If I got on the right wavelength I could play imperious matchmaker, breaking up couples and sending the individuals out in search of new partners or better yet a period of celibate introspection before the next incarnation. Creatures that are free of attachments in their last moments are much more likely to escape the cycle altogether.

MarkO and I decided to put our psychic bond to the test, with a little exercise of a rather unmethodical sort. To exclude the possibility of us both responding to the same external signal we broke the mechanism into its components and set out to test simple transmission in the first instance without physical separation. I would send MarkO an image, after drawing it on a piece of paper. Who knows the frequency of the relevant vibrations and their ability to penetrate walls? Best to start without obstacles. It seemed to make sense, too, not to set arbitrary time limits. We would wait for the completion of the circuit however long it took.

It took no time at all. MarkO had hardly drawn a few lines on the paper before he threw it down and stalked out of the room. The paper had fallen in an awkward position, and I wasn't immediately able to retrieve it. I had to wait until he had returned, still highly aggrieved and indignant, before I could find out what all the fuss was about. The shape on his paper, as it turned out, was very similar to the shape on mine, and you might have thought he would have been pleased by the success of our experiment. Not so. He'd gone upstairs to fetch something that he kept there and now he put it on the table, not throwing it but keeping hold of one edge and then snapping it angrily down, in a way that testified to great resentment. 'There you are, John,' he said bitterly. 'Paid in full.'

The shape on his piece of paper was a regular heptagon, and what he had brought from upstairs was a fifty-pence coin, something that I hadn't remembered him borrowing in the first place. Admittedly amnesia of this sort is highly structured. There's a valve in place impeding the symmetrical flow of consciousness, so that we reliably forget what we owe but not what is due to us. So yes, there may have been a residual awareness of debt tucked away in a distant lobe of my brain, but I was innocent of any sort of personal reckoning. I had dispatched no astral bailiff, even if MarkO was absolutely convinced that I had. 'If you'd sent that picture any more strongly, John,' he said, very deliberately, 'you'd have burned . . . *a hole* . . . in my forehead. It would have *blistered*.'

In fact he hadn't looked properly at the design I had drawn, though undoubtedly it fell into the same category as his, both being equilaterally curved polygons – guilty conscience had done the rest. What I had drawn wasn't a fifty-pence piece at all but a sketch of something I knew about only from him: the three-sided rotor that was at the heart of the Wankel engine, a development he touted as representing the future of car design. His interest in the engineering innovation must have been genuine for him to pass up the name's potential for immature jokes. Poor Samuel Scheidt had not been so lucky, though for all I know he wrote a concerto for every day of the year.

Yes, the differences between rounded triangle and a rounded heptagon are obvious. They leap to the eye. The crucial characteristic they share is less obvious but very striking. Each has been engineered to have a constant width wherever bisected, the triangular rotor to play its part in Herr Wankel's combustion engine, a 'variable-volume progressing-cavity system' (as I discover), the heptagonal coin to be processed smoothly by vending machines. The eye considers a fifty-pence piece to be different in kind from a circular coin, but if constancy of diameter is the only criterion they must be considered identical. The non-human sensing apparatus in vending machines measured its diameter as a constant 30mm and let it through. Pass, friend! Your papers are in order. You may not conform to the norm but you're all right by us.

So our experiment was anything but a failure, even if we had interpreted it differently, and we would need to reconsider the test conditions when we tried again. Being in a room together made the communication if anything too intense, so we decided that I would project an image to MarkO at an agreed time of the morning, while he was doing his milk round. Again, wavelength was an imponderable. If I sent the signal at 6.30, for instance, he should keep his mind open and not be tempted to draw an image until he was confident he had received one. Better a seeming negative than a false positive, when it comes to matters of science.

I sent the signal on the day agreed, wondering where on his route MarkO would be at that point. Sometimes I would have waking dreams, as one 'reality' alternated with another in the early morning, in which I helped him on his round, not doing the heavy lifting, even in dreams, but helping him keep track of orders and sums due. I had sugar lumps with me to keep the horse happy – the horse that had unaccountably replaced the electric motor of MarkO's Morrison milk float.

At first I drew a square on my piece of paper, but then realised it was too simple a shape – I needed to think again, or add some complication without entirely abandoning clarity of outline. A rectangle would be a bad idea, since he might think I was pressing him for folding money. Instead I drew a notch on the upper and lower edge of my square, halfway along, before I transmitted it.

Ideally experiments should take place under controlled and repro-
ducible conditions, but the sort of improvised fieldwork I was doing
with MarkO ruled out any real sophistication of method. On the
morning of our test transmission he came into my flat very agitated and lay on the bed with the pillow over his head. He took a
certain amount of coaxing out. What had happened? I wanted to
reassure him that the experiment wasn't really all that important. If
he hadn't received my signal it wasn't the end of the world. But it
wasn't that. He'd crashed the float again, and this time there were
witnesses.

My first thought was that my broadcast had been too powerful –
he'd had to swerve to avoid a notched square blasted towards him
with fantastic intensity. In fact the accident happened after the time
set for the experiment, just at the end of his day's work, when he was
back at the depot finishing up and probably showing off just a little
about the way driving the float had become second nature to him. He
could do it in his sleep.

The milkmen were supposed to leave their floats connected to the
charging station, but before that they needed to offload the empties.
MarkO was a little late getting back, and there was already a large
tanker parked in the loading bay. Space was tight. MarkO had to
pull in front of the tanker and then reverse right up to it. By now he
was used to the controls and was able to make the best possible use
of the limited space by leaving the vehicles virtually nudging. Then
he offloaded his empties, jumped back in the cab and stamped on the
accelerator, reversing rapidly into the tanker so that he smashed the
brake light and the rear side light of the float. He had forgotten to
switch the controls back to forward after reversing. Broken glass and
unsuppressed guffaws from his workmates – hard to say which was
more upsetting to his self-esteem as a milkman. It didn't help that
the foreman came over to him just then, shaking his head, to say that
he was being assigned to a new route the next week. It didn't mean
anything, or it meant only that Ron was back from the Isle of Wight,
but it still felt like exile. He would be delivering dairy supplies but
to Cherry Hinton, not Alaska – yet after getting so happily bedded
in with his route he felt the change not just as demotion but almost
as bereavement.

With all this distress so recent I hardly wanted to pester MarkO about the results of our little adventure in ESP, but then as if it took all his remaining energy he pulled a piece of paper out of the pocket of his denim jacket and passed it across to me. Here was the transmitted eidolon, the image developed on the plate of a shared awareness. His manner was reminiscent of a wounded soldier bringing news of a battle, whether triumphant or disastrous. I could feel him trying to formulate a joke before real exhaustion swallowed up the exhaustion he was faking. He closed his eyes.

The shape on the paper was a stylised book, or (to describe it a little differently) two parallelograms joined at one edge. Whatever MarkO thought he was drawing, it did bear a resemblance to my figure of a square with notches on the upper and lower edge, but slightly refracted, like a package that has been squashed a little in the post. This was all rather exciting, though I regretted sending so simple a form, and it did occur to me that anyone trying to guess the contents of my head at any particular time would come up with something book-shaped fairly soon.

In a repetition of our first encounter MarkO had fallen asleep, and although I was eager for details I could understand that he needed to recover from a difficult day. I watched over him without too much impatience, and didn't prickle him with mental images to bring him back to awareness. He'd fallen asleep without taking his shoes off, something that I'd been training him out of little by little.

As if he was determined to remind me of that first encounter he stretched with caricatural languor when he woke, rehearsing a slow thrust from the pelvis. Perhaps the Kundalini serpent that snoozes curled up in the coccyx was rehearsing its ecstatic ascent, ready to punch through the third eye at the top of the brain and be free, or perhaps it was more that he was an inveterate tease who couldn't help himself. When he'd made us coffee I asked when exactly he'd received the transmission. 'Six-thirty on the dot, John,' he said with quiet pride. 'It came swooping down on me like a carrier pigeon. Practically dive-bombed me.'

Six-thirty. Oh dear. I'd consciously held back for an extra quarter of an hour before I sent the signal, to avoid contamination of our results by expectation – but who's to say that it's the conscious mind

309

doing the sending? The shape was already in my head, which was I suppose a technical error in the procedure. Six-thirty had been the agreed time, and obviously a basal pulse of the limbic brain had sent the message anyway. The decision to delay the experiment had been irrelevant. I might as well have tried to retrieve a letter after it had been posted, already on its way and irrevocable.

To cheer MarkO up I suggested that we go for a drive and take a look at his new round. Cherry Hinton was more or less a mystery to me, so I drove to the very end of Mill Road and turned right onto Perne Road and carried on until I got to the Cherry Hinton Road, where I turned left and trundled along until I got to Cherry Hinton High Street. The journey seemed to last forever and I wasn't really sure whether I was going in the right direction or not. We didn't reach the delivery area for more than half an hour. There was virtually no traffic in Cherry Hinton in the middle of the day, and MarkO started to think there would be advantages to working outside the city centre after all. He didn't have the details of his route, but there were any number of modern housing estates, quite tightly packed, so that his stops were likely to be conveniently clustered, a real advantage since he hadn't picked up much of Ron's expertise as a geomancer, aficion-ado of the dairy ley lines.

Adding Braille italics to the font of talk

We'd already been thinking of having a pint (half-pint in my case) before we saw The Robin Hood and Little John, but the name on the sign told us we'd found the right place. It turned out that the pub was divided into two areas, with the main bar being the 'Robin Hood' and the snug being the 'Little John', and once again our choice was made for us. We would be snug in the snug, snug as bugs in rugs, snugger than buggers in rugger shorts.

My presence in a bar can be a sort of silent scandal, souring the beer and rousing the cheese mites to storm the ramparts of pickle in the cheddar sandwiches. Perhaps it's normal for a stunned little hush to fall when a stranger enters a pub, though that's not how it hap-pens on *Coronation Street*, unless he's wearing a top hat. There were a couple of old boys in the corner playing cribbage, and they certainly did their fair share of gawping. I couldn't swear it was cribbage. If there's another card game that's scored by poking matchsticks into a perforated wooden block then it could be that.

When MarkO had fetched the drinks he settled me in a position where I was snuggling against him. I managed to slide a hand under the waistband of his trousers. Where there's life there's grope. Groping is an art, like everything else. I do it exceptionally well.

(I can't say I ever fully joined the Plath cult, an influential academic faction in my undergraduate years, but there's no denying that the lady could turn a phrase.)

The equipment at my disposal isn't very sophisticated – a hand with restricted movement – but then nor is my target. Male sensuality, especially in the young, isn't a grand piano – it's more like an Æolian harp, stirred by the slightest breeze, twanging away like nobody's business. I've learned from experience that it pays not to rush things. Once my hand is in the right approximate area, I do nothing until its presence has more or less been forgotten, forgotten by the conscious mind if not the nervous system. I wait a minute then lean inward a bit, so that by the law of levers my arm gains a little discreet movement. Then it's just a question of applying the faintest pressure during conversation, starting by using touch to underline significant words in what I'm saying. Adding Braille italics to the font of talk. Shaping a response.

Not much *vairagya* going on there, *vairagya* being the discouraging of the mind from running in sensual grooves. It's not something I've ever been very good at. With the best non-will in the world I find myself returning to base camp, to the base and carnal.

MarkO told me was getting cheesed off with the milk round, now that the mornings weren't so bright and warm. He'd do Cherry Hinton for a bit, then he'd do something else, something that had less unsocial hours. Perhaps he'd drive a bus and get reacquainted with the joys of a gearbox. I sympathised, though MarkO's unsocial hours suited me well, since they led him to pass out in my flat most weekday mornings. That, essentially, was my social life. I enjoyed keeping watch over his unconsciousness. I felt trusted with something precious. In sleep MarkO took on a general quality – he was like anyone and everyone. Sleep is such a pure state of being, with all the nitpicking of consciousness resolved or better yet rendered moot.

I felt something close to a sense of depleted companionship when he opened his eyes.

There's something sexy to me about men standing with one leg in front of the other, somehow cocked. It's a stance that seems full of carnal implication, an arrested lunge. If it wasn't for that stance darts would hardly qualify as a sexy game at all. The Little John was big enough, just, for a dartboard – well, anywhere is big enough for a dartboard as an object, I'm speaking metonymically, I mean big enough to allow for the game to be played.

MarkO spotted a poster on the wall of the snug advertising the Cambridge Folk Festival, held at Cherry Hinton Hall, either on his new route or just off it. Arlo Guthrie! Loudon Wainwright III! Alan Stivell! I had to break it to him that the poster was out of date, that the Festival had already happened. It had been in the *Cambridge Evening News* – but there was always next year. I made my voice deep and reassuring, to the extent that my chest cavity allows. A public speaker might tap the edge of his lectern – I make debating points with my fingers on the pubic borders. I present my case, and the rhetoric is often rather stirring. Blood supply to the area can be significantly enhanced as the emotional logic builds. Then I can start to strum quite freely the balalaika of a sympathetic thigh. Summer weather doesn't make me randier, I don't think, but when warmth floods my mineralised joints it makes possible a precious little increment of reach. My mobility is marginal – of course it is – but a lot can happen in the margins. That's really where the action is, in any life never mind mine.

I've learned that it's good policy to hold back a certain amount of capacity, so as to allow for the possibility of springing a small surprise on a special occasion. I won't call it a pounce though perhaps I should. When nothing at all is expected, a minor surge of movement must count as a pounce. In any case you can play the most amazing tricks when all your cards are on the table. And if I'm not getting anywhere, or if I've established a beachhead and then got bored, or just feel like another drink, all I have to do is say, 'Can I have my hand back please?', producing a flurry of blushes and apologies from the victim of a crime I wasn't quite motivated enough to perpetrate.

Once you have gained access to a young man's thigh then essentially you have the run of the place. The barbed wire has been cut. All alarms have been disabled. No guards patrol. Verily, every lock in the gaff lolleth open.

The official cigarette of Gay Liberation

In the Little John it wasn't like that. I overplayed my hand, and then we both did. I was comfortable where I was, and I thought I would risk having another half-pint – meaning partly I suppose that I wanted MarkO to have another full one. But my hand was happy where it was in the warm trousered hinterland, and it didn't seem necessary to break the mood. I suggested we ask the barman to serve us where we were, all snuggy in the snug. Perhaps this was insulting to his professional sense of self, though I can't see that it would be such a bad thing to have satisfied your visitors. MarkO had been delivering milk since the early morning. It didn't seem too much for him to have a pint delivered to him now, after the end of his working day.

As I look back at him, I see that the barman had a little shopping list of the elements of his ideal customer, the one he could insult and with any luck expel, with or without physical force. The list read 1) Student, 2) Hippy, 3) Poof. MarkO, bless him, wasn't much of a contender under heading 1), but a very little intellectual pretension goes a long way outside the centre of a university town, and I probably had enough for two, as well as giving off the graduate aroma that suburban ogres can infallibly detect.

> Fee fi fo fum
> I hear the blab
> of a preening B.A.
> (Cantab.)

Point 2) was dealt with by MarkO all by himself, what with his general hairiness, beardiness and lopsidedness of grin. He was a bit whiffy, and yes, I liked it, but one of Bernardette's nicknames for him was Polecat. An aspect of rubric 2) overlapped with 3), since he was wearing conspicuously bright trousers. They were snug round the waistband and thighs (snugger with my hand factored into the equation of fit), then tented out wildly below the knee. That was the

313

fashion, or had been the fashion relatively recently. This was a pair, in fact, of Loon Pants in electric-blue velvet. I was used to MarkO's intermittently flamboyant style of dress, the peacock moments of someone who by prevailing standards of beauty didn't have a great deal to strut about. He was certainly giving the room an eyeful.

There's something about velvet. Its appeal to the eye is an invitation to touch requiring immediate corroboration from the fingers. MarkO's loons weren't high quality – they had probably been bought in the market – but they had a respectably deep pile, which I was exploring. I was also encouraging MarkO to join me in the game. I had noticed that a finger run across the fabric left a visible mark, and the discovery had prompted me to ask, 'Do you think we could play noughts and crosses here?'

'Here in the pub?'

'Here on your loons.'

He didn't see why not. This was to his credit, though it helped that my fingers despite their limited wiggle had sneaked past his defences a little while ago. I had been busy. I had softened him up, in a manner of speaking. His thigh had a certain chunkiness that qualified it for the function of substrate, despite the instability visited on it by our giggling. The marks we made were approximate, so that you wouldn't necessarily guess we were playing noughts and crosses if you hadn't been told. The pile of the velvet, though, made it possible for MarkO to pass his hand across the pile and brush all the tufts in the same direction, very much as if he was wiping the chalk marks off a blackboard, so that we could start the game all over again.

A table or game board is more or less at rest, but the playing surface of our game was agitated not only by the play itself and our hilarity but by MarkO's movements as he reached for his pint, lit a cigarette or dropped its ash into an ashtray. The fact of my leaning against him so as to be able to reach the playing surface meant that I tended to lurch against his crotch as he changed position, a crotch possibly inflated by my scallywag rhetoric and earlier subliminal nudging.

The cigarettes he was smoking were not standard items. Bernardette brought home all sorts of recherché smokers' perquisites from Bacon's – though the word MarkO used most often, pushing against poshness, was 'ciggies', and once or twice he descended the lexical ladder as far as 'snout'. I'd noticed this particular packet when he had opened it in my flat earlier on. The manufacturers were Messrs Wills and the brand name was Passing Clouds. The packet was pink and showed a cavalier smoking dreamily away – never mind that to an actual, historical cavalier a cigarette would have been as unfamiliar as a television. I had no very clear idea of what 'camp' was, but there was no other heading that would cover this image and indeed this product. It looked like the official cigarette of Gay Liberation, though this was not something I was likely to mention to MarkO. He had scribbled over the government health warning with a felt tip, something he always did. Now in the Little John those cigarettes may have played a part in how we were perceived, together with the box of long and fancy Bacon's matches (no doubt intended for pipes and cigars) that he was using to light them.

In a more central Cambridge pub the combination of impromptu cuddle, self-advertising trousers and outlandish brand of cigarette and matchbox would have raised no hue and cry. Even playing a children's game on a responsive pad of quadricipital muscle, its myofibrils under the soft fabric running in a single direction like a puissant velvet in its own right, could have been passed over, but we were in Cherry Hinton and different rules of life applied. From a little distance this didn't look much like a case of friends playing noughts and crosses, more like a grope session in full swing, which was no less true a version of events though MarkO might not fully have subscribed to it.

As intimate as a suffragette

The bartender was jowly and resentful, wet of lip, louring perhaps permanently and certainly now. Some faces are stubborn studies in grievance, shaped by recurrent dissatisfactions. I could see hostility on his face even before MarkO provoked him by treating him as a lower type of employee, a waiter, lacking a barman's dignity and perks. Resentment pools in the lower depths of any hierarchy. Mistake the Queen for her lady-in-waiting and both of them will laugh, but if you mistake the second under-footman for his deputy you've made an enemy for life. The barman produced a tray, pulled the pint and the half, loaded the glasses onto it and came over to our table. As he transferred the pint glass from the tray he sloshed beer carefully onto and into the open packet of Passing Clouds, not just a few drops but a proper surly spill. The rancour of the act radiated out from the cavalier in his pastel pink to smear the whole group. Then he followed up the pretended accident with a needling apology. 'Oops, sorry, mate. I'm not very clever with table service. Not being a waiter.'

The MarkO I knew, or thought I knew, was very capable of finding the soft answer that turns away wrath, and indeed the slyly charming answer that coaxes reluctant laughter from the throat of a foe. I hoped he would make peace by saying something disarming like, 'I'd offer you a ciggie to steady your hands but they seem a little on the damp side . . .' But not today. Not on a day when he had pranged the float in front of what he only realised at the moment of impact was his peer group, entitled to pass judgement on him. He stuck out his chin and said in an ugly rasping voice, 'Is it too much to ask to be left in peace while I have a quiet pint with a friend . . . and a quiet grope,' and here he cupped his hand round my privates, 'and a quiet snog?' At this point he gave me a smacking kiss on the lips, defiant, for public consumption and not sexy at all, about as intimate as a suffragette throwing herself under the King's horse. In other circumstances, any other circumstances, I would have welcomed the contact, but arriving without any warning it was almost the opposite of an event.

It was a horrible moment, but the barman seemed positively gratified by it, pulling the table away from us and saying, 'Time to go, mate.' With the table pulled back we were less screened from public view. MarkO hadn't resisted my earlier recce under his waistband, and now it became clear that his top button had come undone and the zip lowered down all the way. It's possible I suppose that I had managed by sheer luck to pop that button free, though a button is a device that can sometimes seem to have been invented expressly to thwart me. If his trouser-front was held together by velcro — if everyone's were — then my chances of mischief-making would increase exponentially. The day that buttons and zips are outlawed Saturnalia will become fully Johnable. I'll fumble with the best of them. It seems more likely that MarkO had made life easy for me earlier on by discreetly undoing his trouser button, and then had somehow forgotten this little detail. I will admit on principle to having helped the zip on its descent despite the lack of any specific memory, following the example of those legal reports in which the defendant asks the court to take 108 other offences into consideration.

The tableau revealed when the table was pulled back was incriminating in its little way. There wasn't a lot of scope for us to bluff it out, though that never stops characters in farces from having a go. MarkO lifted me up and propped me against the table, and I could hear the sound, covered by a gruff cough, of a zip being pulled up the slide at high speed. If it had travelled any faster it would have been in danger of melting.

To push the confrontation forward MarkO chose a side issue that wasn't an issue at all. 'We're not paying for them drinks,' he said.

'I'm not asking you to,' said the barman. 'I'm asking you to get out – *telling* you to get out. *Shirtlifters.*'

There had been more trouser-delving than actual shirtlifting, but that was a quibble. I felt we were in the wrong as well as being on the losing side, and this double disadvantage limited the room available for manœuvre. MarkO had different ideas.

'A pint is . . . how much? Twelve pence? And you bandits charge seven for a half-pint?' It was horribly true – the cost of drinking was keeping pace with the cost of driving. The necessary fuels of petrol and beer were being priced out of the reach of ordinary struggling citizens, working men and their unworking counterparts.

The barman was distracted enough by this gambit to start defending himself. 'Try washing a hundred glasses and tell me that's over the odds.'

MarkO hadn't propped me in a comfortable position, and in any case I was facing away from the drama, without a proper view. I set about revolving, to catch more of the show, but I only had the crutch, and without the help of my cane all I could manage was a hobbling pirouette performed in extreme slow motion. Lino is not a surface on which I excel. I had to concentrate on maintaining my stability and must have missed a few seconds of the confrontation. It can't have been more than that. But by the time I had completed my precarious rotation the atmosphere had completely changed. The old poisoned air had been pumped out and clean new stuff piped in. MarkO was saying, 'If there's a vacancy I might even apply. It's not a bad place.

I'm doing a milk round at the minute but I can't see carrying on with that in the cold and dark.'

And the man who had come close to threatening him with violence only a minute ago said amiably, 'Come back in a month and there might be something for you. But not if you're thinking of turning it into a queer pub, mind. Plenty of those in town already!' Had I dozed off for a few moments, standing up? Somehow we had got from scandal and riot to MarkO more or less filling in an application form. Of course heterosexual men are freemasons and their every gesture is a secret handshake invisible to the general population. They can sniff each other out anywhere. But why was a barman in Cherry Hinton better informed than me about the gay scene in Cambridge? It seemed very unfair. I knew the Stable Bar, off Trinity Street, but that was about it. I'd have loved to have another place to go. I expect I was better informed about cottages and other places of rendezvous, but I couldn't really play swapsies, offering a schedule of busy times at Four Lamps in exchange for the address of a gay-friendly speakeasy that no one at CHAPs knew about, unless everyone knew about it but me.

'Gay bar! No chance of that,' said MarkO, who had somehow turned himself into a proper bloke masquerading in poofter trousers. 'Maybe I should pay for those beers after all,' he said. 'Don't want to leave a bad smell.'

'I'll top you up, mate, on the house. And sorry about the spill-age. Clumsy of me.' So now the idea of clumsiness, which had been a paper-thin mask for aggression a few moments ago, was being put forward in all matey seriousness. Is this how the world works? Maya normally makes more of an effort to keep things plausible. It seemed likely that MarkO had surreptitiously passed the blame for any dis-turbance on to me. All I could think of was that there had been some bit of dumb show while my back was turned, some shrugging and eyebrow-raising that made everyone friends at my expense. A discreet wink out of my line of sight can make a crash like ultrasonic cymbals. I try not to let my mind run along that dismal track, since my back is so often turned, but on this occasion it was the only real explanation for the swerve that events were taking.

I had liked The Robin Hood and Little John better when we were being chucked out of it. Soon after I had turned myself around in search of better information about what was going on between these sudden friends, the bartender (whom MarkO had started calling Joe) went back behind the bar, and MarkO followed him, leaving me stranded without the supplementary support of my cane, and once again unable to watch the byplay. Was it a coincidence that he had manœuvred himself into my blind spot twice in such a short time? I tried to listen in to what they were saying. They were a little way away, and there were plenty of intervening sounds to filter out, what with darts players, cribbage codgers and jukebox, but I've honed my listening skills over the years. If you're disadvantaged in terms of gathering information, you learn to make good the deficit, acquiring such handy knacks as reading handwriting upside down from the other side of a desk (even doctors' handwriting) and tuning in to conversations at a fair distance. If there was any justice, skilled eavesdropping should act to dissipate paranoia – usually they're not talking about you at all! – but there are times when it confirms every worst fear.

The two of them seemed to be discussing football, of all things. Of course I would have been more surprised if MarkO had started to discuss Old Church Slavonic rather than sports, but not by much. He had expressed only aversion for organised physical activity, for the idiots who chose to take part and the idiots who chose to watch them. Now suddenly he was well supplied with chat about conditions on the pitch and prospects for relegation. He had found another gear, and he was roaring off, away and out of my ken. Seven–nil against Austria! How about that? What a match! What goals from Channon, Currie, Clarke! Any affinity he might have with me was outclassed by the bond he had built up with this stranger in no time at all. It seemed to have given him the ability to repeat names and statistics back to the barman before the barman had actually said them, tapping into a knowledge he didn't have himself, absorbing it for only as long as it took to bounce the signal back to its source. He was a crystal set tuning in to a new frequency, a cat's whisker pouncing on a fresh signal. In five minutes' time he might not even remember those names.

I did another laborious pirouette so as to watch MarkO at work, since getting people to like him did indeed seem to be his work. Who was it that spun around so violently he tore himself in two? Rumpelstiltskin, I think. I knew how he felt.

Nobody asks about the early life of Rumpelstiltskin. Do we really think he wanted to end up in the spinning-straw-into-gold baby-stealing business? Give a dwarf a bad name by all means, but don't be surprised if he lives up to it.

'I'm going now, MarkO,' I called out. 'Your new friend will tell you what bus to take.' I was sure I heard MarkO say in an undertone, 'Don't worry, I can handle him . . .' I set out across the lino, knowing that if he didn't capitulate he would at least have to intercept me with bargaining of some sort. He scampered playfully across to block my passage. 'Come on, John,' he said. 'Just another half. It's nearly last orders anyway, and Joe here has topped up my glass from when he made that little spill, remember?' Yes, indeed, I remembered. It was MarkO who seemed to have forgotten our time of disgrace, back when we were shirtlifters together.

'No, MarkO, I've had enough.' Another beer and enough of you. I set off again, but some demon of compromise made me mutter, as if out of the depths of a bad marriage, 'I'll wait in the car.' Then MarkO got it into his head that he and Joe would carry me there. I could have tolerated MarkO's help – wasn't that how I had entered the pub in the first place? – but I wouldn't consent to being a team project.

I rebelled. 'I can manage. *I can manage.*' I meant business. I can't do kicking-and-screaming, but I would certainly have laid on a screaming component if need be. I would walk. I would saturate myself in embarrassment until it spilled over everyone else, which isn't much of a tactic. I was cutting off my nose to spite my face, of course, since it was the only place my knife could reach. Why shouldn't MarkO have a good time? Because it was my day out too, and his fun shouldn't come at my expense. Of course I had to ask MarkO to fetch my cane, and I couldn't make an exit without the door being held open for me, but those were only dabs of cream on top of the sundæ of humiliation I had whipped up for myself. Then MarkO went ahead to open the door of the Mini for me, and my sundæ glass of bitter juice was full. It ran over.

He went back to the Little John, keeping his side of a bargain that I can't imagine either of us had really wanted to see fulfilled. I sat in the car and waited, wishing I had the strength of character to drive away and leave him to find his own way back to Mayflower House. I've never been convinced by my strength of character, or strength of character in general. The strength of a substance is a meaningless idea when considered separately from the forces acting on it. Character flows, it is viscous. You have to bank on yours setting all the more solidly as the pressure comes, when all too often it exhibits thixotropic liquefaction rather than the hoped-for, the longed-for, dilatancy.

When MarkO got into the car, I asked him if we had finished our business in Cherry Hinton. 'Are you sure there aren't any queerbashers you haven't befriended? Shall we sweep the streets just to be sure?' It mortified me that a kiss, and one I hadn't really been a part of, was enough to label me as the deviant and to exclude me from an expedition that I had actually initiated.

'I don't know why you're being like that, John. Did you want to be beaten up? You should be thanking me for getting us out of trouble.' No, I didn't want to be beaten up, though it felt as if it was happening anyway. He was quiet in the car on the way back to Mayflower House, though not as quiet as I'd have liked. 'There's was no harm in him, no real harm.' Then we weren't going to be beaten up, and there was no call for emergency fraternisation. 'And I'm serious about bar work,' he told me. 'Frankly I'm not much of a milkman, and that seems as good a place as any.' I did my best to give him the silent treatment but it's not in my nature. I'm sure it hurt me much more than it hurt him.

I was upset about the way he had seemed to dump me the moment someone new was in range, but things had gone wrong earlier than that. The kiss had been the beginning of an unravelling. I experienced it as horrible. If MarkO had wanted to 'snog' me, either in private or public, or ideally in some shifting intermediate zone, that was one thing. What had happened was something quite different. 'Snog' is to proper kiss as 'snout' is to Balkan Sobranie. The public snog he visited on me was a Möbius kiss, having only one edge and one surface. It was two-dimensional at best. There hasn't been a lot of research done on the transcendent physics of kissing, but I think I can claim to have laid some of the groundwork on its theory in the Mini as we trailed back from Cherry Hinton that afternoon.

It's possible that I had daydreamed of being kissed by MarkO, for instance in the early morning when I was following his milk round in my mind, but once that kiss had left the world of the possible and become actual it revealed itself as having been impossible all along. I no longer wanted it, though I wished I was still living in a world in which I did. The passionate same-sex kiss of the heterosexual man joined the other unimprovable examples of things that can exist only in language: child of the barren woman, horns of the hare.

A replacement bubble for the spirit level

Over the next week or so it was Bernardette rather than MarkO who came to call. I was both touched and made suspicious by her desire to keep the peace between us, to restore relations by her ambassadorship. She told me that MarkO missed me and didn't know what he had done wrong, also that he missed what she called 'that silly chess you play'. It gave me a little confidence in her as an honest broker that this was obviously not the phrasing as it had issued from MarkO. MarkO took Ultima seriously.

Being alone with Bernardette was quite different from the three of us sharing the room. If anything there was less space. She wasn't a romantic character as that description is normally understood, she didn't fit the category of 'lovey-dovey' so much disliked by my mother and not much more popular with me. But there was something outsized about her presence that made every song on the radio seem like a love song (though of course most of them are, despite George Harrison's best efforts) and every conversation like a love scene in a film, permanently on the brink of outbursts of one sort or another, whether declarations or reproaches. I'm confident this bit of casting didn't come from me.

She moved over to the window, as people do in films, perhaps expecting to draw me tidally after her. There wasn't much of a view from that window, though she could gaze at the Mini if she had a mind to – one of the little amenities of Mayflower House was that I could park right outside the window of my flat. Scraps of romantic dialogue seemed to follow her around, though I'd not noticed it before. Perhaps I was supposed to make a contribution. *Come here, you lovely fool . . . don't you know I smell your hair in my dreams?* That sort of thing.

It was from Bernardette that I learned what had happened on the day MarkO finished his stint on Ron's round and handed the keys back. The foreman asked, 'So did you have any trouble with old Brendan at Number 16, Tenison Road?' And the joke was so old by then, the rite of passage so notional, that the other milkmen hardly even bothered to look at him as they joined in dutifully for the chorus: 'He's quite a goer, is Brendan, him in his winceyette. Slips off easy, doesn't it?' It was easily interpreted in Hindu terms as a *vasana*, one of those ruts in the road where wheels have got stuck many times in the past. Perhaps there's something about places like Cambridge that attracts them, these customs as empty as the Latin grace in any one of the ancient colleges, things that happen now only because they have happened before.

MarkO hadn't been able to work out whether he had misheard the name in the original briefing or if this was a hoary old hoax, the sort of thing that encrusts so many trades, with generations of builder's apprentices being sent out to buy a replacement bubble for the spirit level. Possibly, just possibly, Brendan was a bothersome old goat all too ready to loosen his pyjama cord, drawing back the curtains on a show no one particularly wanted to see. Yet he had paid MarkO meekly enough on Saturday mornings, shuffling back and forth in his slippers and not seeking to prolong the transaction.

'Perhaps MarkO just wasn't his type,' I said, and Bernardette said, 'Yes, I thought that too but it's not really something you can say, is it?' No, it's not, though why someone who was sharing his life with Bernardette would worry about a stranger's sexual indifference was hard to understand, except on the basis that some people's hunger for approval knows no limit.

'John, I'm going to tell you something I've never told anyone. Not even MarkO, in fact MarkO would be the last person I'd tell.' It's the sort of opening that always puts me on my guard. What am I supposed to offer in exchange for a piece of information that I haven't sought but is being labelled in advance as rare, perhaps even beyond price? The intended effect may be to create an atmosphere of trust, which can look calculated in itself. Trust is not something you can turn on like a tap or pipe in like dry ice at a panto. The other way of looking at it is that I am regarded as some sort of cul-de-sac, the place where intimate disclosures come to die, on the basis that I don't have intimates to whom I might pass on whatever the grisly details turn out to be. Bernardette didn't even ask whether I could keep a secret, a formula dedicated to the invocation of untruthfulness which I've learned over the years to counter by saying, no, I absolutely can't. I'm a hopeless case, a complete blabbermouth. I can't help myself. But is that really going to stop you?

And of course I was flattered and intrigued though I tried not to show it. The face-to-face confidence, the potential heart-to-heart, even, these things require so much less work than the complex tracking procedures that most social life demands. I lack the motor adequacy required to keep pace with byplay. The inflexibility of my neck makes it hard for me to follow the foreshortened trajectories of everyday conversational badminton, in which the sally-shuttlecock, dying almost the moment it's struck, needs to be flicked back instantly, before it can touch the floor. I must concentrate frantically on peripheral hearing so as not to miss a syllable of enigmatic conversations made only more tantalising by the fact that they don't go to any particular trouble to exclude me. These factors combine to make a frontal confidence intoxicating, however suspect it may be.

'I told you – didn't I? – that I left school after my O-levels because they wouldn't let me do French as an A-level. Did I really not tell you that? Because my improvement was "too recent". What a thing to say to a schoolgirl. I hated that place. A posh school. Oxford is full of posh schools. French had been taught by a prune, and then she retired and we were taught by Mamselle, who was French herself and could wear a scarf five or six different ways, instead of a Madame who couldn't even get her lipstick in the right place.

'My parents weren't too pleased that I was dropping out, and said I had to get a job if I was going to go on living under their roof. They wanted me to do something secretarial – of course they did. And I would even have tried that if I could have started working right away, but you needed shorthand and typing and it was all a way of forcing me to go to secretarial school, an even worse sort of school. So I got a job at a cash-and-carry, not even a fancy or respectable one. Not a frill to be seen anywhere in the place. In the development at Templars Square, if you know Oxford.' I didn't. I don't. 'Far cry from Harrods Food Hall . . . Horrible lighting, horrible uniform. Can you imagine me in a nylon coat? I hope not. Pale blue gingham.

Zephyrs in the pay of Alberto VO5

'Handi-Save was a basic sort of place, it really was. It made Sainsburys seem ritzy. At least there was no stacking cans on shelves to be done, which was a relief. Not a lot of fetch and carry. Handi-Save saved on everything, pretty much. The aisles were narrow, which saved space. There were no labels on the products, just signs on the shelves next to where they were displayed. Not displayed, really, just bunged, just dumped there. The stuff was left in the cardboard boxes it came in, with the front ripped open so that the madwomen of Cowley could just grab what they wanted. They did seem mad, honestly, scrambling for the tins and glaring at each other then bustling to the till with their trolleys, expecting to be out of the shop in ten seconds flat. The other girls weren't friendly but I'm used to that, in fact I preferred it that way.

'But do you see what we were up against, us girls at the tills, John? They had saved money by not sticking price labels on the individual items, so we had to *memorise* the prices. And there were over a hundred of them. Yes, there was a list but it was creased and tattered, not to mention covered with illegible biro marks where old prices had been changed. A beginner like me was allowed to keep the list handy and look at it from time to time, but it wasn't something that made you popular. My face ached from all the smiling I had to do to make up for being so slow compared to the other girls. The old hands among the customers would choose another queue when they saw the list, or else joined my queue, the cows, just so they could heave a big sigh and choose another when I'd taken a few seconds too long dealing with the shopper in front of them.

'Honestly, John, if looks could cook a person, I'd have been scorched to death by the end of my first shift. I'd be keeled over by the till, sizzling. A few of the prices became second nature, but there were others that just wouldn't stick, and if someone presented me with a tin of, I don't know, something stupid like pease pudding or faggots and I couldn't price it I'd make small talk frantically while I racked my brains or grinned like a madwoman myself and tried to look at the list out of the corner of my eye. By the end of the first week I was in tatters, and then at the end of Saturday's shift they gave us the list of prices that would change on Monday so we could memorise them. Yes, they gave us bloody homework! On our day off.

'I lasted three weeks – three Sundays, really. It was the Sundays that did me in. Then I left the job, which my parents weren't happy about all over again. I wouldn't study and I couldn't hold down the most humble employment. And they weren't the only ones. I was disappointed in me too. I even burst into tears and said, "Mummy, I'm not even clever enough to be a shopgirl!" And she said, "You could never be a *shopgirl*. A shop assistant is something quite different." She meant well but made it worse and not better, far worse, by getting me to see that underneath it all I was just as much of a rotten little snob as Mummy-and-Daddy. The pop festivals and the clothes that made them go tut-tut-tut, the love bite I got at the fairground when I was fourteen, all of it was just a disguise for how ordinary I was.'

After the fiasco of Handi-Save she decided to leave home, though she waited long enough to learn how to drive, working part-time in a library. She quite liked working there, the hush was sexy somehow, though of course her parents wanted her to turn it into a career by studying librarianship. Couldn't she just do it for a bit while she waited for something else? What was wrong with that?

As she spoke strands of her shining healthy hair lifted lightly away from her head, as if they were carried aloft by worshipful currents of air, zephyrs in the pay of Alberto VO5 shampoo. Perhaps she had given her hair a vigorous brushing outside in the corridor just before she opened my door, charging her scalp with static electricity for my benefit, but if so why? And what had she done with the brush? Perhaps her hair was tickled aloft by the atmospheric pressure her glamour created. During her working days at Bacon's I could imagine customers being overcome on a regular basis, encouraged to breathe into paper bags by the volunteers of St John Ambulance until their respiration returned to normal.

There was another brief adventure in retail for Bernardette, after she had arrived in Cambridge but before she met MarkO. Her stint of employment at Joshua Taylor's ended not in panicked flight but active disgrace. On her first day she was put to work in the clock department and had a difficult customer early that afternoon, a woman who inspected a cuckoo clock with great attention and then drew her gloved hand across its bottom ledge. Women, some women at least, still wore gloves then, even if I struggle to work out why. Not gloves for warmth but gloves for status. To show, I suppose, that they did nothing that would make their hands dirty. She looked at the gloved forefinger, saw with grim satisfaction that it was smudged and held it up. 'And what is this dust doing here, young lady? Do you never clean your place of work?' This was unfair, as Bernardette had been in that department for only a matter of hours, and in any case cringing came hard to her. It was against her grain. Like any bird new to captivity her reflex was to peck, and the posh accent that had done her no favours at Handi-Save came into its own. 'Oh no, Madam! That's guano — these clocks pay for themselves in three years.' This had a marvellous instant silencing effect on the customer, even if it only lasted long enough for her to find Bernardette's manager and lodge a complaint against her. She was let go for rudeness, having 'given lip'. The element of cleverness in her reply made things worse rather than better.

It was hardly surprising that a supermarket, even one less basic than Handi-Save, hadn't suited her, since it was predominantly a female environment. She was so very much a 'man's woman', a phrase that you could still hear being used in those days without embarrassment. She drank beer in pints, something that according to MarkO made barmen uneasy. In those days there was something threatening, even in a university town where social attitudes might be expected to be more relaxed, about a woman who laid claim to the larger container. It wasn't even a question of disapproval attached to excessive alcohol intake. The same bartender would cheerfully dispense three half-pints to the same lady, to be drunk one after another against the clock without taking a breath between gulps, and would even look on with admiration. This was a highly specific men-only shibboleth that sought to restrict access to the vessel rather than the associated volume.

I don't know how it is that 'shibboleth' has come to be an accepted word when I have to explain '*vasana*' over and over again. One's from Hebrew and the other's from Sanskrit, which would seem to amount to equal honours in terms of prestige. *Vasana* is the more useful term because more inclusive. Not every *vasana* is a shibboleth but every shibboleth is a *vasana*. I bridle somewhat, as a matter of fact, at the need for italics in one case and not the other. But if I can just keep going *vasana* will become a naturalised English word licensed to mingle freely with the natives, spared the bureaucratic harassment of being made to stand out by the slant of its font, not for added emphasis but in a declaration of its outsider status demanded by the authorities.

Bernardette's glamour wasn't exactly imperious, or not imperious in the way the word is normally understood, though of course there is more than one way to run an empire. There was something oddly offhand about the way she presented herself, as if she was just trying out being beautiful for a day or two to see whether she liked it. A high-class tobacconist's with a stuffy male clientèle suited her well, giving free rein to her regal manner with its lively and even titillating undertone of disdain. At Bacon's her brain wasn't being stretched on a day-to-day basis, but the same could have been said about most women and many men, with me clamouring wildly for attention somewhere on the list.

At Bacon's she was a sales assistant, an entirely different creature from a shopgirl. The element of skill was attenuated, true, sheer mental accomplishment of the sort the girls at Handi-Save could boast. Class-inflected self-presentation became most if not all of the job.

If there's a version of acnestis in the visual field then mine is as enlarged as its physical equivalent. It's very easy for people to manoeuvre themselves so that their faces can't be seen, and this has the odd effect of making me mistrust the expressions that are offered up to me on a plate. Surely if the feeling was sincere you'd hide it away? But that way psychosis lies, or at least neurosis needlessly rampant, licensed to flourish and fester.

As it turned out, I was right to be a little suspicious of Bernardette's confidences about the disgraces in her employment history. She was in search of reciprocal intimacies. Now she produced a glossy magazine from out of nowhere and said she wanted my opinion on something. I groaned inwardly. It was beginning to look as if the only thing my English degree qualified me for was pronouncing on the quality of published poetry. But of course it wasn't that. There was no poetry on offer in those pages. Bernardette plonked the magazine down then stood behind me and riffled through it until she had reached the middle.

I say. *I say!* It was a gentleman in the altogether.

'So . . . what do you think?' Her voice was as neutral as could be expected in the circumstances. 'What's your verdict?'

'I don't know where to look,' I said. '. . . mind you, neither does he.' True, but evasive in the highest degree. 'What is this magazine? Is it legal?'

'It's called *Playgirl* and it's American and quite new, but I think it's legal to buy here.'

'You only think it's legal?'

'I'm not the one who bought it, so I can't say for sure.' She riffled through a few more pages, so that I could see that this was a new sort of woman's magazine, with the images of men without clothes interrupting the usual fare of tips on eyeliner and skirt lengths – the Maxi-versus-Midi wars that were raging at the time, no more an avoidable subject for a certain generation than the Spanish Civil War had been earlier in the century. The unclothed models tried with their expressions to combine the assertive and the dreamy, but there was no ignoring an undercurrent of unease. They might have been flinching from the compromising advertisements with which they were surrounded, campaigns promoting tampons and cigarettes for ladies, slim or mentholated or both. They seemed to be getting a crash course in art history, learning the hard way about the gulf that is fixed between the naked and the nude. They were certainly naked, but they were a long way from nudity. Just men with their bits on show, looking vulnerable and not much else. Obscenity laws made sure their giblets remained in neutral, but a lot more than an enhanced blood supply would be required to turn these into images of power or beauty.

'So who was it that bought it?'

'All I can say about that is that I found it in MarkO's sock drawer.'

'Ah.' Ah. It occurred to me that this might be some sort of ruse, to make me admit to having a hankering for MarkO, though Bernardette

329

seemed too direct for that, not one for subterfuge, rather more a con-fronter than an evader. There was nothing subtle, for instance, about carving verdicts on her lover's musical tastes into the living vinyl. 'Musical differences', so often cited as the reason for groups breaking up, have rarely been so stark in a personal relationship.

'So . . . are you and MarkO seeing each other? Are you "an item"?'

Did she really not know? People believe what they want to believe. Did she really not know that we verbalised our pre-orgasmic tensions together, that we whispered dirty words into each other's ears?

Technically he was a strange man

No reason why she should. The closest we came to any of that was when we sang along to our favourite Gas Works song, 'Verbalise Your Pre-Orgasmic Tensions'. The group had the lyrics printed on song sheets that were given away at concerts, and MarkO had got hold of some – take note, Linda Hoyle of Affinity. Don't leave the fans to guess and mouth nonsense. When it was time for the line 'whisper dirty words into my ear', MarkO would bring his head near mine and would softly breathe 'todger' in my ear (for example) while I did the same with '*lingam*'. I dare say he was as unfamiliar with my word '*lingam*' as I was with his 'todger', but it doesn't pay to adver-tise your ignorance of adult vocabulary in a setting charged, however modestly, with sexual tension. I'd like to think that at least once I breathed 'acnestis' and he breathed 'gazunder', but I can't swear it was so. I never came close to licking his ear, which is really a shame. My tongue once it has got a hearing can be a persuasive instrument.

'Why don't you ask him?' I said.

'I did. He said there was nothing going on. He says he's "curious but not interested", whatever that means. He did say you'd kissed in a pub, but his story was that he wanted to get up the barman's nose more than anything else.'

'True enough. But he kissed me – I didn't kiss him back.'

'I'm not sure that makes a difference. And if there's nothing going on why has he been spending all his time round here?'

'We're friends, that's why! We're on a wavelength. He's tired after work, and he can have a kip here if he wants. He's tired and you're not around. We experiment with ESP, we play superchess. We listen to Supertramp.'

'You certainly love your superchess, I must say.' She'd never sounded so posh, lady-mayoress-at-a-garden-party posh. 'Is it even a real game or did the two of you make it up? When he said all the pieces moved like queens I thought it must be a gay thing.'

'Why would gay people need their own version of chess?'

'How would I know? You can't blame me for wondering. Anyway, when I'm in the room with you I get the feeling of little fishes. Do you know what I mean by little fishes? I call it little fishes when there's something going on, underneath, but you don't know exactly what it is. There's something going on between the two of you, that's all I know.'

I thought so too, but I wasn't any better informed than she was, really. Those little fishes never broke the surface.

'And I really don't want my life turning into that bloody dreary film. Half a loaf is better than no bread and all that. Those old people leading such bloody miserable lives, bloody boring lives, moping around Hampstead.'

Even without her repetition of the adjective I'd have recognised the film she was referring to as *Sunday Bloody Sunday*. If she had made the spool-winding gesture that represents Film in charades and raised three fingers to denote the number of words I would have guessed it on the spot – no bad thing since, let's face it, it's not the easiest thing in the world to mime. At the time 'Hampstead' was a term only loosely connected with geography – we provincials thought every Londoner not sleeping under a bridge lived in Hampstead.

I would have gone to the film whatever its theme out of loyalty to Peter Finch, who was so friendly to me during the shooting of *The Pumpkin Eater* in Bourne End. He would squat on his heels without apparent effort, saying it was something he'd learned from the Aborigines back home, though he couldn't match their endurance. Certainly by Northern Hemisphere standards he had trained his quadricipital muscles to flex and still remain remarkably relaxed, so that he could maintain that unnatural pose, as it seemed, indefinitely. It was intoxicating to meet a grown-up whose dealings with me were on the level and we had some lovely talks. He had offered me a ride in his beautiful car, but Mum wouldn't allow me to go because technically he was a 'strange man'.

When I finally saw *The Pumpkin Eater* I was shocked by how little of the footage I had seen being filmed had made it onto the screen. They had been there for weeks! It had seemed like weeks. I know the film wasn't advertised as any sort of local exposé – 'Peyton Place comes to the Thames Valley . . . Bourne End with the lid off!' – but they could have made more of an effort in that line. It wasn't as if we lacked little scandals of our own. We could hold our heads up. The reason the local vet was so willing to come out in person when an animal was sick wasn't pure goodness of heart, nice though he was. He was having an illicit relationship with a local woman (the wife of a BOAC pilot, often away) and made the most of every chance to make village house calls of the more innocent sort.

I didn't think of the people in *Sunday Bloody Sunday* as being old, as Bernardette did, though of course Peter Finch was in his thirties when I was born and his mid-forties when I met him. I'd like to say that as an enlightened Hindu I could see through the hoax of chronology, but it's also possible that without meaning to I slipped through the grid of the generations created and exploited, above all, by people who want you to buy things. By sheer chance I was invulnerable to the 'knife of advertising', as wielded by J. Walter Thompson and his fellows. What were they going to sell me, a tassel for the bum snorkel? Much of the illusion of belonging to a generation is created by the need to fit in, and the possibility of doing so. My economic nullity was yet another invisibility cloak to add to the pile. Over the years I've been assumed to be every sort of age, rarely within five years of the 'true' one. I seem not to have struck people as either simply young or old, but as some shifting combination of codger and kiddiewinkie.

Sunday Bloody Sunday was about adult compromises and sexual sharing, yes indeed, the whole theme of half a loaf being (or alternatively not being) better than no bread. A gasp went through the audience when the dishy young man and Peter Finch's doctor character shared a passionate kiss. It looks tame now but was daring then. There was another rather shocking moment that retains some impact even now – the heroine makes a cup of instant coffee with water straight from the hot tap, and seems surprised that the result is perfectly disgusting.

Man kisses another man, ho hum. Woman makes coffee straight from the tap . . . oh good Lord, Glenda Jackson, are you even human?

For once Bernardette seemed to need prompting. 'So what you're saying is . . .'

'I'm not sure I'm saying anything.'

'Well, perhaps what you're saying is that you don't want to be in a triangle with MarkO, but if you have to then the third person might as well be me.'

'Well. Maybe. I really don't know.'

'And would I make a good third corner . . . because you like me, or because I'm no real threat?'

A brutal enough question in its way, but she had recovered some of her decisiveness. 'A bit of both, I suppose. I don't even like sharing chips.'

It was taken for granted that I wouldn't mind sharing MarkO, and I could see why she would think so. Bernardette would always be negotiating from a position of strength. Whether MarkO himself was worth the trouble for either of us was a different question.

I felt it would be a good idea to break the mood, whatever the mood actually was, something I wasn't sure of. You don't have to be a cricketer to know the effectiveness of bowling the occasional googly. I recited a few of my favourite lines of poetry at her, in a voice as low and purring as I could make it:

> *Por toda hermosura*
> *nunca yo me perderé*
> *sino por un no sé qué*
> *que alcanza su ventura . . .*

It certainly seemed to stop her in her tracks. St John of the Cross does that, in my experience – he's everyone's favourite Discalced Carmelite, a whole lot posher and less embarrassing than clumsy Brother Lawrence (always the dropper). On the other hand Bernardette may still have been in her own private film, and was now looking down wildly at the skirting board in search of subtitles. I hadn't spoken Spanish for years, and I expect my accent was nothing to write home about.

'You'll have to translate that for me, I'm afraid, considering I'm not educated. No A-levels, you see.' Mock humble, with some well-justified seething underneath.

'Of course – but remember you've got a job, even if you're not educated. It's swings and roundabouts, isn't it? I've got a lovely Cambridge degree and I'm unemployed. Here goes: *I would never be lost / for all the world's beauty / only for a nothing-in-particular / that turned up quite by chance.*'

'You know I hate poetry.'

'I'm not sure you do. You could see that the stuff in Bacon's window was tripe.'

'Anyway, help me with it. Are you talking about MarkO, really?'

'In a way.'

'A nothing-in-particular – he'd hate that. Mind, I'm not saying you're wrong . . .'

This wasn't even the first time I had been confronted with images of male nudity and been called on to confess my own desires, though it can't really be called your *vasana* if it's wished on you. This confrontation at least came closer to my actual interests than the family showdown of summer 1972, when my parents became obsessed with the notion that a magazine in my shoulder-bag, *Jeremy*, showing pale and pretty boys, was mine and represented my secret interests. I suppose I had *Jeremy* to thank for my emancipation from family – what had taken Ramana Maharshi a surreptitious departure, a train ride and arrival at an ancient temple to accomplish had been managed for me by pouting youngsters in someone else's magazine.

At least I was spared Mum following me, as Ramana Maharshi's mother had followed him, first to reproach him while cooking him his favourite meals and finally to be an unbudgeable part of the ashram that grew up around him despite his resistance. I'm not sure I could have stood that.

I'd always been interested in men rather than boys, so the *Playgirl* conversation was far closer to the Śruti-note of my desires, the foundation stone of the imaginary palace, than the adolescents in *Jeremy*, the magazine of pale and incipiently spotty boys that had got me into so much trouble with my parents, who would never believe that it wasn't mine. But just the same, these *Playgirl* men were not what I wanted.

I hadn't seen the last of Bernardette, but her next communication took the form of a note slipped under the door. I suppose there was an element of tact involved, of not wanting to disturb me, except that nothing could be more unsettling than a folded piece of paper, which I was unable to pick up until my home help arrived. Admittedly it was unlikely to say 'Mayflower House is burning down – get out now!' but I found the imposed delay unsettling. Still, there was nothing actively mean about leaving a note. I advertise my own limitations when I make too much of other people's.

That note slipped under the door had a girls'-boarding-school overtone somehow. Perhaps Bernardette had attended some such place, where fervent souls communicate in surreptitious notes: *Dear Caroline (though I dream of calling you Caro!!?), I saved up my squashed-fly biscuits from break all week, and I wanted to give them to you at cocoa time to say 'please will you be my crack' but you were talking to some other girls and didn't see me . . .* though unless Bernardette had pulled off an ugly-duckling transformation on an epic scale it seemed unlikely that she would have sent notes of that sort rather than receiving them. Receiving them in such numbers that it became hard for her to push the door open.

I had been to a boarding school myself, and perhaps I should have raised the topic. My experience had been something of a mottled idyll, what with being force-fed pilchards and held upside down over a stairwell, but the same is true of many people's schooldays – we might have found common ground. Now we'll never know!

The note when Paula retrieved it for me was hardly dramatic. *Don't bother with that idea about MarkO's birthday. Don't see why you should!* I'd actually been having a little trouble with Paula, which was entirely my fault. To start with she had come for two hours three times weekly, but then her schedule changed and she started to come for an hour every weekday. This suited me rather well, and in my blindness I didn't see that she was now being paid for five hours instead of six, on top of which her travel time, for which she wasn't paid at all, was greatly increased. Eventually I was able to see beyond the improvement in my week to the greater burden of hers, and then not only did

I sympathise sincerely but promised that I would help her to a better job, one that made better use of her talents and sweetness of nature.

The suggestion about MarkO's imminent birthday was that I would sell Bernardette the Hacker at a knock-down price for her to give to him. He had always admired the quality of sound. The original phrasing had been that if I ever wanted to get rid of my sturdy little sound system then MarkO would give it a good home, and I can't quite explain why the idea had grown on me, in a way that my present cooled feelings towards the man himself did nothing to alter. It's even possible it was my idea in the first place. By making it a present from Bernardette rather than me I could avoid hypocrisy in the matter of birthday celebrations, those deckings-out of corpses, and could express a quietly insistent part of my own nature.

I was content to say goodbye to the Hacker. It was sturdily built and there was still plenty of life left in it. I had no particular desire to replace it with something more up to date. A quality item like my stereo was an investment. It wasn't worth quite as much as a new one, but it was holding its own in the market – its desirability had developed no more than a slow puncture. These days you can hear the hiss of escaping value as you leave the shop. You're already in a race with depreciation which depreciation will win.

I've always been attracted to self-denial, to the shedding of worldly things, and the fact of straitened circumstances doesn't seem to me much of an excuse for clinging to objects. It's just another trick up Maya's sleeve. Thrift passes for a virtue when it's only a particular sort of worldliness. That was the trap I felt I was caught in. My relative poverty masked an excessive respect for the few things I had, and encouraged a superstitious dwelling on the many I didn't. Poverty can be a particularly insidious obstacle to self-realisation, since it seems to justify attachment to the little one has. Renunciation shouldn't be a privilege reserved for the rich – they've got plenty of those already.

It seemed to me that the vocabulary of dispossession was all wrong. I didn't want to 'renounce' anything – the element of sacrifice seemed to me entirely bogus. In India I had experienced matter-of-fact devotion with no element of the sacrificial, in the shape of a local woman who had said that if I returned she would look after me as long as she lived, and from reading about my guru I had learned that abnegation could be carried out with just as little fuss. Ramana Maharshi let a passer-by walk off with the tiger skin on which he himself habitually sat, for no better reason (and no worse a one) than that the passer-by had asked for it. The tiger skin was never something that he had chosen, it was no more than one of the fixtures and fittings of guru-dom. I envied him the clarity of his decision-making, though making decisions is entirely the wrong description. He could shed possessions so simply, not having subscribed to the fantasy of possession. In fact subscribing in the literal sense was something he didn't do, never signing his name though occasionally making use of the all-purpose OM. And so the supposedly valuable object, rolled up and carried over the shoulder of a stranger, followed its destiny away from him. Did I have the callow thought that I would find it easier to give things up if I too was surrounded by devotees anticipating my needs, usually though not always incompetently? There's no denying it.

It wouldn't be so easy for me to part with, say, my Margaret Erskine Dream-Cloud, that indispensable eiderdown, quintessence of quilt, particularly with winter coming. The Hacker I could manage without, and I even liked the fact that I wasn't on such great terms with MarkO at this point. It purified any tactical aspect of letting Bernardette have my dear little sound system. I needed help, some sort of nudge or cue, if I was to divest myself of attachments without striking a pose in the process, and here it was, help freely offered.

Exactly the sort of fuss he hates

What I wanted, ideally, was a clean break with something I owned, so clean as to reveal the profound truth of its never having belonged to me. Not a painful divorce from an object, not even a separation with a brave face and no bitterness, but an annulment, retrospectively cancelling any connection between me and it. The ego wouldn't let anything happen so smoothly, though. The ego can't do anything without lawyers. It's always working up a case.

There was any amount of hypocrisy in these thoughts, since I wouldn't willingly have parted with the geode I had bought from Miss Duff. In fact I hoarded it as pathetically as any miser in the lit-erature, competing in my smallness of spirit with Volpone and Silas

337

Marner. Paula acted as museum attendant, getting my treasure out of the drawer where it lived and putting it on display for the duration of her shift, putting it away before she left. No one else was going to paw it. And yes, you could make a case for the diode being a sort of crystallised *puja*, even a mineral mantra bypassing not just referential language (as mantras do) but speech itself, but this is special pleading that no jury would accept. My eyes stroked it when my inadequate fingers couldn't, getting a fierce pleasure from its range of textures, glassy smooth and nailfile rough, its range of colour within colour. As a crystal fetishist I paled beside Magnus Hirschfeld's Madame X, but I had to acknowledge her as a distant cousin if not a closer relation. The feeling I had for the object that I had prised from the iron grip of 'Dogs' Duff was not only milder in intensity but different in character, or so it seemed to me. Still, having proposed an indefinite continuum of partialities I can't suddenly introduce sharp boundaries between one condition and another.

The ideal would be to shed things quite naturally, objects, privileges, attachments, without giving the process any thought, to break the imagined link between action and intention. I aspired to emulate my guru, who could say, '*I did not eat, so they said I was fasting. I did not speak, and they said I had taken a vow of silence.*' Aspiration and emulation, though, are just lesser contortions of the will, and what results from artificial renunciation is a hideous sort of striptease, a paraded divestment that perverts any humbling impulse and flaunts itself in the spotlight, shameless. When your spirituality ends up decked out in a G-string, with tassels in the most unlikely places, then perhaps you should have kept your clothes on. I just hoped I could let go of the Hacker without emotional distortion, in all humble fidelity to my less worldly impulses, high vibrations at the very edge of the audible, letting it slip through my fingers without even knowing it was gone or listening for the sound of a splash.

In self-realisation as Ramana Maharshi expounds it the ego doesn't actually disappear but retains a bare executive rôle, palely present in the sky like the moon in the daytime. This did not describe the state of my ego in 1973, when there was no harmony between my need to be noticed, my resentment at being so conspicuous and my desire to evaporate spiritually. I don't doubt that there were people I knew in those days who looked directly at my ego and incurred light retinal scarring.

The desire to shed possessions and attachments is genuine, too strong and persistent in my case to be entirely hypocritical. It's just that the mechanisms for putting the desire into practice are all suspect, being executive, being procedural. Only one part of the self is in the habit of making things happen, and that's the ego, but the moment the ego puts itself in charge things start to go wrong. The ego is a net that is all holes and no string. The ego is the original chocolate fireguard, instantly melted and deformed by the forces it is pledged to resist.

The ego is like a press agent, always calling the papers, murmuring away tirelessly from morning till night on behalf of its client, brokering deals and taking a hefty percentage of the proceeds for its pains, doodling pound signs all the while – *££? £££? ££££!* – on a pad next to the phone. 'Yes, giving things away . . . I know. When you think how little he has to start with. You're right – *shaming* is the right word, exactly the right word. Well, I'm not claiming to be an authority on his motives, and I'd hate to put words in his mouth, but "unconditional love for the whole world" sounds about right. A very strong sense of values, that one. Not at all a common thing in the world as it is now. Pictures? Yes, now that you mention it. All very natural, not posed at all – but now and then you feel the photographer has caught something a little special. Yes, they're recent. Don't say where you got them, though. Don't get me into trouble! Oh I agree, an inside page, definitely. Quite – discretion is absolutely the note to strike. These things have to be done very sensitively or they seem terribly phoney, don't you think? People aren't fools. They can tell when things are done for effect. The last thing anyone wants is anything brash or tasteless in the way of coverage. That's exactly the sort of fuss he hates . . .'

Young people's dental health in pre-Wilhelmine Germany

Bookshops have always been places of enlightenment for me, lay cathedrals. I often popped into the main branch of Heffers, which wasn't architecturally welcoming to people in wheelchairs and was spread over several levels but compensated for the physical difficulties with the coöperativeness of the staff.

I enjoyed a good browse in the religion section, or failing that the natural history shelves. Solo browsing isn't an easy matter for someone with my physical limitations but I could usually recruit a co-pilot, an assistant who might be persuaded to read aloud a sample passage – it was obvious that I needed assistance to retrieve books from the shelves, and though my inability to hold them comfortably wasn't so clear-cut the suggestion was rarely resisted unless the shop was busy. Assistance can develop a nice little momentum. At busy times or when the assistants in the other areas had stocktaking to do, or simply weren't in the mood, there was always the poetry department.

The assistants in charge of poetry shelves, and I'm confident for once that this is a worldwide phenomenon, are invariably softies who have no real expectation that you will buy anything. They're happy enough that you dipped your little cup in the river of refreshment whose tributary naiads they were, and usually delighted to be asked to read aloud, sometimes positively straining at the leash. Once in fact I had to ask for a bladder break when we were about four hundred lines into *The Rime of the Ancient Mariner*. I suppose it's possible that this marathon performance was intended as a deterrent, a way of teaching me a lesson, but I honestly don't think so. The glint in the young man's eyes was convincing, perhaps even worthy of the Mariner himself. Wedding guests in the greater Cambridge area might have been at a significant risk of being accosted.

If he didn't have his hands full with, well, me I wouldn't have put it past him to bring the book along with us. He might have wanted to continue his recitation while I used the staff toilet (a privilege whose sweetness never goes away), either from the other side of the door or actually invading the intimate cubicle with his frantic need to communicate.

Since then I've wondered if the Ancient Mariner isn't some sort of personification of poetry itself, increasingly desperate to be heard but turned away by most of those it tries to detain and enlighten.

I went on using the University Library whenever I could, making sure that the staff never quite forgot about me in case my claims on them turned out to be bogus and I was found out when I needed to fill out a form instead of relying, hypocritically I suppose, on their *vasanas*, their habit of flinging open the books, if not the doors of the building, in welcome.

To keep up my German I read *Effi Briest*, making myself understand the story by an effort of will and treating the dictionary as the recourse of last resort that it is anyway, thanks to the physical size and intractability of my mid-sized Langenscheidt. If *Effi Briest* had a guaranteed place on Thomas Mann's bookshelf then a borrowed copy could hardly bring disgrace to my table during its sojourn there. First, impressing no one but myself, I borrowed an early edition laid out in the old Fraktur print, the heavy blackletter font that makes the simplest proposition look like a row of portcullises or an equation bristling with variables made of barbed wire. I thought I would be able to sneak through this hedge of metal thorns to the meaning of the German but those portcullises kept me out – I'd lost the knack of slipping through, if I had ever had it in the first place. Even with a more recent copy it was a struggle to get to the end, though I enjoyed and even admired it.

Yet the act of reading didn't seem complete when I wasn't able to share its pleasures, and also the occasional puzzlement it produced, with anyone else. For example, it's mentioned as one of Effi's talents that she can eat an apple without needing to cut it up first. For heaven's sake, she's not even twenty at the time! So does that reflect the reality of young people's dental health in pre-Wilhelmine Germany, for this accomplishment to be worth the noting, or is it a case of an ageing author (Fontane being in his seventies when he wrote the book), well past the age of confident crunching, unconsciously imposing his own priorities?

I didn't need to ask Paula if she could tackle an apple whole since I'd seen her do it and had trained her in the art of helping me feed in the same style. Eating hard fruit is a challenge in itself if you can't use your hands, a variation of bobbing for apples whatever the time of year. I need someone to press the apple against my mouth quite hard if I'm to get any purchase. There's something unappealing about this intimate struggle, with my choppers working diligently away while someone's fingers keep up the pressure. The natural response, from the point of view of the fruit-pushing party, is to slacken off, as you might in self-protective alarm while feeding a horse. This is something that I can only try to discourage with inarticulate grunts. Altogether it's a far cry from scenes in films of lovers feeding each other – it's not exactly sensuous. Paula soon got the knack and we would share an apple, by which I mean she would eat the core, a habit that I've never acquired. With her receptiveness to superstitious folklore it was a wonder she had never heard about the tremendous risk of an apple tree growing inside you if you ate the pips.

There's nothing wrong with cutting fruit up for convenience of eating, yet there's a satisfying savagery about addressing a whole apple. I think it must be the residue of the atavistic need to gnash and rend, safely indulged here where no animal life can be forfeit.

The curtain of molecules

On one occasion Heffers contributed to the tingling of my spiritual life without my needing even to enter the shop. This was a case of outright transcendental nudging, italics of greater meaning lending their emphatic slant to the quotidian text. My attention was drawn to a newly published book thanks to some sly salesmanship mediated by divinity. I know all the objections to interventions of this sort – how dare you assume you're worthy of such personal notice? And the response must always be the same: how dare you assume you're not? Don't insult God by assuming he's lost your file.

These things are managed by subtle ripples, nothing crude or overt. I imagine it goes like this: it suddenly occurs to a Heffers assistant on his coffee break that the new book of Indian poetry, with its cover image of a god dancing in a wheel of fire, will look well displayed at eye level (I mean my eye level, naturally, nothing that will impose any further cricking on a neck that is already ninety per cent crick) rather than higher up. Returning to the bookshop window, he finds to his surprise that the book is already in the position to which he had just now decided to move it.

It is Śiva who is dancing in a wheel of fire on the cover of the book, in the sculptural pose known as *nataraja*, a cover designed by Germano Facetti, whose name was so pervasively present on Penguin covers in the early 1970s that he might have passed for an aspect of ubiquitous divinity himself. Vishnu the preserver seems the most likely candidate, considering Facetti's tireless work unearthing and recirculating images, rather than Brahma the creator or Śiva the sweeper-away. It was hard to tell at first glance whether what was being represented on the book's cover was Śiva's wild or gentle dance, *Rudra Tandava* or *Ananda Tandava*. In other words, was he shattering suns and moons or inhabiting the pure bliss of being, which is more his day job?

It has often been said that the wild dance is not altogether wild, since the destruction wrought by Śiva prepares for new creation, but it might also be said that the gentle dance is not so very gentle – certainly from the viewpoint of the dwarf being trampled by the Godhead at the base of the sculpture. Despite myself I feel for that dwarf, though I should know better, and not just because he represents ignorance. I feel for anyone and any thing that is likely to be trampled or tripped over. At least it's unlikely that Śiva would say, 'Sorry, mate – didn't see you down there!'

The assistant is piqued to find the book has been moved without his touching it, and decides to slip off his shoes and climb into the window so as to restore it to its original position, considerably above my natural line of sight. And so it is that as I pass the window display the book is actually being offered to me, virtually brandished, by an agreeable-looking if not actively dishy young man. My progress down Trinity Street is slow, the double take I do is also slow, but I am able to see where his big toe pokes out through a hole in his socks. Then he changes position, with a lurch and a wobble, bodily adjustments both embarrassed and endearing, so as to swing his ragged hosiery discreetly out of sight.

Self-consciousness lends his face an unstable animation, a look that could be mischief or divine possession or (of course) both. It's as if this stranger is passing *Speaking of Śiva* directly through the plate glass to me, trivial cosmic laws suspended so that the curtain of molecules forming the plate-glass shop window, its brittleness only one of the masks of matter, can interrupt their dense swarming and let the book pass through the dividing membrane, to be laid reverently on the backs of my hands. He sketches the beginnings of a smile, but a smile is a big commitment to take on – it often happens that people embark on one and then get suddenly stranded. They lose confidence halfway.

This bookshop assistant settles on the alternative option, anything but disgraceful, of a wink. I welcome his acknowledgement of my presence as his awareness of me dances upwards from lips to eyes and then disappears. I don't mind the way he manages to send a strong signal and immediately cancel it out. That's what a wink does, what a wink is. That's why winking was invented, the need for communication plus 'deniability', a word recently coined or at least recently swimming mysteriously into my ken.

I don't know what the standard incidence of winks is, as exchanged by the general population, so I'm not in a position to offer numerical testimony, but I have the sense of being much winked at. Nothing wrong with that, except that if the winks are always directed downwards then their meaning tends to harden and lose its lightness. It becomes a sign of complicity, sending the message 'You and me against the grown-ups', though I stubbornly class myself as an adult. In aggregate a thousand winks, each one of them sweetly conspiratorial, turn the wheelchair into a pram.

Not this wink, though, flashing through the plate-glass window of Heffers on Trinity Street! Not with its upward trajectory and its cheeky glow − sometimes a glow outranks a twinkle. Never mind that *Speaking of Śiva* has been reabsorbed through the molecular curtain and is about to take its mundane place in a window display. I don't mind that. The job of attracting my attention has been done, and well done. There will be other copies inside the bookshop. I'll buy one of those.

On subsequent visits I kept an eye out for the assistant who had held out *Speaking of Śiva* through a molecular veil that had been plate glass a moment before, but never managed to identify him. Eventually I forked out my 40p for a copy of *Speaking of Śiva* though I didn't read it immediately. The little shop-window miracle I had witnessed outside Heffers seemed a little too good to be true. It wasn't tacky Sai Baba showmanship but it didn't have Ramana Maharshi's fingerprint either, the suffusion of neutral warmth. And the year had contained enough disappointment as it was.

Lacking the power to slip a note under Bernardette's door myself I charged Paula with that errand, though as the gift of the Hacker was supposed to be a surprise I sealed my message properly in an envelope.

I suggested that Bernardette phoned me from Bacon's to arrange a time to collect it. Would she wrap it up? Hide it under their bed? Not my business.

When she came at the time agreed it seemed that she had more important things on her mind.

'Can I ask you a question?'

I said yes without giving it much thought. MarkO had asked no end of questions, some of them downright cheeky.

'What do you think – would MarkO suit a Marc Bolan perm? Loose curls, nothing frizzy.'

I tried to visualise this possibility. It helped that I had seen a picture of Bolan in the form of a full-colour poster in the 'pop' section of the Saturday *Cambridge Evening News*, just one of the ways the paper catered to young people. I struggled to superimpose MarkO's face onto Marc Bolan's, or Marc Bolan's hair onto his.

It was an effort for me to fight off the giggles, since MarkO's attractiveness couldn't co-exist with vanity or primping. His face, broad-boned and unsymmetrical, would make any perm look like a wig. I was already faced with a not-very-lookalike David Cassidy on a daily basis, every time Mr Gerling came to call, and I wasn't sure I could cope with any more homages to the pop charts in my social circle.

It was a compliment to be consulted on this, and arguably it was about time. It had always seemed extraordinary that Bernardette, who could afford to despise mere grooming on her own account, should be free of any urge to smarten MarkO up. Their difference in terms of stylishness was immense. Normally a spark leaps across a narrow gap rather than a crevasse.

'. . . honestly, John. You should see your face! That's not the real question. MarkO's fine as he is, believe it or not. It's just that the real question is so embarrassing. Here goes. Should I . . . take myself more seriously?'

The end of my rough-diamond phase

'Yes.' I didn't need to give it any thought. She had any amount of undeveloped talent. I'd seen her sketch Roger Moore as James Bond with just a few lines of an eyebrow pencil, a caricature that had more life in it than Moore had shown in *Live and Let Die*. I gathered this from the review in the *Cambridge Evening News*, and you should bear in mind how unlikely it was for a Bond film to get a lukewarm review in a local paper. It's fair to acknowledge that the paper's arts correspondents sometimes committed themselves to definite opinions, reactions strong enough to provoke reactions in their turn. I feared for their jobs. Sometimes they might tactically hold two opinions at once, neutralising the net effect in the interest of self-preservation– there was one review whose main headline was 'Flautists Find Perfect Pitch on King's Lawn', while the sub-head ('Spectators Mystified by Shrieks and Ape Noises') took a rebellious stance. Sometimes, though, a definite judgement reached print, seeming – in this context – reckless and even inflammatory.

Then Bernardette had torn up her sketch and thrown it away as if it was nothing. I'd persuaded Paula to retrieve it from the wastepaper basket the next day and we pieced it together then gazed at it in wonder.

'But you don't even know what I'm thinking of doing!'

'The answer is still yes.'

'I'm going to tell you anyway, you know. You're not getting off so lightly.'

Bernardette had visited her parents the previous week. MarkO wasn't thrilled when she told him about it but she reassured him, as she always did, by saying he would never have to meet them if he didn't want to. 'I can always say I'm getting to the end of my rough-diamond phase, that should buy me some time. MarkO is terrified that I'm going to cram him into a suit and try to make him presentable, but I know better than that.

'Anyway, I was in Oxford last weekend, waiting for the pubs to open to meet Ma and Pa – they live in Abingdon – and it was raining so I looked for some shelter. I was wearing some smart suède boots, a sort of dusty rose colour, and I didn't want water stains on them. Suède is tricky to keep looking nice. So I wandered into this entryway that had its doors open and I pretended to look at a wall of notices and announcements. I could feel there was someone behind me so I made sure I looked at the notices harder than ever.

'Then there was a gentle voice behind me saying, "What do you fancy? What subjects do you like?" And I saw there was a notice with FRENCH on it in big letters so I said, "French." And the man behind me said, "Anything else?" So I said, "English," because I speak it already, and that's a joke in case you were wondering. Then he said, "You only need one more – does anything else appeal?" And I looked around and said, clutching at straws, "Anthropology." I didn't know what it was, really, but I'd heard it was easy. And then the little man behind me came round the front and said, "Then that's a BA in General Studies accredited with the University of London. You could start on Monday. Term's already started but you'll soon catch up." I'd wandered into Oxford Poly to keep my boots dry, and I was already almost signed up for a degree. I said I couldn't start that soon, and he said, "I'll give you the paperwork anyway. Keenness is the most important thing."

'So right now I'm in a bit of confusion. I told Ma and Pa, though I still wasn't sure whether it wasn't a joke, and they leaped at the idea. They would absolutely love it if I went back into education. They'd want me to live with them. MarkO's dead against it. He's in a real sulk, though I've told him he could come with me, we'd get a flat together. If there's work for him in Cambridge why shouldn't there be in Oxford? But he won't hear of it. Frankly he's being a bit of a male-chauvinist porker, which isn't really like him. You know that.

'Anyway, I thought you could give me some advice. The forms say I need to send in my A-level certificates, which naturally I don't have. No A-levels. So no certificates. I mean, you must have applied, you must have sent certificates in. Do you think it's worth applying without them or am I just being stupid?'

'Let me think. They obviously want you there, and that must help.'

'They want to have their books full, you mean.'

'I really don't think there's a difference. They want you! When I filled in the forms I was applying for a full maintenance grant – how about you?'

'Oh no. It's almost embarrassing how keen Ma and Pa are on supporting me. They don't even mind if I don't end up living at home, though they'd rather I did. I wouldn't be tempted to take their money if I didn't really want . . . a degree.' It sounded as if she was afraid of

347

jinxing her chances by even using the word, one that she must have thought could never be attached to her.

'Then I'd say, have a go. My guess is that they'll be less fussy about the paperwork if you're only in line for the basic grant.' Fifty pounds a year, it was. 'So you won't be means-tested, and if you're lucky it'll be rubber-stamped before the clerk even has his coffee break. What are you risking? A stamp. You'd better make it a first-class stamp, though. I may even have one round here somewhere.' In fact I had several books. I had stocked up on them at 3p, in advance of the price rise that would make that the price of second-class post, while first class edged up to 3½p, a piece of prudent dealing that gave me a smug internal grin every time Paula stuck one on an envelope for me. I was getting a first-class service for the second-class price!

Bernardette swooped down and gave me a kiss on the lips. I might have enjoyed it if I'd had a little notice, but I understood she was being impulsive. If your neck has no movement an impulsive kiss is a considerable impact to absorb – it's quite a jar – and having your whole field of vision blocked by a descending face, however loaded with glamour, is slightly alarming. Her lips were warm, smooth and very slightly sticky, and I'm afraid that's all I can pass on of an experience that was much coveted in the Cambridge of the time.

'MarkO's really making an effort to get back in your good graces, you know,' she said. 'He doesn't always.'

MarkO was someone it was hard to stay angry with, a characteristic that was outweighed by the fact that he knew it and took care that it should be so. Consequently I fought the tide of forgiveness rising within me and was as petty as I knew how. A while back he had borrowed a book from me, less because he wanted to read it, I think, than out of a desire to impress me and anyone who saw him reading, or at least holding, it. The book was Nietzsche's *Beyond Good and Evil* in the Penguin Classics edition, its memorably lurid cover design showing a woman bare-breasted, both languorous and predatory, dozing but about to pounce – the Sphinx, in fact, as visualised by a Decadent painter. Now I was pestering him to return it, though normally I don't lend a book unless I have already made my peace with losing it.

Before she left Bernardette asked how much I wanted for the Hacker and I heard myself asking £10 for it. I had planned on making it a gift but was unable at the last moment to shed the worldly wisdom (impressed on me by Granny) that insisted on a contribution from any beneficiary. In her view of the world, generosity that imposed no conditions was an egg without salt. So that was a pesky little *vasana* making me fall at the last fence, though which fence it was hardly matters. First or last, it's always the same fence. There's only ever one fence in the steeplechase of being. It's when the ectoplasmic whip of enlightenment is applied to the flanks of pure presence that the fence jumps over both horse and rider at last.

A surprisingly bitter argument about geraniums

Bernardette left happy after our little consultation about her future, and I was happy to have played my part in that. Why point out that if degrees transformed their possessors in the way she imagined then I wouldn't have been on hand to dispense the sage advice she had just received? I had crawled away from Downing like a wounded animal and got no further than Mayflower House. In the end the extraction of the Hacker from 005 was managed smoothly, by arrangement while I was out, even if I couldn't resist pretending to Paula – for a few moments only – that I had been burgled.

For the next few days I was in a strange excited state of non-expectation, ready to rise above MarkO's gratitude without it needing to manifest itself. The gesture would not bring us closer together, and I didn't mean it to. It really seemed as if non-attachment was in my grasp.

Then one day as I was making my way past Mrs Baine's desk my eye was drawn to an item on the notice board behind her. This board was normally of no interest to me, but something made me pay attention and I was drawn in particular to a notice pinned at the very top, not out of my range of vision as such but evading the feeble swivelling powers of my neck unless I aligned myself and the wheelchair just so. Someone was offering a Hacker sound system (one integral speaker, the other on an extension wire) for sale at the bargain price of £40. I was marvelling at the coincidence for quite a little while before I realised what was afoot. That little rodent MarkO was selling the Hacker on for a quick profit! The notice didn't quite say 'one

349

careful owner', but then that wouldn't have been accurate, would it? The owner hadn't watched over his property with the appropriate vigilance.

I was outraged. Exploit my friendship by all means, cheat me out of my stuff if you must, but don't insult my eyesight. I'm not blind yet! Hang your bloody *For Sale* card higher up on the wall, or use smaller lettering. If I can decipher a doctor's scrawl from the other side of a desk well enough to forge it then I think I can manage to make out your wobbling hand from this little distance.

It wasn't exactly that I was vain of my eyesight, just grateful that I didn't need to wear glasses. They're such fiddly things! They might have been expressly designed for unJohnability, impossible to put on or take off unless you can bend your elbows. Maya herself is myopic, and forces her myopia on us bit by bit. I could only hope that by the time I needed to wear glasses I had somehow acquired an attendant or companion to do the honours, or else that spectacles now floated on dainty jets of air.

Mrs Baine may not have had technical knowledge of hydraulics but could see that steam was about to come out of my ears. 'Can I help you, Mr Cromer? Is there a notice you're interested in?'

'Yes indeed, Mrs Baine. Could you hand me down that card with the details about the stereo for sale?'

'I suppose.'

'Now can you tear it in half, please?'

'I'll do no such thing!'

'Then please give it to me, Mrs Baine, and I'll have a go.' She retreated behind the counter, greatly overestimating my ability to snatch and rend.

'Please, Daphne . . .' If I'd plugged her into the mains I could hardly have given her such a jolt as I did by unauthorised use of her first name, learned from the same envelope that had informed me of the correct spelling of Baine, or if I'd correctly identified the wicked Rumpelstiltskin, seeing through the twin-set disguise, and put an end to her baby-stealing ways. But the extreme weapon I had chosen to use blew up in my face. I shouldn't have tried to prise open the strongbox of her character with the crude timber-splintering crowbar of her first name.

I felt I had to explain the situation, and when I did she was outraged. Would she at least let me write a note of protest on the card?
She surprised me by saying, 'Oh, I think we can do better than that,
Mr Cromer. Sometimes there's nothing like red ink to get the message across. I'll get my emergency biro.' I suppose you don't end up
as a concierge without enjoying being a spectator while relationships
are made and broken. Now she had a bit part in her own right, and
lines to speak if she chose to deliver them. It turned out she wasn't shy
of the limelight: 'If there's one thing I hate, Mr Cromer, it's crooked
dealing. There's a special place reserved for crooked dealers, and one
thing I can tell you . . . it's certainly not in heaven.'

What she wrote at my dictation, and then went over with her emergency red biro, was NOT FOR SALE – CONTACT RIGHTFUL
OWNER. We added my phone number, that agile telecommunications Ent that had somehow picked up its roots and made the
curious journey from Downing College unnoticed. The Ents go to
war against the Orcs, don't they? That's my memory of the book, for
what it's worth. No such adversaries at Mayflower House, unless the
local Orcs had slyly disguised themselves as trivial greed and sexual
manœuvring. Mrs Baine replaced the card on the notice board, lower
down than it had originally been, and very eye-catching, stained as it
was with the heart's blood of the emergency biro.

Then I had second thoughts. This was all too public, too melodramatic. Somehow the red emergency biro had got in on the act, when
it was my hand and no one else's that should sign the note of protest.
'Mrs Baine,' I said, 'I wonder if you would be so good as to take down
that card after all. I'll write a note to the . . . person involved.' I do
quite a good line in wounded dignity, though I say it myself, but it's
hard to make sure that the right people notice and out of context it
can look like constipation. I was being a bit rhetorical, admittedly
– it must have years since the formula 'if you would be so good' had
been uttered on those premises, if it had ever even happened (the
building was fairly new). 'Perhaps you'd pass on a note a little later,
to Mark O . . . to the gentleman on the second floor.'

'To Mr Ousby? Very well. So that's the miscreant involved. I wish
I could say I was surprised.' She rose to the refined tone of my denun-
ciation. I realised, though, that whether she acted as amanuensis or

postman I would have to delegate my protest. My desire for a personal confrontation wasn't all-consuming, but it was there.

She was gratifyingly incensed on my behalf. The only time I'd seen her more stirred up was about something that lay much closer to her heart. *The Lady*, her favourite magazine, printed an advertisement for Victory V throat lozenges ('They've got a kick like a mule') featuring Harvey Smith the showjumper, who was best known for making an obscene gesture to the judges after a near-perfect championship round – the name 'Harvey Smith' had become synonymous with the V-sign. She threatened to cancel her subscription, but of course she didn't. People never do cancel subscriptions, it's just something to say. The advertisement certainly looked out of place on those staid pages, but perhaps it boosted sales. There are always women who are keen on men who will be bad for them, and perhaps the same principle applies even to ladies.

Imagine being famous for jabbing spurs into the flank of an animal that already wants to do your bidding! I have an especially vivid sense of the sufferings of horses, evidence of a previous life spent miserably in harness or (more likely now I think about it) an early traumatic reading of *Black Beauty*.

Mrs Baine never offered to pass on back numbers of *The Lady*, and I'm still not sure how I feel about that. Was I fit only for the *Cambridge Evening News* in her eyes?

Ousby. How could I have forgotten this definitively Cumberlandian pair of syllables? I made the assumption that it was MarkO's writing on the treasonous card rather than Bernardette's, which wasn't entirely logical. A woman who kept her fingernails short and wore the man's cologne she had bought for MarkO, knowing full well that he would never use it himself ('Cacharel pour L'Homme,' I think she said, as she offered me an aromatic wrist), need not have a feminine cast to her handwriting, whatever a feminine hand was anyway. People in nineteenth-century novels confidently describe handwriting as being a man's or a woman's – it's not just Sherlock Holmes. Even the duffer Lestrade can get it right! But perhaps boys and girls were taught entirely separate styles of writing at school. The sort of thing that MarkO called so grandly 'transmission of the culture pattern'.

In the end I drafted a letter and left it with Mrs Baine to pass on. *Kindly return the goods you got from me by false pretenses. I'll be away from the flat between eleven and twelve noon for the rest of the week. The £10 that I 'owe' you is in Mrs Baine's keeping.* What could Holmes or even Lestrade deduce from my handwriting? That holding a pen is hard work, but sometimes neither pencil, biro nor felt-tip is symbolically up to the job. One of Paula's duties was to check that my pen was fully charged with ink. In my book the fountain pen of formality outranks even the emergency biro. Challenge someone to a duel using a felt-tip to write the note and your cause is lost before your sabre even leaves the scabbard. I concentrated on forming large regular letters, and forced myself to keep their size and shape consistent — nothing suggests the underlying pettiness of a grievance more than handwriting that is crabbed or drifting. And I know that lined paper is frowned on in calligraphic and duel-negotiating circles alike, but that's just too bad.

As for where I should betake my small body habitus in the time between eleven and twelve, the line of least resistance suggested the haven of the Bot. This wasn't a happy visit. I've spent many hundreds of hours in the Bot over the years and those few may have been the only ones that I really haven't enjoyed. I ended up having a surprisingly bitter argument about geraniums with a member of staff.

I really only wanted to fill my eyes with dahlias and chrysanthemums, perhaps some osteospermums hanging on. When a young employee passed by I asked after Celia, but he had no news of her, or gave me none, and little willingness to believe that she and I might really be on friendly terms. The young man wore shorts just as she had, though in style his were more overgrown Boy Scout than hiking. It should have pleased me that his intonation went down at the ends of sentences. In fact he planted them so firmly in the ground you could use them as stakes for runner beans to climb up, but of course I missed Celia's upward-swooping style of speech, however much I disapproved of it in theory.

The trouble started when I pointed out that the plant he referred to as a geranium was actually a pelargonium. It's an old confusion, dating back to Linnæus, and was sorted out for good and all a long time ago, even before 1800 if I remember rightly. I wasn't expecting resistance! I'm not naïve, I know there's any amount of dirty work behind the scenes at the Chelsea Flower Show, but I relied on reasoned argument being possible at the Bot. In general terms experts are humble and amateurs are gracious, though those in either category who are insecure about their expertise are likely to insist on it. I asked how long he had been working at the Bot, and he said, 'Long enough to know what a geranium looks like.' Maybe, but not long enough to know what a geranium actually *is*. I doubt if he had been there more than a couple of weeks. There were raised voices, it's true, but I said nothing personally insulting about Linnæus, just that he had been a bit hasty to lump in semi-succulents from South Africa, on the basis of a superficial physical resemblance of seed capsule and fragrance, with the geraniums he knew from closer to home. I may have used the word 'slapdash', which I would have left alone if I wasn't in an agitated state from the whole MarkO business, but you can't really say it doesn't apply. Of course they're closely related, both being *Geraniaceæ*, but taxonomy is supposed to recognise differences, such as the asymmetric leaf arrangement pelargoniums used to have before symmetry was bred in, as well as similarities, and wasn't taxonomy Linnæus's baby in the first place? Pelargoniums are much more tender, for one thing – you need to bring them indoors in winter, and to compound the mistake by adding the descriptor 'hardy' to true geraniums is a shoddy way of making that difference clear. Linnæus isn't doctrinally infallible like the Pope, he's entitled to an off day occasionally, and so am I.

I can prove it. In 1973 I still confidently referred to hippeastrums, of which there are any number of species, with the name Amaryllis, whose genus contains only the species *Amaryllis belladonna*. Hippeastrums are originally from the Americas, amaryllis from South Africa. Very much the same story as with pelargoniums and geraniums, and if I had made the error in our conversation that day at the Bot – before it got heated – and the same nervous young man had pointed it out I would infallibly have perked up. I enjoy being set straight on matters of fact. Honestly, I wish it happened more often. I don't see why saying I like being corrected should raise a smile, but it does. I'm being perfectly sincere. Shouldn't the shedding of an error qualify as an occasion for joy? That's much the healthiest way of looking at it. It's a privilege to have your blinkers taken off so that the light can reach you from all sides.

I'm not the only vandal in the building

When I got back to 005 the bartered asset had been restored to its accustomed place on the desk, and so the Hacker came back to haunt me. If not to haunt me then to mock me, lightly but persistently, for the idea that I could behave unselfishly just because I wanted to. As it turned out I had to give up on renunciation for the time being – which I don't think counts as a renunciation in its own right, though you never know.

MarkO hadn't taken away the records stored with me for safekeeping, and there was a kind of inevitability about my choice of first record to play on the turntable's melancholy homecoming. I took the record out of its sleeves, the inner and the outer, with special care, though knowing perfectly well that taking special care at such moments floats lightly over the impulse to destroy. *Oh dear, MarkO, you'll never guess what happened! It turns out your records weren't safe with me after all . . . I'm not the only vandal in the building! Mayflower House is full of them!* I wouldn't give myself that bitter satisfaction, which would only have let him off the hook with its pitiful and asymmetrical tit-for-tat.

I played *Affinity* by Affinity and watched the 'logo' with its endlessly swirling movement that got nowhere at all. I listened to lyrics that were boobytrapped with miserable irony. I do hate irony, don't you? Absolutely one of Maya's laziest inventions. It turned out that MarkO wasn't much of a hater of lies after all, however often he sang along to the lyrics that said so. Leaving me stuck with the dregs, the dreary, left-over role of 'dreamer of sighs'. MarkO wasn't much of a Mr Joy in the end, was he? I knew he would be paying me a visit sooner or later, to pick up his records and to make excuses for himself. It seemed likely that he would still be enough on my wavelength, alas, to be able to detect the moment I was least defended against him.

There were some lyrics I hadn't properly noticed before. *Now where do you belong? In my heart? No no no. Just in this song.* They seemed horribly accurate. When I say I hadn't noticed the lines before, that's to assume they hadn't popped up overnight. Maya loves to say 'I told you so' and usually she didn't, she's just tampered with the records, though it's not an easy thing to prove.

Days could go by without me receiving a phone call, but I had two in rapid succession after the Hacker had finished playing Side One.

Suddenly I was in demand, in a way that seemed almost fishy. The second caller was Granny, none too pleased that the line had been busy when she had tried a few minutes previously. Was it proper for other people to block her access to her grandson with their trivial communications? Unthinkable that anyone would seek to obstruct the workings of her acidulated benevolence. Brezhnev himself could not have been more disgruntled to hear the engaged tone on the Moscow-to-Washington hotline.

'I was worried about you, John. I told myself that I would wait five minutes more and if I still couldn't get through I'd ask the operator to check the line. Anything might have happened.'

It would have been handy if my phone had actually had the power to turn red when Granny rang, so that I had a few seconds to prepare myself, since her normal manner wasn't much more relaxing. She would say, 'Ah, there you are, John,' when I answered the phone, as if I had kept her waiting in some way. As if she had been looking for me everywhere and I had turned up in the most unexpected place.

It has to be faced, I'm afraid, that my grandmother had more of a hand in shaping my personality than my own mother did. When I defend my point of view somewhat relentlessly, as can sometimes happen, I can feel the iron wheels of Granny's karmic wagon deepening the rut in the road, and I understand a certain amount of the dismay I see on the faces around me. Useless to insist that these fierce microorganisms are not pathogens but antibodies gone rogue. Shields with sharpened edges, not weapons as such.

Of course I'm telling this the wrong way round. The first phone call was from George, my dance partner in the strange ideological quadrille of the Cambridge Homosexual Action Project, or CHAPs. We were viewed as a unit at the meetings in Glisson Road, thanks to our having met literally on the doorstep of the house belonging to the Tonys, who played host, on what was the maiden visit for both of us. That evening we had made a pact to go as a pair in future, armoured by each other's company against too much pity and too much ideological analysis. The group imagined us as a couple, though according to the gay liberation wisdom of the time the couple itself was under a cloud, slavish heterosexual imitation and a relic that would shortly be swept away. So we were like two odd socks that might as well be rolled together before being put in a drawer, since no one would be wearing either of them anyway.

Even before George phoned I knew in some dim molluscan way that CHAPs meetings had started up again – just as oysters know, snug in their envelopes of mucous contemplation, when there's an 'r' in the month. I was even well enough attuned to the social calendar of the group to know that I'd missed a couple of meetings. I dithered about phoning George myself, who normally picked me up and delivered me home, perhaps because I wasn't anxious for him to see my new surroundings and my somehow rather crepuscular life in Mayflower House.

Would I be missed at meetings? Would there be a search party organised to make sure I was all right? There seemed no reason to think so. Although at every CHAPs meeting it was made clear that the group didn't cater to students as a priority, there was a definite element of fiction in the notion that this was a local organisation that just happened to be based in a university town. Inevitably graduation took a toll on attendance, and there would be no special curiosity about what had become of me, just another student ephemerid whose mating dance was over. No one would know that this particular ephemerid had exceeded his fated span and was now embarked on some sort of afterlife in Mayfly, sorry, Mayflower House.

George sounded very tentative on the phone that day, since it went against common sense that I could go on having the same phone number when I had graduated and must necessarily have moved to a new address. In those days nobody really expected a patient to survive a transplant operation very long, whether the beneficiary of the surgery was a heart patient in South Africa or a skirting board in peripheral Cambridge, way over by the Elizabeth Bridge, having an existing phone number transferred to it.

Once he'd been reassured that my phone number had been given a new lease of life at a new address he proposed that we go together to the next meeting, though I would have to do the driving, if I didn't mind. His car was in the garage. 'I've got lots to tell you,' he said, and I made out that I was in a similar state, brimming over with the fascinations of narrative, though it was hard to argue for this being true. Since I'd last seen George I had induced temporary death in a mouse

357

by electrocution and projected a regular heptagon into the brain of a jobbing milkman, but there hadn't really been a lot going on.

You'd be the second to know

'What's your address?' Only now did I realise that I didn't know where George lived, beyond the vagueness of 'Chesterton'. For all I knew of it that area of the city might have been founded by Gilbert Keith of the Chesterton tribe and have housed only homespun priests doubling as detectives.

'Why don't you pick us up outside the Haymakers at 6.30?'

'Where's that? Where's the Haymakers?'

'On the High Street. You can't miss it.' Hold on a sec – in fact, hold on a cotton-picking minute (whatever that is exactly). 'Us'? 'Pick us up'? But by then he had rung off and I would have to wait till Tuesday to learn the details. I was thinking of ringing back and asking, but nosiness isn't the most attractive characteristic even when it isn't combined with impatience. Then Granny phoned and drove all other thoughts from my mind, not that she would have minded. She wouldn't have wanted it any other way.

When we'd skirted around the unpalatable fact that people besides her could call me on the phone, though natural justice would have insisted on granting her the monopoly, she got down to business. 'Your clever little Granny has received rather a satisfactory dividend on some shares she had almost forgotten about, and it seems fitting to pass on the benefit. In fact she has sold some Consols. Do you happen to know what the word "Consols" is short for?'

I thought for a moment. 'Consolation prizes?' I didn't say 'for a life of empty acquisition', but perhaps I didn't need to.

She gave a harsh little titter. 'Very good, John. No, in actuality it stands for "Consolidated", a lovely word. Everything should be consolidated, and there's no reason why that rule should not apply to my grandson. To you. If you are in need of help with your rent, as seemed to be the case a little while ago, you will not be averse to some financial assistance, unless perhaps you have won a fortune on the football pools or the Irish Hospitals' sweepstake and have been biding your time to tell me about it.'

'No, Granny, I promise you'd be the second to know.'

'The second? And why not the first, John, if I may ask?'

'Well, Granny, because I'd have to know about it first.'

A pause, and then a merry, surprisingly youthful little laugh. 'John, you're a caution, and I should caution you that I will use that line of reasoning in my future conversations. I shall let you know if it wins me any friends!' Another laugh, but a more perfunctory one. It was as if she realised she had betrayed some principle by showing sincere amusement. If there wasn't a cut-off point in terms of age for the descriptions 'taker of the piss' and 'wind-up merchant' then Granny would have qualified on both counts.

Our conversations always had an edge of skirmish, and if I remember the bouts I won, and forget the ones I lost, that doesn't make me a human anomaly.

Once she said, 'My husband Ivo, as you must know, was a Balliol man.' Must I know it? Must I really? Was I not allowed to forget it the moment I was told, if I was ever told it in the first place? 'So I was rather surprised that you plumped for Cambridge.'

Did she imagine there was some sort of bidding war for my attendance as an undergraduate?

'Well, Granny, all the colleges wanted me at both places, both Oxford and Cambridge, and in the end it came to tossing a coin. Quite a few times, in fact – perhaps you're familiar with the I Ching as a method of making decisions. They couldn't all be the lucky one, could they?'

'John, I detect in your sarcasm a callow strain perhaps characteristic of Cambridge. Oxford would have given you a suaver edge. Never mind, it will serve. I consider myself reproached, not only reproached but lacerated.' Nevertheless she seemed as pleased with me as she had ever been. Now I think of it, this was a draw rather than a victory for either party.

After my success with 'you'll be the second to know' she introduced a new subject, perhaps influenced by my little triumph. 'John, a thought occurs to me. Do you have difficulty going to your bank, as it might be, to deposit a cheque?'

'Well, Granny, it isn't the easiest thing in the world. But it's easier than going to the bank to pay a bill. Psychologically, I mean. The physical effort is the same.' I was in the uneasy position of having scored a seeming success with my last remark, which historically had always tempted me towards extravagant assertion and downfall. 'So if the question you're posing is "Would it be more convenient to have the money delivered in cash to my home address in a little bag?", then the answer is yes.'

'Just the way I see it myself, John. That should present no difficulty. My bank often obliges me in this fashion.' Granny's bank – in other words Coutts. If Williams & Glyn was the junior Coutts, then Coutts was . . . Coutts. Her Majesty the Queen didn't go to the bank to withdraw or deposit money, of course, and nor apparently did Granny. Now, for a fleeting moment in my lifetime, I was being offered a chance to join that company.

'What notes might you like, John? I'd recommend plumping for an assortment.' She might have been talking about a box of chocs. Chocolate creams, tenners, cracknel, five-pound notes. Everybody has a preference, I suppose. When Granny said 'I'd' I would hear it as 'I'ld', as it might be notated in raffish Edwardian literary dialogue, with plush port-and-stilton informality. 'Nothing too high in the way of denominations, though, I'm afraid the people in these parts don't see such things very often. Twenty-pound notes tend to make them goggle.'

It wasn't just the burghers of Tangmere who could have their heads turned. Such a thing might bring on a case of the goggles in me also.

'John, I'll leave you to hammer out the fine print with the relevant functionaries.' If Granny's legal interests could support a whole firm of solicitors then perhaps there was a Tangmere sub-branch of Coutts to meet her financial needs. 'Is there a time of day when you are guaranteed to be in to answer the phone?'

I was always in except when I was able to devise more or less artificial errands. 'Well, Granny, I can undertake to answer the phone any weekday between 9 and 9.30.' It's funny, though Granny had quite a nose for lies it wasn't enough to keep me on the straight and narrow in our conversations.

'I must tell you, John, that the business hours of banking are shockingly short. No work is done, I'm sorry to say, until 9.30 at the earliest. Can you be persuaded to stretch a point?'

360

Graciously I indicated that I would make myself available to the telephone operatives of the cash-delivery department of Messrs Coutts for an extra half-hour.

I missed the presence of MarkO and Bernardette in my life on many counts. I imagined them sprinting across the lobby to avoid me when they heard me start to open my door, or else hanging back while I made my stately progress in or out. Who else would be impressed or even interested that I was having money delivered by a man from the Queen's bank? I could mention it in passing to Mrs Baine, though the whole principle of 'in passing' is that you're moving briskly along and that was something I couldn't aspire to. Easier for me to mention something 'in passing' through the open window of the Mini, but I wasn't going to start giving directions to tourists on King's Parade just so that I could mention my grandmother, her connections with sundry equerries and the fact that I was expecting an imminent windfall. I didn't want to turn into Billy Bunter, the Fat Owl of Greyfriars School, forever bragging about the postal order on its way to him from a titled relation.

In fact it would be a bad idea if Mrs Baine got wind of the delivery. Wasn't I supposed to be the poor relation of the building, the one who had to plead with the authorities to pay his rent in full? Now I might seem to be rolling in it in a very fishy way. A prosecution for fraud would be a useful test of my ability to detach myself from the world, but no doubt there would be other opportunities.

My calendar was almost empty of appointments. I was expecting a phone call from Coutts and I knew that sooner or later MarkO would knock at my door to retrieve his exiled long-playing records and inevitably to make some sort of claim on my sympathy. Naturally I didn't want the two events to coincide, not exactly keen on my life turning out to be both functionally empty and overcomplicated, but I also knew that MarkO still somehow shared a wavelength with me. Consciously or unconsciously he was likely to make it happen.

He brought a can of beer with him when he paid the promised visit, opening the door so soon after he had knocked that there was no point in even knocking, and it was clear that the can wasn't his first. He was defiantly disordered, tearing open the can, burping and wiping his mouth.

'Oh hello, MarkO,' I said, striving for a neutral tone. 'I expect you've come to pick up your records. I wonder if Mrs Baine would look after them? Obviously they're not safe in your flat.'

'Shut up, John. *Shut up!* There's something I need to say and you're going to listen while I say it.'

I wasn't physically frightened. He wasn't formidable in that way. 'Go ahead.'

'John, I'm really sorry. I'm sorry I'm sorry I'm sorry. Honestly I meant no harm. I know you valued it and you trusted me with it. I shouldn't have shown it around.'

Shown it around? I didn't follow. Who had been shown what?

'That book of yours, the one you lent me with the tits on the cover . . . I'm afraid it's been swiped.' I was completely at sea. It took me a little while to realise he was referring to the Penguin volume of Nietzsche he had been so keen to borrow, *Beyond Good and Evil*. It did indeed have tits on the cover, nipple-studded rondures adorning the chest of a predatory-looking Sphinx in an insistently decadent painting (by Franz von Stuck, if you're interested). Naturally MarkO had taken the book with him to work. Letting it be known that he's a bit of an intellectual. Wasted in the job, really, but perhaps he's doing research for a novel. 'I can be a bit of a show-off, John,' said MarkO, 'but I'm not the only one.' Oi! Don't change the subject. Carry on with your story.

My version of 1970s milkman vernacular

Then of course he had to take it into the canteen with him to bruit abroad the fact of his intellectual eminence. As if there wasn't enough posturing in Cambridge already! And in fact his gaffer takes a look at the cover of the book MarkO is reading and gets the wrong end of the stick. I admit that the ghastly shades of yellow and green suggest something unwholesome – they're meant to! This is decadent art, but there are other conclusions to draw. 'Blimey, that looks like a good read!' he says. 'Pretty strong, eh? Strong stuff, is it? Really strong?' All the title *Beyond Good and Evil* suggests to him is that the bint on the cover showing off her tits will be equally free in the minge department once you get the book open. He fancies getting an eyeful and asks to borrow the book, only the snotty little temporary berk says he hasn't finished with it yet. How long does it take to 'read' a book like that? So he nicks it when MarkO isn't looking. Of course he doesn't get what he wants, but he can't give the book back without looking a prat, can he? So it stays nicked.

That's my version of 1970s milkman vernacular, by the way. I expect it needs work. MarkO only gave the bare bones of what went on, leaving me to fill it in. All he would say was that it must have been his gaffer that swiped the book, but there was nothing he could do about it, was there? 'I'm really sorry, John. Sorry about the book . . . and everything else.' And that was it. Hang on – wasn't there supposed to be a specific apology for the little defraudment scheme? Not a kneeling-in-the-snow self-flagellation, necessarily, but something a wee bit fuller than 'everything else'. I was being offered a sort of piggyback apology, one thing lumped in with another without being properly addressed. The stolen-borrowed-book pretext tottering along as best it could under the weight of the unsaid. What did I care about *Beyond Good and Evil*, tits or no tits? It didn't matter to me.

'Everything else?' I wasn't letting him get away with that. 'Like cheating me for example? Selling on the stereo you got at a knock-down price?'

'I'm not proud of that. I know we tried to con you for a bit of Christmas money. Which was mainly Bernie's idea, though her parents are rolling in it, but what she says goes. It was wrong, and I'm glad you've got your stereo back, safe and sound. No harm done. Put on the old Supertramp in a bit, yeah?' I'd never heard him sound plaintive before. 'But I was angry with you – you let me down.'

I said, 'I have no idea what you're talking about.' Unfortunately this is one of those self-invalidating propositions. It feels untruthful even in the ears of the person who utters it in all sincerity. It made my innocence sound bogus to myself.

He stood to my side, knowing after all this time of knowing me that I couldn't turn my head to look at him. His voice was all clotted with resented tears. 'You took my old lady. We were good together, until she got this stupid idea about studying at a Poly and living at home – living at home with her *Ma* and her *Pa*. And you encouraged her. You could have been a friend and told her it wouldn't work, that she didn't have what it takes. But no, you had to egg her on. She has a lot of respect for your opinion.' I had no idea. I wish I'd known! 'Okay, it was pretty mean of us to rip you off, but you got your stereo back, didn't you? And you took away my old lady.

'Bernie's not clever, you know. Not really. She's really not. Did I tell you about the time I had to let her in on the secret that the big hunk of meat in a kebab shop — you know, going round and round on a spit — wasn't some sort of whole joint! I asked what bit she thought it was, to be so big, and she said, "I don't know! The bum?" Lamb bum. Lamb bum on a stick. You think that's student material? Even *General Studies*, whatever crap that is?'

Calling Bernardette 'Bernie' was bad enough, and it was the first time I'd heard him call her that. Calling her his 'old lady' was worse, a sort of blasphemy. As far as I was concerned MarkO had forfeited any claim to Bernardette by referring to her as his 'old lady', as surely as Paris in *Troilus and Cressida* showed himself unworthy of Helen by calling her 'my Nell'. *I would fain have arm'd today, but my Nell would not have it so.* That's Helen of Troy, you twit! Show some respect.

And that was the only benefit I seemed to be getting from my B.A. (Cantab.) in English: apposite internal quotation at moments of boredom or crisis. Better than nothing, I suppose, but not something they put into the prospectus.

Language was changing as was only right, and inevitable in any case. Even the phrase 'old man' wasn't safe — it had gone from meaning Dad ('My Old Man's a Dustman', 'My Old Man Said Follow the Van', any amount of Cockney nonsense) to meaning boyfriend, at least in some circles. Yes, the phrase existed, it had some hippy currency — there were trendy young women who called a boyfriend their 'old man', shutting their ears to the phrase's preposterous associations. 'Old man' and 'old lady' in their new meaning made me think of Pearly Kings and Queens being photographed in their swinging gear after an ill-advised trip to the King's Road or Biba's, the only shop for which I had heard Bernardette express even qualified approval.

'Bernardette was . . . she was the only one who gave me TLC.'

'TLC? What's that?'

'Are you trying to be funny?'

'No, honestly not. What's TLC?'

364

'Tender Loving Care. What she gave me.' Lord knows I love an acronym, but I have to say I was disappointed this one wasn't pharmaceutical.

'But why should she stop giving you . . . tender loving care, just because she's studying for a degree, if she even goes? Why should she stop being your . . . girlfriend?' I couldn't bring myself to say 'old lady'. Enunciating the syllables of 'tender loving care' was enough of a strain on the system.

He moved round so that I could see his face, painfully distorted. 'She's not going – she's *gone*.' He hit the 'g' of *gone* so fiercely that his Adam's apple dived downwards as the sound came out. He shaved his neck every now and then, at Bernardette's prompting or insistence, which gave me an unobstructed view of the cartilage in its sudden descent and more leisurely return to position. I'd never really understood before what people meant when they called a sound 'guttural', though it's part of the technical description of the 'g'-sound (overlapping with 'pharyngeal consonant' and 'voiced plosive'). But as he spoke the word the stopping and subsequent release of breath was brutally abrupt.

'She's gone. And I'm not going after her.'

'Is she expecting you to?'

'She says so, yeah. She *says* so.'

'Then why not?'

He made sure he was looking me square in the face when he made his confession. This made it tricky for me to react convincingly while I was under such scrutiny. This is the converse and corollary of people being able to hide their faces from me so easily, that when they want me to see their expressions (it's usually of woeful sincerity) I can't escape. I suppose I could have tried closing my eyes, but that seemed a bit extreme. I had no objection to looking at his face but I had to keep iron control over my own. Most of the time I have to amplify the expressive messages I send, to convey that yes, in the teeth of the probabilities these communicative signals are emanating from the person with small body habitus, but now I had to turn the volume dial down if not cut the transmission altogether.

'The thing is . . . the thing is . . .' He seemed authentically miserable, putting off the moment that he knew must come at last. MarkO spoke as if there was something clogging his mouth, something – orange peel for instance – not actively vile that wouldn't either go all the way down or come all the way up and out. I suppose it was the taste of himself, sourly regurgitated. 'I haven't been honest with her, and not with you either. Not with anybody really. The thing is—' (the cartilage in his throat made another plunge) '—I'm afraid I wasn't actually an undergraduate here. Not for a year. Not even a term. I've been living a lie.'

Living a Lie – poor MarkO! He was searching my face for signs of shock, when in fact I had to fight a wild urge to laugh without betraying the effort it cost me. Of course he hadn't got into Cambridge to read History! The idea was preposterous, but there had never been any point in challenging him about it. When I had laid a little trap on our visit to Downing, asking whether he'd like to visit his old Selwyn haunts when it was Sidney Sussex that he had claimed as his college, and he didn't correct me, that should have clinched the matter, except that the matter was pre-clinched, clinched more or less from the first. As far as I could make out, the little bit he knew about baroque music was more than he knew about anything else. At one point he had claimed to have been the reserve on his college's *University Challenge* team, but it was as if he could feel the balloon losing pressure even as he tried to blow it up. He changed tack in a hurry, trying to turn it at short notice into a story of comic failure, with his team being eliminated in an early round because someone – not him – couldn't spell 'Mississippi'.

The paradox was of course (one of those ugly paradoxes that wait on the beautiful) that it quite suited Bernardette to have a boyfriend who was so obviously unworthy of her. It looked like a caprice that she could afford to gratify without loss of prestige, rather than a miscalculation, as it might have seemed with a partner lower in status but within reach of her own ranking. In those days there was always a sort of calculus brought to bear on women's sexual choices, one that continued to be imposed from outside even when an independent-minded individual was able to flout it and escape the consequences.

Wear and tear on the frenulum

'The thing is, John, I can tell you, but I can't tell her. And now she's in Oxford, staying with her *Ma* and her *Pa*, and she says I could find casual work there and we could get a flat, but don't you see?

She'll be hanging out with students the whole time, and sooner or later they'll see through me. And so will she.' I tried to contort my facial features so as to suggest that I understood his dilemma and was thinking very hard, but secondary ripples of laughter kept welling up inside me. If Bernardette had believed in his undergraduate career even for a minute then it was a short sixty seconds. She knew and she didn't care, and nor did I. My feeling was that if Bernardette could forgive MarkO for dragging her to see *Steptoe and Son Ride Again* at the ABC she could forgive him practically anything. In fact there was nothing wrong with MarkO's intelligence expect his determination to portray it as academic, perching a mortarboard precariously on his haystack hair. In a university town that was one big game of bluff and counterbluff he had overplayed his hand, that was all.

There were lapses in his ignorance, mysterious openings-out into a larger self, one that was undeceived and undeceiving. But then I had allowed myself to develop a bit of a crush on him, and if a crush was enhancing the clarity of my perceptions then I was the first in human history to reap that benefit.

'Did I even tell you how we met? You ought to know, now that you've spoiled everything. You got your own back, John. Congratulations! Just sitting there like a spider, but you managed to bugger up my life. I was having a solitary pint in the Red Cow by the Guildhall, which in case you don't know isn't really a rough place but not exactly studenty either. She came in and tried to get served but the bartender wouldn't meet her eye. So I went up to her and said, "I'll help you out, lass, he's gone blind. What are you drinking?" It happens all the time in Maryport, single woman not getting served. Nothing she can do – law says the bartender doesn't have to. His discretion. She didn't look too happy but she said, "Mine's a pint." So I order two pints, and the bartender draws one properly in a straight glass. Then he moves towards the half-pint glasses and I thought, "Oh no." Sometimes a bartender will serve a pint in two half-pint glasses when the customer's a woman, just to piss her off.' Not something I've noticed myself. Probably too absorbed in the struggle to get my beer served in a glass with a stem, one I can actually pick up.

'But then he moves past the half-pint glasses and goes to the shelf that has odd shapes, fancy ones for cocktails and that. He grabs one of those shitty Babycham glasses, with the stupid transfer of Bambi prancing on the side – wearing a blue scarf, don't ask me why – then another and another. He's smirking as he fills four of them with bitter and puts them in front of her. So I slide the straight glass over to her and say, "That's yours," and I start carrying the Babycham glasses to a table. Well, it was either that or start a fight with the bartender, and he looked as if he'd like that. As I carry them I realise that she wasn't getting served because she looked like a posh student, not just the being on her own. "Cambridge isn't Maryport, you div!" is what I thought. But then Bernardette comes over and sits at my table to drink her pint. Obviously I've done the right thing by mistake. Guess what she gave me for my birthday? Babycham glass. And another at Christmas. I was on course for a whole set. But right from the start she was so far out of my league that I started saying things that were meant to impress her. Once we were going out I couldn't go back on them, if anything I needed to push on a bit further, and then I was good and stuck.

'And I know her. She's stubborn. Once she's decided against me it's all over. So I may as well save myself the trouble of moving just to get dumped. I've given that witch Baine my notice. I'll move back to Cumbria, where I don't belong either. We all make mistakes, as the hedgehog said as he climbed off the hairbrush.' He forced a smile, but the rancour in his voice tore the delicate fabric of the joke.

I could have told him that any attempt to anchor souls in a carnal union is a foredoomed mismatch of hedgehog and hairbrush, but he'd find out the truth of it in his own time. Admittedly I'm almost as fond of hairbrushes as I am of hedgehogs, particularly the military-style one without a handle that is (as logic insists) the most likely to entice a hedgehog into misunderstanding and heartbreak, but that's an entirely separate question.

Should I have said, 'Don't be stupid—', well, perhaps not using those words, but saying perhaps, 'Think about it! What if she knows already and doesn't care? Isn't it worth at least trying to find out?' If he wasn't going to throw himself on her mercy then he could try to undermine her. Ignoble thought, I know, but from my dealings with Granny I was acquainted with a fair number of ploys. I get the word 'ploy' from Stephen Potter's *Gamesmanship* books, those odd little

Penguin manuals, marketed as droll comedy, when they were hand-books of social and familial guerrilla warfare, struggles for dominance and even survival. The conflict was equally bitter whether it took place at a cocktail party, at a board meeting or on the tennis court. In my time at Cambridge it was R. D. Laing's *Knots*, also published by Penguin but demonstrating seriousness with a plain black cover, that 'everyone' read. This was the pre-eminent guide to surviving relation-ships, though perhaps it was the ones who kept on reading Stephen Potter who got the best of it, taking as their priority not the untying of their own knots but the tightening of other people's, which comes (possibly) to the same thing.

The important thing with a ploy is precision of angle not force of stroke. I remember being mesmerised by a snooker match being shown on multiple screens, some of which must have been fully eight-een inches across, in the windows of Miller's. What a wonderfully abstract game of nudged repercussing globes, Newtonian beyond the dreams of Newton, and though I don't know for a fact that Granny ever picked up a cue it wasn't hard to imagine. With her scrupulously weighted rhetorical strokes she was able to rack up victory after vic-tory, controlling championship play over a matter of decades.

To produce in this particular case the trick shot that might at the last possible moment stop the ball marked Bernardette from toppling into the pocket marked Higher Education, MarkO would need to compliment her and wish her well while also subliminally activating her previous prejudices. Something along the lines of 'Well, good luck to you! You've certainly got the brains for it – though I never thought you'd turn into one of those Newnham ladies . . . you'll be buying Balkan Sobranie cocktail ciggies to match your clothes next!' Honestly, I frighten myself sometimes. It might actually have worked, though MarkO would have needed intensive coaching to screen out reproaches and whimpering.

In fact he had already accepted defeat, or rather he had already insisted on defeat by voting against himself. I didn't feel in the mood to be doling out relationship advice, but I could have told him he should follow her to Oxford. It wasn't me who had pushed her towards that course of General Studies at Oxford Poly. She may already have made up her mind before she broached the issue with me. Lack of confidence didn't run deep in her. Perhaps all she wanted was to hear herself talk about the idea, to try it on for size in 005 Mayflower House, with my flat playing the part of the changing room in a clothing boutique (this was still the heyday of the boutique in all its trendiness) of the mind.

There was nothing keeping him in Cambridge except the fear of being found out. And he had already been found out, though people were too polite to let him know. He was always saying that Bernardette knew her own mind and never changed it, but in this context he was being the stubborn one. I doubt that he would have believed that she had known about his little secret from the first. It wasn't something she and I had ever discussed, just something that I felt was understood between us. He couldn't let himself believe in his good luck, and I couldn't help him there. The thing about *vasanas*, one of the things about *vasanas* at least, is that you have to mend your potholes yourself. You can't wait for the Council to do it.

And that was all MarkO said before he left, except for 'There it is', repeated a couple of times, which didn't get us any further. But that was the point, I suppose. We had gone as far as we were going. That night I laid hands on myself carnally, or did the next best thing, given the limitations of my reach and grasp, by stretching the sheet tight against my cock and getting a tiny but adequate amount of traction from my pelvis. This was an entirely normal activity for a healthy young male, a category that I forgot that I belonged to almost as often as everyone else did. The only thing that could have improved it was a smoother, more luxurious sheet that would minimise wear and tear on the frenulum. When I started on this modest act of *frottage* I thought I was saying an orgasmic farewell to MarkO, a genital revisiting of the valedictory listening that I had given *Affinity* when I was taking my leave, as I had thought, of the Hacker. I imagined a pulsing firework display spelling out GOODBYE, MARKO on the night sky of my limbic brain, with side-sparks from that neglected zone the *nucleus accumbens*, but somehow I overshot and found myself focussing instead on the gaffer at the Co-Op Dairy, an all-purpose Ron who was face-less but no less arousing for that. I imagined the moment when this half-beast, half-*Übermensch* opened his stolen copy of *Beyond Good and Evil* in the privacy of his bedroom, with a hand that had symbolic dirt under the fingernails. An inner voice told me that milkmen normally keep themselves neat and tidy, but never mind that. I imagined his eye falling on the first sentence of the book's preface: 'Supposing that Truth is a woman – what then?' Not quite what he was looking for, this, but not immediately erection-abolishing. Perhaps the woman on the cover of the book was Truth – he'd give her what for. She'd know what was what by the time he had finished with her. How long did it take for him to discover that he was looking not at a properly filthy book but a key work of antinomian German philosophy? How could those lurid tits have lied to him? Yet lie they had.

I wonder why I felt such a surge of triumph as I contemplated the collapse of his manhood. His superior manual access to his plumbing didn't count for much once the water pressure dropped, did it? I seemed to be excited by that. I can only explain it with some sort of appeal to the idea, so well known and long accepted in natural history, of displacement behaviour. A bird threatened by a larger one will take it out on a smaller one, or else peck at a piece of imaginary grain. Perhaps I collapsed one form of failure onto another in the hope they would cancel each other out. But whatever the contortion of sexual logic in my *nucleus accumbens*, not a part of the brain that gets you onto *University Challenge*, I responded to MarkO's piggyback apology with something not far from a piggyback wank.

The images in my head were all of the Unknown Proletarian, distributor of dairy products, but the feeling, the strong surge of baffled energy, was for MarkO. Desire had come skulking up to me wearing a wonky smile on its moon face, and I was smitten. I had lost my footing in the vertigo of affinity. I ejaculated with a sob of longing that would have harrowed the heart of Germano Facetti, or perhaps gladdened it. It's a racing certainty that he was the one who was responsible for designing the cover of the missing book, his gamy choice of picture provoking cross-currents of lust and duplicity at the dairy. Facetti was a little Stakhanov of the Penguin design department, tirelessly descending into the mines of picture research to work shift after shift. I don't suppose the man had a day off in the whole of the 1970s.

The first time that my home help Paula had come across evidence of self-abusive spurtings on my sheets she was startled, not I think a matter of moral disapproval but because like many people she assumed that my relative lack of moving parts extended into the groin area. And it wasn't so, oh dear me no it wasn't so. She gave a sigh that was only routinely disapproving, if disapproving at all. Once or twice when the sheets bore the same signed confession I seemed to catch a look that might have conveyed something along the lines of *Perky little chap. Randy little beast, in fact. Plenty of go in him, I'll say that!*

More flexible people are better at hiding the evidence, though, that's certainly true. Any sort of tissue trick is a bit hit and miss in my case – it's all a bit catch-as-catch-can – and on the night I ventured Beyond Good and Evil there wasn't any suitable absorbency handy. The impulse towards release had come upon me rather abruptly.

I don't remember any similar situation arising with my bedmaker at Downing, but it seems a fair bet that a woman in her line of work measures out her life not with coffee spoons *à la* Prufrock but in sheets so semen-spattered they crackle. Perhaps any such person, habitually dealing with the hormonally overwound, is likely to be battle-hardened, unbothered by anything short of sperm saturation or oceanic bed-wetting.

It turned out that Bernardette had left me a present, giving it to Mrs Baine to pass on. Half a dozen boxes of Bacon's extra-long matches. It was a good job she hadn't left them outside my flat. MarkO might have used them to set fire to the door.

A magical uncosy entity such as a psammead

I was in two minds about whether I wanted the visit of Granny's emissary from the world of money, Mr Moneybags as I was already calling him in my mind, to resemble a top-secret Mission, very hush-hush, or something more like a state visit, something to be bruited about in the most tromboning terms. Granny's largesse wasn't something to be taken for granted. It had some of the qualities of fairy gold that vanishes overnight, or the wishes granted in slightly starchy children's stories by a magical uncosy entity such as a psammead or a phœnix – the desire to visit Atlantis in its heyday, say, or to take a

372

baby with whooping cough to warmer climes. As the tale unfolded such wishes were shown up as having fatal flaws in a way that led inexorably to the conclusion that you should Be Grateful for What You've Got.

This was not a plot development I had ever welcomed in escapist fiction. I felt I had a certain amount of form when it came to accepting limitation, and I powerfully resented it when my desire to explore my imagination without penalty was reproved by the books that had inflamed it in the first place.

Granny made a point of treating me as she would anyone else and often said so, with the implication that she was compensating for the special treatment she imagined me receiving in every other quarter. Possibly she was overrating the degree of that special treatment. Some punches were pulled, I dare say, along the way but a fair number landed squarely on my chin.

It's hard to deny that Granny was addicted to money, but what she enjoyed was its effect on others rather than its private usefulness, its power over people rather than things. It was her language, the way she communicated with the world. Another way of putting it would be that money was certainly her drug, but she was closer to being a pusher than an addict. What excited her was getting others hooked on her supply, and she would be capricious with what she doled out so as to gauge her power to a nicety.

Her approach to money was up to date in its way – I wouldn't have put it past her to have a telex machine in the guest bedroom of her elegant cottage in Tangmere, scorning to disguise it with a chintzy cover as the lower classes were said to do with their loo rolls. Yet in her current dealings with me she seemed to have slipped back in time to a period preceding the invention of the cheque. Why would I want to have money delivered? If it was a substantial sum then having it on the premises of Mayflower House was risky in itself. But then the idea took hold. If Granny had sent me a box of fancy chocolates they would certainly have been delivered by a van with Fortnum & Mason written on the side, and if she sent me a sum of money it was highly likely that the banknotes should be formed into a bouquet and tied with ribbon. Perhaps I could ask the delivery man to bash the stems and put them in water.

The technology of money was making great strides. At first I had resisted being issued the plastic cash card to which as a customer of standing I was entitled. Now I was very happy to be issued with one, and wanted everyone to see me using it and to ask what made it so special. My change of heart came when I learned that the Williams & Glyn card took a different technological approach from its rivals to the problem of information storage. Not for my enlightened bank the inferior magnetic strip used by their competitors. The W & G card had holes punched in it, read by a sensor inside the dispenser. The advantage was obvious – cards issued by other banks could be wiped clean by a magnetic storm or the smallest nuclear detonation, while the W & G punched card was unfazed by such local disturbances and would keep the money flowing. The world might be melting around their heads, but my fellow customers and I could count on burning banknotes emerging from the slot of the trusty dispenser. The bank's preferred term for these machines was 'day-and-night till', welcome or unwelcome proof that capitalism slept with one eye open.

I was excited to meet Mr Moneybags, as much for himself as his cargo. He was plump and wore an overcoat, suitable enough for autumn, with a velvet collar. A coat like that must have cost a lot of money. It stood to reason that particles of the assets he handled should pass into his system, and here I'm suggesting osmosis rather than peculation. He shrugged off his luxurious coat as if someone might be poised behind him to take charge of it, and when he still had it inexplicably in his hands looked round, at first calmly and then with some uncertainty, for a place to hang it. There was no suitable approximation to a hook in sight. His eyes danced to the door handle and then behind me, as if for a moment he was even considering the handles of the wheelchair as possible candidates. It was becoming clear to him that this was not the usual sort of address to which he brought bags of money. 'I wonder . . .?'

In fact he wondered a couple of things. First of all he wondered if he was speaking to Mr John Cromer, then when I confirmed my identity he wondered if he might lay his coat on the bed.

'There's a hook on the back of the bathroom door,' I said.

The rest of the flat had given him shocks enough. He wouldn't risk the bathroom. 'Thank you, the bed will do very well.'

'You're welcome to make yourself a cup of tea or coffee. The kettle's over there.'

'Thank you, I've just had one.' One of each perhaps, tea and coffee, though it was more likely that he was trying to abbreviate his dealings with this room and its occupant. With a lesser visitor I would have sung out, 'I'm dying for a coffee! The Gold Blend's over there.' You could hardly miss it in its giant drum. 'And by all means make one for yourself.' But Mr Moneybags was an emissary of Granny, and even at one remove her authority pulsed through his every startled gesture and unhappy little look. It wasn't a thinkable approach to say, 'Make yourself at home – put on a record if you'd like. Anything but *Neu!* by Neu!. That's hard on the ears, believe me. Don't ask me how I come to own it . . . it's a long story!'

The way it strokes the eye

The money really did come in a bag, but it was a grave disappointment to me when Mr Moneybags produced it, being made of a dull buff hessian. Money in mufti when I hankered after ceremonial attire.

What was I expecting, velvet? Yes, velvet, of course velvet, and with a pile so deep it could take the imprint not just of games of noughts and crosses but games of Ultima. If the bank could pay Mr Moneybags enough for him to treat himself to coat with a velvet collar then there was enough in the kitty for a velvet bag, for heaven's sake, and why not a silken braid to secure it? I'd have settled for needlecord, at a pinch, but please keep those wales nice and narrow. It makes a world of difference to the visual feel of the corduroy, the way it strokes the eye.

But if you're not going to do the thing properly why do it at all? If hessian was luxurious enough for the purpose of delivering Granny's bounty to her underprivileged grandson, who relied on council funding for the roof over his head and even qualified for Supplementary Benefit, then it was hard to see the argument against a carrier bag from Sainsburys. A piece of financial theatre such as this cried out for better stage management.

At least the bag was closed with a piece of wire rather than, say, a strip of Sellotape. It was even sealed with a little blob of metal, though this could only count as a poor relation of a proper self-respecting wax seal, with or without a monogram, either Granny's or Coutts's (I was open-minded about that), impressed upon it.

Mr Moneybags searched a waistcoat pocket and produced a tiny penknife with which he sawed away at the wire, something that I knew, if only by precept (the knowledge passed on by my father), would damage the blade. Should there not be a special instrument for the purpose, or at least one better adapted to it? There were cigar cutters in the window of Bacon's that would have given the wire-severing process a bit of style and a sense of ceremony, something I felt was badly needed to prevent the whole occasion falling flat.

When the bag was open he produced the money in little stacks, some of them blessed with the finishing touch of a gummed paper cummerbund to keep a whole little stack of one denomination intact. Notes of miscellaneous value weren't organised in this proper ransom-money-suitcase or international-drug-deal way, but I suppose that's the price you pay for treating the mighty bank of Coutts as if it was a supermarket sweets counter. Perhaps I had missed a trick in not asking for some of the money in specie rather than notes, which would have required Mr Moneybags to be Mr Travelling Scales also.

He tucked away the little knife in the waistcoat pocket and pulled out a pink rubber thimble. I say 'pink', but it was grubby with use. If, as Shakespeare proposes, lilies that fester smell much worse than weeds, then a soiled pink must be the dirtiest colour of all. I don't mean that Shakespeare was thinking of lilies as pink, but once the freshness of that colour has gone it has nothing to recommend it. Mr Moneybags brought this faintly disgusting object close to the virginal money. It's been a maxim since ancient times that money has no smell – *pecunia non olet* and all that – but I wouldn't want to sniff that thimble too closely just the same.

The very antipodes of tickety-boo

'You don't have to count it,' I said. 'I trust you.' Apart from anything else, I didn't know how much money there was supposed to be in the consignment, so the counting process lost all meaning. There seemed to be an awful lot of it, just the same.

'I assure you that I do have to count it.' He licked his finger and plied the dingy thimble. I was forced to look on as banknotes of a freshness that I had rarely seen were defiled before my eyes by saliva and epithelial sheddings. 'All present and correct. Everything tickety-boo. Now if you will just sign here, Mr Cromer, I'll leave you with the spoils of peace.'

'Can I ask you something, Mr . . .?' If I'd been told his true name I hadn't retained it. 'Can I hang on to the bag?'

He looked scandalised. 'Oh no.' That would not be tickety-boo, that would be the very antipodes of tickety-boo.

'You couldn't accidentally leave it behind?'

'Oh no. Absolutely not.'

'But Coutts must have hundreds of them.'

'Thousands, I don't doubt, but this one came with me and will be leaving with me.'

I found myself in a stubborn mood, though it was unclear to whom I would be showing such a trophy. Nevertheless I wanted it, this banking equivalent of the Turin shroud, bearing the imprint of a miracle, opulence delivered to my door. 'Then I'm afraid I won't sign your docket.'

'Dear sir!' He thought for a moment. 'How vexing. I really can't persuade you?'

'Not unless I can keep the pretty bag.' Which I didn't think pretty in the slightest, but there it was. I had dug in my heels and there was nothing I could do about that. In general it took me longer to put on the brakes of the wheelchair, first the one then the other, than to bring conversation to a halt when I had a mind to.

'I see. Then may I use your telephone? I should take some advice.' I didn't hesitate. The phone was in full view. It would cost me twenty-odd pence for him to make the call (long-distance at a peak time, assuming it didn't last more than three minutes) but never mind that. I authorised the expenditure with some mental effort. The reflex of thrift had become engrained – it couldn't be washed away at a moment's notice just because there was a pile of banknotes on my table, looking for all the world like the proceeds of a bank robbery – no, a *heist*, as seen in a film.

The phone call to Coutts HQ concerned me but wasn't really for my ears, and I did my best to observe the protocol that dictates the creation of a symbolic distance from the instrument, though even if I'd been given a head start I wouldn't have been able to move out of earshot in that little flat. I'd gone a matter of inches before the call was connected.

'Oh hello, yes . . . I'm having a little difficulty, yes. I'm in Cambridge to make a delivery and the payee is reluctant to sign for it. How should I proceed?'

I thought he was getting clearance for the release of the dreary hessian bag with its strong symbolic value, and here he was trying to outmanoeuvre me, and on a phone call for which I was paying. The cheek of it! If I was just 'the payee' then Mr Moneybags was no more than a travelling cashier. Worse, Granny was just a customer. In that case the whole transaction had nothing miraculous about it. I would have to find my money miracles elsewhere, perhaps simply in the act of sliding my Williams & Glyn bank card into the bank's dispenser and having it confirm my identity by a correspondence between the number I dutifully typed in and pre-existing holes punched into its plastic body.

Mr Moneybags was finishing his call, undeterred by my fuming outrage. 'Thank you, I'll do that. Goodbye.' He turned to me. 'It seems that I don't need the payee's signature after all – a witness to the transaction will do. Perhaps the lady behind the desk?' Oh dear. I quite liked the idea of being an enigmatic figure to Mrs Baine, receiving mysterious packages from portly emissaries. Being exposed as a capitalist and profiteer while still imbibing the State's thin milk was quite a different thing.

His C-value was plummeting

'All right,' I said. 'I'll sign.' I should have added 'Damn your eyes!' for melodrama. Mr Moneybags and I were learning about each other, with a certain amount of dismay, I think, on both sides. He watched me very closely as I wrote my name in the place provided, whether out of wonder at my ability to perform a very ordinary task (which happens more often than you'd think) or because he wanted to make sure I wasn't signing it in the name of Walt Disney or Mao Tse-Tung.

Mr Moneybags's expression didn't reflect the pleasure his ignoble triumph over me might have been expected to give him. At some point I realised what this meant – it meant that his C-value was plummeting. In layman's terms, the poor man was dying for a piss. The Continence-value as it falls doesn't describe an asymptotic curve when plotted – one that makes closer and closer approximations to zero. It can hit the limiting axis fair and square, with a splash or a shaming trickle.

'Would you like to use the bathroom?' I said. 'Please feel free. It's clean.' Of course people vary in their definitions of cleanliness, but it's never the wrong thing to say. I couldn't guarantee that my bum snorkel wouldn't be in plain sight, since if it was hidden away it would be no use to me. This object with its elegant Perspex curve might have attracted admiration if exhibited in a case at the Fitzwilliam but was likely to be viewed with suspicion in a bathroom barely on the right side of the Elizabeth Bridge.

It seemed, though, as if Mr Moneybags found the less intimate part of the flat quite alarming enough without passing the threshold of the bathroom. 'No, thank you kindly. I'll be on my way.' He was dead set on taking his nourishing effluvia elsewhere, and my African violets were not going to get a sniff at him.

He picked up his handsome overcoat from the bed and shrugged himself into it. 'Your lapel . . .' I said helpfully, meaning only that it had become turned over as he put the coat on. Whatever our differences, I didn't want him leaving the premises looking less smart than when he had arrived. He looked horrified, as if some contaminant leaching upwards from the bed had defiled the clothing he had so trustingly left there, and he couldn't have pulled it off any more quickly if it had been the poisoned shirt that killed Hercules. He looked from one lapel to the other with desperate worry, and I felt silly saying, as firmly as I could, 'It wasn't lying properly. We must keep you looking smart, mustn't we?', a nannyish statement which I have to say went down no worse than anything else I had said since he had arrived, and perhaps rather better. If I'd started with that tone by now I might have been the possessor, proud and a little embarrassed, of a buff hessian moneybag.

Perhaps it wasn't too late. 'You should go to the loo while you can,' I said. 'You'll regret it if you don't. And don't put your coat back on now, silly! Do it after you've finished.' And off he obediently toddled, leaving me to wish that I'd had the sense to add, 'And give that horrid pink thimble a good scrub while you're in there. It's disgusting!'

When he returned all his huffiness seemed to have gone, and a good thing too since bad feeling in a confined space is particularly oppressive. Of course this was partly the serenity that comes with a newly restored C-value, but I think there was more to it than that. He put on his coat calmly and said, 'I'll wish you good day,' as nicely as Granny could have wanted. Some people just need to be organised, not left to their own devices, they're just not the ones I'm usually drawn to. Granny would have patted his bottom as he passed, and in his altered mood I might even have got away with it myself, but he was moving too fast for me. He receded, taking with him his hessian bag, the diminutive Turin shroud that I had coveted so much, bearing as it did the granular imprint of Granny's holy money.

I didn't need to count the money myself, just to take a look at the receipt he had left behind. It came to six hundred pounds, and not £600 in that chimæra 'today's money' but six hundred 1973 pounds, sterling English-money pounds. To put it another way, six months of MarkO's wages as a temporary milkman was sitting on my desk awaiting transfer to a safer place. Granny's largesse swelled my liquidity in terms of cash while shrinking my self-esteem. I had fallen out with MarkO over ten pounds. Yes, there was principle involved (it was in there somewhere) but my sudden prosperity gave me a retrospective impression of rankling pettiness.

A Marc Bolan perm

I had expected altogether too much from a three-cornered friendship with MarkO and Bernardette. If my task in life was to square the circle, to find a way of being looked after that didn't take my independence away, then I was getting way ahead of myself by dreaming of sphering the triangle. I had been misled by an unrealistic botanical role model of domestic harmony. Under the Australian soil *Rhizanthella gardneri*, *Melaleuca uncinata* and *Thanatephorus gardneri* might be able to make a go of their alternative lifestyle, but that didn't mean you could bung any old tuber, shrub and fungus in a drawer and leave it there, expecting on your return to find a thriving ecosystem in place, even if the trailing roots of the broom honey-myrtle might over time, when viewed by a sympathetic eye, have taken on the likeness of a Marc Bolan perm.

Only afterwards did I see that the bone of contention between us, the modest Hacker stereo set-up, with its integrated turntable, amplifier and speaker connected by a wire to another little speaker, symbolised the fantasised arrangement of a couple finding a use for an additional element. In this analogy I played the unglamorous role of the supplementary speaker, not strictly necessary for the production of sound though contributing a certain illusion of dimensionality. I remembered what MarkO had told Bernardette about his attitude to men: that he was curious but not interested. Just my luck! It might have been the only realistic self-assessment he ever made. Over a little more time I could see that my position wasn't so very different. In asymmetrical relationships, as mine tend to be, it's hard to spot continuities however blindingly obvious they might be to an outside observer. I didn't want to spend my life with MarkO. I didn't necessarily want to spend a night with him. I just wanted something to think about in the mornings.

Would it have been so bad to let the little runt get his grubby hands on the Hacker? It feels pleasingly wrong to use the phrase 'little runt' of someone markedly taller than I am, but if I have to wait until it's technically appropriate I'll never get to use the words, and that can't be right. Words can't be off limits just because they never quite fit.

I waited for Gas Works to become the sensation that MarkO had predicted, and when it didn't happen I felt sorry that they should have been cheated of what they deserved, but quite glad on my own account. I didn't much want to share them with the world.

So with the best of intentions Granny had cast a raking retrospective light across my recent emotional history, making me seem like something I hardly felt myself to be, a child of privilege slumming it. When I say 'with the best of intentions' I should probably say 'without any specific or immediate desire to undermine'. For once Granny's gift hadn't come with strings attached, but then it didn't need them. Those six hundred pounds, soon bundled into a drawer but still glowing as if radioactive, sank through the layers of my life as destructively as a depth charge. I felt shock waves of affluence, and an instability out of all proportion to the modest economic power conferred. For the time being I couldn't think of myself as poor, but I was only 'comfortably off' in the most paradoxical way. I had been hoping for a cushion, a financial cushion, but by an administrative oversight so many cushions had been delivered that I could hardly move around in my own home.

I wrote Granny a thank-you letter with just a little too much sugar to be convincing, a hint of God-bless-us-every-one that even she despite her nose for nuances and distortions of ingratitude was unlikely to detect. She phoned to say, 'Really, John, there's no need for thanks. It is my indulgence, my caprice, to spread my good fortune around.' And this was true to the point of incontrovertibility as a statement of fact, without being particularly truthful. If I hadn't sent her a bread-and-butter letter, with the butter on it laid inches thick, then every living representative on the family tree would hear about it, and even a few dead Cromers might catch the echo.

When it was time for the rendezvous in Chesterton to pick up George and whoever else made up the mysterious 'we' or 'us' he had referred to, I was ready for it. George had said since the first meeting he had been to (which was the first for both of us) that he would only go on attending to keep me company, and only until he found a boyfriend, someone 'calm and sensible', little enough to ask in most contexts. My guess was that this was what had happened over the summer, though I did my best not to jump to conclusions. If there was one thing my recent experience had taught me, it was that not every curved regular polygon of constant diameter is a fifty-pence piece.

From this distance it seems strange that two grown homosexuals should feel the need of each other's support when attending a meeting dedicated to meeting the needs of their own kind, but CHAPs was not at heart a support group. It was a forum, a marketplace of ideas, and in any marketplace there will be those who attend for the pleasures of haggling and those who want to run their errands and go home in peace. 'An independent forum where issues of sexual and political liberation could be freely discussed and worked through' – that was the formula that was recited at the beginning of every weekly meeting. The group had met only fortnightly when I first attended, but the frequency had since been stepped up, presumably to keep pace with the issues of sexual and political liberation as they multiplied. On that first meeting we had been notionally welcomed by our hosts (the Tonys) but no one had come to make it more personal. Later we had noticed the change of atmosphere when a glamorous newcomer attended, but even then there was a sense of inhibition, a fear of being seen to give special treatment or, putting it more bluntly, to pounce. A comely new arrival (likely to be an undergraduate, though the group sought to appeal outside the university) might spend his first meeting feeling almost invisible, until a late-blooming effusiveness showed itself at the very end, in long-held squeezing handshakes and pleas to return soon, soon and often.

George was waiting outside the Haymakers in Chesterton, and he had company, as I had anticipated, a strapping young man in a sober dark suit. George got in beside me and the stranger climbed into the back seat.

Tureens have had their day

It had been so long since there had been anything approaching a crowd in the Mini that I should have been delighted rather than (I admit it) at my most begrudging and mean-spirited. 'Could the gentleman in the back – I'm assuming it's a gentleman – please move so that he can see my face in the mirror? Then I can see him and say hello . . . Hello there! And George, if you don't mind opening your door again so that the interior light goes on, then visibility will be much improved. Now I can see him properly.' At that time of year, with the days still having a fair amount of length to them, I was laying it on a bit thick, admittedly, but when people are slow to master the basic principles it becomes necessary to resort to some strategic exaggeration.

After a few seconds a pink young face, desperately grinning, swam into the angled oblong of the Mini's mirror. 'Sorry, John,' said George from the passenger seat, 'I should have given you some warning. This is Robin. We've been seeing each other over the summer. Can I close the door now?'

'Feel free. And it's autumn now, so if you're still seeing each other I assume things are going well.'

'For God's sake don't put a jinx on it, John!'

I don't like sentences that have God and superstition in them at the same time. It seems to me that people need to make up their minds, but all I said was, 'Touch wood if you can find any.' If Granny and I had invested in a Morris Traveller rather than a Mini – the ones with the curious half-timbered design – there might have been some wood trim to be found somewhere, but I left it up to him to improvise.

There was a soft burp behind me, not emanating from George although he voiced the apology for it.

'I'm sorry, John, we were a bit early so we decided to have a quick drink. We slipped into the Haymakers for a sharpener. We've supped some ale.' Blimey! They certainly had supped some ale. It was still early evening – they must have charged in the moment the pub cracked its doors.

'I can't wait to hear how you two met,' I went on, 'but I find it hard to concentrate on conversation when there's driving to be done, so I'll put on some imaginary earplugs till we get there. You two feel free to natter away all you like . . .' George must have thought it strange that I had this sudden difficulty in processing more than one stream of brain activity at a time, and though talking while driving doesn't necessarily bring out my best efforts in either department I'm not as strongly opposed to it as I am to conversation at mealtimes. It's also true that chatting with an intimate acquaintance, which seemed to be George's category, makes less in the way of mental demands than talking to an invisible stranger, but that didn't wholly account for my attitude.

I was a bit jealous, I suppose, not sexually or even emotionally but still put out by the prospect that George would be spending Tuesday evenings at home in future, though why I should need protection in the insistently welcoming space of a CHAPs meeting was hard to explain. Perhaps it was the insistence of the welcome, its doctrinaire quality, that worked against its success. Almost immediately I changed my tune, saying, 'Traffic seems to have thinned out a bit . . . I can relax. In fact I'm taking the invisible earplugs out in your honour. So tell me, how was it that you met? I'm agog.'

'Well, I was at work in China and Glass and in comes this lad with questions about . . . about tureens, of all things! Well, John, tureens have pretty much had their day, even as wedding presents. It's quite a while since I've seen one on even a posh wedding list – it's just not how people live nowadays. So when this one here kept asking questions about cubic capacity and whether they were ovenproof up to mark 9, well . . . eventually I realised he was shopping for something else.'

'You took your time!' That was Robin chiming in, making his own contribution to the creation myth of their relationship, without properly explaining it to an outsider. Didn't the story begin a bit earlier, with Robin getting his first sight of George, either in Eaden Lilley or somewhere else, and then thinking up a way of approaching him?

There was something disturbing about the feeling underneath the words being spoken. Harmony in conversation has an unsettling effect on me. I don't trust it and it makes me tense.

Uncomplicated emotion was as strictly rationed in my family as sweets were in wartime – and yes, I just about remember sweet rationing, though my early life involved the rationing of more important things. In the bed-rest years I was only allowed half an hour of reading a day. I'd certainly have swapped my sweet ration with my brother if Peter had been in a position to give me more reading time in exchange.

I found myself wanting to test this harmony, to drive some sort of wedge between the pair of them, so recently united. Oh dear, was this a genetic inheritance from Granny manifesting itself? I have to take responsibility for it either way. The obvious target was the difference in their appearance, George tanned though still looking washed out thanks to bright-coloured clothes rather too young for him, Robin's almost ridiculously pink-and-white complexion boosted by the contrast with his sober suit.

'Robin, I know George will have told you meetings aren't always the greatest fun in the world, but at least they aren't formal . . . you don't need to dress for a funeral, you know!'

'Funny you should say that, John . . .' cut in George. 'Robin works for a family firm of undertakers. P. W. Weyman in Abbey Walk. Established nearly a hundred years.' Pride in his boyfriend had a transforming effect on statements that would normally seem short of glamour. All this made perfect sense to me – a soul close to the end of its cycle of rebirths, its passage through eighty-four hundred thousand vaginas (it tends to be vaginas rather than wombs in Hinduism, one day I must really try to find out why), ready to dismount the treadmill, will naturally choose a life where death is both omnipresent and nothing special. Business as usual, as it so clearly should be.

'And did you always want to join the family business, Robin?'

'Oh no. It's a family business, too right, it's just not my family. My family are railway people. We've been shedmasters time out of mind.' Even better! I had no trouble understanding his desire to break his family's railway tradition to become an undertaker. Family is an accident and an irrelevance, and the mystical insight that the body likewise is an accident and an irrelevance would move him quite naturally to spending time with the dead and offering real comfort to those who imagine themselves bereaved. My own awakening came when as a child in hospital I saw smoke from an incinerator being snatched away by the wind. I wouldn't begrudge another seeker being roused to self-realisation by the louder spiritual trumpet-blast of a crematorium chimney. Who could sleep through that?

I had no idea where shedmaster stood in the employment structure of the railways. It sounded both grand and rather forlorn, a high estate and a dead end. My main reference point in that general area was the Fat Controller from the *Thomas the Tank Engine* stories, and I couldn't think of a sensible question to ask.

I concentrated instead on the marked difference of skin tone between the two of them. To judge by the physical evidence George had been basking for long hours in the sun, while Robin had spent his holidays visiting Santa in Lapland. 'When are you going to take the risk of spending a holiday together?'

'John, we're well past that stage. We had two weeks on a Greek island.'

'You wouldn't believe what went on,' Robin cut in. 'You would not believe your eyes.'

'The shower block was like Piccadilly Circus. Robin went for a wash-up one evening, innocent as can be, and got quite an eyeful.'

'I ran – didn't even wait to wash the soap off.'

Beside me George kept craning his head round, as if he had no better use for the flexibility of his neck than making sure his boyfriend hadn't disappeared from one moment to the next. 'His boyfriend' – the English language seemed to bridle at the phrase, not rejecting it outright as defective but somehow wanting it returned for further inspection before allowing it to circulate as valid.

This was a love-in, a honeymoon prolonged beyond the standard duration, and it filled me with mixed feelings, not to mention a renewed urge to stir things up just a little.

'Forgive me if this is a personal question, but why is one of you so pale when the other one is bronzed to within an inch of his life?'

'Robin didn't get into the swing of Mediterranean heat, I have to say. Long sleeves, long trews, hat at all times, though I have to admit he ditched the jacket and tie. He doesn't approve of tans.'

'You know it's not that . . . it's just . . .'

'I tell him it's because he wants to keep his peaches-and-cream complexion.'

'You know it's not that! A tan on you is fine. But on me it wouldn't be right. Just not right. Not respectful.'

I didn't follow. 'I don't follow. Whyever not?'

'Well, it's about what's proper at work. The bereaved don't want to see an undertaker looking too healthy – it's not polite.'

It wasn't a subject that I had given any thought. Why shouldn't morticians be free to inflict voluntary skin damage on themselves in homage to an illusion of healthy colouring?

But when I turned my mind that way I could see what he meant. Undertakers are not just the technicians of mortality but psychopomps, whose job is to accompany the dead at least part of the way they must go. I even thought he was right. You don't want pallbearers who look as if they can hardly stand up by themselves, let alone when they're toting a coffin, but it's just as wrong if they look as if they could take on the Grim Reaper in a tug of war and win.

Was it then that I realised that a message was being sent? Here was I meeting someone who actually adorned corpses for a living, just after the botched attempt to mark a birthday with a present!

George said, 'You could always get a tan and then put on some make-up, tone yourself down a little.'

Robin seemed genuinely scandalised. 'That would be worse. Much worse!'

'I suppose you're right – better keep the make-up for the dead bodies. They need all the help they can get.'

'George!'

This wasn't a real squabble but mutual grooming and preening lightly disguised. The pretended protests and grievances were only corks bobbing on a tide of endearment. The implied cry of 'How could you say such a thing?' was no more than a variant pronunciation of 'Aren't you wonderful?'. I have to say my uneasiness increased. In my birth family both harmony and discord had been much more deeply buried – 'little fishes' indeed, many of them poisonous – and I instinctively distrusted anything that came close enough to the surface to be identified.

To connect directly with the flywheel of history

By this time we were parked outside the Tonys' house on Glisson Road, where CHAPs meetings were held, though none of us seemed to be in a hurry to leave the car and enter the premises. This could be put down in Robin's case to fear of the unknown, and in George's case (and mine) to adequate familiarity with something not obsessively desired.

A figure rode up gravely pedalling a solid bicycle, young rather than old though his big head was entirely bald and he wore spectacles with thick lenses. Every mighty piston-stroke of his legs seemed to connect directly with the flywheel of history. He was so swathed in chains as to look like a travelling escapologist. He dismounted from his machine, then used the chains to fasten it to a lamp post, looping them through the spokes of both wheels so as to secure the bicycle both as an entity and a set of constituent parts. Behind me Robin let out a little gasp, as if he was sighting something of a rarity beyond belief, the Yeti or a species of Bolivian peccary long believed extinct. 'Is that . . . Ken?'

Yes, it was Ken, the leader of our group, by self-election rather than acclamation, referred to behind his back as 'Our Beloved Leader' with varying degrees of exasperation. Both George and I flinched, not exactly courting that gaze, a gaze that was severe though also somehow bewildered.

There was never a suggestion in the group that we should have a whip-round for a toupée on Ken's behalf. But some of us were tempted to set up a fund for contact lenses. If his forbidding aspect was softened someone might fancy him (he was stocky and strong-looking, and there are always people who go for that) and take him off our hands. In any case, if he came out from behind his heavy specs, blinking at the newness of the light, he might also lay aside the bottle-bottom lenses of the ideology that he wore. When it came to the intricacies of gay politics, this was an optician who didn't believe in the necessity of an eye test. He was happy to read the small print on our behalf.

Ken removed his bicycle's lights from their mountings, the front light with plain glass and the rear one with its red lens – in Cambridge at that time I imagine dinner guests jocularly brandishing these items on arrival, saying, 'I didn't know whether you wanted red or white, so I brought both,' before producing their actual offering of wine to be admired or else looked at with withering connoisseurship.

Ken stowed his bicycle lights in a rucksack, then seemed to have second thoughts and fished out his front light again, as well as a small black-bound notebook like a policeman's, with a loop of elastic to fasten it. He shone the light on a page as if memorising notes, then put both lamp and notebook away, pulling a handkerchief from the rucksack and giving his thick glasses a polish. He tucked it away again and visibly squared his shoulders before knocking on the Tonys' door. Without waiting for an answer he turned the doorknob and let himself in.

I don't know what George's reaction was to this little tableau but to me this was an utterly unwelcome revelation that Our Leader needed to steel himself before meetings at which he was by common consent the intimidating element. I wouldn't have believed it if I hadn't seen it with my own three eyes. How was it possible that he felt the need to square his shoulders before joining a group that more or less quailed before him? We complained a fair amount behind Ken's back, and I think overall we probably felt a bit sorry for him, but no one really questioned his authority as our champion against the patriarchy.

If George had suggested we should scarper I might have said yes, if only for the bliss of playing truant for once. Truancy! The word had a powerful sacrilegious charge to it, as it must to any scrupulous student – scrupulous in my case until the undergraduate years, but then I wasn't alone in thinking that going to university was a reward for education rather than forming part of it. Truancy is in its way a temptation of the privileged, however little they think of themselves in that light, since you can only abscond from your education if there's a serious expectation that you will show up to be taught. I'd have loved a taste of that wicked joy, but if I'd never turned up to a lesson at the Red Cross Memorial Hospital at Taplow there would have been no consequences. It's true that we pupils of the invisible school that coincided interdimensionally with the hospital known as CRX were short of the mobility required to absent ourselves physically from lessons, but there was always open to us the subtle truancy of pretending to be stupid, though that option never appealed to me personally. The Vulcan School was different, and Burnham Grammar was different again, but only because I forced those institutions to expect something from me.

In our turn we nerved ourselves to enter the Tonys' house. A delicious savoury aroma greeted us as we crossed the threshold, as it so often did at meetings. Without the reinforcement of their tasty snacks Ken's unravelling of the patriarchal fabric would not have been enough to keep people coming back. Once we were inside there was the usual kerfuffle, with people blocking our progress, some of them with their backs turned, and then any amount of embarrassment as they were nudged or whispered at until they scampered wildly out of the way, as if I was holding if not personifying a red-hot poker.

Naturally a large proportion of the members had been on their travels over the summer. There was a wide range of holiday destinations, with the dream holiday for most being San Francisco, second prize going to Amsterdam, less difficult and expensive to get to, but there were exceptions. Our leader Ken warned us not to expect too much from America, where the radical discourse was rudimentary. Gay activists over there were anxious to secure 'rights', above all in the marketplace – essentially the right to be exploited on the same basis as everyone else – as if it wasn't necessary to pull the whole degraded enterprise of society down. Americans wanted to sugar the pill of sexual dissidence rather than let it do its salutary work. By analogy our sexuality would work on the body politic in the manner of a worming tablet.

Ken himself had travelled over the summer, but in search of knowledge rather than pleasure. He had gone to Paris to further his research. ('We were doing research, too,' murmured someone behind me. 'There's a lot of research to be done in Brighton.') He didn't seem all that satisfied with his progress, though it took some time for the reasons for his disappointment to become clear. He had prepared the ground with the various thinkers he wanted to interview on the subject of sexual transgression and transgressive sexuality, several of whom seemed to be connected with the École normale supérieure, an institution whose name Ken breathed with something like awe. If this school was normal how was it also superior? He didn't explain – and 'normal' was not normally a neutral word in his vocabulary but close to a term of abuse. Ken had been encouraged by these luminaries to get in touch the next time he was in Paris, though as it turned out they were without exception spending the summer in California, no doubt doing research of their own.

He had tried to make the best of things by cutting his Paris visit short and spending ten days in Amsterdam. As a group I think we hoped that the city had somehow managed to seduce even this visitor, who seemed not to have a hedonistic bone in his body. It didn't seem impossible that, properly coaxed, he would show us snapshots of himself holding hands with a blond waiter and wearing an expression of poleaxed bliss, or (failing that) at least one of him perched grinning on one of the suggestive bollards for which the city is known. But it seemed that in his suitcase when he returned, where the hash-brownie crumbs and sticky magazines should have been, there were only pamphlets expounding revolutionary theories of sexuality. That wasn't the sort of stimulation that we wanted on his behalf, though he was eager to incorporate these new ideas into our discussions, which were really only lectures with token questions.

The beginning of the academic year was a time when a few new people might come along to a CHAPs meeting, and this evening there was a newcomer with the distinction of having nothing what-ever to do with the academic world. This should have been cause for celebration, given the group's embarrassment about the dominance of its university contingent, but the new arrival wasn't the fantasy of working-class youth that we collectively longed for – bear in mind that E. M. Forster had died only a few months before I arrived at Cambridge. On bright days his diffident ghost could still faintly be made out perched on the low wall outside King's, murmuring 'Pretty things! Pretty things!' as the young people passed by, undismayed if one or two sat on his polite shade to eat their ice creams. Jim was from a background that lacked privilege, but not in an earthy way. He had recently retired from the Air Force, young to be retiring rather than young as such. He was altogether a mismatch with the group, to an extent that made me look like a rank conformist.

Big Ben Was Wrong

When sexual acts between men had been partially decriminalised in 1967 members of the armed forces had explicitly been excluded from this loosening of the law. If anyone at a meeting inadvertently said 'legalised' rather than 'partially decriminalised' he would rapidly be corrected, and not just by Ken. Figures would be produced to dem-onstrate that the rate of arrests and convictions had gone up rather than down with the change in the law. You could make a case that homosexuals in the forces were being oppressed beyond the ordinary, since the prohibition relaxed elsewhere still applied to them, but it wasn't a case anyone would make at a CHAPs meeting. Never mind that when Jim joined up there was no legal permission anywhere. He was beyond the pale. It wasn't just that no one present could imagine wanting to join the armed forces. This was self-hatred expressed on the level of career choice.

He was 'nice-looking', which I suppose is a deadly enough descrip-tion. His ears stuck out a little, his nose was a little snub, he was a little red in the face, though I hate to pass on this sort of detail when I know all too well how the little fixed judgements of body habitus shut off the realities of perception.

At that first meeting Jim didn't do much to rescue himself from the disgrace of the uniform he had chosen to wear until his retirement. There was a cartoonist whose work Dad particularly liked called Bateman, H. M. Bateman to be pedantic about it, and very much a reference point for that generation, who did a number of drawings on the theme of 'The Man Who . . .' about people who do the fatally wrong thing. Bystanders in those cartoons turn puce or faint dead away at some terrible lapse in decorum. British humour at its most piquant, celebrating the admirable sense of proportion we have about, well, our lack of a sense of proportion. They were classic vignettes: 'The Man Who . . . Lit His Cigar Before the Loyal Toast', 'The Man Who . . . Didn't Like the Leonardo Exhibition', 'The Man Who . . . Said Big Ben Was Wrong'. And now, to bring the series up to date, Jim made his own contribution, 'The Man Who Attended a CHAPs Meeting' – the Cambridge Homosexual Activism Project, no less, an independent forum for the free discussion and working through of issues of sexual and political liberation – 'Wearing a Tweed Sports Jacket'. With a little triangle of red handkerchief peeping out of its breast pocket.

His outfit was completed by a pair of corduroy trousers and some dully gleaming brogues. I had had a glimpse of those brogues and those enticing cords earlier on, and wondered who it could be that was wearing them, but then I was broad-minded about such things, or clueless if you prefer that term. The sleeves of his shirt protruded the regulation inch beyond the cuffs of his jacket. There was even a glint of what might be cufflinks. If so they were surely the first cufflinks on those premises for years if not decades. The Tonys were not dressy people. There was a fair chance they had made wills stipulating interment in their favourite dungarees.

Sooner or later new arrivals would be funnelled my way at meetings, but Jim came over to introduce himself of his own accord. His hand came forward with reflexive assurance then became abruptly tentative, as often happens when people realise that I can't follow through to complete the ritual of greeting. Luckily, though, as a military man Jim had other resources and could shift with fair smoothness to a salute. It had something a tiny bit wonky about it, that salute, to take out the starch, a hint of *Dad's Army* sloppiness or Benny Hill foolery.

I enjoyed being saluted, still do, since after all – as I told Jim – Dad had saluted all of us whenever he came home, long ago, before I was even ill. Naturally I wanted to know his rank. He had been a Squadron Leader, and was impressed in his turn that Dad had been a Wing Commander. We were having one of the few natural and animated conversations I remember from CHAPs meetings, so of course one of the Tonys had to come and break us up, before we got around to talking about exciting things like postings.

The Tonys didn't do anything as suburban as showing slides of their holidays. They tended instead to incorporate aspects of local cuisine in the catering they did for CHAPs meetings. So I knew they had spent time in Provence the moment water biscuits smeared with an aromatic black paste started to circulate. On the plate was a little card proudly announcing *Tapenade*. A voice in my ear said, 'We tried making it without the anchovies but it's really not the same.' I was politely being warned by one of the relentlessly catering Tonys that as a dyed-in-the-wool vegetarian I was being excused participation in the nibbles. Never mind that I was starving. Never mind, either, that those biscuits with their pungent granular topping were a lot less laden with bad karma and the dreadful prospect of numberless rebirths than what was left for me in the oven five times a week. I was trapped – my home help knew what a bad vegetarian I was, or rather she thought I wasn't a vegetarian of any description but simply a flesh-consumer of the type considered normal. At CHAPs meetings I passed for exemplary in terms of my dietary choices if nothing else, and since I fitted in so poorly in the gay-liberation world order I somehow felt I owed it to the group to make more of an effort as the representative of another minority. I could hear Jim crunching on the delicious snack as he was led away.

The password is 'tureen'

I don't remember what Ken spoke about that evening, but it wasn't in him to make things too easy for beginners. The patriarchy was certain to have featured, in a relentless analysis that seemed very unlike understanding. Were all our heterosexual friends really tools of the patriarchy? What, MarkO and Bernardette? MarkO might be a tool but he wasn't a tool of the patriarchy. I didn't want my life to be a reproach to anyone else's, and I didn't want my erections to be a critique of the norm. They had enough on their plate without taking on extra responsibilities.

There can't have been actual spotlights in the Tonys' house trained to pick out simultaneously the shine on his bald head (he had been alopecic since his teens) and the glare of his thick glasses. That would have been an elaborate lighting effect, when the Tonys were aiming no higher than what everyone aspired to, a Habitat or Casa Pupo smartness – I forget which of those shops was the more desirable, and they probably changed places on the ladder of consumerism every now and then just to keep people on their toes. Yet in my memory Ken's scalp and the lenses of his spectacles were signal lamps flashing separate and possibly contradictory messages, Morse code not easily transcribed into words, a broken dazzle related in some way to enlightenment. Related, yes, but not closely, perhaps only in the way of a distant cousin. The person no one can quite place at family gatherings.

Looking back on the image of Ken nerving himself to join a CHAPs meeting after he had parked and impregnably locked his bicycle, I rejected the evidence of what I had seen, or reinterpreted it in a way that took away the unthinkable vulnerability. I decided that his state of mind must be similar to what a preacher might experience, confronting Sunday after Sunday the weak faith of his flock.

At some point another fragrant snack was passed round on trays, labelled with as much pride as the first. This was *pissaladière*, cut into wedges. If anyone else was serving the regional delicacy of that name to the group there would have been any number of lazy jokes made about the piss-elegant pretensions of what was really no more than Frenchified pizza. But the Tonys, staunch in their pair-bond, however contrary it was to what was prescribed by Ken's theories, were too central to the functioning of the group to be mocked. 'We tried making it without the anchovies,' said a voice in my ear, only this time it wasn't the same voice – it was the same ear though a different Tony – 'but it's really not the same. It's just not the same.' Once again the pretended vegetarian was having his bluff called. 'Maybe,' I said, '. . . just this once . . . I should try it? Just out of politeness? I know how much trouble you've taken.' Cooks love appreciation, as is only natural. But the Tonys weren't going to let me betray my principles for a mouthful of ashes, however delicious that mouthful of ashes. I felt sure that these were ashes altogether superior to the ashes I was usually served, but I could only watch as the tray was borne away.

As we were leaving, George gave Robin a brief but passionate kiss on the mouth. I think everyone was startled (and that included Robin) since George had been such a quiet presence during the whole of his previous attendance. He hadn't shared personal experience and kept his eyes on the floor much of the time to avoid the dreadful possibility of Ken searching him out.

It wasn't hard to tell what message he was sending, and it confirmed my suspicion that this would be the last CHAPs would see of him. He was broadcasting it pretty freely, saturating the frequencies: *Look what I picked up, and not on the meat market either – in the China and Glass department of Eaden Lilley. You should try it sometime! The password is 'tureen'. Till then, enjoy your brainy wrangling!*

In the car, George seemed in awe of his own boldness. 'I can hardly believe I did that. Were you very shocked, John?'

'Not shocked, no. But I do think it means you won't be coming back.'

'Well, you never know. How many farewell tours did Sarah Bernhardt do?'

'I haven't a clue.'

'Nor me. But there were quite a few.'

He was doing all he could, I suppose, to avoid leaving me with a feeling of abandonment. He was trying to console me. I could almost hear him saying sheepishly to Robin, later in the evening, 'I think I softened the blow. Poor John. He'll be fine, though . . . won't he?' He must have been used to dealing with disappointed customers, with ladies adamant that the Waterford crystal must have been cracked before it left the shop because they're always so very careful with precious things and it was a mystery where the receipt could have got to. And of course I'd be fine. Wasn't I always?

'And how about you, Robin? Did you enjoy yourself?' I could hear the unrealistic wheedling note in my voice. I was hoping against hope that Robin had been in some way converted by what I guessed to be his first taste of gay liberation. Then we could continue to attend as a trio, turning Tuesdays into a sort of family outing. I was far gone in fantasy.

'Well, it wasn't as terrible as I was expecting. The food was good – those toasty things were very tasty, though I've had better pizza than that piss-whatever-it-was-called.' In his professional life I dare say he was starved of treats. My guess is that serving delicious food after funerals would be adjudged as much of a display of bad taste as a bronzed mortician. 'But that Ken of yours! Does he ever have sex, do you think?'

I didn't much relish 'that Ken of yours', though I supposed George was included in the possessive pronoun, and after all it was a question that we had asked each other often enough. Sometimes we thought it likely that he did, though it was hard to imagine the stream of dialectical materialism being interrupted by an orgasm for more than a few seconds. A pause of raucous panting perhaps before normal service in terms of patriarchy-unravelling propositions resumed.

'And why does he look like that? It's horrible. Why would anyone shave their head?'

'It's not that,' said George. 'He lost his hair after measles when he was little, didn't he, John? You told me about it, and you even knew the medical word for hair loss.' Even without being able to see him I could sense George fluffing up what remained on the top of his own head, a robust remainder but still a remainder.

'Alopecia. But you're the one who told me about the measles.'

'I really don't think so. I'm positive I heard it from you.'

This was a puzzle. Admittedly I encourage people to think that I have a monopoly on medical information, but I had a distinct memory of George telling me the explanation for Ken's baldness, even if I was the one – guilty! – to supply the technical term.

Robin wasn't convinced. 'If he lost all his hair, how do you explain those eyebrows? He looks after them a bit better than Mr Denis

Healey does, I'll say that for him. But I'm telling you, *he shaves his head*. I haven't the faintest idea why, but that's what he does.'

'But wouldn't there be little bits of stubble? I don't know, shaving cuts, dried blood?' I could hardly believe we were having this particular discussion. One way or another, Ken was taking possession of the evening.

'Not if he's been doing it for years. He must have got good at it over time.'

This was a new idea, shocking in its force. Ken looked the way he did because . . . he wanted to look the way he did. George and I, and (as we imagined) the rest of the group, had attributed his intense intellectual persona to the combination of that bald brain-box and the heavy glasses behind which his eyes looked so small. A matter of making the best of a bad job. The vision of Ken lathering up his bonce and giving himself a going-over with the old Wilkinson Sword was downright disturbing. The image fitted in with something monastic about him that should have appealed to me but didn't, very much didn't. This was not Brother Lawrence, not by a long chalk.

'Where am I taking you to?' We were back in Chesterton by now. 'Give me some directions, please.'

'Just drop us by the Haymakers. We're in need of some refreshment, aren't we, Robin? Stop in yourself, John. Would you care for a half?'

Even a half could render a small body habitus liable to penalties if tested by breath-analyser – and no pub serves quarter-pints. I fought against the contraction 'breathalyser' as long as I could, and only ended up thinking I might as well have capitulated right away for all the good my resistance did me. Same with new pence and new pee, same with people pronouncing 'flaccid' as 'flassid' just because onomatopœia prefers that sound's mimicry of slack tissue, though there's no other English word where a double 'cee' is pronounced as 'ess', is there?

Well, is there? The correct pronunciation is not arbitrary, not assidental. We can't let sonorous appeal trample all over the rules of pronunciation, though of course we already have. It's a *fait accompli*, beyond the scope of any appeal to the British Council for Pronunciation and Phonic Enforcement, which doesn't even exist though it so obviously should.

I left them to their beers, though if what they had drunk earlier qualified as a 'sharpener' then these could only be blunteners. And despite the example of Sarah Bernhardt this was (to the best of my knowledge) George's one and only farewell tour.

At meetings after that his name wasn't really mentioned, perhaps because he had been a misfit among misfits (the wrong sort of misfit) from the start, without my obvious excuse, or because the final message he sent was so clear. Is there something called a kiss-off? If so that was his parting gesture. It would be wrong to say that Jim took George's place on any deeper level, but he certainly tended to sit next to me thereafter. I suppose it's possible there had been hints that he should try to console me for the break-up of a couple that had (as it happened) never existed, but I doubt it. He so obviously lived in a world of commands rather than hints. And he didn't give off any of the faint neighbourly glow I detected from George, the sense of a boundary that was neither crossed nor defended. Jim's sense of himself as a separate physical entity was much stronger, though he was friendly and even remarkably open, open about his rather closed-off life, not hiding his surprise at the new things around him.

'That kiss last week, eh?'

'What about it?' Though it was demonstrably in its way a public event.

Better than no kiss at all

'I don't know what I thought. I mean . . . I know there's a film with two men having a great big smacker, open mouths and everything, caused a real fuss, I know, but I didn't catch that. I'm not much on the flicks.' At last – someone who hadn't seen *Sunday Bloody Sunday*. Ignorance cheerfully owned up to can be positively refreshing in a world (or a university town) where people are always madly playing up their knowledge. 'I'd never actually seen men kiss before. Is it a sexy thing? I'm in two minds. It takes some getting used to.' I was in two minds myself, about whether he was calm or really quite het up under the surface. This was a question that often came up with Jim, who was somehow relaxed and unrelaxed at the same time. His retirement was run on a schedule and he didn't want to get behind.

399

'I'm not sure it's anything unless you're doing the kissing.'

'Good point. I expect you think I'm very backward.' Well, yes, but he was being very forward about it. And kissing between men was a rare bird in those days. I should have been more forward to Jim about my own lack of experience. Once in Market Hill I had seen a record cover displayed on the stall of Andy's Records showing two men kissing with apparent passion in pouring rain. Andy's brother Billy took it from the rack for me, slightly puzzled because it wasn't the sort of record I usually asked about. Billy was the slightly rattier of the two brothers but they were both lovely boys, lovely to me certainly, and would come over to help me cross the cobbles if they weren't busy with customers. For about half the year, working outdoors as they did, they wore RAF-surplus sheepskin flying jackets, which could only make them seem family. 'What's it about?' I asked him, really meaning the cover. He turned it over in his hands a couple of times and said, 'Well, it's the soundtrack of a film, isn't it? A gangster film by the look of it.'

'But why are they kissing?'

It wasn't really a question that lay within his competence to answer, but Billy did his best to oblige me.

'I think maybe one of them has betrayed the Mafia gang and the other is passing on the death sentence, letting him know he's for the chop. So it's the kiss of death.' Heavens! The scrapes some chaps get into.

'But which is which?' In the frozen moment chosen for the cover of the LP they seemed equally committed to the desperate act. Of course Billy could only shrug. How was he supposed to know? I was trying to make sense of the world as my education had insisted I do, turning everything into subject–verb–object when that sort of clarity is the exception not the rule. Billy returned the record to its place in the rack, leaving me with the thought that perhaps the kiss of death was better than no kiss at all.

A fair number of CHAPs members kissed in greeting and farewell, but though this wasn't a peck on the cheek it was definitely a peck on the lips, as generalised as the kiss of peace practised in the heartier sort of Christian service.

Jim told me he hadn't had much sex but was sure he'd get the hang of it and catch up. He might have been talking about the layout of an unfamiliar instrument panel. 'I'm not unrealistic,' he said. 'I'm not exactly a catch, but I know I've got something to offer.' He was philosophical about the accident of legislation which meant that his chosen career denied him legal expression even after decriminalisation was afforded to others, saying it was just the luck of the draw. Well, maybe, but postmen and window-cleaners weren't ticket holders in the same lottery. What had they done to deserve fuller, richer or at least less hypocritical lives? Perhaps karmic resignation is part of the training that is given to air cadets.

After that first meeting Jim made some attempt to make his turnout more appropriate (the tweed sports jacket was retired, for instance) but never managed to get it right. In a way, he wasn't supposed to, but he was meant to try, to find some impossible middle ground between embarrassingly fuddy-duddy and mutton dressed up as lamb. The task of reconciling the contradictions of the group's ideology fell to him, to the individual. We saw sexuality as unbounded by prohibition, restriction and taboo, though we hadn't stopped being faintly horrified by the idea of substandard flesh following its desires and seeking satisfaction. Sometimes when Ken was addressing the ranks I would see his eyes drawn to the side of the room where Jim and I might be sitting side by side. His gaze would be pulled helplessly along, past me, until it rested on Jim's corduroy trousers, worn with a rather scruffy brown leather bomber jacket. Once or twice his eyes seemed to shift back and forth between the two of us, as if undecided which of us was the more hopeless case. I was reticent about my sex life, not wanting to boast about my little adventures, and perhaps Jim was pursuing a similar strategy.

Jim had more than one pair of cords, in tones of salmon and ochre. I like cords, but there are cords and cords, and I found that on any particular evening I instinctively preferred the ones he didn't happen to be wearing. After his first, tweedy *faux pas* he always turned up in that bomber jacket, which was particularly mocked by the membership, something I thought unfair. I had to bite my lip, not something I really have a gift for, to avoid asking the obvious question: as the only person attending meetings who might at some point have flown a bomber, was he not entitled to wear a bomber jacket? But then we would have been back to square one in the wrangle about military service and self-oppression.

The northern white cedar springs to mind

He was referred to as 'Captain Jim', without malice, out of politeness with just a hint of mockery. It made him wince just the same. In the army, with its more reticulated hierarchy, 'Captain' doesn't have a lot of weight, but in the RAF there's only Group Captain, and that's a different matter, outranking as it does Squadron Leader (Jim's retirement rank) and Wing Commander (Dad's). An army captain is small beer but a Group Captain is a big cheese in the Raff. Jim didn't want to be thought of as inflating his own status, even passively by not correcting an error, though he and I were the only people in the group who understood the ticklishness of it. I don't imagine he lost sleep over it. He wasn't the losing-sleep kind.

It was extraordinary on how many levels he didn't fit in. He might almost have represented an outstandingly clumsy attempt to infiltrate the membership, devised by outsiders who had no idea about what was being impersonated. He didn't look like a gay man, whatever that means, though he also didn't *not* look like a gay man either. Whatever *that* means. You could just about imagine him in an earlier period slipping half a crown to a guardsman in a public convenience as an inducement to perform, or to allow the performance of, unspeakable acts. Otherwise he had a sort of consistent dullness of finish, a refusal to sparkle that would routinely assign him to the tribe of straight rather than the tribe of gay.

In those days a service career brought with it a sort of flattened, all-purpose poshness. Jim's way of saying Chewsdy for Tuesday ('See you next Chewsdy') was already being laughed at, or at least smirked at. People in the group started using that pronunciation themselves, and after a while it became a free-floating affectation, cut loose from its roots in mockery, all thanks to Jim's refusal – though refusal suggests too much in the way of conscious choice – to let it get under his skin. Those who joined the group later could have no idea that it started out as a joke at a particular person's expense. It became naturalised, like a tree of foreign origin happily growing on British soil (the northern white cedar springs to mind). The inverted commas that called attention to its status as silly were worn away by constant use.

Did Jim say 'Ack Emma' and 'Pip Emma' to mean morning and afternoon? I can't swear to it, though having a father who had been in the Raff meant that those expressions wouldn't have struck me as particularly exotic.

Military training has its benefits. Jim could sit there during an exposition of radical ideas without moving a muscle, absolutely immune to the fidgets in a way that few of us who attended could match. No doubt he would be equally impassive in a briefing whether the mission was to drop incendiary bombs on Dresden or food parcels over Biafra. A poker face come in handy. It wasn't to be expected that he would respond enthusiastically to denunciations of the patriarchy when the patriarchy signed off on his pension cheques.

This of course was an issue in itself. According to dogma anyone who joined the armed services was opposing his own liberation, joining the ranks not of his country's defenders but of the self-oppressed. That swarming, numberless horde.

Another such victim of his own internalised attitudes was a student in his third year who had perhaps procrastinated a bit, not being in a hurry to address his sexual nature. This was Francis, problematic in terms of the group both because he had an on-again, off-again relationship with religious belief, and because he was as camp as a row of pink tents. 'Camp as a row of pink tents' – that expression was fresh then. Those imaginary tents still had the early-morning dew on them.

As a group we wanted camp and the self-hatred it represented to be eliminated, or at least to die off of its own accord. As individuals we must have known we would miss it when the last piece of bitchy cleverness had been uttered and the world had been defanged.

We should have been crafty and delegated Ken, on his next ideological shopping trip to Paris, to ask the powers that were for a ruling about whether effeminacy was a miserable hangover from an earlier period or a heroic provocation of patriarchal values. To put it in more concrete terms, were we allowed to laugh at John Inman on *Are You Being Served?* None of us dared. It was all very well deciding on a worthwhile course of action, but no one would be willing to bell the cat, the bald and thickly bespectacled cat who pounced on our errors of radical thought and toyed with them, releasing them only to pounce again as they dragged themselves towards the refuge of the skirting board.

Francis had changed his course of study from Theology to Archæology and Anthropology and then switched back again just as abruptly. Academic turmoil doesn't always correspond to personal crisis but in this case it definitely did. Francis had lost his faith in his first term and decided that in good conscience he couldn't go on studying something he didn't believe in, though he was told he wouldn't be the first to do so and not even the thousand-and-first. The switch to Arch and Anth was an attempt to take actual belief out of the equation, but this solution was overtaken by a more drastic one. He would read theology after all but against the grain, seeking to highlight the injustices done to women and minorities. Somewhere in this set of decisions and reversals had come the realisation that his changed course of study was felt to be an easy option, with a First in Archæology and Anthropology easily outclassed by a 2.1 in Theology. One thing that hadn't changed was his need to have his cleverness recognised.

Tiffs with divinity

The paradoxes hadn't gone away, since he wanted to agitate for the inclusion within Anglicanism of those traditionally outside the fold, while no longer believing its teachings to be true. This was a precarious if not impossible balance to strike if his ambition was to admit a broader range of people into a delusion. He wanted religious belief to be at the heart of his course of study so that he could dissent or even apostatise from it. From week to week he changed his position, sometimes thinking that God rejected him and sometimes insisting that he rejected a God who didn't live up to His own gospel of love. Sometimes God and His pronouns required the tribute of capitalisation (I have an ear for such things), sometimes the deity was dethroned and slammed back into lower case. Francis wanted to raze the established church to its foundations but also to impose lady priests on it, to horror and hilarity in the theology department. I'm afraid 'lady priests' was the phrase they all used.

In between these tiffs with divinity there might be reconciliations and even brief honeymoons. Sometimes he thought that love between

men was holy as long as it wasn't expressed physically, and sometimes that sexual relations between men would earn forgiveness as
long as there was fidelity on both sides. He'd had any amount of pastoral care from the college chaplain as well as his personal tutor. Some
personal tutors fulfilled their function better than others – it was a
required part of an academic's administrative duties, and not everyone
is up to the task of humble listening since cleverness often clogs the
ears. Someone was even sent from the Porter's Lodge to check up on
Francis every day or so, in a way that suggested he was on some sort of
suicide-watch roster. He had the feeling everyone was waiting for him
to crack up completely and be carted off to Fulbourn. Then they could
get back to their lives. What's a nervous breakdown between friends?
Nobody minds that, it's dithering that gets on people's nerves.

All of this information filtered through to me very indirectly, but
CHAPs was in its way as efficient a gossip-processing plant as the sewing circle that had provided my mother with her social life in Bourne
End when I was a child. By the time Francis was finally led over to
me I felt I had been fully briefed about his predicament in all its com-
plexity. I understood, too, how little help the group would offer him
as a spiritual being. I think everyone but me was waiting for him to
abandon the folly of belief. They would listen with a certain amount of
patience to his torments, as long as he ended up shutting the door on
God. As if that was a possibility! I was eager to show him that there
were other ways of looking at the whole question, other ways to con-
jugate desire and divinity. I had a little homily of my own prepared.

I put out my hand a little bit and he touched it very gingerly
without shaking. I'm good practice for greeting royalty – the feath-
erweight touch is just the approach the Queen prefers, or so we are
told. Then I announced myself in formal terms to ease the tension.
'John Cromer,' I said, 'doubly oppressed.' This description was more
or less the only reference that had been made to me within the group,
when Ken in the course of a homily had referred to the patriarchal
values thanks to which 'someone like John is doubly oppressed'.
Mentioned in passing, to make an ideological point, yes, but at least
I was mentioned. Oppressed by reason of being gay and also by virtue
of disability – my moment, I suppose, of glory, of having a double
helping of untouchable status slopped in my bowl. Francis gave his

name in return, but I have to say he seemed a little thrown. Perhaps he was possessive of his own twofold oppression, by the straight world for being gay and by the gay one for having the impertinence to feel connected with all creation. Of course I had that trump card up my own sleeve ready to play.

His breath was sour, not from halitosis (that invention of marketing) but from depression medication (not then an invention of marketing) and just possibly from the altered biology of depression itself.

My plan to help Francis didn't involve telling him that God Is Love or alternatively trying to convince him that his animal instincts were things to be ashamed of, but simply telling him about the rather different way things were managed in the pantheon of my religion. In Hinduism the gods are rutting like brainless teenagers most of the time and no one thinks it calls their divinity into question. For heaven's sake, the goddess Rati, she who presides over sexual pleasure, was even born from drops of sweat! In one episode of the cosmic soap opera, Śiva had been having enthusiastic carnal congress with Parvati for years – *years* – without climaxing. The suspense was killing practically everyone, the other gods couldn't get on with their lives, so a deputation was sent to resolve the deadlock. Can there be an unstoppable Tantric chain reaction of withheld orgasm capable of destroying this world and every other, shattering not only the four elephants that uphold the world but the infinity of turtles that uphold *them*? No one wanted to find out.

Suburban adultery hound slinking around Olympus

There's no good moment to interrupt a god in flagrante delightful. It showed surprisingly good manners on Śiva's part that he bothered to open the door when he heard knocking during the eternal tantric moment. The visitors were about to ask politely when he was finally going to get his rocks off so that everyone else could please get some sleep when Lord Śiva abruptly ejaculated. Not quite such good manners on his part, perhaps, but never mind that.

One of the visitors, Agni, the spirit of fire, was quick off the mark, lunging to swallow the divine seed as it spurted. It was strongly perfumed with jasmine, or so the texts say, but also so hot that he needed to dive down into the Ganges to cool off. Śiva's semen burned the fire god's mouth! Not bad going. It still had some heat in it, though, even when spat into a vast watercourse, more than the river could absorb, and the Ganges boiled. For fear of evaporating completely Ganga, the god of the river, managed to throw the mouthful of superhuman seed onto the bank (where the city of Varanasi now stands, if you're interested). Later, though, when everything had cooled down, that spat-out mouthful of sperm, prudently invested, gave birth to a new god.

Six wise women sat by the godly load, attracted by its glow but also soothed by its warmth in the chill of the evening. Mysteriously it entered all six and made them pregnant, with the gestational novelty that they gave birth, collectively and without the customary delay, to a single being. This was Skanda. Sometimes he sports six heads in honour of his multi-uterine origins, as I suppose he may do on Mothers' Day cards. (There would have to be special ones printed, with teams of crack proofreaders on high alert to make sure that apostrophe was properly placed, not lazily restored to its usual position.) The name Skanda means, by some accounts, 'spurt'. And 'spurt' in my etymological lexicon endlessly cross-references with 'spirit'. For spurt see spirit. For spirit see spurt. 'By some accounts' – certainly the most frequently recurring phrase in anything written about Hindu cosmology. Cosmology means by derivation words about order, but the Hindu version of it likes the order to be richly seeded with chaos and contradiction. The traditions seethe with variants much like the Ganges itself when Śiva's sperm, released at last after being so long withheld, brought it to its boiling point.

The whole saga makes randy old Zeus seem like a sordid philanderer, doesn't it? Suburban adultery hound slinking around Olympus disguised as this, disguised as that, hoping against hope that no one tells on him to Hera or else there'll be trouble come dinnertime – real risk of her spitting in his Ambrosia creamed rice. But whether they're lurid or merely seedy these powerful figures, Greek and Hindu, are not there to be emulated morally, any more than thunder and lightning are to be considered a blueprint for conduct. Gods will be gods. It's none of our business, and if we ourselves get up to sexual activity that's slightly out of the way, aroused by crystal as we may be or longing to run a pair of hairbrushes through the locks of strangers, then frankly it's none of theirs either.

I think I expounded Hindu scripture respectably enough, though of course any specialist in the field would enjoy riddling my pitiful expertise with bullets of pedantry – there's no gunslinger so trigger-happy as a scholar with academic territory to defend. Yet somehow I didn't achieve my goal. It's frustrating when you know you have something important to pass on but somehow can't convey your meaning. This of course is the whine of the Ancient Mariner, ever renewed, never finding adequate response.

I can only think that there was a very limited overlap between the words I emitted, words bearing the message of comfort I so much wanted to convey, and what Francis was able to take in. It's possible that I garbled my presentation.

I'd neglected to observe one of the cardinal rules of life in a wheel-chair, to wit, settle your pigeon. Settle your pigeon! Don't assume that someone in your general area will stay put just because you've started talking, however eloquent you may judge yourself to be. A lot of soothing must be effected before any actual communication can take place. Francis was perching next to me, and everything about his posture shrieked provisionality. I should have waited until he had settled in properly before I could expect him to listen. Normally I know better and work to relax my audience. Apart from anything else, it's a precondition for being heard rather than nodded at. On this occasion I didn't prepare the ground. I didn't verify, either visually or with a discreet poke, that Francis's quadriceps were fully relaxed, rather than poised to boost him upwards at a moment's notice.

To judge by the expression of alarm on his face, what he heard wasn't an exposition of the vibrant tangle of sexuality taken for granted in the Hindu picture of the universe but something closer to a cryptic obscenity. It wasn't really surprising that he should recoil. Those tensed quadriceps of his became fully engaged and his perching position changed to headlong flight.

I was crestfallen at the failure of my attempt to soothe Francis's religio-sexual qualms, but I certainly wasn't expecting to be scolded by the one-man committee that Ken constituted. He seemed scandalised, saying, 'You can't say such things, John. You just can't.'

I realised my cross-cultural message of reassurance had been badly garbled but decided to play the innocent, asking, 'But what did I say that was so wrong?', and it was a good job that I did. Ken said, 'You told him you were deeply depressed! And you know how fragile Francis is. Everyone is always saying so.'

'But that isn't what I said! I said I was *doubly oppressed*. Don't you remember?' In general my enunciation doesn't pose a problem. It sometimes happens that people don't want to hear what I have to say but that's a different matter entirely. 'You're the one who told me so, you're the one who raised my consciousness. It's thanks to you I know that I'm oppressed by being gay in a difference-hating patriarchy and also by being disabled in . . . a difference-hating patriarchy. I didn't spell it out, but that's what I meant, and I'm sorry if Francis misunderstood.'

Ken may not have been convinced by my quoting his gospel against him, but he had at least to consider the possibility that I was telling the truth, and anyway I had used the word 'patriarchy' twice in a single sentence, something he was bound to find soothing.

It was unfortunate that Francis had misheard an introduction that was meant to be disarming and light-hearted, and his fragile state of mind no doubt played a part in his mistake. But it was true of the group as a whole, perhaps even the departed George, who had come the closest to being an actual friend, that its members took deep depression to be my natural state, simply because it was what they imagined they would feel if put in my place. They could see my life only as a sum of lacks.

However clearly I wrote my message on the wall, however bright the poster paint I used to colour it in, it would always be read as *Killjoy was here.*

Even so I had to take some responsibility for the failure of the conversation with Francis. My instructive commentary on sexuality in Hindu religious thought, garbled in transit, had arrived in his consciousness an unholy mess. If he'd been asked to give a précis of my little cross-cultural presentation, what could he possibly have come up with? *'God ejaculates the moment you open the door – and it doesn't half burn your mouth!'* Something mad-sounding along those lines.

If I'd been given another chance to cheer Francis up I would certainly have tried to be less entertaining and colourful, suggesting merely that the instinct to worship and give thanks is fundamental and not something to apologise for. That's the Śruti-note, the foundational tone, and everything else including desire for bodies is just an overtone in the harmonic series.

After the mishearing of 'doubly oppressed' as 'deeply depressed' I would have certainly learned to avoid a phrase that people found somehow baffling, though when it had been said by Ken at that memorable original meeting everyone had nodded gravely at its self-evident and searing truth, but in any case no one who could be thought at all fragile was allowed near me after that. Persuasion is my only power, and power is exactly what it isn't. It's very easy to keep me at the edges of a group. I imagine it was feared I would give advice about the precise number of sleeping tablets required to ensure a lethal dose, perhaps even propose a pact. I shouldn't be flippant. Student suicide is a real scourge and a real headache for the authorities.

I don't know if there is any truth to the idea that university students are inveterate suicides, but I remember being told that Oxford and Cambridge were the first places to be supplied with natural gas rather than coal gas, to keep the mortality figures down. Killing yourself with natural gas takes patience. You have to stick at it, persevering until you're breathing in gas instead of oxygen. It's asphyxia instead of actual poisoning, which is how coal gas works, filling your lungs with carbon monoxide and knocking you out in record time. With coal gas, death is waiting in the wings and has his lines off pat, needing no prompter.

I could understand Francis's sense of being urged towards disintegration. No sooner had he thrown away a piece of paper with the Samaritans' emergency number than another one was slipped into his pocket, and all these individually reassuring messages had a cumulatively oppressive effect. Everyone steered him away from the brink of psychological collapse while somehow also nudging him towards it. After a while he felt that he was doing the wrong thing by not properly cracking up. He was letting people down. I once heard him say, 'Maybe I should just get on with it, and let everyone visit me in Fulbourn.'

Fulbourn was more than the name of a settlement near the city. Just as King's College Chapel, with its teats of stone upturned to suckle the academic sky, represented Cambridge in its entirety, so Fulbourn (or rather its psychiatric hospital) took on the lesser synecdochical task of symbolising the turmoil that threatened to overwhelm the student mind.

Once I had thought about it, I was able to realise that there was more than a whiff of hypocrisy in Ken's scolding of my conduct as regarded Francis. Hadn't he himself floated the idea at least once that what was lazily termed mental illness was a 'contested site' of a great potential instructive richness? Everyone in Paris, apparently, loved a contested site. Schizophrenia above all was a sort of involuntary critique of bourgeois values, a cortical rejection of the status quo. The brain threw off its shackles, and if it felt lost without them that was only to be expected.

Francis made costume choices every bit as eccentric and meaningful as Jim's. It was Francis's invariable habit to wear a shirt and tie under a jumper, even if the strangulated knot of the tie was not always visible beneath the collar of the round-necked jumper. In this way he insisted on a layered restriction concentrated on the throat, as if to emphasise that his most important task was to hold back from speech, or at least not to say anything personal. Despite the symbolic barriers to his communication, there was no question of him just keeping quiet, as many of us did. Francis's curious way of dressing didn't attract mockery, voiced or silent, the way Jim's did, and perhaps the fragility of his psychological state had something to do with that. Jim seemed robust. He could take a joke, though it seemed against the odds that he would ever make one.

No one had ever accused Jim of being a conversationalist, whereas Francis's tongue regularly ran away with him, and sometimes with the rest of the group. He introduced a benign tension into meetings, with the permanent possibility that caustic heretical sallies would disrupt the exposition of Marxist–Keninist thought. 'Marxist–Keninist thought' itself was an early and welcome addition by Francis to the word-hoard of the collective. I'm not sure Lenin ever had the initial letter of his last name restored to him, except when we were on best behaviour. It was confiscated more often than not. Vladimir Ulyanov would have to learn to get along without it.

Francis became the group's consecrated wit or wag, the mocker-in-chief, often funny though only occasionally kind. A sharp tongue protects its owner, that being the main reason for its acquisition of an edge.

Perhaps it was just because Jim tended to sit next to me at meetings that I found myself taking his part willy-nilly. His frankness about how little experience he had had should have counted in his favour yet the mood was a little dismissive. His honesty as well as his history in uniform appealed to me, but I could see it wasn't doing anything to improve his standing in the group. He was unabashed about how little his sex life had amounted to up to this point, yet he seemed to lose respect by the admission. In a forum where honesty was touted as the be-all and end-all, he reaped no benefit from his openness and would have done better, in terms of popular acceptance, to make up some sordid episodes.

Surviving on crumbs

From the group's point of view it was as if he'd squandered a legacy, which is I suppose a way of looking at youth – but legacy, the passing on of one generation's property to the next, seems a patriarchal enough idea in all conscience. What's the Marxist–Keninist line about that? Doesn't it get squandered in any case, youth, one way or another? It's what economists call a wasting asset. Youth is wasted on the young, just as mobility is wasted on the able-bodied. They really don't appreciate it.

I was young myself and you could say I wasn't getting much of a return on my investments. But look at it another way: the chronic frustration that was imagined to be my condition of life was a useful contribution to make to the group. Best to keep quiet about any exploits and experiments to maintain the equilibrium of the membership, who might not mind surviving on crumbs so much as long as they could be sure I had nothing in my belly.

No one at CHAPs was betting on Jim's finding what he wanted, partly because they couldn't imagine what it might be. Someone (which usually meant Francis) made a rather unkind comment about his programme of making up for lost time, this delayed adolescence or sedate kicking over of the traces, saying he was sowing his wild oats. No, I'm being silly, that's just the standard phrase, it doesn't begin to work as a joke. What Francis said was tame oats. Tame oats! That's more like it. The general feeling was that Jim had retired from the RAF – and shouldn't his sex drive have been pensioned off as part of the same package? Given indefinite leave to do watercolours, to potter about the herbaceous borders wearing corduroys of any colour it happened to fancy but not to bother the world at large.

I didn't know whether to be relieved or alarmed that Jim seemed to take his welcome at CHAPs so much at face value. It would be wild exaggeration to say that he was accepted by the group, but you could not have deduced that from the way he behaved. Perhaps one group really is much like another. I wouldn't know. I've been part of so few – it's not my area of expertise. Perhaps the differences between an officers' mess and a radical gay group pale beside their similarities, and Jim felt as much at home in the one as he had in the other.

At first I assumed that Jim would fade away after attending a meeting or two, and I rather pumped him for personal information aligned with my own little interests while I could. I had underestimated his stolid persistence, and the power of habit, the uniform people wear after they've taken the uniform off.

'Can I ask you a question, Jim?'

He was immediately on his guard, though he gave a little laugh and said, 'Ask away.'

'Do you have a hairbrush?'

He laughed again, with more confidence. 'Do you mean do I have one with me now, or do I own one? Most people have hairbrushes, John! Most men, and all women too, I expect . . . Yes, I own a hairbrush.'

'What does it look like?'

'Let me see. It's oval, no handle. Bristles on a sort of pinky cushion. That's all I can tell you. I've had it for a long time . . .'

I was dangerously excited. He was describing the Mason Pearson brush in the military shape that had been one of the delights of my bedbound childhood, a possession of Dad's that Mum sometimes used soothingly, arousingly, on my hair, charging me follicle by follicle with the static electricity deriving from a father who wasn't there most of the time. While she brushed my scalp tingled with the worship I felt for the father who was so often away that it felt almost wrong when he entered the room and was present in person.

'One little perk of those brushes, John, is that they come in a box with a brush of their own.'

What!? I was so thrilled I could hardly breathe. *What?!?* I'd seen the full panoply of incredulous punctuation in the boys' comics I'd read or seen others reading in the *Eagle*, the *Tiger*, the *Victor*, but never really understood the depth of need it answered. With the help of my brother Peter I had trespassed into the taboo zone of the marital bedroom long enough to find and play with Dad's wonderful Bakelite tie press, which you wound up almost like a clock, but had failed to spot this specialised brush with its elevated ontology, a brush too refined to brush anything but brushes. 'How does it work? *What does it look like?*' If he had produced technical drawings I might not have thought it too much.

We behead Scheherazade

'I'm not quite sure what you find so thrilling, John, but I'll do my best to fill you in. Let me see. It's square, or rather rectangular, it's made of wood, a bit rough, the bristles are coarse and much longer than the bristles of the actual brush. They're . . . you'd have to say the bristles are in tight bunches but the bunches aren't close together . . . so, quite widely spaced. What you do is you put the proper brush face up and the cleaning brush face down and you rub them together – I suppose actually you scrape the cleaning brush across the proper brush. Do it a good few times. And hairs are transferred onto the cleaning brush. Do you follow?'

'And how do you clean the cleaning brush?'

'Well . . . actually you don't. You just pull the hairs off the bristles.' I was disappointed that there wasn't an infinite regress of brush-cleaning brushes, but then that may have been my attachment to Hindu cosmology speaking, its love of layers, the elephants that support the world, the turtle under the elephants, and then the infinity of turtles beneath. And to those sceptics who say, 'Why turtles?', I would point out their clear load-bearing superiority over creatures as fidgety as elephants.

I had another question. 'How about a tie press? Do you have a tie press?' Another object that had seemed to me as a child excitingly charged with Dad's essence, the nature he teasingly withheld. Recessive as he was, his traces often spoke more loudly than his presence.

'Now you're asking. Don't have one, don't need one, wouldn't want one. Was never much for ironing, put my trousers under the mattress at a pinch. As for ties, I hang 'em up neatly and if they don't pass muster then . . . that's too bad.' So that was a disappointment, and the wistful erection I'd been nursing since we started talking about Dad's hairbrush gently subsided. It had never had a lot to say for itself, as erections go, had never been an urgent or clamorous thing, and it had been at its peak for some reason when Jim described the two brushes being brought into contact belly to belly, their fibres caught up in each other, but that's no reason to exclude it from the historical record. In terms of the Œdipus complex, it has to be said, I have a long way to go even now.

This was an outstandingly strange conversation to have had with anyone, let alone someone I had just met, yet Jim seemed entirely unfazed by it. I had asked him technical questions that he was in a position to answer, and I'm confident he didn't give it a moment's thought.

It so happened that I had childhood memories of another military Jim, Jim Sheaffer, on whom I had a crush, or even the Ur-crush, the crush of crushes, the crush that told me what a crush was, the possibility of living richly inside an unfulfilled need. Jim had been kind to me when I was bedbound. I prefer 'bedbound' to 'bedridden' because the idea of being ridden by a bed is so silly, but I was certainly bound by the bed, and by the promise I had made not to move. Jim Sheaffer gave me his luminous watch, not just to look at but to keep, and the ecstasy of tenderness I felt then had never quite dissipated, first love being subject to the most gradual possible rate of radioactive decay. Now my eyes were drawn to the new Jim's wrist, to the wrist of Captain Jim who wasn't a captain, and though it wasn't hairy (as Jim

Sheaffer's had been) I couldn't stop staring at it, at both the wrist and the watch.

'I can see you like my watch,' he said, 'so shall I tell you how I learned to do a handbrake start, on a hill? This watch had a lot to do with it. It's a funny story!' Silently I gave him permission to speak, on the usual legally binding terms, namely *This had better be good*. I may not be good at running away and I can't put my fingers in my ears, but I'll make my feelings known just the same. Power lies with the listener, not the teller of the tale. We behead Scheherazade every time we close a book short of its last page . . . or at least we give her pretty neck a nick.

Luckily hers is a large family.

Jim's company had been unloading supplies from a warehouse awkwardly placed on a hill. This was in Rhodesia. When Jim tried to drive off uphill, the lorry kept rolling back a bit, and the more his commanding officer shouted at him the less he seemed able to get the clutch to bite cleanly so that he could take the handbrake off and move away smoothly up the gradient. Then his CO said, 'Give me your watch,' and said he was going to put it behind one of the rear wheels of the lorry. 'And after that, somehow it was easy. I got my watch back and believe it or not I never had trouble with that particular manœuvre again.'

'I'm sure you didn't. But do you think he really put your watch behind the wheel of a lorry? Perhaps it was all a bluff.'

He stayed entirely still for a long moment. 'I never thought of that.' Furious internal activity. 'I'm not sure it matters. I just needed something to help me concentrate. That certainly did the trick! I've never been so glad to get something right, and to get my watch back.' He gave its dial a fond repeated tap, using two fingers, twice and then twice again. His long-serving watch had earned the right to its own salute.

I recognised this style of idea, the mystical nudge that doesn't have to be real to be effective. Ramana Maharshi's comparison was with a sleeper dreaming about an elephant and waking with a start. The elephant wasn't real but it woke the sleeper up – and my guru goes on to explain that this is a parable about the functioning of, yes, a guru, not in any absolute sense a real entity but real enough to administer the beneficial shock that triggers self-realisation. On the other hand Jim couldn't qualify as all that awake if it had never occurred to him that his superior officer might be telling a fib. The elephant of unquestioned authority still trumpeted in his dreams without disturbing his sleep.

An easy person to avoid

Jim retained a regimented mentality even when theoretically integrating himself into civilian life. He let his regular weekday hours be known: he would be at the Whim on Trinity Street every weekday at 1030 hours for coffee, at The Eagle on Ben'et Street (though maybe it's Bene't Street? apostrophes do'nt always stay where the'yre put), whose Scotch eggs found favour with him, at 1300, and at the Mitre on Bridge Street from 1900 hours. It was somehow in character that he preferred real-ale pubs though his drink of choice was cider. If this was connoisseurship it was at second hand, or perhaps it represented a siding with traditional values that were making a curious return to favour on the back of the counterculture. In principle publishing his schedule like this made it easy for people to meet him, though it also made him an easy person to avoid. I would happily have met him by arrangement, but he made no individual overture. Putting up a notice on an imaginary message board was ample notification, as far as he was concerned. That was his social life taken care of, the schedule made known. From then on it was up to everybody else. Jim would no more have left the shape of his week to chance than he would have neglected to polish his chestnut-coloured brogues every day. The group soon realised that he would attend every Tuesday meeting unless prevented by a medical emergency.

At one early meeting Jim started to take notes when Ken spoke. It was as if he couldn't help himself, being used to briefings and the need to get everything exactly right. One evening a Tony discreetly nobbled him on a related matter, rather to my surprise. The Tonys gave the impression that the only thing that could go wrong at meetings from their point of view was the food running out.

'You do a lot of nodding while Ken is talking,' said Tony, 'and I do wish you'd stop. It's giving him ideas.' Jim's was a crisp little nod, a message-received-and-understood nod, bearing no necessary or even likely correlation with actual receipt and understanding, but it was more than enough as a response to encourage and even inflame our leader, who may have felt starved of endorsement in the ordinary run of things.

'Do I? I'm sorry about that. Habit of a lifetime. I don't even know I'm doing it, but I'll try to stop.'

'He really doesn't need encouragement. It doesn't seem to bother him that people are going cross-eyed with boredom.'

'I'm not sure I'm even bored, exactly. I'm not used to that university way of talking. Maybe that's all it is.'

'Well, actually, I think it's a bit more than that.'

When he noticed Jim taking notes Ken was briefly thrilled and then alarmed. Here was the rapt attention he craved and was so often denied by his audience yawning, fidgeting or trying to eat homemade cheese straws in total silence, but he soon became suspicious. When he had finished speaking he came over to ask Jim why he was taking notes. Jim tried to explain that he just wanted to make sure he had understood what was being said, but Ken wasn't content with that, and asked him simply to listen, please. If he was having trouble with any particular point Ken would be only too pleased to clarify it.

We all of us lived in fear of Ken's obfuscatory clarifications and would certainly have deterred Jim from asking for any, in the unlikely event that he was actually interested. We also knew what was really on Ken's mind, and the reason for the sudden eclipse of the pleasure he had showed in someone listening closely for once. He was afraid someone was going to steal his ideas. By the time he had discovered that Jim wasn't much of a thief, nor much of a man for ideas, new or old, good or bad, he had committed himself to a ban on amanuensis activity, though he might have liked to change course and go back to having someone take his words down. Too late for that.

In due course Jim explained his note-taking habit, to me rather than Ken. 'It's a trick I picked up in the Raff. Useful. If it looks as if you're taking notes no one will ask you questions.' It made sense that he wouldn't want to risk being interrogated on his understanding of sexual politics. So he would look just as serious as he could while he wrote in his little notebook *tub marge, small Hovis, two (2) tins corned beef* as Ken developed his themes, Ouroboros themes with a tendency to swallow their own tails and chew them many times. Many, many times.

It was at about this time of the autumn that Mrs Baine brought me an official letter, wearing a sombre expression as if such a thing could only be bad news. Well it wasn't rent arrears, that much could be taken as read. It was obvious that she would have liked to be there when I opened the consequential envelope, but I managed to dismiss her with an air of unconcern, modelling my behaviour I think on Holmes's dealings with Mrs Hudson, preoccupied rather than haughty, not insisting on protocol but mindful of a gap that can never be closed while Victoria is on the throne. Sometimes I think that the ideal *ménage à trois* would resemble 221b Baker Street, allowing me to pursue my hobbies, self-medication among them, with a biographer-cum-doctor in attendance and a home help on call day and night – a lot more workable than the version with the temporary dairy roundsman and the tobacconist's glamorous assistant that had come so badly unstuck not long before.

A concierge without curiosity would be an unnatural thing, someone not to be trusted, and I hadn't been surprised to see Mrs Baine once or twice discreetly sniffing the envelopes that arrived for the residents. I even approved of the fact that she made no exception for manila envelopes, the ones that would normally contain only bills and business correspondence. She sniffed those too. Perhaps a perfumed love letter had been slyly disguised as a final demand – though her nose might not find it out if she could confuse the dope smoke with the smell of garlic cooking. Over time I saw her sniff quite a lot of things, but I'm hardly likely to sit in judgement when I'm something of a sniffer myself.

A small glass of the Bristol Cream

If anything she took more interest in business correspondence than the personal kind. In her eyes a final demand might actually be a form of love letter, the sentiments turned inside out but still decipherable. 'Why don't you love me (pay me) any more? I haven't changed. I'm still the same. You're the one who has been untrue.'

Above all she was drawn to letters with the Lytham St Anne's postmark. Of course there are people who live on the Fylde coast, and I don't mean to suggest that they're unable to write letters, but it was understood that to all intents and purposes Lytham St Anne's had a population of one, and that one was not a human but an electronic being.

I had a grand total of three Premium Bonds, sitting in a drawer in Bourne End, and I don't seriously doubt that Mum and Dad would have sent on any notifications that I had won a prize. In a seven-floor block such letters arrived fairly frequently, and clearly Mrs Baine found it frustrating not to know how big each payout was. Would they be cracking open the champagne in flat 026 or just have a small glass of the Bristol Cream? Whenever she referred to ERNIE, the vast computer that made the selections, I corrected her, pointing out that the original ERNIE had been put out to grass and replaced by ERNIE 2 in 1972. I couldn't help myself. The pupils of her eyes did a strange waggle dance when I first passed on this information, but to do myself justice I didn't claim it was important or interesting, merely that it was true.

ERNIE, or the Electronic Random Number Indicator Equipment. It wasn't just the Cambridge Homosexual Activism Project that had to fudge things fairly drastically in search of a catchy acronym.

This was a different sort of manila envelope that held her attention. 'Don't get your hopes up, Mr Cromer,' she said. 'No champagne today. I've seen this sort of letter before and it's not normally good news.' She produced by a remarkable flexing of the facial muscles a gloating frown. 'Thank you, Mrs Baine,' I said, adding 'That will be all' so loudly in my head that she took the hint, though it was screamed at her on frequencies bypassing what the human ear can hear.

When I opened the envelope I could hardly believe my eyes. I could have jumped for joy. Exciting letters are like prime numbers – after a while the gaps between them seem to get longer and longer, until you think the next one will never come. The last prime-number year before 1973 (itself a prime) had been 1951, a long wait. And now I was being offered a chance to participate in the civic process. Jury duty! A dream come true. It felt as if I had won some sort of jackpot, as one of the twelve good men and true through whom justice would manifest itself in Cambridge Crown Court.

The next time I passed Mrs Baine – though given our respective rates of progress it's more likely that she passed me – I told her of my good fortune. She reacted very oddly, saying, 'Oh well, never mind. These things are sent to try us.' 'Oh no, Mrs B,' I said, 'you've got that the wrong way round. Try looking through the other end of the telescope. We're sent these things so that we can try them.' In my excitement I didn't make sense and certainly failed to communicate effectively with Mrs Baine, who said doubtfully, 'If you say so, Mr Cromer. Perhaps they'll excuse you once you've explained your circumstances.' What on earth was she talking about?

Paula wasn't much better, I'm sorry to say. She told me that the summons to serve that I had received might well be a mistake, and she could certainly ask around at Social Services. Perhaps a letter could be written on my behalf. I wouldn't need to lift a finger. Well really! People don't deserve to live in a democracy if they refuse to oil its wheels, keeping their lily-white hands free from the engine grease of its running.

On the other hand, if it had been Paula that was called for jury duty I might not have been so blithe about it. Yes, Cambridge Council would lay on a replacement for the duration of her absence and not raise objections. And yes, as I saw it, there was no great degree of difficulty involved in what she did for me. Yet I have to acknowledge that I had become used to her little ways, as she had got used to mine. I needed to keep in mind the possibility that meeting my needs for a few hours a week was not the dream job that it might seem at first sight.

Niminy-piminy junior penalty

I refused to have my exhilaration squashed by the discouraging atmosphere around me. To serve on a jury was a privilege of citizenship that was denied to the very young and the aged and could be taken away for bad behaviour. I can't really claim that the worst part of having the prison gates clang behind you would be the accompanying shout of 'And you needn't think you'll be serving on a jury any time soon!' Nevertheless it was part of the punishment, the stripping away of a right that was at its core a privilege and a responsibility.

I had more or less despaired of getting a criminal record myself, let alone a prison sentence. I would never serve a *stretch of bird* in the *hoosegow*, properly *banged-up in chokey* at Her Majesty's pleasure, but would inevitably be let off or given some niminy-piminy junior penalty. Even if I killed someone with full premeditation, gloating over the vileness of the deed, any competent barrister would be able to argue the sentence down to house arrest, and after a little good behaviour I'd be just as free as I had been before I coldly took a life.

I wanted full exoneration or condign punishment, not a patronising letting-off. Yes, let's allow 'condign' out on day release from its diction-ary confinement for a walk in the sun of usage, though still shackled to the warder-word of 'punishment'. A prison sentence and a criminal record, those rites of passage, certificates of full moral accountability, might be out of my reach, but I could at least be part of the process that awarded them. As juror I would show that I didn't hold a grudge against the system of criminal justice for its ignoble exclusion of me from the full consequences of wrongdoing. In fact I couldn't wait. The form I received gave a lot of leeway for deferral and even being excused, which seemed to me quite wrong. Why would my employer (suppos-ing I had one) seek to stand in the way of my performing so vital a civic function? Such dragging of the feet should surely be penalised rather than encouraged. I was so keen to play my part that I contemplated delivering my acceptance in person rather than trusting it to the post, but even I could see that I was getting overexcited.

I waited for my jury service date as if it was a lottery draw and I had a lucky ticket. I'm not normally subject to nightmares, but in the tense interval between jury summons and designated day I had some-thing remarkably like one — not the standard oppressive courtroom dream of being arraigned for something you have or haven't done but a subtler vision of dread, with the discovery that every single defend-ant on the docket had changed his plea to guilty overnight, leaving me with nothing to do but go home and weep for the wasted oppor-tunity. Where was my rage for justice to vent itself now?

I was puffed up ahead of time with my civic sufficiency, my func-tionality as a chemical reagent of human motive, living indicator paper of guilt and innocence. I would be required for the whole day, and the orange cardboard wheel that I was used to leaving in the Mini didn't allow me to announce so long an absence. I would be tempted to leave a note saying that I would be away for 'exactly as long as the administration of the Queen's Justice requires me', though I doubt if the administration of Cambridge Crown Court would have compensated me for the breaking of the windscreen by infuriated crowds if I had.

Lack of parallelism in the ocular axes

On the Monday morning which I had been anticipating so keenly I was there outside the Guildhall half an hour early, having allowed too much extra time for rush-hour traffic. An elderly usher with pronounced heterotropia came scuttling out to tell me I couldn't park there. He might have been a parking warden except that they don't wear black gowns. I told him that indeed I could park there for a whole list of reasons, starting with the fact of my having disabled parking privileges, continuing with the fact that I had been invited. Not just invited but summoned. His manner softened and we reached an agreement. I tidied the Mini away a little distance, for form's sake, neither abating my rights in the slightest nor setting a precedent. If I'd known the phrase 'without prejudice' I would have used it. This was parking without prejudice, privileged but not entitled. I felt that the heterotropic usher and I understood each other. I re-parked the Mini without prejudice let alone rancour. This chap's heterotropia, the lack of parallelism in the ocular axes vulgarly known as 'wall eye', was only slightly disconcerting. It may have been a childhood condition, though it's also something that can come on in middle age. None of my business. By this time I was well used to being stared at, but also to being looked through as if I was invisible, and there was something oddly refreshing about talking to someone who seemed able to do both things at once.

'We'll get you out of here in a jiffy,' he said. 'I'm sorry you have to come inside, but I'm not allowed to bring the form out to you.' Form? What form? Think twice before you express doubts about my paperwork. It took me a while to realise what form he was referring to. He took it for granted that I would want to be excused. When I asked why he thought so, he said, 'I mean, your special circumstances.'

As far as I knew my special circumstances corresponded in every respect to the ordinary ones, in that I had been summoned for the purpose of being empanelled. Wasn't that special enough to be getting on with? It seemed alarming and almost treasonous that officers of the court should join the general conspiracy to block balanced representation of the populace in administration of the law.

'What do you mean, special circumstances?' I asked, and then of course he was stuck. He couldn't exactly spell out difficulties that I was ignoring, any more than I could have said, with any politeness, 'What's the matter with your eyes?'

In the end it all worked out rather well, though it was clear that there were many people reluctantly attending who would have loved to fill out the form I had been offered so as to be excused. One man was wearing a tracksuit and dark glasses, which (as the usher whispered to me) was often what people put on to indicate they were on drugs and thereby incompetent to play any part in the administration of justice. 'Does that work?' I asked, as impressed by the ruse as I was shocked by the desire to opt out. 'It can do – no one wants to take a chance and have a case go haywire. We keep them kicking their heels, though. It wouldn't be right to send them straight home, would it?' He was beginning to make a little bit of a pet of me, something that happens fairly often when I start off on the wrong foot with someone. There's some sort of self-correcting mechanism that overshoots and works in my favour. 'The judge we have here is very tough on drugs, in point of fact. His son overdid it, you see.'

'You mean took an overdose?'

'Yes, overdid the dosage. So he comes down on druggers like a ton of bricks, and it's best they not be on the jury when he does. And there's something else I should warn you about, sir . . .'

'Oh, what's that?'

'The defence has what are called perfunctory challenges – they can just say they don't want you on the jury if they don't like the look of you. They don't have to give a reason, and there's no appeal against it. That's why they're called perfunctory challenges. They're allowed quite a few, so don't be surprised if it happens, and don't take it personally.'

Perfunctory didn't seem the proper term, but I wasn't going to challenge an officer of the court. 'I'll do my best. But why would anyone not want me on a jury?'

424

Again I put him in a tight spot, daring him to name a prejudice that wasn't supposed to exist. He hesitated, and for a few moments his eyes seemed to diverge even more than they did normally. 'Well, sir, it's just . . . that they may think it's too much of a strain for you.'

'Oh, I'm tougher than I look. And it'd be a shame to make the trip and not get the chance to do my duty.'

'That's the spirit – I'm just warning you that you may be excluded . . .'

'Like anybody else.'

'Like anybody else. It's part of my job to explain how the system works. So don't be surprised if you're on the bench for a fair old time.' On the bench? For a dizzying moment I thought he was using the phrase in its legal meaning. Was there by any chance a citizen-judge tradition dating back to the time of Henry IV, which once invoked would lead not just to my empanelment but actual embenchment? Then I realised he was borrowing the phrase from football. People are always drawing analogies from the world of sport, and I know it's supposed to be reassuring. Lowest common denominator and all that, but if you're excluded by the lowest common denominator then you're excluded in spades – which I suppose is a reference to bridge, a game I don't play either but somehow it doesn't matter. I could play it if I had nothing better to do.

He meant that for the time being I would be a reserve player and not on the pitch itself. In this version the courtroom became a field of symbolic conflict where the referee's colours are scarlet and ermine and he keeps his knees out of sight.

Just as well. If I'd been fitted with a full-bottomed wig at short notice I might have died of happiness on the spot . . . on the other hand, putting both sides of the argument as is only right in a legal setting, there could be no better way to step off the treadmill of reincarnation. I might have disappeared with a curious perfume and most melodious twang, like the spirit manifesting itself not far from Cirencester that Aubrey mentions in *Brief Lives*. Then the young man in the tracksuit with the dark glasses might have found himself serving after all, after they'd shone a torch in his eyes to make sure he was really faking intoxication by drugs.

In fact the process of empanelment went without a hitch. I was pleased to find that the usher who had been helpful, on balance, despite his warnings about the odds I faced as a potential juror, was sworn in as our jury bailiff. I remember his Christian name was Timothy, which he encouraged me to use or at least made no objection when I did. He came over to introduce himself to the group, and to explain his duties, but he also made a point of having a little personal chat with me, which I appreciated.

'No sign of those perfunctory challenges,' I said.

'Are you sure you've got the right word? They're called *peremptory* challenges, seeing as how you don't have to give reasons.'

Glue extra tailage on a lyrebird

'My mistake,' I said, though I knew the word 'peremptory' perfectly well and was sure he had used the other one. I didn't take issue with him about it, because he seemed a helpful sort of chap. I'm always on the lookout for slightly drab individuals, easily overlooked, who may turn out to run the show, even if their official position is a humble one. Such people can make all the difference in the world to my passage through an institution or a tricky negotiation. Everyone has eyes for the peacock, but it's often the peahen who organises the peacock's calendar. It's a mistake to be dazzled by plumage.

Who'd be a male lyrebird (to shift species) rather than a female? There's no upper limit in the female's eyes to the sexual value of a male bird's long tail, except the likelihood of a predator grabbing it when the beauty-encumbered male tries to take flight. Even physical impossibility is no deterrent. Glue extra tailage onto a lyrebird and the females ogle relentlessly on, never reaching the point of saying, 'Come off it! That's not real!', any more than human males do when they leer at the female chimæras in their magazines.

Timothy was a peahen with possibilities.

'I suppose I'm safe now, then? No danger of being disempanelled? Sounds painful!'

'No risk of that, sir. Safe as houses.' He knew my first name and I could have encouraged him to use it, but there's nothing wrong with having a little starch in the laundry, some crispness to collars and cuffs. 'One thing I thought I'd mention, sir. Juries seem to be getting a bit . . . wayward recently. Hizonner has even said "skittish". I remember a time, not so long gone, when you had to remind the members of the jury come verdict time that they needed to choose someone to speak for them. Didn't stop them having a proper discussion. Not any more. It's all squabbles. Everyone wants to be foreman, they want to put questions of their own. Hizonner blames telly, it's always that for him but I'm not so sure. Some juries get bees in their bonnets about the whole foreman business, and there's nothing I can do to get the bees out. So, sir, just for the record, there doesn't need to be a foreman chosen right away. A foreman can be a lady and the sky won't fall. It certainly doesn't need to be the first person empanelled, or the one who sits nearest the judge – it's just the other way round, we make sure the foreman has the place nearest the judge when the verdict is given. So sit tight and don't let them push you around.' For a moment he seemed confused by what he had just said, and no wonder. If I didn't let anyone push me around I wouldn't have much of a life, would I?

'Here's an idea, sir – if you want a private word, just say you need a lavatory visit, and I'll see to it.' I wasn't wild about this idea. I had nothing to apologise for in terms of my C-value. There were already enough people who thought I stood in permanent need of drainage, holed below the waterline, when in fact I could hold my own very decently. If anything I urinated less than most, since I didn't pop into the facilities frivolously to rid myself of a few drops.

Still, I like conspiracies as long as they include me – so few of them do! 'Are you supposed to do this? To have separate dealings with a single juror?'

'Absolutely not, sir.' Then it was settled.

I can't say I was an immediate hit with my fellow jurors when we were in a position to take stock of each other. They too might have been happier if I'd applied to be excused, but that was just too bad. If the accused was entitled to a fair trial then wasn't I?

One of my fellow jurors waiting to be empanelled, a dignified middle-aged man with a carnation in his buttonhole, surprised me by expressing the wish to swear on the Old Testament. In fact there was general amazement, if I can claim to deduce such a thing from its peripheral indications, the jerking back of multiple necks, a communal gasp finding expression in the overlapping syncopation of individual diaphragmatic spasms. What could possibly be the

427

reasoning behind such a choice? He might have been Jewish without wanting to say so explicitly. He might have disapproved of forgiveness on principle and wanted an eye for an eye, no matter what. Was the Old Testament the only part of the Bible he knew? If so he might not want to commit himself to a legal obligation without reading the rest of the small print. Sequels can spring surprises, though I have to say that they generally don't, that's not what they're for – though I have to admit that the New Testament is the exception that proves that particular rule. He was told he could Affirm rather than Swear, dispensing with a holy text of any description, but he turned down the offer. For him it was the Old Testament or nothing, and he was excused jury service on that basis.

There was a noise of muffled protest from a lanky young man with a thick paperback bulging out of his jacket pocket. He had just been sworn in himself, and I don't think it's too fantastic to translate his protest into English as 'I wish I'd thought of that.'

I was content to Swear, on the basis that this was a social convention rather than an act of faith, though I might have felt differently if I'd had the forethought to bring a *Bhagavad Gita* along with me. When the young man brought his book out into the open I saw that it was Frank Herbert's *Dune*, a classic of science-fiction fantasy and not quite a holy book in my eyes though it had been the basis of a cult at my grammar school.

Since shared tastes are always a good way to make friends I started talking to him about how much I liked the opening of the book. It's a memorable scene, a rite of passage that is also an episode of torture, in which the hero's mother takes him to be interviewed by a powerful sisterhood. I could even remember the name of the sisterhood, the Bene Gesserit. If this was Latin then it could only be an example of that strange tense the future perfect, meaning perhaps 'he will have done well'. The boy (Paul Atreides! the name came to me as I was speaking) must put his hand in a box and not take it out, no matter what. If he does the Reverend Mother – I think she's the Reverend Mother – will prick him with the poisoned needle she's holding against his wrist and he will die. The box is a box of pain, instant and absolute but somehow also growing. I could remember the name 'gom jabbar' but not whether it was the name of the box or the name of the needle. *Gom jabbar* sounded Arabic, as I'm sure it was meant to, cultures and traditions swirled together in the raspberry ripple of cosmic fantasy.

Everyone who reads *Dune* is Paul Atreides for the duration, young or old, male or female, brave or cowardly. That's how reading works, age and gender no more than points of view that the body corroborates with whatever mixture of eagerness and reluctance.

I remembered another detail. 'Paul can feel the flesh of his hand burning off and the bones charring. The only way he can survive it is to imagine that the pain is everywhere *except* the box. He uses his mental powers to make a picture of the universe in which he occupies the only safe place.' The young man blinked a few times but said nothing whatever, though he seemed to be humming faintly. Yes, some of the words sounded exotic, Latin, Arabic or – surely – ancient Greek (Atreides), but I was speaking English just the same. From this young man's point of view I might just have been a patriarch of the Romanian Orthodox Church speaking Old Church Slavonic. I was a young man too, but that was a detail that often escaped my conversational partners.

Of course the reading of science fiction and fantasy is compatible with the possession of social skills – of course it is! There's hardly any need to say so. It's also an obvious refuge for those who lack them. I was trying not to judge my fellow juror too harshly when I suddenly wondered if the book I was describing might not actually be one of Isaac Asimov's *Foundation* novels, and not *Dune* at all. The *Foundation* trilogy also had its vogue at Burnham Grammar.

Mistake or no mistake, I was getting nowhere with this young man. He had angry-looking spots evenly distributed all over his face, except for a clear patch on one cheek, to which his hands kept returning, not to bestow caresses – as you might expect – in a spirit of wondering joy, but to give it a good old scratch. I was used to resistance, to awkwardness and the challenge of a long-drawn-out campaign of charm, but this was different in kind. There was no response of any sort, an absolute refusal of social exchange. Every now and then he put a hand up to his neck and scratched it fiercely, as if there was a tick there needing to be dislodged. Perhaps to his way of thinking I was that very tick.

In fact only one of my co-empanellees made any effort to welcome me. In his case it was almost as if he was running for office, on some relatively lowly level. This was a schoolteacher, though a distinctly posh example of the breed. He was called Philip Anthony, as if his family went back to a period before surnames had been invented, and he sported a tweed jacket over a Fair Isle sweater worn with a tie. The jacket not only had brown leather patches at the elbows but a brown leather strip stitched onto the edge of its cuffs, strange reinforcements for areas unlikely to encounter much friction. He wore a signet ring, too. He taught geography at the Perse School, which in Cambridge terms is as close as you can get to being a master at Eton without leaving the county.

The habit of screaming is partially repressed

When I say that he was running for office, I suppose I mean he hankered after a little immediate glory. I had no thought of aspiring to the empty ceremonial position of foreman – I was more than happy to play my humble part in the group. Egotism is a tireless fisherman, always laying out its lures, and I knew better than to be tempted into taking a nibble at that particular seductive spoon as it swirled in the water. Prestige can have a very distorting effect, and it seemed all too likely that the position would interfere with my intellectual access to the case before me. Still, I took an idle pleasure in the word itself. Foreman. It had a pleasingly down-to-earth feeling about it. You'd expect a jury to have a spokesman or a president or even a chairman. A foreman sounded more blue-collar than white, seeming to call for the wearing of overalls rather than a three-piece suit. A foreman wearing a tweed jacket with all the squirearchical trimmings didn't seem quite right, but never mind that. Wouldn't a foreman be more likely to roll up his shirtsleeves and keep a pencil tucked behind his ear? At the Co-Op Dairy MarkO had had dealings with a foreman, and I envied that. It seemed unlikely that I would ever have a foreman, a 'gaffer' whatever that meant exactly, and with Philip Anthony putting himself forward so suavely my only chance of being a foreman myself was evaporating minute by minute. No one would say of me, 'You'll have to take it up with the gaffer – he's very particular, is the gaffer.'

Still, it was for the best. I was content to sit back and let the egotists fight it out. I would lie low and abide by the group's decision, only venturing an opinion if explicitly asked for one. I absolutely didn't question Philip Anthony's eminence and his right to take on the rôle of foreman of the jury. It's a job that involves nothing much more than the ability to count up to twelve and the understanding that the word 'Guilty' means something different when the word 'Not' is placed in front of it, and I didn't covet it. Let him enjoy himself. Let him preen to his heart's content. All he needed to do was to look the part, and it was obvious that he had all that sewn up, all stitched up, at the elbows and cuffs of his jacket. I couldn't have competed with that even if I had wanted to. I couldn't come close – I was near enough as it was, inhaling the cigarette smoke that those tweeds had breathed in and now breathed out.

And then a single word put in an appearance and made me wonder if I wasn't being a bit feeble. The word was 'graduate'. Mr Philip Anthony said, with a self-deprecating grin, 'Well, I'm a graduate, perhaps that makes a difference. It's a silly thing, and it couldn't matter less, but there seem to be times when having a degree comes in handy.' As if the person designated to communicate with the judge needed to have a bit of class, the blessèd knack of rising above the riff-raff.

In the 1970s it was only about ten per cent of school leavers who went on to higher education, so Mr Anthony wasn't outraging the laws of probability by imagining himself as the only graduate among the twelve. He must have looked at his fellows and decided that they were no sort of threat – so far I had only been able to observe a matronly lady engaging in some form of handicraft and a scruffy young man with a thick science-fiction paperback in his pocket. On the other hand, it was a risky assumption to make in a world-famous university city, not all of whose graduates, as I had reason to know, were snapped up by the City, the Civil Service or the Atomic Energy Authority and whisked away to glory elsewhere.

I spoke up. I couldn't help myself – though self-enquiry insists that this sentence be rewritten, or at least freshly typeset, to reveal its hidden assumptions about choice and personality, as follows: '*I*' *couldn't help 'myself*'. I decided I had no alternative, and of course I had the option of deciding otherwise and keeping my trap shut. I said, in a manner at least as offhand as Philip Anthony's, 'Actually, I have a degree too. From Cambridge of all places. Of course it's a silly thing, and it couldn't matter less, but there seem to be times when it comes in handy.' It seemed unlikely that I could defeat this smoothly beaming fellow on the home ground of his privilege. It was as unlikely an outcome as crushing someone to death with an egg box though perhaps there are cases of that on record.

His immediate reaction was supercilious, or perhaps I should say superciliary. The communication of emotion by eyebrow movement is something about which Darwin has interesting things to say – he traces it back to the compulsion to scream in infancy and the tendency of the eyes to become 'gorged with blood'. The muscles surrounding the eyes become strongly contracted as a protection, and this action persists as an accompaniment to distress or confusion, however slight, into adulthood, a time of life when (as Darwin so beautifully puts it) 'the habit of screaming is partially repressed'. But when I laid claim to graduate status Mr Anthony's eyebrows did not take on an oblique distortion symmetrically, so as to communicate grief or anxiety. Only one of them moved, and then it was elevated rather than drawn down. What that shifting area of expressive tissue conveyed was something less drastic but not altogether trivial, namely a disbelief in my educational qualifications. He was good enough to perform this action in my full line of sight, to give me the benefit of his doubt.

Since qualifications were really all that my education had given me, I felt bound to defend them. 'And where did you study?'

He blushed to the roots of his Fair Isle sweater. 'Bristol, actually.' I had drawn blood without meaning to, according to the codes of the time, since Bristol though a perfectly respectable educational institution did not dine at the high table of the country's universities. Philip Anthony recovered his poise enough to ask the name of the Cambridge college that had awarded me my degree, and when I said 'Downing' the asymmetrical activity to be observed on his face made a sidelong movement from eyebrow level to lip. The faint distortion there, the incipient curl, testified to an entrenched scepticism. It was as if I had made a lucky guess in naming a college that, without being one of the university's landmarks, might plausibly exist. I had a sense

432

that this struggle was being followed with fascination by the other jury members, even if they weren't visible to me, and since the communal mood had never been propitious and might turn decisively against me, I felt the need to secure an advantage, any advantage, while I could.

A degree enriched with marrow-bone jelly

'Tell you what,' I said. 'Let's have a little game. I'll tell you the Latin motto of Downing College, and you tell me the motto of Bristol University, Latin or otherwise. Let that decide things. Does that sound fair?' He nodded slowly, with his eyebrows almost on a level. It seemed to me that something new was being conveyed by this micro-muscular adjustment, perhaps grudging respect.

I thanked my lucky karmic stars that I knew what Downing's motto was, thanks to my recent visit with MarkO and Bernardette, though I hadn't known it during the three years I had actually been a student there. Otherwise I would have had to rely on bravado and made one up. I could have done worse than claim *Bene Gesserit*. 'He will have done well' – a defensible motto for an educational establishment vain of its students' later success in life. I would have convinced my audience or else lured the *Dune* reader out of his silence, either of them a desirable result. I hadn't decided whether his silence was seething or serene, though the strong smell of cigarettes didn't suggest serenity. 'The motto of Downing College is *Quaerere verum*. "To seek what is true."'

'Not bad. Very nice, in fact. Admirable. And the motto of Bristol University is . . . *Qui facit per alium facit per se*, usually taken to mean "He who does things for others does them for himself." So we end in a draw, unless everyone votes on the merits of those mottoes. Was that what you had in mind?'

If we had a vote then it wouldn't be about the merits of the mottoes. I was confident that the Downing motto was philosophically superior, as well as superlatively appropriate for a jury, since the one he quoted suggested that all human activity is essentially selfish, not an inspiring sentiment even if true. Any vote would be a referendum on the candidates themselves, and in a popularity contest he was undoubtedly the favourite. I consoled myself with the fact that I had at least made him work for the empty honour he so coveted.

Then something struck me as I thought about his motto for a moment, and something about it seemed not quite right. Not just the sentiment but the phrasing. Something troubled me about those last two words in particular. 'Hang on a mo,' I said, and I saw his pupils tremble. 'Isn't that in fact the motto of the Perse School rather than Bristol University?'

A complexion can do only a limited number of things, and Philip Anthony's, having exhausted the possibilities of blushing, was now exploring various sickly shades of white. The adjective 'shamefaced' seems to fit, even if it didn't originally refer to the face, being a variation of 'shamefast' – held tight in a vice of disgrace. Philip Anthony's pupils might not even recognise him as the same man who could with confidence list the tributaries of the Orinoco. There was a group exhalation of breath, the sort of noise that comes from everyone and no one at the same time, a little omni-susurration that meant *That's torn it.*

I don't know how I could be so sure of my ground. The quibble on '*per se*' and 'Perse' offered a hint but no sort of proof. Is it possible that I had read about it in a back number of the *Cambridge Evening News*? That glorious publication offered sanctuary to a wide range of snippets on the strict understanding that they contain nothing of inherent interest or use, but perhaps something had slipped through the net and armed me for single combat. There can't have been many duels fought in Latin since the Middle Ages. It was suddenly clear that this one was over almost before it had started, and that I had won it.

On a glandular level I can't deny I was exhilarated and gloating, though I was also wondering why I had opened my stupid mouth in the first place. 'The thing is,' Philip Anthony was saying miserably, 'I couldn't remember the whole Bristol motto, in fact all I could remember was that it had *Vim* in it, and I couldn't just say *Vim*, could I? Sounds like scouring powder. *Vim vim vim.* Absolute non-starter. So I said something I could actually remember and now I feel a complete fraud. And now of course, the moment it can't do me any good, I've remembered Bristol's motto. It's *Vim promovet insitam . . .* which means, I think, "It promotes the inborn force." Something like that.'

'What promotes the inborn force?'

'Well, the University of Bristol. Can't be anything else, surely? I'm not making it up! But you're the Latin expert – that must be what it means, don't you think?'

Why was he asking me? My Latin credentials were pretty tatty and he was the one whose inborn force had been promoted. I liked the real Bristol motto even less than the Perse one he had offered in the first place – it had the ring of an advertising campaign, not for scouring powder but actually dog food, to wit the 'Prolongs Active Life' slogan of Pal. Perhaps a degree from Bristol was enriched with marrow-bone jelly.

I could completely understand the poor man's thought processes, but I could hardly retreat, could I? I tried to think of ways to cushion his landing, but couldn't think of one. I couldn't simply say it didn't matter since it certainly mattered to him. I found myself saying something that went entirely contrary to my ideas of the administration of justice, the sacredness of the jury system and the charged neutrality, the privileged servitude, of the foreman's arbitrary but consecrated function within that system. A little voice emerged from my throat to say, 'Let's toss for it.' I had taken pity on him without particularly meaning to.

At this point the control of events passed from me swiftly and irrevocably. Time moved forward in a sort of hiccup. It was as if the coin to be tossed was in his hand already. I don't doubt that the process of flipping and then calling was above board. I'm sure it was. In fact Philip Anthony manœuvred me so that I could see the coin where it had landed and confirm that he hadn't cheated, a sensible precaution for someone who had so recently been caught cheating.

It seemed that after an agonising moment of free fall we were back exactly where we had started, in no time flat. Philip Anthony was officially the foreman of our jury, and I had the distinct impression that I was seen as an upstart and even a bit of a weasel, though (let the record show) I had been entirely truthful while he had fibbed. The roles imposed on us were respectively graciousness in victory and magnanimity in defeat, and we played out this rigmarole without overt gloating on his part nor grinding of teeth on mine.

Then he took pity on me, repaying the favour I had done him when I proposed that infernal coin-toss. 'Tell you what, John . . .' I imagined he was going to propose another round of coin tossing so as to give me another chance, a shot at the best of three, but instead he said, '. . . suppose we were to take turns?' A little pity goes a long way in my book, but this was so obviously a sensible suggestion that I only went through the motions of needing to think it over. Admittedly it was slightly intoxicating to feel so many faces scrutinising mine for signs of assent or refusal, a bombardment of attention at a time when my opinion was rarely sought and often swept aside even when I tried to express it.

The selfish drama of reflexive opposition

I had only wanted this near-sinecure when someone else had claimed it as his right, but I found I could be persuaded to rise above the selfish drama of reflexive opposition. 'I don't see why not. Unless our jury bailiff has any objections. Timothy?'

'These matters are entirely for the jury to decide, sir.'

'Then it's settled,' said Philip Anthony. 'So why don't you go first?' he said. And there was no opposition from this corner, from this Cromer.

Philip Anthony leaned forward to say in an undertone, 'I really don't mean to throw my weight around. To tell you the truth I've ducked jury service twice before, thought I'd get it over with this time.' He spoke as if confidentially, though I couldn't see for myself whether we were really in a little zone of privileged speech, as his manner implied. I've spent enough time and energy honing my eavesdropping skills to know that remarkably little conversation is genuinely out of range if you really want to hear it, and I wasn't altogether convinced by this charade of secrecy. 'Doctors are exempt,' he went on, 'even bloody pharmacists are exempt! Teachers just have to hope the Head thinks they can't be spared.' Which apparently was not the case with Philip Anthony, the poor lamb. Not this time, anyway.

Was I the only person in the whole lawless city, hotbed as it was of bicycle theft and fraudulent intellectualism, who saw jury service as a privilege rather than a nuisance?

After all this epic kerfuffle about leadership of the jury the first case we were called upon to determine should by rights have been an anticlimax. In fact it was a corker, or I should say rather a horrifying glimpse into the breakdown of contemporary society. Violence had broken out between two groups of youths outside a nightclub, and injuries had been sustained. The charges to which the defendants had pleaded Not Guilty were of grievous bodily harm, actual bodily harm and affray. Any little incident or expression of opinion might have struck the crucial spark between the two groups, clashing allegiances in the matter of football teams or a further dismal episode in the long antagonism between 'town' and 'gown'.

I was settled at one end of the seating for the jury, with a reasonable view of the proceedings, though naturally it would have been a much better one if I was able to move my neck more. For comfort I needed a cushion, but I had long since learned that people overdo it with cushions on my behalf. They think that if one is good then four must be better, and it saves time and frustration if I'm firm from the very beginning and spell things out. 'Timothy – I'm going to need a cushion if you can find one. Just the one, mind.' When James Bond wants his martini shaken not stirred nobody turns a hair, and his was the sort of assurance I was aiming at when I made the request. Eyebrows may be raised at the whims of the super-spy, of course, but that's all right. I don't mind eyebrows.

'Right you are, sir.'

When the judge made his entrance everyone stood up except me, though the *Dune*-reader waited just long enough before shambling to his feet to give an impression of insolence. In his attitude to me Hizonner was caught in a logical impasse in what might be called the equilibrium of deference. If I didn't rise to acknowledge him then he must be standing to acknowledge me. He even gave me the faintest of nods, as his gaze moved over, with the hint of a frown, to the youth who had been slow to show his respect.

The judge started the proceedings with a sort of manifesto. He said: 'Her Majesty's Justice will not be administered on the basis of a three-day week if I have any say in the matter – we will sit by candlelight if need be. However, with the government and the trades unions apparently embarked on a suicide pact of some sort the decision may not be mine to make.' I couldn't help feeling that this was largely rhetorical. There had been warnings of power cuts to come, but nothing in that line had yet happened.

Then the case proper got under way, with prosecuting counsel laying out the case for the Crown, that sublime metonymy, and delineating the origins of the conflict for our benefit.

'Ladies and gentlemen of the jury, you will hear that one remark in particular, one shouted insult outside the Sensations discothèque on that fateful day, precipitated the altercation. That insult was – if you'll forgive me – "shortarse". The gentleman so addressed was not disposed to ignore this jibe about his height. Naturally in the population of the British Isles as in any other country there is considerable variation of stature, and it is a sad fact of human nature that extremes tend to call forth ridicule. It is perhaps significant that the defendant, to whom the remark was in the first instance addressed, was not merely an individual whose stature was somewhat below the average but someone whose restricted inches constituted an aspect of his daily life and one might almost say his identity. His was a working world in which extra height would have had an inhibiting if not a disqualifying effect. In fact he was one of a group of stable lads from Newmarket out "on the razzle", as the saying is, that night.

'It is a mysterious fact that none of the other participants in the brawl has been identified, though you will hear evidence, from a lady who was closing up the Blue Lagoon chip shop opposite the Sensations discothèque, that there were perhaps two dozen young men involved altogether. When the police arrived the only parties remaining were the injured man Mr Wade, who was still unconscious, and the defendant Mr Millon, who was being discouraged from leaving the scene by a nightclub receptionist of the type known, I am told, as a "bouncer". The defendant claims never to have met any of his vanished confrères before, though the same witness testifies that his associates were all of slight stature, plausibly fellow stable lads, young men whose avocation as you may know tends to go along with being of rather less than average height. You might reasonably suppose that the rough and tumble of modern life would have the effect of inuring such young men to such unsympathetic commentary, rather than predisposing them first to savage fisticuffs, in which all joined.

'The defendant Thomas Millon punched Mr Andrew Wade, causing him to fall to the ground. It was later proved that Mr Wade's jaw was broken by this punch. Then later, after a short but definite interval whose timing will prove to be of considerable importance, the defendant picked up a brick that happened to be lying on the roadside a few paces away and used it as a weapon, inflicting serious injuries to his head. His claim is that he was acting in self-defence, having seen a knife in the possession of Mr Wade earlier in the evening and knowing him to be an abattoir worker who would be well versed in the use of a blade. I should point out that no such weapon was found on the person of the victim who suffered the two successive assaults.'

As comforting as the smell of wet dog

At about mid-morning exhibits started to be distributed to the jury, containing among other things witness statements, medical reports and X-rays. They were made up into a bundle, and indeed we were asked at intervals to consult our 'bundle' and extract from it particular documents. I was in heaven, particularly as Timothy hovered by my side to provide assistance in finding the appropriate exhibit or the right page in the sheaf. I don't know if the Akashic Records as envisioned by theosophical thought, the compendious plenum in which everything that has ever been done, thought or felt is archived for eternity, will turn out to be a staffed or an unstaffed facility, but a library certainly needs librarians and if that isn't a library I don't know what is.

Then came the lunch break, though I think it's called something rather grander like a recess. I asked Timothy what the routine was. I had made my way from the car to the court without benefit of the wheelchair and I didn't have much of an appetite for further travel. I didn't want to fall asleep during the afternoon session, even if dozing was a general temptation rather than a danger lying in wait for me in particular. Timothy said he would bring me something to eat – I could stay where I was. 'I'll be back as quick as you can say Sam Robinson.'

'Don't you mean Jack Robinson?'

'Never met the feller.' I have to admit I closed my eyes and dissolved the world for a while. Perhaps I was already asleep.

I was woken by the smell of soggy pastry, which in the right circumstances can be as comforting as the smell of wet dog. Timothy

439

had brought me a little pie. 'I brought you some lunch, sir, save you rushing around too much. I'm your tiffin-wallah – that's what they call it in India.'

'Really – you've been to India?' I was suddenly wide awake.

'No, sir. It was something my father used to say.'

'So he'd been there, at least?'

'No, sir, it was just something he used to say. If I brought him a couple of biscuits to have with his tea he would always call me his tiffin-wallah. I don't know where he picked it up.' I'd played the trump card of My Expedition to the Subcontinent so often that I was sick of it, and would only have brought it into play now if there was a real overlapping of interests.

I examined the pie. Was it a vegetarian pie? It was not. Timothy would have had to be a mind reader to set out in search of such a thing. Were vegetarians even allowed to serve on juries (I would have slipped through the net on the technicality that I had been eating meat for months)? In its own way justice is a carnivorous business, demanding a bite for a bite if not an eye for an eye. The legal system doesn't condescend to the forgiveness of sins, and though the New Testament is a lentil burger (not that anyone pays much attention) the Old is a T-bone steak hardly touched by the grill.

I'd forgotten to bring along my cutlery that day. I had more than enough to do getting ready without that, and carrying eating irons with me at all times hadn't really bedded down yet as a necessary reflex. Timothy helped me eat without drawing attention to the fact, chatting away while he cut up the pie. I expect I could have managed with an ordinary fork once the pie had been reduced to bite-sized pieces, but I didn't volunteer. It was a toss-up between the awkward-ness of having my rather bespoke eating style observed by a stranger and the awkwardness of being spoon-fed, or rather fork-fed. It was also in my mind that I shouldn't miss this chance to see if hetero-tropia adversely affected depth of vision. I wouldn't have minded the odd jab in the lip or cheek in the service of optometrical fieldwork, but there was nothing at all wrong with his aim.

In any case Timothy seemed to be taken up with his own thoughts. 'It's taken Sidney . . .' he said, and I waited politely for him to finish the sentence. It had taken Sidney an age to queue in the canteen for my pie? Was that it? I didn't even know who Sidney was, another usher presumably. Hadn't met the fellow, though sorry in a general way to have put anyone to trouble.

It seemed only polite to make conversation. 'How did you get into this line, Timothy? Being a court usher and so forth.'

'It's more of a second career sort of thing than a first, sir, really. I don't expect people leave school dreaming of being court ushers or jury bailiffs. It's a good line of work just the same. I used to work in snakes and lizards.'

'What's that you said? Snakes and lizards?'

'Don't be silly! Weights and measures. That's where I worked. Snakes and lizards! Whatever next – you should get your ears tested.'

But I knew darn well he had said 'snakes and lizards'. It was the same trick I had learned to use myself, when I disoriented my conversational partners by seeding subliminal obscenity, though Timothy lacked my baseness of mind.

He carried on regardless. 'I was in Weights and Measures for a stretch of years, and then someone thought I'd be right for this, and maybe I am. You just need to know a little bit of law and keep your eyes open.'

'So you're the chaps who pounce when someone sells apples underweight or takes money for a mouldy fruit pie . . .'

'That's us, sir, or that was us, when I was in the job. Now someone else does the pouncing when traders take advantage.'

As we know ladies are demons

'Why the change of career, Timothy?' Trying not to say, you had a job already. Wasn't it a bit greedy to be wanting another one? Not two at the same time, obviously, but . . . have a heart! Spare a thought for the rest of us. Effortless leaping from job to job makes the chronically unemployed look bad.

'Well, sir, I decided it was time to throw in the towel when the new sales tax was on its way . . .'

New sales tax? I must have missed that. 'Oh . . . do you mean VAT?'

'That's right, sir. Whole new system of taxation introduced because we're now in the Common Market, brought in on April Fools' Day, not that I make too much of that.' He gave a little snort, just the same, the sort of playing-along laugh people more often make to mark other people's weak jokes than their own. 'Replaces the Purchase Tax we all know and don't much love, and a real headache, particularly for small businesses. New forms, three-monthly returns . . . It's not as if it wasn't already hard enough to mount a prosecution for infringement of trading laws, but the new system makes it ten times worse.'

'How's that, Timothy? I don't follow.' It's wonderful what relief I get from acknowledging ignorance. My chakras positively fizz with the release of pressure.

'Well, sir, let's suppose that a lady shopping, say, in Haverhill picks up a bar of Cadburys milk chocolate with a label that says *Extra Value*. It could be a gent, of course, but as we know ladies are demons for chocolate. Her chocky costs 10p for 4¼ oz., a sum she's content to pay knowing as how it represents extra value. She places her simple faith in the company's word. They're respectable people, Cadburys. She can depend on them. Then she sees in the display next to it another bar, also Cadburys Dairy Milk chocolate, making no claims as to value but priced at 9p for 4⅜ oz. It's a bigger bar, it costs less . . . she's flabbergasted. She tells the lady at the till, but the lady just folds her arms and says, "Buy one or t'other, buy 'em both, buy neither one, it's all the same to me."

'Redress is not to be had in the shop, nor even courteous acknowledgement of the problem. So this lady – the first lady, the one who went shopping for chocolate, comes to us, comes to Weights and Measures, and we investigate and find that she's quite correct. This constitutes a false description under the Trades Description Act. A customer seduced by the idea of extra value would be worse off. We have a case on our hands.'

'"The game is afoot," as Sherlock Holmes says.'

'If that's how you like to put it, sir. But when after a great deal of preparation we arrive in court we are told by Cadburys' counsel that it was never the firm's intention that the two bars should be simultaneously present in a single shop. The change in the tax régime required a revision of product sizes and prices. The "extra value" was as compared to earlier production not the later, larger bar. Cadburys had no control over individual shopkeepers and whether they rotated their stock properly or not. If there was an offence in this instance it was committed by the shopkeeper who improperly displayed the two bars on the same rack.'

'And what did she say?'

'What did who say, sir?'

'The shopkeeper lady who folded her arms and was so unhelpful. The one who had somehow forgotten about the customer always being right.'

'Sir, there was no lady. There was no chocolate improperly labelled or displayed. You asked me why I stopped working in Weights and Measures and I'm telling you. I could see the sort of palaver we were letting ourselves in for with the courts and I got out while the going was good. It was time to down tools and get shot of a lot of unnecessary complication. Sod this — as I said to myself at the time — for a game of soldiers. Now do you understand, sir?'

'Y-e-e-s,' I said, reluctant to admit how easily even the most trivial or hypothetical narrative can get a grip on me. *And-then-and-then* — it's not so much the bedtime stories themselves that bewitch us, more the illusion of sequence they build in our minds. Maya's first spell is cast in the glow of the night-light.

If there is ever a prosecution mounted against Cadburys, for short weight or anything else, and the firm's representatives are under oath, I hope at least that someone will ask why they feel the need to say 'dairy milk'. It's the sort of reassuring statement that brings any amount of turbulence and uncertainty in its wake — what other sort of milk is there? *What is it that you're not telling us?* Insistent questions in the Watergate era, but the suspicions have never really gone away.

'So I've gone into another line of country and learned a few procedures. Not to mention another little bit of law to go with them.' Without a change of tone he said, 'My wife and I have an understandment. She spends weekends with her sister in Oulton Broad, and I don't.'

I didn't know what to say, but as between the secrets of a marriage and geography I chose geography. 'Is Oulton Broad over near Lowestoft?'

'Near enough, I'd say. Maybe too near. One of these days Lowestoft is going to eat it up and swallow it down. And if that ever happens, mark my words — there won't be as much as a burp to be heard.'

I spent the first part of the afternoon in a state of stunned torpor. If I want to summon up this state of aggravated mental absence I need only replay in my mind a phrase that was repeated any number of times, by both barristers and the judge himself in one of his occasional interpolations: 'an altercation outside a discothèque'. The three legal men spoke those words again and again with great deliberation and a curious intonation, as if they were competing to pronounce them in the poshest and most alienating way, to remove them as far as possible from the world that the defendant and the man he had hurt actually lived in. They stressed the 'sh' sound in the middle of 'altercation', as if urging themselves to silence mid-word yet still going on paragraph after paragraph, and they bent the last syllable of 'discothèque' completely out of shape. The grave accent seemed to license an elongated drawling vowel uncatalogued by phonetics.

The darkling pie

In the middle of that endless afternoon I was probing my teeth with my tongue, wondering just what unspeakable fibre had become lodged there. Did I dare to ask Timothy if such a thing as a toothpick might be part of the emergency kit that was no doubt issued to every court usher? Then suddenly it struck me all of a wallop. Not 'taken Sidney' at all, *steak and kidney*! He was telling me about the exact composition of that supremely tamasic lunchtime pie.

While Western dietetics presents consumers with a bewildering variety of elements to consume, restrict or avoid – protein, vitamins, fats, calories, carbohydrates, roughage – the Hindu philosophy of food dogmatically divides nutrition into three mutually exclusive categories, sattvic, rajasic and tamasic, and then elaborates the categories so as to blur the boundaries.

Lately my diet had been low if not entirely deficient in the spiritually desirable category of sattvic nutrition, the sprouted grains, the fresh fruit, the nuts, high in the over-stimulating rajasic (tea, coffee, potatoes, cheese) and ominously heavy on the impure and corrupting tamasic – sugar, meat, onions, wheat. Over time items migrate between the categories of rajasic and tamasic but the sattvic list is reasonably constant, though sattvic food that has been fried in oil or generally overcooked can be dragged down into the rajasic category according to some Ayurvedic practitioners. Rajasic food should not be eaten after noon since it tends to clog the digestion. There is no time of day at which tamasic food may be regarded as wholesome.

Tamasic food leads to a duller, less refined form of consciousness and over time, of course, to the utter destruction of body and mind. Signposts of warning along that dreadful route include stagnation of thinking, irritability, lability of mood, laziness. I was certainly experiencing a dull form of consciousness that afternoon, stagnation of thinking brought on by an accumulation of karmically catastrophic nutrition. I wanted to be at the opposite end of every scale from the injured abattoir worker attacked by Mr Millon, but he and I were locked in a dance of animal death that would require both of us to live any number of more lives before we could dismount from the treadmill of birth and rebirth.

You don't need to adhere to a particular philosophy to understand that eating meat has a corrosive effect on the carnivore, creating dogmatic thought patterns and emotional inflexibility. The proof of this certainly seemed to be mounting up – now that I ate meat my vegetarianism was becoming steadily more aggressive and uncompromising. My intolerance of carnivores had become noticeably harsher since I had joined their ranks.

If I'd stuck to the sattvic high road I wouldn't have taken so long to understand the meaning of Timothy's remark, though of course if I hadn't accepted the darkling pie he wouldn't have made it in the first place. 'Taken Sidney' – I still didn't know if this was a joke or a true unconscious spoonerism, but at least I had cracked the code.

A few things pierced the dull form of my consciousness. One of them was a stylised noise I heard on two separate occasions when the policemen who had taken statements from the injured man and the defendant – one conducting the interview and the other transcribing what was said – testified that they had not got together to make their evidence hang together more than it should. The first time I wasn't sure, though the implication of scorn and disbelief was strong. The second time it happened, coming at the corresponding point in the second policeman's testimony, there could be no doubt about it. I thought to myself, 'Hold on, I've read about these! That's a mirthless laugh, that is.'

The judge noticed it too, and his gaze was drawn to me for a moment, presumably because I had already registered in his mind as anomalous. Then it swept over the jury, but didn't succeed in fastening on the culprit, the lurking dissenter from trust in the forces of order – the youth with *Dune* in his pocket, as my peripheral hearing confidently proclaimed him to be. I hadn't caught his last name when he was sworn in, but his first name was Simon. Naturally I had my own name for him – he could only be Sci-Fi Si.

As an undergraduate I had gone along with the self-consciously revolutionary politics of my generation, not just passively but with some energy, to the point where I took part in the occupation of the Senate House, having been sneaked in through a window, and earned a place in the official report on that fracas by being dropped on a staircase when the oppressive forces of The Man cleared the building early one morning, rightly calculating that revolutionaries sleep late. I had a better claim than most to regard myself as a victim of casually oppressive authority. Yet I was almost as shocked by the scorn shown for police integrity as the judge was.

I think I must have lolled somewhat in the course of that afternoon, drifting off the roughly vertical and even slewing a little in my cushioned seat. I was able to notice that one of my fellow jurors was engaged in some primitive sort of handicraft. She was a large woman wearing a scarf whose scarlet, barely less vivid than Hizonner's robes, could only have been chosen in a spirit of homage or rivalry. In one hand she held a wooden shape like the handle of a skipping-rope, and with the other she was winding yarn around four pins fastened to its top, then gently hooking the loops in sequence over the pins.

A thick woven worm

I say 'primitive' because this technique, known as French knitting, was traditionally taught to children as an introduction to what wool could do. The device in her hand, often painted to resemble a female figurine, was called a Knitting Nancy. In its standard form the handle shape is painted with a rudimentary face (dots for eyes, little circle for the nose) and sketched-in clothing. This one was a little different, shaped like a red mushroom with white spots. She told everyone who would listen, and plenty of people who would rather not, that it had been made for her in a woodwork class by her nephew, who had based it on the cover of one of his old Tintin books.

While we were waiting to be sworn in this woman, wearing a poppy in anticipation of Remembrance Day, though the scarlet of her scarf made it hard to see at first glance, had asked if I wanted a poppy of my own. She was sure she had a spare one in her handbag and it was a nice tradition to keep up, wasn't it? People are always offering to deck me out in their opinions, perhaps shrewdly relying on my incapacity to remove such things once they're installed. I told her I only ever wore the white poppy.

'The white one? Whatever's that?'

'It's the style of remembrance favoured by pacifists, as a way of commemorating loss without endorsing the violence that caused it.'

'I've never heard of such a thing.'

'It's actually a tradition almost as old as the red-poppy one, started by some women's guild or other between the wars.'

'I've never heard of such a thing,' she said again, as if that settled the matter. And so we got off on the wrong foot, which was entirely the right foot to be getting off on in this particular case. As a matter of fact I've never worn the white poppy in my life. I've never even seen one, but that's beside the point. A smattering of knowledge about the history of non-violence in the West had given me the weapon I needed to deflect this unprovoked assault on my autonomy.

And here she was, a grown woman appearing in public with a Knitting Nancy! There's no getting away from the childish nature of the device and the associated technique. Doing it up to resemble Albert Einstein rather than a mushroom would do nothing to elevate the reputation of the craft. This contraption bore the same relationship to proper knitting as a toy piano does to a concert grand. Slowly it extrudes – I'm tempted to say excretes – a thick woven worm from the bottom of the wooden tube. This textile waste product could then be sewn into larger decorative or functional forms by those with nothing better to do with their hands and their lives. And this lady was winding and hooking yarn in her lap the whole time, though she wasn't fool enough to do it in the judge's line of sight. If jury service didn't provide enough to occupy her mind there must be something wrong with her mind.

Someone smelled of mothballs but I couldn't be sure of who it was. I very much wanted it to be the lady with the Knitting Nancy, but I didn't want to jump to conclusions, that being very much the potential weakness of the jury onto which I had been empanelled.

My attention was drawn and then held by the next witness, the lady who had been closing up the Blue Lagoon chip shop opposite the nightclub. From the first she was oddly defiant, even truculent in a simmering sort of way, though counsel for the prosecution approached her with a juiciness of tone that would have seemed overdone in a West End play. 'Is your name Joanne Koukis?'

She bridled at his words, though he had spoken in the most honeyed tones imaginable. He was a Silk and silkily he went about his business. He could charm the birds from the trees, but he couldn't charm Joanne from the chip shop.

'And why shouldn't it be?' Her tone was close to belligerent. 'I married a Greek, well a Greek Englishman, didn't I? He was born here. He's not foreign.'

The barrister for the Crown was a little taken aback. Did she not realise they were on the same side, trying to put a nasty piece of work behind bars? 'I don't doubt it for a moment, Mrs Koukis. And on the night in question you were shutting up the Blue Lagoon restaurant after close of business?'

'Not just shutting up – cleaning every surface. Has to be done every day.'

'No doubt. But when the *altercayshion* started outside the *discotairk* you were able to see what went on? You had an unobstructed view?'

'Who says I didn't?'

'My dear Mrs Koukis, no one says anything different. I'm just wishing to establish your situation for the benefit of the jury. You could see everything clearly?'

'Didn't I just say so? When the shouting started I turned out the lights. Plate glass can be broken, you know. I didn't feel safe with all those yobbos out there, all of them as bad as each other. They don't come into the Lagoon, that's for sure, none of them. They know they won't be served.'

'Quite right, Mrs Koukis. So you were in an ideal position to see what happened.'

'Didn't I just say so? Not that I was poking my nose in, if that's what you're implying.'

'Of course not, Mrs Koukis, anyone would have done the same.' It was odd the way statements intended to be soothing had an inflammatory effect in her case. She stood there righteous and somehow wounded in advance, arms folded in front of her.

Nevertheless she confirmed what she had said in her statement about there being an interval of some minutes before the punch to the head and the picking up of the brick. Counsel for the prosecution sat down with a small smile, but he looked a bit done in just the same, as if he was the one who had been interrogated and wasn't quite sure what he'd confessed to.

Counsel for the defence stood up to cross-examine, displaying from the start an artificially puzzled demeanour, as if there was something he didn't quite understand. Lawyers are a bit actorish, aren't they, I mean the barristers, the ones who can play to an audience. This one was basing his performance – of course this is all guesswork – on someone sighing noisily on a train and sucking the end of his biro, just so that everyone can see there's only one clue in the crossword that he hasn't filled in, which will make the triumph all the sweeter and more public when he can slap his forehead in self-deprecation ('Of course! Silly me! How could I be so blind?') as the enigma yields to him at last.

His delivery was hesitant, as if he had no particular idea where the line of questioning was leading. 'Mrs Koukis . . . in the statement you made to the police you said that after the defendant had struck Mr Wade on the jaw, causing him to fall to the ground . . . he did not immediately take up the brick that resulted in the second injury. I wonder, can you be sure of that?'

'Sure as eggs.'

'Mm. Experiments have shown that human beings are not always accurate judges of the passing of time. I might for instance take out my watch' – and he let us have a glimpse of a pocket watch, attached to his waistcoat pocket by a gleaming chain – 'and count off two minutes exactly. But if I asked you to tell me when those two minutes were up, you might be very far off in your calculations.'

Mrs Koukis stared him down. 'I'll take my chances,' she said, with no particular emphasis. Perhaps two minutes was the time it took for chips to go crisp and acquire the proper dark colour, and consequently a chronological unit very familiar to those who run fish bars.

A customer had helped himself to a saveloy

'The experiment was offered as an example, nothing more,' said counsel for the Crown. Was he perhaps a little rattled by her intransigence? 'More to the point, distressing events can be hard to absorb in their proper order. No one is suggesting that you were being untruthful, but perhaps the second event followed close on the heels of the first.'

Now Mrs Koukis's angry integrity came close to boiling over. It was as if a customer at the Blue Lagoon chip shop had reached over while her back was turned and helped himself to a saveloy. What is a saveloy, exactly? On second thoughts don't tell me, really I'd rather not know.

'I know what happened and when it happened. I was so upset that I phoned my husband, and while I was talking to him I was watching what *him*, him in the dock, was doing, and I said to him, him being my husband, "The little bastard's just lit a ciggy. He's taking his own sweet time, but I bet he's not finished." Then he – him in the dock – picked up the brick and stood over the other fellow and I couldn't watch what happened next, but we know what happened now, don't we?'

At this point counsel for the defence was not so much rattled as reeling, with all the answers somehow slipping off the grid of his crossword, leaving it blank. Still, he did his best to neutralise the setback. 'But Mrs Koukis, why didn't you mention this in the statement you made at the time? How can the ladies and gentlemen of the jury place any confidence in your evidence when you produce something like this at the last minute?'

'I didn't like to mention it. It's not something you want to say in front of a policeman, "bastard", is it? It's not nice.'

After two such hammer blows, counsel for the defence subsided into his seat, rather than wait for her to land a third.

Being on a jury is an inherently dramatic situation – it's surprising the whole set-up hasn't been turned into a film. Hang on, though, I think there's a Margaret Rutherford film, maybe even one of the Miss Marple ones, where she serves on a jury. She has quite a funny line, if only I could remember it. I can just see her wonderful face, both indomitable and woebegone.

Prosecution counsel rose to his feet on joints freshly oiled by recent success and consequent excitement. 'Is it possible that your husband will remember this telephone call?'

'Just ask him! He can't come in today, though – someone has to run the shop, you know. We're not all free as birds, not like some people.' Her look of accusation spared no one in the court. 'But he won't have forgotten. He gave me a good old telling-off for using bad language. He's not Greek, not a bit of it, I wouldn't want you to think that, he was born here, though his parents brought him up in their ways. And he's good to me.'

At this point counsel for the prosecution was at his silkiest, as well he might be. He had been served up on a plate everything he could have desired: a damning witness with an unobstructed view and a husband ready to corroborate if needed though not exactly eager, will-ing to attend as long as someone could be found to keep an eye on the deep-fat fryer. Counsel was almost purring when he said, 'Dear lady, I should hate to imagine anything else,' and sat down with a sigh of satisfaction. She rewarded him with a queasy look, as if half mollified, half ready to take offence all over again at being called a 'dear lady'.

At this point counsel for the defence asked for an adjournment so that he could consult with his client, which the judge granted. Since the afternoon was more than half gone he dismissed us altogether for the day, saying that we should return the next morning without fail. As if we would miss a day in court after the sting in the tail at the end of the first day's business! Admittedly there hadn't been any proper dramatic development of the small explosive revelations that had come from the witness box, but if my fellow jurors shared my commitment we would all be setting our alarms good and early on Tuesday morning.

I was a little crestfallen that the curtain should have come down just when the drama was picking up pace, and grateful when Timothy brought me a cup of nasty tea and produced from his pocket, wrapped up in silver foil, a brace of Cadbury's chocolate fingers. He wanted me to eat them both, but I insisted that we have one each. It was obvious that when he had got ready for his day he wasn't catering with me in mind. Cadbury's or Cadburys? That apostrophe is as moot as they come, the very mootest among the moot. The name used to be embossed on every square of their chocolate bars, but I never paid enough attention to it to remember whether it had once included the apostrophe, the evanescent mark (as any proofreader will tell you) long since licked off by the rough tongues of those relentless kittens over the years. Sainsbury's or Sainsburys? It's essentially the same question, and yet I don't care.

It must have been at about this time that I started to wonder if I hadn't perhaps been something of a bigot when it came to apostrophes. 'Sainsbury's' – that's obviously right, with the word 'supermarket' being understood. 'Sainsbury's chairman' – there's no difficulty with that either. But when correct usage seems to demand 'Sainsbury's chairman's Achilles's heel' you have to ask yourself a serious question: *Where is it all going to end?* If Achilles long ago gave up his apostrophe (along with the 's' that came along for the ride) without feeling the need to sulk about it, then shouldn't less temperamental nouns follow his lead? The stern protocols of punctuation must allow for some softening.

I can't liken these internal debates very convincingly to the throwing off of mind-forg'd manacles which so preoccupied Blake, but finally the weakened mental link went *ping* and in my small way I was free, lighter by a single foreshortened shackle of printer's ink.

Timothy was as thrown by that afternoon's development in court as any of us. 'That's certainly put the cat among the pigeons. I wouldn't be surprised if things move rather quickly now.'

'How do you mean?'

'Well, it's not easy to say you were acting in self-defence when actually you had a good think after you'd knocked the other fellow down. And a judge is likely to come down hard on someone who tried that defence and got caught out. There'll be some pressure brought to bear on young Mr Millon.'

'I still don't follow.'

'We'll have to wait and see, won't we? You mustn't try to put words in my mouth, sir.' I didn't see why not. He had put forkfuls of pie in

452

my mouth at lunchtime, and was following up with a chocolate finger even while we were speaking, so it would seem like a fair exchange. And of course it was the intimacy of feeding me that had led him to be so indiscreet. It's hard to keep information behind the normal barriers when the normal barriers aren't in place. I began to see that there could be advantages to combining eating and talking, though I'm normally dead set against mixing the two and my digestion would gladly take the witness stand to testify in its own defence, backing me up strongly on the wisdom of my normal practice.

'Oh, one more thing, sir. I've had a word with Hizonner about you being the jury foreman and he's content – I wouldn't say mad keen, but content – for you to deliver the verdict without standing up.'

'Oh, I think we can do better than that, Timothy,' I said. 'You'll help me get roughly vertical, won't you?'

'Certainly, sir. He'll like that. Hizonner is a stickler.'

That was fine by me. In my little way I stickle too.

'We can have a little practice tomorrow, can't we, Timothy?'

'If we have time, sir.' There didn't seem any great hurry. Timothy had already told me that the case was listed on the docket to last four days, so we had time in hand to rehearse the ceremonial choreography.

When I was reunited with the Mini at the end of the day, it had an honour guard round it, to make sure no one interfered with it or questioned its bona fides. Not members of the Household Cavalry but traffic cones, every bit as good. I began to feel that my commitment to the justice system was being on balance more rewarded than penalised.

Back at Mayflower House I was bursting with the events of my day, regretting that I hadn't built up relationships with the other residents that would allow me to mention, quite casually, that I was a judge of the facts in a criminal case (that was how Timothy had explained to us the rôle of the jury), a briefly serving but brightly shining cog in a glorious machine. The best I could do was approach Mrs Baine behind her counter in hopes of a chat, but she was fixed in a strange position, staring at her left hand with a pencil in her right. 'I'm sorry, Mr Cromer, but unless it's urgent I'll keep on doing what I'm doing.'

'Of course, Mrs Baine,' I said, though I can't deny I felt a little small.

'I'm doing my homework for the evening class in art I'm doing at Seacat, if you must know.'

At last someone who understands. Yes, I must know. *I must know!* Keep me as well informed as you possibly can. Hold nothing back.

Seacat was really CCAT, the Cambridge College of Art and Technology. 'Drawing your own hand is harder than you think,' she went on, and abruptly lost all the points she had abruptly gained. Please avoid that form of words, 'harder than you think', since you have no idea what it is that I think. I felt a fizzle of disconnection, though I listened politely enough. 'Last week we had to do a drawing of one of our hands, which was hard enough. This week we have to do it again, only wearing a bracelet this time. It's practically impossible! It just doesn't look right. But if I move my hand I'll have to start all over again. So what is it I can help you with, Mr Cromer?'

'It's really nothing, Mrs Baine. Don't let me disturb you.'

'Another time, though, ask me about Lasko. That was quite an adventure!' Lasko. I made a mental note of the name.

It seemed that everybody in the building, everyone in the whole city even, was busy improving themselves except for me. Improving themselves is the wrong way of looking at it. Mrs Baine, Baine of my life, why improve yourself when you can Realise your Self? There are no barriers to that except imaginary ones – mind-forg'd manacles again – so much harder to see than the bracelet she was trying to render with her pencil. She was like someone who always goes in and out the back way because she had once dreamed the front door was blocked by boulders.

The next morning I was so early at the Guildhall I had time for a nap. Admittedly I didn't realise I had been napping until Timothy rapped softly on the window of the Mini.

May the Best Yob Win

'It's all change this morning, sir.'

'How do you mean?'

'Change of plea. Hizonner will explain what's involved.'

'But is that allowed? Changing your plea?'

'It is indeed. Fundamental part of the process.'

454

'But why would someone do that?'

'When things are going badly it can make sense. Saves time and public money, which goes down well with judges and can make for leniency. And, speaking hypothetically, it may turn out that the defendant has a criminal record as long as your arm, but then again so does the other chap, and another time things could have gone the other way.'

I wasn't at all happy and didn't pretend otherwise. Was it pitifully obvious that I wasn't thinking about the defendant at all, not remotely concerned with the right and wrongs of the case? It must have been. Timothy said gently, 'You still get to deliver the verdict, sir.' Yes, but we wouldn't be deciding it. We wouldn't be *retiring to consider our verdict*. We wouldn't be *deliberating*. We would just be doing what we were told. As foreman I was always only going to be a mouthpiece, but now I wasn't going to be the mouthpiece of the twelve, of Philip Anthony and Knitting Nancy and Sci-Fi Si. I would be the ventriloquist's dummy into which Hizonner threw his voice, so that I could say his words back to him and he could officially hear them as legally binding.

I tried, not for the first time, to elevate pique into principle. 'But Timothy, you told us we were the judges of the facts.'

'And so you are, sir, judges of the facts as presented to the court.' So much for the sovereign power of the jury, bastion of liberty, last line of defence against the forces of oppression! We were judges of the facts as they were presented to us, not of the facts as we might work them out and understand them ourselves. The whole wobbling system made Hindu cosmology with its load-bearing elephants and turtles seem sturdy and well balanced.

'Tell me, Timothy, has a jury ever ignored a judge's direction to acquit?'

'Not to my knowledge, sir, and I'd appreciate it if today wasn't the day the rot set in. I've got double rations of chocolate fingers with me and I'd hate to have to eat them all myself.'

I took the opportunity to ask about Knitting Nancy. 'Should that lady be knitting, Timothy? Is that sort of recreation allowed?'

'Well, she's being discreet about it, isn't she? One chap in the summer came in with a little radio so he could listen to the cricket. We soon put a stop to that. I had a word with her about it, but she says it helps her concentrate and I'm keeping quiet about it unless Hizonner sits up and takes notice.'

'Do you know what the lady does? I mean what she does in life?' Silly phrase, really. Where else would she be doing it? Whatever it was.

'Well, her husband is high up in Januarys.'

I'd seen that name in the *Cambridge Evening News*. 'The estate agents.'

'That's them.'

'And she just sits at home all day doing French knitting?'

'I don't think so. She works in a shop, though to hear her talk you'd think she owned it. Says she's going to be the manageress of the branch of Dorothy Perkins that's opening up in town.'

'She should be running a small country. Maybe not one I'd want to live in.'

'As you say, sir.' It occurs to me there was a bit of Jeeves in Timothy, a Jeeves gone slightly wrong. Perhaps he never left home without a copy of *The Code of the Woosters*.

People who haven't read Dickens tend to associate knitting with wholesomeness. If Knitting Nancy didn't have the active malevolence of Madame Defarge it may have been in part because she lacked skills as a knitter, the adroitness with her needles that made it possible for Madame D. to record in stitches the names of her enemies marked out for death.

Knitting Nancy did no more than mark people out to be the recipients of insipid Christmas decorations, but in my book that was more than enough. She cultivated the other women on the jury, and my eavesdropping skills told me she was promising them knitted angels for their Christmas trees. She took one out of her bag to show off. It was a horrible pinky thing. An angel is not a sugary confection but a bringer of terror and disorientation, before whom shepherds have the good sense to cower. It's not mentioned how their flocks react, but it can hardly be good for their digestion or bringing lambs safely to term.

I expressed my concerns to Timothy. 'She's suborning the jury! She's buying their favour with French knitting! She wants them to toe the line and vote the way she wants.'

'That's a hard charge to make stick, sir. I'm not sure there's a lot I can do about it. I suppose you could say she's just being nice.'

'You could say that. I certainly wouldn't.'

Sometimes she looked at me with a glint in her eyes, and I knew she was measuring me for mittens. On the whole I'd rather be measured for a shroud, whether crocheted in a folksy manner or otherwise. The worst of it was that in a bitter Cambridge winter I would probably wear them. I might even thank her, though it would be through teeth as comprehensively gritted as one of the city's main thoroughfares during a cold spell.

When she learned of our case's sudden swerve Knitting Nancy showed no more than a prim disapproval at the hairpin bend of procedure, merely muttering, 'This would never happen in Fulchester,' wherever on the map Fulchester might turn out to be. The person most upset was Sci-Fi Si, who actually made me rather glad we weren't going to judge the facts since he saw the facts so differently. 'Can they do that? How can they get away with it? The whole system is buggered!'

He would have found the defendant Not Guilty. Not because he accepted the story that the blows were struck in self-defence, but because this was no more than a Saturday-night free-for-all, a 'ruck', 'barney' or 'dust-up' rather than a criminal assault by one individual on another. They were just letting off steam though admittedly things had got out of hand. 'It could have gone the other way, couldn't it?' he said. 'We don't know that the other bloke didn't have a knife – his mates would have made that disappear. I'm actually impressed that a shortarse like that could land his punch. You've got to admire that, haven't you?'

Well no, I had no possible reason to admire it. So perhaps it was for the best that I wasn't required to steer deliberations about guilt and innocence, given that one of our number would have been standing up for no higher principle than May the Best Yob Win. It would have ended with a majority verdict of Guilty, I suppose, but it would have been a long and purgatorial wait. I imagine that Sci-Fi Si would simply retreat into his book, while Knitting Nancy and Philip Anthony would bicker endlessly about his smoking.

Smoking was forbidden in court but permitted in most other spaces, including the jury room, as she was horrified to learn from

457

Timothy. It's true that Philip Anthony's tweeds retained the smell of smoke so strongly that it was hard to know without looking if he had a cigarette lit at any particular moment. If they had been passed on to him by his father then they might well be impregnated with half a century's worth of poisonous fumes. Still, Knitting Nancy's suggestion that there should be segregated juries, smoking and non-smoking, was hardly realistic. How would a forty-a-day man accused of murder get a fair shake from a jury that regarded smoking itself as a crime? 'I'm a great supporter of ash,' she said, and I managed not to mutter, 'You could have fooled me.'

'Ladies and gentlemen of the jury,' said the judge, 'the defendant is "in your charge". That is the legal technicality, and it means that you must be involved in the proper resolution of a case even when, as is the case today, your decision as to guilt and innocence is not being sought. The defendant, as you will remember, was charged on two counts – the counts representing the two injuries considered separately – of causing Grievous Bodily Harm under Section 18 of the relevant Act, that is, of causing serious injury with intent. He has now chosen to plead guilty to the same offence but under a different section, Section 20, where the offence is considered less grave because there was not the intention to do the harm, and this will be considered when I come to pass sentence.

'The prosecution is content to accept those guilty pleas. For what it's worth my own judgement accords with this decision. On my direction, therefore, you will return a verdict of Not Guilty on the charges under Section 18. Have you chosen a foreman to pronounce your verdict?' He let his gaze wander over the dozen of us, though Timothy had placed me so that I was nearest him and he knew about my . . . let's call it election already. Rigmarole upon rigmarole!

'We have,' I said, with as much hauteur as I could muster.

'I will ask the foreman to stand.' For a moment I was tempted to sulk, to stage a one-man sit-down strike that would make no difference but might appease my frustration at the hollowness of my allotted rôle, but Timothy was waiting and I let him do the honours. 'How do you find the defendant Thomas Andrew Millon on the two charges under Section 18 of the Offences Against the Person Act of 1861, Guilty or Not Guilty?'

I wish I could say that I shouted out, 'Hanging's too good for 'im! He's a little bastard just like the chip lady said!', but of course I didn't. I said meekly, 'Not Guilty, My Lord.' And that was my first stint as jury foreman done with. Would I ever get another crack at it? It was over to Philip Anthony for the next case. As a functionary I had been superseded. Collectively as a jury we were sent home until the next day and the next case.

Why weren't we disbanded as a jury, to be thrown back individually into the jury pool to be re-empanelled in due course in a different permutation, as procedure dictates? Sometimes Maya makes these slip-ups, as if defying us to notice them and unmask her, but you have to be quick to catch her cooking the books. She doesn't keep receipts.

Timothy's promised chocolate fingers furnished elevenses rather than afternoon tea, and all the crunch seemed to have gone from them somehow. It was as if they had been dunked before the event, held below the surface by a person or persons unknown until all the cocoa joy had melted away.

The defendant, by the time the verdict was delivered, did a good job of mustering his face into an expression of sneering contempt. I wish I hadn't noticed how different he had looked the day before, when the damage done to his chances of walking away by the chip shop lady had begun to dawn on him. Then he was defenceless and close to tears, back to being what he had been not so long before, just a boy who wanted to spend all his time with horses.

Still, the next day, when I saw that our case involved nothing more serious than petty theft, I felt almost sorry for Philip Anthony. After the twists and turns of R. v. *Millon* it hardly seemed worth our time. I made sure that Timothy installed me in the back row and at the other end from Philip Anthony, which was perhaps rather overdoing the scruple. I hardly needed to give him free rein to play jury foreman in any style he saw fit, without reference to my own performance, since it hardly qualified as a performance at all. I had uttered half a dozen words, amounting (a group of two words, then a group of four) to a pair of formal statements. Really no need to murmur 'break a leg' – he wasn't taking over from me as Hamlet at Stratford.

I wasn't expecting the next case to be actively interesting, and I felt that this was as it should be. Without anticlimaxes where would climaxes be? They wouldn't know what to do with themselves. Besides, if jury service was as exciting as crime fiction people would be bribing the officers of the court to be admitted to juries, rather than taking extreme measures to avoid the experience or enliven its tedium, dressing like drug addicts or whiling away the hours with a hefty book or a rudimentary handicraft tool.

The nougat of wisdom enrobed

There seemed plenty of anticlimax in store for us. A young woman, a law student, was accused of stealing a book from Bowes & Bowes. She didn't deny that she had looked at the book, which had been mentioned by a lecturer on the morning of the alleged offence. She had never intended to buy it. The lecturer had said it was rather a bad book. Her explanation was that it had somehow accidentally got into her bag, between other books. The store detective, who had been keeping an eye on her, had triumphantly retrieved it, and here she was. Or rather, that was how she had come up before the magistrates. She was here because she had pleaded Not Guilty on that occasion and opted for a jury trial. We were to be her judges and her vindication – judges of the facts merely, of course. The judge proper, the judge of flesh and blood and robes and wig, would direct us on the law.

Before this second case got under way I asked our jury bailiff for some background information. 'I don't want to seem ungrateful, Timothy,' I said, 'but after all the excitement of the last case this new one seems a bit . . . nondescript. Wouldn't this sort of thing normally be dealt with by magistrates?'

'Well, sir, you're right and you're wrong about that. The defendant has exercised her right to a jury trial but such a thing wouldn't normally come up in front of Hizonner. The problem is that the new Crown Court system is new – new-ish – and there are teething troubles. One of them being that there is no court of first or second degree in the county, though (as you may or may not be surprised to hear) the crime rate in Mid-Anglia is higher than it is in Norfolk, Suffolk and Northamptonshire . . .'

'So courts are classified like burns? Are first- and second-degree cases less serious?'

'That's right, sir. So this case was scheduled to be heard in Peterborough, with police and other witnesses having to make the trip
there as often as was necessary, which is a great waste of public
resources. But then a fraud case that was supposed to be heard here at
the Guildhall collapsed and there was some extra court time suddenly
came available. We did what we could at short notice.

'As I expect you know, sir, there's a shake-up of the county system under way. On the morning of April 1st next year we'll wake
up in a new administrative area that includes Huntingdon and
Peterborough, but unfortunately that won't solve our little problem
about courts being located in inconvenient places. Not unless someone has a word with the Lord Chancellor. You don't happen to know
the gentleman, sir?'

'I'm afraid not, Timothy.' Even if he was a regular at Four Lamps I
wouldn't be able to put a name to the face.

'And nor do I. We just have to put our faith in the workings of
government.'

The defendant, Thomasina French, needed us to save her reputation and her professional prospects, which made sense. A guilty
verdict on a charge of shoplifting in the Magistrates Court would
mean that her career in the law was over before it had properly begun.
At intervals she directed pleading glances at the twelve of us, the
judges of the facts, more or less in rotation. She made sure that we
all received our allotted portion of mutely eloquent appeal, as if her
eyes were simpering humanoid searchlights controlled by the sophisticated sort of remote-control computer system we all marvelled at
on *Tomorrow's World*. Really, the things they think up! We live in a
golden age of invention, and much of it is British. Pye Electronics,
proudly Cambridge-based, lead the field.

The judge received a modified version of the same treatment. She
gazed at him as if she had never before seen such a confection, the
nougat of wisdom enrobed in the milk chocolate of compassion, and
it was clear that his lordship didn't mind her phantom fingers creeping their way through the rustling tissue paper of his robes towards
his soft judicial centre.

Defendants take trouble about their clothes. The way they dress
is the first signal they send to judge and jury – and if this was true

of Mr Millon in his blue suit and fat tie, how much more so of Miss French. She had put real thought into her appearance, impersonating not just an attractive young woman but an attractive young librarian. Someone who could be trusted, not just in general terms but with the most valuable book on earth. Byron's diaries rescued from the fire, the manuscript of *Love's Labours Won*, a Gutenberg Bible signed by both God and Gutenberg, none of these would be diverted by her from the proper stretch of shelving.

She was beautifully groomed but made no attempt at sexiness, with her hair pulled back by a tortoiseshell clip. Even so, she had combined two elements that would have worked well separately but clashed in combination – a plunging neckline and a choker necklace. So where is it exactly that you want the judge to look, dear heart, up at the sparklers or down at the softer attractions? Because in between you are undefended. Those awkwardly exposed inches make you look like a bit of a ditherer, which in this particular context is worse than being either a prude or a tart. Is it knows-a-thing-or-two or butter-wouldn't-melt? You look either too bold or too coy. Between wanton and demure there is no overlap but rather a gulf fixed.

The bundle of documents we received as jurors was much slimmer than what we had been given in the heady days of *R. v. Millon*, plump as it was with X-rays and medical reports. This wasn't much more than a leaflet. There was a small handful of witnesses for the prosecution, including the shop assistant on duty in that department and the store detective who had seen the dirty work in progress (if the work was indeed dirty, as alleged). She had summoned the police, who also testified.

The store detective herself was mousy and inconspicuous, though these are close to being qualifications for the job. She didn't know what to do with her hair and gave the impression of complete indifference to the impression she made. It was as if she had dressed without taking a personal interest in the procedure, putting on whatever had been laid out on the chair by her bed by some third party.

There had been advertisements for store detective jobs in the *Cambridge Evening News* from time to time, though the copywriters had come up with no greater attraction than 'Each day will be in a different store within easy reach of home.' Not much glamour there!

It's a rather forlorn pitch for what should by rights be a fascinating form of paid snooping. I won't say I'd seriously considered it as a line of work for myself, though I can't deny it crossed my mind. I've often thought that extreme conspicuousness is a specialised sort of invisibility, but obviously that wouldn't wash in this context.

The first surprise of the trial came from the first words she spoke, identifying her employers, even if everyone but me took it in their stride. She worked for the W. H. Smith chain of newsagents, and W. H. Smith owned Bowes & Bowes. Yes, you heard right – W. H. Smith owned Bowes & Bowes! W. H. Smith the high-street prudes pulled the strings of Bowes & Bowes the august and open-minded academics, whose premises at Number 1, Trinity Street could claim to be the site of the oldest booksellers in the country. It was like finding that Dr Jekyll and Mr Hyde were the same person, or at least divergent personalities housed in the same body – something that certainly came as a shock to the first readers of Stevenson's novel, since it's only revealed late on in the book. Never mind that these days everyone is in the know long before they embark on the first page. In general 'embark on' seems the right word to use for readers of fiction, floating away in the fullness of their freedom from the shores of what Maya insists on as fact.

So the same store detective went from one premises to the other, from W. H. Smith to Bowes & Bowes and back again. It gave me a warm feeling to know that I might be under surveillance at any time in those shops, watched to make sure I didn't slip an atlas into my pocket and make a bolt for it.

These toffs need to be taught a lesson

The store detective's evidence seemed clear and unambiguous. She had seen the book furtively slipped into Miss French's shopping bag, not falling by accident but inserted by design. Counsel for the defence set about undermining the impression of truthfulness she had produced.

'So tell me, Miss Laidlaw—'

'Miz.'

'I beg pardon?'

'Miz. Ms Laidlaw.'

'Of course.' By a miraculous piece of face-choreography he managed to bestow an indulgent twinkle on the witness, while also sending a tight little smile in the direction of the judge, to convey the message *I'm afraid we've got one of those.*

'"These toffs need to be taught a lesson." Do you recall saying those words, Miz Laidlaw?'

'No, I don't . . . and anyway I thought she was supposed to have fainted. How could she hear when she was out cold on the floor?'

In response counsel for the defence resorted to pantomime. 'Excuse me, Miz Laidlaw, I'm looking through my bundle and I can't seem to find a certificate of the relevant medical expertise in your name. Should I call the clerk of the court to account for its mysterious disappearance?'

Her expression became sullen and she lowered her face. 'No.'

'Then perhaps you will answer the question rather than treat us to your opinions about semi-conscious awareness and what may or not be registered upon it. Did you say those words – "these toffs need to be taught a lesson"?'

'No.'

'Have you ever expressed such a sentiment?'

'Not to my knowledge.'

'But you have used the word "posh" in the past? You're not claiming, I take it, that today is the first time you have heard it? I notice you didn't need to ask what it means.'

'I know what it means. I must have used it myself. At some point.'

'Very good – this constitutes progress. Now I put it to you that you have turned misunderstanding into vendetta simply because you took a dislike to the defendant on the basis of what you assumed to be her class.'

'I did not.'

'What did you assume about the defendant Miss French? That she was privileged in ways you are not, that she had professional prospects denied to most people?'

'I have prospects.' She almost stuttered as she explained, 'I'm studying at the College of Arts and Technology here.' CCAT alias Seacat again, unglamorous engine of advancement for the less fortunate.

464

'I congratulate you. And what subject are you studying?'

'Catering.'

Counsel affected a puzzled frown, as if he been expecting her to say 'cuneiform' or 'the rococo'.

'Nevertheless a gulf may be said to subsist between your circumstances and those of the defendant, who stands to lose those prospects on no better basis than what you said you saw.'

'The book was in her bag.'

'That is not contested and has been explained. But tell me more about that day and your impressions of the defendant. How was she dressed?'

'A lot less [inaudible].' She swallowed the end of the sentence.

'I'm afraid I couldn't hear that, Miz Laidlaw, and I suspect My Lord and the ladies and gentlemen of the jury were in the same unfortunate position. Would you be kind enough to repeat what you said more audibly?'

She raised her head from its lowered position. 'A lot less cleavage. A lot less cleavage than today.'

'Oh.' Counsel seemed taken aback. 'Indeed. Well, perhaps the weather was cold.'

'Warmer than today, sir. It was quite a bit warmer than it is today.'

The pause, though ghastly, was brief, and counsel recovered himself. 'I suspect we're allowing ourselves to be distracted by inessentials.'

Nevertheless the next time the defendant appeared, after a short adjournment, she had changed her top for a less revealing one, which married better with the choker necklace. Perhaps she had dashed home to rummage through her wardrobe or else had made an emergency application to Marks & Spencer – is there a special aisle for demure defendant knitwear? Perhaps there should be.

When counsel for the prosecution rose to re-examine the store detective, he was all smiles. 'Miz Laidlaw, do you happen to recall who founded the educational institution that has become the Cambridge College of Art and Technology?'

'Oh yes. It was John Runcorn. They're very proud of him.'

'John Ruskin, exactly so. The great Ruskin. And where was it originally housed, do you know?'

'Well, I think . . . in the Guildhall.'

'Precisely. In this very building.' Despite the detective's garbling of Ruskin's name, the prestige of Seacat was being wiped clean of the condescension with which it had so recently been sprayed.

The judge must have seen that counsel was about to sit down, having finished his questioning, but nevertheless interposed to ask where exactly this argument was tending. Was it crucial to the case in some way not immediately evident to the mere expert observer?

'No indeed, My Lord. I merely wished to establish that this is a city of students, all of them deserving of respect.'

The judge gave a sour little snort and announced the luncheon recess – lesser workers may break for lunch but judges recede. The barrister's rather edged comment, not helpful to his own interests in court, viz. keeping the judge sweet, seemed to show that he had more or less given up on a conviction. I sent him a mental message to persist in his push for justice. If he was trying to play on egalitarian instincts in the jury he wasn't making any headway, as far as I could see. Sci-Fi Si hadn't even signalled his cynicism with his mirthless laugh (patent pending) when the police gave their evidence, perhaps assuming in advance that privilege would look after its own.

Knitting Nancy said, as the witness left the stand, and loudly enough for her to hear, 'I wish that girl would keep her hair off her face.' A crushingly middle-class comment on manners and style, certainly, but some way short of a political position. I didn't know where I stood myself. In the class war I was somehow on both sides of the barricades, waving a white flag just as vigorously as I could manage.

Philip Anthony didn't head off smartly in search of food as he had previously done. He seemed to be loitering, almost as if he wanted to consult me. 'I wonder if I might have a word?' he asked at last, for all the world as if we were colleagues in the common room of the Perse School trying to unpick a stubborn knot in the timetable.

He took up the closest he could to a deferent posture, which isn't easy when you're talking to someone in a wheelchair. He went down into a squatting position, though it was clear that it wasn't a comfortable one and he put out a hand every now and then to steady himself, either against the wooden wall of the jury box behind him or the wheelchair itself. 'I thought that you'd be the chap to talk to,' he went on, and I made agreeable noises. 'I've spoken to the other jurors, and I couldn't get them to see what I was driving at. They're a mixed bunch, if I can put it that way. I thought you and I might see eye to eye about a worrying aspect of this case.' Not just eye to eye, I fancy, but graduate to graduate – he might just as well have held out his rolled-up degree certificate and touched its tender tip to mine.

My idiolect had gone to the dogs

'I wonder if I know what you mean,' I said. But in fact Philip Anthony and I said, more or less together, 'I'm sure you've noticed the—', and though he said 'discrepancy' and I said 'anomaly' it was clear we had been struck by the same omission.

Best to make sure we were talking about the same thing. 'Perhaps you mean the curious affair of the disappearing witness, Mr Freeman?'

'I felt sure you were following the case with proper attention, John! If I may use your Christian name – and please, do call me Philip.' I tried to oblige him, but the two names had somehow coagulated and become a single compound entity, as if he was a Roman emperor or a child being given a full formal scolding by Nanny – 'Philip Anthony, how many times do I have to tell you? You know better than that.' The component parts couldn't be separated.

'It certainly seems strange,' he went on, 'that a person in a position to corroborate the defendant's testimony, or else to undermine it, hasn't been called by either side. That gives us something to think about, surely?'

We would never know unless there was a proper investigation. We asked ourselves why on earth this man had not been . . . and here Philip Anthony produced after a struggle the word 'subpœnaed'. I could do no better than follow it up with the horrible coinage *affidavitised*. He should at least have been affidavitised. Once that word had passed my lips what grounds did I have for objecting to nasty word forms like *toileting*? My idiolect had gone to the dogs, there was no question about that.

'I was wondering,' said Philip Anthony, 'if we should perhaps send a note to the judge on the subject.'

467

'Aren't we only supposed to discuss the case in the jury room, as a group?'

'No harm in us comparing our reactions, surely?'

'As for the correct procedure to follow . . . here's the man to tell us.'

Timothy had arrived with my pie, accompanying it with the no-longer-mysterious formula, 'It's taken Sidney . . .' In fact the words, the pie and the person were the most welcoming parts of my short life as a juror. Timothy's manner changed immediately. 'Hello, sir,' he said to Philip Anthony politely, and then, to me, 'It's good you've got company.' Philip Anthony stood up from his awkward position and made rather a show of stretching his back, I thought. Anyone would think he'd done a shift in a coal mine, but then it's hardly my specialist area.

I had accepted the first pie as a gift, but honour demanded payment thereafter. The awkwardness of urging him to go through the purse in my shoulder bag for change was a bit of a comedown from the summit-meeting tone of the discussion with my new friend – I might almost say 'my learned friend' – Philip Anthony. I couldn't fail to notice that Timothy was ill at ease in this new social grouping. I put it down to the way it revealed a sort of favouritism in terms of his duties as jury bailiff. Timothy might conceivably act as pie-wallah to any or all of the other eleven, but fork-wallah? Not likely.

He might have liked the fork to turn suddenly telescopic, extending itself by a few precious inches to lessen the intimacy of the feeding process. The public transfer of nutrition can be a ticklish business – try regurgitating food into your chick's beak in full view of passers-by and see what they have to say about it.

It seemed best to press on with the matter in hand.

'Philip Anthony and I are concerned about a point of procedure. Perhaps you might help us with it?'

'I'll try. But bear in mind that I'm not legally trained as such.' Then he rather spoiled the impression he was trying to make by adding, without seeming to be aware of its lack of connection with what had gone before, 'My wife and I have an understandment. She spends Christmas with her sister in Oulton Broad, and I don't.'

Philip Anthony looked a bit blank, but it would take more than a lapse in conversational logic to disqualify Timothy from acting as a lay advisor on legal matters. 'At any rate you know more about the law than we do. Who is it that subpœnas a witness?'

'You're not using the right word there, sir,' said Timothy. 'It's important to use the right words. They're very hot on that.'

'And what is the right word?'

'Witness summons.'

'So who issues a witness summons?'

'The silly sister.' This certainly didn't sound like the right word, and both of us said, 'The who?' at the same time, and in the same exasperated-graduate tone.

This time he came out with a word significantly closer to 'solicitor'.

'But which solicitor? The one for the Crown or the defendant?'

'Can be either.'

'But what does it mean if neither does it? We're wondering why the man who was in the bookshop that day and talked to the defendant isn't part of the case, one way or the other.'

'It might mean a lot of things, sir. It might mean that the chap supports her version, but the defence doesn't think that'll clinch it in her favour.'

'Even though it makes the store detective look unreliable?'

'It might only mean that the chap doesn't remember, or isn't sure of the date – something like that.'

The Sidney part of the Taken Sidney

Until now Philip Anthony had been asking the questions, and I felt it was high time I had my say. 'But might it mean that he *doesn't* corroborate her testimony, so the defence is keeping quiet, and meanwhile the prosecution is being a bit dozy and hasn't spotted it?'

'It might mean that. But you're not arguing the case. That's not the jury's function. You can't ask for a new investigation!'

I dare say I sounded a bit sulky. 'I thought we were supposed to be the judges of the facts. It doesn't feel like that, I must say.'

'Judges of the facts that go before the court, yes. We've been through this, sir. That's as far as it goes – and His Honour won't thank you for putting your oar in, I can tell you that.'

Philip Anthony took back the reins of the conversation. 'But you'd pass on a message if we asked you to?'

This was the only solution to the procedural dilemma but not necessarily something Timothy wanted to hear. Throughout the conversation he had been feeding me those forkfuls of pie, though after the first day I had brought along my own cutlery. His gentle manner made the process seem natural, even if I didn't enjoy having Philip Anthony as a witness to it. Perhaps this is how people start to become institutionalised, when help with a chore seems worth the abridgement of freedom that comes with it. Or perhaps this was merely tamasic thinking, a classic stagnation of consciousness – the pie talking. There may be nuances of degradation within the broad category of the tamasic, just as there are more or less damaging cigarettes, though smoking is harmful in any version. It stood to reason that offal, the Sidney part of the Taken Sidney, was the worst and meatiest meat, the equivalent of the high-tar cigarettes that the government was at that moment committed to phasing out, to the chagrin of a few hardened lung-destroyers and the relief of everyone else. Regulations being imposed on the industry were sounding the knell for the passing, among many other brands, of Passing Clouds.

Timothy's fork stopped in the middle of my field of vision while he summoned up all his reserves of character to keep Philip Anthony at a suitable distance. 'As jury bailiff and officer of the court, sir, I am the proper channel of communication and will of course pass on any message the jury – the whole jury, not individual members of it – chooses to entrust to me. But just now I'm having my lunch break. If you don't mind.' The loaded fork came towards me with an agitation displaced from what he was saying, so that he came close to piercing me in the lip.

At this point I burped, a very modest soiling of the public air, certainly as compared to the tobacco miasma that shrouded Philip Anthony like a bespoke fog of foulness, but causing an understandable recoil from my conversational partners. Quite apart from the issue of tamasic intake I had been breaking my normal rule about not eating while talking, or the other way round. The two activities place very different demands on the brain and compete for control of the key activity of breathing. If I talk while I'm eating I swallow air and

470

then I burp, which makes people think I'm badly brought up when it's really only that I'm trying to do two incompatible things at once.

Philip Anthony seized the moment to leave, muttering something about seeing me later. Timothy's fork regained its equilibrium once we were alone again. 'Your friend there . . .' he said. 'Your friend . . . is . . .' By now I was aware that Timothy's word-finding apparatus didn't always function smoothly, and I endangered my lip all over again by biting it to stop myself from finishing his sentence. Then I gave up and provided the missing piece: '—rather too fond of the sound of his own voice? Isn't he just!' I've often been on the receiving end of this treatment, with 'help' from people who don't actually have any idea of where my sentences might be going or what they would do when they got there. It was fun being on the other side of things. I quite enjoyed the view from the prompt box – I could get used to it.

Except that the prompter in his box needs to be in sure possession of the text. Timothy took up again where he hadn't quite left off: 'Your friend there . . . he's a bit of a pillock, isn't he?' For the moment there was nothing wrong with the word-finding apparatus at all.

When we were settling for the afternoon session Philip Anthony vented a little frustration at the impasse we found ourselves in, but gave it a personal turn. 'What was all that about silly sisters and Oulton Broad? Is that usher friend of yours a halfwit?'

'No, not a bit of it,' I said. 'He's from Weights and Measures.'

Which wasn't exactly whole-witted either but had the advantage of a decisive cadence. Sometimes a cadence is all we have to plead for us. Excellence of cadence is the reason the Authorised Version clings to its place on my bookshelf when much of my allegiance has leached away into other scriptures.

That afternoon it was the defendant's turn to make the move from dock to witness box, to be sworn in, to lock her eyes onto the barrister representing her, with only the occasional sidelong glance, pitched in a key of luscious trust, at the judge. When her eyes rested on the jury it was clear she had made the decision to look at Knitting Nancy exclusively, woman to woman – even Woman to Woman – though there had been other females empanelled. Perhaps she had the knack of singling out the floating voter in a crowd, the scrappy patch of soil where an emotional appeal might somehow take root.

471

There were no surprises in her testimony. Her counsel asked her to reconstruct, if she would, the sequence of events that had led to her leaving the premises with a book for which she hadn't paid and indeed had never intended to take away with her. Yet for some reason she was allowed to re-enact this crucial set of movements with the bare minimum of props, shuffling some files that were handed her to represent books and dropping them into an imaginary bag. That's not a reconstruction, that's pantomime! It hardly even qualified as going through the motions. I was in no doubt that counsel for the prosecution would demand a more stringent, more realistic re-enactment.

If he was going to pounce, though, he wanted to lull her into a false sense of security with some very tame cross-examination.

'Law books are expensive, are they not?'

'I suppose so.' She gave a wan smile. 'They aren't given away, I'll say that.'

'There is, moreover, a robust market, above all in a university city such as Cambridge, for second-hand or indeed brand-spanking-new law books, is there not?'

'I really wouldn't know.'

Then he sat down! He was letting her off the hook. This wasn't cross-examination as Ironside practised it. And I couldn't say whether it would cut any ice in Fulchester, being ignorant of the practices of that mysterious part of the world, but it didn't cut any ice with me.

It looked very much as if the scheming miscreant in the witness box was being allowed to have it all her own way and to produce an entirely unrealistic charade to back up her story. The charming piece of byplay we had seen bore no relationship to the transfer of bulky objects in space. The defendant was being allowed to repeat the crooked dealing of which she stood accused in the first place, but this time in full view of the court. A miscarriage of justice was under way, with the appointed guardians of legal process spellbound or dozing, and there seemed to be no one prepared to stop it.

Counsel for the prosecution seemed to have stopped trying, simply because the judge had so obvious a preference for New Hall, Cambridge, founded 1954, over Seacat, founded 1858. So what? So ruddy what? Were we not sovereign, we jurors?

472

Hang on, I don't mean Ironside, do I? I mean Perry Mason. Same actor but a different rôle. Ironside wasn't a lawyer. I must have been hypnotised by the wheelchair, I suppose – proof that it can happen to anyone.

When I heard a noise like a bicycle tyre being let down I thought for a moment that I was unconsciously voicing the hiss that greets the villain in a pantomime, in this case Class-Based Injustice twirling its mustachios. In fact this was Philip Anthony soliciting Timothy with an orgy of attention-getting phonemes, namely that time-honoured plosive-plus-sibilant-plus-unvoiced-dental-combination *pssst*. Despite the warning we had received about Hizonner's hostility to such initiatives he had scribbled a note, which he wanted Timothy to convey to the judge. As jury bailiff Timothy was in no position to object.

Hunched over the lurid mushroom

The judge frowned, and kept the frown in place when he spoke. 'The foreman has indicated that he would like what he terms a "proper" re-enactment of events in the bookshop that morning.' I tried to support the proposal by calling out softly, 'Hear! Hear!'

'Am I to take it that this is a request made on behalf of the whole jury?'

'It is,' I said, more firmly, and for once that seemed to clinch it. It would have taken more gumption than Knitting Nancy, Sci-Fi Si and the rest could muster at short notice to take a stand against the assertion of unanimity.

'Very well. On this occasion I am minded to indulge the ladies and gentlemen of the jury.' Bloody cheek! He wasn't indulging us, he was listening to us. Perhaps the old goat should make a habit of it. 'I take it that the book in question, and perhaps even the shopping bag in question, is on hand? If not then substitutes of the appropriate dimensions must be found. We will take a short adjournment so that suitable action can be taken.'

While we waited in the jury room for the signal to return to court, Nancy gave us a piece of her mind. That's not a paraphrase but her own words: 'I'm going to give you two a piece of my mind.' She didn't deign to look at us but worked frantically at her French knitting, hunched over the lurid mushroom as she wound yarn at high speed round the pins and hooked it, wound and hooked it again. The progress of the woven worm emerging from the spool's bottom was almost visible to the naked eye. We might have been watching a Rumpelstiltskin, dogged rather than demonic, making do with inferior equipment.

'So that was the whole jury wanting something, was it? You've got a nerve to speak for us without a word of warning.'

Philip Anthony's life as a schoolmaster hadn't completely obliterated his long-ago days as an unhappy schoolboy, and he duly adopted a hunched posture of misery and guilt. Or perhaps he was reaching back even further through the karmic mists and reliving a previous existence as a dog much scolded. 'I just thought . . .' he said but broke off, as if knowing in advance he would be interrupted if he went on with the sentence.

'You thought you'd show us how a university degree makes people think they're more important than anyone else. You've certainly done that.'

Luckily Timothy came to tell us the hearing was ready to resume before she got any further into her stride, and before I got the secondary scolding that was no doubt coming my way, my due drubbing for the offences of being in lawful possession of a university degree and aiding and abetting a legitimate enquiry. I like to think I would have stood my ground better than Philip Anthony, but I dare say that's wishful thinking. There should be a special word for thinking that contains no element of wishfulness, but if there is I don't know it.

The second reconstruction was quite unlike the first, which contained so little realism that it hardly qualified as a reconstruction at all. It had been like a party game, literally a charade, a set of gestures disconnected from reality. With an actual book to manœuvre Miss French made rather a hash of picking it up between two others and slipping it into her bag. When she bungled it, so that the book fell to the floor, she singled me out for a fiercely resentful look. The eyes she made at me then were very different from the ones she made at the judge. The pose of simpering slipped, and what came flashing through the eyeholes of the mask was not benevolent.

After that, well, hadn't we all seen what we needed to see? The chances of an honest mistake had dwindled to nothing. Then the judge intervened to put some questions of his own. Was he right in thinking that her father was a distinguished archæologist? He was. Had she in fact worked for him on a dig in the Middle East? She had indeed, between school and university. He had been attached to the British School of Architecture in Iraq. Was it also the case that when the alleged offence had been committed she wasn't short of money? Also true. He thanked her. That was all.

Outrageous! This wasn't anything to do with being judge of the law – he was indicating his own view of the facts. He was leaving us to connect the dots, hypocrite that he was, but he was clearly suggesting that this wasn't the sort of person who would do such a thing, usurping our function. As if we were there to decide not whether she had done it, but whether she resembled a typical offender. I was seething with the class consciousness that I had acquired thanks to becoming a council tenant. I wasn't much less rancorous than Madame Defarge herself, though she had more of an excuse since after all her family had been wiped out under the *ancien régime*.

Larceny bred in the bone

And it wasn't as if this little biographical detail showed the defendant in any very favourable light. In fact, didn't it make things worse? An archæologist is only a thief who has the slyness to wait until the claims of the original possessors have no living champions. The basic difference between Howard Carter and the bodysnatchers Burke and Hare, all three of them deserving that sinister description 'resurrection men', was that Carter had the good manners to wait a few thousand years, confident that there would be no next of kin to kick up a fuss. It was almost ominous that the defendant had served as accomplice to such a barbaric exercise in depredation as an archæological dig.

In *R.* v. *Millon* I didn't remember the judge asking the defendant if he had shaken hands with the Queen Mother on one of her many visits to Newmarket, nor (come to that) if he had brushed out the tail of a past winner of the Cheltenham Gold Cup, though these queries would have been exactly as germane to the matter being decided as his leading questions about her supposedly respectable father.

Lawless appropriation and disregard of rights obviously ran in the family, larceny bred in the bone. The grave-robber father was being produced as a character witness for his book-thief daughter, the ghoul vouching for the pilferer – and on the judge's own initiative, too, Hizonner not just putting his thumb on the scales of justice but leaning on the pan with the full weight of his large body habitus. Whatever next!

Hizonner wasn't even the last character witness of the day. I found it altogether baffling. Miss French wasn't being accused of being the sort of person who might be expected to steal a book, by people who knew her in contexts far removed from book-stealing, but of making off with a particular book on a stated day, as she had been seen to do. The general admiration had no bearing on the particular allegation. Yet we had to listen to her personal tutor from New Hall, who I have to say looked rather cagey, as if she was hedging her bets, not wanting to be dragged down into the pit of infamy in the event that we found Miss French guilty, and didn't produce quite the ringing endorsement that perhaps had been hoped for. No such problem with the last witness, since it turned out to be the dear old vicar who had christened her all those years ago and had more recently prepared her for confirmation, coming all the way from Somerset to model the defendant's character all in alabaster while she feigned a squirm of embarrassment. Perhaps we should have heard from the midwife who had delivered her, whose testimony would have had exactly as much relevance, to declare under oath that she had emerged from the birth canal clutching a posy of baby's breath.

And that was more or less the case for the defence. The argument seemed to be: here are some people who have not seen butter melt in the defendant's mouth. This proves, as a matter of scientific fact, that her oral temperature is too low ever to allow the semi-solid emulsion churned from cow's milk, when ingested but not swallowed, to pass into its liquid state. I didn't agree. Even in a world with a low level of convincingness this was shoddy work. The inspectors at the reality factory were falling down on the job. This batch would not pass muster and must be sent back.

The judge announced an adjournment till the next day. I had half thought we would be hearing counsels' speeches and the judge's summing up so as to be sent out to deliberate, but I suppose there wasn't enough time. Fondly I imagined that we would all find the defendant Guilty chop-chop and go home, but Timothy warned me there was likely to be a fair amount of what he called 'argy-bargy'. There always was. It's in the nature of juries to wrangle. And at least by the time we started the next morning Nancy's wrath might have died down.

As Timothy helped me back to the Mini I took the opportunity to pick his brain a little more. 'Hizonner seems very keen on Miss French, doesn't he? I'm surprised he's in favour of women studying law – he's not most people's idea of, um, a progressive sort of character. I'd have thought he'd have liked the law to stay a bit of a male preserve. Like a London club, if you know what I mean.'

'You're wrong there, John. You're not doing Hizonner justice. He's all in favour of women's education, as a matter of fact. Thinks we have a lot to learn from other countries. It's important that girls get to know how the world works. I've heard him say so. He thinks we're stuck in the Dark Ages, with wives having no idea what their husbands do at work all day. That can't be healthy.'

Oh. Well that's all right, then. For men university offers an intellectual adventure and a professional advantage; for women it's something rather different, a finishing school with a reading list. But female graduates make better company at dinner – so fling wide the doors of the houses of learning!

The next morning Knitting Nancy was clutching a folder distinct from the court documents. I was afraid she was about to distribute rudimentary knitting patterns in the hope of turning the jury room into some sort of craft centre, improving the shining hour with the creation of a product more tangible than justice. She showed no particular interest in either of the culprits she had blamed for the procedural irregularities of the day before.

Thursday morning's session in court held some surprises for everyone, I think, perhaps even the judge. Counsel for the prosecution made his closing speech with a new and unexpected emotional colouration playing over it – sorrow. I suppose he was trying to counteract the barely veiled sympathetic attitude of the judge. According to him it was a cause for regret that this promising young woman, enjoying

477

all the advantages, should have thrown away her integrity and in all likelihood blighted her future for the sake of a book she could have afforded to buy without needing to go short on the necessities of life. It gave him no pleasure, or so he made out, to maintain that her guilt had been clearly demonstrated by the evidence given before the court. Nevertheless we should beware of misplaced sympathy. Everyone was equal before the law, and we should have no hesitation in convicting someone who had perhaps given in to a momentary impulse but had nevertheless committed the crime for which she must answer today.

I suppose this was as close as he could come to indicating that the judge was an interfering old reptile whose maunderings we should feel free to ignore. I didn't need to be told.

Then the barrister representing Miss French responded by dwelling on the absence of motive, emphasising that his client could indeed have afforded the book. Why would she throw away everything she stood to lose? And why would she choose trial by jury unless she was determined to prove her innocence? – though, as he added immediately, she wasn't required to do any such thing. She had nothing to prove, the burden of proof fell entirely the other way, on the Crown, and the Crown had fallen short. Meanwhile her fate lay in our hands.

The judge summed up the evidence, with perhaps a little less emphasis than he had placed the previous day on the defendant's social standing and how much she stood to lose if she was convicted – to which the answer could only be 'She should have thought of that!' Perhaps in his mind the fragrance had been sufficiently diffused not to need a further squirt of perfume, though he seemed to have any amount of it on hand. Then he told us about a thing called doubt, a word that people often used in casual conversation but had a different meaning in law. While chatting, he suggested, someone might for instance say that he or she – though in the circumstances 'he' seemed the more likely pronoun! – doubted whether Cambridge United football club would win the Football Association Cup in the current tournament. That was the sort of doubt we encounter every day, amounting to an open possibility. But on the day of the final in the coming May, there would be no reasonable doubt about who had won, who had scored the crucial goal, whether the team responsible was Cambridge United or indeed Wolverhampton Wanderers or

Oldham Athletic. He was aware that the judge in a court case might seem to be like the referee on a football pitch, despite (and here he twinkled rather than loured) the difference in 'get-up'. Yet the fact was that the jury – we the jury – being judges of the facts, were equivalent to the referee, while he (the judge of the law) was no more than a perambulant version of the Football Association's regulations.

He seemed to have stumbled into a minefield of analogy, from which there was no easy way of extricating himself. I imagine that, since he was required to say something similar in every jury trial over which he presided, he had been fatally tempted to vary the set phrases, and was now left with no road home. There was perhaps the theoretical possibility of an appeal being allowed by a higher court on the basis of misleading sporting comparisons.

'You may feel, ladies and gentlemen of the jury, that the defendant's innocence – guilt or innocence – has been so clearly demonstrated that there is no need for you to retire before giving your verdict. I am aware that although everyone is equal before the law, not everyone is equal in their ability to move with ease from one place to another. May I ask if that is indeed the case?'

Outrageous! Enormity upon enormity! Not content with putting his plump finger on the scales of justice, His Lordship was loading the wheelchair onto the pan as well, with me in it. Although he had been careful to say 'guilt or innocence' it was perfectly clear that he intended us to acquit. This 'young lady' 'with prospects' who had 'everything to lose' should walk free.

There was indecisive shuffling around me from the jury box, but I said, 'By no means,' just as clearly and evenly as I could. There are limits to the volume and depth producible by a voice housed in a small body habitus, and I've often thought that the single greatest improvement to my life would be the possession of a properly reso-nant voice, a sonorous and persuasive instrument. On this occasion, though, I managed to achieve a sort of diapason effect. Perhaps it was no more than a fluke of acoustics, but for a moment my words seemed to manifest the jury palpably in sound as the emanation of a twelve-person'd will, something along the lines of Donne's 'three-person'd God'. An egregore, to use the beguiling term strongly featured in the bumf the Rosicrucians sent me in hope of membership fees, an occult entity made up of conjoined streams of thought. I came to love the word 'egregore' though it had a troubling dark colouration when I first became aware of it. Only after a while did I track down the disagreeable association, with Mr McGregor, he who baked Peter's father in a pie in *The Tale of Peter Rabbit*, a stark tale of terror that has somehow failed to make a vegetarian of every single person who has ever read it.

This jury would not make a snap decision based on the assumption that posh people were nice. The justice train would not stop even if the judge stood in front of it waving his address book. This jury would deliberate as tradition demanded.

He waffled on, telling us that we should aspire to unanimity in our verdict. A majority decision, though less desirable, was permissible, but only after we had deliberated for a minimum of two hours. Two hours was not a very long time, little longer than the time required for a football match, but we would find – in the event that we were unable to agree on a verdict – that it passed very slowly. We were entitled to ask the jury bailiff for refreshments on a reasonable scale, but he regretted he was unable to offer us orange quarters at half-time.

Again he hinted – addressing Philip Anthony as our representative – that we need not even retire to consider our verdict. Philip Anthony was as taken aback as I was, as we all must have been, and looked round rather wildly for guidance. This time the reasoning was economic, not based on mobility. The judge explained that it was not always necessary for a jury to retire when the verdict was clear, and of course any saving in court time was a saving on the public purse. This was insult on top of injury, not to mention travesty on top of misrepresentation! After his own praise of the defendant's father, whose fascination with exhumed remains I seemed to be the only one to find sinister, he could only be implying that we didn't need a moment's thought before acquitting Thomasina French.

Reservoirs of trodden foulness

At least when I had been the jury foreman I hadn't been required to speak unprompted, in fact it was rather the other way round, my complaint being that I was merely being called upon to repeat a set formula. Philip Anthony had no script to read from, though in the end he managed to blurt out some sort of response. 'My Lordship Your Honour,' he said, slightly scrambling the approved fawning forms of address, 'we do need to.' He must have realised that the formality of the setting required a fuller expression, and once having started ended up going rather to the other extreme. 'We do need to retire to reach a verdict. To deliberate, to consider the evidence we have heard, to examine the facts and come to our own conclusions.' Those last words may have represented a little flare of protest, a timid defiance of the pressure we were under to acquit Thomasina, unblemished rose of Somerset. Even so, this was not the rôle of jury foreman as he had imagined it, and I'm sure he would have swapped back with me at a moment's notice.

'Very well,' said the judge. 'I'm sure you are all aware of the desirability of a unanimous verdict. In due course you may return a majority verdict, but only after you have tried every avenue that might lead to consensus and have concluded that it is impossible. I will instruct you at a later time if this Court is willing to accept a majority verdict.'

It was Philip Anthony who pushed me to the jury room. In fact as our jury service went on he seemed to gravitate to a position behind the handles of the wheelchair, though whether that made us a graduate élite or a pair of pariahs was anyone's guess. I heard someone behind me say, 'I hope he knows more about law than he does about football. Cambridge haven't a bloody hope.' Sci-Fi Si, I presumed. Knitting Nancy was also unimpressed by the majesty of the legal system, as it was displayed in Cambridge Crown Court. 'They wouldn't last a week in Fulchester, not one of them.' That was her opinion – she didn't care who knew it. 'Honestly . . . they're just not up to snuff.' By this time, I couldn't wait for her to piss off all the way back to her beloved Fulchester, wherever it was on the map that Fulchester might turn out to be.

We were to be left in the jury room essentially to stew in our own juice. The prescribed period of deliberation was a pressure cooker designed to render down our stubborn differences into a meltingly tender mélange of unanimity, like the *bœuf en daube* in *To the Lighthouse*. Under these ideal conditions our verdict would fall off the bones of contention, and justice could be fed and satisfied using only a spoon.

But how I hated the jury room of Cambridge Crown Court! I hated its floor covering in particular – hated it from the moment I set wheels on it. There was certainly dirty work carried out in that chamber while I was there in the course of discharging my civic duty, but the dirty work had started long before and it started at ground level.

Carpet tiles. The words are innocuous in isolation, and even when combined they don't seem so very threatening. The floor of the jury room was covered with carpet tiles of coarse maroon fibre, perhaps fifteen inches square. You didn't need to touch them to know they were synthetic. That message travelled unimpeded up my crutch and my cane to arrive in each lobe of the brain simultaneously. A cringe in living stereo! Carpet tiles were devised to combine the bad points of both carpets and tiles. There is no other way to account for them. Creating a degenerate hybrid must have been the entire objective of the design. Carpets are invariably reservoirs of trodden foulness while tiles abolish the visual unity of flooring. At least proper tiles are securely stuck down – carpet tiles by contrast rest lightly in place (or used to rest, if such things can safely be relegated to the past), held by no adhesive more reliable than lengths of double-sided tape. Over time, inevitably, they have their edges curled up by scuffing feet.

I assume carpet tiles were cheap. Might they actually have been given away? Some things, as everyone knows, are bad value for money even when they cost nothing.

There were two carafes of water on the table, and a dozen glasses that didn't look particularly clean. Timothy told us that he would be outside, and that we should knock on the door if we had reached a verdict or had a reasonable request to make. I'm sorry to say that there was a slight emphasis on 'reasonable'. He would knock in his turn, and enter, after two hours. At that point the judge would appreciate and indeed expect a bulletin on the progress of our deliberations.

Philip Anthony opened his folder of documents as suavely as a government minister consulting his portfolio then let out a sharp squawk of alarm. 'What the hell's this?' he asked, holding up a sheet of paper, some sort of photograph in reproduction. 'Does anyone else have this? This doesn't belong. How did it get in here?'

He waved the sheet around but I couldn't see any detail. Then Nancy spoke up. 'There on the left, that filthy thing – that's a cross-section of a lung from a heavy smoker, a smoker like you . . . Mr

Foreman. And on the right, that's a normal lung. A lung like mine as long as I can breathe fresh air and not have to inhale smoke.'

She had played rather a cruel trick on Philip Anthony – I'd say a neat trick if I hadn't developed a strange solidarity with the man – by slipping some anti-smoking propaganda into his bundle of documents.

'What are you talking about? And how dare you put this nasty picture in with court papers?' *How-dare-you*, though, is one of those slightly treacherous expressions that sound feeble if they aren't delivered with commitment and gusto, and gusto was beyond Philip Anthony's power to muster just then. 'Have you no shame?'

'I've told you often enough. It's not my fault if you don't take it in. I'm a strong supporter of ASH – Action on Smoking and Health.'

Oh, now I get it – not 'a strong supporter of ash'. A strong supporter of *ASH*. By the sound of things an anti-smoking pressure group. News to me, but likely enough. These catchy acronyms, though, they have their disadvantages, don't they? I flatter myself I can detect capital letters when they're used in casual conversation, but a whole word in upper case sometimes slips right past me.

'Every puff you take on those cancer sticks gets you closer to the lung on the left, but I don't see why you should take me with you. Yes, I said "cancer sticks". That's what they are.'

Towards a European gold standard

Disconcertingly Sci-Fi Si chuckled and said, 'Coffin nails – that's what I call them.' I say disconcertingly because, after all, he had been rolling cigarettes on his little machine rather neatly and efficiently throughout the week. He must have been building up a stockpile since his actual consumption was nowhere near as heavy as Philip Anthony's. I hadn't heard the phrase 'cancer sticks' before – perhaps even a coinage by the good people of ASH. 'Coffin nails' was a more established phrase, an example of the gallows humour that goes strangely quiet when the gallows is actually in sight.

'But Nancy,' said Philip Anthony, 'what has that got to do with the jury and what we're here to decide?' Of course you're right, he didn't call her Nancy, he couldn't have because that wasn't her name, but I've forgotten the real one. And yes, I could make one up for more plausibility, but it seems simpler to stick with the one I've made up already.

She didn't back down in the slightest. 'You seem to think it's quite normal expecting me to breathe foul air for a matter of hours in a room whose windows only open a crack.'

ASH hadn't penetrated my consciousness, but then I dare say there would have to be coverage in the *Cambridge Evening News* for that to happen. There were still regular advertisements for cigarettes on those pages, mainly Benson & Hedges. 'A little gold does you credit' was one little slogan, 'Towards a European gold standard' another. All very subtle – tobacco advertising was becoming increasingly cryptic now that the blatant equation of smoking with such things as glamour, pleasure and freedom was being outlawed. Journalistic hypocrisy has no limits but the *Cambridge Evening News*, depending on the advertising budgets of tobacco giants, would tend to put a brake on its coverage of the opposition. It's true that those advertisements included the words 'Every Packet Carries a Government Health Warning', as if this was something to be proud of, an accolade along the lines of the Queen's Award to Industry rather than a legal requirement.

Nancy hardly seemed to be thinking about the case at all. 'Cigarettes cause lung cancer. It's as simple as that. You need your lungs every minute of the day, and cigarettes cause cancer. Look at the packet, there in front of you. What does it say?'

'Well, if I must.' He read it aloud like a dutiful schoolboy. She had touched that nerve. I don't suppose you can become a schoolteacher if the schoolboy inside you is altogether extinct.

'"Warning by HM Government. Smoking can damage your health." It doesn't say anything about cancer,' he said, but the words came out sulkily.

'Cancer is what it means. You must know that. Lung cancer. Cancer-cancer-cancer. You can't ignore it. Smoking leads to cancer, cancer leads to death, cancer leads to lungs like these. Do you really want lungs like the cancer-ridden ones I'm showing you now? Do you have a wife? Do you have children? Do you really not want them to have you around, because a stupid habit has given you a fatal cancer?'

There's no way to reconstruct it, the shock value in that decade of the taboo word that she was wielding like a sledgehammer. Most people were not medically aware, and in a way they took care not to be, though ignorance about medical matters is a luxury no one can afford. They need not know their axilla from their maxilla or their anus from their ulna, but they certainly knew what words they didn't want to hear. It was common practice to keep people in the dark, not to pass on a dark diagnosis – bad enough that they knew they were dying without telling them they had cancer into the bargain. If they couldn't be spared the disease at least they could be spared the word. In this context Nancy's free use of the word 'cancer', 'cancer' repeated and repeated until it spread right through the conversation, was a highly effective shock tactic. It was a battering ram making a dent by dint of repetition even though the target area was reinforced and well defended. I'm confident that there were people who died of cancer in Addenbrooke's that year who heard the word less often from their physicians in the last weeks of their lives than we in the jury room did in the course of that minute and a half.

It was rather pulverising to be on the receiving end of, I have to admit, but I was grateful to Nancy for rooting out a *vasana* – one of the seven billion (or so) deadly habits Hinduism substitutes for the frankly rudimentary seven deadly sins of Christianity.

I had a lot of medical interest and a fair amount of medical knowledge, and I could see that oncology was potentially a rich specialty. What is metastasis, after all, but a cellular *vasana*, the compulsion to repeat without understanding, an inability to do something once and have done with it? Even so I flinched at the repetition of a word that I subconsciously avoided. It was a clear case of *transmission of the culture pattern* – and I found I could think of that hand-me-down phrase of MarkO's with a certain fondness, while free of any compulsion to use it myself except on special occasions.

Even so, Nancy's assault on Philip Anthony's smoking, and his refusal to acknowledge the risks it posed to his health, seemed excessive. Having only two smokers on a jury, or any other group of twelve, was a statistical freak on a par with having ten redheads out of the dozen. It was extraordinary, and it would have been a more logical reaction on Nancy's part to rejoice in the sinners being such a small

485

minority than to push the vice she hated up against the wall. Where it would only ask for a last cigarette anyway.

Pain turned inside out and pushed away

I wanted to return the favour. You pulverise my rut and I pulverise yours. That's fair dos. So I took the opportunity to ask her, in the gentlest possible tones, and relying on the fact that people tend not to find me intimidating, if she herself had lost anyone to cancer. There was certainly anger being directed towards us – and by 'us' I mean Philip Anthony, fully in the firing line, who was getting both barrels, while my exposure was less. I was merely being peppered with buckshot. But it seemed obvious that this anger was no more than pain turned inside out and pushed away from its source. This tender approach didn't work particularly well. 'So you think I need to have "lost" someone,' she said, 'to care about poison in the air? Wanting hospitals not to smell like ashtrays? Anyway, I'm going to sit over here by the window, where the air is a little less stale. You'll have to speak up, I'm afraid, but we must all make sacrifices.'

A deputation of her disciples pulled their chairs over in that direction too, in a strange little tide of secession.

It was highly probable that Nancy's pressure would rebound anyway. All too often nudging and nagging stimulate stubbornness rather than compliance (I speak as someone who has had to rely on nudging and nagging more than most). Philip Anthony would only be put on the defensive, and defensive people build earthworks, thereby turning shallow, effaceable ruts into deep trenches and mighty abutments, even if it means acting against their own long-term interests. He might end up smoking more rather than less. It was highly likely he would cut off his nose to spite his face – admittedly the only form of plastic surgery that can safely be performed at home. I say, that's rather good! I must write that down.

Philip Anthony made a desperate appeal. 'Nancy, I promise I'll look at anything you care to show me after we've reached a verdict. But can we get back to the matter in hand, please? Court time is precious – you heard His Honour say so.'

Nancy gave a sniff but softened slightly. 'I'm listening.'

'One thing we should really discuss is that John and I have a theory about what was really going on in the bookshop that day.'

'Have you indeed? And what's that?' The question was poised somewhere between curiosity and the urge to mock.

'Well, we think – don't we, John? – that the missing witness is the key to the whole affair.' His invoking of my support showed how unsure of himself he actually felt. If he had felt that our reading of the case was likely to be a triumph he would have been that much less willing to share the credit.

'Oh, you mean David Kelly? The boy mentioned in our documents, the one we haven't heard from?'

Philip Anthony was crestfallen, though it should have been reassuring that we had all noticed the same point. Despite our differences we were performing the task civil society asked of us by sifting the evidence.

'That's right. We think that he put her up to it and has now left her in the lurch. John here knows all about organised gangs that steal books for students on demand . . .'

'I wouldn't quite say that . . .'

'. . . and he thinks she may have got mixed up in it and is trying to protect him. Perhaps he's using threats to stop her spilling what she knows.'

'*Of course* she's protecting him! You'd don't need a fancy education to know that, you just need to have eyes in your head. She's sacrificing herself for him, though he doesn't deserve it. She's worth ten of him.'

It took Philip Anthony and me a little moment to absorb what was being said. How close we were in our imaginings, the three of us, and how far apart! Philip Anthony and I felt we had unmasked the ringleader of a seedy racket but Nancy had gone off on a different tack and diagnosed a tragedy of love. Where we saw Fagin she saw Heathcliff. 'You mean . . .?'

'I mean he's probably got a string of girls in his power.'

Perhaps Svengali, then, rather than Heathcliff. I made a mental note that we should ask for a medical report after Miss French was convicted, to see if she had been brainwashed in some way.

'Oh come off it, Nancy. This isn't a woman's magazine story.'

'If you say so. It certainly isn't a boy's adventure – you've been reading too much Sexton Blake. And you're certainly not an expert on the complexities of a woman's heart.'

Pedro the bloodhound, welcome

To my way of thinking the shift in her emphasis from diseased lungs to conflicted heart was rather abrupt. I also thought mentioning Sexton Blake was a low blow, since he was generally acknowledged to be a sort of poor man's Sherlock Holmes. If I had a soft spot for Sexton myself it was only because he didn't just have a companion in the Dr Watson rôle (Tinker), someone handy in a fight though also in charge of the archives, but also a dog. Pedro the bloodhound, welcome – it's hardly a team, crime-fighting or otherwise, without a dog. The times of my life when I haven't had a dog have been almost as much hard work as the times without a mantra.

Take the *vasanas* out of a dog and there's nothing much left, and yet I feel that my love of dogs is not in itself a *vasana* but more in the nature of a mystical insight. If the habit-bound encrusted themselves with more habits would they become free? It can't be that. Maybe dogs are assembled from the *vasana*-trimmings that fall from the reincarnation machine as it churns away, though is loyalty actually a *vasana*? These are deep questions, and dogs probably know as much about it as we do. The root meaning of *vasana* is 'smell', the smell of past lives. Perhaps that's it? Though if dogs are supposed to transcend the tyranny of the nose then karma doesn't seem to have been thought through as a system.

'So, Nancy,' said Philip Anthony, trying for a conciliatory tone, 'how do you make sense of the whole incident?'

'Well, who can say how these things start? But it's a tangled web and no mistake. Didn't you think it was strange that a well-off law student was stealing a law book? Not just any book but a law book?' I hated to admit it, but now that I gave the matter some thought there did seem something overdone about breaking the law by stealing a law book. What was the exact title of the volume? It must be somewhere in our bundle. 'From the beginning it looked more like a dare to me, or else some sort of test of love . . . here you have a well-brought-up girl breaking the rules to show she wasn't a child but a grown woman. But then of course she flubbed it and got spotted by the store detective. After that it became another sort of test: whether she would keep her mouth shut or betray him.'

'Then why did she mention his name at all?' It was Philip Anthony who came out with the words, but he certainly spoke for me, and I don't often say that.

'Well, I can't claim to know everything, but perhaps she was hedging her bets. Waiting till the last moment before she made up her mind. By the way, did you see her peering round the court, looking out for someone she knew?'

'No, I missed that. Did you notice, John?'

'No, I didn't either.'

'That's because she didn't do it. She controlled herself. I'm sure he slipped into the court, that's only human nature, but she didn't let on. She's learning the ways of the world, that one.'

'But that's insane!' This time neither of us voiced the words, though I'm confident that we both thought them.

I don't know whether in the course of his duties at the Perse School Philip Anthony was ever called upon to take assembly, but if not then at least he knew in general terms how it was done. He clapped his hands together to signal his authority and said, 'We must take a tally of votes. John? You first.'

Why me? Why ask me? I havered for about three seconds, but havering is not my forte. 'I say Guilty.'

'And I say Guilty also.' The foreman and I were on the same side, at any rate.

At that first count we were divided six and six, with Sci-Fi Si joining our party, on the root principle, presumably, of teaching toffs a lesson. She was guilty in class terms, a separate matter from personal criminal liability.

Philip Anthony tried to break the deadlock with an appeal to logic. 'A Guilty verdict means we think the defendant stole the book, Not Guilty means she didn't. Can we at least agree on that?'

Nancy almost purred. 'It's not always so black and white, don't you think?'

'It is that black and white! That's what we were sworn in to do. We're to judge the accused by the facts.'

'But you've said yourself that there are things we haven't heard about.'

'That's not under our control. We must simply return a verdict.'

'And my verdict is Not Guilty.'

'But you know quite well she did it.'

'Of course she did it. But she's learned her lesson, hasn't she? She's had the fright of her life and had to dig out that sweet old vicar, who would rather have been anywhere else, as anyone could see.' Personally I thought the old boy was enjoying his day out, but really, who's to say? 'You don't imagine she's going to make a practice of stealing books, do you? Not after this she isn't, I can tell you that.'

'That's still not what we're supposed to decide.'

'You have my answer. Now the ball's in your court. What are you going to do?'

'Try to talk you round,' he said, without enthusiasm for the task ahead, the long haul of persuasion against the odds.

Then he turned to me and asked, 'How long do we have to wait before we can give a majority verdict?' I assume this was a way of thinking out loud, since we had both (and indeed all) been given this information at the same time.

'After two hours we can ask the judge for further instructions.' But we hadn't got a majority verdict yet anyway, not even a simple majority let alone the eleven-to-one or ten-to-two majorities that were required. So that was a fat lot of good. In practice Philip Anthony's idea of talking the opposition round was to push the wheelchair towards someone in Nancy's party and more or less dare them to walk away while he argued the case. I wish he'd asked me before he did that! I'm not fanatically opposed to being used as a pity bludgeon but I do like to be consulted.

It was altogether odd. Some of us wanted her convicted and some wanted her acquitted, but we all thought she had done what she was accused of. Was this really how the legal system was supposed to work?

I suppose it was the wheelchair that licensed the unconventional disposition of the jury in the room assigned to it. We had gone rather open-plan, what with Nancy starting a trend for sitting away from the table and Philip Anthony roving the room on a charm offensive that was significantly short on charm.

Autoglossotomy is a wonderful word

As for the other members of the jury, I realise I haven't even sketched their outlines, but I don't see why I should try to individuate them when they made so little effort in that line themselves. Yes, I'm sure they all had star signs and preferences in crisps, but don't expect too much in the way of detail from me. I remember a green handbag, a grey wool tie and a tatty back number of *Gramophone* magazine, but for all I know these were taken at random out of a prop box when jurors arrived at the Guildhall and returned to the same place at the end of the jury day. There was also a lady's folding umbrella which splashed chilly drops onto the back of my neck one morning – something that might seem to argue against the prop-box hypothesis, except that realistic styles of theatre never know when to stop. There was a student production of Kyd's *The Spanish Tragedy* in my time as an undergraduate that made headlines for all the wrong reasons. Admittedly making headlines in the *Cambridge Evening News* was no great achievement – a letter delivered to Melbourn (Cambs.) after a long detour to Melbourne, Australia, all thanks to the sender inadvertently adding an extra 'e' on the envelope, could and did do the trick.

With Tragedy being a compulsory paper in Part Two of the English tripos, putting on out-of-the-way plays was a canny move, but the director had decided to pull out all the stops for the shocking moment when Hieronimo bites out his own tongue. Autoglossotomy is a wonderful word, but having to explain its meaning every time you use it takes all the fun away.

So he bought a piece of ox tongue and had it pickled so that it would last the length of the run. Unfortunately the pickling affected the texture and one night, flung by the actor with too much brio, it bounced and then landed on the lap of a lady who fell backwards and banged her head. I dare say there's a single word that means falling and banging your head, and I expect it has 'cephalo' somewhere in the middle, but perhaps it's better not to go in search of it. People always say that no one likes a know-it-all, though I have to own up to a certain sneaking affection for the breed.

At the end of two hours Philip Anthony took a second count of our votes. We were now nine who wanted to acquit as against three to convict. As far as winning hearts and minds went, we would have done better to sit quietly with a book, as Sci-Fi Si had done – he was now more than three-quarters of the way through *Dune*. He and I had finally exchanged a few words. I'd asked him what he did for a living and he'd said, 'I'm a hospital porter. I'd offer to give you a push but I'm off the clock.' The remark could be either mean-spirited or rue-fully charming, and even after replaying it in my mind I wasn't sure which it had been.

Philip Anthony produced a bottomless sigh and knocked on the door to signal to Timothy that he should come in. 'How are you get-ting on, sir? And have you reached a unanimous verdict, may I ask?'

'No, we have not. And we haven't even got a majority verdict that's worth its salt. We're deadlocked nine to three.'

'Even if you had, sir, you'd be jumping the gun. Hizonner will ask you to retire for a further period before he will accept a minority verdict. That's what's laid down. Further instructions, yes, but they're always the same further instructions. And you've got a little time in hand. Hizonner hasn't finished with his lunch. I'll let him know you're ready for him then I'll bring you some refreshments.'

Then he came over to me and murmured, 'It's a pretty sorry-looking plate of sandwiches – you'll be better off with a pie. But don't worry. I'll see you right.'

'Whatever you say, Timothy. I'll be guided by you.' My tiffin-wallah was certainly being conscientious.

Nancy made a point of asking him to empty the ashtrays, saying she might not be able to stop certain people from smoking – though then again she might – but she certainly didn't have to share the room with their nasty leavings. Timothy agreed politely.

When Timothy brought the pie I greeted it as an old friend, though nothing so tamasic could possibly qualify as a friend to an enlightened digestive system. 'And this if I'm not mistaken is Taken Sidney . . .'

But then his face fell. 'Taken Sidney? Oh no, sir, you couldn't be more wrong. Taken Sidney! Nothing like. It's Licking a Cheek.'

Timothy was right about the judge's instructions. We were instructed to deliberate all over again, to seek that which could not be found, namely unanimity of opinion. In a way we were all agreed, agreed that Miss French had done what she was accused of, we just didn't agree that this made her guilty. We were unravelling the principle of jury trial thread by thread.

There was a lavatory attached to the jury room, though it had no window. I can't say if this was a peculiarity of the Guildhall or standard practice – I suppose otherwise a jury could be tampered with if there was discreet access from outside, visual or physical. Wads of cash might be thrust through the smallest opening, messages passed even through the glass.

Now Philip Anthony asked me if I wanted to use the lavatory before we took up our deliberations again. I was none too pleased by the slur on my C-value. It wasn't as if I'd been caught short at any point in either trial. Timothy had made himself discreetly available for that purpose, and I suppose the knowledge that assistance was available had an altogether soothing effect on my bladder. You could practically hear it purring.

'I'll just take you to the loo, shall I?' It was obvious that he wanted some sort of discreet pow-wow. Really, there's no upper limit to the time people think is appropriate for me to spend in lavatories, and though this has served my turn any number of times it can occasionally be irksome. 'I'm just taking John to the loo,' he said, making his clandestine purpose even more obvious.

He pushed me into the lavatory, dragging a couple of squares of carpet tile along with us. Then it turned out that the light bulb had blown. Philip Anthony left me there to alert Timothy to the defective amenity. He must have left the door open somewhat, as a compromise between leaving me without privacy or else plunging me into darkness. There was a creaky little extractor fan, so at least I couldn't hear what was being said in the jury room, and if I imagined it was about me then that was a little *vasana* all my own.

The hygroscopic properties of honeycomb confectionery

'I'm sorry, John,' Philip Anthony said when he came back, 'that odd little usher can't find anyone from Maintenance for the moment, so we'll have to manage as best we can. I vote we close the door for privacy. I've got plenty of matches so we won't be completely in the dark. I'd ask the chap who rolls his own if he has a lighter – quite likely, don't you think? – only I wanted you to myself to work out what we're going to do. We need a new approach.

'How about this? We go on arguing for conviction but offer to add a rider recommending clemency.' His eyes flashed wildly in the light of the matches he lit one after another. I don't know if that's normal for a geography teacher seemingly obsessed by a trivial court case and trying to hold on to the empty position of jury foreman. I'd need a larger sample to be sure. Making a judgement on the basis of a single case would be like biting into an atmospherically softened Crunchie and saying, 'Gosh, that's ever so nice' without the slightest whisper of methodology, and with no control Crunchie waiting in the same fridge at the same temperature to make possible at least some rudimentary analysis of results.

'I'm sorry, Philip Anthony, but I don't see that plan working.'

'Won't wash?'

'Won't wash.'

'Expect you're right. I wish you'd call me Philip, by the way.'

'I can't seem to manage it.'

'I'm sorry. I dare say that's my fault.' He may have thought I was using formality to maintain a chilly distance, still bearing a residual grudge about being replaced as jury foreman. At that moment he couldn't have been more wrong. I was happily retired.

We were certainly outclassed as tacticians. We made a rather awkward exit from the lavatory, after Philip Anthony had almost burned his fingers on a match while he turned on the tap in the little sink. This was to suggest that I was washing my hands after having a pee, though if the others in the jury room were even listening they must have known this was the realm of sound effects rather than acts plausibly accomplished with the one-handed help of Philip Anthony in the dark. Then of course the splashing made me wish I had taken that pee after all.

494

When we came back into the main part of the room it was immediately clear that something or everything had changed. The atmosphere was quite different, and not because we were about to be accused of staging a lavatory visit under false pretences. The chairs grouped by the window had been returned to their original placement.

'What's going on?' asked Philip Anthony.

'We're making some changes,' said Nancy. 'You're no longer the foreman, for starters.'

'How's that? What do you mean?'

'We had a vote while the two of you were all hugger-mugger.'

'You can't do that!'

'We recorded you two as voting against the motion – did we get that wrong? Perhaps you agree that things were getting out of hand when you were in charge.'

'But that's not how it works. It can't be!'

'I don't see why not.'

At that moment there was a knock at the door and Timothy slipped in, leading a man with overalls who carried a little step-ladder. This was Maintenance in person, coming to replace the defective bulb.

Philip Anthony appealed to Timothy for guidance, saying, 'This lady tells me that there's been a vote and she's the new foreman . . . that can't be right, surely.'

'I've explained to you, sir, such things are a matter for the jury . . . and the only time a foreman is actually necessary is when you deliver your verdict.'

'But she called a vote while I was still foreman! That should have been my decision.'

'This is entirely a matter for the jury, sir. I won't be inter-fering.' Which may have been a neutral description of the situation, though I thought I could detect an undercurrent of for-God's-sake-don't-drag-me-into-it.

'Well, at least tell me what rules of order are being followed here.'

'Never mind that,' cut in Nancy. 'Usher, will you please take these nasty things away.' She pointed to the ashtrays on the table, both laden with ash, the ceramic one that Philip Anthony had preferred and the tin one that had been left for the use of Sci-Fi Si, though he had shown no sign of minding the class-based distinction implied. 'There'll be no more smoking in this room.'

'That's not for you to say! In any other committee . . .'

Timothy was clearly losing his patience. 'Excuse me, sir, but a jury isn't exactly a committee. And I'll be leaving you to it.' He pointed to the ashtrays and Maintenance duly gathered them up. Timothy as he left sent a reproachful glance my way as if I had been tirelessly fomenting unrest. Was this how I thanked my tiffin-wallah and his tamasic largesse?

'That woman is poison,' muttered Philip Anthony and pulled a chair away from the table and over by the window. He sat there sulking, as if to underline by an exact exchange of positions the neatness of Nancy's coup. Whatever else you could say about her, she was a terrific plotter, almost in the Iago class and quite wasted on so small a stage, able to mount a putsch at a moment's notice.

And there she was, Knitting Nancy, enthroned and formally in charge. Of course it's possible that she had harboured territorial ambitions of that sort from the start, that she had set her cap at the curious position of jury foreman from the moment that the jury summons landed on her doormat. I think it's more likely that an opportunistic impulse was involved. She would never have dared to depose Philip Anthony while he was in the room, rather than the no-man's-land of the lavatory. Unless I'm flattering myself then my presence too would have been a deterrent, if I hadn't been pretending to urinate at the time, in darkness hardly relieved by the flaring of successive matches held aloft in a geography teacher's uncertain hand.

There were three of us at last count who were holding out for a Guilty verdict. As long as we didn't weaken we could at least block a majority vote for acquittal. If we stayed firm for another couple of hours we might achieve the tiny victory of deadlock, with Hizonner having no alternative but to call for a new trial. On the other hand if one of us threw in the towel she would be acquitted ten to two. I didn't know how much resolve to expect from Sci-Fi Si, who had ended up in the odd position of allying himself with the poshest-seeming pair among his fellow jurors, in order to prevent a toff from getting off scot-free.

His production of cigarettes went into an odd overdrive when smoking itself was banned. He seemed perfectly happy to add to his stock without being in any hurry to indulge. If he was addicted to anything then logically it was the habit of rolling, not the habit of smoking. My own family had enjoyed or endured a winemaking phase, inspired it has to be said by me, which might have gone on indefinitely if it wasn't for the piling-up of the end product, which no one wanted to drink. It wasn't that we thought it was bad, but drinking home-made wine was an entirely separate activity, and we never acquired the habit. If some benign creature had poured away the bottles in the night, and washed them up, we would have continued to profit from a project that was of great benefit to the cohesion of the family. It was only with the end product that the problems started.

Nancy carried on implacably with her French knitting, making no attempt to lead discussion of any sort. In the end I couldn't help asking her about it. 'Aren't you going to talk us round?'

'Why bother trying? Everything's been said, hasn't it? I think I'll just wait and see what happens.'

This was plainly a war of nerves, and if there was one person in the room who could be described as 'living on his nerves' it was Philip Anthony.

Clearly he hadn't enjoyed the discovery that a jury foreman could be replaced as easily as a light bulb. Now the spotlight was squarely on him and his tobacco habit. That was the word used at the time, habit, with the graver indictment of addiction being reserved for grander delinquencies.

Nicotine withdrawal has a physiology all its own. He must have wished there was something he could put in his mouth to allay the cravings, something that could go direct into his bloodstream, even, but such things were not thought of. In those days if you decided that smoking was a filthy habit and was 'cutting your wind', or simply costing too much, you were supposed to smoke your last packet and never buy another. Simple as that. Go out with your friends and never think of asking them for a puff on one of theirs.

There is a physiological process involved, a cascade of interlocking neural systems, but people didn't think in those terms at the time. Everyone knew that the only thing necessary was willpower. Character.

'If I'd known there was going to be martial law imposed I'd have had a good old smoke before we came in here. You'd have allowed that, I expect?'

'It's a free country.'

'I wonder sometimes.'

'Don't take your bad temper out on me.'

'It's just I didn't get much sleep last night, and all because of that bloody woman.'

'You mean Miss French? Or do you mean me?'

'Of course I mean her,' he said, almost too fast. 'This is all her fault.'

Philip Anthony was working himself with her assistance into a negative affective state, otherwise known as a tizzy.

'You smoke in front of your pupils, I suppose?'

'Well . . .'

'Not setting much of an example to children who look up to you.'

'Some do, some don't. It isn't a popularity contest.'

Nancy was needling him, baiting him. The physiological effects of withdrawal can hardly have set in so soon after his last nicotine dose, but psychology is different. That was where she put her claws in.

The back number of *The Gramophone* was making the rounds of the group in a desultory way. When it reached Sci-Fi Si he picked it up eagerly enough. I suppose he was hoping that it would fill the looming void left by *Dune*. I wondered if I should tell him that there was a sequel, in case he wanted to stock up on reserves of narrative. He might have time in the next break to nip to the library and borrow *Dune Messiah*, though sequels rarely satisfy.

He was genuinely shocked to open up the magazine and find that there was no coverage on those pages of anything he would call music. He was incredulous, and perhaps he had a right to be – even the *Cambridge Evening News* had its pop pages but *The Gramophone* put its fingers in its ears when it came to young people's music. Sci-Fi Si betrayed his exasperation by the savagely disrespectful way he turned the pages, as if they should by rights be torn clean out if they didn't contain a review of the latest Gentle Giant album, or a list of Gas Works' concert schedule if he had better taste. When he'd finished riffling aggressively through it he dropped it on the floor.

Stiffly Philip Anthony stood up from his chair and approached the table. 'Have you finished reading that?' he asked Sci-Fi Si, pointing at the magazine on the floor.

'What do you think? Help yourself, mate.' Philip Anthony returned to his seat and made great play of reading every article and every advertisement. It's normally only in dentists' waiting rooms that magazines are subjected to such fiercely empty scrutiny, a forcing of concentration that lays down no memory trace.

'So what will it be, gentlemen?' Nancy said at last, sounding for a moment like a pub landlady. 'Does one of you three change his vote and we can all go home, or do you stick to your guns and the judge tells us to wait another two hours? Mr Anthony, you don't look comfortable. Perhaps it's time for a cigarette.'

'I can have one while the judge is getting ready – you must have noticed it takes a few minutes to produce him out of his box. And another one while everyone is getting settled back in here. I'll be fine.'

'And you still say you're not addicted? Smoking does rather seem to rule your life.'

'I enjoy it and it helps me concentrate. Anyway, I'm thinking of cutting down.'

'No time like the present. Skip those two cigarettes, the ones you mentioned, and you'll be off to a flying start.'

'I'll choose my own time, thank you.'

'So you're holding out for Guilty?'

'That's right.'

I couldn't decide whether she really wanted to pressurise him into capitulating, in terms of the case, or had been led astray by sheer enjoyment of the situation.

I would have anticipated Sci-Fi Si being an easier mark than Philip Anthony, but she seemed to have an instinct in such matters.

'And what do you say, Simon?'

'I'll stick with Guilty.'

'Toffs needing to be taught a lesson, is that it?'

'Could be. Maybe I'm enjoying the show.'

'And you, John?'

'Do you need to ask?'

'I think I'm supposed to.'

'I haven't changed my mind.'

So Nancy sent a message to the judge to say we were ready for more of his valuable instructions. She heaved one of her sighs, those hearty lungfuls of disparagement and regret. I couldn't resist saying, 'Don't tell me – this couldn't happen in Fulchester.'

'I should say not. They keep things moving pretty briskly there.' I didn't see how the administration of justice could vary very much from region to region, nor why she should be privy to the fact even if it was, but I didn't ask any questions. Her self-importance was quite ardent enough without me fanning the flames.

A dozen assorted dolts

'Ladies and gentlemen of the jury, have you reached a verdict on which you are all agreed?'

'My Lord, we have not.' Hizonner produced an expression of sourness and surprise, which must have been for show. I can't imagine Timothy hadn't kept him informed.

'And is there a likelihood of your being able to reach such a verdict after further deliberation?'

'I'm afraid not.'

'Then the court is prepared to accept a majority verdict of eleven to one or if need be ten to two. Are you able to deliver such a verdict?'

'Alas no, Your Honour.' Hizonner now treated himself to an expression of scandalised outrage. It conveyed disgust of a developing, unfolding sort. There were stages to it. If his earlier expression had suggested he had put in his mouth something he had been assured was a mint humbug, when it turned out to be an oyster, now he was discovering that it was a bad oyster to boot. How could these dozen assorted dolts plucked from the electoral roll fail to see the shining innocence of Miss French when it leapt to the eye? Who did we think we were? If we were appointed to be judges of the facts then we had been comprehensively waylaid by delusion somewhere along the line.

'Then we must hope that a further period of deliberation will at least produce an acceptable consensus, must we not?'

Philip Anthony was last into the jury room after we had heard Hizonner's latest instructions, and from the time he took he must have smoked at least two cigarettes in a show of defiance. He had regressed from schoolmaster to disobedient sixth-former in a remarkably short time. He slunk in with none of the assurance with which he had begun the week, and it seemed to me that he wasn't keen to meet my eyes. I'm not mad about 'slunk' but 'slinked' is worse, and there's a thunderbolt reserved for me if I ever say 'dove' for 'dived'. Perhaps I should just have said 'sneaked', but 'slink' with its overtones of conspicuous invisibility has all the advantages.

He was becoming bedraggled, somehow, was Philip Anthony, bedraggled on the inside – it's a good thing tweed doesn't moult or his jacket would have been falling off him in clumps. He couldn't settle. He kept looking at his watch, shooting his cuffs with an air of purposefulness that seemed slightly mad in this context, as if hoping it was moving faster than the clock on the wall, which with any luck had actually stopped despite its continued ticking. He fiddled with his cufflinks, then leaned back in a position of exaggerated ease and folded his hands behind his head, but he couldn't maintain the pose for more than a few seconds. It was easy to feel smug about the advantages ankylosis gives me. My body would never let me down like that! It's very good at making sure people don't know my feelings.

Nancy wasn't exactly conciliatory, that wasn't her style, but at this point she didn't try to badger me. If anything she was seductively pragmatic. All she said was, 'Don't you think it's time to stop, John? You've made your point.' People are always telling me I've made my point, which they seem to think is proof positive of an open mind. In fact it's almost guaranteed to mean that someone has decided not to listen. 'Just suppose you wear us all down – and I'm not putting it past you! What sort of sentence is the judge going to give her even if she's convicted? She's not going to suffer, which seems to be what you want. Is it worth making a stand just to make yourself unpopular? Give it some thought, that's all I ask.'

'That's not up to me,' I said. 'I'll vote according to my conscience, thanks all the same.' Then she left me alone, to stew (as she may have thought) in my own juice, though it was Philip Anthony who seemed to be deliquescing into a sort of squirearchical broth.

Then Sci-Fi Si took his turn, lowering his voice so that Nancy was out of earshot. He worked the little cigarette roller tirelessly, even while he was speaking, not quite expert enough to lift his eyes off the mechanism for more than a second or two. 'That old girl's running rings round you, mate.' There was no denying it.

Ordinarily I adored the word 'mate' and wanted nothing more than to find someone to call 'mate' who'd call me 'mate' back, and yes, no doubt there was mating bound up with this matiness. I'd heard the word first on the lips of the ambulance men who had transported me to Bath station on my way to CRX, and it had never quite lost its bloom. But now for a little while I went right off it.

'You're on a hiding to nothing,' said Sci-Fi Si. Another dispiriting phrase, meaning 'you haven't a chance' though I've forgotten how it means that.

He seemed if anything perked up by the situation, gaining energy as Philip Anthony's leaked away. 'You're enjoying this, aren't you?' I asked.

He shrugged and stuck out his tongue to give a flange of paper a precise lick. 'I don't know I'd say that. I've had worse days. I'm sticking with Guilty. I'll give you and Mr Chips some company.' And of course he had his book, even if he was on the last pages, something that always makes me feel a little anxious. Booklessness has always been a terror of mine. In those days I dreamed of carrying a hundred miniaturised volumes around with me so that I could never be caught short, but not everyone feels the same way.

There's a silly little book by Henry James, *The Sacred Fount*, about a house guest who tries to detect sexual entanglements in the weekend house party by trying to spot a man known as a wit who runs out of quips while a woman reputed as dull suddenly shines in repartee. Or a celebrated beauty who seems to be losing her lustre while a very ordinary-looking man is suddenly sleek and commanding. The reason for these changes is that there's a sort of hydraulic process at work in couples, an exchange of qualities, and at the end of the book he gives his hostess the lowdown about who's up whom (if you'll pardon my English). She tells him he is entirely mad. As I say, a very silly book.

But by the rules of *The Sacred Fount* Philip Anthony and Sci-Fi Si were going at it hammer and tongs, one drooping while the other perked up, though I think we can agree it's unlikely.

Every chance of a rosette

Every trade has its tricks, and as an undergraduate I soon learned that basing an argument on an obscure book scored more highly than anything more in the mainstream. *The Spanish Tragedy* scored more highly than *Hamlet*. References to *Felix Holt the Radical* were roughly three times more likely to get a tick in the margin of an essay than those to *Middlemarch*, for instance, irrespective of the quality of your reasoning. Besides, *The Sacred Fount* has so many fewer pages in it than *The Portrait of a Lady*.

Finally Philip Anthony made an approach of his own, giving me a feeble smile and asking if he could take me for a tour of the room. If there was an award at Crufts for Supreme Champion Hangdog he would have every chance of a rosette. At least we didn't have a repetition of the lavatory conference that had gone so badly wrong. He went through the charade of pushing me round the perimeter of the room, stopping in front of pictures hung too high for me to make out what they were. For form's sake I asked him what the pictures were. 'That's a view of the Backs.'

'And this one?'

'That's Castle Hill . . . I'm sorry, John, but I'm throwing in the towel. I'm voting to acquit. We've put up a good fight but there's no point in carrying on indefinitely for no reason. It's shooting my nerves to pieces, and I'm not going to give that ghastly woman the satisfaction of watching me bite my nails for another two hours of waiting, with nothing to show for it.'

Et tu, Philip Anthony? Then fall, Justice, fall Probity, fall the Rule of Law.

'So instead you're going to give her the satisfaction of watching you abandon your principles. But you still think she's guilty?'

'Of course she is. She's a worthless little schemer but someone else will have to give her the comeuppance she so badly needs. It's not our job.'

Obviously it was our job, but I didn't say anything. Let him talk, let him wind himself in knots. This specious acquittal gave him more than enough rope to hang himself with.

'John, are you listening?'

Yes, I was listening, but my mind was also working overtime.

I was properly preoccupied by the betrayals involved, both personal and civic, while also frantically composing an apt pastiche of a couplet from *The Rape of the Lock*. I murmured the lines under my breath for practice, to make sure the scansion passed muster.

'What's that, John?' asked Philip Anthony.

I cleared my throat and repeated my ersatz Pope more audibly. *'The Snobbish Judges Other Toffs Invoke / And Trulls Walk Free That Jury-men May Smoke.'* The 'other toffs' I had in mind were the distinguished archæologists and parish priests who provided the supporting cast of the drama. My couplet wasn't in Pope's league but then it didn't need to be. It would serve. Although this was hardly a comic moment, comedy was what it demanded. The presence of outrage, after all, does not require the absence of wit. Isn't that in fact the principle on which the whole genre of satire is founded?

'Don't be like that, John. Please don't sulk. They were always going to wear us down. It was only ever a matter of time.'

Maybe so, but what sort of excuse was that for giving up the ghost? And I was hardly sulking – I was in mourning for civic trust, morality in public life. As one of two against ten I had felt fortified though hardly optimistic, bolstered by company almost as much as by conviction. Now, as one pitted against eleven, I was faced with a fierce assembly baying to acquit, a lynch mob in reverse ready to spring a scheming minx from jail, pelt her with rose petals and send her laughing on her way.

If the jury had briefly seemed to constitute a twelve-person egregore it had been a momentary alignment, a non-physical entity that lacked staying power. It had dwindled to three dissidents standing up for the jury system and then dissolved like a spoonful of sugar stirred into tea.

Finally I was confronted by something close to Nancy's full firepower, the *Wille zur Macht* masked in the ordinary run of things by dowdy choices in clothing and shoes. It was an alarming experience, though it was also like being court-martialled by a tea cosy, condemned to the electric chair by a box of crystallised fruits.

'So, John, you're in a minority of one,' she said, as if that position held any terrors for me. 'Philip and Simon have both seen sense, not before time. Are we really going to sit here for another couple of hours, or are you going to change your vote? It's really up to you.'

'What does it matter?' asked Philip Anthony. 'You've got your precious majority verdict, haven't you? It's in the bag.'

'But didn't you hear the judge say how much to be preferred a unanimous verdict was? "Much to be preferred", those were his actual words. And there's no reason on earth we can't oblige him.'

I didn't say that I had met worse tyrants than this, that I had been held below the surface of the hydrotherapy pool at CRX by Miss Kruger, that Judy Brisby had force-fed me pilchards and dangled me over a stairwell at the Vulcan School. I didn't even say, 'Do your worst!' as Sexton Blake might have, though it's possible that I thought it.

'Can someone please fetch something from my bag?' The shoulder bag that rarely left my shoulder, mere inches away but easier of access to others than to me. My tone of voice was level, or I imagined it was level, but there was a definite sense of urgency, as if I'd shouted 'Scramble' on an airfield in wartime. Philip Anthony was the first to reach me, and asked me what it was I wanted. 'A book. A paperback book.' He looked disbelieving. What did he think I wanted, smelling salts? He retrieved the book, still seeming rather perturbed.

She knocks George Herbert into a cocked hat!

Why shouldn't I read a book? The business of the jury had boiled down to the marking of time. Direct participation was no longer required. Sci-Fi Si was engrossed in the last pages of *Dune* and, besides, reading no longer seemed the dereliction of duty it had on the Monday. Before the beginning of my jury service I had asked Paula to put a book in the shoulder bag, a light one, something digestible and more importantly easy to carry. A book is a packed lunch for the mind – better yet an eat-as-little-as-you-like buffet equivalent – and I had no doubt that I would have need of nourishment sooner or later.

Now in intellectual terms, and even though this body was weighed down with tamasic stodge, I was starving.

The book was *Speaking of Śiva*. From this distance I can't say for sure that I didn't point it out to Paula, but this may have been the book's second opportunity to push itself forward, to secure my attention at a moment that was both propitious and unpropitious, in the middle of a worldly swirl badly in need of blotting out. Some books don't take no for an answer. I was going to be the centre of attention no matter what, and twiddling my thumbs was an impossibility. I might as well pass the time reading a collection of poems by twelfth-century Hindu mystical revolutionaries.

If someone had taken a photograph of the scene in the jury room, with one person engrossed in a Penguin Classic having a rather specialised appeal while eleven others gaze or stare at him, I feel sure it would warm the cockles of Germano Facetti's heart. I would have liked to hold the book's cover up so that everyone could see Śiva in his dance, but that's not a viable position for me. That's a shame – as a jury we could have voted on whether this is the *Rudra Tandava* or the *Ananda Tandava*, the wild or the gentle cosmic trampling, while Nancy in her invisible microcosmic juggernaut trampled on justice.

Breaking a book's back isn't exactly civilised behaviour, but leaving it unread out of a misplaced qualm is the greater offence against reading. At first I was very conscious of all those eyes trained on me, then I forgot all about them. The book swallowed me whole. People always talk about the blessed Tardis from *Doctor Who*, as if it was somehow remarkable for something to be bigger on the inside than the outside. Have they never opened a book? That's what I'd like to know.

Occasionally Heffers would set aside their standard advertisements in the *Cambridge Evening News* and produce something more ambitious, drawing attention to a particular book. I remember one in particular for *The Great Gatsby* that signed off with the delightful words:

Wrap yourself in blankets of excellent prose at 51 Trumpington Street.
Good night, old sport.

Presumably this was to mark a reissue. There must have been a film version announced – that's how these things work. As for why the 51 Trumpington Street premises were particularly well suited to the book I have no idea. And Gatsby has so many friends already! He hardly needs to fish for more. *Speaking of Śiva*, on the other hand, made no particular splash and could have used a little push to establish it in the mind of the literate public, those lacking the advantage of a personal shop-window-melting annunciation.

What line would I have taken myself, if I'd taken on the job of publicising *Speaking of Śiva*? I wouldn't have wasted my time appealing to specialists or people with a pre-existing interest, I'd stake everything on crossing into new territory. I'd say, 'Undergraduates reading English – are you still writing the same stale old essays about the Metaphysical Poets? Then buy a copy of *Speaking of Śiva* before your supervisor does! Make vibrant connections between cultures and historical periods. Get to know Mahādēviyakka, the Lady Godiva of militant twelfth-century Śaivism, whose love of God makes Donne seem wishy-washy. Professor Knights says she knocks George Herbert into a cocked hat!'

Naturally L. C. Knights, King Edward VII Professor of English Literature, said no such thing, though he might be persuaded to if a pretty girl was sent to interview him on the subject and batted her eyelashes in the appropriate rhythm. Perhaps advertising might have been a good career for me after all. I have the unusual advantage of being uninterested in or unable to use most products on the market, and can observe the mercenary manipulation of appetite from a position close to neutrality.

If these lines had been offered as part of an undergraduate session of Practical Criticism, that Cambridge speciality of specialities:

> Like a silkworm – weaving her house
> with love from her marrow –
> and dying in her body's threads
> winding tight, round and round –

only one student in a hundred would fail to identify them as being by Emily Dickinson, and the one exception would be someone who hadn't read Emily Dickinson. But this is Mahādēviyakka, writing seven hundred years earlier. And yes, I've cheated with the punctuation – those dashes – but punctuation of old texts is always more or less of a cheat, and editors are pedants who take liberties.

I know there's a famous Ramanujan, a mathematician whose theorems were somehow transmitted to him by the Hindu goddess of his locality, but for me only one being bears that name, the A. K. Ramanujan who translated the poetry in *Speaking of Śiva* and wrote its Introduction. Attipate Krishnaswami Ramanujan.

It wasn't just Mahādēviyakka. There was also Basavaṇṇa (with subscript dots hanging under those 'n's, freckles of suspended meaning), founder of the Lingayat sect, whose boldness makes Walt Whitman seem rather a wallflower – 'O lord of the meeting rivers,' as he puts it, 'I'll make wars for you / but I'll be your devotees' bride.'

And how about the ending of poem number 848?

> . . . sir, is it really right to bring out into the open
> the mark on our vitals
> left by our lord's love-play?

Blimey. That's really the only possible response. *Blimey!*

Yes, the devotees are called Lingayats, but don't get too excited. In order to receive Śiva's blessings Lingayats must wear a stone symbol of the Godhead in a silver casket around their necks, but this isn't quite *linga* as in *lingam*, the male organ that features so insistently in the *Kama Sutra*. The *linga* is technically a votary aniconic object and not a sexual symbol, no more than a lens, a prism through which prayer can pass. It's not an object to be venerated in and of itself.

His head became the temple bell

Where to begin, with this world of transgressive devotion? The four poets in the book used a style of verse lyric called the *vacana*, not a rigid form but a short utterance often with the sort of shock value we associate with Zen koans. I know, just when you've got used to *vasana* meaning an inherited habit, the smell clinging to an earlier incarnation, along comes *vacana* to muddy the waters. Each *vacana* poet signed the poem with a ritual formula addressing Śiva – 'O lord of the meeting rivers' for Basavaṇṇa, 'my lord white as jasmine' for Mahādēviyakka.

If these poets were rebels what exactly were they rebelling against? They had the sense of worship gone stale, and temples that had lost their original connection with the human body. The temple-building ritual starts not just with the breaking of ground but with planting a pot of seed. The holy structure is sown, even inseminated, not just built. So when the saint Ghaṇṭākarṇa (the name positively swarms with subscripts) gave himself whole as an offering to Śiva his body became a temple threshold, his limbs the frame of the door, his head the temple bell.

The *vacana* poets in *Speaking of Śiva* turn this logic on its head. If the temple represents a body then the body is already a site of worship and no temple is a devotional requirement. The floor is yours, dear Mr Ramanujan: 'The Virasaiva movement was a social upheaval for and by the poor, the low-caste and the outcaste against the rich and privileged; it was a rising of the unlettered against the literate pundit, flesh and blood against stone.' *Power to the pariahs!* might have been their watchword. Śiva is the supreme god in the poems, destruction taking precedence over mere creation (Brahma's portfolio), let alone maintenance in being, which is Vishnu's. What is being destroyed is the inessential.

I know it's wrong to be interested in writers' lives over and above their work, but there were tantalising biographical hints in the book. Mahādēviyakka may well have been married young, and to an unbeliever, the local chieftain, though as Mr Ramanujan drily puts it, 'some scholars dispute the tainting fact'. Later she wandered restless and god-intoxicated, throwing away both modesty and clothing. She covered herself only in her long tresses – my excuse for the comparison with Godiva.

Mahādēviyakka was both naked and hidden. When challenged about this coy flaunting she compared her hair to the husk of an unripe fruit, not yet ready to fall off. In this duel of words she managed the same feat of exposing and withholding herself simultaneously.

And how about Allama Prabhu, unquestionably a mighty saint? One tradition relates that he was a talented temple drummer, the son of a dance teacher, who fell in love with and married Kāmalate, whose name means 'love's tendril'. I thought at the time that I'd love to be known as love's tendril, and I can't say I've changed my mind.

'John' seems to mean by derivation 'Yahweh is gracious', all very nice but lacking a certain oomph and not exactly exclusive (not that I care about that). In the late Middle Ages the name was given to one out of every five English boys. Twenty per cent of the male population was christened John! You could throw stones at a crowd and be pretty sure of hitting at least one John.

Then Kāmalate was stricken with a fever and died. In his grief Allama wandered like a madman, his memory erased, looking for her wherever he went. One day, sitting in a grove outside a settlement, he scratched idly at the ground with a toenail. He saw something gleaming and unearthed the tip of the golden cupola of a buried temple, protruding from the ground 'like the nipple-peak on the breast of the Goddess of Freedom'. But when he had the place dug out, there was no Kālamate there, just the closed door of a shrine.

Hang on a sec! 'Had the place dug out'! Moments ago he was a crazed amnesiac, now he's directing building operations. All of a sudden madness has fallen from him, his memory has been restored and he is calling out the JCBs, or (to respect the historical context) a few hundred labourers with primitive tools. Of course this is the way time works in parables – and any narrative in which a temple's topmost point appears just below ground level has already left realism of any humdrum sort far behind.

I've shown a consistent preference in the matter of spiritual guidance for the down-to-earth over the flamboyant, for Ramana Maharshi (described by Somerset Maugham as a shrewd old peasant) over Sai Baba, and certainly for Allama Prabhu over the various Siddhis he so sweetly showed up, using his chosen tools in unpredictable combinations: mockery, invective, argument, poetry, loving kindness and sheer presence. Admittedly being down-to-earth is a relative term when you're dealing with mystics, but I know which side my faith is buttered or indeed ghee'd. Allama Prabhu's *ankita* or signature phrase was 'O Lord of Caves', after all. You can't get much more down to earth than a cave. Ramana Maharshi himself spent several years in a cave in Tiruvannamalai, so deeply withdrawn in austere contemplation that he ate only when food was put in his mouth.

On that first encounter with *Speaking of Śiva* I did something I rarely do. I browsed, instead of respecting the integrity of the book's arrangement. I bounced from footnote to text and back again, and everywhere my eye alighted there was intoxicating nectar. In Brother Lawrence I had found the older brother I lacked, in Mahādēviyakka my missing older sister. I found it so much easier to find common ground with Mahādēviyakka than I did with, say, a Jane Austen heroine. Mahādēviyakka struggled with her condition as a body, experiencing rejection, indifference and qualified acceptance in turn, she struggled with being a woman, with a worldly existence tyrannised by social roles, above all with being human but confined to a single place and time. Forgive me for finding Austen's heroines a bit one-dimensional. No offence, Elizabeth Bennet, but your wedding invitation will never have pride of place on my mantlepiece. If it isn't mystical union isn't it just social climbing?

In the period after the sundering, with MarkO's departure, of what was never conjoined, my mood was not an easy thing to characterise. Somewhere between Rilke in his most elated desperation, perhaps – 'Who, if I cried, would hear me among the angelic orders?' – and Brother Lawrence's 'Useless thoughts spoil all.' I have to admit that dear Rainer Maria tends to be a bit pulverising as a source of material for meditation. That's what made *Speaking of Śiva* such a treat, such a banquet of many courses, with enough food left over to fill a multitude of doggy bags.

Mahādēviyakka was as close to me as my jugular vein. Sorry, that's from the Qu'rân. We syncretists are always mixing up our sources, ending up with a swirled spiritual ketchup that sometimes burps messily out of the bottle.

She lit up the Guildhall from within with the sheet lightning of devotion and desire. Why should I be the only one to benefit? An advocate, for example, able to see beyond the confines of English jurisprudence, infused with the deeper understanding I was drawing from the book, could use it to mount a spirited defence of some poor sod up on charges for cottaging: 'My Lord, my client maintains that these spurting acts were analogies of the mystic ascent, mere rehearsals for the bliss of union. He asks for 11,664 other counts of voluptuous devotion to be taken into consideration . . .' 11,664 being 108 multiplied by itself.

The last time I looked into the question, there wasn't whole-hearted agreement about the etymological closeness of 'spurt' to 'spirit'. There were arguments for and against. Personally I haven't the slightest doubt – a spiritual leap is as magnificent an ejaculation as a solar flare, consubstantial with it. Why wouldn't such a truth be woven into the fabric of language? Though I could also derive some pleasure of a sheepish sort from the idea of the two noun roots and overlapping notions becoming surreptitiously intertwined, like strangers' fingers in the back row of a cinema.

Certainly when I held *Speaking of Śiva* in my hands, poetry far spurtier and more rampant in its spirituality than anything I had pre-viously come across, it seemed to me that my transgressive inklings had been altogether too tame. I'd done my best to outrage the decen-cies and fallen far short. My blasphemies had been insipid all along. Holy men, of a particular sect admittedly, had gone much further along that path. That was a good lesson to learn. I should have been much bolder in trusting the link between the knot in my groin and a more generalised impulse to participate in worship. There are worse dowsing rods than the genitals. They may at least show you where to dig. Where to ask the question 'Who is it that asks the question?'

I seem to remember that Doctor Who's Tardis had windows or portholes of some sort, and obviously I was aware at intervals of what was going on in the jury room. I wasn't even the only one reading, until Sci-Fi Si finished *Dune* at last and pushed it away from him.

I was both in the jury room placing myself as a bulwark against a frivolous acquittal and grappling with ideas of a dark mystical melting. I felt I was in two realities at once, and when that happens it's all very distracting and sometimes rather entertaining, but what you're really being told is that neither of these worlds is real. I wasn't far from taking up Alice's cry of 'Why, you're nothing but a pack of cards!', also made in a courtroom of sorts. Alice doesn't follow this insight as far as realis-ing that she too is no more than a playing card, but she's on her way.

The undemanding version of this, hung up in poster form in many a student residence, is the story of the philosopher Chuang Chou dreaming that he was a butterfly and then, when he woke, wondering if he wasn't actually a butterfly dreaming of being a man. The posters stopped short of the next bit of the quotation, where he makes the dubious suggestion that there must be a difference between a man and a butterfly. A difference to whom or what? And just as he was getting so close to the heart of things!

I took one last look at my bundle of documents, for form's sake. It made me look less like a naysayer, a mere malcontent. One detail leaped out at me. Miss French had made off with the second (updated) edition of *Simmons on Criminal Responsibility*. To swipe not just any law book but that particular title seemed bizarre. Could it be that Nancy was right, and that this was a dare rather than a crime as such? Never mind. It was rather late in the day to be prying open a closed mind and pretending that I had been unprejudiced from the start.

By the time the two hours were finally up, Philip Anthony had been pacing back and forth for at least the last thirty minutes. Somehow he managed not to fall foul of the rucked-up edges of carpet tiles, and perhaps that's the esoteric justification for the existence of carpet tiles in the first place, that they make it hard if not impossible to lay down a rut. This is *vasana*-proofing of a humble sort.

It seemed inevitable that Nancy would give me some sort of final telling-off, after the judge had been notified that we had reached a verdict at last. I stand up well to scolding on the whole, having had my fair share.

She started off with an exaggerated sigh, something people do to put on record how patient they've been, usually when they haven't. 'Now that the proceedings have dragged on a lot longer than they needed to, John, I hope at least you're satisfied?'

'More or less, I suppose. I'm not so sure about Lady Justice, but I've done what I can for her.' Nancy gave a sniff, and although this was the season for coughs and sniffles it was clearly a comment made without the use of words rather than a symptom as such. The sigh and the sniff were the orb and sceptre of her pusillanimous dominion.

As we were about to leave that dratted jury room at last I could feel a miniature kerfuffle behind me. It sometimes happens that more than one person wants to push the wheelchair, which is better than having no one do it without being asked. One volunteer is better than two pressed men, as Dad used to say, and a multiplicity of volunteers only consolidates that arithmetic. At the same time, as one of the volunteers was highly likely to be Philip Anthony, trying to make peace with a gesture that I wasn't being given a chance to reject, I had my preferences. I can't always identify the hands that seek to grasp the wheelchair, but this time it was easy enough. I set out to recruit a replacement without voicing an objection. 'Oh Timothy,' I trilled. 'That's so kind of you. You always push me so smoothly. There's never a jolt!'

Despite which, as I was pushed out of the jury room a curled square of carpet tile somehow scuffed itself up and became caught in the axle of the chair. Timothy took a little while to wrestle it free from where it had caught in the spokes. It was as if that chamber of conflict was reluctant to let me leave, or else the wheelchair wanted a souvenir.

I prompted Timothy to park the wheelchair a little distance away from the jury box, and at an angle. This gave me an improved view, and enabled me to see the faces of most of my fellow jurors, but it also pointed up my estrangement from the decision-making process when it was time for the verdict to be delivered. If the judge didn't already suspect the identity of the solitary dissident from the majority I was making it abundantly clear.

I watched Nancy's face when the verdict was delivered, suspecting that she would be sending some sort of message to Miss French. I wasn't disappointed. She telegraphed a complex facial message: first a gracious nod, as if to convey that this exoneration was her personal gift, which wasn't as far from the truth as I would have liked it to be, and then a slight exasperated shake of the head with raised eyebrows. The best transcription I could make of this facial semaphore was 'You silly girl! He's not worthy of you – don't throw your life away.'

Margaret Rutherford does the Twist

But Thomasina French didn't seem grateful for this complex communication. She slid her eyes slyly towards the body of the court. Perhaps Nancy was even right, and Fagin–Heathcliff had come to inspect his pupil's progress.

Did the judge tell us that she was leaving the court without a stain on her character? I can't vouch for it, though it's as much of a set formula as 'you may kiss the bride' at weddings. Oh, and I've just remembered Margaret Rutherford's splendid line in the Miss Marple mystery, where (as I've also remembered) she dances the Twist at the end of the film. The trial where she serves as a juror is at the beginning of the film, it's a sort of prelude. After the event a policeman says to her, with ironical intent, since her intransigence will result in a new trial, 'I gather there was one very stubborn soul on the jury,' and she replies with a lovely innocence, 'Oh no, inspector, I assure you – many more than one.' That was in the days before majority verdicts, those shotgun weddings of justice and expedience, were even permitted. No wonder the system had to be changed, with Margaret Rutherford on the loose. Majority verdicts are sometimes the only way to bring crime and defendant stumbling down the aisle, locked together in a clumsy embrace, towards the signing of the register.

I was both drained and excited by the encounter with Mahādēviyakka and the other *vacana* poets, and merely drained by my dealings with Nancy. I almost fell over as Timothy helped me transfer to the Mini from the wheelchair. 'You won't be long for your bed, will you, sir?' he asked as I started the engine. As I let it warm up, my mind idly tugged at what he had just said. Long for my bed? Long *from* my bed? Longing for my bed. Procrustes' guests were sometimes long for their beds, true, but he soon cut them down to size. This is why the brain needs a mantra! To soothe the Brownian motion of consciousness, the constant tiny adjustments required to constitute a world and keep all the plates spinning. I yawned so deeply I came close to dislocating my jaw.

Timothy cleared away the cordon of traffic cones, and then seemed to remember something all of a sudden. He came over to the Mini and rapped on the window, as if he had an urgent message to pass on. I wound the window down laboriously and he said, 'My wife and I have an understandment. She lives with her sister in Oulton Broad and I don't.' He gave a nod and walked away.

On the Saturday after my week of jury duty I went to Heffers to see if *Dune* was as I remembered it. I could have borrowed the book from a library but this approach was definitely more sociable. By then I was confident that I hadn't got it mixed up with the *Foundation* trilogy. In fact I can't remember a single character or incident from those books, reason enough for their lesser vogue.

515

The shop sign on all Heffers premises (the children's bookshop, the paperback shop) omitted the capital and added an inexplicable colon, so as to produce *heffers:* – I've tried to write it that way out of politeness, but I can't bear it. Politeness can only go so far. The dots were enlarged to form unsightly blobs. The only consolation was the way the 'f's in the font used by Heffers snuggled up to each other, a pair of quietly consenting consonants, voiceless labiodental fricatives whose curves fitted together with the ease of long intimacy. Pixillated late-night revellers passing those shop fronts on their way home might glimpse the compound glyph turn over in its sleep, those two matching allographs moving in lazy elbowing unison to produce momentarily a snoring double 'z'.

It was the first time in all my Heffers visits that I'd asked for a reading in the fiction section, but after all there's no real reason for Poetry to monopolise the fun. It was a day when I was mysteriously confident that I would get my way, though it's also true that the disability makes both instant agreement and alarmed dismissal more likely, with the middle range of response less in evidence. I chose a female assistant for the job, on the basis that she was relatively unlikely to know the book and might have her eyes opened to its merit. The fact that she was young and pretty was strictly speaking irrelevant. I gave her a little pep talk about not being bothered by tricky names, coaching her in the ones I remembered (Bene Gesserit, gom jabbar, Atreides). Poor girl – it was something of an obstacle course, even so. On the first page she had to negotiate 'Muad'Dib' and 'Kwisatz Haderach', but she settled in and her voice gained in confidence. I stopped her after the Reverend Mother tells Paul to take his hand out of the box and shows him that it is undamaged, since the pain was caused by nerve induction. She also says that for some reason she made the test last longer than it should have done, almost as if she wanted him to fail it. No one has ever withstood so much pain.

There was scattered applause from the stacks around us, Saturday-morning customers distracted from their browsing but beguiled just the same. Some of them were keen to know what the book could possibly be, and one bought a copy on the spot. That's fine by me – happy to help literary culture on in any way I can. The assistant who had obliged me by doing the reading processed the sale and then asked, 'Is it all as good as that?'

'Well, no, it isn't, not really,' I said. What was I supposed to say? There's no point in overselling things. It only leads to disappointment. And don't get me wrong, there's plenty to enjoy, what with telepathy, a naturally occurring hallucinogenic drug, colossal worms that dive through sand, but that was the passage that got its hooks into me as a teenager. The special boy, the mother who protects him and exposes him to danger, the pain that cannot and must be mastered – no wonder the passage struck a chord, but everyone at my school must have found something different in the book, their own point of connection, and I suppose that's the trick. One funny thing, though, was that though there was quite a lot in that first chapter about Paul's inculcated mental discipline, with references to lessons like the need to 'strive for flow-permanence within', the idea of making the box of pain the one safe place for him in the whole of the universe wasn't there. Now Maya is a great one for cooking the books, of course, and she changes her story all the time. Even so, perhaps the idea of reversing the perspectives, putting the world in a box and at the same time turning the box into a world, was something I'd come up with all by myself.

While I was there I paid a call on the children's department and had a good look at the cover of the Tintin adventure book *The Shooting Star*. As I had thought, it was a very unconvincing giant mushroom, with patterning on its outsized cap that nature would never consent to. Knitting Nancy's Knitting Nancy, on the other hand (I freely admit that the short-term convenience of a nickname can sow confusion later on), was a much more convincing representation of a real fungus. This was that splendid cosmopolitan mushroom fly agaric or *amanita muscaria* – 'cosmopolitan' meaning only that it grows in a wide variety of locations. I didn't need to toddle across to the religion shelves and find John Allegro's *The Sacred Mushroom and the Cross* to confirm my suspicion that Nancy's nephew was having fun with his tiresome aunt. The book had raised a ruckus on publication by linking the early history of Christianity with fertility cults in the Near East whose rituals made use of the mushroom and its hallucinogenic properties. Nancy hadn't specifically said that she would be spending Christmas with him, but I could only hope that they were, and that he would be preparing a special mushroom gravy. I'd certainly rather join them than spend the time with my own family, though Mum knew that her gravy was one of her secret weapons.

Malabar for the Derby

That week of being a juror was my first experience of a proper work schedule, though it wasn't even a full week and the days were not long. The last time that my time had been so strongly structured I was a schoolboy. Since then I had increasingly been left to my own devices. Unusual pressure calls for unusual release — is that Boyle's Law? Probably not. I'm not good on gases. Normally a visit to Heffers would have been enough of an outing for a Saturday, with or without a command performance of Romantic poetry or classic fantasy prose. As it was, I had an urge to visit Four Lamps though it was only early afternoon and unlikely to be a peak time or anything like. Somehow I was confident that something would happen, or could be made to happen.

There's a famous D. H. Lawrence story about a boy who can predict the results of horse races, not always but sometimes. It's called 'The Rocking-Horse Winner'. Young Paul lashes himself into a frenzy while he rides his rocking-horse in the attic, and sometimes the name of the winning horse comes to him. It's a true vision — when it first happens he doesn't even know anything about which horses are running. It's simply that a name comes to him. He starts to make money, though there's nothing selfish about his motives. It's all done to placate the greedy house in which he lives, which whispers its demands for cash in a voice that no one else can hear, and to make his mother happy. Sometimes the vision is blurred and he gets the result wrong, but sometimes it's unmistakeable, as it is with Malabar for the Derby. It was Malabar to win the Derby and no mistake.

This Saturday felt like a Malabar-for-the-Derby day to me. The correspondence between me and young Paul was tenuous, of course. The wheelchair was consciously designed to minimise rocking, yes, Mayflower House had shown its greed by demanding £12 weekly but its appetite for lucre was static, and nothing that happened at

Four Lamps was likely to please my mother. Nor would I want it to. Nevertheless the feeling of impending certainty was very strong. I had no immediate knowledge of events nor control over them, but the sense that those things would arrive very soon. It was at Four Lamps that this would happen. I was experiencing something like a hunch at one remove, the certainty that soon I would be having a hunch I could rely on absolutely.

The only man in sight was standing still, with his back to the lavatories themselves, something that suggested either great firmness of purpose, in surroundings where people were expected to accomplish their hygienic tasks without pause or detour, or a complete unawareness of where he was, a sort of fugue state. He was tall and lanky, with a big nose, his eyes cast down. He wore dark-blue overalls and the sort of footwear I've heard called monkey boots. I don't know how to explain that working clothes weren't sexy at the time, they were just what people in particular trades wore to work. It so happened that Aldous Huxley was wearing jeans when he made his experiment with mescaline, but corrected the mistake by describing himself as wearing the proper bohemian-intellectual's uniform of a tweed suit when he came to write his adventure up. My fascination with the tight black trousers of waiters was an eccentricity that marked me out, but I would have been mystified if anyone had worn tight black trousers in the hope of being mistaken for a waiter.

Perhaps this was the Malabar that would romp to victory in the Derby, though he seemed oddly absent, not to mention rather spindly for a thoroughbred. Now was the moment to test the theory, and to saddle up the horsey, see if the fetlocks are sound (if that's what you do) or at least determine whether he answered to Speedy Gonzales or Dobbin. No time like the present.

I said, 'I think you should take me home.'

He lifted his head to look at me, slowly and deliberately, as if coming out of a trance or else sinking deeper into one. 'Of course. Do you want to leave now?'

Oh dear, he thought I was asking for help returning to the Mini and Mayflower House. 'I mean you should drive me to your home.'

'Of course. That's what I thought you meant.' The instant agreement to unreasonable demands seemed to show there was a real chance of it being Malabar for the Derby. I might be backing a winner. Still with an odd sort of delay effect, he said, 'I can bring you back here later, if that's all right.'

That was all right and more than all right. As for the madness of letting myself be separated from my car, of trusting my welfare and indeed survival to someone I knew nothing about, well, sane conduct hadn't led me anywhere I much wanted to go despite my having stuck with it for years. It was time to try something else.

'Which is your car?'

'The Mini. Over there.'

I tried to look where he was pointing but couldn't see anything that I would call a Mini. 'That's not a Mini.'

'Mini Clubman Estate, I should have said.'

This eerie lack of resistance or protest made me think I should go further down the path of danger. If the reckless man will persist in his recklessness he will be perfectly safe – really, Blake's visionary aphorisms have a lot to answer for in terms of the behaviour of my generation. 'I won't be needing the wheelchair, thanks. Take it back to my car – the Mini over there.' I didn't say 'the proper Mini'. The *mini* Mini.

'Do you want to give me the keys?'

'No need. It's not locked.'

'But don't you want me to lock it in the boot?'

'No need. It'll be fine. Hurry up.' It was Derby Day, and I was going all in for Malabar.

He propped me up against his alien Mini, so much less compact that the name, I felt, should have been forfeit. When he came back after stowing the wheelchair he helped me into his car in silence and with an extraordinary concentration on my comfort and well-being. This shouldn't be so unusual as to call for comment, but I can't help that. If you're busy talking while you manoeuvre me, so that I wonder how long it's going to be before you bash my feet, you're not likely to get the cream of my attention. 'Now you should get in and drive,' I told him. He made no protest. Perhaps he too was betting on Malabar.

He started the car. I reminded him to put on his seat belt.

'I don't usually.'

'You do today. It's a good habit to get into. Clunk click, every trip.' Sooner or later the government must surely make it compulsory, and it made sense for people to get into the habit of compliance. My Mini wasn't equipped with such newfangled accessories, though it must have been one of the last to be exempt from the requirement. Obediently he clunked and clicked.

'How about you?' he asked.

'I can't.'

'I'll help you – I'll do it for you.'

'That's not what I mean.' It was true that I couldn't fasten a seat belt unaided, but I was talking about something different. 'How is a seat belt supposed to work?'

He seemed confused by such an obvious question. 'Well, it stops you hitting the windscreen.'

'And how does it do that?'

'It . . . sort of holds you across the chest.'

'Agreed. But where does the belt come on me?' On my small body habitus.

He stretched the webbing across experimentally. 'Um . . . your chin, or just below.'

'Meaning that in the event of a crash my body's forward travel will be arrested by my windpipe. No thank you! I'll take my chances. Now drive. But carefully.' We set off.

'Where do you live?'

'Trumpington.'

'Very nice.' It's not always easy to keep the note of royal-family condescension out of your voice at such times, I find. 'And what do you do?'

'I'm a licensed victualler.'

'Delighted to hear it.' I relished the Dickensian word, but really all I meant was that I'd always rather someone was licensed than not. 'But aren't you a bit young to be a licensed victualler?' In reality I had no expectation of the median age in a profession I was only just now hearing about. He was certainly ten years older than me and in a roundabout way I was trying to close the gap.

'It's my uncle's business, but he wants me to take it over. He's got girls.' It was said with the neutral tone of a vet diagnosing worms.

'And you? What do you do?' I appreciated the courtesy of the returned enquiry, when most people could only imagine I spent my time staring at the walls.

Past form as taker of the piss and wind-up merchant

'Me? I'm a graduate member of the University.' He nodded with respect or perhaps inattention. I was continuing my policy of saturating every morphic frequency with this fledgling fact until it took to the air by itself. Perhaps it was working.

He started to speak, in a dreamy tone not fully explained by the need to concentrate on the road while in charge of fragile cargo. 'You might not think it, but being a licensed victualler is a very responsible job. I have a lot of responsibility. I'm always chasing up orders and dealing with breweries and publicans, sometimes it's a real struggle. People say I'm lucky not to have to deal with the public, but I'm not so sure. So in my leisure time I like to let someone else take charge, it's only natural . . . I like to please people.'

'Don't we all!' I said, though peripherally aware that my past form as taker of the piss and wind-up merchant bore witness against me to a certain extent. Sometimes I liked to drive people just a little mad – then, assuming they were still on speaking terms with me . . . *then* I wanted to please them.

'You haven't quite got it. I *really* want to please people. Really. It's what I enjoy. In my spare time, when I don't have to make all the decisions, I really want to please. To let someone else have the wheel. I want someone else to take charge, and I want to please . . . a man.' He seemed to include me in the category of 'man', which isn't always the case. 'One thing, though. Can I use the toilet when we get to my place? I couldn't go when we were at Four Lamps, and I've got a righteous bladderful just now.'

Nobody had ever asked me before whether he was allowed to use the lavatory in his own house, yet it seemed clear that the correct answer was not 'Of course you can use the toilet. In fact I'll be in there with you. You're not the only one with a bladderful, you know!' I needed to say something that played into his idea of what was going on. I was all-powerful, and he was a lower order of being, if not a worm by his own wish then certainly a minion. Powerlessness has its nuances, as I have reason to know. Helplessness is something else again – not much nuance there.

It was as if he was conjuring with his invocations a phantom that could be condensed from the vapours of his fantasy so as to take my place in the passenger seat. ('On' the passenger seat feels more accurate when your bum lacks the flexibility to touch down properly, and even 'on' seems wrong – 'over' is more like it. Don't get me wrong, I've got nothing against my hip replacements, wouldn't be without them, but if your knees remain fixed you'll never really rhyme with the furniture.) And why not? Was it really more unlikely than travelling to India unaccompanied to pay my respects to the holy mountain Arunachala, with no guarantee of a place to sleep, in a venture that seems in retrospect the very definition of the phrase 'on a wing and a prayer'? Was it really more difficult than things I did on a regular basis, such as keeping district nurses away from my toenails and anus with lavish bolts of mental electricity? If this man had cast me in a rôle perhaps he knew what he was doing.

As a child I had once said I wanted to be an actor, and my father, breaking his own typecast rôle of ironised passivity, had defended the suggestion against exasperated opposition from Mum. 'What part could I possibly play?' she wanted to know. 'How about an old lady in an upright wing chair in a corner upstage?' That was Dad's suggestion. Mum thought that this wasn't much of a part, very far from a starring role, but he stuck to his guns, saying that my character could direct operations like a general on a battlefield. 'He gets it from my Aunt Molly, of course,' strategising in his own way by attributing an appetite for drama, which I might seem to share with his mother-in-law, to his side of the family. For a moment or two he revealed the possibility that he was not as unaware of domestic cross-currents as he usually seemed, perhaps took care to seem.

Now I would need to show more than a hint of thespian flair if I was to avoid being left by a bus stop in Trumpington. In fact what I needed was the skill of a director rather than an actor.

'I'm Frank, by the way,' said the man who wanted me to be in control. 'Frank by name . . . and devious by nature.' A very practised way of introducing himself, and I imagine well suited to the opening stages of encounters with strangers. '. . . but you can call me anything you like. And what should I be calling you?'

I'd overheard one of the men at Four Lamps giving a different name every time he was asked to label himself, which I found very exciting. I was sick and tired of hearing everyone wheedle this phantom creature 'John', plastering him with his name from head to toe until he almost recognised himself under that disguise. I too could fly the net of naming. And just wait till it got around that there were two young Mini drivers in wheelchairs haunting the urinaceous bowers of Four Lamps! I ran through a list of suitable names – Charlie, Toby, Luke – then said, 'Dominic. My name is Dominic.' Where had that come from? It absolutely made me homesick for Charlie, Toby and Luke, in fact I wasn't far from being homesick for John. 'But people generally call me—' and then I piled blunder on blunder. 'Om.' I swear I meant to say Dom. That initial consonant just went missing. It evaporated. After his self-realisation Ramana Maharshi never signed himself by his previous name, but only as Om. Did I know that? Of course I knew that! Emulation of the guru can as easily be humility as egotism but I know where the *vasanas* converge, no mere rut but a pothole that the Council never seems to do anything about, it'll break my axle one of these days. I was ashamed of myself, while also knowing that no bad behaviour on my part could coerce my guru or force him out of hiding. I have a certain amount of envy for those whose belief systems allow for the possibility of blasphemy and the punishment it calls forth. So much easier to deal with a vengeful God than a Cheshire Cat.

This dithering wouldn't do. 'But don't call me that either. Don't call me anything.' Even so I realised that this was in the circumstances some way short of a satisfactory answer. 'Just do as you're told.'

The effect was extraordinary, a sort of simultaneous tensing and relaxing plainly visible even at the wheel of a car. Frank tuned in immediately to the current of command that he had invented and apparently needed to submit to. So far the experiment was almost alarmingly successful. It was Malabar by a head, no, by several lengths. Malabar first, the rest of the field nowhere. He was putty in my hands. Strange phrase, and I can't say I've ever handled putty in the first place. So really the only way I can get a grip on the analogy is to reverse it, and to say that having putty in your hands must be like treating a lanky licensed victualler as if he had no rights in his own car. As if his status was lower than a chauffeur's.

The small change of mage and huckster down the ages

'Here's something to think about,' I said. 'Everything is different in your house. It isn't the same place as the one you left. Everything has been turned upside down and inside out. The whole world has been reversed, north and south, east and west.' On second thoughts it would have been better to stick to up and down, since reversing left and right isn't much of a drama, but these were not second thoughts and hardly even first ones, no more than fumbling moves towards a magic trick to be worked without rehearsal. 'What was up is now down, what was ceiling is now floor. The heights have been drowned in the deeps.' The small change of mage and huckster down the ages. I was still in need of warming up, of clearing my throat. Was the attic now the basement? I had no idea, not having entered the premises and not knowing whether they contained either feature.

I didn't need to raise my voice in volume, nor deepen it in pitch. Those were the very things I needed to avoid. The resonances already existed in his head. I only needed to strike the right note, soft as anything, and the response would be waiting. The response was already there.

It was like blowing across the wide lip of a milk bottle to bring out the fruity bass note that it turned out to contain. My brother Peter was far better at holding the bottle, but I was the one who could coax out the note. You're not blowing down the bottle top, you're blowing across it, and gently does it – you don't need to exert yourself too much.

'And forget about your bladder. You don't have needs any more. That's all in the past. You have duties now.' This ridiculous chain of assertions was met with a leisurely expiration of breath, a long sigh of satisfaction. Which was all very well, but he'd still be needing a wee, wouldn't he? I would have to include that factor in any kinky playlet of my devising. Who'd be an improvising actor–manager? If I could bring this unlikely project to some sort of happy conclusion I would expect approaches from the Edinburgh Festival.

'When we arrive, I'll stay in the car until you've made arrangements. Run a bath right away. Not too hot, not too cold.' As if
anybody ever wanted a bath to be anything else – never mind,
the crucial thing was to appear demanding. 'I'll give you eleven
minutes.'

I thought 'eleven minutes' was a nice touch. Had he noticed I wasn't
wearing a watch? Didn't matter. As an undergraduate I had worn a
watch only on special occasions and not at all since then. Watches
aren't much use to the unemployed, not to mention the nascently
unemployable. Still, the notion of precise timing is potent in itself
– even now I like to schedule things by the quarter-hours, making
arrangements for, say, 10.45 or 3.15. It keeps people on their toes. 'Do
you understand? Don't keep me waiting. And I'm not planning to get
cold, so leave the heater on here.'

'I understand.' If he didn't have the nouse to have a wee while he
was running the bath then we were both in trouble. *Entre nous* the
word is supposed to be spelled 'nous', but not under my roof. In my
house it's spelled 'nouse'. We were also in trouble if I didn't come up
with some way of building up a promising situation from the elements to hand, viz. an unfamiliar house and a stranger who seemed to
be a blank canvas yearning for dabs of pigment but presumably had
a definite design in mind. The bathroom when he took me there was
clean, modern and almost fanatically tidy. Steam rose from the bath,
but a small fan mounted in the wall worked to clear it away. There
were towels in two sizes and two shades of blue, with the darker ones
on a towel rail and the paler set on the end of the bath waiting to be
used, next to a matching flannel. Lined up on the bath's edge was a
row of plastic bottles, three of them, green, pink and blue. Bubble
bath! I had to admit he had used his eleven minutes – or however long
it had actually been – well.

'I didn't know which one you'd want.' I indicated the middle bottle and he took off the cap, passing it under my nostrils to release an
agreeably dusty smell of rose. 'That'll do,' I said. He tipped a stream
of viscous liquid into the bath. 'Stop. That's enough.'

'May I help you off with your clothes now?'

'No, you may not. The bath is for you. But first you need to prop
me up – over there, by the towel rail.'

526

In the car, during those eleven minutes, I had considered both of the ways the scene might play out. Him bathing me had any amount of *Arabian Nights* flavour to it, but in the end adding nakedness and the complete helplessness of immersion to the risks I was already running would have taken any possible thrill out of the experience. Any contained body of water bigger than a sink is likely to remind me of the fear I felt in the hydrotherapy pool at CRX. And in fact switching the rôles was perfectly compatible with the psychological drama he seemed so keen on. In this version I was still in charge, inspecting the property on offer to see if it met my standards. 'Take your clothes off.' He did as he was told, but not before he had swapped the towels around so that he wasn't using the ones reserved for a guest. Play-acting had its limits, apparently. People are strange – but we knew that already. Then he stripped efficiently and without hurry, to stand before me in the same blankly expectant pose he had adopted in Four Lamps, loosely upright, eyes cast down at the floor, except that of course he was naked now. 'Get in.'

Again he followed the instruction with a neutral readiness, though he was too tall to be able to stretch out in the bath. Even so he relaxed in the water, as people who haven't been invited as children to contemplate their own drowning at the hands of those charged with their safety and well-being tend to do. He went as far as to duck his head under the surface, raising his knees higher to make the position more comfortable. Such ease is understandable and I bear no grudge, in fact I should point out that I've enjoyed many hundreds of baths without undue tension. It was still a little surprising to me that anyone should feel safe in the water when there's anyone close by, even a person with negligible hurting power.

At my physical peak as I was then, I could manage quite a purposeful traipse around a room, and I undertook one now – I had to get close if I was to have any sort of view, for plausible 'inspecting of the property'. I even managed to hoist the crutch up onto the side of the bath, for use as an improvised probe, though at the cost of knocking the waiting towel onto the floor. He kept his eyes averted, in a way that I was slow to understand didn't represent distaste but exaggerated respect, as if he wasn't allowed to look. In return I was free to examine another man in his physical prime without the usual limitations on my visual appetite, an appetite which under the circumstances remained stubbornly moderate. I wasn't crazed with sensual curiosity about these reddened knees and giant feet. I quite liked the chunky thighs – I can't help assessing strangers on the basis of their ability to carry me up flights of stairs. If we were standing side by side they wouldn't be far from my eye level, not that I am (or would be) complaining.

Constricting preputial hood

I poked dutifully at his groin with the crutch, to see if he was in the mood. He was in the mood. Down there below the waterline it was definitely a case of Up Periscope. 'Soap yourself,' I said, confident that he wouldn't mistake this for an instruction to, for instance, start scrubbing behind his (prominent) ears. Justifiably he took 'self' to mean 'genitals', as it does in the phrases 'touch yourself', 'play with yourself' and so on. Not quite what Ramana Maharshi had in mind when he spoke of self-realisation, but he would certainly have had something fresh and enlightening to say on the subject. Frank shifted his hips from side to side, not with the pleasure I foolishly ascribe to working joints but in something like discomfort.

'Is it all right if I skin my cock?' he asked. I had never heard the phrase and had no idea what it meant. It sounded very unpleasant. There had been no spoken commentary accompanying the acts I had witnessed or participated in at Four Lamps, and when I wasn't directly involved I didn't have much of a view. How to react? The rôle I had been allotted ruled out admissions of ignorance or uncertainty. With great power comes great responsibility, yes, yes, not a new thought but striking home just now with some force. Reluctant permission seemed the best option, so I said grudgingly, 'If you must,' and waited to see what would happen.

With a wince and then a sigh of relief he adjusted his penis, and now I could see what was going on. He had a tight foreskin, a potentially problematic conformation of tissue, so that his arousal had been causing him pain as well as pleasure. Now he was able to ease the foreskin down – perhaps the soap helped? – so that the glans emerged from its constricting preputial hood or cowl. For the first time since

528

we had entered his house he looked straight at me, grinned and said, 'I should have seen to that before I got too excited.' I had become eerily used to the rules by which he played, and this moment of stepping out of character took me by surprise. It was as if a piece of furniture had called me by name. Then he looked down again and everything was as it had been before, though the rocking of his hips in the water was much more relaxed now.

Had I really not seen an uncircumcised male organ before? I hadn't seen many penises in the flesh, and the easily available representations of them (on the walls of Four Lamps, for instance) were designed to inflame rather than instruct. I was aware that there were two factions of male humanity, as it were, and had even heard a pair of jocular terms used to distinguish them. Roundheads and Cavaliers. How had this strange piece of slang come my way? Its origin could only be Jimmy Kettle, a fellow pupil at Vulcan School, older than me and infinitely more sophisticated, not to say cosmopolitan.

I'd become sidetracked, as I watched a licensed victualler play with himself in the bath while an extractor fan purred away, doing its job of sucking away fragrant steam from a well-equipped bathroom. But then from the moment I'd noticed his slight genital anomaly I had lost all erotic concentration. You don't have to have taken the Hippocratic oath as such to feel the need to help a fellow human being, and phimosis as a condition is bound to repay study. What it came down to was that my therapeutic drive was a stronger force than my sexual curiosity, though heaven help me if anyone at CHAPs learned that in my book a diagnosis outranked an orgasm. Even the crutch idly patrolling my host's groin area had more in common with a medical probe than an amorous one. It stirred the waters with no more than a casually titillating intent.

At some point, though, this wayward probe became entangled with the chain attached to the plug, and I accidentally pulled it out. In normal life I could have done a swift U-turn, saying, 'Sorry! That wasn't supposed to happen – can you put it back, please?' Under the special conditions prevailing I would have to find a way forward, dressing accident in the robes of design.

'Stay where you are. Let the water run out.' This was of course one more attempt to buy time, though there was a certain pleasure in watching those bony legs emerge from the dwindling bubbles. If Frank's posture was a little hunched over it was only because he was too big for the bath. There was no sense of his flinching from my gaze, though 'gaze' raises my interest to an exaggerated pitch. It was certainly a privilege for me to witness something mildly unusual, though no more unusual than a flight of birds blown off their usual migratory routes. Once the bathwater had entered its final phase of gurgling he started to shiver. I managed to drag the towel from where it lay on the floor and to push it bit by bit towards a place he could reach, telling him to dry himself. If there was an interior voice telling me how absurd it was for me to be managing the bath time of an able-bodied stranger, given that Cambridge Council didn't expect me to be responsible for my own ablutions, then I made the effort necessary to drown it out.

He stood up and dried himself off thoroughly, paying the proper attention to his genitals and perhaps a little more. I had time to consider the next step in this strange ritual, both improvised and pre-ordained. Someone once said or wrote (Samuel Butler a likely candidate) that living a life was like picking up a violin for the first time and playing a solo in public, having to learn the instrument as you went along. I could feel the force of that analogy, but so far my audience (my audience of one) hadn't booed me off the stage, and I decided to be encouraged by that.

I liked the look of his little pot belly, which had possibilities as a pillow. Even visually it was a relief from the sharp bends and angles of his body. I was about to suggest a change of position that would let me take advantage of this amenity when he swooped down and picked me up, without causing too much discomfort. Gentleness and a decisive approach don't often go together, but I have to give him fair marks for both.

He set me down on a sort of sofa that was all leather and steel and altogether remarkably uncomfortable. I was about to say that I couldn't keep my balance under such conditions when he subsided onto the floor himself, facing me with his legs crossed and wrapping his arms around my knees. 'May I touch your feet?' He was already tugging at my built-up shoes, and I had a right to be nervous since there's a knack to taking them off or putting them on, and clumsy handling is so painful.

I wasn't so sure I could bet on Malabar for the Derby after all — highly fancied on the day, yes, but there are some formidable fences along the way, aren't there? And the going can be tricky. Those shoes were ordinary, in the sense that I wore them every day, and also special, made on a numbered last and conforming to a very individual interpretation of what a foot is or might be. They were made of a cream leather — the idea that you could ask for shoes that weren't made out of another mammal would not have met with much understanding then.

Those shoes were as expensive as any pair that Prince Charles has ever worn, though I wasn't expected to meet the cost myself. A new pair was provided gratis every year. To add to the demands I make on the State I need to have a new last made every few years, since my feet though unmoving are oddly changeable. There seems to be some strange rule in force, dictating that the less you use your feet the more they go their own way.

On this occasion it seemed wiser to accept a little pain than to disrupt the strange rapport. And then he handled my operation of removing my shoes beautifully, showing an intuitive knowledge of the slight degree of rotation needed to slip past consolidated bone without jarring it. I may be making too much of this, and there's certainly such a thing as beginner's luck. Still, there have been many beginners in the business of removing my shoes, ever so many bungling apprentices. No beginner has happened on so much luck, either before or since. Of course I can't discount an element of professional habit. Someone so involved with the drinks trade on a daily basis may have expected everything to behave like a corkscrew until proved otherwise.

At this point in the afternoon, rightly or wrongly, I began to think that in this privileged moment absolutely any risk would come off, and that I could take the most outrageous chances in perfect safety.

I would tower over him. Somehow I would tower over him — I would find a way. And then the guru jumped on the disciple's back, as happens in a Hindu teaching parable, to administer the shock of enlightenment, my mind cleared and I suddenly saw how it might be done. I would tower over him *from below*. I would focus my hypnotic charisma until the gravitationally determined vectors consented to swap places. Reality is suggestible, being no more than a suggestion itself. Essentially this would be a refinement of the up-is-down routine I had tried out before I had even entered the house, but if he hadn't said 'Stuff this for a game of soldiers, mate' then, why would he say it now? Well-adjusted fantasists are capable of some finesse and even practicality in the staging of their dreams.

I'd never seen such a record collection. He had LPs in their hundreds, and a turntable in a casing of grey Perspex on a sort of plinth. I could see that the tone arm was balanced by a little weight at the end of a wire. Is it even still called a tone arm on such a superb hi-fi? Perhaps a sonic gantry of such distinction automatically receives the accolade of a grander name. Underneath was an amplifier, equally sleek, with an array of dials that the reigning boffins of the Cavendish Laboratory itself would not have been ashamed to twiddle with.

I wondered if music would enhance the mood or disrupt it. While I was desperately trying not to dither, which is a form of dithering in itself, he said, 'Would you like some music? Just tell me what you'd like to hear. I've got a bit of everything. You have only to ask. Your wish' – he really did say this – 'is my command.'

Impossible to resist such a challenge. 'All right, then. Max Bygraves' *Greatest Hits. Volume One.* The one with "Gilly Gilly Ossenfeffer Katzenellen Bogen by the Sea".' The Malabar-for-the-Derby feeling was still strong. I didn't even know if such an album existed, let alone whether that particular song appeared on it, but so far this afternoon every time I had pushed against the walls of possibility they had been good enough to recede.

Nor did they stop receding now. It was as if Frank had known what I was going to request – which was absurd, since I'd hardly thought of the song since CRX days, and our silly competitiveness about getting our favourites played on the radio. There was a fervent Rosemary Clooney faction, to be sure, and pockets of devotion to Tommy Steele and Danny Kaye, but in any properly run referendum Max Bygraves would have carried the day, not just in the ward but across the whole hospital, perhaps the whole Home Counties.

Frank went straight to a section of shelving far from the stereo itself and pulled out a record. He slid the inner sleeve from the outer, and then the vinyl disc from the film-lined inner sleeve, with the automatic precision of a surgeon donning gown and gloves before proceeding to theatre. He lifted it on his fingertips and laid it with reverence on the turntable.

The first song can't really have been 'You're a Pink Toothbrush, I'm a Blue Toothbrush', can it? But it was. Part of me just wanted to listen to the song, to wait for the moment that dares to rhyme 'whistle' with 'nylon bristle', but there was a task in hand and it required my attention.

'Lie me down here on the carpet, and mind you make me comfortable – that cushion over there will do.' The carpet was wonderfully thick. Who could have guessed that licensed victuallers lived so well?

I wonder if Frank understood how utterly in his power I was, at the moment when I was preparing to exercise my symbolic ascendancy over him at the maximum voltage. Even when I was in my physical prime, getting up off the floor unaided would have been a major enterprise. It's not everyone who realises the virtual impossibility of my getting up from floor level by myself, but since I can't lie down there in the first place without doing myself a damage, why should they? It's not high on the list of blindnesses that give able-bodied people a bad name.

He was still naked, apart from the towel around his waist. 'Now stand there and I'll tell you what to do. Know your place.' Such a loathsome phrase, the opposite of everything I believe in, but I delivered it with as much bleak authority as I could muster, and there was definite recrudescent stirring under the towel.

I was about to give more specific instructions when it occurred to me that not-quite-clinical phimosis was likely to raise its troublesome head if I didn't make allowances for the not-quite-patient. I had seen a blue tube of balm in the bathroom which would serve my purpose. Is there balm in Gilead? I really couldn't say, but there was certainly balm manufactured by ICI and available from every corner chemist.

'Get the Savlon from the bathroom.' It's hard to make any sentence with 'Savlon' in it sound fierce, but I did my best to mask the tender concern implied. When he came back I said, in the same implacable tone, 'Now I want you to skin your cock. And put some Savlon on it.'

Frank's glans when it emerged from its sheath was shiny and a dark purple until the cream he was applying softened its shade. It wasn't easy to decide what was excitement and what inflammation, but then from a medical point of view these are divergent descriptions rather than separate states. I doubt if he was in active need of the antiseptic agents in Savlon (cetrimide and chlorhexidine gluconate, both of them ICI discoveries), as opposed to the lubricant relief offered by the cream in which they were suspended, but they were doing him no harm.

'Start to play with yourself, and be sure to look up at me while you do it.' *Looking up* in this context being what laymen and gravity would call *looking down*, but we were tinkering with the givens, taking the components apart and reassembling them in a new way. But then it struck me that I was making things altogether too easy. If he had wanted a wank without rules or structure he could have had one at Four Lamps.

I began to wonder if it had been such a good idea to choose Max Bygraves as the musical background to our erotic adventure. Frank almost certainly had the *1812 Overture* in multiple recordings. To me there was no mismatch involved between the sexual scene we were improvising and the simple wish-fulfilment of the songs. Yes, they had nostalgic associations, but innocence is not a particularly strong element in the lives of children who live in a hospital. There the struggles for survival and dominance may be expressed in terms of who must sleep in what was labelled the 'death bed' or whose letter gets published in the *Busy Bee News*, but they are no less intense for that. Conversely there was nothing in my adult world of stubborn longing and no less stubborn sense of connection that had not been there from the beginning, the need to inhabit an Other that was not Other. To my way of thinking, the trysting place Four Lamps on the edge of Midsummer Common and the song 'Gilly Gilly Ossenfeffer Katzenellen Bogen by the Sea', though done by different hands, were both valid sketches of Paradise. But I wondered, in the event that the next song was 'Gilly Gilly Ossenfeffer Katzenellen Bogen by the Sea', whether it would be possible for my new friend, however devious by nature (though Frank by name), to sustain an erection once he heard the children's choir – Max even calls them 'kidlets' as the song begins – that is such a beguiling feature of the song, alternating with the lead vocal in the opening phrases about the tiny house (a tiny house) by a tiny stream (a tiny stream) where a lovely lass had a lovely dream. One more time, though, I was bound by the decisiveness of the rôle I had taken on and debarred from having second thoughts.

Luckily the next track was 'The Ballad of Davy Crockett', sung in a gruffer style and with the carolling children less dominant a presence. 'Stop!' I said, to freeze Frank's strumming hand. It was surprisingly effective. As a bed-bound child I had fantasised about action at a distance and the power it would give me, though at the time it had taken the form of a giant metal ball that I had manœuvred round the room with my mind to general astonishment. This wasn't a bad approximation.

'Wank! . . . Now stop! . . . Now wank!' When I saw his lips draw away from his teeth in discomfort, I would insert another command into the series out of consideration, though consideration was almost a betrayal of the rôle I had taken on. 'Savlon!' I would say, in a softer but still authoritative tone of voice, as if this was the dentist telling a patient to rinse. I would have been happy to play with my new toy indefinitely, but I became aware of a moaning that at first seemed disembodied. I thought that perhaps this was an animal shut in another room, a small dog perhaps longing to join us, but soon it became apparent that, bidden or unbidden, he was coming.

He was reaching his climax, whether I encouraged it, forbade it or pretended it wasn't happening. It made sense to behave as if this was all taking place on my command. Perhaps this is standard procedure on such occasions, in any case, following the golden rule that if a dog comes towards you, then you should whistle for it, and if it starts to run away you should certainly shout, 'Be off with you! Scram!' I said, 'I'm telling you, I'm instructing you, I'm commanding you, I'm ordering you—' but the stream of domination-particles with which I was bombarding him was simply too strong. He was already coming before I could muster that verb in its infinitive form.

His orgasm erupted from under a diffused blob of Savlon, and I suppose the cream he had been applying (not freely but under strict supervision) may have added to the apparent volume of ejaculate, but I'm confident that there was an objective plenty of seminal fluid outflung. In any case the presence of a surrounding layer of emollient was as likely to muffle the explosion as to amplify it. Information on the subject must be available somewhere, in the Akashic Records if there's nothing nearer.

And by this time I think the whole towering-below-him idea had become deeply embedded in what we both experienced. I wouldn't have been surprised if his ejaculate had travelled in any direction whatever, a swarm of human seeds chasing its own tail. All bets were off. It was as likely to fly upwards and splatter on the ceiling as fall anywhere else.

The cosmos breathed peacefully with us for a few moments. Then he said, 'That was *bloody lovely*,' putting on a stylised accent (Welsh, I think) that let him disown the emotion almost before it had been expressed. Then he disappeared. I don't mean that he made any particular effort to disperse himself, he just vanished from my line of sight. It's easily done, especially when I'm lying on the floor. The world is full of magicians, packed with Jeeveses shimmying in and out of the room.

The humming of his realigned chakras

When he came back he brought a flannel with him. I thought he was going to mop up his shed genetic information, which for all I knew might be encrusting my socks, but instead he separated the woebegone velcro flanges of my trousers and started to administer a very expert thank-you wank. The flannel was not too moist and not too dry (it was damp but not wringing wet), neither too hot nor too cold – above blood heat but comfortably so. It was the very face-cloth that Goldilocks would have chosen if she had wandered into the Bears' bathroom. She would have made a beeline for it, for that flannel and no other.

This was the moment that Max and the children's chorus starting singing 'Gilly Gilly Ossenfeffer Katzenellen Bogen by the Sea'. Perhaps the very song Goldilocks would have selected on the Three Bears' jukebox. I soon realised that I was in the hands of an expert. I can't pretend I was able to exercise the discipline on my own account that I had imposed on him. The tiny house, the tiny stream, the lovely lass (who might be a lad), the perfect flannel, the skilful squeeze . . . it all became too much.

As I approached the point when the cell wall of time weakens and allows for a degree of mystical osmosis, when even a spine that lacks movement can feel the tingling of the Kundalini serpent that nests in every pelvis as it prepares to uncoil, he started to give the flannel that he had wrapped round my cock a series of rapid rhythmic squeezes. The mechanism involved must be similar to what happens when a mother, holding the hanky to help a child with a cold to expel nasal mucus, squeezes the wings of its nose while telling the child to blow. Simultaneous pressure from outside and in, the squeezing fingers allied to the expulsion of breath through the nose, results in a thoroughgoing emptying of the congested cavities.

Yet there was virtuosity involved, over and above hydraulic expertise. Frank played an arpeggio counter to the one my sphincter muscle was already busy strumming – with who knows how much help from the pubococcygeus – on the liquid surface of my brain. Perhaps the sensitivity of his own parts made him especially considerate, or perhaps he was just (not a phrase you often hear these days) one of nature's gentlemen. Never in my rich masturbatory existence of rubbing myself against textiles had I experienced frenular excitation at such a pitch. Of course it's a place, just near the tip of the penis, where the nerve endings are packed in as tightly as wires in a telephone exchange, as tightly as sardines oiled in a tin of pleasure. The difference in the sensation I experienced was not a matter of the contrast between the loose damp weave of a wrung-out flannel and the closely massed threads of a sheet, though of course the flannel was significantly nubblier and more ruckled. It was all in the fingerwork. The pulsations that were induced by it interrupted and intensified each other to produce a syncopated ecstasy. How do people learn such things?

The experience of timelessness, the moments both stretched and compacted, didn't exactly last long. Timelessness doesn't work like that. I wouldn't have been surprised if my backed-up semen had exploded like my favourite part of a firework display, the whizzing and screaming of girandoles and tourbillons as they fly off in peripheral zigzags – but of course he kept the flannel where it was, to catch and quench in terrycloth the last concatenated sparks. The sensation was so delicious, in fact so bloody lovely, that for a moment or two that afternoon I was almost tempted to believe in the reality of the body.

537

For a while we just lay there, or rather I lay and he crouched between my legs, as our sighs of repletion overlapped and then, pleasingly, began to synchronise with each other. I wondered how best to suggest the requisitioning of his little pot belly for me to lie my head on. Not for the night, I wouldn't want that, just for a little while, so as to eavesdrop on the humming of his realigned chakras and also, it has to be said, to experience the luxury of a pillow that doubled as a hot water bottle.

Then Frank gave an artificial chuckle, a ruse not so different from his adoption of a Welsh accent earlier on, another way of brushing off the intensities that had passed so cracklingly between us. 'It's all just a bit of fun,' he said. 'I don't take it too seriously.' It seemed to me that he took his specialised form of pleasure very seriously indeed. It was profoundly embedded in his nature. Magnus Hirschfeld would have milked him for a whole chapter, and the *Kama Sutra* itself might make room for a discreet supplement in honour of his discoveries. Frank may not have expected me to believe his disclaimer – the underlying reason for diminishing the significance of our strange encounter was that he wanted me to keep quiet about it. Who did he imagine I would tell? Our MP? Mrs Baine?

I've had plenty of foreplay in my time – I think it still counts as foreplay even when there's no actual play to follow, don't you? I can manage very well on a snack selection from the sensual buffet. But I sometimes feel I've been cheated of afterglow, and there was no reason why we shouldn't have got all nicely post-coital on this special occasion.

I was disappointed that Frank had retreated from the intimacy that between us we had created. It felt like a missed opportunity, especially as the last song on the record was 'When You Come to the End of a Lollipop'. I would have liked to exchange a smile with him at the line in the song that describes how it feels when the pleasure is over (your heart going 'plop') since we knew so much better. There was no doubt in my mind that Max Bygraves blessed the doings of all his listeners, kidlets of every age – the ones singing on the records must be older than me by this time, after all, and misbehaving in their chosen ways.

It was time to resume our lesser selves. 'These are *advaita* shoes,' I said, knowing perfectly well that this could mean nothing to him. *Advaita* meaning non-duality, pure consciousness not subscribing to the apparent forms.

'What that means is . . . turn inward.' Turn inward, ask, 'Who am I?' and realise yourself.

Gravely he nodded and repeated what I had said. 'Turn inward.' Of course the spiritual lesson is only there when you're putting my shoes on, not when you're taking them off, but everything can't be a parable or we'd all drown in an overflow of meaning.

He was as good at putting my shoes on as he had been at taking them off. Malabar had won the Derby by any number of lengths and was taking a well-rewarded stroll in the winners' paddock.

'What's your tipple?' he asked. 'What is it you like to drink? I want to give you something to remember me by.' It didn't seem likely that I'd forget the afternoon one way or another, with or without the reward he promised.

'I like the odd half of beer. Abbot Ale, Tolly.'

'Not sure I can help you there. A keg wouldn't be much use to you, would it? I don't think so.' He was right there. 'I could phone around and get you set up with a barrel, I suppose, worse comes to worse. I'm sure I'll think of something. You won't go home empty-handed. But I can certainly get you a discount. I can save you a packet of money.' This was to assume that expenditure on drink was a significant part of my weekly budget, which it wasn't.

By this time I had twigged what 'licensed victualler' really meant – he supplied the pub trade. So what he was offering wasn't exactly a full range of groceries, which might have been useful, tinned goods to tide me over between visits from the home help (so long as the home help opened them). He only handled the sort of victuals that come in boctuals. Not at all what was on my regular shopping list. I'm not immune to the siren song of the bargain, far from it, but in those days I had to be practical and avoid the temptations of hoarding. Did I really want to share a very limited living space cheek by jowl with hogsheads and magnums?

After he had deposited me in the passenger seat of his Mini Clubman he opened the back and loaded something substantial in there. And when we got back to Four Lamps he set about a double unloading, with great expertise I have to say, first of me into the front seat of my own Mini and then of three large boxes into the back seat. 'You don't have to give me anything,' I said, almost pleading,

539

unable to keep it out of my mind that I would need help unloading at the other end.

'It's my pleasure.' The word itself had a disarming effect. If he wanted to give me a present I could hardly say no. When had I last experienced such a brute onrush of pleasure as the one that had derailed me earlier? If anything I should have given him a gift, but what and how?

When I got back to Mayflower House I was planning to leave the boxes where they were. Paula could bring them in on her next visit. But I had underestimated the acuity of Mrs Baine's concierge nostrils – somehow she had sensed the whiff of novelty, perhaps even the change in me. I can't state as a fact that the Kundalini serpent had uncoiled its whole length that afternoon, thrusting ecstatically through my pineal gland and drenching me with soul nectar from the fourth chakra down, but I wouldn't rule it out, and perhaps she was sensitised to such things by loneliness, frustration or just possibly a recent chakric drenching of her own. It doesn't do to discount unlikely events, and perhaps it was Derby Day across the board.

There was definitely a spring in her step. In a way that was anything but characteristic she came out and asked if she could help me with anything, and it seemed churlish not to let her undertake some light portering duties. I can see the attraction of her job myself, the constant licensed trespass into other lives and privacies.

'What's in the boxes, may I ask, Mr Cromer?'

'Of course you may ask, Mrs Baine. What does it say on them?'

'Well, on this one it says Cheese and Onion Crisps.'

'Then I dare say it contains cheese and onion crisps. And the others?'

'Gordon's Gin.'

'Then I expect that's gin.'

'Don't you know? Where did you buy all this stuff?'

'I didn't. I was given it. For services rendered. So I don't know what's inside. But the boxes don't look as if they've been tampered with, do they? So I expect it's crisps and gin.' It wasn't hard to sound offhand about the packages Mrs Baine had toted in. Frank was following his own logic of largesse, and I couldn't physically stop him from acting on it.

Perhaps I should have told her that this consignment of spirits and nibbles constituted the wages of sin. I was reaping the rewards of a life of vice and these were the immoral earnings I had racked up. I had sold my body or my commanding mind for a mess of liquor and snacks, and at a good rate of exchange since I had been paid in pleasure too.

There was undoubtedly a girlish element manifesting itself in Mrs Baine, not normally a part of her repertoire. 'Well, all I can say is – if you're having a party, do try to keep the noise down . . . unless you invite me, of course.' And after all, she knew the tiny size of the flat. It was congested by a single visitor, and high volumes on the Hacker made the little fridge buzz alarmingly, as if it had been a loudspeaker in a previous life and couldn't stop itself joining in.

Mrs Baine was all for opening the boxes right away. Her curiosity was a raging beast and she offered to fetch a knife to end the suspense. I managed to hold her off, and in due course it was Paula who had the privilege of revealing my booty, if privilege it was and if booty it was. Why am I pretending there wasn't a certain thrill to be had from the opening of the box? A little bit of Christmas-morning anticipation. As to whether a premature Santa would decide I was a good little boy or a bad one, that was hardly for me to say.

The jumbo box of crisps contained no surprises, unless perhaps a bag of ready salted had infiltrated the cheese-and-onion packets somewhere below the top layer. Paula and I shared a packet on the spot, unequally, and I have to say that I was already tired of the flavour by the time I had finished my little portion. After that there were only fifty-nine left to dispose of. Crisp-crumbs lurked in my substandard beard to remind me at intervals of their presence, both savoury and unsavoury, for the rest of the day.

The boxes of gin were altogether more thrilling.

Frank had given me the Gordon's gin in tiny little bottles. Miniatures! Was this a comment on the good and potent things that come in small packages? I didn't care. There were four dozen of them in each box. To spell it out, that's 50 millilitres multiplied by ninety-six, or a little under five litres. Somewhat more than a gallon in imperial measure, and 40° proof.

Paula was giggling as she took them from the box and created a parapet of green glass on the countertop, then a phalanx and finally a sort of rampart. We sang 'Ninety-Six Green Bottles A-Hanging on the Wall', but only a snatch of it, otherwise we'd have been there all day.

What with the miniatures of Gordon's gin and the catering drum of Gold Blend, and the extra-long matches from Bacon's that were my inheritance from Bernardette, my kingdom was combining elements of Lilliput and Brobdingnag in a way that I found very pleasing. I tried to convey this to Paula without being either horribly highbrow or patronising, saying, 'It's funny, some of my things are tiny and some are enormous, it's like . . .' and before I could go on any further she said, 'It's like *Gulliver's Travels*, isn't it? Giants and tiny people.' Which didn't follow in any obvious way from what I had said. She was washing up at the time, and I couldn't see her face, but just for a moment we were our own little egregore of perfect mental unity. I can't test the French saying about no man being a hero to his valet, but it almost certainly applies to home helps. Either way, there was nothing to stop me idolising her just a little. This exchange made my attempts at telepathy with MarkO seem very approximate, and if she had glanced at my face just then she would have seen that I loved her.

The array of little green bottles stood as memorial to a triumphant episode. If the 1970s had a more magnificent emission in store for me than the one effected by a licensed victualler's flannel then I was entering my prime as a sexual adventurer and this would be my favourite decade. There was a break in the clouds of the Kali Yuga, the dark ages which according to Hindu cosmology will last for 157 million days in total, though we've barely got started and it's probably best not to keep count.

Not everything is a parable, true, and it's not every story that points a moral. But if there was anything to learn from this delightful episode, it was perhaps that despite what most people thought, despite what I thought myself, I didn't actually enjoy getting my own way. Being in charge is a chore and a bore. Or perhaps the lesson was that I only really enjoyed getting my way if it didn't happen too easily. I had an appetite not just for token resistance but the real substantial thing.

I saw Frank a couple of times after that at Four Lamps, adopting the same position, both upright and somehow hunched, his eyes downcast, like a battery-powered toy waiting for someone to switch it on. He didn't acknowledge me. Of course it's possible that he winked at me when I had moved just too far to catch it. Fat lot of good that is! I'm ready to believe that light can bend round corners, but I know for a fact that a wink can't. Connivance and complicity, though their ends be devious, move in lines that are straight enough.

I'll be the First to Roast

I went back to the Guildhall the Monday after my adventure with Frank, somehow having managed to forget that we jurors had not only been disempanelled as a group but discharged as individuals. Our official term of duty was two weeks but we had been honourably discharged after only one of them. Timothy the jury bailiff broke the news as gently as he could that I was no longer officially a judge of the facts, though of course we all judge facts in a private capacity day in and day out. I could read real compassion in his eyes, and I began to think that his motive in trying to discourage me from jury service the previous week had not been the prejudice against disability that I had assumed. It seems pretty clear that administering the Queen's justice can be an addictive business, and perhaps from long experience he could spot the susceptible ones, those with a lowered resistance to its effects. It would be years, perhaps many of them, before I could qualify for a second dose of the drug.

I started to think that serving on a jury shouldn't just be a civic duty, a fixed tax on the time and decision-making powers of the populace, but a proper job. It was one I felt I could do and do well, on a full-time basis. I had leisure, I could follow argument, I enjoyed the pageantry of the court without being intimidated by it, and I was on the side of the weak against the strong, being weak myself. But perhaps this was only the reasoning of an addict unwilling to contemplate the giving up of his habit, desperate instead to ensure continuity of supply.

One early evening in November I was startled by a sharp report not far off, immediately followed by a cry. I hadn't been asleep, though not in any very advanced state of awareness, and my heart lurched so much that for a few moments I thought I was the one who had been shot. I hesitated to call 999, but only for a moment. It seemed to me that access to a telephone was not just a privilege but a responsibility. How would I feel if I learned that someone had bled to death only a hundred yards away from me? That I had heard the fatal shot and done nothing to alert the authorities? I remember that it was hard work getting the number dialled, dragging the finger-wheel of my telephone set round through more than 300°. It required exactly the sort of effort that is more or less beyond me, a surge of purpose, elbow- and shoulder-powered, and I had to make several attempts before I managed to string those three 9s together. Of course I used a pencil, but even so it kept slipping out of the 9 hole, so that I had to start all over again.

I understand the arguments against the choice of 111 as the emergency number, and the likelihood that toddlers experimenting in imitation of their parents would paralyse the switchboards of the nation, but you have to factor into the calculation the critical seconds that may be lost, the agonising wait for the rasping finger-wheel to return three times to its starting position before a cry for help can reach an ear that might be able to do something about it. I was determined to see the task through, knowing that someone's life might depend on it. Did I consider the possibility of serving up an actual item to the *Cambridge Evening News*, a headline that earned its keep? Not really.

The laborious process of composing the number took more time than the wait for an operator to answer the call. 'What service, please?' said the voice. It seemed obvious that what was wanted was a police car with doctors in it too, or an ambulance containing some constables, but in the end I just said, 'Police, please. Someone's been shot. I heard it.'

I gave the address of Mayflower House and said the police should meet me at the emergency assembly point.

'And where's that? Where's the assembly point?'

I suppose I shouldn't have been surprised that the operator didn't know, though isn't it exactly the sort of information the emergency services should have on hand? I had familiarised myself with the details of fire drill more or less the day I took up residence in Mayflower House, as everyone should. There's no excuse for being unprepared.

'It's the car park.' It's usually the car park.

I had my own personal drill prepared in the event of a fire in Mayflower House, which was to shout, 'Help! Disabled person trapped inside!' as loud as I could. An emergency by definition is a moment when people think only about themselves, and I wasn't going to be any different. I would shout out my message at ten-second intervals for two minutes, then abbreviate it for greater impact and to save breath, shouting out instead, 'Help! Trapped cripple!' Self-respect could wait until I had been assisted to safety, wrapped in a blanket and given a little tot of brandy. I wouldn't drink the whole tot. With a small body habitus the line between medicinal application and wallowing in spirits is easily crossed.

It's the continence question, the C-rating, arising in a different form, isn't it? I'm not inherently more combustible than anyone else, but have a lesser ability to outrun flame (and anything else). If you want me evacuated you'd better lend a hand.

I have a marked aversion to the idea of burning alive, which suggests I've been on the receiving end of the process in a number of previous lives. I certainly felt a grievous solidarity with the widow in a top-floor council flat – '"I'll be the First to Roast" she says' – whose plight was made public by the *Cambridge Evening News*. Her only escape route was through the flat below, by way of a trapdoor concealed under a mat in her kitchen.

For years I would insist on seeing the instructions for fire drill in more or less every public building I entered. If the information was uncomfortably high on the wall then I would ask for it to be read aloud to me. There's nothing selfish about that, since the safety of all depends on the vigilance of each, and the instructions (when you could find them) invariably stressed the importance of knowing what to do, even if I seemed to be the only one taking my duties seriously. Supermarkets were often the least obliging, which I found strange. If I was incinerated in the disabled toilet (assuming the supermarket had the good manners to offer that amenity) just because the fire precautions hadn't been properly formulated or adequately observed, and no one had thought to check on me – my cries perhaps muffled by a no-expenses-spared approach to lavatory soundproofing – then it wouldn't look good for that year's dividend, would it?

It's possible that in those days I was a little bit obsessed. I couldn't pass an extinguisher without checking when it had last been inspected and last tested. Was it suitable for all types of fire? There's no point in pinpointing the weaknesses of a building's defences just as your hair starts to smoulder – it needs to be done in plenty of time or not at all. Nowadays I'm more relaxed, and though cremation is in my calendar I hope to see my fair share of the presence and action of flame before it happens.

I hadn't made it as far as the car park by the time the police arrived, though I had got as far as the lobby. There were two of them, though one of them was twice the size of the other, a real man-mountain. I had heard no siren, but reasoned that such things are only called for when there is a lot of congestion. 'Good evening, sir,' said the older one, who had a little grey moustache I thought very suitable. 'Shall we sit down in your room and talk about what you heard?'

I thought this was a mad suggestion. You don't call 999 in order to have a chinwag – it's life or death. Isn't that the whole idea, the whole justification of the system? 'Officer, we need to keep moving,' I said. 'There's no time to lose. I think it would be best, Sergeant, if your constable here carries me to the car. Perhaps you'll be kind enough to take my crutch and cane.' I caught an expression of dismay on the constable's face, but I don't let little things like that stand in my way. 'It's an emergency, Constable – that's why you're here.' I didn't exactly drop the crutch and cane for the sergeant to retrieve, nor let myself topple into the constable's arms. Luckily such desperate measures weren't called for in the end. And why should they be? These were public servants. There should be no need to blackmail them into taking action by asking how they would feel if it was their sister lying out there bleeding, dead or dying. For some reason I thought the victim was a woman. I could almost see her face.

Yet even when we were in the car there seemed to be delays. The sergeant made no move to turn the engine on. In the meantime I explained to the constable that he would need to prop me up if I was to see anything much out of the windows, and in the end we snuggled up pretty comfortably. I could imagine melting into the side of this mountain, just as the goddess Parvati melted into the holy mountain Arunachala, leaving her outline etched in bliss. The sergeant said, 'Now about this noise . . . Constable, do you have your notebook to hand?'

546

The constable squirmed against me to retrieve it from his pocket. 'Sarge, we may as well drive around a bit, eh? Let our friend John here see what he can see.'

'He's not likely to see anything much, though, is he? That's what I'm trying to establish.' Even so he started the engine and we pulled away. At this point I can't say I was impressed with modern police practices. Dixon of Dock Green would have torn them off a strip in a fatherly sort of way, for wasting time and for disrespect to the tax-payer. 'Our friend John' indeed! I'm your employer. He wasn't in a position to know that my tax record at this point was a field of virgin snow without a fiscal footprint on it anywhere.

We had only gone a few hundred yards before the fatherly sergeant pulled over and turned the engine off. 'Now, sir, about this report you heard. This detonation.' His voice was still fatherly, but I suppose it was more like a real father than a fantasy one. This was someone who might put you across his knee and give you what for, though I dare say people fantasise about that also.

'Yes,' I said timidly, though still a little thrilled.

'How did you know it was a shot from a gun?' It sounded like the shots on television programmes, that's how. This didn't seem the right answer to give, though the reason wasn't clear. Were citizens really not supposed to raise the alarm unless they had wide previous experience of gunfire and could vouch for it authoritatively, perhaps identifying its calibre by acoustic comparison?

'It had the right . . .' I searched for the word, 'timbre.'

'And can you hear anything now?'

'Um . . . yes.'

'Perhaps I can ask you to describe what you hear.'

'Reports. Detonations. Lots of them.'

'I see, sir. Are they like what you heard earlier?'

'Not really. There was just one, and it was . . . deeper.'

'And who do you think is causing all these detonations?'

'Um . . . the IRA?' It was the best explanation I could come up with at short notice.

'Now, let's see, sir. What day is it?'

'Monday.'

'What month?'

'November.'

'And what day of the month?'

'Let me see. The fourth?'

'Yesterday was the fourth, as a matter of fact. Today is the fifth. Does that tell you anything, sir?'

As the sentences unwound I began to realise just how badly off the mark I had been, and I started to shiver. 'I'm getting rather cold, gentlemen. My disability makes it hard for me to maintain my body temperature.' I always know I'm on the ropes when I mention disability. 'Could we turn on the heater please?' In fact animal heat was coming off the constable in glorious waves that no mere heater could hope to match.

There was some justification for my mistake. No law prohibited the letting-off of fireworks before the 5th of November – it wasn't like shooting red grouse on the 11th of August, if opening fire on blameless specimens of *Lagopus lagopus scotica* is still a cult activity – there wasn't even a bye-law, but in those days it didn't occur to people that possession of a rocket and a box of matches at roughly the right time of year was all that was needed to summon up the incendiary spirit of Guy Fawkes. I'm not saying that a few children didn't wave sparklers in the privacy of their back gardens on the evening of November 4th 1973, but there was no general conflagration. People didn't jump the gun, and the truce in the sky held good until the sun went down on the 5th.

My amnesia was also obviously driven by the fact that Firework Night was the only festival the Cromer family did well. In my mind I had pulled the plug on celebrations nationwide. If I wasn't going to mark the occasion then neither was anyone else. I had abolished it mentally, and then lacked the means to interpret the sharp and sudden noises that mysteriously survived my silent embargo.

I decided to shift my ground. 'I wonder . . . if someone was taking advantage of a noisy evening, this particular noisy evening, to settle some sort of gangland score with . . . *gunplay*, and someone phoned in to report it, only the call wasn't taken seriously, then I suppose it wouldn't look good from your point of view, would it?' I hadn't changed my mind about the victim being a woman, but there are such things as tactics.

The only answer was a sigh. 'Tell you what we'll do, sir. We'll go for a little drive hereabouts and see what we can see. We'll roll the windows down, in case you hear another bit of gunplay, as you put it. Then we can pinpoint where it's coming from. And my constable here will give you his tunic to keep you warm, won't you, Constable?'

The constable lifted me from my position (I was trying to migrate into his lap with pure unaided willpower) and wedged me against the back seat while he left the car and took off his tunic. His superior murmured, 'Doesn't feel the cold, lucky sod. Big strong chap, he is, wins cups for putting the shot. Practises with cannonballs. In training for the Commonwealth Games.' As this enormous man impassively took off his tunic, his superior asked softly, 'How much would you say he weighs, at a guess?'

I tried to answer sensibly. 'Thirteen stone?' It seemed an enormous amount. Could the earth's crust withstand such a load?

'Not even close. Seventeen and a half. None of it fat, mind you.'

'No, I can see that.' The constable tucked his tunic round me and we set off. The car was well and smoothly driven, yet I found myself toppling over softly time after time towards him, until he more or less accepted his fate and hoisted me on board, so that I was getting his warmth in two forms, if not all three of the possibilities – radiation, convection, conduction. All the marvellous ways a policeman may be partially converted into British Thermal Units.

I set myself to return some of that warmth in social form. There are subjects of conversation that take some igniting – you can feel you're striking spark after spark and still the tinder refuses to catch. A conversation about fireworks is not like that, least of all one on Bonfire Night itself. The flame of pyrolatry seems to burn deep in every breast, and combustible material goes up with a whoosh as if it had been soaked in paraffin. Differences of opinion however real are essentially mild – I don't think even the fiercest advocate of Roman candles, for instance, ever wanted Catherine wheels knocked off their pins.

Hard to know whether this adulation of cleansing fire is just the id seeking the destruction of the world, as usual, or a longing by the ego to see itself burnt out. Arson at first blush would seem to be the supreme expression of destructiveness, the quintessence of id, but periodic wildfires are necessary for the health of a forest and in Hindu cosmology destruction has a high place. Has any arsonist ever stood up in court and argued, quoting Nietzsche, that the urge to destroy is also a creative impulse? It might be worth a shot. As a juror I might be moved. I can find in myself quite a deep affinity with the setter of fires who loves the flames for themselves. The desire to watch the fire brigade when it turns out in all its uniformed glory, though I also share it, seems much less likely to have Śiva's blessing.

How much do I need to apologise for being frightened by loud noises at night? On the other hand, they needed to be careful. If they made wasting police time such an enjoyable affair they'd soon be swamped with frivolous complaints.

Enlightened dog-breeders, when the new owners come to pick up a puppy, present them with a square of blanket from the basket where it has lain with its mother. The only thing that could have improved my little excursion in the police car that November the 5th would have been a cut-out square from the constable's tunic. With that next to my pillow I could have slept peacefully through any firework display, any explosion controlled or uncontrolled.

All England seemed to be bending

With MarkO no longer a presence, I lacked a factotum for small household adjustments, particularly at weekends, when the home help didn't come. Filling the kettle hardly counts as a chore for a visitor, but it certainly does for me, and as for the packaging on cheese, it was diabolical. That impregnable plastic had me weeping more than once, from hunger and frustration, if I had forgotten to ask the home help to make at least a preliminary incision.

I was being reminded once again of how unnatural a state is independence, how artificial lives are when not in constant dialogue with others. The light abrasion of unavoidable daily human contact prevents or delays the formation of mutagenic barnacles, the origins of personality disorder and mental illness.

Still, it's hard to deny that I was at a loose end in a fairly profound existential way. I read something about circadian rhythms in a colour supplement at the doctor's, and wondered if that was the explanation for my energy seeming so undependable. I tried to create little projects for myself without achieving any real momentum. The world gave me back no echo.

I managed to fill my time, just the same. It's not so hard. Once I noticed a spider in the bathroom with a deformed abdomen, and phoned the BBC about it. At first they tried to tell me it might be pregnant – as if I didn't know the signs of pregnancy in spiders! So then they encouraged me to send it in, and I did, spending good money on proper padding for the journey after sealing the spider in a tube (along with some flies gathered from its web) and of course paying out a substantial amount for postage. 'Encouraged' isn't quite the word. Grudgingly they seemed to accept that there wasn't a lot they could do if I wanted to send them a spider with anomalies, and they had to be reasonably polite to someone who paid the licence fee. They weren't to know that I paid nothing, perfectly legitimately, since I didn't own a television.

It showed how much progress Paula had made that she was willing to pack an arachnid and a few insects into a humble cardboard tube, actually the core from a roll of toilet paper. Her hand shook as she deployed the roll of Sellotape, but the task was completed. Not knowing how much time would pass before the tube was opened, I couldn't be sure there would be enough moisture in the flies themselves and so included a little wad of cotton wool soaked in water, on general principles. That spider travelled to the BBC like a pharaoh into the afterlife, with food and drink for the journey. Even so, it seemed pretty furious when I put the stopper on the tube. I would have included slaves, too, if I could, but I did the best I could with the materials available. That's an epitaph you never see on a gravestone, though it is anything but dishonourable and could apply to so many of us: *He (or she) did the best he (or she) could with the materials available.*

I enclosed a note in the envelope suggesting that the Natural History Unit, obviously the appropriate department to receive the package, should check for the presence of toxins. It was no secret at the time that most of the spiders in Cambridge were on drugs. There was a real craze for blowing dope smoke over them, or giving them outsized doses of acid, so as to see how their spinning skills were affected. To which the short answer is: not for the better. Really it's a wonder that any flies were caught in the city at all until the craze subsided. Of course flies had a relatively low I.Q. in those days, and no one ever thought of making flies hallucinate. Even with the doors of perception flung wide, and a hot wind of distorted images scouring through them, spiders retained the intellectual edge.

I never heard a dicky bird from the BBC, not even an acknowledgement of the trouble I had put myself to, let alone a refund of the cost of postage. Then one day Mrs Baine's sister's car key broke off in the ignition hardly ten minutes after she had listened to Uri Geller bending spoons on the *Jimmy Young Show*, before she had even had a chance to turn it. The next morning she found that her father's watch, which had been in a drawer for years, had started ticking. I volunteered to contact the University's metallurgy department on her behalf – an event like that should be properly looked into, without gullibility or closedness of mind. I may have implied some sort of connection with the department, not much of a misstatement given the rampant interconnectedness of all things. Uri Geller seemed to me pretty shifty, but that's exactly the sort of petty prejudice that should be set aside until the data confirms or refutes it. I left a message with the department but the higher-ups didn't have the good manners to return the call. And they call themselves scientists!

Geller's broadcast had certainly set Schrödinger's Cat among the pigeons. The whole BBC switchboard lit up like the burning bush. All England seemed to be bending. A lady from Harrow who was stirring soup found that her ladle was suddenly starting to bend. In Surrey a girl's gold bracelet lost the battle to retain its shape and buckled under the psychic pressure. A watchmaker's tweezers had done the same, rendering them useless as professional tools.

When there was no reply from the metallurgy department I suggested to Mrs Baine that we should document the event properly and try again. The Lazarus watch, restored to life in its drawer, was not a phenomenon for which evidence could be mustered, but perhaps she could get hold of her sister's broken car key for me to cast an eye over? She said she would try.

The next day she showed me the broken key. Keys break from time to time, that's a fact, but when I examined the broken edges of the two parts of the key I could see a line of vitrified material, suggesting not only very high temperatures but a high degree of localisation, and that too is a fact. Then I had an idea. If Mrs Baine was doing a drawing class at Seacat might there not also be a photographic course or at least a camera club using facilities at the same institution? We needed documentation, and they were the fellows to provide it.

Mrs Baine undertook to 'put out feelers', a satisfyingly insectoid turn of phrase. I could imagine her as a beetle burrowing into soft wood. She got an encouraging answer from the teacher of photography at Seacat, who said he would make the broken key the subject for a class project. This sounded ominously arty to me, but I could hardly say so in advance. Then it seemed to take a frustrating amount of time before there were any tangible or visible results. Materialist interpretations of the universe are hanging by a thread here – hurry up with those scissors!

The results were even worse than I had feared. Those fragments of key were subjected to any number of formal and technical experiments. They were blurred, even smeared in the prints that Mrs Baine spread out before me. There were fancy double exposures, in a number of colours. One student had gone to some lengths to make the fragments look spooky, giving them a sort of otherworldly halo. 'What in the world is going on here?' I asked her. She said she'd asked the same question herself, and the answer, apparently, was that the photograph had been 'polarised'. I wondered if perhaps she'd got the word slightly wrong. Might the right one be 'solarised'? Whatever the name of the process, one thing was certain: these photographs were useless for our purposes.

Mrs Baine seemed remarkably calm about this setback. 'Well, we tried,' she said. 'We did our best.'

I wasn't having that. 'I don't think we did. There are no breakthroughs without persistence. What if Alexander Graham Bell had lost all interest in *Staphylococcus*? What if he had stopped leaving out Petri dishes of mould near open windows?'

She thought for a moment. 'Well, Mr Cromer . . . I think he'd still have invented the telephone.'

Oh dear! That's the drawback about getting up on your high horse in a hurry. You can find that it's April Fool's Day in Thomas Hobson's livery stables and the ostlers, laughing madly behind their hands, have mounted you on a donkey. A well-rested donkey, mind you, a donkey fresh as any daisy.

In fact my blunder lowered the tension, which might otherwise have led to Mrs B taking umbrage. Umbrage is a fiercely addictive substance. Doses that were disorientingly strong only a short time ago must be increased tenfold to produce anything like the same thrill of righteous indignation. So my mistake was a fortunate one. Not everyone responds well to a scolding – I haven't always shone in that department myself.

We shouldn't be in too much of a hurry to detect here an utterance of the guru mingling with human breath to produce the subtlest of changes. There's still such a thing as blind luck.

Without too much resistance Mrs Baine agreed to try again with the camera club. With rather more resistance I decided to offer a cash prize of £5 for the clearest photograph of those key fragments, which should include precise measurements and focus on the zone of melting where the molecular pressure had been most intense.

I had barely made a dent in Granny's nest egg with my little spoon, and I felt the expense was justified. Even so, I found it shocking that it was necessary to offer a bribe to guarantee evidentiary material of sufficient quality for an investigation of considerable significance, but that seemed to be the world we lived in. Those were the conditions prevailing.

Another week went by, of course, before there were any results, but then they were remarkably different. These photographs were bleak and dark – they would have been suitable for Wanted posters, if fragments of ignition key could be sought by the authorities. The set with the clearest details won the prize. I paid up without regret, and sent the portfolio of photographs to the Department of Materials Science and Metallurgy, using recorded delivery so that there could be no possibility of their not arriving. Not just to the department but to its head.

I had made a note of the top man's name when I had made my initial failed assault on the Department's fortress on Charles Babbage Road, which I imagined to be made of steel with copper turrets. It's always a good idea having an individual name to ask for. Ideally you should practise saying it, until it seems to live in your mouth, so that you speak it with such embodied fluency that it will never occur to his secretary that you aren't old friends. She may even think she has put you through to him on any number of earlier occasions. But it's worth doing even if you put the phone down the moment you have been given the information and then call back immediately. You may already have passed from one zone of the secretary's brain to another, less well defended, simply by dint of having articulated the magic syllables of her employer's name. Though she disclosed it to you mere moments before, it may still have in her ears the ring of 'open sesame'.

I waited a day or two and then phoned the Department to make sure of the package's arrival. I said I had no need to speak to the Professor, I just needed to make sure an important package had been delivered. Coldly the secretary on duty confirmed the fact and then reverted to a silence that was, well, if not metallurgical then certainly metallic in its coldness and hardness. Normally I'm fairly good at warming and softening such persons, but my powers seemed to have deserted me – and in the long run, if I was suddenly able to bend spoons but not ears I would have got the worst of the bargain.

I long to stet those hyphens

I'd ignored Christmas 1972, spending it in Cambridge rather than at the address I was supposed to call 'home', but I wouldn't be allowed to get away with a second offence against the festival. I felt no atavistic tug, though I couldn't help noticing the empty build-up to the empty celebration started earlier every year. Christmas itself is the first day of Christmas, and the 'twelve days of Christmas' end with Epiphany on January the sixth, with Twelfth Night on the fifth being technically the eve of Epiphany. There's no argument about that, the church calendar for 'Christmastide' is perfectly clear about the limited extent of the season, but nobody minds people jumping the gun a bit by putting up the tree and decorating it even before the proper day, Christmas Eve. A little leeway is one thing – but there were shops in Cambridge that had put up their tinsel before December had got properly under way, weeks ahead of the day itself. I was shocked, and I can't have been the only one. What next, New Year's resolutions in July?

I still resisted the idea of a family celebration, but I had a proper home address of my own now and could perhaps afford to be gracious. In any case the forces ranged against me were formidable and coördinated, in a way they hadn't been the year before.

Co-ordinate, coördinate. I've thrown in my lot with the diæresis, but every now and then my eye rebels and I long to stet those hyphens. It would help domesticate the look of it if, for instance, Coöp supermarkets led the way, but I can't quite see that happening. They'd be more likely to coöpt the idea if it became generally accepted elsewhere.

Little silken nets were being woven around me, with a decision already taken that I was not party to, namely that I would spend Christmas at Bourne End with what was alleged to be my family. Everyone is always saying that blood is thicker than water, but there is no shortage of anti-coagulants available, and my Hindu faith had thinned mere hæmoglobin connection to the point of non-existence. Yet those many silken strands of supposed connection, so weak individually, have the power to bind in combination, just as Gulliver was pinioned in Lilliput. It takes a lot to make me see myself as a giant among the little people, Brobdingnag being so much more my home address, but that's the whole force of the fable. The most effective mantrap contains no metal, has no moving parts, even, and makes no sound. It doesn't even let you know that you've been immobilised, it merely condenses a cloud of inanition round you until you think, not 'Help! I can't move!', but *I never wanted to be anywhere but here.*

Possibly this pitches the whole Christmas question too high, but it's a mistake to insist on a sense of proportion in circumstances that are themselves hopelessly skewed.

There was as much manœuvring and machination about my attendance in Bourne End for Christmas as there must have been at historical moments when the fates of nations or religions were decided, let's say the Congress of Vienna or the first Council of Nicæa. Crucial to the diplomatic effort was Bourne End's most evolved soul Joy Payne, unique in being able to claim both me and my parents as her friends. She was able and willing to talk to all parties, to help people dig themselves out of entrenched positions. If anyone could get everyone to hammer out their differences, then get us all round a table on the 25th of December, it was her.

I don't know why she took on the thankless position of Cromer family liaison officer. I didn't ask. When I was little I loved her because she lived in a house on the Abbotsbrook estate called Otters Pool (no apostrophes to be seen in the name), and I think I would have loved Cruella de Vil herself if she had lived in a house called Otters Pool. The front door was painted a strange salmony pink that I associated with Shippam's fish paste. Joy didn't mind the association, she even said with a straight face that she had given the painters instructions to match the colour of the jar. Later I thought of her as embodying neighbourliness of the desirable sort, not because she had no problems of her own but because unlike Mum she could see over them. She wasn't nosy and she wasn't in a hurry to volunteer information about her own life. She just had a knack for putting other people first. I wasn't used to people whose first response to a request, to life in general, was Yes, Dear or Of Course. Her husband Guy was high up in Vauxhall Motors, maybe even the managing director. He went to art dealers and bought paintings, just because he liked them. That was outlandish enough in Mum's eyes, but then he gave Joy a drawing that cost £700, which scandalised Mum. It wasn't even a painting! A painting was one thing, if you had cash to throw around, but a drawing? The cheaper materials involved were enough in Mum's eyes to nudge him over the edge of eccentric behaviour into something more worrying. Of course the element of financial recklessness was only part of it. The emotional lavishness that went along with it was guaranteed to make her uneasy.

The highlights of Joy's weekend were Mel Calman's little-man cartoon in the *Sunday Times* and Katharine Whitehorn's column in the *Observer*. I suppose that's one of the perks of being married to a car company executive, two newspapers on a Sunday (for those who care about such things). Expense no object! Thrift be damned. It's only money, after all. If Guy could be picked up every morning from Otters Pool by a chauffeur and driven to Luton, and be delivered back to Bourne End after work, then Joy was entitled to push the boat out in her own small way. Guy would buy Joy presents and arrange treats even when it wasn't her birthday. He once took her to London for a Swingle Singers concert. Joy was mad for the Swingle Singers, but Mum was baffled. She had heard them more than once on the radio and was always saying what they did wasn't proper singing – 'I mean, they don't sing words, it's all "bum". A "bum" for every note. Bum bum bum. That's not singing, that's . . . bumming.' Her disapproval was remarkably strong. She seemed taken aback by her own vehemence, or perhaps worried that she had invented a horrible new word.

It wasn't unusual for Joy to phone me for a chat, though I don't remember her doing it when I was an undergraduate. The number stayed the same when I moved, of course, or rather moved with me, thanks to the miracle of administrative conjuring that had been worked for my benefit. I was blessed. In those days a tree taking a stroll like the Ents in *Lord of the Rings* was hardly more startling than a telephone number following you from one address to the next.

I may have been a little jealous of Joy's children Nicola and Stuart. I remember Stuart went through a stage of being a fussy eater. That was all anyone said – 'fussy eater' – but it must have been a bit more serious than that for Joy to go to the doctor and then a consultant. Stuart would fill his cheeks with food at meals, hamster fashion, and then spit everything out into the lavatory bowl. The family doctor didn't take it seriously, and in his defence 'eating disorder' wasn't a phrase you heard in those days. Joy didn't go to our splendid GP, Dr Flanagan, known to us as Flanny, I think because Guy wasn't convinced that women doctors knew their stuff and favoured another partner at the practice who had the extra qualification of being male. If so Guy got it exactly the wrong way round. Flanny was very much on the ball, while some doctors particularly in late career rely on notions that are distinctly antiquated. What the Paynes' chosen doctor told Joy was that Stuart had 'outgrown his strength' and that the trouble would sort itself out. Joy didn't agree, and made her own decision to consult a specialist.

I'm not sure the consultant went to the psychological roots of the problem, and perhaps he didn't have to. The allopathic tradition turns diagnosis into an end in itself – it still counts as a diagnosis when you describe someone's condition as 'idiopathic', even though that only means you can't explain it and it belongs to them alone!

What he suggested was for Joy to leave biscuits around, not whole packets but individual biscuits, a biscuit here, a biscuit there, all around the house, a squirrel trail so that he could be discreetly tempted to nibble rather than closely watched to see whether he ate a full meal or not. It seemed to work. The trouble passed. Naturally the GP, when he asked later on about Stuart's progress and learned about his improvement, said, 'Didn't I tell you so?' as if he had been vindicated rather than ignored and sidestepped.

Her daughter Nicola was unwavering in her determination to be a vet, though no one could quite understand how she had come by this vocation since there were no pets in the family. Joy loved nature too much to keep it indoors. I wonder what she made of the menagerie at Trees, though she was far too tactful to say anything. Mum pumped her love at much higher pressure through animals than people, which was just as well. A full dose of her love, in a home that wasn't shared in my childhood with a floating population of dogs, cats and birds, and I would have exploded. 'I wasn't exactly quick on the uptake,' she said. 'It took me quite a while to realise that her imaginary friend Sandy – did I tell you about this already? – was actually a horse. I kept wondering why Sandy liked hay as well as ice cream. And of course I was wondering if this was boy-Sandy or girl-Sandy. But *horse*-Sandy . . . I didn't have an inkling. Am I a rotten mother, would you say, John? When I was tucking her in I'd ask if Sandy was in her bedroom with us and she would roll her eyes and say, "Of course not! Honestly, Mum, you're not thinking. Sandy can climb stairs all right, but how's she supposed to get down again? She wouldn't have a clue, and she'd be terribly frightened." And all I registered was that Sandy was a girl after all, Sandra perhaps or Alexandra but definitely not Alexander, and what that might mean or not mean, if you see what I . . . mean. Too many "mean"s in that sentence! So muggins here wasn't thinking about hooves one way or the other, neither boy hooves nor girl hooves (I suppose I should be saying colt hooves and filly hooves!). Mind you, I told her, if you're going to be a vet you're going to be up to your shoulders in a cow sooner or later. Are you sure you can cope? I mean, this is a girl who wouldn't pick up a dead bird from the garden during Bob-a-Job week — well, if you're a girl guide not a scout it's called Willing for a Shilling, please don't ask me how that sounds — she wanted five shillings for it. But she said yes and so far she's been true to her word.

'Apparently they give you special gloves, long, long ones like the swankiest evening gloves, up to the shoulder. But not velvet I shouldn't think.'

Joy Payne's activities as telephone intermediary, honest broker trusted by both sides, started long before Christmas, perhaps in October. Her status was so high she could get away with something that is morally obnoxious, namely the apology at second hand. 'John, I know Laura is sorry about what happened during the summer last year, whatever it was, I don't know and don't want to, haven't asked. Still, you mustn't expect her to apologise. It's not in her. I'm always saying sorry, mostly for things I haven't done, but everyone's different, aren't they? I said sorry to a kingfisher recently, while I was swimming. "Sorry if I startled you," I said. Of course it was long gone by then. Dennis may be sorry too, though I wouldn't bank on it. Mischief runs quite deep in him, doesn't it? — though he'd always rather egg someone else on than take the risk himself. Sorry, John! This is no way to be talking about your parents.'

Often enough apologies are insincere even when they're made in the first person, but they lose all possible value when transmitted by a third party. Still, and only because it's you, Joy, I'll make an exception.

It's one thing to pass on a cheque made out to you and endorse it in someone else's favour, but even in the 1970s that was something you couldn't do with an apology. It's first-person or no person at all. Of course the moment I've said that, my mind starts emitting a little whirring noise and I get to wondering how you could make such a transferable system work. It might be rather nice to build up a hoard of second-hand apologies and then cash them in when you've put someone's nose out of joint. All the embarrassment about saying sorry would be gone in a flash — along with the last little remnant of sincerity, it's true, but the system was on its last legs anyway. What would you call them? Indulgences, I suppose, borrowing the religious terminology that applied before the Reformation. Secular indulgences.

There could be a going rate set by the government, and the money could be used to fund . . . I don't know, schools? Hospitals?

Everyone knew Joy was mad for swimming in the river, and loved to lurk in the reeds blending in with the other wildlife. She said the happiest moment of her life was when a family of moorhens came by, and one of them pecked at a bit of weed that had stuck to her bathing cap. I felt a little throb of envy for that moment of privilege, her inclusion in the natural life of the Thames, though she had certainly earned it.

'Do you remember Chi Chi the panda? She died last year.' I remembered the name, though I had never seen her in the flesh – in the fur. 'I mourned her, you know. I really did. I thought I was having one of the episodes that get me into trouble. But I'm just daffy about animals, you know that. I don't approve of them being kept in cages, not normally, but Chi Chi was a little different or the Zoological Society wouldn't have taken her on – she'd been taken from the wild long before. She just needed a home.

'She'd been there more than ten years, and I wanted to send a condolence letter. Can you imagine, John? A condolence letter – who did I think I was going to send it to? Chi Chi's family? Some pandas in the wild who would be much better off if they never saw a human being? I could send it to the zoo, to the keepers, but really, there wouldn't have been much point to that. It's their job after all. But then I thought me a thought, and I remembered something I'd heard from Nicola. All her friends are vets, trainees rather, and it's quite a little grapevine. News gets round. So in the end I sent a nice sympathetic letter to some Boy Scouts in Cornwall.

'I'm sorry, John, I'm not explaining it very well . . . but what's the thing everyone – almost everyone! – knows about pandas?'

'That they're fussy eaters?'

'They're fussy eaters, that's right. Bamboo shoots aren't something you can get at the corner grocer's, and I'm not sure even Harrods Food Hall could rise to that particular challenge! But then a retired military gentleman living somewhere called Menabilly cut some shoots from the bamboo thickets and took the chance of sending them to the zoo to see if Chi Chi approved. And she did! So from then on this Captain Billy Menabilly – I'm sorry, John, that's not actually his name but it's how I remember what the place is called – became the certified supplier of bamboo shoots to Chi Chi the giant panda. What an honour!'

Writing letters to pandas about Boy Scouts

'Yes, what an honour! So much more inspiring than getting the royal warrant to supply Her Majesty with soap . . .'

'I'm not sure we should say so, John, but I dare say you're right. Then Captain Billy got the local scout troop to help, so they would cut the shoots on a Sunday and deliver them to their pack leader, who would take them to the railway station at a place called Par first thing Monday morning. Have you seen a film called *The Titfield Thunderbolt*, John? No? It's a charming little film about a village trying to keep its train service from being replaced by buses, and I know perfectly well there aren't any steam trains running any more but still I imagine the Titfield Thunderbolt carrying Chi Chi's bamboo shoots from Par to Paddington. Isn't that silly?'

'Then when poor lonely Chi Chi died I thought the Boy Scouts must be lonely too, so I sent a sort of condolence letter. I think I addressed it to "The Scouts Who Love Pandas, Cornwall" or something equally mad, but it reached them and they sent the nicest letter back, signed by all of them and including a picture. It turns out they have special panda badges that they wear on their scarves. The Polkerris troop. Pretty name.

'As you can imagine, I haven't told Guy about such an odd piece of behaviour, so I'm asking you – is it a little crazed of me to write to Boy Scouts about pandas?'

'Crazed' seemed a good word in this context, suggesting as it does the tiny cracks in a glazed surface, potentially giving lustre to the patination, but I felt able to reassure her, flattered to be considered some sort of arbiter of sanity. 'I'd have done just the same, Joy, and I'm sure they were thrilled to hear from you.' Of course my great advantage as an amateur Doctor in Lunacy was that I had no power whatever to enforce an unfavourable verdict.

'Thank you, John. I take that kindly. Maybe I'm on more of an even keel than I feel sometimes.'

I wouldn't have worried about Joy Payne's sanity even if she was writing letters to pandas about Boy Scouts. Who knows, perhaps that's what I should have told her. She was subject to emotional illness, but that's a different matter, and there was a lot of it about, both in Bourne End and the wider world. You could say she was in real difficulty if I was her closest confidant, but that wasn't how I saw things, and I hoped she spoke as freely with others as she did with me.

I could feel myself becoming stronger from being relied on, and perhaps I wanted more of that, but it wasn't clear where I was going to get it. I loved it that Joy had no gift for the social lie, and never pretended things were fine if they weren't. By rights this characteristic would have been enough to make her unappealing to Mum, who set such tremendous store by appearances. Perhaps Joy seemed to belong to some sort of elite, not necessarily of class, who were allowed to express themselves without reservation. I also enjoyed Joy's hospitality, which was never overdone, always seeming spontaneous. She had a knack for making food appetising, and made sure there was always a bit of visual flair to the plate. She would always leave a bit of the green top on when preparing carrots for cooking. She'd add greens even to a poached egg – a scattering of chives from the garden. Parsley too is an aphrodisiac of a subtle sort, rousing the appetite in its own indirect way. There's nothing trivial about dressing a plate, making it appeal to the eye as well as the palate. Joy knew that the ungarnished life is not worth eating.

She suffered from depression mania – was that technically what it was called then, or had she slightly misheard the diagnosis? Needing professional help wasn't exactly respectable in the 1970s, not in Bourne End anyway. Joy was frank about it. I certainly remember her saying that she'd been put away for being too happy as often as she had for not being happy enough.

Somehow Joy was whole and broken at the same time. She had had a wide range of treatments. 'Did they give you LSD?'

'Is that the electricity? Because I had some of that.'

'No, Joy. Little pills that make you see things.'

'Yes, I expect I had some of that, dear. I've had most things.'

She told me about the time she was treated at St Thomas's Hospital in London by the brother of Sir Malcolm Sargent, the conductor, as an inpatient. He drugged her down into a coma (she used those matter-of-factly dreadful words, 'drugged me down'), and then left her there to sort out her own problems in an induced vegetative state. It was a therapy much in vogue in the 1960s, apparently. To me it sounds like a case of 'Zombie, heal thyself', but the theory was that in a comatose state people disengaged from their problems, along with everything else, and when consciousness resumed they were somehow refreshed and better able to deal with things.

She even said it seemed to work. She woke up less frayed than when they put her to sleep. Again, 'frayed' was how she put it – 'I get frayed at the edges, John dear, and I cope for a little while and then somebody needs to do something. I can't see my way out of it by myself. I'm at the bottom of a hole in the dark and there's no ladder.'

She didn't think the coma did her any harm. 'Mind you, dear, it was a bit hit and miss. I felt a bit better, but one poor chap didn't wake up at all. He choked somehow, I think. Is there something called chyle? I think he choked on that, whatever it is, or it got into his lungs.' Chylothorax is no joke. Awake or asleep, you don't want chyle seeping into your chest cavity, and if you're deeply asleep in the basement of a hospital who's going to notice? 'The nurses were very quiet for a while after that.'

That took me back, to the nurses being very shocked and subdued after Mary Finch, my best friend at CRX, died after her parents were given the wrong dosage of medication when she went home with them for a long weekend. The mood of suppressed horror lasted for days, and I think seeped into us all. But the idea of the induced coma as a treatment took me back even further, to my bed-rest years, which were really only a sort of waking coma. I was prescribed bed rest in the 1950s, and a very bad idea it was too, though at least I was an inpatient, told to lie still under Mum's care and in my own room, not in a hospital.

Look under Pascal's name in a book of quotations and you're bound to come across this one: 'All of humanity's problems have a single cause: not knowing how to sit quietly in a room.' I beg to differ. In fact, begging is too submissive a posture. I demand to differ. As a child I spent a few years alone in a room – mainly alone, with just enough company to accentuate the solitude – lying quietly rather than sitting but still following the medical advice of the time as well as your directives, Pascal, and if I'd gone on doing it much longer I would either have died or melted into Mum's side the way Parvati melted into the side of holy mountain Arunachala, only without the consolation (if it is one) of becoming a site of pilgrimage.

Bed rest was a particularly bad idea because my condition had been diagnosed wrongly, so that I spent more than three years in bed having my life dictated by this course of action – more precisely a course of inaction, and not remotely resembling a course of treatment. My consumption of books was rationed to half an hour a day to make sure I didn't become overstimulated, making reading seem like a refreshing burst of REM sleep bringing dreams of other worlds. It was a régime that might have benefited rheumatic fever, which I didn't have, but positively increased the damage done by Still's Disease, which I did.

The practice of 'bed rest' which had taken up a lot of hospital space in the 1950s and '60s immobilised people in the hope that inactivity would improve their condition. It was only reluctantly that the National Health Service stopped the practice, out of entirely unfounded fears that mortality rates would go up. Despite it seeming immobile itself, there's a certain amount of faddishness in the NHS, or as Granny always called it 'the Scheme', which may have been a neutral early description of the system but certainly made it sound shady, as if this was another South Sea Bubble likely to burst at any moment.

Only a few years after the National Health Service abandoned the practice of 'bed rest' in hospitals, relying on inactivity to improve their patients' conditions, psychiatric medicine revived the idea as a treatment for mental conditions. I realise that this observation doesn't really reflect my particular understanding of the shared unreality of the notions 'body' and 'mind', as revealed and transcended by the Hindu practice of self-realisation, but I don't think being put in a chemical trance is much like meditating.

The labels have been switched on the voting machine

Perhaps coma therapy for the mind was copycat medicine in a different way, inspired by the practice of inducing a coma in patients

565

suffering a physical crisis. It sounded pretty extreme, as Joy explained it. 'He wrote a book about the mind and how he thought it worked, not that I've read it – perhaps you should get it from the library.

'I slept for a month, but the thing is, there was nothing in that month I was looking forward to. I was glad to have it taken away, and there were plenty of months I'd have waved goodbye to just as happily. I don't remember anything about it, though they wake you every now and then to wash you and feed you and take you to the lavvy.

'I'd have taken a permanent sleep pill, if you see what I mean, if he'd offered one. Something to make it all stop – so why not have a month's holiday to sleep it off? I was sleeping a lot of the time anyway. When I go off the rails I either sleep all the time or not at all. I have a personal question to ask, dear, though I'm not sure I should . . .'

'Ask away.'

'Have you never wanted to make everything stop?'

'No, I haven't, Joy, though I can't really explain why.' Even during episodes of great pain I've never thought that I wanted to die, though I've often wondered, why is there still an 'I' there? 'There' rather than 'here' – an oddly neutral query, with a certain distance built in. Is that the same thing as wanting to die? I wouldn't think so.

It would have been more truthful to tell Joy that when the thought comes along I just know it wouldn't work. My objections to suicide aren't moral so much as mechanical. I just know it isn't effective. It's like the Ghost Train rides in funfairs that Dad and I used to watch so closely, since I wasn't allowed to ride. It would have shaken me up too much. But there's a pair of doors that gets flung open, and the car seems to leave the ride and come out into the open air, but actually the track does a sharp U-turn so that the car heads back inside. To me that's suicide. It's a pretend escape that never leaves the track.

The trick is simple but cunning enough. The labels have been switched on the voting machine. Anyone who presses the button marked Death has to go round again any number of times, passing through eighty-four hundred thousand vaginas and, yes, we've established it's not my lucky number nor anyone else's. It's only by pressing the Life button relentlessly that you can earn death proper.

'Well, I'm glad for you, dear. And it's a funny thing, too,' she said, 'but since then I haven't been able to listen to anything Malcolm

Sargent conducted. I know it's silly – he had nothing to do with putting me to sleep, which did me good anyway. He's just waving a stick in front of people who know what to do anyway. I'd love to see them try without a conductor! I can't really see they wouldn't get to the finishing line without help. Still, if I've been listening to something, tapping my foot, and they say that was "Pomp and Circumstance" played by such-and-such an orchestra conducted by Sir Malcolm Sargent, it gives me a bad moment, even if I enjoyed the music while it was on. I like "Pomp and Circumstance".'

Anyway, Joy Payne thought the treatment did her good, and that had to be enough for me. One thing that made it stick in my mind was the whole 'brother of Sir Malcolm Sargent' business. In those days a scrap of knowledge that I couldn't follow up was like an itch I couldn't scratch, and it's a statement of medical fact to say my itches mainly fall into that category, though I can reach some surprising places using a kutchi, a stick from the neem tree, whose branches are lightweight and have naturally occurring right-angle bends, so that it's easy to find one that fits my hand and gives me that precious extra bit of scratching power. A library is a whole forest of neem trees.

It turns out that the sinister psychiatrist's name was Sargant rather than Sargent, so there was no direct connection with the conductor. But I have to say that to my knowledge it was the only thing that Joy Payne ever got wrong, so I move a vote of forgiveness for the puzzlement she caused me over the years. If that was the worst distortion visited on her by her illness and the treatment she had for it, then my ideas about her underlying strength of character are only confirmed. It was one of Sargant's ideas, as it turns out, that 'good previous personality' in a patient made the treatment more likely to be successful. I don't like the sound of that. 'You can't make a silk purse out of a pig's ear' was one of his favourite sayings. I'd say that's the opposite of my philosophy. The best purses are made from the most unpromising materials.

The nurses were nice, according to Joy. 'I made friends with one of them – though actually she made friends with me. We still exchange Christmas cards. She must have seen me at my weakest, at my worst, and she became a friend. A sort of friend.'

Dolphins always seem to be smiling, don't they?

Nursing care could make all the difference, in one way or another, in the basement of sleepers that must have seemed more than halfway to a morgue. Some people were hard to wake up when the allotted time had elapsed. One died through inhalation of vomitus when he was fed too much, unconscious and unsupervised. Another died of peritonitis. You also have to watch the other end of the digestive process, viz. defæcation. Potentially incriminating papers went mysteriously missing in a number of cases, but Sargant had kept notes in his diary and there was something of a scandal.

The '60s had been a great period for radical experiments on willing subjects, willing and not necessarily over-informed. Dolphins were given LSD. It's hard to say whether they derived any benefit. Dolphins always seem to be smiling, don't they? 'McKee pins' or hip replacements probably qualify as an example of this semi-philanthropic research craze, the devices installed with such difficulty – hammered into me, to be blunt about it – that for so many years underpinned my disimmobilised state and every change of position.

It made me think about my . . . let's not call them sufferings. I was installed in high-minded institutions, CRX and then Vulcan School, where the presiding powers were as benign as anyone could wish. It was at the lower levels that cruelty flourished, carried out by minor devils who were never noticed by the higher-ups. Joy's case was different. It's hard not to think that William Sargant was an unstable character with some sort of Messiah complex, even if he thought that Christ himself, given the proper therapy, would have gone back to the family trade of carpentry and been fulfilled by it. What child of a Methodist family thinks like that? His brother ended up as bishop of Mysore, proof enough that they were a rum old bunch.

What kind of psychiatrist looks for simple physiological solutions to complex disorders of mind and mood? Leucotomy, insulin coma therapy, ECT – slice, stun, fry. Hardly the holy trinity of medical interventions. In my experience good doctors don't mind patients who have something to say for themselves. Bad ones prefer their patients docile, and there's nothing much more docile than a patient in a coma, unaware in her artificial sleep that the doctor is engaged in a competition with an Australian colleague, a sort of gentleman's bet, to see who can keep someone in a deep coma for longest.

Yet the bitterness of Sargant's régime, the 'doing good by stealth' that meant in practice giving multiple sessions of ECT to patients who didn't want it, but couldn't object because they were asleep, 'drugged down' in Joy's phrase, was neutralised, at least in part, by the loving care that the nursing staff were able to offer to the patients in their helplessness. I'm not sure that I'd want to get a Christmas card from someone who first saw me unconscious in the narcosis ward, who fed me, washed me and took me to the lavatory, for weeks before I was awake and we could be introduced, but then I'm not a fan of Christmas.

Perhaps 'good' and 'evil' always come to some arrangement, with rot at the top offset by wholesomeness at the bottom, or the other way round. I suppose an organisation that was corrupt from head to toe would simply collapse, without needing to be touched from outside by as much as a finger, and one that could boast integrity in every cell would make the angels huffy at the trespass on their territory and bring about the end of the world ahead of schedule. What most often happens is a sort of stalemate between the kindness and the cruelty, with the result that the organism stumbles on baffled and bleeding, like most entities in the world that we know.

Joy and her children all played recorders, not just making squeaks but proper sounds. They even gave little concerts with their consort – this sounds confusing, but apparently it's the technical term. Joy's was twice the size of the children's and produced an appropriately deep and cooing noise. She held it in front of me once and invited me to blow into it. I liked the result though it made me uneasy, as if I was impersonating her voice rather than playing an instrument. She didn't take the mouthpiece away immediately but wanted me to improve at it. She was quite insistent that I work on the position of my mouth to get a properly rounded note. It didn't seem to be a relevant concern that I was unable to hold the instrument without help – there must be no shirking. For a moment I got an inkling that it might not be exactly relaxing to have parents who wanted you to make something of yourself. I imagined Joy sticking mouthpieces in her children's mouths the moment they woke, as if the recorders were wooden thermometers and she was trying to take their temperature.

The parents of children who play the recorder have to have a high tolerance for nasty noises, at least in the early stages, but it was another instrument that tested the Paynes' patience. 'That boy of mine Stuart used to play the mouth organ – harmonica – or he thought he played it, anyway. It was one of his crazes. He just blew and sucked at it, which is what everyone does, really. Everyone but Larry Adler. It was driving Guy potty, so he beckoned Stuart over and said, "Do you want me to show you 'The Flight of the Bumblebee'?" Well, Stuart couldn't resist an invitation like that. Then the moment Guy had the thing in his hands, I suppose you'd have to call it an instrument, he didn't try to play a note on it, just threw it out of the window with a flick of the wrist, saying, "There you are . . . 'Flight of the Bumblebee'. Now buzz off." I had to laugh, though I doubt if Guy was being original. I didn't marry a comedian, wouldn't want to. Bless him, he probably got the idea from someone on television. I can just see Jimmy Edwards doing that in *Whack-O!*, can't you? But then I saw Stuart's face and he was mortified, utterly mortified, so I ended up helping him search for the damn thing among the rhododendrons.'

Mum and Dad were flesh and blood but Joy was voice and heart. Her voice was deeper than Mum's, with the texture that's called contralto, bringing a flavour of Kathleen Ferrier. If anyone could *blow the wind southerly*, it was Joy. Her efforts to bring the Cromers together had a subtly undermining effect, as she showed me without meaning to, in fact meaning to show exactly the reverse, that family was what she was and what my parents were not. If adoption was a unilateral procedure she might have found herself saddled with an extra child, the laggard last in her little procession of moorhen chicks, as I piped feebly behind the others on my recorder mouthpiece. It would be just the mouthpiece, unscrewed from the body of a wholly impractical instrument, but I knew she would always come back for me if I kept making even the feeblest sort of sound.

Topping up the dog's bowl with vodka

I could more easily tell you Joy's favourite piece of music ('Slaughter on Tenth Avenue', less upsetting than its title seems to suggest) or favourite writer (Raymond Chandler) than I could tell you Mum's preferences in either realm. Why, I even stopped trying to persuade her that this most American of writers had been educated at a posh English school, though that detail was almost certainly put down as part of the biographical sketch in her Penguin copies of *Playback* and *Killer in the Rain*. Love could ask no more. I know Mum borrowed Georgette Heyer books from Bourne End library, not the romances but exclusively the detective stories, and even then she said she could take them or leave them. They passed the time.

Joy didn't immediately broach the subject of Christmas, talking about everything under the sun and then adding it as an afterthought. She certainly went around the houses! Perhaps she was dragging her feet, not really wanting to be used as a cat's paw in a charade of rec-onciliation. 'By the way, Laura and Dennis really want you to come home for Christmas – though I expect you're like me, John, and can't bear the waste at that time of year – the sheer amount of food every-one thinks they're supposed to want . . . Still, I know Audrey wants to see her big brother.' She'd said exactly the things that might have per-suaded me. Now I wanted to have Christmas in Bourne End, but not with the Cromers, with the Paynes. We could sit round the Scrabble board and really enjoy ourselves.

There was one Christmas Eve that the Cromers spent at Otters Pool with the Paynes. Joy's husband Guy had plied Peter and me with whisky – we were only teenagers – until we were in no fit state for Midnight Mass. Our heads were swimming, but I was hardly likely to tip out of the wheelchair, was I? Meanwhile Peter, performing the brotherly duty of pushing me in it, could unobtrusively support him-self, benefiting from my stability while he supplied mobility.

Peter's whisky had come in a tumbler, but Guy knew me well enough to give me a glass with a stem. He'd filled it up pretty much to the brim, though. At that stage I hadn't yet come across drinkers who splash the stuff around just to camouflage their own consump-tion. There are plenty of people who play the hearty host just to make their own drinking habits seem moderate, only stopping short of top-ping up the dog's bowl with vodka.

Joy came at the Christmas question from a number of angles in subsequent conversations. One was 'I know Dennis was asking what you might like as a Christmas present.' Bribery really comes into its own at Christmastime, doesn't it? This seemed quite an unlikely conversation on the face of it. I could imagine Joy asking Dad what he was thinking of getting me, and Dad saying, 'I don't know. Do I really need to get him something?' And Joy then using her tact to mould the conversation into a more obliging shape. It made me reconsider the idea that Joy was a saint. Joy Payne is a saint – everyone said so, and up to this point I had felt no need to disagree. But saints don't have elbows. They don't nudge things along. Prayer is not a higher form of nudging, unless I've gone about things the wrong way all my life.

Here she was on the phone, still trying to broker reunion in a family of irreconcilables, carrying around with her the pain of successive breakdowns but clinging to wholeness and refusing to let others be sundered without protesting, even when that sundering was their dearest wish.

'Oh, and Laura wants to know if you're still vegetarian.'

'Of course I'm still vegetarian.'

'Well, I thought so, but I promised I would ask. Why does she say "vegeteerian", by the way, John? Do you know? It's not a difficult word, and I've set her straight any number of times.' Paradoxically this healthful word, this titbit of sattvic wholesomeness, stuck in Mum's craw like the rankest gristle. She had set herself to tempt my appetite when I seemed to be fading away, but now that my vigour was assured she wasn't going to cater to what she saw as whims. How long does a whim have to hold firm until it is recognised as a principle?

My sense of myself as vegetarian was unchanged that autumn, despite my body's regular intake of meat. In a way I was being given a clue to something which sometimes puzzles people about Hinduism, even some Hindus: how can Krishna be described as celibate when he so constantly cavorts with milkmaids? The orthodox explanation is that for someone living in Brahma (as Krishna does) contradictions simply dissolve. States of being are never so absolute as to exclude an overlap, necessarily creating such anomalies as the celibate sex maniac or chop-chewing gravy-slurping vegetarian graduate member of the University he has left for good. In Hinduism, after all, there are (or have been) devout cannibals, members of the Aghori sect and caste who invert every ritual, setting excrement and corpses at the pinnacle of their system of values, smearing themselves with cremation ash, shaping human bones into jewellery and using skulls as begging bowls, and all to assert the same primordial truth as the mainstream of Hindu faith, that everything is holy. If everything is holy nothing can be unholy, as every mouthful of human carrion seeks to assert. Aghoris, like the radical twelfth-century poets I admired so much, are devotees of Śiva – clearly a deity who faces in all directions, not just forwards and backwards like the Roman Janus but upwards and downwards as well, licensing any amount of reverent desecration. He's the joker in the pack, except that the Hindu pack is all jokers.

With the help of this change in the frame of reference, my eating without protest the tamasic food that my home help served up shifts from a great and repeated betrayal of my principles to a rather niminy-piminy misdemeanour, the merest suburban indiscretion on the level of diet. Admittedly either Śiva or Krishna would have the gumption to tell their home help not to do it again, after she had innocently served him inappropriate food, without worrying too much about the embarrassment she would feel once she had realised her innocent slip-up. I had been more straightforward in the past, roundly denouncing the authorities at Downing for serving me steak under a thick camouflaging layer of tomatoes and vegetables. Why this late-arriving cowardice or feeble scruple? It isn't a sufficient explanation to say that I had felt more secure as a student, somehow included in the privileged expectations of the group, than I did now as a graduate without prospects. In any case, as so many have found before me, *anything for a quiet life* is not in fact a recipe for peace, either inner or outer. If I had contemplated my father's life with proper attention (to look no further) I would have grasped the truth of that.

Joy was asking, 'Is there something I could suggest as a present for you?' The thing that came immediately to mind wasn't an object but an experience. It had that little claim to eminence over the standard debased Christmas wish list.

If you were born on the 27th of December, you'll always feel upstaged in the nativity stakes. Anyone with a birthday hidden away between Christmas and New Year is likely to bear a calendrical grudge. To minimise trauma prospective parents (I'm only talking about Christian countries here) should be warned off coupling, ideally from mid-March to mid-April, the danger zone when it comes to Christmastime births. Who will speak out for us overshadowed ones, huddled beneath the manger? Generous-minded Robert Louis Stevenson did what he could, transferring his own November 13th birthday to an unlucky girl born on December 25th. Not a legally binding document, I imagine, but perhaps an illuminated scroll to make official-ish some early celebrations, not spoiled by the obligation to share.

Perhaps my feelings about Christmas are the feelings of a disappointed lover. I once had a pure love for it, not for the presents but the communication system that secured them: the Christmas lists that Peter and I made which were then burned so that the smoke would reach all the way up, or across, to Santa Claus in Lapland. I loved the idea of the meaningful smoke coming out of our chimney, just as I loved the Red Indians for their smoke signals. The white man's telegraph couldn't hold a candle to the Red Man's smoke. It took quite a time before I tumbled to the deception. When Mum checked the list 'to make sure there were no spelling mistakes' she was doing rather more than that. I was disappointed, but only in Mum and in Christmas, not in the mystical power of smoke.

On the phone to Joy, I started to make my wish. 'I want . . . I want . . .' My voice sounded strangely childlike, but then I was expressing a childhood wish, something I'd never brought into speech before. I wanted to look out of the peephole in the front door of Trees, to imagine myself as the eye of the house. The peephole was concealed behind a little sliding panel in the door, and naturally enough I had never been able to look out of it. To exploit it required a formidable array of physical skills, either enough tallness to peep through it unaided or the ability to clamber on a stool, as Peter and Audrey had been encouraged to do from childhood. Either way, a free hand was needed to pull the panel across and look out. I could drive a car, I had achieved a Cambridge degree of a discreditable sort. Why could I not be helped to look out of the front door of my childhood home, through an aperture designed for the purpose?

All I Want for Christmas Is a Pygmy Sphygmomanometer

My voice died away before I could reveal my secret wish. What it came down to was that I didn't have confidence in the welcoming committee. My secret was tender and I wasn't in a hurry to have it trampled. I trusted Joy but I could hardly tell her what I wanted for Christmas and then expect her not to pass it on. I changed wish midstream. 'I want . . . there's a book that's just been published called *The Natural Mind*. It's about drugs. That's what I'd like. A copy of that. It's by Andrew Weil, W-E-I-L.'

'We-e-e-ell,' she said, almost as she was choosing to misunderstand the author's name. 'Why don't I suggest that Dennis gets you a book token? Then you can choose for yourself.' This was very disappointing, coming from Bourne End's most evolved personality. A book token is a crime against the love of reading. I'd rather be given a book I end up hating than be told to make my own stupid choice. Without the electrical charge of the donor's taste such a gift means less than nothing. The book token is – was, I suppose I should say, since they disappeared long ago – the bored palace eunuch on duty in the seraglio of literature, telling you to look around and choose something you like the look of. Boys or girls, the eunuch doesn't care.

I wouldn't commit myself, not to a book token and not to a family Christmas either, though I could feel the pressure mounting. The silly thing was, I badly wanted to see Audrey, feeling guilty about the absence of contact even though it wasn't my choice, and if Mum had played a waiting game I might even have suggested coming home for Christmas myself.

Joy said, 'If you do come, as I hope you do, you have to expect your mother to have changed, you know, John. Laura has seemed a bit feverish lately, though Dennis won't see it. They're a little stuck in their ways, wouldn't you say?' More than a little, I'd say. 'They have their little routines, which they don't exactly enjoy but can't seem to keep away from. Have you noticed that Laura will always ask if the kettle's boiling, and Dennis always says, "The kettle's not boiling, my dear, but the water inside it is"? You'd think they'd both of them like to change the record, but it never seems to happen somehow. Anyway Laura has been a bit unlike herself, to my way of thinking at least, as if she was running a fever, but she says she's perfectly fine, that she feels better than she has in ages. But the thing is, she's started wearing make-up. I mean, she always did, but it was just a touch. No different from the other Bourne End ladies – no different from me! Now it's really quite obvious. It's as if she wants it to be noticed. Not like her at all. The Laura I know isn't like that. For a while I thought she was trying to show Audrey something in a roundabout way . . . that it was quite easy to look a bit – I'm sorry, John – a bit tarty. Young girls can be hard to talk to about such things, and of course they won't be told. They have to know best! So I thought that perhaps Laura was doing what teachers do when they want to get a message across very vividly and they use a Visual Aid. But it's not that, and it's been going on for quite a while now. I just wanted you to be a bit prepared.'

A Mum preoccupied with her appearance was certainly something to get used to. She disliked women who traded on sex appeal and was happy with her own relative absence of curves, with being 'straight up and down'. Her priority was to be neat and tidy, and if she ever put on a pound of weight that impertinent pound soon had cause to regret it.

The moment I was off the phone with Joy I realised what I wanted, far more than a trendy book on the healthiness of experimenting with drugs, something that I knew already. I should have asked for a pædiatric sphygmomanometer, so I could take my blood pressure properly at home. Still's Disease has any number of cardiovascular implications, and small body habitus means that adult sphygmomanometers are just too large to do the job. Perhaps I should have tried singing 'All I Want for Christmas Is a Pygmy Sphygmomanometer' to the tune of 'All I Want for Christmas Is My Two Front Teeth', though the syllables spill over however hard you try. And yes, I know 'pygmy' is somewhat insensitive, though species of animals with small body habitus (hippos, frogs, shrews) can receive that designation without scandal. In any case there's no appeal against the attraction of assonance, though I can't deny it's a bit of a mouthful.

I asked if Peter would be there at Christmas. 'Oh no, dear. I gather he's in Australia operating his mechanical digger. He's earning a lot of money, apparently, and he won't be home till he has got enough put by for a flat.' I knew this already, from Peter's laconic and even crabbed communications, but I was hoping that he would change his mind. A lot of the sting would have been taken out of the impending Christmas if only my brother was there too. He'd been the witness and sharer of my early life, and if he had been able to shed the family without letting go of me then I know that would have been his choice.

Secretly I thought it was a bit lazy on Peter's part to go all the way to Australia – imagining that by going to the far side of the world he was somehow freeing himself from the *vasanas* that had shaped him. It's a classic mistake to suppose that you must go to the jungle, or the outback, to realise yourself. You can realise yourself anywhere, and it was my plan to bring a truly opposite spiritual attitude (and by 'truly opposite' I mean slyly opposed to the very notion of an opposite) to Bourne End with me. The Mini was a pocket Antipodes, more distant from the world of Mum and Dad than Peter was managing, while I myself was the Southern Hemisphere in little. Or a gloriously paradoxical planet that was all Southern Hemisphere, spherical yet imperturbably unipolar.

Once at the end of one phone conversation Joy said, 'I'll love you and leave you, John – isn't that what people say? Such a funny way of putting it, though, almost a threat. Perhaps between us we can come up with something a bit nicer. Any ideas?'

'How about . . . loving you more than leaving you?'

'That's rather lovely, John. Let's use that from now on.' So we did.

Granny got in on the act with the Christmas deliberations, not because she had much time for the festival but because she disliked being excluded, and machination was her element. If I couldn't see what she had to gain then that in itself was no small part of her advantage. It might be a caprice of hers to weld links in the family chain together the better to pry them apart later. Westerners come over all surprised when they're told that Ganesh, the god who presides over the removal of difficulties, sometimes also installs them first, but haven't we all known people like that?

Her actual ideas about festivals certainly diverged from convention, both from social custom and from Ramana Maharshi's view, which describes celebrating a birthday as being like adorning a corpse. Why, she asked, did people persist in sending flowers on that one day, so that the house looked like a florist's and she ran out of vases, instead of organising things properly and sending bouquets at regular intervals throughout the year? And why this obsession with chocolate? 'You would think the world at large would know at this late date that chocolate is a substance that means nothing to me. I have never made a secret of my weaknesses, and my vice – such as it is – is liquorice.' The thin coating of self-parody, habitual with Granny, took away the taste of her egotism in her own mouth, if not in mine.

The stone money of Yap springs to mind

Granny was fluent on the phone, but it was always a mistake to be lulled into too receptive a state by her confident diction and delivery. You might find you had signed a contract without reading it, and no good can ever come of that. I had learned to be especially wary when she seemed to be rambling, straying very far from the point, which was usually a sign she was setting her snares.

By this time in my life I had probably spent more time hearing Granny's voice transmitted through a wire than dealing with her in the flesh. I suppose her generation, and her class, grew up with some familiarity with the instrument. I remember her saying, '*I shall call you on the electric telephone* – that's what we used to say in my young days. We found that rather amusing. Very few people had telephones in those days.' The ponderous phrase was probably in distant mockery of her elders, slow to get used to this new means of communication.

For most people, for practically everyone, phone calls were not relaxing experiences, what with every minute and part-minute charged for, even for calls of the shortest distance, calls between neighbours. As a child, it's true, I had been given the privilege of telephoning in the family grocery order each week, as a way of keeping me in contact with the wider world, and the phone was my lifeline first on A6 Kenny staircase and then in 005 Mayflower House, but I didn't go overboard with outgoing calls. Even when Mr Moneybags' delivery meant that I was fairly flush financially and could have afforded to call the Met Office to ask why the local weather forecast was so often wrong I resisted the impulse.

School friends of mine at Burnham Grammar School who lived almost next door to each other had rigged up a walkie-talkie between their bedrooms, slinging a wire over the roofs, just so they could chat for free. I suppose there were other advantages from their point of view, including the ability to talk without being overheard by parents and siblings, on top of the unfading pleasure of saying 'over' and 'over and out' over and over again.

One morning Granny telephoned while I was getting a bath, and naturally enough Paula rushed to the phone trying to wipe shampoo off her hands and played for time as calmly as she could, saying, 'Would you be kind enough to phone later, please, madam? He's having his bath.' Bathing me was part of Mr Gerling's portfolio rather than Paula's, but I liked it so much better when she did it.

I couldn't blame her for a single syllable of what she said, but I could also see that two of those syllables wouldn't go down well. Granny exacted deference but reserved the right to be treated as an equal, and the word 'madam' and its implications rubbed her up entirely the wrong way. Suddenly the grandson in whom she was indulgent enough to take an interest in had become a Noël Coward leading man, an exquisite idler whose maid fobbed off callers, both those who knocked on the door and those who used the phone, while he lounged in a yellow silk dressing gown to open his fan mail, pausing to smell the pages to see how alluringly they had been scented. To my cost I knew that Granny would indeed call back, and that I wouldn't enjoy it when she did. I would be on the back foot from the first word and was unlikely, for the duration of that conversation, to regain the upper hand.

'John, do you have a moment?' Paula wedged the telephone receiver in a bearable position with a bean bag – otherwise long calls would leave me shaking with pain.

'Of course I have a moment. I have any number of moments.'

'Splendid – because I rather received the impression that you were busy. You might not have time for your little Granny. Young men have a lot on their plates, I understand that, they may not have time in their busy lives for mere family.'

Yes, mere family. Ghosts and cobwebs of unreal affinity. Every ounce of spiritual feeling I had opposed itself to the grip of family, yet I found myself squirming and simpering, 'Not at all, Granny. I am at your disposal.'

And then of course she said, 'There's no call to abase yourself, John. Without self-respect life has no value.' That was Granny, Granny all over. First she required capitulation then gave me a scolding for not standing up to her.

Granny enjoyed a certain amount of spoofing when it came to other people's habits. She and her best friend Alice (though friendship seemed too stable a relation to please Granny for long) would exchange birthday and Christmas presents, 'like Elizabeth' as she explained, literally exchanging them on a ritual basis without ever unwrapping them. Those presents circulated like some exotic and unworkable currency – the stone money of Yap comes to mind. Granny's present was a coffee pot, and she was fairly sure that Alice's was a goffering iron. They carried this consciously absurd ritual to such a point that if they were not going to meet on or near the relevant dates of birthday and Christmas they would wrap the object whose turn it was (on top of the wrapping that was their permanent state) and put it in the post. Less determined women might decide at some point that their mild satire on other people's sentimental habits had mildly backfired, if it meant that they spent hours in a queue waiting to post a present that was supposed to show up the ridiculousness of celebrating personal ties with gifts, but they kept at it.

I imagine she disliked the unthinking celebration of birthdays and Christmas on the basis that a generalised benign fog obscured the clean outlines she valued in transactions both inside and outside the family. She preferred to give presents at other times than the designated festivals, not wanting her very calculated generosities to be mistaken for mere diffused goodwill.

In fact Granny took enough pleasure in the ritual to mention it more than once, and she must have realised that I didn't know who it was she meant by 'Elizabeth'. The obvious candidates (Windsor, Bowes-Lyon, Taylor) seemed unlikely mockers of present-giving. When I admitted my ignorance she just sighed.

'Sometimes I despair of your generation. Do the young not read?' Apparently 'Elizabeth' was the author of *Elizabeth and Her German Garden*, a favourite book of Granny's youth, and it wasn't only the birthday-present wheeze that she remembered from it. The heroine of the book describes a husband as being like a sofa that turns into a bed, in that it doesn't work particularly well as either a sofa or a bed. The suggestion I suppose is that the sofa represents the companionable side of marriage, the bed its more torrid aspect. To spell it out: the rôles of husband and lover are incompatible. Trying to combine them only results in awkwardness. I remember, too, that the husband in the book was referred to as the 'Man of Wrath', a joke that wasn't entirely a joke. The evidence, though, seemed to suggest that Granny had nothing to fear from Ivo's temper, only his unreliability.

Alice had been Granny's 'matron of honour', a term that she explained was correct usage for the chief bridesmaid if she happened to be married. Granny was very big on correct usage, at least on the surface. She let slip at one point – except that there was no letting-slip involved in such a calculated disclosure – that it was not part of a matron of honour's duties to break off sexual relations with the groom. As she put it, 'I don't know if Alice stopped sleeping with Ivo after we were married. I never asked.' She didn't exactly say it was none of her business, but that was certainly the implication. It sounded as if there was rather a lot of rearranging of the marital furniture going on in Granny's set. It can't always have been easy to sleep for the creaking.

Sometimes she referred to Alice as 'Craven A', something that I eventually asked her (with the usual sinking feeling) to explain. 'Oh surely you know Craven A, John – "For Your Throat's Sake"? With a black cat on the packet?' I did not. Not only did the young not read the right books, they didn't remember cigarette advertisements that were popular before they were born. Alice's last name was Craven, which I suppose gave the nickname some colour. 'And what was so special about Craven A cigarettes, Granny?'

'Why, the cork tip, of course. Not a filter, just a tip.'

Again the sensation that I was on the edge of a cliff of ignorance, fairly begging Granny to tip me into the void. 'But what's the point of a tip that isn't a filter?'

'Well, before non-stick papers you might find a bit of your lip had stuck to your cigarette. The cork tip made sure that did not happen. Of course men were more vulnerable – the wearing of lipstick makes unwanted adherence to your cigarette unlikely. And it's men who are the great complainers. Ivo smoked Craven A and so did I, even when he was in Africa "making our fortune" as he so fondly imagined. I may even have a packet in a drawer somewhere.' I thought it should stay there.

The gentlemen of the law warm their hands impartially

The fact that Ivo wasn't Mum's father was that strangest of things, an open secret in a closed family. She had told me on my eighteenth birthday something that was for her a terrible secret and to me a complete irrelevance. Perhaps she made the same disclosure to Peter when he came of age. If so she was likely to have been just as disappointed by his reaction. He was a great shrugger, an instinctive dismisser of overloaded emotion. He may not even have paid enough attention to realise how much it explained about Mum's psychology, the conformism that was in stark contrast to Granny's conviction that she could go her own way and not suffer, or not suffer in the long term.

At least Granny didn't bear her out of wedlock, even if conception occurred in the absence of a husband. She had the strong protection that married status conferred in the years between the wars, and after all no one could prove as a matter of fact that Ivo hadn't interrupted his attempts to establish a coffee plantation to pay a flying return visit to the marital home at a legally providential moment. She was safe as long as she played the game. She could ride out any threat of scandal on condition of paying lip service to respectability, which turned out to be just what she couldn't do. Did she actually tell me, 'I couldn't go through with it, John. Your little Granny rebelled!'? Perhaps I filled in the blanks, since for once it was easy to reconstruct the missing pieces. 'If you compromise when you're in a strong position that's all very well, but if you make concessions when you're at your weakest you're sunk.' That has the true ring of Granny logic, distilled almost into a theorem. She had planned to register Mum as Ivo's, but then at the last moment she gave the real father's name, putting her disgrace on record. I could imagine her sweeping the mantelpiece clear of invitations, with a small, well-formed hand – wearing an evening glove, why not? – sweeping away not just invitations that had already arrived but the prospect of a whole five years' worth of pasteboard and social life. Her hands were one of the few items in her self-inventory that passed muster, and she took good care of them. Despite her description of herself as my 'little Granny', she was above average height for a woman. She would have liked to be smaller, so as to live down to her hands.

She had been brought up on goat's milk after being sick drinking cow's, and had been fed pineapples grown in a conservatory. Granny claimed to associate the taste of pineapple with the relief of Mafeking, the luscious pang of the fruit in her childish mouth corroborating the good news that imperial pride had been redeemed. She must have been four. I had another grandmother in the wings, but Dad's mother was a marginal figure in the family comedy, while Granny aspired to centre stage, feeding the other actors their lines when she didn't have a speech of her own to make.

Her privileged upbringing had given her the toughness required to manage when privileges were withdrawn, a difficult period coinciding with Mum's childhood. While Granny prospered in hard times, Mum somehow absorbed adversity into her bones. The lack of proper ego-food and social sunlight during those crucial growing years had given her character something like a case of rickets.

Five years' worth, because it took that long for the invitations to start flowing again. Ivo 'stood by her' – except that the stock formula doesn't really represent what happened. He had nowhere else to stand except beside his wife, since 'Ivo's coffee adventure' as she called it had been a disaster, bringing not riches but a rich portfolio of debts. Both 'her people' and 'his people' left them to stew in their own juice. His health had broken down, too, in a way that she left mysterious and that may even have been mysterious to her. 'Ivo was never going to make old bones, even before,' she said, without saying why she thought so.

Somehow the reconstituted family held its own and earned back a sort of respectability, with the added prosperity that came from renewed links with both sides of the family. It may be that after her time out in the cold, socially speaking, Granny came to prefer the warmth of a hearth to the wildfire of passion without shelter. Most forceful women who manage to tame the man they have chosen are disappointed by the result, the fizzling triumph of uncontested dominance. Granny seems to have been an exception. Perhaps I should refer to her as 'Barbara Mildred' rather than Granny, since obviously she wasn't a grandmother then. The birth of a son, my Uncle Roy, set the seal on Barbara Mildred's new life. The birth of a male child, in a certain social stratum, seems to send hasty schemes of disinheritance into reverse like nothing else, to the quiet delight of those solicitors who get paid both coming and going as testamentary dispositions crackle with dismissive rage or kindle with renewed affection. The gentlemen of the law warm their hands impartially on either source of heat.

In the course of one phone call Granny said, 'I am led to believe, John, that your mother especially wants you to spend Christmas at Bourne End. She's a difficult woman, as we both know, and whether it's better to humour her or contest her wishes and hope that she sees sense seems to be . . . as the expression goes, a toss-up.'

Granny certainly made a habit of intervening, but changed sides at will, sometimes driving a wedge between me and Mum and Dad and sometimes appointing herself reconciler-in-chief. She took credit for eliminating a mysterious obstacle to their getting married, claiming to have found and paid for the 'top man' who had overcome Dad's qualms or medical worries, but she wasn't particularly impressed by the union she had brought about and seemed to feel only intermittently that she had an interest in its survival.

'So why don't you spend Christmas with me, up home? I don't know how jolly it will be, but you'll be warm. I can teach you the rules of mah-jongg, if you don't already know them.'

Imagine your little Granny serving granules!

That 'up home' was very characteristic, not a phrase I've heard on anyone else's lips. She seemed to imagine her house as an absolute eminence, from which you went downwards in any direction. People, posh people, always talked about going 'up' to London, not because they were travelling from south to north, if they were, but because you went up to the larger place from the smaller. Class isn't just a matter of accent and vocabulary but syntax and grammar, even punctuation. Nothing keeps out the rabble like a barricade of semi-colons, and these, likewise, were the prepositions of privilege. Granny's reference

584

points followed the 'up to London' model, but her conventions were her own. I could imagine her, post-mortem, going to her long rest, perhaps tactfully refraining from calling St Peter 'my man', but certainly insisting she was going 'down' to heaven. She was expected.

Granny's rules were no easier to accept than Mum's, but her invitation was not something that could be refused. If need be she would send a car to fetch me. I wasn't attracted by this rather John le Carré touch. Would I return if I got into the car Granny sent? The Grandson Who Came in from the Cold might never be seen again.

'Did Laura ever mention that we used to have new potatoes at Christmas lunching?' I don't think I'm wrong in remembering her pronunciation of the word 'luncheon', itself obsolescent. 'I expect you're wondering how your clever Granny managed that. It just takes a little forethought. You fill a tin box with new potatoes when they're in season and simply dig a hole in the garden and bury it. As long as they stay cool, as they do, and are kept out of the light, as they are, then they keep more or less as long as you like. This is not at all like the Chinese and their hundred-year-old eggs, and I personally would not try to keep them more than a few months, but having new potatoes on Christmas Day is such a treat. It sets the seal on the day, and would no doubt have given Laura happy memories, if she was only capable of amassing such things. I heard something on the radio the other day, John, which rather struck me. "It's never too late to have a happy childhood," someone was saying. You might pass that on to her. Perhaps Laura will be laying on Christmas new potatoes in her turn, though I can't quite see her planning ahead as the treat requires.

'As I say, John, you are entirely welcome to spend the festival with me at Tangmere. Your Uncle Roy may pay a visit at some point, and I'm sure you would enjoy spending some time with him.' No mention of whether he would enjoy spending time with me, which was even less likely. I didn't know whether to take the invitation to spend Christmas with her as a serious threat, if I didn't dance to Mum's tune, or as a test. Perhaps she was trying to discover how much subservience corresponded to a delivery of £600 in a substandard bag. The idea of spending time with my Uncle Roy was not appealing. He came first with Granny from the moment he was born, and I had seen at first hand how little time she had for Mum, the mere first-born daughter, but Roy was unable to relax into his position as the favourite and fought off any suggestion of sharing. Perhaps birth order is more important than is generally recognised and a second child is always born into the cold shadow of the first. From Roy's point of view I was one more claimant on his mother's attention.

Did I block some of the light from falling on my brother Peter, in the couple of years before illness put me in a shadow zone of my own? It's not something I can know, though I'm fairly sure that Audrey, arriving quite a few years later, had mother love shone on her altogether too fiercely. If it didn't burn her skin then it did something stranger, rendering her immune in the short term.

'I haven't been given the notice that would be required to produce new potatoes on Christmas Day, but I'm confident that something can be arranged. You may not believe that your little Granny does her own shopping, she can scarcely believe it herself, but in the Village Stores here there is offered a product, or at least a substance, called Smash. Instant mashed potatoes, of all earthly delights. I'm told they're "granules". It might be rather amusing to serve you some of those with your vegetarian spread, your beanfeast. Imagine your little Granny serving granules! Perhaps they will want me to appear in an advertisement for the substance. Stranger things have happened.' They must have, but I couldn't think of any offhand. 'Tinned peas and carrots, perhaps, for your main course. Tinned fruit and tinned custard for dessert. A return to wartime rations! Don't worry about bringing a tin opener, John, the kitchen is well equipped.'

As the family found its equilibrium with the reconciliation of Granny and Ivo, and bedded down into seeming conventionality, the only absolute loser was Mum, was Laura, whose childhood coincided with exile and a poverty that was more than relative. Barbara Mildred and Ivo really did get by on next to nothing in the late 1920s and early '30s. It's even possible that burying new potatoes in a metal box was a good investment in terms of Christmas jollity, though jollity was a notion Barbara Mildred would have regarded with suspicion. Perhaps Roy liked them – that would have been reason enough.

With two agents in the field working on their behalf there was no call for Mum and Dad to get directly involved. Admittedly Granny was a rogue agent if ever there was one, capable of shifting allegiance just for the fun of the thing, but Joy Payne would never put her own interests ahead of the Cromers. Her ego corresponded, as closely as is possible in a life without detectable austerity, to the Hindu description of the enlightened person's, shining without the slightest selfish heat, like 'the moon in the daytime'.

Relied upon to deliver more death than love

Yet Mum and Dad did get involved, in a way that I found quietly shocking. There was nothing as straightforward involved as picking up the phone and saying, 'John? I know Christmas is as unreal to you as the horns of the hare or the children of a barren woman — something that exists in language but has no more deeply rooted existence — but do you think you might put your principles aside for a few days for Audrey's sake? She doesn't know why you're staying away and it's not something we've been able to explain to her.' Of course the moment I've put those words into their mouths I realise how impossible it would be for either parent to deliver them. Dad could never have been so direct nor Mum so calm. It's actually these unrecognisable, undeluded people who resemble the horns of the hare, the children of the barren woman.

What they did sounds so simple. They sent a telegram. No, that's wrong, what they sent was a 'telegram'. Mrs Baine was as excited as if that capricious deity ERNIE 2 had showered me with the unlikely blessing (since my little handful of Premium Bonds was held hostage in Bourne End) of a payout.

She came dancing along the hallway and knocked on my door, calling out, 'Telegram for you, Mr Cromer — heavens, I don't know when I last saw one of those!' Almost before she had entered the room she was tearing open the outsized yellow envelope, something that I wouldn't normally have stood for. On this occasion, though, in the frenzy of her impatience she seemed if anything to be doing me a favour, since her excitement had sparked my own. She pulled the telegram form out of the envelope and handed it to me, though I feel sure that in the split second of its being airborne and on its way towards its designated recipient her eyes had pounced on its message.

Concierges have their little ways. I even sympathised, having taught myself long ago to read doctors' handwriting upside down from the far side of a desk without seeming to pay any particular attention.

The message read CHRISTMAS + IS + COMING + THE + GOOSE + IS + GETTING + FAT + COME + HOME + SON + ALL + IS + FORGIVEN + LOVE + DADMUM. Everything about it was disordered. The sentiment was distorted enough, with its mixture of phoney good cheer and blackmail so perfectly setting the agenda for Christmases everywhere. It was the ending that created the maximum of dismay. Not the proximity of 'love' and Mum and Dad – Mum used the word freely in conversation, if only to denounce 'love stuff' on stage and screen and anywhere else. Those Georgette Heyer detective stories she borrowed from the library, though less well known than the Regency romances, could be relied upon to deliver more death than love. I suppose she felt personally betrayed by the word 'love' or what it promised, a betrayal more than confirmed when I joined the ranks of the treacherous. Dad never said 'love' in person but he would put it at the end of the postcards he sent us when we were children. He put it on record that he knew the word. Well, it was more than that. He could see his feelings more clearly when we weren't around to confuse him.

But who on earth or anywhere else was this appalling entity DADMUM? The griffin and the manticore, hydra and centaur, every chimæra in the bestiary of the impossible seemed more harmonious than this hybrid. No proofreader confronted with a botched stretch of text could have felt the need to open a space in the middle of that shockingly compacted portmanteau word more desperately than I did. It seemed so wrong. Of course it's customary in telegrams to jam words together for economy's sake, but was there really a special rate for sixteen words, so as to warrant the abridgement?

Mum and Dad shared a bed, yes, but she felt the cold and he was hardy. If she was shivering even with a hot water bottle then he was sweatily throwing off blankets in his sleep. She banned him from sleeping naked, though – I have to ask – how do I know this? It was as if their metabolisms were insisting on their incompatibility. They had no instinct to turn towards each other for warmth, since one already had too much of it and the other too little. No flaming sword placed between them was needed to underline the point. They turned away from each other with perfect naturalness. For them to produce three children there must have been at least that many incidents of DADMUM, but I found it hard to imagine many more. There were moments of DAD-and-MUM, of course. I'm not making out there weren't amicable episodes now and then. But we in the household were well used to DAD   MUM, to DAD   MUM, even to DAD

           MUM. I have to say, though, that there was a strange periodicity, phases of rupture alternating with what you might call unsought rapprochements, half-reconciliations that were inadvertent but somehow inevitable. However often Mum retreated to her base of operations in the kitchen, or Dad barricaded himself in the garden shed, they would seek each other out on a pretext. He would bring in some rhubarb, or she would claim to have lost track of something though it was clearly labelled on the spice rack. Their incompatibility was glaring but neither had the talent that is required for sustained estrangement.

Cooks were not adventurous in those days, and Mum's spice rack amounted to a very modest run of jars. She would unscrew the tops of the little bottles of almond and vanilla essence to shake out numbered drops of flavouring into cake mixes. Her fingers dipped freely into the angelica, into the ground nutmeg and cinnamon and the caraway seeds, reached confidently into the jar of whole cloves to stud an onion for bread sauce, but hesitated over the curry powder. This was kitchen nitroglycerin, dangerous in the smallest quantities. Even white pepper was gingerly tapped out of its container. She wasn't yet altogether confident in the language of herbs, though I'm sure Joy Payne was already fluent, accustomed to their different accents. Mum used dried sage and mint without anxiety, but the level of the oregano in its little glass jar never seemed to go down.

In cases of kidnap the abducted person can sometimes manage to sneak into the ransom note they're being made to write some private message that will give the authorities or the anxious family some sort of clue. This was exactly the opposite of that situation, though hardly

589

less distressing. The message absolutely violated the characters of the people purported to have concocted it. It could have nothing to do with them. Where it was, they were not, and the same proposition applied with no less force the other way round. Where they were, it was not — yet here it was, somehow claiming to be signed by them.

'Isn't that lovely?' cooed Mrs Baine, having read the message, or having re-read it, over my shoulder. The satisfaction in her voice didn't convey her real emotional response so much as the pleasure she could anticipate, from passing on the suggestion that I needed my parents' forgiveness for sins unspecified. This was a nutritious item that could be chewed as cud, ever stale, ever fresh, endlessly recirculated in the multiple stomachs of gossip rumination.

The only sin that might properly be held against me was my inadvertent subscription to *Contact* magazine. In the late '60s this enlightened organisation would send you a free sample. This was wildly exciting, above all the 'Personals Sexion'. My sample copy was followed by others; in fact they never got around to charging me. Copies followed me to Downing, sent on by Mum even after our rupture. She can't have known what it was, perhaps mistaking it for Major Howell's eccentric and indispensable seed catalogue, which I'd taken the trouble to have redirected, or else was striking a pose of martyred dutifulness. For months those copies of *Contact* she sent on were the only contact we had. I'm sure the magazine would have gone on sending me free copies right up to the day when (for no very obscure reason) the magazine folded. Perhaps they grasped the basic principles of business at the exact moment the bailiffs came a-knocking. It's often the way.

Little Bo-Peep trying to calm her panicked sheep

I hated that telegram, not a telegram at all but no more than a sickly mock-up, and I hated Mrs Baine's whipped-up froth of excitement about it. The fakery was obvious, as much on the level of technology as emotion — I didn't much mind the insult to family feeling, since no such thing exists, but I resented the insult to the telegram. This debased replica of the real thing was delivered by the ordinary postman, there was nothing remotely special involved in the way of procedure. Yes, it came quicker than it might have done, quicker than first-class post, almost as quickly as a phone call — since presumably Dad (or someone) had paid good money to dictate it over the phone. He would have spent less, something that normally appealed to him, by phoning me direct and talking man to man. Talking man to man was supposed to be a good thing but in my experience it was something men did very little of.

I could remember the excitement that was caused when a real telegram arrived at the Vulcan School for the rich boy Abadi Mukherjee, when his father (who owned the Appa Corporation) sent him one on his birthday, and the bustle of its arrival. In theory the great occasion in those years was the visit the Queen Mother made to the school, but that was a crude event by comparison. The telegram form with its enigmatic compressed wording pasted on in strips was passed round like a holy relic. Did a messenger come to the Castle on a bicycle, a specialist operative with no other duties, a telegram boy? Even if we didn't see one we believed that such a person existed and had ridden at top speed, pounding the pedals and ringing his bell to clear the road of less urgent traffic. I could almost see Little Bo-Peep trying to calm her panicked sheep while the rider of a penny-farthing toppled into a hedge in his desperate attempt to get out of the way.

We associated telegrams with excitement and good news, which shows our innocence. Older people, having lived through a war, could only have a more complicated response. Death revealed itself in Morse code down a wire. Reprieves also, of course, but no one of those generations could receive a telegram without a lurch of the pulse, though we at Vulcan could have survived indefinitely on a diet of them. When Abadi's telegram arrived we hardly noticed (I speak for the group) that it wasn't our own birthdays that were being celebrated. The glory might be spread thinly but there was more than enough of it to go round.

On the other hand, we wouldn't have felt deprived if the Queen Mother's visit hadn't come off. We might well have preferred a telegram, along the lines of the helpful sign at the official reception in *The Young Visiters*, displayed next to where bishops 'and other searious people' are eating ice cream, that reads *Her Majesty Is Indisposed*.

As I remember it, when the birthday telegram arrived at Vulcan in my schooldays it came in a small brown envelope rather than a big yellow one. The slip inside it on which the strips of message were stuck was unassuming. It had a job to do, and pageantry was no part of it. The 'telegram' I was sent in the run-up to Christmas 1973 was much bigger, and the folded card inside bore a bright design. I think it was an autumnal landscape in orangey yellows and browns.

Would it have been better or worse if the design had been more crassly seasonal, crowded with robins and snowmen? It made no odds to me since the whole thing was a fraud. The Post Office (not the General Post Office any longer, the veteran institution had been reduced in the ranks) had devised a profitable little sideline, but I wasn't fooled. In the age of the teleprinter the whole thing was a nonsense. There had been no Morse code involved, none of that exciting dot–dot–dash, the stuttering dance of impulses down a wire. Even though I preferred smoke signals to electrically transmitted messages, there was still room in my heart for the telegraph. It should be allowed some dignity in its retirement. No one would have blamed Mum and Dad for having a superstitious dread of this form of message. Instead, unaccountably, they were trivialising it. I was the only one who saw it as an intrinsically serious means of communication, not to be turned into a gimmick. Everyone was humouring me about this supposedly special message, and I hated it, hated both the 'telegram' and the humouring.

The worst part of it was that I felt I could detect Joy Payne's influence, sweetly intended but in this case badly misfiring – 'Dennis, the last thing I'd want to do is interfere, but why not send John a telegram about coming home for Christmas? Isn't that just the sort of thing he loves . . .? If there's a chance of it bringing him round I'd say it was worth a try.' Her loving fingerprints were all over that telegram (the telegram that wasn't one), and I wished I was able to scrub them off or pretend I hadn't noticed them.

It was as if everyone was determined to find out how many turns of the screw it would take before the family vice finally squeezed the consent out of me. I had more or less decided to return 'home' for Christmas, so that the campaign to make me do so became redundant, yet there seemed to be no stopping it. There's no point in knocking at an open door, let alone charging one with a battering ram, which just proves my point about the insanity of family. When this very situation arrives in silent comedy films the besieged heroes open both front door and back as the battering ram approaches. The momentum of the invasion party's charge makes them plunge right through the house and over a little hill behind it, never to be seen again. There's no doubt that this, or its equivalent, would have been the spiritually advisable course of action, a withholding of resistance that stood implacably apart from agreement. Nor would my guru (my guru *in absentia*, though it was the mootest of points who was absent from whom) have disdained an analogy drawn from cinema, since Ramana Maharshi was so fond of using them himself.

Whether or not Joy Payne was implicated in the fiasco of the telegram, she was the obvious person for me to tell that I was throwing in the towel of Yuletide resistance.

'Mum and Dad really took me by surprise – they sent a telegram.'

'Oh, was that fun?'

'Great fun.' It pained me that Joy should have joined a conspiracy, even one that thought itself benign – don't they all?

'But you're still not on speakers with Dennis and Laura?' I wondered at 'on speakers' – had she perhaps been reading Nancy Mitford?

'Still not.'

'So should I pass on the joyous tidings on your behalf?'

'Feel free. Though I have some conditions. Do you want to get a pencil?'

'Oh dear. Is it a long list?'

'Not long, no, and I mean no disrespect but it's important to get the message across in full.'

'Very well, dear. I make no claim for my secretarial skills, though I can usually pass on messages fairly accurately . . . but I'll try not to take it personally. I expect that's for the best.'

'Much best.'

'Hang on a minute, then.' I waited for her to return to the receiver. 'Fire away, John.'

'Item first – I will stay two nights at Trees and no more. Item second – I will not be a part of any religious observance. Item third – I will bring no presents and will accept none.'

'Can you repeat that last item, please?'

'Of course – I will bring no presents and will accept none.'

'But surely you'll want to buy something for Audrey, if no one else?'

The moment she said it I could feel the force of what she was saying. But wasn't it the thin end of the wedge to make any sort of exception? That's the thing about family. Tremendous leverage can be exerted once a crack has been opened up. The crevice becomes a chasm.

'I'll have a think about that. But Mum and Dad have to agree to it just the same.'

'It's a tall order, John. Anything else while I've got my pencil handy?'

'One more thing,' I told her.

'Yes, John?'

'I'll be bringing a parrot.'

'What's that?'

'I'll be bringing an African grey parrot.'

'Yes, I thought that's what you said! I'll have to ask Laura about that. Perhaps you're looking for an excuse not to come . . .'

'Of course I am, Joy, but I can't find one. Still, if I do come I'll be coming with a parrot. And that's definite. Make sure Mum knows what she's letting herself in for.'

After all, if I agreed to Christmas at Bourne End I needn't worry about Granny summoning me to Tangmere.

Its plutocratic absorbency perhaps giving it the edge

The proposal to bring a parrot with me wasn't a long-thought-out plan, but nor was it an idea plucked from the air. I wouldn't have made the undertaking without being fairly sure of seeing it through. I had indeed been spending some time with an African grey parrot named Phyllis, belonging to herself (as animals do) but placed in the uncertain hands of Major Spinks, the manager of Mayflower House and its most privileged resident, with the benefit of a large flat on the ground floor adjoining his office. My flat could have fitted inside it four or five times, as I could see on my first visit. The Major and I were known to each other, of course, and in an evening emergency (when Mrs Baine had gone home) he was the one to summon, as I had found in the matter of The Mouse That Wouldn't Die. I don't mean to imply that all adult men who buy Variety Packs of cereal have lost their bearings in life, but there was certainly a haunted quality to him, suggestive of bereavement or marital breakdown. In those days the two afflictions were much closer in their emotional spectrum than they are now, but for the life of me I couldn't get Mrs Baine to tell me which of them it was that had derailed the Major. Mrs Baine was a gossip of a shamelessness that was close to admirable, but she had her limits. This was tattle that would not pass her lips. The code of *omertà* between concierge and manager could not be violated, and so I was denied the only information that actually interested me between those walls.

When I heard that he had bought a parrot I was concerned. To my mind he didn't have the social or personal skills to offer such an exquisite creature a suitable home. A dog or a cat would have tamed him in their very different ways, a dog offering companionship and a bottomless fidelity, a cat consenting to co-existence without granting any detectable privilege. Birds weren't explicitly banned and therefore must be allowed, but I wondered if he had given any thought to how Phyllis took in the world. How would she cope? How was her talking coming along?

From the first I had expressed interest in Phyllis's progress, passing messages through Mrs Baine, who was the Major's representative on earth, or at least behind the counter in the lobby of Mayflower House. I hinted broadly, then less broadly, that I would appreciate a display of her skills. Luckily it's almost unheard of for a parrot owner to refuse a visit from an interested party, and we set a suitable time. I was taken into his flat-cum-office, where her cage, naturally enough, had pride of place. He took the cover off it and opened the door. She hopped out and looked at me.

Phyllis's cage was furnished with the basic amenities for a captive with feathers. There was a cuttlefish bone and a water pot, a bell to ring, a little feeding dish and a forlorn suspended garland of millet. There was even a mirror, though it didn't look as if Phyllis could see herself in it from her place on the perch. The only detectable touch of luxury was that the bottom of her cage was lined with salmon-coloured sheets of the *Financial Times*, its plutocratic absorbency perhaps giving it the edge over other papers. Or perhaps it was just that back numbers of the Pink 'Un were passed on to the Major, just as I was a reluctantly addicted recipient of the *Cambridge Evening News*.

'Major, shouldn't Phyllis's mirror be hung where she can see herself in it?'

'It used to be. She looked at herself the whole time, which I didn't think was healthy. It's not as if she's going to forget what she looks like! I put it back up once in a while, though. It seems to cheer her up.'

'She's beautiful. No harm in her knowing.'

'She's a nice little thing.'

Poor Phyllis's life was being drastically controlled and regimented. I was brought up in a house where budgies had been trained to take seed from Mum's mouth and even to pull the cat's whiskers, but they weren't asserting themselves, just fulfilling Mum's wishes. At the time I thought this was natural, and it took a book of Kipling's to change my mind. Not Rudyard, mind you, but his father Lockwood, author of the magnificent 1892 volume *Beast and Man in India* – having gone to the trouble of creating the confusion I should at least show willing and clear it up. Here was a man who could confirm from personal experience the foulness of pythons' breath, even if most of what he writes about snakes is about the part they play in Indian folklore – Hindus, for instance, being required to mourn a snake they have killed as if it was a dead relation. I moved on to more technical works about the reptilia.

The passage that so struck me was about parrots – he's talking specifically about the parakeet *Palæornis eupatrius*, whose depredations in the fields and groves of India are tolerated, according to the dear old boy, because they are credited with having brought seeds of fruit and grain from Paradise after the Flood. Their beaks are so sharp that they can't be kept in wooden cages, but their sufferings in metal ones – 'one cannot but grieve for the captive slowly roasting in his tiny oven-like prison' – don't seem to be a matter of concern to their keepers. 'Leaving the general question that is sure to arise some day,' he goes on, 'as to our right to imprison creatures for our pleasure at all, the confinement we inflict should be at least as little irksome as possible; but it is hard to persuade people that creatures have rights, and a polite smile is the only answer to a plea for these prisoners.' He remarks that the phrase 'parrot eyed' is used in India to describe a deceitful or ungrateful person, on the basis that a captive bird, however fussed over, is only waiting for the day the cage is left open. And quite right too. So it should.

Mum's favourite budgie Charlie had been parrot eyed in that sense and had made a dash for it when he could. Phyllis was a more complex character. Her grey plumage was as varied in tone as a pair of men's striped formal trousers, though the underside of her tail feathers was a startling scarlet, something that no trouser lining can match (red socks, obviously, don't count). Her eye seemed to take me in whole, though she turned her head as if to reassure herself that she wasn't seeing things. Is it a myth that vulnerable prey animals have eyes on either side of their heads, with limited overlaps of the field of vision (but magnificent peripheral coverage), while predators require depth perception for effective hunting? All I can say is that Phyllis didn't look much like prey, however limited the overlap in her visual field. She seemed to perch pretty high up the food chain.

The Major produced a peanut and said, 'Hello.' Phyllis said 'Hello' back to him, was offered the peanut and ate it. I felt that we had been introduced and waited for proper conversation to begin. Then the Major said, 'Would you like me to do it again?' and I realised that as far as the Major was concerned, at least, the performance was over. Weeks of 'training', to call it that, had produced the most rudimentary exchange of word and treat. The limitations were all in teacher rather than pupil, but they were no less absolute for that. I felt like a parent turning up to the school concert to find that his child is being applauded for locating middle C but not encouraged to make any more substantial excursion into music.

Parrots don't really talk, of course, lacking vocal cords, but they can produce an extraordinary range of sounds, both in mimicry and spontaneous expression. They let pressure build up in the glottis, trachea and œsophagus, controlling its release by means of tongue placement and adjustment of the beak. Phyllis wasn't much of a talker, but then neither was the Major. Two understimulated creatures each waiting for the other to make the first move – if this was the pattern of the Major's relationships it wasn't surprising that he should be living alone. It could hardly be a consolation for Phyllis that her captor had locked himself in the cell by her side.

I don't think Freud ever got around to asking the question, 'What does a parrot want?', but surely the answer would be the same one as when the subject of the question was 'a woman'? She wants to have her intelligence respected. She wants people to talk to.

'Parrots are very intelligent birds . . .' I said hopefully.

'Remarkable creatures.'

'. . . and I believe the African grey is regarded as the most intelligent of all.'

'Well . . . after all, we've only made a beginning. There's time.'

Not if Phyllis dies of boredom before she learns another word there isn't. Some things are better left unsaid, though they're usually the more interesting and informative ones.

A Rosetta Stone with nothing whatever written on it

'I wonder, Major, if you could let me in on your teaching methods.' At this point, really, I was trying to train the Major rather than presuming to educate Phyllis directly. All things considered this might be the harder task of the two.

'Well, John, I showed her the peanut and said "hello" just as clearly as I could, and I held it out and kept on saying "hello" till in the end she said "hello" and then I gave her the peanut.'

'Fascinating. And what is it that you've taught her, do you think?'

'I've taught her how to get a peanut, that's for certain!'

That, of course, was the whole problem. 'But what is it that she understands?'

'Well, think about it . . . she knows that if she says "hello" she gets a peanut. Isn't that enough?'

Enough for you, maybe. 'I wonder. What do you think she thinks "hello" means?'

He blinked as he took in the complex imbricated thought. 'She might think it means . . . sorry, I've lost my thread there. But she might think it means . . . I suppose, peanut.'

So, to sum up, at this point Phyllis had a vocabulary of a single word, and she had been conditioned on a systematic basis not to understand what it meant. She would confuse the ritual greeting that starts a human conversation with the legume seed, *Arachis hypogæa*, that was supposed to entice her into joining it.

'H'm,' I said. 'Do you think we could start her education from scratch, somehow?' This was the time for me to exert my prestige, if any, as a graduate member of the University. If the Major or Mrs Baine had been kept in ignorance of my eminence, widely broadcast as an emergency signal on every morphic wavelength there was, then it was the purest accident. I needed to be somewhat tactical. It's always a mistake to extrapolate from a small sample, but I felt I knew something about the psychology of men with a background in the armed forces – Dad, obviously, but there have been a fair number of Majors in my past. Though trained to obey orders unthinkingly they subtly kick against control, even though they would have been shocked to learn that they harboured the slightest rebellious impulse anywhere in their beings. 'We can't change horses in mid-stream, obviously . . .' I said, but it was already too late. The Major had jumped from one waterlogged nag to another without giving it a moment's thought. Already he was holding up a peanut in front of Phyllis and saying, 'Peanut.'

'Hello,' said Phyllis with her usual flatly definite intonation, imitated as it was from the Major.

The Major closed his fist around the peanut. 'Not "hello", Phyllis, "peanut".'

She raised a claw that clenched on nothing. It was as if she was trying to grasp some elusive thought, hoping to snatch it from the surrounding air. She produced a rapid partial rotation of the head so as to offer us two profiles in succession, one beady eye and then another, but she said nothing. Between us the Major and I had given one of the world's most talkative animals a solid nudge towards mutism. The originary linguistic transaction, the moment that actually introduces the novice into speech, had turned into a trap from one day to the next. Suddenly the stepping-stone to expressive communication was treacherous, slick with moss. What was this object being held out to her, unchanged since yesterday but charged with a new, unsettling power? There are beings much less intelligent than *Psittacus erithacus* that can spot a trick question when they see or hear one. Were we showing her the way to communication in words or blocking her path? Perhaps we were teaching her two languages on different days. How was she supposed to know?

The Major did his best to cajole her. 'Say "peanut", Phyllis. Be a good girl and you get the tasty peanut.' But it wasn't even certain that she knew when she was being addressed by name.

'Excuse me, Major, but do you usually call her Phyllis? I mean, I know her name is Phyllis but does she?'

The Major thought for a moment. 'John, you have a point. Phyllis, your name is Phyllis. Phyllis. Say "Phyllis" and you get the tasty peanut.'

Impulsively he had introduced a third meaning for the treat, if not a third potential language for her to wrestle with. One had been based on the importance of greetings, another on the naming of foods. The new one required her to conceptualise herself as an object of knowledge with a name of her own. That peanut was becoming as cryptic, as fraught with missing meaning, as a Rosetta Stone with nothing whatever written on it.

The practical aspect of training a parrot was becoming trickier by the moment. I felt the need to step back from the educational tussle and to find out more about this disordered household.

'Tell me, Major, how does Phyllis spend her day?'

'Well, John, I have to say she doesn't get up to much. She hops about a bit. She flutters about a bit. That's about it. She likes her food, I'll say that, but she doesn't have a lot of go.' It was as if Phyllis wasn't pulling her weight somehow, though it wasn't clear what her duties might possibly be.

'And she drinks regularly?'

'Oh yes, she drinks a fair bit. I keep topping up her dish. She's a thirsty girl.'

'Are there places she favours?'

'Well, yes. She'd spend all her time in the bathroom if I'd let her,' he said. Again there seemed to be a whisper of criticism. 'Particularly fond of my toothbrush, for some reason.'

I thought for a moment. 'Major, could you by any chance afford a new toothbrush?'

He blinked a few times. 'I dare say so. I expect I could.'

'Then why not buy a new toothbrush and put the old one in the cage with Phyllis? It would give her something of yours to remember you by – when she's shut in the cage and you're somewhere else.'

'That's actually not a bad idea, John. In fact that's exactly what I'll do.'

Belatedly it occurred to me to ask if the peanut offered so lightly to Phyllis as a way of luring her into the world of the spoken was by some horrible chance a salted one.

The Major looked puzzled. 'It's just an ordinary peanut.'

'Yes, but what sort of ordinary peanut? The sort that comes from a packet bearing the words "Roasted Salted" on it?'

I don't know whether I had found the perfect vocal frequency for scolding, in which case I should have tried to remember my exact intonation and made it part of my permanent repertoire, or whether he had a history of being hen-pecked, but the Major offered no resistance. 'It might be,' he admitted rather quietly.

Professor emeritus of bird education

'How large do you think her kidneys are, Major? Look at her, for heaven's sake! Her kidneys are ever so much smaller than this peanut, don't you understand? She's not a "thirsty girl" so much as a creature whose electrolytic balance is being sabotaged on a daily basis by the person she trusts above all others. Not that she's got much choice!'

By rights this homily should have got me banned from the Major's quarters. Instead it earned me the status of professor emeritus of bird education, with a specialism in parrot linguistics. From then on I was invited to his rooms at intervals to assess the progress of Phyllis's language learning, progress that was so slow as to be barely measurable, as if I was sent by some sort of inspectorate with oversight over avian welfare nationally. The old toothbrush had duly been placed in her cage. She seemed enchanted by it – and a thoroughly dishonoured, splay-bristled object it was too. The rapt attention she paid it could almost be interpreted as a parody of attachments generally. Plainly this was a deflection of the love impulse, but then the love impulse was only ever a deflection of the spirit's urge to worship, and though there are unworthy partners in love there are no unworthy objects of devotion. Devotion doesn't dwell in the chosen object but shines transfiguring light through it.

I'm not sure it's right to say that Phyllis preferred the toothbrush to the Major, though it had a shorter list of disadvantages. In terms of responsiveness there was little to choose between the toothbrush and the ex-military man – they were neck and neck – but the toothbrush would never scold her nor bring on the arbitrary nightfall of a cloth pulled over the cage.

Without quite meaning to, I had become a sort of advisor to the Major on subjects some distance from the amateur training of parrots. I suppose I had already done my bit for his oral hygiene by requisitioning his sordid old toothbrush so that he had to buy a new one, but Phyllis must take much of the credit for that. Between us we had done something to stop the rot, not of caries or gingivitis as such but of self-neglect. Now it seemed time to intervene again, in a household (rather a grand term in this context) where staring into space seemed to be the main activity on both sides of the species barrier. I was hoping that this barrier, like so many, would be porous to slyly migrating particles and the osmotic action of a mutual attunement.

It seemed important to get them both moving. A sedentary life is something to be avoided by those with the means of doing so. No slackers! I suggested that the Major teach Phyllis the difference between 'here' and 'there'. Or 'over here' and 'over there'. By 'over here' we meant 'come towards us for your lovely peanut'. By 'over there' we meant 'do nothing while we bring you your lovely peanut'. Perhaps it was always on the cards that for Phyllis the hard task would be sitting still, while the Major heaved something of a sigh whenever the curriculum we had devised between us required him to ferry a peanut across the room.

As the Major set off on his grumbling way Phyllis would shuffle tensely on her perch, taking her weight on each claw in rapid alternation so that the cage rattled, positively bouncing in her excitement but still bound by the rules of the game. She seemed to have understood them remarkably quickly. If I hadn't periodically insisted on the need for this pattern of behaviour I think they would have been entirely happy with the other part of the training programme, in which Phyllis flew from her cage to collect her peanut from the

Major's hand then returned to her perch for the next cue and the next flight. Birds' wings in a confined space generate an extraordinary amount of draught. The papers on the Major's desk would flutter in the breeze of her passing. I had to be stern, to insist on there being an element of balance. Otherwise Phyllis would have done all the work.

Pathos can be cranked up to quite Dickensian levels

Wisely, Joy Payne didn't jib at my final stipulation, that I would be bringing this bird not mentioned in 'The Twelve Days of Christmas'. 'Righty-ho, John. I've got all that. I'll talk to Laura and Dennis and let you know what they say.' Neither of us resorted to our fond ritual sign-off, about loving more than leaving, and perhaps that indicated a slight unwonted tension between us.

In late 1973 there was a strange parallelism between the illusory realms of politics and of family. Just as the government and the unions were on some sort of collision course so the Cromer powers were massing to overrule my desire to be left alone. I could only hope that the two crises would cancel each other out – there was a fighting chance that the petrol rationing made necessary by the energy crisis would make it impossible for me to make the journey to Bourne End.

I'd already gone through the process of getting my ration coupons, but there was no need to bruit that about. There was a system for applications based on the first letter of your surname, so that A–Ds were expected to turn up on one particular day, E–J the next and so on. I was comfortably in the first group to be called, but there's no excuse for accepting good treatment if better treatment might be available behind a door that just needs a nice little push. Getting those doors swinging is always a good move – you never know when you're going to need a shortcut. If you don't know the right name to mention, the right extension number to ask for, one that will be answered right away by someone with the ability to make things happen, you won't get far.

My use of a car was recognised as necessary rather than frivolous, so that I was entitled to an issue of coupons on a priority basis. The way the system worked was that you picked up your coupons from the Post Office branch where you drew your benefits, the only trouble being that there was a Scottish woman in that particular branch who went out of her way to make life difficult for me, or so it seemed. To her it must have seemed that I went out of my way to gum up the works. Certainly she can't have enjoyed the way I was invited to jump the queue as a matter of course – 'Let him through, he's only a little chap!' – so that I had hardly entered the premises before she was expected to dance to my tune.

Sensing trouble ahead, or else subtly fomenting it, I telephoned the main Post Office number and explained my difficulties. Talking on the telephone has always been my secret weapon, from the time that I earned the right, as a child, to place the family's grocery order. Voices without bodies conjure up bodies finer than the ones we know. They told me not to worry, and said I should just get my coupons when it was convenient for me.

'What if there's trouble?' I asked.

'Why would there be trouble? There won't be trouble.'

'Yes, but what if there is?'

'We're here to help you. You'll see.'

'I don't think everyone is in on the secret.'

'Then say Mr West says it's all right.'

So I really enjoyed the way the scene played out with Mrs Disobliging at the Post Office. She took great pleasure in informing me that I'd come on the wrong day and wouldn't be able to pick up my entitlement. I looked very crestfallen and made as if to leave. One of the advantages of a generally slow locomotion is that I can really draw things out when I want to. No one will ever say, 'Get a move on, Tiny Tim! For Gawd's sake shift yer carcase!', and the pathos can be cranked up to quite Dickensian levels. Oliver Twist should take lessons – he'd have got all the gruel he wanted if he had taken the Cromer course in wheedling. Then I turned back, still in extreme slow motion, plucky however outclassed, to fight my little corner. 'You're saying that I can't be dealt with today?'

'That's what I said.'

'Not under any circumstances?'

'You have to come back on the proper day. It's the same for everyone. It's alphabetical.'

'So there are no circumstances under which you would issue my coupons today?' I was really playing it out.

'I keep telling you, you've come on the wrong day. It's your own fault – I don't see what I can be expected to do about it.'

'I see. My mistake. You're only doing your job. You're obviously not prejudiced against me in any way, are you? You're just treating me like any other customer, any other member of the public.'

There was a little pause before she said, 'That's right.' She could hardly contradict me, but agreement felt like weakness, and nobody likes to have their side of the dialogue anticipated.

'It's just that I made a phone call before I came out, and Mr West said it would be fine. He said there wouldn't be any trouble, why should there be? It's just I was told I should mention his name if there was . . .'

The moment I came out with the name she flinched and went bright red. It was as if I had slapped her, which I'm ashamed to say was rather the effect I was after. Then she couldn't issue those coupons fast enough. She more or less flicked them at me and it would have served me right if they had taken my eye out as they skittered across the counter.

And after that was there a hint of grudging respect in her manner towards me, as if in the endless war of attrition between shop assistant and customer she had at last found a worthy adversary? No, there was not.

Mr West had come up trumps, but I knew not to bandy his name about. It only takes a little over-eager resorting to the Mr Wests of this world before they have a minor breakdown, or can't be reached on their old extension number, or put on a falsetto voice and pretend to be their own secretaries.

You had to provide documentation to get your petrol coupons, and obviously I had been prepared for that. A driving licence was acceptable, and so was the logbook of your car. Poor Mrs Baine had left her car unlocked while she ran an errand. It was unattended for only a minute or two, but when she came back someone had nicked her tax disc, also an acceptable document, peeling it clean off the inside of her windscreen. Why had she been so careless? 'Be fair! I didn't think there was anything in the car worth stealing.' But there was.

What with all this to-do about fuel rationing (secretly enjoyable, at least to me), I thought I would be able to cancel returning home for Christmas, pleading *force majeure*. I couldn't be expected to honour oppressive traditions when the whole world economy had turned against me, could I?

After all that, I don't think petrol was ever actually rationed, though the queues at the pumps and prices went sky high. I think I speak for the nation when I say we were aghast at the idea that the price not only reached but passed 50p a gallon, but life went on and driving with it. Sunday driving was officially discouraged though not prohibited. I was quite prepared to ignore an unofficial frown. There was a voluntary 50 mile-an-hour limit in force every day of the week, but a voluntary limit is no limit at all. My rate of progress was always sedate rather than headlong, so that my driving retained the unhurried quality of Sunday driving whatever the day of the week it might happen to be.

Their catapults don't miss

I think I have still those coupons, rancorously issued thanks to the intervention of Mr West. I know they surfaced at some stage. I doubt if they're worth anything, even if this was the first exercise in rationing since the restrictions brought in during the war were lifted, in fact for that very reason. I expect everyone tucked theirs away counting on their rarity value in the future, and when everyone does that the far-sighted course of action is actually to chuck them out as soon as an opportunity arises.

I certainly had a guilty conscience about Audrey, left to Mum's tender mercies and to Dad's fitful interest. I had written her a letter after the bust-up of the previous year, which was returned unopened, readdressed in Mum's hand. I even wrote to her school, but when you've written *Audrey Cromer c/o Junior School, Convent of the Nativity of Our Lord, College Avenue, Maidenhead, Berkshire* on the envelope, you already know the message isn't going to get through but will be returned on Mum's instructions. The nuns in the watchtower will inevitably train their searchlights on the carrier pigeon fluttering exhaustedly towards them with its message of peace, and their catapults don't miss.

I had phoned the house once or twice, hoping against hope that it would be Audrey who answered the phone, but Mum got there first.

I tried to disguise my voice when I said 'Wrong number', but its timbre is distinctively light (all part of small body habitus) and she said rather sharply, 'Who is this?' The second time I fumbled the phone on its way back to the cradle, so that she had time to say, 'John? Is that you? Who is it that you want to talk to?' before the line went dead. 'Back to the cradle' indeed! It was the pull of the cradle that I was trying so hard to fight.

Even before the Christmas-reunion pressure built up I had given some thought to the possibility of seeing Audrey at the end of the year. Apart from anything else I knew nothing about the group my little sister belonged to, thirteen-year-old girls. I didn't keep up with Audrey's schooling on a lesson-by-lesson basis, far from it, but Joy Payne kept me loosely up to date. I knew that Audrey liked History except for the dates, Geography as long as it was rivers and mountains and not trade, Domestic Science except for pastry and French except for the verbs.

I'd asked Joy if Audrey had grown, a question which she interpreted rather narrowly as a question about puberty. 'I don't think so, John. When I last saw her she looked to be filling out, but when I asked her about it she just said, "What God has forgotten we stuff with cotton." Don't let people tell you that human nature changes. We said exactly the same thing in my day.'

If Audrey had characteristics and habits that made her stand out from her age group I didn't know what they were. The area was a sociological blank as far as I was concerned. It absolutely wasn't my world, and I had no one who might be able to inform me about it. I would need to do some research. Normally 'research' to me means something that happens in a library, but I would stoop to seeking first-hand information if need be. I'd have a stab at fieldwork. Eventually I made an expedition to a newsagent's on Mill Road, hoping at least to find out what magazines thirteen-year-old girls liked to read, if not what they thought. I hadn't entered those premises before, having no need to – national newspapers were a closed book to me and back numbers of the *Cambridge Evening News* kept me marvellously shielded from events in the wider world, even if my radio-listening habits had a tendency to take the shine off my ignorance.

As I pulled in by the kerb I could see a solid woman in a nylon work tabard standing outside the shop. I took her to be the owner

— employees usually hide their moments of leisure rather than advertise them, as she seemed to be doing. The woman stretched luxuriously in the sun of early September and produced a roll of Toffos from the pocket of her smock. If it was a September sun then this must have been in September, though the fiction of sequential time takes a lot of keeping up and the month isn't something I could swear to. She took two from the roll, unwrapped them and then put both in her mouth.

I was about to attract her attention but then thought better of it. I knew from experience that until softened by body heat and the lubrication of saliva Toffos strongly oppose the production of speech. I didn't buy them for that very reason. In due course, naturally, mastication transforms the stiff texture of the sweet into something melting and chewable but it can't get to work until the other two processes have made a start. My mouth isn't enormous, though more or less exempt from the smallness of the body habitus, but it certainly isn't half normal size, so she was taking a real risk by doubling the recommended dose. I had briefly been afraid of choking the first time I ate one. Choking on an uncoöperative toffee may not be the worst way of passing from one life to the next (if this is not to be the last, more's the pity), the sweet sensations on the tongue taking away some of the supposed bitterness, but I'd rather not find out. Death, whether you classify it as event, non-event or anti-event, amounts only to the stirring of our spoonful of personality, whose crystalline structure we make so much of, into the circumambient tea.

Finally I judged that her chewing had become fluent enough to permit conversation. I had lowered the window of the Mini before setting out, which is supporting evidence for a date in September. 'Excuse me,' I called out. 'Can I ask a question?'

'Course you can, love. Care for a Toffo?'

Immediately we were in the tricky area, the potential minefield, of welcome rituals. Tread carefully as you approach the threshold dividing acquaintanceship from something less easy to dissolve. If you bring mouldy beans to a potlatch in the Pacific North-West of America, or if you give your Cambridge supervisor a bottle of the cheapest possible wine (Hirondelle, though I know it only by its reputation for stripping dental enamel) as thanks for his enrichment of your studies, then you're unlikely to make friends but your gift will not be turned away. I gave a grave nod, powered from the hips, and said, 'Yes please.'

Fellow sufferers from an idiopathic lockjaw

She approached the window of the Mini and unwrapped the sweet for me, something that was understood to be part of the original offer. Such operations are very fiddly, though I liked the way the folded-over wrapping left lines on the surface of the toffee, proof that its current tooth-resisting texture was no more than an interval between two episodes of melting, one in the factory and one in the subtle furnace of the mouth. To have the sweet popped directly between my lips, as was also necessary, added an extra intimacy to the exchange but also an element of the sacramental, as if the toffee should be spared profanation by unnecessary contact.

Any hint of holiness in the transaction was annihilated by a blast of synthetic banana flavour, though the bilious-yellow cast of the sweet as it travelled towards me should have prepared me for the shock. In my innocence I had imagined that Toffos were synonymous with the taste of toffee, that they lived and died by their delivery of it, but in the feverish world of the early 1970s a hunger for novelty had ousted honest appetite. Jaded palates had dragged us all down. With my palate and metabolism reeling I hardly noticed her trotting round the Mini and getting into the passenger seat. Apparently her customers could wait for their sweets and magazines.

'What is it you want, my love? Something from the shop?' With my mouth locked as it was in its first struggles with the sweet I couldn't articulate, any more than a snake that has unhinged its jaw so as to accommodate a goat can make small talk with its fellows. 'You just enjoy your sweet, my love. Won't be long before the kiddies come screaming along but things are quiet just now. Take your time.' Although she had only just freed her own talking apparatus from the clagging effects of toffee she peeled two more sweets from the roll, unwrapped them and put them in her mouth. I can't deny there was something companionable about this drawn-out moment of shared silence, clogged satisfaction, something close to oral stasis. We were fellow sufferers from an idiopathic lockjaw, toffee-induced. The mingling of our breaths intensified the intimacy, though our eyelines weren't able to cross.

Finally she said, sated and almost drowsily, 'What flavour did I give you, my love?'

'Banana.'

'I've got a blackcurrant and a mint.'

'Is that nice? It doesn't sound nice.'

'It makes a change. I'll say that, it makes a change.'

'Don't you have your favourites? And flavours you'd rather avoid?' Like banana, for instance.

'Not really. I take 'em as they come. I pick up a different sort of sweet every day, and they're all nice.'

I thought this was evidence of an evolved spiritual being. For someone who sold sweets to have no preference among her wares showed a freedom from *vasanas* that was little short of astonishing, when her clientèle was so tyrannised by preferences and aversions. There's no shorter route, after all, to creating mayhem in a family than the gift of a 'selection box' of chocolates. If Iago had thought to leave a box of Quality Street in the General's bedroom discord was guaranteed – there would have been no need to wait for a handkerchief providentially dropped. It stood to reason, then, that this lady would be a reliable witness to the foibles of her customers.

'Now what is it I can get you, my love?' she asked when she could speak again. 'I can bring it out to you if you like.' I had just about reached the stage in my dealings with the Toffo that teeth weren't at risk of being wrenched from their sockets if I actively chewed rather than letting warmth and saliva do their softening work.

'It's really a question I'd like to ask.'

'Then ask away.'

'What magazines do thirteen-year-old girls read?'

She frowned. 'Thirteen, you say? Girls of thirteen? At a guess I'd say that's half still on *Bunty* and half have already moved on to *Jackie*. You can tell the *Bunty* girls from the *Jackie* girls at a glance, nothing easier. After that it's mainly *Jackie. Jackie* makes all the running. And if they grab their *Jackie* and start flicking through it before they've even left the shop I know they've sent a letter to "Cathy and Claire"

– that's the problem page – and they're hoping they've got a reply, poor souls! Who'd be young nowadays? A few of them buy the *Melody Maker* – they're usually the ones with pierced ears – though I don't think they're interested in reading it. At 8p it's twice as much as *Jackie*. They really only want boys to see them with it. And none of them can dance, that's what bothers me. They just bump about! That's the style these days. Have you seen *Top of the Pops* lately? No wonder they can't meet boys if they can't do the proper jive.'

I found this whole exposition pretty shocking. I had no idea there were thirteen-year-old girls in Cambridge with pierced ears. 'Is it legal, pierced ears on a girl that young?'

'Couldn't say, and a hairdresser won't do it . . . but a needle and a cork do the trick. That's what most of these girls do.'

'Gosh, I see.' I didn't really, not understanding where the cork came in. Does the cork go behind the ear, to make sure the needle doesn't go into the neck? That must be it.

Her mention of jive dancing stirred up some murky old memories. Jive was the dance that Teddy Boys did, and when I was at CRX and supposed to move from Ward One to Ward Three I was convinced, on the basis of something a nurse had said, that Ward Three was full of Teddy Boys. In my nightmares Teddy Boys broke up the fun of the Teddy Bears' Picnic with their quiffs and their flick knives, stamping on all the little cakes in their crêpe-soled shoes. I had been quite frightened enough by 'The Teddy Bears' Picnic' as a song, the first few times I had heard it. The music started off sinister before it turned jaunty, and the song seemed to be in two minds about going yourself, egging you on to watch them, catch them unawares, while also warning you in quite definite terms that it was safer to stay at home.

An undertone outshouts a megaphone

By 1973 Teddy Boys should have been long gone, and the jive with them. Yet I had seen a little group one sunny evening marching along King's Parade in those long jackets with the velvet collars, escorting women in puffy dresses. They were too young to be proper Teddy Boys, and perhaps they were just students on their way to a May Ball, but if there was a jive revival in full swing I would hardly be the first to know.

'Then there's a bit of a gap before they're ready for *Over 21*. One thing I can tell you is that the people who buy it are either fifteen or forty-five. It's all do-it-yourself facelifts and "romantic destinations". A few of the girls buy it, but it's a bit dear at 20p so they club together and take it in turns to read it. Or be seen with it. I s'pose if you're carrying *Melody Maker* you're saying you're one of the lads, and if it's *Over 21* you're saying you're a grown woman.'

Wasn't there a novel in which a group of poor young women bought a Paris dress between them and wore it turn and turn about when they went on dates? Independently Cambridge schoolchildren had found their way to a comparable arrangement, though at a humbler level of glamour and expenditure.

'Every now and then *Jackie* has some pretty good things in it, I have to tell you. There was a question for "Cathy and Claire" a little while back – "I've just moved to a new part of the country and have no friends. How should I go about meeting boys?" And Cathy and Claire said, "Why not join a woodwork evening class? We can't guarantee you'll be the only girl there, but there won't be much competition. Of course the rest is up to you . . . just don't break too many hearts." Cunning, I thought, downright sly. Good chance of it working. In fact I was thinking of giving it a try myself.'

'Oh I see, did you just move here?'

'It's been five years. But I'm a single lady now.'

The mood of the conversation had darkened, insofar as that was possible with a steady supply of glucose irradiating us, leaping over the blood–brain barrier as if that vital protective hurdle wasn't even there. I could hear regret in what she said, but it was hard to attach it to a cause. 'I lost my husband a couple of years back,' she said, but before I could frame a suitable form of condolence she went on with – 'and if anyone finds him they can keep him. Good riddance to bad rubbish.'

She chuckled. 'I'll tell you about it if you like.' Our tongues were wagging companionably in a syrup of caramel, and it was as easy to gurgle 'Why not?' as anything else.

'We met at a party in a grand house out of town. I didn't know anybody – I only went because my Mum did some of the catering and there was a swimming pool. And this man was showing off his party trick, which was timing a minute exactly. Someone got out a stop-watch and pressed it, and bang on sixty seconds later he opened his eyes. Big grin on his face. So I spoke up and said, "I can do that too." I used to do a lot of swimming, took part in galas, and it helps if you know how the time is going exactly. It comes with practice.

'He pushed me in the pool. If it had been a man stood up to him, he would have jumped in after and held me under. Instead he jumps in and asks me out on a date.

'When we got married, there were so many cars they blocked the whole city centre. They just sat there sounding their horns like mad, and the buses couldn't get through. I was young and stupid, and I thought it meant everyone was happy for me. It was all planned – it was a big V-sign to the whole town. I didn't know what family I was marrying into. I wasn't allowed to come to the pub on a Thursday, but plenty of wives put up with worse. Turns out that was when they planned their jobs.'

'Their jobs?'

'Burglaries. I'd only married into a family of villains. The rule was no violence, but someone forgot and there was some jail time needed serving. Only he scarpered. Someone else was put inside, and it was the same routine – cars blocking the roads outside the court, sound-ing their horns like mad, buses not getting through. I've not seen him since. My family and friends, the ones I'd kept, thought I was protect-ing him, and that I'd join him when the stink died down. Nobody believed I didn't know anything about anything. So sod them all. Sod them every one.' She said this with any amount of satisfaction. It can't entirely have been the Toffo talking.

Burglars! How exciting. The larcenies I read about in the *Cambridge Evening News* were either student pranks or connected with drugs. Two students from St Catherine's College – Cat's – with drink inside them might make off with one of the stone pinnacles from the roof of King's College, planning to place it in front of the Guildhall as a practical joke, before being intercepted by the police, who discovered fresh chip marks and damage to the securing pin, though the culprits insisted they had been 'very careful' with it. Or a thief might steal drugs from a chemist on Hills Road, the haul including Mandrax, durophet, Drinamyl and pethidine, leading the police to say, 'We are obviously looking for a pretty thin chap,' able to squeeze through the eight-inch gap between security bars. Might it not in fact have been a chap-ess? And yes, that ugly coinage (*chaps and chapesses*) had a mercifully brief currency in the 1970s, an elephantine way I suppose of acknowledging the trend towards open-mindedness in matters of gender without pretending to feel comfortable about it. Why shouldn't it be a woman rather than a man who slipped through the bars, slick as an eel? An eel with another eel's teeth fixed in its own flesh, his or her own flesh, the tightening jaws of a chemical need.

Even without the lulling effect of confectionery I don't normally have trouble getting people to tell me their life stories. I prefer to hold back on my own, as a rule. Little surprises are much more effective when they come from out of the blue – an undertone outshouts a megaphone. I was a heroin addict for a few years. My dog Bobbysocks died of rabies. I don't believe in evil, even after meeting it, one sunny afternoon at the end of winter, outside Four Lamps. There's a sandalwood tree that has kindly been designated to provide for my funeral pyre – I could point it out to you. And very nice it will smell too.

'How old do you think I am?' she asked but answered herself right away, 'I'm thirty-six.' Perhaps she had asked the question in the past and not got the flattering answer she was counting on. If so she had learned her lesson. 'It would do me no harm to lose some weight, I know that, and working in a sweetshop doesn't help – it's called a newsagent's but without the sweets side of things I'd be making a loss. Still, a woodwork class would work out cheaper than an introduction agency. At one of those I'd end up with old buffers who play golf all day.'

I wasn't completely convinced but decided to play along. 'You may not end up with a husband but the chances are good you'll end up with a knife box.'

'But that's what it said in *Jackie*! That's word for word.' There are times when morphic resonance goes haywire, aren't there? No point pretending it doesn't. The delicate osmotic mechanism turns into an inebriate let loose in a telephone exchange, connecting miscellaneous parties willy-nilly and laughing wildly at all the misunderstandings created. 'Are you sure you didn't write it?'

'Of course I didn't write it! I'm not Cathy and I'm not Claire either! Why would I be here asking about girls' magazines if I wrote for *Jackie*?' I'd once submitted a story to *Woman's Own*, true, but that's different, and it had been turned down anyway. And I'd only mentioned knife boxes because Peter had made one at school and brought it proudly home, though it hadn't met Mum's standards for the kitchen and had ended up in Dad's shed, full of miscellaneous nuts and washers.

She wasn't going to retreat further than she had to. 'You could be doing market research.'

'Well I'm not.' Though I'd probably say yes if I was offered work in that line. Phoning up strangers and asking about their preferences in washing powder – it would be a dream come true, just as long as I could ask about other things as well.

'Then are you a student? You could be doing, I've heard it called, course work?'

'I'm not doing course work, but that's because I'm a graduate member of the University.'

'Is that the same thing? I'm not sure it sounds right . . . so are you a student or aren't you?'

'Of course I am.' I was slightly crestfallen that morphic resonance was getting distracted by inessentials and doing such a patchy job of getting the word out about my status as an insider. 'And as for meeting suitable men, wouldn't a jive class be a better bet, if you can find one? I'm sure you already know the moves.'

'You might just be a godsend, you know, my love.' I didn't doubt it, though the gods send so much, don't they? 'I've even got the dress tucked away somewhere. Once upon a time I'd do the splits as soon as look at you. My husband wasn't much of a dancer, though. And can I get into the dress? That's what worries me.'

'Well,' I said, 'you can either have the dress altered or alter yourself to fit it. No more Toffos for a start!' Clearly I'm an agony aunt *manqué*, and the list of jobs I'm suited for is growing so steadily that eventually it will be longer than the list of jobs from which I'm disqualified, though that's the one everyone seems to be fixated on.

'No more Toffos,' she said, with an intonation, I have to admit, closer to mourning than the making of a good resolution, though mourning is part of that. Still, it seemed to me that someone who had emancipated herself from caring about the flavour of what she put in her mouth was well on the way to indifference to the act of eating itself, though perhaps that's a naïve perspective. Not that she was ever likely to spend years in a dark cave as my guru did, so abstracted from the body as to forget the necessity of food and drink, chewing and swallowing unresponsively whatever his disciples put in his mouth, but she might well lose enough weight to become a late-blooming man-magnet in a dance class or jive revival jamboree.

A balancing dose of masculine terror

I hadn't realised that a sullen crowd of schoolchildren was building up outside the shop. I have to build up the scene from scraps of peripheral vision and the words spoken. Sometimes Maya needs help with her homework, knowing what a temptation it is for us all to fill in the blanks. The lady in my passenger seat had locked up and turned the sign on the door from Open to Closed, but her customers hadn't taken long to sniff her out. I only became aware of the situation when a child, having recognised the truant shopkeeper, rapped on the windscreen with a coin.

Did I see her or did her shallow but unanswerable grievance pierce my consciousness by some other means? No great effort was required to visualise the face as Audrey's, streaked with resentful tears. Blood is thinner than water but perhaps pre- and peri-pubertal tears are a fluid in a different category, possessing some viscosity beyond the normal. I might have my reasons for staying away from Bourne End, but expecting Audrey to understand them was an impossibility. Perhaps that was the moment, even before any external pressure was applied – and the multiform Lord knows there was plenty of that – that the tide began to turn in favour of a family Christmas, an institution so desperately hated that it must, deep down, have been loved as well. Christmas, like the Russian Count in Kleist's *Die Marquise von O*, both saviour of life and destroyer of virtue, would not have appeared to me as so much of a devil if it had not, at its first appearance, seemed an angel.

'So, my love,' said the lady in my passenger seat, 'do you in point of actual fact want to buy one of those magazines? Don't worry if you don't. I've had a nice break.'

'Yes, why not? Give me a *Bunty*, a *Jackie* and an *Over 21*.' For a moment I felt like a child splurging his allowance on sweets.

Unsurprisingly her arithmetic was instant. 'That'll be 28p.' A shocking sum, though I should have been prepared for it. I had no idea adolescence was such an expensive time of life! In those days, and depending on where you chose to drink, you could get close to two pints of bitter beer for that amount of money. The case was often made by my friends at Downing that I got units of alcohol at half price anyway, in terms of the physical effects, that being an incidental benefit of my stature. In effect I was being subsidised in my tippling by small body habitus. This was not a logic I welcomed or encouraged. I've also been told that small body habitus allows me to get away with a bossiness that would be intolerable coupled with a more imposing physique, but of course I have no way of testing that hypothesis, and I suspect it's possible to be intimidating even without the physical force to back it up. When people do something out of fear, it's not because of something that is going to happen if they don't. Something is happening already.

I told her how to retrieve my purse from the shoulder bag and she helped herself to 30p. 'Keep the change,' I said, a phrase that allows even a small chest to swell with lordliness regardless of the size of the sums involved. In those days I would try to shift my voice down in register, or failing that to use the deepest part of it – not very deep – for enhanced masculine impact. This put me in the same position as my trusty Hacker, trying against the odds to impress the world with my audio output. A woofer gets more traction on the ear than a tweeter, the human ear rather than the bat's, there's no getting round it. I'd love to have a voice so deep it makes the windows rattle, but that's not on the cards this time around, this (fingers crossed) last time around.

'I'll have to deal with the little . . . treasures now,' she said as she got out of the car, though I think the first word that had risen to her lips was 'horrors'. 'I'll send one of them out with the mags.'

Sure enough a minute or two later a sheaf of magazines was thrust through the window of the Mini to land roughly in my lap. A voice called, 'The lady says to tell you these are on the house.' The statement was followed by a projectile that bounced painfully against my arm before disappearing from sight. I squirmed round, hoping to get a glimpse of my benefactor and assailant, but I was too late, though my squirming must have been relatively rapid. She had gone. If squirming is one of your main means of locomotion then your abdominal muscles may not be the envy of the world but they certainly do their job.

If I hadn't seen her I could certainly conjure up her appearance. The relevant images in my mental library (snub nose, pigtails, little round glasses) were drawn not from life but from drawings, drawings of St Trinian's and its inmates, though considering how much I had suffered at the hands of female delinquents at CRX I had no need of fictional exemplars of cruel girls. Boys on the other hand had shown themselves to be nice far more often than not, yet still I had been petrified of Teddy Boys lying in wait for me if I moved to Ward Three. I must have felt I was owed a balancing dose of masculine terror.

I was able to shuffle the magazines onto the passenger seat, but there was no question of retrieving the missile thrown at me immediately afterwards until I had help in searching the Mini's footwell. It turned out to be a packet of Toffos, in the standard toffee flavour, so perhaps my expression as the banana flavour exploded in my mouth had conveyed a message impossible to misunderstand. One of the toffees was missing, which at least explained why they had been flung at me. The girl involved hadn't want it to be noticed right away that there had been a charge for delivering the item, exacted in kind.

In the end the magazines themselves, as opposed to the information about their varying readerships, were not particularly useful. I have to admit that I found them so hectic as to be unreadable. Even *Bunty*, by far the most sedate, seemed mildly frenzied. I had become used to the infinitely slow exposition of events preferred by the *Cambridge Evening News*, in whose pages a dispute over the exact style of window installed in a block of flats by council architects (the 'Shelford dormer affair') could rumble on for many months.

All along I had been hoping that the energy crisis would let me off the family hook as far as Christmas was concerned. Surely it was legitimate, when vast impersonal forces mobilised against each other, to be deterred from something you didn't want to do in the first place?

Paula had coached me in readiness for power cuts, not only bringing candles and boxes of matches but making sure I had a torch and a supply of reserve batteries. She would regularly drill me in lighting candles with my eyes closed and urged me not to change the place I kept the torch. In any case there was a sense in Mayflower House that I was likely to need help in such an emergency, however little I saw myself as especially vulnerable. It happened once or twice that Major Spinks knocked on the door of the flat, asking quite insistently if I needed help, and it was all I could do to keep him outside with reassuring calls of 'I'm perfectly all right!', not wanting him to see that I'd spilled matches in all directions and had knocked my torch onto the floor into the bargain. I did my best to shepherd the matches into corners where Paula wouldn't see them, but the intense friendliness that charged our professional relationship didn't blind her to her duties as home help. She shook her head and tidied up. My real fear, of course, was that when a power cut did happen Mr Gerling the district nurse would set off across Cambridge from wherever he happened to live (I took care not to know) and arrive with cocoa and a hurricane lamp.

Christmas was coming, no doubt about that. The Major gave me a Christmas card, Mrs Baine gave me a Christmas card, and when I said I didn't have one to give them in return they murmured ever so sweetly that they wouldn't expect it, not giving me time to explain. It made me seethe. How dare they not expect it! What a nerve to mistake boycott for failure, simply discounting the possibility of my having an opinion on the matter. I'd sodding well send Christmas cards if I wanted to, thank you very much. If I could make a piece of toast I could write a Christmas card, if I actually wanted to. I had a home help to buy the bread that made the toast, and she could just as easily buy Christmas cards for me to write if I considered that a desirable activity. It infuriated me that my protest against a culturally enforced and utterly empty gesture was interpreted as a simple matter of physical incapacity and passed over in supposedly tactful silence.

I had a right to be vile old Ebenezer Scrooge if I chose, same as everyone else, but no. Everyone automatically cast me as Tiny Tim, without thinking to ask permission. In fact Paula was no different, bringing a card herself but with no expectation of getting one in return. In her case I could see active goodness of heart was involved, and I forgave her the tender-minded trespass.

Greater than the average mousewife's

Joy Payne didn't send a card but would certainly have one ready to give me in Bourne End, and her too I would forgive. It was part and parcel of her generosity that she should accidentally squash the idea that I could shelter from family behind world events. She volunteered to come and fetch me, if I didn't feel like driving. I said no. It wasn't that I was too proud – I'd accepted lifts from her in the past, after all. She was good company on a journey, short or long. I just wanted to be sure that I could leave the family premises under my own steam if things got out of hand. Why would they? Why wouldn't they?

No one ever doubted Joy's desire to help, and her husband's being an executive with Vauxhall Motors gave her an access to the refined product of petroleum fractionation rather greater than the average mousewife's. I apologise for that mean-spirited though very satisfying coinage. Advertising can be properly insidious – I had absorbed it thanks to a campaign for PeeKay kitchen appliances in the *Cambridge Evening News*.

'MOUSE*wives say* . . . *"You're right, dear, we can't afford a freezer."*

'HOUSE*wives say* . . . *"We can't afford to be without a freezer." And they are right!'*

No, Joy, I'll manage on my own, but thanks just the same.

I had been prepared for resistance but the Major made no objection to my taking Phyllis with me for the two nights I had agreed to stay in Bourne End. Perhaps he didn't want to admit that any sort of attachment had developed between him and a parrot, acting out an exaggerated independence as damaged creatures are apt to do. From Phyllis's point of view a little excitement seemed preferable to a continuation of monotony. The Major could hardly have contrived a more deadening environment for an intelligent bird if he had taken to reading her the *Cambridge Evening News*, day by day and page by page. If there was to be any wallowing in self-pity done that Christmas the

Major must do it alone. *Homo* allegedly *sapiens* was not entitled to cast a pall over the existence of *Psittacus erithacus* just because he happened to have a case of the seasonal blues himself.

The Major helped me arrange things in the Mini for the journey to Bourne End. Before he installed Phyllis in her cloth-covered cage I asked to see her provisions. Proudly he produced a plastic tub and snapped off the lid. Inside were what looked like fibrous little logs, dark brown in colour.

'What are these?'

'Fru-Grains.'

'But what are they? It sounds like a breakfast cereal.'

'Well . . .'

'You mean it *is* a breakfast cereal?' I should have known better than to trust a grown man who lived off Kellogg's Variety Packs when it came to understanding the dietary needs of a bird. Did he even know there were foods that you didn't shake into a bowl and slosh milk over?

'Well, yes, it's a breakfast cereal, if you like. But you said that parrots ate fruit and grains, didn't you? In the wild. And these are Fru-Grains – fruity grains, that means. Fruit and grains, all in one. Full of goodness, doesn't it say so on the packet? I was only going by what you said.'

But you said! How many times have I heard that? You said, John, you said! Yes, *I said*, and you weren't listening. You couldn't be bothered to pay the necessary attention.

'But Major, there's any amount of sugar in this stuff! First salty peanuts, now sugary cereal – it's a wonder Phyllis has lasted this long.'

Perhaps I shouldn't have reminded him that he had a history of administering massive doses of undesirable additives to the small, defenceless body in his keeping, restricted in its displays of emotion by virtue of being a bird, however pseudo-articulate or para-articulate, fluffing up its feathers to appear formidable when threatened, squashing them down ('adpressing' is the striking word Darwin uses) when frightened so as almost to disappear. He became just a little sulky. 'Well, John, I wasn't born knowing these things,' he said stiffly. Then, with a rush of concern, 'Do you think she looks under the weather?'

He pulled the cloth off her cage and we both looked at her. I had to acknowledge that her eye was bright and she seemed alert, even full of mischief, as if she had been told she was being introduced to a new environment and couldn't wait to explore it. 'No, Major, she seems fine. I think you've got away with it. But the Fru-Grains must stop. I'll take them with me if there's nothing better – but I may be able to find something more suitable where I'm going. Don't be afraid to go back to the pet shop where you got her and ask for advice. I'll go with you if you like.'

He seemed a little mollified. 'All right, John. I might take you up on that. But you should know that I give it to her dry. I don't add milk.'

I should think not!

'I was thinking, John, maybe she should have something to sleep in while she's away. I have an old sponge bag if you think that would pass muster. It's perfectly clean and nice. Sleeping bag sort of affair.'

I was amazed that the Major could be so unaware of a creature's needs and habits when he was, after all, responsible for accommodating them. 'Major, how do you think Phyllis sleeps? Do you think she curls up on the ground?'

'Not necessarily.' He was suddenly vague. I've noticed this in other people with a military background, my father included, the reflex to beat a retreat from a firm belief as soon as correction looms.

'Not ever. If you ever find Phyllis "sleeping" on the floor of her cage, call a vet immediately.'

'I think I'm more likely to call you, John!'

'That would be a mistake, Major. I'm not Doctor Dolittle.' I had only a smattering of knowledge, but in the country of the clueless a smattering is enough to make you Secretary of State for Education and Science. 'I can't ask her what's wrong, or at least get an answer if I do.'

'Understood. Now, John, if you don't mind me asking . . .'

'Go ahead.'

'How does she do it? How does she sleep standing on her perch and not fall off?'

'Well, Major, there's a mechanism in her leg, at what would be the ankle level of a human being, and it works like . . .' I scrabbled about for a workable analogy. '. . . like the catch that stops your umbrella from collapsing once you've put it up.'

'How wonderful!' Yes indeed, wonderful. Imagine my surprise when it turned out to be true.

The Major had reinstated the mirror so that Phyllis could look at herself unconditionally and without interruption. Whichever theory you subscribe to, that parrots recognise themselves in the mirror or merely think they have company, her need for existential confirmation was acute. 'Sanity' may be the wrong word to use when assessing a non-human creature's ability to function in its chosen or allotted setting, but I felt that her sanity or some equivalent measure of equilibrium was hanging by a thread in her world of garbled messages and breakfast cereals fizzing with sugar. Whether by being visually present to herself or by being fooled into thinking she had the company of her kind, Phyllis stood in desperate need of her existence being corroborated.

I'd given some thought to Phyllis's sleep patterns over the coming days. Parrots being equatorial, they sleep roughly twelve hours a day in the wild, irrespective of the season. In a summer far from the equator they should be put to bed while it is still light and left to sleep long after the sun has risen. In winter the arrangements were likely to be simpler, but there was the complication that she would be expected to be awake in the evenings to socialise, if that isn't too ridiculous a word to use in this context, with its drinks-and-nibbles overtones, for a bird being introduced to the Cromers in their native habitat. I had decided that it would be better for Phyllis to travel without the cloth on her cage, and then have some rest in artificial darkness after we had arrived. There can be no equivalent in the jungle to travelling by car, whether sighted or unsighted. I explained my logic to the Major, who replied rather wearily, 'You know best.'

Rather oddly, he seemed to find it harder to be separated from his old toothbrush than from the parrot. It was as if he needed something to remind him of her while she was away enjoying a jaunt with me. This was an unlooked-for inversion of the original reason for the gift. It took a fair amount of coaxing before he surrendered the dishonoured object into my custody.

Maya, or a defective memory, draws a veil over the journey down to Bourne End, though I know I arrived after dark. The speed limit of 50 mph for all roads, including motorways, had been made mandatory earlier in December, but I've never been much of a boy racer even when I'm not trying to guarantee a smooth ride for a caged bird. When I arrived at Trees I took the precaution of turning the car round, tired as I was, to make sure I was ready to make an efficient getaway. This was a precaution I'd neglected in the past, with the result that my departure the year before, my glorious expulsion from an Eden crawling with snakes as far as the eye could see, had required a series of emergency manœuvres, which included ramming the garage door open from inside while in reverse.

There were on–off flashes of light visible in the shrubbery, semaphore soliciting my attention. Was this 'Season's Greetings' spelled out in Morse code? Even without the hushed calls of 'John? John?' it could hardly be anyone but Audrey. To reassure me that I wasn't dealing with an impostor she shone the torch on her face from underneath, but the effect was eerie to the point of being counterproductive since I almost didn't recognise her. The effect was more Halloween scare than Christmas cheer. Then she came towards me holding a finger in front of her lips, saying, 'I'll take you in by the ramp. Mummy mustn't hear. We have things to talk about. To *discuss*.' The more grown-up word underlined the seriousness of the sibling reunion.

An extension had been added to Trees to accommodate my needs, creating a bedroom for me and Peter that could be accessed directly from outside by way of a ramp and gave entry to the kitchen. Yes, this made life easier for me at that address. It also sent the message that I would never be so well catered to anywhere else as I was there, which had the effect of turning Liberty Hall (Bourne End division), for all its amenities, into a subtle sort of prison.

Before Audrey and I could set off, though, the front door opened and Dad came out with the light behind him. I didn't know what sort of greeting to expect from my father after a year and a half of estrangement, but he had not lost the power to disconcert, saying

624

'Oh, hello!' as if he was fairly sure he knew me from somewhere, even if he couldn't immediately remember where it was from. He didn't walk right past me, he certainly acknowledged my presence, and it's true that the Cromers are not an effusive people. I myself am both effusive and infusive, combining characteristics of the kettle on the hob as it sings away, waving plumes of steam, and the teabag radiating flavour in the privacy of its own mug.

Audrey moved to head him off. 'Daddy, can you keep Mummy busy while John and I have a serious talk in his bedroom?' Dad didn't reply but gravitated towards the Mini and peered in at the parrot cage. He opened the car door and inspected its occupant. 'What a magnificent chap.'

'Not much of a chap, Dad. Her name is Phyllis.'

'Very intelligent creatures, I've heard, as well as beautiful.'

'Yes, Dad. She understands the positional use of language, which is extraordinary.'

'You must tell me all about that later.'

'Please, Daddy!' Audrey put in. 'I'm counting on you. Keep Mummy busy.'

'Hadn't I better take this lovely bird – Phyllis, I think you said – into the house? I'll put her into the boys' room. Then I can come back this way, and yes, keep your mother busy if you like. But I should warn you, she's very on edge.'

'Thank you, Daddy.'

It seemed very unfair that the phrase 'your mother' counted as neutral, though if I had referred to the same person as 'your wife' this would, rightly, have been seen as outrageously provocative. How would he like it if I'd said something along the lines of *Your wife is always on edge. She's never anything else. Why do you think that is?* He met her before we did, after all. He should be in a position to know.

Yet he melted away and could never be cornered. Dad behaved all that Christmas as if he had been recruited for a parlour game and had moments ago been handed a card bearing the description *Family man, father of three*, taking on the script in a spirit of fun, though the words on the card had no more defining application to him than if they had said *Cannibal* or *Player of the banjo*. This was often the way family life took him, bringing out a mocking performance of conformity, and I can even find it admirable, the refusal to mistake the rôle he happened to be playing for his deeper identity, except that if he wasn't Dad then who was he? Nothing to do with us. Why was he here, then? Was it that he had nowhere else to go? The terms of his presence had always been confusing. He was a sort of honorary absentee however often he was around. Christmas is one drawn-out party game, that's understood, and it starts long before the party games designated as such, but charades can't be the true meaning of the festival, can they? Perhaps we would be finding out.

If the charades had started early for everyone, what did Audrey's card say? It might turn out to be *Try to make everyone better friends.* Peter's? *Miss a turn.* How about mine? *Don't play their game.* I wasn't putting on much of a show. Mum of course would be clinging tight to the same piece of pasteboard that had governed her behaviour for twenty-odd years now, grubby and tear-stained though it was: *Martyr to her disabled son, 'wonderful' with him, 'no life of her own', 'never a complaint'.*

I couldn't wait any longer to take in hand the improvement of Phyllis's diet. 'Dad, is there any bird food in the house? Any Swoop, any Trill? Or some sunflower seeds? Maybe you can find some nuts, but they have to be raw and unsalted. See what you can do.'

'Affirmative.'

'John? John? There's a packet in the larder with "Bird's" written on it. Shall I get that?'

'I shouldn't think so, Audrey. That'll be custard powder, won't it?'

She gave it a lot of thought before she replied, 'I s'pose.' In that household, for all its shortcomings, she had probably never been served custard that wasn't home-made, and free-pouring into the bargain, however often she protested that the custard poured over the puds at school was so much nicer, all lovely and thick. Flavour and texture can't meaningfully be separated from each other. Viscousness and free-flowing liquidity can each of them produce enchantment or disgust.

People who revisit their childhood home invariably report their surprise at how small it seems, compared to how it is remembered. This is explained by the fact of their having grown – but I am in a position to argue against this hypothesis. Trees in Bourne End seemed small when I returned there for Christmas in 1973, though my dimensions thanks to Still's Disease have not much changed since childhood. This effect of shrinkage is properly explained as one of spiritual distance. With practice the past, to the extent that it even needs to be remembered, becomes a miniature scene of purely neutral interest, like a picture engraved on a peach stone. Good workmanship, yes, that's agreed, but no claim to the status of reality even in the lower tiers.

There was a female presence in what Dad referred to as 'the boys' room', but it was only Miss Pearce, Mum's old dressmaking dummy, around whose hard but adjustable body so many other women's dreams had been draped in the heyday of Mum's sewing circle. Audrey helped me lie down on the bed, though I kept my shoes on. It's a bit of a business for me to get calced and discalced, and I would need to be on stage in the family drama before long. 'Would you like a fizzy drink, John?'

'No thanks.'

Phyllis was installed by the bed, and I authorised Audrey to cover her cage with the cloth. Since Phyllis was going to be awake past her usual bedtime I was letting her nap for an hour or two. 'In the tropics,' I explained, 'where parrots are from, night and day are the same length all year – I expect you've done that in geography.'

'Yes,' she said, though I have to say she didn't seem too sure. 'Of course.'

'Just make sure that the cloth covers the cage completely, would you? If there's even a chink of light she'll stay awake. We can wake her up later, but we'll need to be a bit careful. She'll be a bit grumpy at first.' Parrot owners who bother their companions prematurely can find ourselves on the wrong end of a sharp beak.

Animals need to get their bearings, and not all of them find it easy to lower their guard in new surroundings. I wish this courtesy could have been extended to other visitors, for instance me. To pick up my script as a family member right away placed great demands on my nervous system. A rest period in a darkened room would have been no end of help.

I told Audrey that Phyllis was an African grey parrot, *Psittacus erithacus*. 'Sit-upon arithmetic,' she said politely. 'No, Audrey, *Psittacus erithacus*.' Again she said, 'Sit-upon arithmetic,' not in a tone of contradiction but as if she was repeating exactly what I had said. I had to accept that I wasn't the only wind-up merchant in the family. Mind you, living under the same roof as Mum would be enough to make anyone earn a Girl Scout badge in passive resistance. Audrey was learning to manipulate, and why wouldn't she? – having so often been manipulated herself.

She lay down next to me and administered a sort of abstract hug, making sure not to apply more than the mildest pressure where our bodies touched. How had she learned to do this? We weren't at all an embracing family. Away from 'home' I myself pursued gropes more keenly than hugs. Yet there was comfort here, undeniably. Her skin was cold from being outdoors, but she warmed up remarkably quickly, heated no doubt by the hidden furnace of adolescence, the secret fires that would drive her from the arms of *Bunty* into those of *Jackie*, if they hadn't already.

In spite of her presence the room still smelled of Peter. I asked if she heard from him, feeling that at least one of her brothers should be attentive. It turned out that he sent a postcard from Australia to each of us in rotation, in a way that was dutiful enough but also seemed mocking of that duty. He wrote a card a week, and so we each of us in the family got a card a month. From what Audrey said her cards and mine were virtually identical. Were Mum's and Dad's cards any different? Ours contained lists of the vehicles Peter drove at work and also lists of the milkshakes available in the local milk bar, with marks out of ten for deliciousness. Blueberry, guava, coconut. Passion fruit was his favourite, despite the pips that lurked at the bottom of the goblet, lying in wait to ambush the teeth or the spaces between them.

British milkshakes at the time were pink or brown or whitish, dull shades to match their tentative flavours. It was easy to imagine a single glutinous substance being siphoned off in batches and tinted with different colours, leaving wishful thinking on the part of the consumer to provide the rest of the illusion. It's pink so I suppose it must be strawberry. Brown? – logic suggests it's chocolate. To me, that's what drinking a milkshake was all about, and I wasn't sure I wanted the guesswork taken out of the experience and replaced by brute sensation. I did idly wonder, though, what a passion fruit milkshake could possibly look like. Red is always supposed to be the colour of passion, but that seemed improbable.

I asked Audrey if Peter ever asked about what she was doing. 'Well, he signs off "hope you're well and happy". Does that count? John, we're wasting time. *She* could come in at any moment and there's something I need to show you. It's a sort of present for you, except it's yours already. It's under the bed. Aren't you curious?'

I was, just a little. Then she froze. There was a stealthy clinking outside the door that connected with the kitchen and then a soft tap on the door. 'I've brought you some tea and a couple of mince pies, Jay. I'll leave them here. Come out when you're ready. I know you and your sister have a lot of catching up to do!'

This was as un-Mum-like a statement as could be imagined. She was obliquely announcing a new dispensation. She wasn't going to press her claims, and against all precedent she would treat a closed door as a locked one. She would – of all things! – respect my independence. But what was the clinking noise?

'Oh, that's just her new shoes. Clicky heels, and they've got little chains across the fronts. She's bought a lot of new things lately. Perhaps we're rich. And the little chains mean I can keep track of her.' Another break with tradition, and the habit of keeping quiet and trying to overhear. We'd never succeeded in belling the cat, and now the cat had belled herself of her own accord. It was all very odd.

Even when the novel sounds had died away Audrey approached the door very cautiously, as if it was on the cards that Mum might have slipped off her shoes and come back noiselessly on stockinged feet. She brought in the mug of tea and the mince pies. 'No, you don't,' she said suddenly after she had put them down, and swooped on a cat that had profited from the open door to slink in. 'Out you go. You can meet John later.' Before putting the cat out into the kitchen she held the cat where I could see it. It was of an unfamiliar breed with blue-grey fur, strikingly beautiful, and pregnant, having something of the Siamese in line and carriage, and green eyes of an unusually intense shade.

I asked Audrey about this new resident. 'She's a rare and very special cat, and the kittens will be worth millions.'

'Millions?'

'A lot of money, anyway.'

'What makes them so special?'

'They're from Siam, which is now called Thailand, but they're not Siamese cats though they're almost as yowly. Their eyes are a lucky colour, a special sort of green like young rice plants if you know what those look like. Which I don't!'

Mum had good taste in animals, and a knack of persuading weak ones to survive. Needing to be needed was part of it, though this is an impulse that soon runs into trouble. Kittens don't stay dependent for long, and mother cats aren't known for wanting to share.

'Mummy took me to see *The Mousetrap*, John. Shall I tell you who the murderer is?'

'Thanks but no. I'm not in a hurry.' I'll get to that bloody show before I die, and I promise to be surprised by the unmasking of the culprit, however many times the secret has been revealed to me. A solution without a problem is so much more discouraging than a problem without a solution.

I said I wouldn't be eating my mince pie, and Audrey tried to persuade me that I should. 'You probably think it's got meat in it because they're called mince pies, John. I used to think that, but it's perfectly all right. Mummy told me. There's no meat in them.'

'Actually there is. They're made with suet — fat from animals' insides.' A meat product if not meat as such. I knew Mum would never buy in such things (it would take a much more serious family breakdown for her to resort to shop-bought), and her recipe was a traditional one.

Audrey made a token 'ugh' noise, but she was already halfway through eating the first mince pie. In practice her disgust didn't slow down her progress, nor deter her from tackling the second one, after I had confirmed that I didn't want it.

Mum knew me too well to imagine that I would fall at the first fence, the mince pie test for vegetarians. I knew she would be biding her time, working on something less obvious. Surely she wouldn't be so simple-minded as to try winning me back with the full repertoire of tempting treats of my bed-rest years, like a neglected wife wearing her wedding dress on an anniversary, hoping against hope to rekindle a spark that is no longer there? Scrambled-egg boats and bananas cunningly sliced within their peel – I felt confident I could resist their nostalgic spell.

'Are you sure you don't want a fizzy drink, John?'

'No thanks.' Audrey frowned her disappointment, though I couldn't see why it mattered one way or the other. Hospitality should know when to take no for an answer.

She dived beneath the bed to retrieve a loose-leaf binder with a blue plastic cover, decorated with flowers done in biro and princessy faces in felt tip. She opened it and carefully pulled apart the spring-loaded claws holding the punched sheets in place. Even with the precautions she was taking the mechanism made a loud clack, and out of reflex we both listened out for Mum's approach. She handed one particular sheet across, with an excited and eager expression, as if she was offering some trump card or treasure, some missing jigsaw piece.

I inspected the sheet of paper she had handed me. It took me a little while to recognise it as a drawing I had done years before. It was a likeness of a young woman, short-haired, raw-looking somehow, almost cross-eyed in her intensity. I say 'likeness' because though my drawing skills are limited I had managed to catch something of a face that had made a deep impression on me. It was done on a small scale since I can't make large gestures, and over near the edge of the piece of paper so that I didn't have to reach too far to do it. I had based it on a photograph in the *Radio Times*, but I'd seen that face in motion, gripped by a wide range of conflicting feelings, so that it was more than the imitation of a photograph. Her voice was a big part of the impression she made, and you can't draw a voice. I can't explain why the catch in George Harrison's voice made him seem like a phoney, while the catch in Judi Dench's made her seem so real. It's just one of those things.

'Where on earth did you find this?'

'Mum was going to throw it out. It got a little crumpled but I pressed it between some books and I've been hiding it in among my schoolwork. I had to punch holes in it – sorry.' She had protected the holes with reinforcing circles. They looked like flattened Polo mints. I remembered the dispenser of those little rings, a device made of nothing more substantial than cardboard that is one of the few machines I have ever been able to operate more or less on even terms with everyone else. There are few loves as pure as the love of stationery. The dispenser was a little box containing a roll of waxed paper tape, the laminated reinforcing washers arranged in a row, so that they almost touched. The waxiness of the paper tape prevented the circles, made of a material that was some sort of plasticated textile, from sticking too fiercely. If you were silly enough to pull the paper tape straight out, you would get a length of tape with the little life-belts still attached, but if you had the sense to pull it slowly round the corner of the box then the greater stiffness of the ring would make it rise proud of its backing, offering itself humbly for the intended use while the waxy paper hugged the cardboard corner. The ring's next home, on a dry surface, would be more permanent.

There had been times before I was expelled from the family home, or had expelled myself, when I would help Audrey organise her schoolwork using just such a dispenser of reinforcing rings. I would prepare a number of reinforcers, letting them rest on my fingers, an adhesive edge just giving them sufficient purchase, until she was ready to slip the next sheet of paper over the curved metal prongs of the loose-leaf binder. In my mind, though not perhaps in hers, those adhesive rings were the albino cousins of the flesh-coloured plasters made by Dr Scholl that Mum used to cushion her toes in tight shoes, from the flat yellow packet with the cellophane window. Perhaps the two types of ring were turned out by a single factory somewhere, from different materials but using the same machinery.

Makeshift portholes punched through the parietal bones

My little sister — the strange formula arrived uninvited — had looked after the drawing well. A teenaged girl's need to doodle is a powerful thing, and Audrey hadn't been able to resist it altogether, but she hadn't done much more than extend the lines of the name 'Judy D' into interweaving loops and tendrils, this time using ball-point pens of different colours — red, blue, green.

'You'd written it "Judi" with an "i" but that isn't how it's spelled, is it? I wrote it the proper way, but maybe I shouldn't have?'

'She writes it Judi with an "i" but it doesn't matter.'

She put on a severe expression, suitable for the discussion of grown-up matters. 'It does if she's your girlfriend. Is she your girlfriend?'

It wasn't a question I had anticipated. Audrey hadn't learned much about family happiness under the roof of the House of Cromer, but she hadn't learned to stop playing Happy Families in her head. 'Well, no, she isn't.'

'Have you Broken Up with her? She looks nice.' I supposed that meant she didn't look pretty!

'No, she's not my girlfriend and never was. I've never even met her. She was on the telly, a long time ago now. You were little.' We were whispering, though I had no idea why we needed to be, but Mum was good at getting that sort of mood going. She had licensed this contact between us, but it was deeply engrained in her to be suspicious of anything in which she wasn't included. The effect wasn't hard to predict. We became conspirators against her whether we wanted to be or not.

Talking to a Stranger had been shown on Sunday evenings for a month, four television plays covering the events of a single dramatic weekend. I must have been about sixteen. How enthralled we became with that other family on screen, the Stevenses I think it was, whose travails reflected ours in ways that we were under no obligation to recognise.

Those television plays united us in a way that church attendance had failed to do, and Sunday became a day of concentration rather than rest. It was Judi Dench, playing the resentful, mixed-up daughter, who fascinated me from the beginning of the first episode, and it was her likeness that I had set myself to capture. In the end I had made a reasonable job of notating in soft pencil her harsh unpretty beauty.

There was so much turbulent emotion on the screen. Anger and confusion were brought to the surface in a way we could never manage. It was bad enough that the Judi Dench character didn't know who had made her pregnant. She claimed it could have been any one of five or six possibles. This could have been bravado on her part

– may as well be hanged for a tart as unmarried and pregnant – but Mum wasn't going to risk it when she could go to the kitchen and make tea until those particular storm clouds blew by. The arrival in the story of a West Indian ex-husband was also a bit of a facer.

Audrey had been a troubled sleeper as a child, and the associated disruption could sometimes be annoying. On the night of the first episode Dad and I had reason to be grateful for it. She started calling for attention at another crucial juncture, saying she'd had a bad dream, and Mum went to comfort her. It was Mum staying in the room that would have been the real nightmare. She would have heard the devastating speech where the daughter says that she (or her brother) should have been a cripple, a little crippled kiddy, so that their mother would really have something to sacrifice herself for. That got us where we lived all right, in a moment of appalled understanding. Dad and I didn't gaze at each other in horror, our gazes held back in my case by an ankylosed neck and in his by chronic emotional disengagement, but we didn't need to. I'm not built for sidelong glances, but the optical apparatus as such need not be involved in such things.

Trepanning is normally an operation performed near the top of the skull, but in this case makeshift portholes were punched laterally through the parietal bones of father and son, requiring them to acknowledge for the duration of the scene that they were thinking the same thing.

Mum's psychology had been laid bare in living black and white on our twelve-inch telly. And all this was in the first episode! We were either going to turn off the disgraced set for violating the family silence and never speak about the play again or we were going to wait impatiently for the next instalment, and think over what we had learned at some later date.

Audrey, lying by my side, was restless and started exploring her face unhappily with her fingers.

She had been out of the room when those startling plays were shown, yet something of their atmosphere had been transmitted to her. She knew that the girl in the drawing meant something to me, and she had drawn a conclusion, even if it was one that belonged in a fairy tale romance. At least I could assume that her mind hadn't been filled by Mum with lurid lies about my sexual proclivities – or worse, dull truths.

'Oh *sugar*! I shouldn't have eaten those mince pies. I'm breaking out already.'

I found myself lagging behind the logic of these remarks and struggled to find my bearings. It was ages since I'd heard the 'minced oath' or minced expletive *sugar* for shit, both chiming and clashing with the sweetened mincemeat in the little pies. The phrase 'breaking out' was linked so strongly in my mind with the previous year's drama that I could only think she was talking about an escape of her own. 'Of course you must break out, Audrey. But you're a minor. They'd only bring you back.'

She sounded almost frightened – but then talk of freedom always brings something fearful with it to the confined. 'I don't know what you're saying, John. My *face* is breaking out, look!' She leaned over me, and no doubt with the appropriate magnification I would have been able to see the irregularity of texture to which she referred, the clogged misbehaving pores. 'Eating sweets and sweet things makes it worse.' She scolded herself in a voice not her own.

It was one of those moments, subtler than *déjà vu*, when a sort of compaction of subject-matter – the feeble double meaning of 'breaking out', the coincidence of minced oaths and minced pies, sugar as a euphemism for *shit* and sugar as a contributory factor in problems of adolescent complexion – makes it seem as if Maya is asleep at the wheel, failing to do her job of making reality convincing. These apparent doublings and overlaps are really hidden discrepancies waiting to be teased out. There's a line in an Ibsen play where a character says, 'I only pulled at a loose thread and the whole sleeve unravelled.' I could swear it was Mrs Alving in *Ghosts*, though I can't find it in the text. Perhaps it's not there any more. It may have been deleted for fear of offering too broad a hint about the flimsy tissue from which everything is woven, or loosely knotted – blown together, as Mum used to say, with some contempt, of poorly finished clothes. Even the cathedrals in stone are no more solid than the models of them that people make from matchsticks. It's all the same skimpy stuff.

Despite the apparently crossed wires between us, Audrey showed the next moment that she was responding to the underlying theme of what I had said, about freedom and confinement. 'John, what's a remand home? Mummy says that if I don't behave she'll send me to a remand home and I won't come back. Can she do that?'

I was tempted to say, 'This – *this* is a remand home, where you've been sentenced after a hasty bit of womb-choosing. Alas I can't spring you.' Though I have no remembered knowledge of the process involved in choosing a womb. It can hardly be done against the clock, there where there are no clocks. The system may even be first-come-first-served, a Hobson's Choice between incarnations. As Celia at the Bot had explained to me, Hobson's Choice wasn't an arbitrary rule imposed just to be disobliging. The reason people weren't allowed to choose a particular horse was because then the favoured ones would be denied the chance to rest. But then wouldn't people be entitled to say, 'I didn't choose to be born'? Which won't wash with me. I don't think so. They still chose to be born, even if they didn't have a range of options to plump for. They could have said no – couldn't they? The whole area is necessarily mysterious.

Instead I said, 'Of course she can't do that. That's not for girls who don't do what their mummies say. That's for really bad girls who are in trouble with the law. You haven't been robbing banks, have you? I think I'd have heard about it.'

She gave a little laugh but still seemed unhappy. 'Of course not, silly. But sometimes Mummy picks up the phone and says she's going to phone up a remand home and have me taken there. Then I'll wish I'd done what I was told.'

'That's all nonsense. I promise you she can't do that.' This didn't seem nearly enough reassurance. I had to do better. 'Don't forget, when you were born I was in the same hospital. In a different ward, but just round the corner. I've always been here.'

'No you haven't.' She was right to point out my hypocrisy. In fact she didn't go far enough. How could I play the born-in-the-next-ward card if I believed that wombs in general were no more than parachutes? To be folded up and hidden, by those being dropped into the unknown territory of a new life. And as we see when we look around us, there are many who never get free of the silken cords, whether their landing was soft or hard.

If I couldn't help in any meaningful way, I should at least offer distraction. 'Audrey, I have a present for you, too. It's in my shoulder bag.' A nice light present, easily portable even when the porter was me. 'In an envelope.'

She took out the envelope with her name on it, which was gratifyingly fat, even bulging. I had asked for favours to make sure I could hand over a goodly stack of the things. I'd even accepted favours, to swell the supply, from sources that I'd rather have turned away.

Audrey looked surprised rather than delighted. Dismayed, even. 'And if you have a rummage in the bag there are a couple of completed books.' She did as she was told, and pulled out two little booklets, their pages swollen with adhesive that had wet the pages then stuck them together. They wouldn't lie flat. By now she looked downright mystified, just stared at what she had retrieved and said nothing.

'You do collect them, don't you?'

'Who said so?'

'Joy mentioned it.'

'Joy Payne?'

'Yes. Did she get the wrong end of the stick?' Or did I? I tried to think back.

'I don't want a toaster. Is that what Joy thinks?'

There were double or even quadruple Green Shield Stamps on petrol, and competitions to win 10,000 of the things. Wests Garage on Newmarket Road had something they called the Green Shield Stamp stampede, offering to give away six million. Six million! You might not be able to buy a house, even with that many Green Shield Stamps, but you could probably build one out of them.

'You didn't mention them to Joy?'

'I hardly speak to her. I mean, she's nice, but . . .' She shrugged helplessly.

'Maybe Mum said something to Joy, and I misunderstood.'

'I'll have a think.' She frowned in a way that may conceivably have increased cortical blood flow but is more likely to have meant simply that she wanted me to know she was concentrating. 'Oh . . . I think

I remember. There was a lady in High Wycombe dressed in green and yellow frills who everyone was taking pictures of, and she was a Green Shield Stamp princess or something like that. And Mummy was asking what I wanted to be when I grow up, maybe a nurse or a secretary, so I said I wanted to be a Green Shield Stamp princess – though she was really called a Personality Girl – and have my photo taken for the newspapers. I just wanted her to stop asking me what I wanted to do, I didn't mean it. Green and yellow frills, honestly! She looked awful.'

'And did it work? Did it stop her pestering you?'

She grinned. 'You're so lucky. You don't have to put up with people going on asking what you're going to do.'

'You're right there.' I hope I sounded convincing, since it is genuinely what I think. In that department I have dug my own ruts. No one laid down a groove for me, no matter how shallowly indented. Everyone assumed that my future was a gradient uniformly inclined, a shallow slope that would lead, and sooner rather than later, to the Day Room. The place where they wheel you when they've fed and wiped you and then leave you in front of the television, not asking which channel you want to watch, or even if – unthinkable! – you'd like it turned off.

The whole Green Shield Stamps fiasco, the stampede that didn't get past the starting gate, was mortifying mainly because I had recruited so many people to help, including Paula and Mrs Baine. Then somehow Mr Gerling had got wind of it. His were the full books of stamps, evidence of long evenings running his tongue over glued surfaces, though if Audrey had really collected the blasted things she would have preferred doing it herself anyway. A pre-filled book of stamps seems as pointless as a paint-by-numbers kit that has already been filled in when you buy it, which is a depressing thought when you consider how null both these activities are even when undertaken in their full form. Now I was indebted to Mr Gerling for a favour I hadn't sought and would have refused if there was some mechanism available for doing so. Life would be so much simpler if you could veto an obligingness that is only a feint masking the itch to take liberties.

With Every Good Wish for a Freeze-Dried Christmas

It was lucky that I had invested in Biba cosmetics from Josh Tosh, more or less at random, after trying to describe Audrey's colouring to Bernardette without being sure whether she would be choosing complementary shades or ones that were brutally contrasting, so that Audrey could make herself stand out as every woman should, though Bernardette herself had so little need. 'John, they're gorgeous!' She kissed me. 'Dead grown-up. I'm not sure I'll be allowed to use them, though . . . and if I show them to Mummy she may "confiscate" them. Then use them herself.'

'Chance would be a fine thing!'

'No, I'm serious. Wait till you get an eyeful.'

I was quite happy to give her the make-up on the quiet. I hadn't brought presents for anyone else, but Audrey would know she had been remembered. I hadn't wrapped the cosmetic pots and pans, by which I mean I hadn't asked Paula to wrap them, but I've never seen the point of wrapping paper. A child who needs help wrapping presents for other people, and also help unwrapping what they give him, soon realises that the currents of obligingness and greedy impatience alike have been diverted so that they no longer pass through him. I hadn't wrapped my present to Paula, but then I didn't need to. All I needed was to indicate the catering-size drum of Gold Blend, from which only a few spoonsful had been taken, and to say, 'That's for you,' though I had gone to the trouble of writing a little note that read *With Every Good Wish for a Freeze-Dried Christmas*. That was what I wanted on my own account, a dehydrated event to mark the end of the year, with family relationships reduced to inert granules.

'*Now* will you have a fizzy drink?'

'No thank you. How do you feel about this move to High Wycombe?'

'The schools are better there.' This was obviously not something she would know for herself. She must just have started at the senior division of the convent school. Not a time for upheavals.

'That can't be why they're moving, though.' High Wycombe being not much more than five miles away. All the upheaval of a move without a real change of scene, just rearranging the *vasanas* on the deck of karma's *Titanic*.

'Mum says she wants to go out to pubs.'

'There are pubs here, and she doesn't even like to drink.'

'The pubs here are too suburban. She wants some proper nightlife.'

'And Dad? What does he want?'

'He never says.'

'No more he does. Tell me about the kitten you're getting, then.'

'Well, to start with it'll be like *A Hundred and One Dalmatians*, because Korat cats have blue eyes when they're born, just like the puppies being born without spots. You're supposed to say "the cat is in kit" when they're expecting, did you know that? Except Daddy always says, "I don't know if the cat is in kit, but the kit is certainly in the cat." Isn't that funny? So I'll have to wait until she's grown up before she has the lucky eyes, like dewdrops on a lotus leaf, whatever that looks like, but I'll love her from the moment she's born.'

'I'm sure you will.'

'John . . . do animals have souls?'

Oh dear. One more reason to avoid family life is that there can be minefields within minefields, invisible pitfalls lurking next to the pitfalls that you can see. 'W-e-e-e-ll . . . what does Mum say?'

'She says they don't, but we'll meet them in heaven anyway. John, why do you say Mum when I say Mummy?'

'Why do you say Mummy when I say Mum?'

'It's what she's called!'

'But not by me . . . and I was here first.'

I had hoped that this little excursion into family habits of naming had let me off the hook in terms of animal eschatology and religion in general, but no such luck.

'Well, Mummy says you don't believe in the same God as we do.'

'There are lots of different ways of getting to the same place, aren't there?'

'You mean like animals and people ending up in heaven though animals don't have souls?' I didn't know whether this was a lucky hit or a sign of ferocious intelligence well hidden. Either way I needed to change the subject.

'In my religion there are lots of gods and some of them are ladies. Parvati. Lakshmi. Sita. Wouldn't you like a lady god to pray to?'

She giggled. '*Our Mother, who art in heaven . . .*'

'Why not? I like the sound of that.' I didn't much, but let that pass – I wasn't all that enthusiastic about that Prayer when it was the Lord's rather than the Lady's. A prayer is supposed to focus the worshipper's attention on divinity, when what I really wanted was a mantra able to dissolve the lens.

'Well, there's a Mother's Day but there isn't a Father's Day . . .'

'So perhaps they even out. God's a man but mothers get a card, if they're lucky, one day a year. Is that it?'

'I don't really know. You're the clever one, John, everybody says so. Who goes to your heaven? Is it animals as well as people?'

'There's no heaven, really. Hindus – I'm a Hindu, remember? – don't hope to be born again. We hope to disappear.'

'"Or come back as an animal," Mummy says. So you must believe that animals go to heaven too!'

'No I mustn't. I just told you Hindus want to disappear.' Already I had coarsened my belief system. If you *want* to disappear you're showing you haven't lost your ego. The wanting is the problem, not the vehicle of that want. 'The thing is, Audrey . . .' I reminded myself uncomfortably of MarkO emptily pontificating when righteously stoned. She didn't seem to be listening anyway.

'The thing is, Mum and Dad—'

'Mummy and Daddy.'

'They're not our real parents. No such things as real parents! It's all a trick. Do you understand?'

'Yes, John.' But she sounded very vague, almost as if she was falling asleep. In fact she yawned so deeply that she gave a little yelp. 'Now I've made my ears pop! What were we talking about?'

I should have known better than to have a serious conversation lying down. The horizontal position doesn't suit orderly thinking. That's the reason I've always held out against having a phone next to the bed. If I conduct conversations from the horizontal I end up saying yes to arrangements that I would be better off refusing.

Hardened to the sufferings of potatoes

I ventured into territory I had told myself to avoid, the events of the previous year, when Audrey mysteriously intervened to rescue me from a strange sort of ordeal. Without thinking I said, 'What happened with Prissie after last year?' Prissie was the neighbour who had lent a hand when Mum and Dad were keeping me prisoner in the house, or trying to help me through a bad patch, depending (I dare say) on who got to you first with their version of events.

'Sent to Coventry. That's not a real place. I mean, it's a real place but that's not what it means. She still lives next door but I'm not supposed to talk to her.'

'I understand.'

'Now, John, perhaps you'd like a fizzy drink.'

'No thank you. I just had some tea.'

'Please can I make you a fizzy drink?'

'You want me to have a fizzy drink even if I don't want one?'

'Well . . . yes.'

I should have twigged long before. It had taken me ages to catch on. Mum and Dad had invested in a 'soda stream' fountain and she couldn't wait for me to sample the product.

'You know what I'd really like, Audrey? A fizzy drink. Christmas Eve isn't Christmas Eve without a fizzy drink. Why will no one bring me a fizzy drink?'

'John, you are silly,' she said as she left the room. The tone of fond dismissal would very likely serve her well in the years to come.

At the end of the conversation I had that faint sense of overdose that is the true indication of the made-up status of family. I hadn't seen Audrey for over a year, we had talked for only a few minutes, and yet already I felt we had run out of things to say. She was my sister, of course, 'my little sister' if you insist, but what did that mean? That we had chosen the same womb at different times, and for reasons that were not clear to us now. It wasn't much to go on.

Who was this girl? I was like someone reading a Russian novel and going back every few minutes to the list of characters printed at the front of the book, bristling with polysyllabic patronymics, in an effort to understand how the Princess Audrei Dennisovna could possibly fit in with the rest of St Petersburg high society, or alternatively the sordid life of the streets. It took real mental effort to remember that this was my ten-years-younger sister, still legally a prisoner at Trees though she had helped me escape my own confinement there a year and a half before. I had certainly thought about her in the interval, but perhaps I hadn't thought about her enough. Obviously there's a difference between transcending worldly ties and not wanting to admit they're there.

If the new soda stream had pleased the whole household then it was a rare gadget indeed. So few products received the Cromer equivalent of the Royal Warrant, and the most resistant to new applicants was (or had been) Mum. She was in a cleft stick of her own carving, torn between her love of the bargain and the belief that 'you get what you pay for', a formula that administers a salutary jolt of emptiness as admirably as any Zen *koan*.

It was almost a ritual of my parents' marriage that Dad would buy Mum a supposedly labour-saving device for Christmas or her birthday, not at all expecting her to change her domestic habits to include it but offering her instead the pleasure of demonstrating how useless it was. Improving on her domestic equipment was not a possibility – and that was his present to her.

The Kenwood Chef was regarded with particular mistrust, on the basis of its having usurped a noble name. There had already been an earlier Kenwood with a proper pedigree, the coffee maker that yielded its place on special occasions to the fragile glamour of the Cona (whose glass was so very thin – Mum kept a spare). The Kenwood Chef with its array of accessories was treated with almost as much suspicion as the Tichborne Claimant had suffered in the 1870s. In the course of Mum's testing the Kenwood Chef showed ominous signs of promise. Naturally it could never aspire to the rank of Chef, but it might have something to offer if renamed the Kenwood Kitchen Hand. Would Mum have to acknowledge its usefulness? The machine had an accessory for peeling potatoes, and it was clear that this would decide the issue. It was a metal bowl whose sides were lined with carborundum or some substitute for carborundum, at any rate a surface that resembled grey pebbledash. Rotating at the bottom of the bowl was a disc covered in the same material, equipped with a central shaft driven by the motor of the Chef. This disc was flat except where the underlying metal had been bent up at regular intervals, so as to provide a series of little slanting ramps. You put potatoes and water into the bowl, lowered the neck of the main machine to engage with the shaft, turned on the engine and hoped for the best. The potatoes were stripped of their skins, flayed even, by the moving carborundum, in a chamber of relentless abrasion that the Inquisition itself might have considered excessively cruel. They had nowhere to go, with the raking flanges of those little ramps bumping them upwards every second or so, to expose new surfaces for the torturing.

Good and multiform Lord! I seem to be talking myself into an extreme Jainist position, accepting that a tuber is the repository of an infinite number of lives and therefore forbidden as a foodstuff. Hypocrisy within hypocrisy – I was as hardened to the suffering of potatoes as Mum was herself.

It was the sight of the device in action that put an end to the Kenwood Chef's chances. The bowl lurched and chuntered with a thunderous rumbling. Mum may have exceeded its capacity, but as she said, you don't want to use a machine when you're only cooking a few potatoes, and I feel she was within her rights as a consumer. To prevent splashing while the machine did its work there was a strange rubberised skirt you fitted over the bowl, but this drastically limited the user's ability to see when the potatoes had reached a satisfactory state of nudity. Again, Mum may have 'forgotten' to check on the machine's progress, though ordinarily her sense of kitchen timing was a matter of pride to her, and if she had taken the Kenwood Chef to her bosom she would soon have learned the niceties of its operation. But her delight when she saw the potatoes when they were rescued from the process was complete. They had been whittled to little nubs that were almost translucent. So the Kenwood Chef was packed up and stored in Dad's shed, yet there was no sense of vexation on her part, and the man himself made no protest. It was as if the Kenwood Chef had simply leapfrogged over its life of domestic service and been granted an honourable retirement. The whole transaction was made up of negative elements, from Dad's trespassing into kitchen affairs to Mum's rejection of his gift, yet there was a strange residue of pleasure on both sides, despite the expense, something that one of them would under normal circumstances have been sure to mention. It couldn't properly be called a waste of money when it gave both parties a satisfaction as deep as it was strange. Such are the mysterious inner spaces of a marriage, that crossroads of ruts.

Further back in the shed was an appliance that had seen a certain amount of use and wasn't altogether disgraced: the Hoover Constellation, a pioneering vacuum cleaner that rode on a cushion of its own exhaust air, a sort of housework hovercraft. Mum had actually liked the machine. It was the animals that couldn't get used to it – there were always animals at Trees – and why should they? Floating around the way it did, 'like a spook' as she put it. It had to go for their sake.

Never been anywhere near the rooftops before

Audrey came back to the bedroom very soon, and empty-handed. 'Mum says we're not allowed fizzy drinks in bedrooms. Honestly!' She gave the sort of sigh that the walls of Trees must have heard any number of times. In fact if you pressed hard against them there would very likely be a visible leakage of frustration and discontent, not all of it Audrey's.

'Well then, I suppose you'd better help me get up.' It made perfect sense that I should be required to engage with the chronic unreality of family, and the acute unreality of 'family reunion', in order to be served a fizzy drink I didn't want.

Dad came in, as smoothly as if he had been summoned, to transfer Phyllis in her cage to the sitting room. He had silently appointed himself parrot warden. I could hear the whisper of the cloth being removed, and then the creak of metal. I'd started to say, 'Don't open her cage just yet, Dad. She'll need to wake up in her own time,' when there was a flurry of motion over by the cage. 'Otherwise you'll get a nasty nip.'

Dad said in a calm voice, 'Yes indeed, John, I've just found that out . . . by the experimental method. So much easier to remember than a precept handed down. She really is a magnificent creature.' He carried her out of the room with something like reverence.

In the kitchen I had my first sight of the new changed Mum, and a further exposure to the sound of her shoes. What were they saying, those insistent heels and little chains? 'Don't ignore me'? It was hard to say. The visible changes weren't drastic, but perhaps they sent the same message. She had always used a little make-up, but now she had ventured into the unknown territory of wanting to produce an effect. It was almost as if she had overheard Bernardette's credo that a woman should make a statement every time she entered a room. There was a purple shade on her eyelids, and her mouth was pinked with lipstick. The eyeshadow had a metallic glint that I seemed to remember from the make-up counter of Josh Tosh. The effect wasn't outrageous. It didn't scream from the rooftops, but then Mum had never been anywhere near the rooftops before. She had barely raised her head above the parapet of 'makes an effort'.

She had always worn earrings, true, but in the past they had been studs rather than hoops, and though what she was wearing were demure hoops, not cackling-barmaid hoops, hoops they were. The next time Audrey was in my line of sight she raised her eyebrows as if to say, '*Now* do you see?' Now I saw. And it was only now that she had changed her style that I realised just how set in stone it had been for so long. I had to agree with Joy Payne that, though Mum's approach to cosmetics was wayward, this was unlikely to be a conscious attempt to warn Audrey against the pitfalls of misjudged glamour.

I know there's always supposed to be a tension between teenaged girls and their mothers, one sending out shoots, coming into bloom, the other fading in the vase of obsolescence – but Mum wasn't exactly sexual, if that's something a son can presume to judge. Even so, the passing of time was very vivid to her, and she had always said she couldn't imagine being fifty, a landmark that was only a couple of years off.

'So there you are, Jay!' Mum said. 'You're looking thin, I must say.' She had the habit of saying this to the world at large, so that if anyone said the same of her it would look like tit for tat. She had never carried much weight, but now she was decidedly skinny. 'How was your journey?'

'I can't say. It's not over yet.' Mum just blinked, though she was entitled to make a much stronger protest at this supremely inane pronouncement. Really, what a time for me to turn twaddlemonger!

'There are plenty more mince pies, Jay.'

'He didn't eat any,' said Audrey, adding in an exaggerated childish tone, 'I cannot tell a lie,' though my refusal was no sort of secret and if she hadn't learned to lie in that household she was putting herself at a severe disadvantage. 'And I shouldn't have, 'cos I'm breaking out.'

'*Because* I'm breaking out, Audrey. Try to speak properly.'

'Yes, Mummy.' The acceptance of correction was purely tactical. 'John, I've had a brainwave! Tell you what — let's play Careers.'

Brainwave is a strong word, but there's no doubt this was a welcome suggestion in its context. Admittedly in the conventional understanding of the Christmas festival board games are aligned with the phase of satiety rather than anticipation. They have — in other words — Boxing Day written all over them. Audrey pressed for us to play on Christmas Eve instead, either out of native impatience or because I would be leaving on Boxing Day (earlier rather than later if I had anything to do with it), making it seem a matter of now or never. I was happy to go along with the idea. Board games have the attraction of being so eminently Johnable. Give me a dinky little cup and a pair of dice and I'll take on the world.

We Cromers were a disordered bunch, there's no doubt about that, but at least we had the bare minimum of common sense required to avoid playing Monopoly. There has never been a family so free of tension as to be able to endure the agonies of unchecked capitalism, as represented by that game with appalling fidelity.

Our preferred board game was much more conducive to serenity. It was called Careers, though blessedly distant from the world of careers as I had encountered it, or perhaps merely brushed past it. There was no square marked 'Appointment with the Disappointments Board', let alone 'Filmed Interview with J. Walter Thompson — learn to wield "the knife of advertising"'. The game's novelty was that there was no prescribed way of winning. At the beginning of a game each player wrote down what combination of money (£s), fame (★s) and happiness (♥s) constituted his or her goal in life. The total of the formula had to be sixty, but it could be composed of twenty money-units, twenty fame-units and twenty happiness-units, or fifty of one and five of the other two. So in the course of play you couldn't guess from where your opponents' counters landed, with the various units accumulating or being taken away, how close they were to winning the game. There was no unambiguous race to the finish, as there is in Ludo, where the centre of the board is the goal to which all efforts tend.

Not how you impale customers on the knife of adverting

Our set of Careers had been much used. It was scuffed and there were the usual substitutes for missing tokens. In fact players could elect to have as their representative a little racing car that had somehow strayed from a rejected set of Monopoly. We could only hope that it didn't carry with it spores of the greed that made the original game so destructive.

I was grateful that the transmission of the Cromer culture pattern had favoured so innocent, so herbivorous a game. It seemed odd and even perverse for Careers to describe itself on its box as being 'by the makers of Monopoly', namely John Waddington Ltd. of Leeds and London. Wasn't that exactly the sort of connection that should be passed over in silence, strenuously denied, even, rather than admitted without shame? It was like marketing a pot of strawberry yoghurt as being 'from the inventors of steak tartare'. That's not how you impale customers on the knife of adverting – which should be melted down and reforged as a runcible spoon anyway, for maximum utility at table.

Once upon a time there had been a pad of printed forms on which the players could write their individual formula for success in life, and other relevant details like level of 'salary'. No longer – it had been used up donkeys' years ago. But scraps of paper did just as well. I suppose it would be possible for players to have more than one scrap filled out in advance, so as to tailor their formula retrospectively to the scores they accrued in the different currencies of the game . . . but that is a Monopoly style of thinking, and none of us would stoop so low.

Even before we started playing Mum was reminiscing. 'Do you 'member the way Peter always chose hearts, everything hearts? Sixty of them, every time.' Of course we remembered. It was entirely in keeping with his character. But we had also noticed that Peter was far away, and that ♥s were no longer his exclusive currency. He had switched at least part of his attention to £s.

Players' tokens, moving round the outside ring of the Careers board as the dice dictated, might land on white squares (rectangles, really, like paving stones) giving access to career paths, whether 'Farming' or 'Expedition to the Moon', that were rendered in visual terms as twisting garden paths, or perhaps simplified digestive systems, leading away from the perimeter and then returning to it after a series of turnings with ample opportunity for bonuses or forfeits along the way. By Christmas of 1973 I had forgotten that the rectangle granting admittance to each career spelled out the requirements for each option. So to have a career in Hollywood a player would need to have previous film 'experience' (which only meant, to have propelled his token through the two-dimensional pipework at least once already) or to pay £1,000 for new clothes. These stipulations were laid out with a bijou mark, inexplicably dear to me, thus: *Must have: ¶ Film experience; or pay: ¶ £1,000 for new clothes*. The precision of the punctuation here, those exquisitely calibrated colons and semicolon, suggested a familiar figure being involved in the final layout of the game, to wit the English Literature graduate down on his luck. More to the point, I wondered if my first exposure to the incomparable pilcrow hadn't been by courtesy of Careers rather than the Bible, as I had always imagined. Fancy that – the King James Version pipped at the post by John Waddington Ltd.!

There were eight career paths leading off from the perimeter of the board, and with seven of them you got an Experience card when you returned there. The exception was University, where when you, I suppose, 'graduated' your income rose by £2,000. Dad had the good manners to wait a couple of turns after my Careers graduation before he asked, 'How are you off for money, chicken?' I didn't answer directly, partly because I wondered if he knew about Granny's strangulated largesse and my visit from Mr Moneybags. £600 wasn't £2,000 a year (which must have been quite a salary jump when the game was new), but I still had most of it and I wasn't about to complain.

'Dad, I'm rolling in it,' I said, indicating the pile of Waddingtons money by my side of the board, the yellow One Thousands and dark pink Ten Thousands, whose currency wasn't named on the notes though the board gave figures in pounds. I had made a killing with a 'bumper crop' during my brief farming career and had pocketed £5,000 – the squares committed themselves to a currency even if the banknotes were coy. I knew from Dad's use of the word 'chicken' that his enquiry was not about the game, and was sincere. The endearment stuck out like a sore thumb, or like a tender one, although there's a certain amount of synonymical overlap between the adjectives. On the other hand, it didn't necessarily mean that he planned to help. He just wanted to know. Technically he was the Banker of the game, but I can't imagine that being a factor either way.

I had been the first player to go to university in that particular game, and had naturally chosen a medical degree. There wasn't a wide range of options – if there had been an English degree on offer I might have plumped for it out of pure cussedness. You could only choose Law, Engineering or Science apart from Medicine, but everyone always chose Medicine. A Careers M.D. paid nothing to move on if he landed on the Hospital square, and received payments amounting to half their salary from the other players if they were laid up, after (for instance) falling off a cliff while Uranium Prospecting in Peru, and didn't want to wait for a lucky roll of the dice to be discharged. I'm not sure we noticed that this was not the way the National Health Service operated, evidence that Careers was adapted from an American original, if not taken over with the minimum of changes, mainly in the Politics career path, with references to 'Sensational maiden speech' (6 ★s) and 'Lose in by-election' (Go to Park Bench), along with 'Judge beauty contest' (providing 2 ♥s, for no reason that I could imagine). Monopoly, to give credit to the monster, had so effectively imposed itself on the geography of London that many of my generation would have maintained even under torture that our Park-Lane-and-Bond-Street version was the true and original one.

Phyllis was failing to pull her weight socially

Careers is not a game that calls for concentration and is infinitely the better for it. Mum and Dad kept wandering away from the game but didn't stray out of earshot and could be summoned back to the notional competition with a minimum of effort. Mum's absences were naturally prompted by events in the kitchen, though I noticed that she checked her appearance rather often, as she left or entered the room, in the mirror of her powder compact. There was something newly frank about these confrontations with her reflected image, not merely defensive – as they had once been – but almost eager. It was as if she was looking for the first sign of some far-reaching change, as if it might be the shedding of a skin, which starts in snakes with the loosening of a single rostral scale.

Dad, on the other hand, responded to the mild magnetism of Phyllis in her cage. I was positively glad that Phyllis had served him notice with a reproving beak, earlier on, of her independent existence. Initially my bringing a parrot along to the Christmas celebrations had been received as an outrageous violation, but now I could sense that the mood at Trees had undergone a shift, moving closer to disappointment if it hadn't reached that state already. The ability to talk is regarded as a marker of intelligence in birds, which is fair enough, but it can also be a sign of intelligence to keep your beak shut. Family is such a perverse organism that I felt I was becoming unpopular not for the original reason (imagine bringing a parrot along when you're invited for Christmas!) but because she was a let-down in terms of entertainment value. It was as if Phyllis, who hadn't yet spoken – she didn't say more than a handful of words the whole time we were at Trees – and didn't even squawk, was failing to pull her weight socially. Anyone would think the household had been promised a boisterous rendering of 'Ding-Dong Merrily on High'.

Mum certainly seemed distracted, though she was well used to dividing her time between family life and the schedules of the kitchen. Did she like the noise her infinitesimally dangling earrings made when she moved her head? She must have, just as she liked the little clankings her new shoes made when she scurried between sitting room and kitchen, constantly repeated evidence that she actually existed.

Mum was flustered as usual from having taken on too much. Any guru worth his salt would diagnose that as her arch-*vasana*, the rut that contained every other rut as the spiral groove in a long-playing record contains all the subsidiary encoded patterns. She saw everything in terms of tasks, though no one but her could see the element of the compulsory. She heaped coals of duty on her own head, then seemed to want compliments on the smell of burning hair.

It's hard to say whether she rebelled against the rôle of wife and mother she had chosen, though I had never heard her express a desire to return to nursing. I did once see her smoking while she hoovered the sitting room, and I noticed that she dropped ash directly on the carpet. She wandered away and hoovered at some distance from the disgraced area for quite a while, as if she hadn't spotted it, before eventually steering the vacuum cleaner around it in a spiral, a tightening hygienic noose, until she had swept the ash up again. Perhaps this counts as rebellion, from someone furious in her docility.

Mum wasn't particularly competitive, but at least if she played the game she put some energy into it, otherwise the game wouldn't have given anyone any pleasure. Dad was more of a hindrance to proceedings, sometimes neglecting to fill out his slip since (as he said) he couldn't make up his mind what he wanted. Perhaps he never had, in the game or out of it.

Privately I felt a bit suffocated by the illusory attachments – money, fame, 'happiness' – that were all I was offered. I had toyed with the idea of a board game called Karma, where it's serene indifference rather than the spirit of competition that is rewarded with points, but even if I could iron out that wrinkle in the fabric of the rules there's no getting round the fact that the best way to play Karma would be to sit in front of the board without moving, and really, you don't need a board for that. Perhaps all Careers needed was a fourth symbol in play to represent self-realisation. 'Om' or 'Aum' would be the obvious choice, represented in Devanagari script as a rather beguiling cursive ligature, though to Western eyes it looks more like the number 30 (scrawled by someone none too sober) wearing a fancy hat. Naturally the game would need substantial revision to accommodate the new set of priorities, perhaps with squares marked 'Receive the guru's *darshan* 3 Aums' or 'Earn enough to eat by begging as a *sadhu* 5 Aums' adjoining 'TERRIFIC shore leave in Pango Pango 8 ♥s' and 'YOU are the 1st Human to land on the moon . . . 16 ★s'.

Several times since 1969 I had argued that such an outrageous number of stars should be whittled down, now that Neil Armstrong had scooped the jackpot of fame once and for all. Later walkers on the moon would be famous, yes, they would be pointed at in the street, very likely they wouldn't have to buy their own drinks in the pub for the rest of their lives, but they could hardly hope to outshine the pioneer. I had been shot down in flames every time. There was a strange family solidarity when it came to defending these entrenched habits, mere marks on a printed board, on the basis (I expect) that if you make one change everything else is up for debate – an eminently sensible position, and a definite step on the path towards self-realisation.

I made the suggestion again on Christmas Eve of 1973 (does there come a point where the determination to uproot *vasanas* becomes a *vasana* in itself?) and suddenly there was no opposition. 'It does seem a bit silly to pretend nothing has changed, doesn't it?' Mum said, and Audrey chimed right in with 'It's a bit silly.' I suggested we lower the amount to 4 ★s, and that too was immediately agreed. Dad found a biro and made the alteration there and then. I had to consider the possibility that the Cromers really were a-changing along with the times, even Mum. I had suggested 4 ★s as an opening bid, and would have allowed myself to be persuaded at least as far as 6 ★s, which was what you got in the Hollywood career path if you landed on the square that said *Marry foreign prince(ss)*, with 2 ♥s thrown into the bargain. I might even have gone as far as 8 ★s, the fame quotient corresponding to a ministerial appointment on the path of Politics. It was disconcerting to have a point cleanly conceded, in a way that eliminated the need for wrangling.

At one point when Mum was staying put, for once, between turns Audrey sniffed a couple of times and said, 'Mummy, is something burning?' Mum gave a couple of uncertain sniffs of her own. She must at least have considered the possibility that Audrey was trying to get her out of the room, but she dare not snuff out the incendiary suggestion without making sure, even if her nose did nothing to confirm it. The moment she was out of the room Audrey picked up the Careers form Mum had made and showed it to me with a frown of worry. At first I couldn't see what was bothering her. Mum had done what the rules of the game required from her and formally listed what she wanted out of life – the supremely unrevealing 20–20–20 split again, though we nagged her and Dad to vary their choices, simply to give the game a little more bounce.

A poultice of his own devising

I always gave my desiderata a slight twist of encryption, which Audrey hadn't yet been able to decipher, though she was intrigued by the odd combinations I chose, such as 1–2–57. After the game she would pester me to tell her how I had chosen my numbers, for all the world like an old lady at the bingo. Naturally I was showing off to her, 'like an old toad' as the saying went, though no reason has ever been given in my hearing for the age of the toad being relevant. If there was any justice then consideration of the ten-year age gap between me and Audrey would have stopped me preening, but no such luck. Preening in birds removes parasites and realigns feathers for improved performance in flight. I could hardly put forward that excuse.

It wasn't Mum's list of targets that Audrey wanted to show me. Underneath it she had written the phrase 'A kind of loving?' twice over, adding an extra question mark to the repetition. I doubt if Audrey knew this was the title of a novel, and there was no guarantee that Mum did either. It certainly wasn't what she was thinking of when she wrote it down – she wasn't reminding herself to look for something on her reading list in the library. As a book *A Kind of Loving* had the reputation of being gritty, and grit was not what she wanted from literature. 'What does she mean?' Audrey mouthed at me.

I had no idea. She could have been asking the question about any one of us, even Peter on the other side of the world. Her real list of desires in life could have included a husband who paid attention, a daughter who did what she was told and a son who had the faintest inkling of what she had done for him. Any or all of the above.

There was no point in agonising with Audrey over what Mum might have meant when she wrote those words, in a message to herself that would self-destruct as surely as the tapes in *Mission: Impossible*, even if they didn't go up in smoke directly but were crumpled and then thrown in the fire. It would be a better idea to distract her.

'Shall I tell you how I choose my numbers?'

'What do you mean? What are you talking about?'

'Careers. The game we're playing, in case you hadn't noticed! You've always wanted to know my system, haven't you?' System being rather a grand word, but it got her attention.

'Yes,' she said, sounding very guarded, as if this might be a trick. She had grounds for being suspicious.

'Now's your chance. But you'd better put that slip of paper back where it was.'

'Sugar! I better had.' I don't know whether she habitually spied on Mum, or just on the new Mum, who seemed to be going just slightly off the rails.

'Now, before I explain, can you tell me what day it is?'

'Monday.'

'And the day of the month?'

'Christmas Eve. You can't have forgotten!'

'And if you put that date into numbers what would you get?'

'Twenty-four and twelve.'

'And what were my targets in the last game?'

'Salary £24,000, hearts 12, stars 24 . . . it can't be that simple!'

'Oh but it is. I always start with the day and the month, and then the other figure is whatever brings the total to sixty. You were always going to rumble me today anyway . . .'

'How do you mean?'

'24 plus 12 needs another 24 to make 60. Not an easy thing to disguise, even if I moved them around. You'd have spotted the pattern.'

'Don't think so. I didn't have an earthly.'

'Anyway I tried to throw you off the scent by turning the 12 round to make 21 − plus 24 needs 15 to make 60.'

'But that's cheating!'

'I don't see how. Breaking your own rules isn't cheating. And I always had reversed 24 = 42 in reserve − plus 12 needs 6 to make up the count.'

Audrey was now indignant, and it was more than just the annoyance of an audience member discovering how simple the trick was all along. At family gatherings emotions inevitably take distorted forms. Factor in the extra pressure of Christmastime and every bit is off.

Then Mum was back, ruffled and still anxious despite the false alarm.

'What are you two talking about?' she wanted to know.

'I'm explaining my system for choosing the winning formula in Careers.'

'Of course you are . . . you really expect me to believe that?' Her mood was darker though still heightened in the new way. I tried to remember if I had ever seen her like this. If so it must have been before Audrey was even born.

'Audrey, whatever made you think something was burning? I went right into the garden to make sure. There's nothing.'

'I promise I could smell something, Mummy. Maybe it was the parrot.' She giggled. 'It's got a funny smell. Not a *nasty* smell, John,' she said, as if I might take offence on Phyllis's behalf, 'just a funny one.'

'I can be trusted not to leave anything to burn, even at Christmas,' Mum said, with the grimness that the season more or less insists on. 'I've done it often enough. Dennis, are you playing or aren't you?' Dad had spent the short interval while play was suspended for Mum's kitchen-safety inspection looking at Phyllis in her cage, but now, with a fair display of willing, he rejoined the family party.

'Daddy, you've left the cage door open.'

'Well spotted, chicken.' I felt a faint pang at his extension to another family member of an endearment I thought of as mine by right. Did he use it when talking to Peter? I couldn't remember. 'I thought it was about time the animals in the house got to know each other.'

'Dennis, have you gone quite mad? She'll make mincemeat of that poor bird.'

'Not at all, m'dear. That will not happen, I promise. If parrots can survive so well in the jungle it's because they're good at assessing the danger in any given situation. Just set aside your sentimental ideas about nature and keep your eyes open.'

'But Dennis, we can't just sit back and let them fight it out. It's not even John's parrot – what will the owner say if she never comes back?'

If it had been anyone but Dad behaving in this way, I would have thought it was some sort of revenge on Phyllis for the nip she had given him mere minutes before. I was confident that such motivation was not in Dad's mind, and it wasn't often that I could be sure of what he was thinking or not thinking. He seemed to hold no grudge, rather the reverse, as if he was pleased with the clarity of her responses. Animals were only the agents of Dad's mischief, which was directed towards the human company, and particularly at Mum. But then he had been brought up by a mother who hardly noticed her children but could describe a worm in a jar as 'a perfect lamb'. This was Nice Granny, as dim and pale as the other was fiercely distinct.

'That's a formidable beak, m'dear. The cat recognises that – she's not stupid. She's also not hungry, she's not threatened. I guarantee she will keep her distance. She's curious, that's all.' It's possible that he had a motive beyond mischief for the whole little drama. He may possibly have been seeking to draw out the family toxins with a poultice of his own devising. I'd like to think so.

It was strange. Mum was the one with intimate knowledge of birds and cats, but she seemed to panic confronted with the situation Dad had engineered. 'Dennis, think of the kits she's carrying!' she cried.

'Nature's more robust than you think, m'dear. This cat could do a forced march for a thousand miles if she had to and still give birth to perfectly healthy kittens.' Perhaps he had been issued with a supplementary parlour-game card, this one reading *Impish child-man – likes nothing better than getting a rise out of 'the wife'*.

I suspected he was right about the relatively low danger of the animals harming each other, though he was certainly trying to provoke a human reaction. He was playing with fire, a much less respectable activity when no actual flames are involved. He was having some success with Mum, but if he was trying to get the cat and the bird worked up he wasn't succeeding. They seemed to know there was a symmetry of power involved, with relatively little likelihood of contested territory, as if in this Buckinghamshire kitchen they were the equivalents of a whale and a polar bear.

Not remotely worth the double amputation

It was Audrey who seemed most worried, holding tightly to the cat with the inevitable result that it squirmed free. 'They'll kill each other!' she cried softly. 'I can't look,' though of course she could and did.

It seemed a better plan to distract rather than reassure her, so I asked, 'What's the cat called?'

'She's Phœbe.'

'And do you know how that's spelled?'

'It's with a pee eff, no I don't mean that! It's spelled with a pee aitch not an eff.'

Phœbe and Phyllis sounded like nymphs out of a pastoral, though the record suggests that things don't always go smoothly for nymphs.

Who'd be a nymph? Fending off the advances of a cyclops or a god is par for the course, and there's a surprisingly high risk of being turned into a shrub or a star.

'And what comes after the pee aitch? Go on, show me how it's spelled.' There was plenty of scrap paper around, left over from Careers.

'I'm thirteen, John, not six.' Just the same she made a start but got stuck after the pee aitch.

'Shall I do the next bit for you?'

'I suppose.'

I wrote the 'œ' digraph as clearly as I could, but of course she wouldn't have it. 'You're doing it wrong! Is that an "o" or an "e"? I thought you knew how to spell.'

'I do, and it's both. "O" and "e" squashed into one letter.'

Phœbe's name was bound to appeal to me. It couldn't not. Those fused vowels seemed to wink at me like the optical 'Vari-Vue' illusions of my childhood, achieved by the lenticular printing of plastic, so that the images changed as you viewed them from different angles, though with a little effort you could get the angle exactly right and be able to see both versions at once. I'm disproportionately attached to digraphs like 'æ' and 'œ', where the vowels both melt and cling to their separate identities. They're like moot points in type, and moot points are hands down my favourite kinds of point.

These are true linguistic ligatures, not merely typographical ones like 'fi' or 'fl', which are visually satisfying streamlined forms but don't tell the story of the component letters as 'œ' and 'æ' do – separate in Latin, merged in the Middle Ages, teasing themselves apart again in modern times (though not on my watch). In American usage something appalling happens and the 'e' swallows the 'o' altogether, so that 'fœtus' becomes 'fetus'. It's as if an evil twin had somehow digested its rival in the womb.

'Why don't I do a drawing of Phœbe for you, Audrey? I'm out of practice with drawing but I used to be rather good.' I gave her an exaggerated wink so that she understood I was sending her a special message.

'If you like.' She pretended not to care one way or the other but furnished me promptly enough with the pencil and paper. All I did was draw a rounded triangle shape, adding cocked ears and curly whiskers like broken guitar strings. I left the eyes till last, then did one of them as 'o' and the other as 'œ'. 'Do you see? She's winking at us.'

'Cats don't wink.'

She was right about that, complicity being alien to their natures, or at least the acknowledged complicity that winking represents. They don't blink, either, at least the way we do, having a different approach to lubricating the eye. 'Maybe it's her third eyelid.' The *palpebra tertia* or nictitating membrane. 'I expect you've seen it sometimes when she's just waking up. It comes in from the side.'

'Then she'd have it in both eyes, not just one, wouldn't she?' I did my best to make good the omission by replacing the 'o' with another 'œ'. It wasn't a good drawing, but that wasn't really the point.

'Daddy, is this "o-e" thingy real or is John making it up?'

'I've seen it, chicken, but it's not common these days.'

'It needs defenders, Dad,' I put in. 'You wouldn't want red squirrels wiped out just because there are more of the grey ones now, would you?'

I should have known better than to have known better than Dad. The chances of him responding to a direct challenge of that sort were very slim. 'Do you see, Audrey, the animals have settled down? Peace has broken out.' I wouldn't quite put it like that. Phœbe was lying on her back with her eyes closed on the other side of the room from Phyllis's cage, lashing her tail roughly every ten seconds, but there was no chance on earth that she had forgotten about the new arrival. Sensibly Phyllis was keeping to the back of her cage. 'Time to give your bird something to eat, John?'

'I don't see why not.' I decided not to quibble over the phrase 'your bird'. 'Is there an apple in the house?'

Mum was in the kitchen but showed that she was listening by calling out instantly, '*Of course* there are apples in the house. We've got russets and some Golden Delicious.'

'Jolly good. Perhaps someone would peel and core one, and take a slice to Phyllis. She's wide awake now – she won't be giving anyone a nip. Scout's honour.'

'Affirmative. Audrey – man the fruit bowl. We'll dob, dob, dob, won't we?' said Dad. It took me a moment to identify the abbreviation of the Scouts' motto 'do-our-best, do-our-best, do-our-best'. I should have thought twice before invoking scouting when I was neither knowledgeable nor particularly interested. Dad said, 'But no creature of quality is going to be given a Golden Delicious if I have anything to do with it. Taste of nothing.'

Again a burst of exasperation from the kitchen. 'Dennis, they're the only ones Audrey will eat!'

'Oh I see. So, Miss Cromer, do you think parrots eat Golden Delicious apples in the wild?'

'Affirmative, Daddy.'

'Then she'll feel quite at home, won't she? Which do you want, peeling duty or slicing duty?'

'I'll peel and you slice.'

As a group we moved to the kitchen. There were times when Dad could behave like a proper dad, almost as good as a father on a television programme. I don't know how Audrey felt about that, but when I was her age I had found it maddening. If he could do it at all, why couldn't he do it all the time? It seemed to make things worse, knowing that he could play the part perfectly well but chose not to. It didn't matter much to him. But perhaps the television version of Dad put in an appearance more often for Audrey's benefit than he had for me or Peter.

When the apple was ready, Dad and Audrey took it through to Phyllis, though Dad vetoed the idea of watching her eat, saying it wasn't polite. Animals too have their dignity.

While they were out of the room, Mum came up behind me and put a hand on my shoulder. Either she was making out that she had forgotten how to behave around me after so long, or she really had. Neither thought brought pleasure. I imagine it's a bit oppressive for anyone to have someone speak to you from behind, but if you're not able to turn around the thing is beyond doubt. At least the clanking of her shoes – department of small mercies – meant that she didn't make me jump.

The teeth of punctuation protocol

'We're having a lovely stew, Jay, but I'm not going to try to tempt you – I know better than that. We know all about your willpower. I thought you might like a cheese sandwich and a few pickles. Not too much on the plate! I haven't forgotten.'

'That's fine, Mum. That'll do nicely.'

'You can't expect me to make a hot meal for one – that's not reasonable. It's not as if I don't have enough to do at Christmastime.'

'But I don't expect you to. A cheese sandwich will do fine. It's just what I feel like.' Somehow she had managed to let it be known that I was a real fusspot, as if it was more trouble to make a sandwich and open a pickle jar than to cook a stew with dumplings made from scratch. How had she done that? She knew how to cut sandwiches so that they were Johnable – she could do it in her sleep. She never fed animals tinned food, so it was a racing certainty that she bought and boiled up bits of rabbit for Phœbe. But no, somehow I was the demanding one, the one whose needs bent everything out of shape. If I sniffed hard enough I could probably have smelled rabbit. I see no reason for rabbit meat being more tamasic than any other, yet the miasma lingers on the premises of its preparation indefinitely. Perhaps the logic is this: a cat that kills and eats a rabbit incurs no karmic consequence. To conspire with a butcher to kill a rabbit and feed the corpse to a hunting animal is an act of rampant perversity.

I was grateful for the cheese sandwich, just the same, when we sat down for dinner. I didn't mention that there was such a thing as vegetarian cheese, made without rennet. There were limits to my hypocrisy. In those days vegetarian cheese cost an arm and a leg, and it wasn't remotely worth the double amputation. It had no flavour whatever and I never bought it myself.

The table talk wasn't exactly fluent, but somehow we managed. As a conversationalist Dad never took any trouble, any more than he did with the general business of fatherhood. He did nothing to maintain relationships yet we could always take up where we left off. He might say, 'There's a *Drosophyllum lusitanicum* I've been bringing on – it's early days but I have high hopes of it . . . we can take a look at it later.' Or 'I've been testing compost against horse manure – I think the results will surprise you.' It wasn't always the garden, though it usually was. 'You'll laugh, John, but I'm trying to grow an avocado from a stone. Yes, I know, the odds are a thousand to one against, even with a greenhouse, but I'm enjoying my foolishness and ask you not to give me too rough a ride.'

Mum's approach was very different. Her idea of how to talk to me was to say something that was like a problem in emotional algebra, made up of a whole series of substitutions for what she might actually be feeling. 'Old Mrs Roberts – you remember old Mrs Roberts – she was asking me what I'd heard from you. I didn't know what to say.' And how was I supposed to react to that? You can't make a useful reply to a statement that says nothing at all.

I remember Granny saying, as if it was nothing, 'It was such a disappointment to me when Laura turned out not to be clever.' A very matter-of-fact statement, not encouraging speculation, but neutrality of tone was a rarity with her and necessarily revealing. It was like a prepared statement read out by a politician, after which there will be no questions taken. There was obviously so much more to say. In terms of the mother–daughter relationship, Mum opting out from being clever was the only form of defiance open to her that was compatible with survival. Her intelligence lay all around her, she just refused to inhabit it. To be not-clever was a sustained act of passive resistance on her part and also a terrible Pyrrhic victory, particularly as it entailed being a little unsure about what a Pyrrhic victory might actually be. How was she to know that the constant electric shocks she received in her childhood were intended to promote growth and not sterilise it? The pain of being dismissed as lacking intelligence was terrible, there can be no doubt about that, but it was as nothing compared to the destructiveness of being treated by Granny as a rival. It should be noted in passing that Granny found no difficulty in treating people as threats without granting any claim to equality.

'No brains,' said Granny, 'and no common sense neither. Do you know, when I told her she should never go out with a man who carried a raincoat on a sunny day, she had no idea what I meant.' That 'do you know' was fully parenthetical, and licenses the omission of a question mark in the teeth of punctuation protocol. 'I had to spell it out for her.'

'Oh dear!' I felt I needed to do better than poor Mum in understanding what this advice, which sounded like a failed proverb, was supposed to mean. 'I suppose someone who carries a raincoat on a sunny day is being unnecessarily cautious and perhaps generally expects the worst. It's probably not a good idea to have someone as a friend who is so pessimistic.'

'Not pessimistic at all, John. Rather the reverse. Good heavens – how can anyone be so innocent in this day and age? A man who carries a raincoat on a sunny day is planning to lay it down on the ground *and then to lay you down on top of it.*' I felt sure I could have worked out the riddle if given time, but Granny wasn't one to let the conversational tempo slacken. No point in giving other people the time to gather their scattered forces. 'All in all, Laura was lucky that nothing worse happened to her than your father.' The way she phrased it made it difficult to frame a question that would clarify this secondary enigma, without the disloyalty that would be involved in asking what could possibly be worse than Dad.

Rather than wait for Mum to raise the subject of the proposed house move, which I suppose she would have done eventually, I jumped straight in. 'Audrey tells me you're planning to move to High Wycombe.'

'Oh, it's no secret. I thought Joy Payne might have told you – I know the two of you are very thick. Some people don't have to worry about phone bills!'

'Audrey tells me the schools in High Wycombe are better. Will she be changing schools right away? I thought she had only just started at the senior school in Maidenhead.'

'So she has. We'll see how it goes, John. You can't rush decisions about education, after all . . .' As opposed to decisions about where you're going to live. At least it was being admitted that the move wasn't being undertaken for Audrey's benefit.

'What is it that you are looking for in a new place, Mum?'

'High Wycombe is a proper town, JJ. There's a lot going on. Not like here. There's nightlife. There are restaurants.'

There was a restaurant or two in Bourne End too, but Mum hadn't been at ease in them. When an Italian place, the Piccolo Mondo, had opened its doors, she was told that 'they put this powdered cheese on everything that smells like sick – and when the waiter came over with this enormous pepper grinder and started swinging it around I didn't know where to look'. Admittedly her informant had been Ring, our cleaning lady of old, who would have hated to be considered sophisticated, but it was a long time before Mum could be persuaded to eat there. It hardly seemed that she was ready for the step up from the Piccolo Mondo to the wider horizons that High Wycombe represented.

'You're not the only person who likes going to the pub, you know, John.' I couldn't remember Mum ever having frequented pubs, though it has to be admitted that her tavern opportunities had been much reduced, in my early years, by the demands my body made on her. When I was in CRX, though, she had more freedom, and it seemed fair to say that this was a new appetite, or just a case of tit for tat. My own recent pub visits had hardly been rewarding, either to the Stable Bar, Cambridge's 'meat market', or the Robin Hood and Little John in Cherry Hinton, but she wasn't to know that.

If there is a Mrs Wogan

'And what's your tipple these days, Mum?'

'Well . . . in cold weather I do like a Whisky Mac.'

What a fib! I'm surprised the half-full bottle of Stone's Ginger Wine didn't rattle a protest from its neglected place on the pantry shelf. It's no secret that you can't make a Whisky Mac without ginger wine, and this particular bottle had been bought during the bitter winter of 1962–3. It still had a lot of the sickly stuff left in it.

I had to admit, though, that Mum was trying a new tack. Her character card had worn out and fallen apart like an old library ticket, but when it was reissued it looked different. Now it said *Unnatural son means unnatural mother. His place is with me – where else would it be? If he would only come home and say he was sorry I'd . . . well, I'd tell him to get lost. I'd show him what rejection feels like.* This was no longer material for parlour games but for a masterclass in acting. No wonder Mum couldn't get her new character to come off. It would demand extraordinary interpretative skills to make so much contradiction cohere. It would have been a lot easier for her to stop performing and wonder what a character actually is, and who wanted her to have one, but that wasn't Mum's style. She was wedded to the rôle of someone wedded to her rôle. What would she be like if she started asking who kept passing her these scripts? I made a real effort to imagine it, to imagine her without her insistent her-ness, but I was tired after all the driving and couldn't get the picture to come together in my head.

'You may not like everything that comes with moving to a bigger place, Mum.'

'And what's that supposed to mean?'

'Well, there are bigger fish in bigger streams, that's all . . . What if you're doing a bit of shopping in town, and suddenly you find that the person in the queue next to you is . . . Terry Wogan.'

She gave a snort. 'I don't think people like that do their own shopping. I don't even think Mrs Wogan, if there is a Mrs Wogan, does her own shopping.'

She knew all too well what I was hinting at. Bourne End was a desirable place to live and attracted a fair few celebrities. There had been the actor Jon Pertwee, but he hadn't intimidated her, partly because he laid the flattery on so thick, not flattery of her but of the house, saying that he couldn't imagine how he had missed such a gem when he was house-hunting and would always be interested if we moved on. Tom Stoppard was a different matter. During his residence in Bourne End she had been terrified of running into him in just such a set of circumstances, and it hadn't been possible to reassure her by telling her how unlikely it was that *he* did his own shopping. She had grown pathologically fearful, and had come very close to a nervous breakdown.

'When did the Wogans move to High Wycombe anyway?' she wanted to know. 'I think I'd have heard about it.'

'It was just an example, Mum.' My trump card had not done the trick and I needed to do a little back-pedalling. 'But there must be celebrities there galore.'

She wasn't impressed. 'Well let's just suppose Mr Terry Wogan does live in High Wycombe and he does do his own shopping. If I met him I might have the manners to say "Good morning" and nothing more, but if tried to turn on the Irish charm I'd just say, "Fiddlesticks! I know you've got umpteen million listeners on your breakfast show, but if you want umpteen million and one I suggest you stop sounding so pleased with yourself. And don't talk over the beginnings and endings of the records you play. That's not what people want to hear. That's not why listeners tune in."'

Perhaps there was some basis for Mum's idea that she had changed and was ready to make more changes yet. This was a creditable performance of self-possession on her part, though it was unclear how much assurance and fluency she would hold on to when the moment came and Irish eyes were smiling into hers.

'And how do you feel about moving house, Dad?'

'Well . . . I do as I'm told.'

This remark was received by us in startled silence. I think we all boggled a bit at the notion. Was he playing a part? It was always possible that he was telling the truth, the truth of things as they seemed to him, however little it corresponded to our own impressions. Mum just jerked her chin up and raised her eyebrows, as a way of saying, 'You know what he's like.' In a way we did. We knew what he was like, but we could never work out what this likeness to himself amounted to.

I played what I thought was a trump card that could not fail. 'What is it you're looking for in High Wycombe that you haven't got here? It's a shame to get a garden the way you want it and then move somewhere else, somewhere you'll have to start from scratch.' I felt sure that Dad had too much invested in the garden to walk away from it without heartbreak.

'Actually, John, the part I like is getting everything established – after that it can be a bit routine. I won't mind a new start.' Another trump card had fallen flat. All in all we seemed to be playing in No Trumps. 'Though it annoys me that the witch next door will get what she wants. What she has always wanted.'

'Who's that?'

'Magda Freeman. She's always had her eye on this place.' Magda might not have been in the saintly category as far as neighbours go, but she was hardly a witch. She had forgiven Mum, for instance, for shopping her to the National Society for the Prevention of Cruelty to Children. Mum had been appalled by the way she treated her son Pippo, who wore little or no clothing out of doors whatever the weather, though the régime in that household was Spartan rather than abusive.

'Can't you sell it to anyone you like? Don't forget – Jon Pertwee wanted to be told if ever we decided to sell.'

Mum made a dismissive noise. 'Oh, he's too grand for Bourne End since he played that silly doctor.' It was a good job Peter wasn't in the room when this blasphemy was uttered – it's even possible that its aftershocks reached him in the Antipodes. Was Jon Pertwee a better Doctor Who than Patrick Troughton? Didn't matter. We had spoken to him. He had spoken to us.

'She's offering a good price,' said Dad. 'As I say, she always had her eye on it.'

Up to that moment I was free to think that all this talk about moving to High Wycombe was just that. Talk. But if negotiations had been embarked on, however informally, with a potential buyer, then I had to acknowledge it was taking on some sort of shadowy reality.

'Magda won't let the garden go to pot, I'll say that much for her.'

'*Daddy! Daddy! There's someone in the sitting room!* I can hear them talking.'

'Dennis – did you hear that? There's someone in the sitting room.'

Anapæstic sigh of wonder

Are all householders so jumpy? It seemed wildly unlikely that the house was being burgled on Christmas Eve. Admittedly I myself had dialled 999 when someone bumped against my door, but I was woken from a deep sleep and I had panicked. In any case shared accommodation has a different atmosphere, an inherent pregnability. But how could an intruder have breached the front door of Trees, or the back one come to that, without being detected?

'Dad, I don't think we're being burgled . . .'

'Leave this to the grown-ups, John. I'd better go and investigate.'

'Dennis – take this with you.'

'A bread knife, m'dear? I don't think that will help. Never mind – give it to me. It will serve. And get out the toasting fork, you know the one, from the back of the drawer. Now give it to John.'

'But Dennis . . .'

'This is a man's business, Laura. You need to stand back. Stay in the kitchen, and whatever you do . . . don't open the door.'

Dad had given me a big wink at some point during this rigmarole, but Mum seemed to take it perfectly seriously, though she didn't go as far as arming her menfolk with bread knives and toasting forks. She had lived through a war, through real danger – could she really not tell play-acting when she saw it? Dad was having a lovely old time, and we needn't waste money on tickets to the pantomime this year.

'Audrey, do you have the cat with you?'

'Yes, Daddy.'

'Hold on to her, whatever you do.'

This at least was sensible advice. 'Audrey,' I said, 'we're just going to see what Phyllis needs — the parrot. That's what's making the noise.'

Dad took the handles of the wheelchair and pushed me to the sitting room. Behind me he said, 'Don't think you've spoiled my fun, John. I was just about to let them in on the joke.'

From where we had been, in the kitchen, it wasn't possible to make out what Phyllis was 'saying'.

'Dad, what do you think she's saying? Is it "over here" or "over there"?' Phyllis was repeating the call about every thirty seconds.

'Is this the positional use of language you were talking about earlier?'

'Affirmative.'

'Fascinating.' It was extraordinary how present he could be when something genuinely interested him. 'I think she's saying "over there". What do you think?'

'Same here.'

'What do you suggest we do?'

'I suggest you stand at the other end of the room from her cage.' I told him the appropriate position to adopt. He held his arm out level, fist lightly balled and knuckles down, the way the Major did. The way Phyllis and I between us had taught the Major to do.

'Now say "over here". You don't need to say it loudly, just copy the way she says "over there". Long–short–long, with a higher note in the middle.' What is that, an amphibrach? My knowledge of Greek prosody is pretty feeble. It's either that or a cretic.

'O-ver *here*.' We waited and nothing happened. 'Shall I try again?' he whispered.

'Why not?'

'O-ver *here*.' Before he'd finished saying it Phyllis was in flight. As she landed on his wrist Dad let out a strange sound that I can only render as 'oh-oh-*oh*', an anapæstic sigh of wonder that tried, with total lack of success, to pass itself off as a chuckle. But why would amusement ever be an appropriate reaction to such an event? Phyllis didn't even look at him from her perch on his arm, which in this context was a far greater compliment than meeting his eyes. He said, 'You liked your apple, didn't you?' though he didn't really imagine that acknowledgement of being fed was the basis of the transaction – animals can't be polite any more than they can be rude. It was just his way of controlling emotion. He stayed quiet for a few more moments. Then he said, in a completely ordinary tone of voice, 'That's the best Christmas present you could possibly have brought me.' At least one person was enjoying the festive season, and despite a slow start Phyllis might yet turn into a social success.

'Do you think I should wait for her to fly off, John? Or shall I carry her back to her cage?'

'Try that, Dad. If she doesn't want to go there she'll stay where she is.' In fact when Dad took her to her cage she hopped off his hand very happily, as if she was satisfied with the whole little expedition, and the first stage of training Dad up as a domestic taxi service.

It seemed possible that Phyllis had opened up a direct route to Dad by the sheer unexpectedness of her actions.

'Dad, what's happening with Mum?'

'Well, you know what she's like.'

'Yes, that's why I'm asking. This isn't like her – the make-up, the earrings, wanting to go to pubs.'

'Well, if she wants to kick over the traces I don't see why she shouldn't.'

Kick over the traces? The phrase had all the wrong overtones, suggesting as it did a genteel surrender to impulse. Joy's bridge partner Trevor, for instance, normally so dependable, might be so unbearably excited by a corker of a hand that he abandoned Blackwood altogether (whatever Blackwood is or was) and bid by the seat of his pants. That was kicking over the traces as we understood it. This was different, a systematic abnegation of personality. I wouldn't expect an outsider to understand, to draw drastic conclusions from noisy shoes, make-up that missed its mark and not-quite-inconspicuous earrings, but Dad was an insider. Wasn't he? 'It doesn't make any difference to me, Dad,' I said, 'but there's still a child in the house. Don't forget about Audrey.'

'She goes to school with the nuns, doesn't she? I expect they'll keep her in order.' A remarkably casual line to take, I thought, but I was hardly in a position to challenge it. Yes, she was at school with the nuns, but she was at home with Mum. And with him.

'What will you get out of moving to High Wycombe?'

'I suppose I'd like somewhere I could be a bit more separate. Your mother isn't the easiest person to live with.'

'She looks after you.'

'If you want to call it that. And I look after her.'

'She puts food in front of you.' And you eat it and say nothing. I don't think I'd ever heard Dad either compliment food Mum had served up or express reservations about it, which was a fine example either of mutual attunement or mental cruelty.

'She likes to cook.' Indeed she did, but that didn't mean he was doing her a favour by eating what was put in front of him. Even I knew that, and I was meticulous in my withholding of thanks. I was the ingrate-in-chief.

She couldn't half make your ears pop

In the absence of expressed appreciation Mum was forced into making small talk about the food she had cooked, reduced to the miserable status of someone fishing for compliments. 'I think I left the beans in too long,' she might say, or 'I'm not sure I'll try that recipe again,' or 'Those chops had a lot more fat on them than usual, don't you think, Dennis?' However she pitched the comment or enquiry Dad would give a response of scrupulous nullity. 'They weren't too bad, m'dear.' 'It makes a change, m'dear.' 'You know best, m'dear.'

'So how will you manage to be more separate? Are you thinking of setting up on your own?'

'As you say, there's a child to be considered.'

'And in the meantime – would a bigger shed help?'

He laughed, really quite boyishly. 'Wouldn't do any harm.'

Though the shed he already had was pretty substantial. Two sheds, maybe? But that would only work if Mum didn't know about one of them – not a practical solution to the imbalances of a marriage in its third decade. And that was as close as I got, in the charmed little interval that Phyllis had made possible, to winkling out of Dad the secrets of his domestic life.

Finally Audrey strode out of the kitchen with Phœbe in her arms, having overridden or ignored whatever threats Mum had made to keep her there. She was carrying the cat at arm's length in front of her, like an anarchist about to throw a bomb.

'What have I missed? I know I'm missing something!'

'Phyllis took a little flight, that's all.'

'That's all? Where did she fly?'

'Only across the room.'

'And where did she go?'

'Well, she more or less landed on my arm.'

'Can you do it again, Daddy? I didn't see it happen – please?'

'I don't see how, chicken. And I didn't do anything. The bird made it happen. It's not a party trick – she did it because she wanted to.'

'But she may want to do it again.'

'We'll have to wait and see.' Audrey had heard that formula often enough to realise that its six syllables really added up to one – *No*. 'Don't sulk, Audrey.'

'I'm not sulking.' There were tears in her voice. '*I'm not sulking.* I just terribly wanted to see it.'

'Then why don't I tell you all about it while we get you some more pud?' Dad said. She gave a sigh that, dropped in the Thames, would have sunk like a stone. She slumped her shoulders, let go of the cat, and Dad shepherded her back towards the kitchen.

'Oi!' I called after them. 'I thought we weren't leaving Phœbe and Phyllis alone together . . . and someone should pick up any bits of apple that Phyllis didn't eat.' That stopped them in their tracks. And while we're talking of creatures that occasionally need to be looked out for, how about giving me a hand back to the kitchen too? Was I part of this family or not? They should make up their minds. Luckily this second suggestion didn't need to be brought into words to be taken care of.

I'd learned about the advisability of removing uneaten fruit while doing a bit of research on parrots' habits in Heffers. On those premises I could browse undisturbed for hours on end. Perhaps word had gone round about my tendency to provoke impromptu poetry readings (that memorable 'Ancient Mariner') and even that I was a sort of Ancient sub-Mariner myself, sworn and deputised. I was left unbothered.

Mum and Dad would be going to Midnight Mass at St Mark's. They always went to Midnight Mass at St Mark's. You didn't need to think of it as worshipping if you didn't want to, it could just be a chance to see some familiar faces, particularly if you had been away for . . . what? A year and a half? If I didn't want to come then that was perfectly all right, though it would be nice to go out as a family for a change . . . For someone who wasn't piling on the pressure she couldn't half make your ears pop.

It would be fair to describe Mum as a churchgoer rather than a worshipper. It was the going to church that was important to her, not any dialogue with herself she might undertake once she was there. A lapse of attendance would be a more serious matter than a lapse of faith, though admittedly the one might mask the other.

Dad accompanied her only rarely. Though there were any number of past Cromers who had graced, or not actively disgraced, the ministry, his nature seemed purely pagan. The streak of nature-worship in him was strong and unsentimental. Admiring the way baby birds left the nest at the first available opportunity, he thought his children should follow that example. Rat parents too were impatient for their offspring to move on and start a new colony. He was an advocate for drowning unwanted kittens the moment they were born, before they had a chance to get round you. Don't bother trying to find them 'a good home' if you've got a bucket of water handy. That's home enough.

Dad lived as much in a world of phenomena and sensations as in one of moral values. When I had asked him about God once, he told me it was the name of a Force representing 'all the good in the world'. Reading Dylan Thomas's poetry, and above all 'The force that through the green fuse drives the flower', I thought that Dad and he were on a wavelength, that the same Force drove them both.

In fact Dad owned a set of long-playing records of Thomas reading the poems. They were housed in a box that was made of a cardboard with the feel almost of a textile, more than paper though less than cloth, specially reinforced like the sound holdings in a library, required to stand up to the rough handling of the public. He could certainly have borrowed such an item from the public library in Bourne End. That he set store by owning it himself seemed to suggest it was in some hidden way close to his heart. You don't borrow a holy book from the library, you want to be in a personal relationship with a copy you don't need to share.

I could see the attraction of the poem's ideas about a Force that could drive water through rocks. I even have a shrewd idea that Dylan Thomas capitalised 'Force' in the holograph of the poem, though whisky stains soon smudged it and made the initial cap hard to read. I can even believe he capped it up again in the proof, only for smears of cigarette ash to make it illegible a second time.

If the readings on the records were a disappointment to me, it was because Thomas sounded English rather than Welsh, not to mention sober rather than intoxicated with the spirit of poetry or anything else. I felt I had a right to expect a proper wild Celtic bard. Was this really the chap who sucked whisky through a key-hole with a straw when locked in his dressing room to stop the shakes? Ovaltine more like!

My original *pianissimo* ending was the right choice

Dad's age (he was around fifty) certainly seemed green, since he was spry and dry, upright and bright-eyed. Mum's animation seemed hectic and unstable by contrast, though I would hesitate to ascribe any osmotic interplay to them along the lines of *The Sacred Fount*. A circuit diagram of their relationship was likewise hard to imagine, since Dad seemed capriciously to dim her current by withholding his own. Perhaps an analogy with plumbing rather than electrics would be closer to the truth, and their marriage was like the sort of oddly organised house where you can't flush the lavatory while the washing machine is running.

By opting out of the church service I had allowed Audrey to duck it too, and she wanted to repay the debt. In Cambridge I was used to putting myself to bed and getting up without help so that having her hovering by the bedside made me feel self-conscious about the whole slow procedure. We agreed, in a reversal of our history as siblings, that she would come and tell me a bedtime story before putting out the light.

'What story would you like, John?' she asked, trying to sound stern and schoolteachery, but adding that she wasn't at all sure that she could remember any.

'"Oranges and Lemons", please,' I said.

'That's not even a bedtime story! It's just a nursery rhyme.' I had my reasons for the choice, just the same, and she agreed in the end. She may have guessed why I so particularly wanted to hear it.

When we were playing our original older brother–little sister parts, and she was drifting off to sleep, I would say the last words of the nursery rhyme very softly, though frankly they're horrifying. 'Here comes a candle to light you to bed, and here comes a chopper to chop off your head . . .' I could have left them out altogether, but I'm a word child, book child, print child, as well as having a strong feeling for completeness, shown at its least popular on family expeditions to the cinema when I insisted on sitting tight until the last of the credits had rolled by.

Then one night Audrey struggled against sleep to say crossly, 'That's not how it goes. Do it properly.' *Doing it properly* turned out to mean creating a lovely dreamy mood, and then breaking it into little bits by roaring out the last line. Before then I hadn't understood children's need for a homœopathic dose of terror, since in my own childhood there were adequate supplies of the real thing. There had been torture, mental and physical, laid on at CRX, and a certain amount of both at Vulcan School also, though the régime there had a softer side. On my first night there I would have been badly frightened if it hadn't been for the broad hints given by an older boy, who must have noticed my frazzled nerves, that the apparition of the 'Grey Lady' of Farley Castle wasn't anything to be scared of.

From then on, when I recited that particular nursery rhyme, I would have to decide whether Audrey was really drifting off, in which case my original *pianissimo* ending was the right choice, or whether she was shamming and would feel cheated if she was deprived of that delicious jolt of terror.

Now our rôles had been reversed. I did my best to pretend I was crossing the border to the Land of Nod, and in due course (when the chopper came for me) I produced what I thought was a creditable scream of alarm, but I'm not sure I really gave Audrey value for money.

Then I ventured onto more delicate territory. '*There was a crookèd man* . . . do you remember how it goes on?'

Uncertainly she repeated, '*There was a crookèd man*,' then added, '*who walked a crookèd mile* . . .'

674

I joined in with her, then gingerly we carried on with the rhyme together.

'*He found a crookèd sixpence . . .*'
'*Against a crookèd stile . . .*'
'*He kept a crookèd cat . . .*'
'*Who caught a crookèd mouse . . .*'
'*And they all lived together in a little crookèd house.*'

I have to give Mum the credit for teaching me that rhyme as a child. I loved it. The strange adjective became domesticated by repetition until it sounded utterly right. Who wouldn't want to be crookèd? I certainly did, and I was crookèd already. The word in the rhyme absolutely needed the accent worn so rakishly by the 'e'. I only knew two words with that archaic accented suffix, crookèd and blessèd, and I blessed them both. It would be awful if anybody thought it was 'crooked' as in 'crooked a finger', just as the wonderful word 'wicked' would lose all its power if it just meant having a wick, like a candle, even if it somehow managed to live its life on the page without the benefit of diacritical headgear.

I made Mum repeat the rhyme again and again, joyful but also anxious. Was I really being told the proper version? It would be dreadful to find out that I was being soothed and spellbound by something that had been revised to spare my feelings. Perhaps one day I would learn that everyone else knew a different version, that it was really supposed to go 'they all fell downstairs and it jolly well served them right', but every time it held good. The integrity of crookèdness was not lesser than the forces that come down so hard on the crookèd ones.

After Audrey had crept away, rather overdoing the walking-on-tiptoe act, I thought, I was tired but not sleepy. I lay there on the edge of unconsciousness, dangling out of habit. So many nights in our teens I had waited for Peter to return from his shift as a *commis* waiter at the Spade Oak – I think calling you '*commis*' is a sort of consolation prize for not paying a proper wage. Lying there, I wasn't anxious but perfectly content. It seemed natural to lie there with sleep lapping at the edges of my mind without quite submerging it, while I listened out for him with half an ear connected to a fifth of a brain. I couldn't give in to sleep until I heard his key in the lock and his footsteps in the hall, but I was always unconscious by the time he reached our bedroom. It was a strange relay race, one in which I kept dropping the baton of consciousness in a happy fumble before I had the chance to pass it on . . . but then Peter was already awake, so the analogy too goes out like a light and is snoring away in no time flat.

It was at the back of my mind that Peter might turn up for Christmas unannounced. He had done something of the sort while I was in India, just turning up. He had said, 'See you in India, Jay,' before I set off but I hadn't taken him seriously. Now he had said nothing to indicate that possibility. His letters came like clockwork, twice a month, but they never had more than a postcard's worth of message on them and mainly listed the vehicles and pieces of machinery he was driving in Australia, right down to number plates and chassis numbers.

As a boy his faith in machinery, in models and in actual vehicles, was already strong. He bought one toy that he never took out of its box – a Corgi model of a car transporter with *Écurie Écosse* written on the side. He was perhaps a bit old to be playing with model cars, but not too young to worship and I think he found his mantra earlier than I did. I don't think he ever knew what the words 'meant'.

He had gone through a bad patch at one school, not by direct bullying but by the torturing of the lizard he kept as a pet, but had been rescued and rehabilitated at a Quaker school called Sidcot not far from Bristol, where his gentleness seemed to blossom. He was a model pupil except for one strange episode when he absconded very early on a Saturday morning and hitch-hiked to London. His destination was a specialist establishment in High Holborn called Bassett-Lowke, apparently a famous shop for model trains and cars altogether too fancy and faithfully recreated to be called mere toys. He stayed there for four hours marvelling, unpestered by assistants who knew a true devotee when they saw one. This was a pilgrimage not a shopping trip. Not for nothing did the shop call itself the 'Mecca for modellers'.

Peter didn't have a prayer mat and I doubt if he went down on his knees except to look at boxes that were displayed near floor level, but this was a schoolboy version of the *hajj* just the same. Perhaps the assistants recognised in him the perfection of a certain subtype of boy, the one on which their livelihoods depended. After an hour or so they brought him a cup of tea and a biscuit, but he let the tea go cold and needed reminding to eat the biscuit. Eventually one of them fired up a Mamod model traction engine and asked if he'd like to make it run. The traction engine was green and red, but a very particular green and red, both of the hues being dark and faded-seeming, a colour scheme shared by Meccano although the manufacturers were, as far as I know, only loosely connected. Perhaps there was a stock of post-war paint needing to be used up, going cheap, and that was enough to set a tone for the period in boys' minds, those retentive receptacles.

As Peter told it, he said yes out of politeness rather than real desire – it was him humouring the staff and not the other way round. Those traction engines were in a special class, to my mind at least, and it was remarkable that he was able to resist the temptation. Unlike, say, a clockwork car or an electric model train (the fanciest electric ones had the extra gimmick of an oil you dropped into the funnel to generate puffs of 'smoke') these traction engines were powered by steam, from a water tank heated with a spirit burner – the same force that drove the full-sized engine. It was a working miniature not a simulation. Obligingly Peter took the Mamod engine out onto the pavement of High Holborn and put on a bit of a show for the passers-by.

When I was in India for those weeks in 1970 the wheelchair, in a culture where prams were unknown and toys with wheels unthinkable luxuries, was an object not just of curiosity but veneration. It turned out that images of the local divinities were paraded around on makeshift trolleys on high holidays, and I benefited from the association, being seen as a little trundling god. The introduction to *Speaking of Śiva* mentions similar rituals, making the case that from the point of view of worshippers 'spiritual beings draw the chariot, which only seems to move by human traction'. The movement of the Mamod engine on the London street was less mysterious, unless you factor in the activity of the gods appointed to watch over toyshops, who had summoned a boy from clear across the country, not to mention the mystery of the water in the little boiler over the spirit burner which expanded more than a thousand times over to make the metal chariot chunter across dirty pavement.

After four hours Peter hitch-hiked all the way back to Sidcot School, where he confessed to the misdeed of going absent without leave. By some oversight or laxness of administration his absence had not in fact been detected. No action was taken against him, and I suppose you could argue the matter both ways. It was a moot point whether he had betrayed the ethos of the institution by absconding or vindicated it by owning up to a misdemeanour without being caught. There seems to have been a feeling on the part of the school that he had behaved more honourably than not. The Society of Friends has had a sort of dove-grey respectability for so long it's easy to forget that the Quakers started out as rebels, refusing to pay tithes or swear oaths. The logic behind the refusal of oaths was that it created a special category of truthful speech when their unsworn speech was truthful as a matter of course. Honest people need no special dispensation from lying. Perhaps Peter showed that he had imbibed this principle when he denounced himself for an infraction that no one had noticed.

In conventional terms mine was the unenviable life, but I wouldn't have swapped fates with Peter, not exactly overshadowed by me but perhaps undershadowed, his accomplishments nullified in advance by my inability to compete with them. Younger brothers aren't necessarily meek, though meekness may be their strategy in life, but Peter seemed to have had no great hunger to push himself forward. Independence seemed to lie well within his reach, but if in fact he had to go all the way to Australia to escape the clutches of family (my clutches too, such as they are) then I shouldn't begrudge him the adventure, even if I couldn't thrill to the technical specifications of the machines he drove once he got there, as he might have liked me to do.

This Christmas Day I wasn't really waiting for Peter. Changing a plan wasn't really in his character. I had only been surprised when he turned up in India because of the practical difficulties. I had learned from that, but there had been nothing in those rather odd letters of his about 'see you at Christmas'. If there had been I would be expecting him with confidence. I would be telling Mum to put the kettle on, even if there was a wildcat strike putting every Australian airport out of action.

The one that lived in Ivy's mouth

Something else was keeping sleep at a distance. A faint friction between word forms in my conversations with Audrey was beginning to nag at me. At thirteen she still called Mum 'Mummy'. So when had I stopped using the more childish form of the word? I must have used it up to a certain point. Were there circumstances that might make me recoil from it? I'll say there were!

I couldn't remember directly, I could only reconstruct, but that's the way memory works. The knife cuts away the hole it has made.

On the children's wards of the Canadian Red Cross Memorial Hospital at Taplow a boy who called his mother 'Mummy' rather than 'Mum' had betrayed his class origins and must be punished. There was an autocratic régime in power led by the corrupt little Robespierre known as Ivy. During Ivy's Terror the boy who called his mother 'Mummy' might as well have called her 'the dear old Mater' or 'the Progenitrix'. The only guillotine at CRX was the one that lived in Ivy's mouth, but no sharper blade was needed to enforce her rule.

Language was intensively scrutinised on those premises for the class allegiances it betrayed, and I had been lucky not to be caught pronouncing nougat *noogah* rather than *nugget*. The names of sweets, how to say them, these were things that could be unlearned. They didn't lie close to the molten core of the brain's word-hoard. *Mummy*, though – *Mummy* was different.

The tender word, first word on my tongue, presumably the word that brought me into speech.

I'd chipped the namby-pamby suffix off this foundation stone of language, without needing to be told to get the chisel out. I shed it in an act of lexical autotomy in the same way that a lizard sheds its tail, perhaps misunderstanding the evolutionary logic of that gambit. The lizard sheds its tail when attacked, hoping to confuse predators by offering them two targets. With any luck they will pounce on the still-twitching tail and give the creature itself time to escape. I had done something much less useful, shedding my tender tail even before I could be attacked. It did not grow back.

It was only in the special circumstances of a long-stay children's ward, where I was judged by the standards of a primary-school-aged revolutionary tribunal, that it was possible for me, the son of an Air Force pilot and an ex-nurse, to be assessed as posh. It's true that there was more distinction in the previous generation, at least on the maternal side. Dad had parents, of course, but Mum could almost be said to have 'people'.

I gave up my first and oldest word in the hope of being safe from Ivy's gang, and although I suppose I could have gone back to it when the threat had passed I never did. The all-clear never sounded in my head, and all that I had left in my mouth was the stump of a word. Mum-my. Mum-my. I couldn't get rid of that hyphen, and the amputated tender segments refused to be rejoined. I could no longer call her that in my mind, though I had for years.

The same operation had been carried out on 'Daddy', but that was different somehow, done as much for symmetry as anything else. A boy who called his father 'Daddy' at CRX wouldn't have had a good time, but the word advertised only class, not emotional vulnerability. He was posh but not pathetic. It was odds against that a boy who called his mother 'Mummy' would survive in any form his mother could recognise.

Was there more to it, even? I don't remember feeling abandoned, and I had been encouraged to look forward to CRX, which was touted as a school rather than a hospital, but there are devastations with no edges to them, so that they leave no record – for the very reason that they take up all the available space. Perhaps it was out of revenge as much as fear of my fellows that I amputated the possessive adjectives from 'My Mum-my', fore and aft, to produce 'Mum', disowning any sense of owning or being owned. She was no longer mine and I was no longer hers, not as I had been, even though I lived for her visits.

I could have started calling Dad 'Daddy' again without anyone noticing, I dare say, without internal turmoil or outward hesitation. 'Mummy' was a different matter. Not that 'Mummy' is a word that necessarily brings sincerity with it. Audrey had a knack for bending the word just slightly out of shape, stretching out its final syllable or caricaturing the vowels in a way that could never be proved to be mocking.

The grass blades became daggers and cudgels

In the morning Audrey brought me a cup of tea and propped me up comfortably, either because she had taken me under her wing or because Mum had sensibly deputised her as a way of rationing direct contact between us.

Even before Audrey took the cloth off Phyllis's cage she was making noises. I'd emphasised that the cloth must be arranged to create complete darkness or she was likely to wake up, but either my instructions had been ignored or the cloth somehow had slipped.

They were outstandingly odd noises, like a car starting up after a long period of disuse, and it took me a while to work out what was happening. It must be that parrots are attuned to particular times of day, and that they accordingly reproduce the sounds they have heard at the same time on other days. Theirs is a delicate recording mechanism, self-programming but lacking in curiosity as such. That's the best explanation I can come up with for Phyllis's morning repertoire. She started the day with an extraordinary display of raucous coughs, lengthy episodes of hawking and spitting, and the words that she mimicked to accompany them were 'Oh God', delivered in a tone of flat despair. It seemed safe to deduce that the Major was very far from a morning person. The cough was distinctive and I felt I could pick him out, on the basis of Phyllis's performance, in the heart of a coughing crowd.

Dad's Christmas-morning routine was more serene, though there was an undertone of mild mischief-making. When Audrey had helped me to get comfortable she pushed me in to join him. She herself had to help Mum by cutting little crosses in the stems of the Brussels sprouts, whose number she estimated at a thousand.

Dad seemed to be enjoying the instability caused by my visit, the return of a barely-half-welcome prodigal son, one who was likely to respond to the sacrifice of a fatted calf, and even the offer of suetted mince pies, with a lecture on the proper ethics of eating. He was having quiet fun of a strange sort, putting on a seasonal LP but stirring things up just the same. He selected 'In the Bleak Midwinter' from the track listing, turning up the volume to the level that traditionally gets complaints from parents. It would certainly be audible in the kitchen. Sitting room, kitchen, hall. So many spaces for the incalculable forces of family to swirl back and forth through, rushing past me but somehow sweeping me along despite my best intentions and long-before-New-Year resolution to absent myself spiritually.

'This is your mother's favourite carol, you know, John. And doesn't the choir of King's College Cambridge make a lovely noise? Did your college have a choir, John?'

'I expect so, Dad. We had most things.' It's possible we had a more searching father-and-son conversation about my university career at some point, but I can't remember one. 'If this is Mum's favourite carol perhaps she should come and have a sit-down with us so she can listen to it properly.' Though she already had the radio on in the kitchen.

'Oh, she has far too much to do for that. The turkey needs trimmings and the trimmings need trimmings too. And when I say this is her favourite carol, it's probably truer to say that she's learning to like it.'

In another man his mood would have suggested a sherry breakfast. Dad was perfectly sober, just slightly excited by the opportunities offered for misbehaviour presented by my return. Audrey would indeed pour him a ritual glass of sherry before the meal, but he might forget to finish it. Still, he twinkled in front of me like a minor official of carnival, not the Lord of Misrule but the Lord of Misrule's usher, carrying the ceremonial bladder and tickling stick on his behalf. 'High Wycombe here we come. Last Christmas at this address, last Christmas in Trees, last Christmas in Bourne End – enjoy it while you can. We'll still be in Buckinghamshire, of course. So it's not all change.'

'When did you decide this, Dad?'

'I'm not sure that I did. But you know me, I'll go along for the ride.'

'I'm sorry to keep asking, but this is a big change and needs to be taken seriously. I don't mean to make waves, and I promise to keep to safe subjects at table. I just wish I felt you'd thought this through.'

'Honestly, John, do we ever "think things through"? If we'd thought things through, do you think I'd be here? Do you think you would?' He evaded the question for once with a plunge into profundity rather than trying to change the subject.

It didn't in fact take Audrey all that long to install crosses on the sprouts, and then she was all for playing Careers again. The game is described on the box as being for two to six players, but as a *pas de deux* it's a pretty melancholy affair. Dad agreed to take part, if not to

682

concentrate. Every few minutes he would get up and put the needle of the gramophone player back to the start of 'In the Bleak Midwinter'.

After revealing my system to Audrey I didn't find it hard to predict her targets (they would be 25–12–23 in various combinations), though that sort of inside knowledge doesn't make a huge amount of difference in ordinary play.

At the end of the first game she couldn't wait to grab my slip and see what I had written as my targets. Her face fell. Naturally I had changed my system. It was now based on the Kali Yuga, the Hindu Dark Age that had started in 3102 BC and is due to last until the year 428,899, so don't hold your breath. 31 plus 2 plus 27. She couldn't make head nor tail of what was behind my choices, though I comforted her by promising to reveal my new system at Christmas 1974, if we dared contemplate a repetition of the event in progress. As her older brother I took seriously my obligation to tease and tantalise.

The beginning of the Kali Yuga marks the death of Krishna, which came about when a hunter shot an arrow into his foot, mistaking it for a deer. Krishna forgave the hunter before dying, having lost the will to live, or its divine equivalent, after the extinction of his whole clan, the Yadavas, in a fratricidal brawl. The Yadavas had gone to the seashore *en masse* for a celebration, but then what had started as friendly banter turned vicious, and so they beat and stabbed each other to death. They weren't armed, since this was supposed to be a party, but as bad luck would have it the reeds along the shore had absorbed the powdered metal ground down from a cursed iron bar (to which Krishna's son Samba had given birth), so that the grass blades became daggers and cudgels. It's a long story. Of course it is! It's in the Mahabharata. Perhaps the whole episode is best understood as a warning against family gatherings, and the tendency on such occasions for the most innocent subjects to take on a murderous edge.

Then Dad said he'd like to show me the garden. In late December this was always likely to be a thin errand – I like wintersweet and mahonia as much as anyone, but they don't exactly put on a glamorous display. Fragrance is their contribution. At least he was considerate enough to wrap me in a blanket against the cold. So I wasn't surprised that he said, 'There's something I'd like to ask you, chicken.' I was going to hear the real story of the sale of the house and the move to High Wycombe. Except of course I wasn't.

'John, I've been thinking . . . will we be pulling crackers later?'

'Of course we will, Dad! Christmas cards, Christmas carols, Christmas pudding, Christmas cake, Christmas crackers . . . there's a definite pattern emerging. I think it might be Christmas.'

'I know that, John. No need to be clever-clever. But is it wise? I was thinking that this year we could skip the crackers part of the day.'

Over my unreborn body we will! For me Christmas crackers were not optional but an absolutely integral part of the festival. I would have given up all the other traditional elements on the list rather than miss out on crackers. 'Why on earth shouldn't we pull crackers?'

'I'm only thinking of your splendid bird. I'm only thinking of Phyllis.'

'What's Phyllis got to do with it?'

'Think about it, John. Here is a wild animal, prey animal rather than a predator, easily frightened. If she feels she's in danger then either she'll find herself shut up in a cage with nowhere to go or free to fly around in a complete panic. We can't leave her out here in the cold, can we?' He produced a convincing shiver of sympathy and leaned over to tuck the blanket round me more snugly. 'So what do we say? That our pleasure in pulling crackers is more important than her peace of mind?'

Stuffed festive tubes designed for no other purpose

Yes, that's exactly what we say if it comes to the crunch. I was dancing to the family tune in any number of ways already, and I wasn't going to budge on this. 'There are plenty of sudden loud noises in the jungle, Dad.'

'I'm not so sure there are, chicken. But I suppose she's your bird.' This was definitely not the moment to reiterate my conviction that animals belong only to themselves. 'Would she be less frightened with the cloth over her cage or more so, do you think?'

For the first time I began to regret bringing Phyllis along with me. 'I think she'll feel safer in the dark. We can make sure she's in the far corner from the dinner table, by the window.'

'I suppose we could go into the kitchen to pull our crackers. That would help.'

I was surprised by my own dogmatism, my inflexible attachment to the pulling apart of stuffed festive tubes designed for no other purpose. 'As you say, Dad, she's my bird. She'll be fine.'

Dad didn't exactly say 'On your own head be it', but it's a sentiment easily communicated without recourse to words.

Mum had been busy. That was the message her new shoes were sending, after all – the clopping of those heels advertised how far she travelled in the house on her thankless errands. She insisted that they should be thankless and wouldn't have been mollified by being told her efforts were appreciated, though many had tried. But as we re-entered the house it was impossible to ignore the barrage of delicious aromas that greeted us – atavistically delicious, but that hardly made the effect less powerful. The stomach has no conscience. If the stomach had a conscience then we would all consider the consequences of our choices, though I don't exclude the possibility of vegetarians and vegans ganging up on Jains for being so smug.

I tried to concentrate on the less tamasic elements of the composite bouquet my senses were taking in, but the nose doesn't have much of a conscience either, and salivation is not a subtle mechanism. I was being bombarded with the smell of Christmas and the taste of home, and it's true Mum had a tendency to overplay her hand. I needed to focus my recalcitrant senses. Was there an innocent savoury thread somewhere with a hint of spice? Could I detect an intimation of marmalade? When Audrey offered me yet another fizzy drink I jumped at the chance and asked for the strongest flavour of syrup available, blackcurrant as it turned out. Not only did it block some of the signals emanating from the kitchen but it allowed me to pass off any possible tummy-rumbling as a side-effect of carbonated drinks.

When Mum came in she was carrying a seasonal display in a dry vase, sprigs of holly spray-painted silver with miniature baubles attached. 'Audrey, have you folded those napkins as I asked? Don't forget, you're the one who wanted to put on a special show. You volunteered.' It was as if Mum was singing a familiar, comforting song, even a carol, in the bleak midwinter. The twelve *vasanas* of Christmas.

At my request Audrey brought in my own cutlery for use at the meal. As Mum washed them up she noticed the inscription on them and asked me what the D C C stood for. I had half a mind to say, 'It couldn't be plainer, Mum – Don't Celebrate Christmas,' but settled for the truth in the interest of harmony. 'It stands for Downing College Cambridge, Mum.'

'Oh I see. Wasn't it nice of them to let you have a set!'

'Yes, wasn't it?' My mother had a low opinion of me in various departments but she had yet to identify me as a practitioner of petty larceny.

Mum had marked the occasion by using a white tablecloth and lighting red candles matching the crackers whose moments of glory were just around the corner. I was even beginning to get used to those cloppy new shoes of hers. What she lost in noiselessness she gained, I suppose, in the symbolic statement made by those rapping heels and clinking chains, that her life was a treadmill and that she was always running to stand still. Never mind that she refused to dismount from the treadmill she had built from scratch. She advertised, with the help of these percussive instruments worn on her feet, the cost to her in nervous energy of keeping the household running.

It was hard to go along with the idea that she was spreading her wings when every movement was accompanied with a miniature clanking, as if this was the Grey Lady of Farley Castle dragging her chains behind her. Those shoes gave a horribly strong sense of what it might be like to be Laura Cromer – to be in her shoes, as people are always saying. Constant activity to catch up with herself, forever running to keep still. The overlapping rhythms of heel and chain were the equivalent in sound of a Heath Robinson machine, its normal functioning hard to distinguish from collapse.

When we were finally at table I did my best to play along conversationally so as to keep the family temperature low. Even so I tried to resist making too many trips down memory lane, whose ruts can trip up the best of us. 'Do you 'member,' Mum said dreamily, 'when that beautiful swan paid us a visit? I'm sure you 'member that, Jay.'

If she hadn't prompted me directly I might have behaved better. I'm not proud of myself, but I have to own up just the same. 'The butterfly,' I said primly, 'has no memory of the caterpillar.' What a load of old tosh! Soulful bilge, and just the sort of phonius balonius that put my back up when anyone else came out with it. Honestly – where did that come from? I have no idea what it thought it was doing coming out of my mouth. By rights it should have got me sent to my bed with no pud. It would have been one thing if I'd really risen above attachment to that glorious episode, but I merely covered it over with an indifference I didn't feel. I was affecting disdain for the sublime memory we shared.

One summer a great swan had waddled in through the open back door of Trees, done a great green poo in the kitchen and then swanned out of the front door. What an honour! Mum, Dad and I didn't know what we had done to deserve such a visitation. Only Audrey seemed to think it was offensive, held her nose and ran out of the room. Of course she was young, and perhaps a little frightened.

To dispel the sanctimonious pong I had created I did my best to find a friendlier wavelength. 'And how about the ford – are people still coming a cropper?'

'Two last week,' said Dad. 'They never learn, do they?'

People were always getting their cars stuck in the ford and knocking on our door – we were the nearest house – for help getting them out again. We would turn out to help, though Dad always said we could have charged and made a mint. I insisted on being part of the team, or at any rate not being excluded from it, which is only human nature, from which likewise I am not to be excluded. There's always someone offering advice when a driver is in a tricky position, reversing out of a tight parking place, say, someone who calls out 'Left hand down a bit – no, *left*!' whether they know what they're doing or not. There was no reason it shouldn't be me.

Over time I had become a sort of repository of miscellaneous expertise, a walking instruction manual for activities I could never master myself. How to tie a running bowline. How to open a tin of corned beef using that dratted little key, with the minimum expenditure of blood. That's all a bit too much delegation. In my mind there's a definite difference between being unable to participate in any particular activity and being made to feel left out. When Peter had a craze for playing ducks and drakes, skimming stones across the water all the way from the house called By the Pool to the house where Jon Pertwee lived, it didn't occur to me that we weren't all doing it. Dad and I would follow in Peter's wake, with Dad drawing on his æronautical experience to analyse the forces in play and the variables to be factored in. He calculated the ideal angle of incidence of the spinning stone meeting the water surface to be 20° or a little less, perhaps 18°. The flick of the wrist, meanwhile, must be pronounced but not overdone – the analogy was with flicking an old-fashioned thermometer, firmly enough to force the mercury down past the kink in the glass neck, but without risking breakage of the fragile wand itself. One more piece of expertise I could pass on but not put into practice. But I could look out from the Tan-Sad invalid carriage for suitable candidates on the ground, hoping for a rounded piece of slate to catch my eye. Its triumphant flight would be our joint achievement, not just Peter's. Dad and I were boffins, like Barnes Wallis, who invented the bouncing bomb – though of course pilots like Guy Gibson are also remembered – and hadn't I been given the middle name of Wallis in his honour? In our dreams Peter and I could skim stones just as well as each other, skim them clear across the Thames, to leave lovely deep dimples shining darkly in the water that would close up in their own good time.

Because you are morbidly obese

Gibson might well have been on Dad's shortlist for middle names for me. The choice of Wallis perhaps showed an intuition on Dad's part that I would be a backroom boy of some sort, scribbling equations on the back of an envelope rather than opening the bomb-bay doors. And if I'd been christened John Vade-Mecum Cromer it would certainly have prepared me better for life as a walking handbook of out-of-the-way skills and tasks.

'And what's the news of Rolo the cat?'

'Oh dear,' Mum said, 'that's such a sad subject. It started off as a party trick, 'member, and then it got out of hand.' Rolo was the pub cat at the Heart in Hand on Cores End Road. Rolo wasn't his name, which was really Charles (insofar as humans know such things, v. Eliot op. cit.), but he became known for his way of eating Rolos, impaling the soft toffee cup on his claws and licking languorously away at it. The name stuck to him as firmly as the confection itself stuck to the clenching of his paw.

'He started to get very fat, so the landlord put a sign up saying PLEASE DO NOT FEED ROLOS TO THE CAT, which may not have been all that clever because it only gave people ideas who hadn't seen it happen. Anyway Rolo – Charles, I should say – became very fat. He became diabetic. Towards the end he had swelled up so much he looked like a . . . what are those things called, for children . . .? There's a craze for them.' Lesser husbands would have made helpful suggestions, but Dad sat back and waited for her to find what she was looking for. 'You know, for children to bounce along the street on. A Space Hopper, only a Space Hopper with tabby stripes. That's exactly what he looked like, I'm afraid, and it was all too much for his system and then he died.'

There was a long moment of silence before Dad chimed briskly in. 'In my opinion, m'dear, that animal should have been stuffed and put in a glass case.'

'*Dennis!*'

'Hear me out, Laura,' he said, as if she ever did anything else. 'On the glass case there would be a sign saying *This is what happens when you sentimentalise Nature*. Imagine turning a cat into a performing animal – a cat, of all creatures!'

'But that would be cruel.'

'Can't be cruel to the cat, m'dear, since it's dead. Can hardly be called cruel to the customers in the pub if it helps them to change their ways. The real cruelty is rewarding animals when they accidentally behave like human beings. You've kept a lot of dogs in your lifetime, m'dear – would you ever teach one of them to shake hands to get a treat? To roll over and play dead? Of course you wouldn't! You know the difference between training animals and corrupting them.'

Of course she wouldn't. And in the case of Rolo the cat I felt there was an element of mental torture over and above the physical distress. Nothing could be more degrading for an animal as scopæsthetic as a cat, conscious without needing to use its eyes of every glance that came its way, than the knowledge of being looked at not because you're aloof and unknowable but because you are morbidly obese.

'Laura, you're sentimental too in your own way. Nature is tougher than you think. Just because an animal seems beautiful to us doesn't mean it needs an extra amount of looking after. Phœbe, who is at this moment writhing round my leg and hoping against hope for a titbit, is in the pink on the régime I suggested, which means she is fed every two days. Her kits draw on her just as well, or even better, when she isn't digesting on her own account. We agreed we would try it for the next two weeks, and if she's doing anything but thriving we'll go back to your way of doing things.'

'Yes, Dennis. We agreed. I'm being very fair-minded.'

'And Audrey, I'm counting on your coöperation – no treats.'

'No treats, Daddy.' I thought in fact that she was very likely to do as he said. Unquestioning compliance on her part was an anomaly, but so was Dad in the rôle of authority figure.

By this time I had eaten my splendidly foreshortened main course, the small portions of potatoes, sprouts and carrots that would have been dry in the absence of gravy without the presence of bread sauce. Bread sauce – how can something that tastes of so little taste of so much? The poached ghost of an onion, the breath of a clove – otherwise it's not anything to write home about, just a basinful of breadcrumbs taking a long warm bath in a pan of milk, with a bay leaf standing in for a loofah.

It's often said that more couples have separated over whose turn it was to take out the bins than over the breaking of their marriage vows, though it wouldn't be an easy statistic to verify. In the same way more families may have been kept together by bland food rich in associations, by bread sauce and by custard, than by good resolutions and consultations with experts.

I had stuffing too – Mum had put a separate vegetarian version in the oven, away from the contamination of the turkey flesh. Likewise my potatoes had been boiled rather than roasted in dripping.

'*Now* can we pull our crackers, Mummy?'

'Not before pudding – you know that.'

Mum and Dad had been brought up with the protocols of their generation, bread-and-butter before cake and all that nonsense, and it was obvious to them that the boundary between celebration and rampage must be tightly patrolled. Christmas was no sort of excuse for anarchy.

'Mummy, you said this was a special Christmas because John was coming home – maybe we should ask him what he prefers? He may want us to pull our crackers right away.'

Clever girl! Though I didn't fancy her chances of rewriting the rules of the celebration simply by invoking my status as prodigal.

'John? What do you say?' Mum's voice contained a warning that I shouldn't presume too far.

'Well, I wouldn't mind waiting a while before we have pudding.' It wasn't altogether that I was siding with Audrey by trying to create a gap that might profitably be filled with tiny explosions, with scattered trinkets and mottoes, with jokes that would actively disappoint if they raised a laugh and not a groan. I could wait for the cracker-pulling hour, myself, but then I could wait for pudding also – for hours, for days if need be. I was sated already. My stomach fills up very easily, and after that every extra mouthful feels oppressive. I really don't see the point of eating for the sake of it.

'I'm full up already.' No more than the truth, though perhaps I shouldn't have said so out loud. Certainly Mum was dismayed by the remark.

'But JJ, you can't be!' There was something close to panic in her voice. 'You've hardly eaten a mouthful.'

'More than enough to satisfy this body's needs.' The falsity of the festival seemed to be bringing out an equal and opposite falsity in me, the tendency to turn every little thing into a self-satisfied homily.

'You *have* to have some pudding, JJ! It's Christmas.' If I had wanted a demonstration of the bullying that lurks in the heart of family welcome I couldn't have asked for better. Perhaps there was an element of tender concern in the ultimatum, but it was still an ultimatum.

'What makes it a meal, if you *have* to eat it?' Why doesn't it count as a punishment, or a mild form of torture? *I sentence you to roast turkey and all the trimmings, and may God have mercy on your karma – usher, take him down!*

'You're being utterly ridiculous, John! Utterly. I'll bring you your pudding, and if you really don't want it you can leave it.' She calmed her voice and attempted a transition from reproach to seduction. 'But it's your favourite.' How many times have I heard that! How many times have I had my choices overruled in the name of my own supposed historical tastes! 'It's your favourite' – supposing that the statement is true it doesn't need to be made, and if untrue then it falls to the ground refuted. If we weren't allowed to move on from our original preferences we would none of us have been weaned. As Mum left the room I caught a look of complicity between Audrey and Dad, a look that said, 'Little does he know.' Clearly I was in for a surprise and a treat.

Something rubbery and bright yellow

The collision of these three things, surprise, treat and (whether I liked it or not) 'my favourite', promised a real pile-up at the dinner table. Nevertheless as Mum returned there was a fragrance in the air that I couldn't help recognising and confusing with past contentment. The smell in my nostrils was congruent with some antique intuition of how things should be. Here, surely, was Queen of Puddings, its layers of blandness brought to life by an interposed grouting of jam then sealed under meringue. Raspberry jam is traditional in some households and in most recipe books, but what I knew from childhood and could now smell as an adult was definitely marmalade.

Mum set a ramekin in front of me and placed my trusty sundæ spoon next to it. This unassuming portion was perfectly calculated to resurrect appetite and to allay most of my doubts. Still, I had to be sure. 'There isn't suet in this, is there, by any chance?'

'Don't be silly, JJ! Of course there isn't. Who would put suet in a Queen of Puddings?' Who would put suet in anything? That's the real question, but any last suspicions were swept away in an upwaft of sweet enticing steam.

I didn't expect anyone else to be given the treat of a ramekin, but I had taken it for granted they too would be eating Queen of Puddings. Instead they had bowls laden with Christmas pudding (incorporating suet, if 'properly' made) and proper thin custard. Custard should always be thin rather than thick, but it's no good explaining the fact to those lost souls who have been dulled by prolonged exposure to something rubbery and bright yellow.

'Did you have yours earlier?'

'Did we have our what earlier?'

'Your Queen of Puddings.'

'Oh no, JJ.'

'Did you really make this just for me?'

'Why, don't you like it any more? You should have said!'

Oh, it wasn't that, as well she knew. Preparing a single miniature pudding is a challenge on the technical level, rather like making furniture for a dolls' house, but there was no question of the feat being beyond her powers. She measured by eye, and was perfectly capable of adding just enough egg, for instance, to do the job, saving the rest (thrifty as she was) for another recipe. So what she was saying when she served that little ramekin was not so much 'Here's a lovely little Queen of Puddings – I haven't forgotten that it's your favouritest!' as 'I am the uncrowned Queen of Puddings'. *Remember when we were each other's favourite? Remember when I kept you alive with little treats like these?* Though she had never devised anything as wonderful in its little way as this tiny delight with its castellated peaks of toasted meringue, Queen of Puddings as it might be served at a banquet hosted by Queen Mab.

I could feel Mum not looking at me as the sundæ spoon broke into the yielding crust, revealing something sweetly melting under the illusion of crispness. I began to feel that I had been too uncompromising during the main course of the meal, when I had repudiated the gravy jug on its approach to my plate of vegetables and bread sauce. She had respected my insistence on separation – might I not safely have yielded to her desperate need that we be sharers? At least to the extent of allowing a little trickle from the gravy boat of peace to descend in blessing on my potatoes. She wouldn't have known how little of an exception I was making for her benefit, since I was hiding the extent to which I was a carnivore in vegetarian's clothing. My diet on this visit, even if I had let it be clouded with a little gravy, was closer to vegetarianism than the way I lived, at least on home help days, in Mayflower House.

I didn't deny Mum her moment of triumph, but that moment seemed never-ending, with the members of my family all smirking at each other over the lowering of my defences. I had to call a halt to that. 'Stop looking at me, please. Get on with your lives. Can't you let a man enjoy his pudding in peace?' Nevertheless the meal, narrowly defined as 'the time when we were actually eating', was a success beyond expectations.

Finally, *finally*, crackers were authorised. Is there a better use of a shock-sensitive chemical solution than for impregnating the explosive strip of a Christmas cracker? As a child I had loved proper fireworks but was often fobbed off with the indoor kind – but there's nothing second-rate about Christmas crackers. They're not also-rans. They hold their own, in the more muted arena of the dinner table, with your Roman candle, your Bengal flares, your devil-among-the-tailors. The silver fulminate in the impregnated strip (though there are other formulas) gives up its energy with a snap and a spurt of joy. The Indo-European root *Spar* summons up a constellation of meanings from 'vibrate' to 'breathe', with 'moving to and fro' or perhaps 'palpitation' the underlying idea. It gives us the words 'spear', 'spur', 'spurt' and even, ultimately, 'spirit'.

It was always understood that I would approach the moment of cracker detonation in my own way. Don't invite John for Christmas unless you're prepared to make Christmas Johnable. If there's no room at the inn for heaven's sake say so! Put up the sign that says No Vacancies. Is there a more discriminatory activity than cracker-pulling? It's a contest of brute strength visited on a festival whose welcome is supposed to be universal. *The God of Love and Sacrifice is born . . . now, whose arm is the strongest? Winner gets a toy.* Usually it's an unJohnable toy, too, such as a set of three rings to be assembled in a particular linkage. Puzzles whose only common factor is the requirement of dexterity, jokes printed on slips whose only common factor is remoteness from mirth.

If something is unJohnable then unilateral action must be taken to restore the proper balance of things. I can do quite a professional job of disassembling a Christmas cracker, having had a fair amount of practice over the years. It's a sort of merry autopsy. I unfurl the cocoon of crêpe paper and cardboard to reveal its packed innards: the motto, joke, toy and tightly rolled tissue-paper hat. These I briskly extract and lay aside as being of secondary interest. Moving with a surgeon's unhurried efficiency I detach the white cardboard strip whose central inch or two, though demurely grey, is steeped in explosive chemistry. Thereby I remove the heart and spine of the thing from the thoracic cavity in which it has lain.

Mum knew what I was up to. There was nothing secretive about it. She was close by, even if she was going back and forth on kitchen errands. She even picked up the tissue-paper hat from the anatomised cracker, unfolded it and put it on my head, which was an outrage and also a tactical mistake. Even putting a crown on someone's head without permission is just another violation of autonomy, and implying that I have an obligation to get into the Christmas spirit is just another piece of presumptuousness. I won't have it. If I can't control what goes on my head what can I control?

Paper hats are all one size, so the hat fitted. Still's Disease plays havoc with the joints but the skull itself isn't articulated, and my head size is not something that strays from the norm. Am I supposed to be grateful for being a standard measure for once, to the point where I must carry around on my head anything, from tiara to deerstalker, that has been put there? I couldn't dislodge the paper hat with shakes of the head, nor reach it by hand, but at a dinner table there are knives within reach that usefully extend my range. After a few attempts I was able not simply to remove it but to slit the fragile tissue so that it was unfit for any future shaming coronation. The three kings don't turn up for a good while after the Nativity anyway, if that's what the paper crowns are supposed to denote, and the whole thing is an unholy mess in terms of iconography.

It's true that I was departing from the norm in terms of Johnable Christmas crackers. The nude central strip would put up much less resistance to being pulled than the cracker in which it had been hidden, but the unwelcome element of competition remained. Yes, I could pull it, but anyone pulling against me would be using much less than their full strength. Why should I pull it at all, if they were going to be pulling their punches? I wanted to move the Christmas cracker into a different category, into the gloriously non-competitive area of the firework display, where everyone just goes *ooh* and *aah* and the ego itself melts in wonder.

That was the rationale behind my action – my action being to push the chemical strip directly into the flame of the candle in front of me. I don't mind admitting that for once I had given very little thought to the strictly scientific aspect of what I was doing. A chemical reaction powerful enough to make a loud noise when subjected to sudden tensive stress, from two opposed human arms, was much amplified by being raised at short notice through a great many degrees of temperature.

From one point of view a candle at a festive meal is a source of warm and flattering light, relied upon to soften hard edges and ease stubborn emotions. If enemies would only eat together by candlelight they would soon find their enmity soothed. In a season dominated by news of fuel shortages, as was the case in late December of 1973, it is also a reassurance that absolute darkness will not befall the celebration even if electrical power is cut. Seen from another perspective it is a miniature cauldron of scalding wax waiting to disseminate mayhem.

I can't deny that the explosion from my cracker was very loud. I was prepared for it, unlike the rest of the company, and yet . . . I wasn't prepared for it. 'Explosion' is a fine term but a very inclusive one, encompassing a wide range of detonations. A supernova is an explosion and so is a sneeze.

Red wax was splashed quite widely on a white tablecloth, and I can't pretend that I had foreseen either the specific visual impact or the general effect on the company. Audrey gave a little scream, Mum dropped a vegetable dish onto the table and even Dad, allegedly good in a crisis, cried out, 'What the hell was that?'

Everything was turned upside down, though with families there's no right way up. Did it make matters worse that I had sabotaged Christmas, as it must seem to Mum and perhaps even Dad, with the help of props from Christmas itself, with a candle and a cracker? It could hardly help my case that I had stabbed Santa Claus in the back with his own Ho-Ho-Ho.

If I had properly understood the potential consequences would I have made the extra effort and lifted the explosive strip a little higher, so that scalding wax was not part of the detonation? I don't know. Little blobs of molten wax had landed on my left eyelid but I didn't make a fuss about that, though I had no means of removing it. Why do people find it so hard to maintain a sense of proportion?

People talk about 'burning your boats' as if it was a laborious procedure to set the whole flotilla of attachments ablaze. So much accelerant to be sloshed over the timbers, so many flaming arrows to be loosed across the bay. In practice it can be done very simply. Simply holding the impregnated incendiary strip from an unravelled Christmas cracker into the flame of a candle does the job more than adequately. Perhaps there was a smouldering that had been going on for years, but that's a different question and a different point of view.

Mum picked up the vegetable dish, possibly disappointed that it was intact, put her hands on her hips and muttered bitterly, 'I don't know why I bother! Why do I even make the effort?' As happened so often in her case, this was a profound speculation couched in frustratingly shallow terms, turned outwards in protest and reproach rather than inwards where it might bear fruit. It was a shrewd self-diagnosis, but diagnosis should be the starting point, rather than a baffled terminus of enquiry. She only needed to turn the thought round by 180° to flood her own heart with understanding.

At the same time the vade-mecum, knack-stacked part of my mind was working on the immediate problem. There were always ways to remove household stains. 'Is there some white spirit in the house?' I felt sure there would be. 'Or some blotting-paper? I know there's a trick you can do with an iron.'

'Oh shut up, John,' she said. 'For once just shut up.'

Dad said, 'Keep your pucker up, m'dear. Gentlemen have a pecker, ladies have a pucker.'

'*What* did you say, Dennis?' It seemed very clear that Dad was taking a leaf out of my book in terms of muddying the conversational waters with deniable innuendo. Not that I claim any sort of right of possession, 'my' book being everyone's in the circulating library of morphic resonance, where there are no overdue fines and no worries about copyright.

'I said, "Keep your pecker up."' And Mum, knowing there was more to it than that, swung round and stared in bafflement at the bird cage, Phyllis being as far as she knew the only possible pecker in the room.

I felt sorry for Audrey, firstly for having to live in this house, and then being uprooted from it, leaving the only home she had ever known, even if it was to be resettled only ten miles away, given a pedigree kitten as a bribe, a bribe with the ability to purr, admittedly, which is not something to be underestimated – but she would have to wait at least a year for its eyes to take on the lucky colour, just as she would have to wait until she had eaten pudding her system didn't want before she was permitted to pull a cracker.

There were *vasanas* as far as the eye could see. The family road was rutted beyond belief, and forward travel was impossible for any one of us till the bulldozers of self-realisation had done their work and cleared a path. Despite our Buckinghamshire postal address we were all denizens of Rutland. Already I felt that the wheelchair was stuck up to its axles in the residue of old decisions, decisions that might not have been bad when first made but that clogged any future action by being endlessly repeated. *Vasanas* are the gossamer threads that collectively keep big-souled Gulliver trussed and helpless in Lilliputian bondage, though the filaments are hardly detectable one by one.

I don't know which of us was first aware of another sound in the room. It may not have been a person. Phœbe the Korat cat landed with a thump on the table in front of me and picked her way fastidiously through the debris. I'm willing to accept for argument's sake that she jumped up there, though it fits just as well with observed reality and the atmosphere prevailing to suppose that she was dropped from the ceiling by an invisible hand, so as to land with that other-worldly impact. Her presence, and her fierce concentration on the parrot cage, seemed to suggest something about the whole rigmarole of that Christmas and its attempt at reunion, that it was as futile as any treaty between cats and birds.

The very cream of her toes

Phyllis was saying something. We all shushed each other and tried to listen. 'Over here.' It was definitely 'Over here'. As for whether the cloth had been imperfectly closed round her cage again, leaving a gap at the back, or whether sudden loud noises in the jungle night do indeed wake parrots up, I couldn't say.

Phyllis repeated her two words, at a greater volume but with no added emphasis. Parrots may resort to capital letters but will hardly stoop to italics. 'Over here. OVER HERE.' Her understanding of positional language had not faltered under stress. She didn't want to repeat her trusting flight of the day before. She wanted someone to go over there, to where she was – it was as simple as that. I might be the person with whom she was most familiar, the person she might seem to be summoning, but it seemed sensible to deputise Dad.

'Dad, she wants you to go over to her.'

'And what do I do when I'm there?'

'Talk gently to her. Just as you would with any other animal.' It seemed extraordinary that Dad could imagine himself out of his depth, when his feeling for animals was so much more reliable than his feeling for people.

'Aren't you a lovely creature, though, Phyllis? What a beauty . . .' His voice tailed away. Then he said, 'I say,' though actually he didn't. He said nothing else, just 'I say' again. Then, after quite a long pause, 'Perhaps you'd better take a look, Laura.'

'Why, what's happened, Dennis?' Mum sounded panic-stricken. 'Can't you just tell me?'

I didn't see why I should be excluded from the conversation.

'Dad, is she all right?' I asked, calmly as compared to Mum but admittedly with a little anxiety. My credentials as a bird expert were anything but solid, except in the eyes of the Major, but I could reasonably hope to keep his parrot alive and in good health for three days and two nights.

'Oh yes,' Dad said. 'She's all right.'

'Then what's happened?' In an entirely deceptive show of shared priorities Mum and I spoke the words in unison.

'Can I see? Can I see?' Audrey too was jockeying for position, and positively jittering with disordered excitement. She cried, 'Polly wants a cracker! Polly wants a cracker of her own to pull! Polly wants a cracker and a paper hat!'

It had seemed to me over the previous day that Audrey's mental age fluctuated wildly, though much of that impression can be put down to my ignorance of girls her age and how they behave generally. This, though, was regression by any measure. She knew perfectly well Phyllis was not Polly and had said nothing of the sort. Phyllis had neither expanded nor distorted her vocabulary under the pressure of an emergency but had used a formula that was familiar to her – but the garbling of the message by Audrey was hardly surprising.

It was always going to be through her that the family tension was discharged. This isn't a matter of maturity, narrowly defined, but of something closer to amperage. As a general rule the youngest person in the group is the one whose fuse is most likely to be blown when the load on the collective circuits becomes too great.

'Pipe down, Audrey!' Dad said with a firmness that was not usual. 'Pipe down, girl. You don't know what you're saying.'

'Dennis, what has that bird done?'

'Well, my dear, she's made rather a meal of your curtains.'

'What are you saying? Those are my best curtains.' Of course they were her best curtains! It could not have been otherwise. If a visitor dropped or spilled anything it always ruined her best carpet, as she would say later, though insisting at the time that the stain would come out in a jiffy. If someone accidentally trod on her toes in the queue at the baker's it was always her favourite foot and the very cream of her toes that had been made to suffer.

Now Audrey made the sensible decision to commandeer the wheelchair and approach the huddle by the birdcage. Her curiosity was disguised as helpfulness, which was fine by me since it allowed my own curiosity to be indulged.

Dad was holding up neat strips of the dark-red curtain material. 'She hasn't eaten any of them, I don't think. At least I hope not. But she's done a certain amount of damage.'

Perhaps it had been unwise – and I hadn't been consulted at any stage, so need take no responsibility – to put Phyllis's cage in a position from which she could reach the curtains, since the cloth intended to blanket her in soothing darkness didn't go all the way down at the back.

'She was nervous, Dad, she was frightened by the noise. Surely you can see that?'

The incisions in the curtain material were remarkably clean. I can only assume that carborundum was one of the ingredients of the Fru-Grains the Major insisted on feeding Phyllis, to give her beak such an edge. It cut out as neatly as a pair of dressmaker's scissors, something that in another context Mum might even have admired.

But not now. 'That's it,' she said. 'That's *it*! Take your ruddy car, take your bloody parrot and go back to effing Cambridge!' As it must have seemed to her, a two-pronged assault had been carried out on treasured textiles, the white tablecloth and the red curtains, by me and my accomplice Phyllis, if she was not in fact my familiar.

Mum's fury was real, but more blocked than released by the expletive she couldn't quite bring out. When Audrey said 'Sugar!' instead of 'Shit!', she was paying lip service to the niceties prevailing, whether they were house rules or school rules. In theory there was nothing to stop Mum articulating taboo words in full, but everything in her opposed it.

My generation, supposedly freer of qualms, had its own lingering inhibitions, its own tendency to snigger. When a group called Jody Grind released an album called *Far Canal*, we were amazed at their daring, though you had to contort your rough regional pronunciation of the title pretty far north to make it sound, as was the whole idea, like *Fuckin Ell*. When advertisements for Joe Cocker's single 'Delta Lady' appeared in the underground press there was argument aplenty about whether what it showed, when viewed from far enough away and the right angle, was really as rumoured a lady's delta. No one could quite believe that Al Stewart used the word 'fucking' in a song ('Love Chronicles', it was – I've always had a bit of a soft spot for Al Stewart), even for non-expletive purposes, so as to make the case for a particular sexual act being less like fucking and more like making love. The needle had to make repeated journeys through the grooves to establish to everyone's satisfaction that Al Stewart had indeed done what D. H. Lawrence had done forty years before and used the word to mean what it was supposed to.

Mum would not have wanted to imitate any of these cultural figures but might have got some relief from the articulation of obscenity, at the cost – arguably worth paying – of her entire shell cracking, the gross and subtle sheaths alike giving way, to allow a new person to step out of it. Though she talked so much that Christmas about starting a new life, and her appearance and behaviour were in several ways jarringly different from what we were used to, this particular transformation was not what she had in mind. She wanted to move to High Wycombe, not to Mars.

I don't enjoy drama but have a very limited ability to leave the stage. Luckily Mum clip-clopped out of the dining room, in the shoes that seemed in her mind to symbolise the freedom of a fresh start, despite the fact that they were festooned with little chains. Before she did, I had a moment of insight that took the form almost of levitation. I looked down on my family, myself included, from above. We looked suddenly smaller, shrivelling in the pickling liquor of bare observation. This wasn't a conscious exercise in methodical diminishment (itemising bodies for instance as fathom-long carcases) as recommended by the *Satipatthana Sutta* but an involuntary bolt of understanding along the same lines.

Dad was a Peter Pan surprised to find himself sharing a bed with Wendy Darling, and I could feel Mum's deathly tiredness underneath the changes she was so desperate to make. Audrey only wanted to be held in Dad's arms and be safe. I was able to look down on these petty people with trittophthalmic clarity of vision as they harried and cajoled the tiny monster in the wheelchair, both theirs and not theirs to manipulate, both able and not able to resist or absent himself, who had terrified a parrot for the sake of a little illusory excitement and wasn't even regretting it just yet.

'Trittophthalmic' is my own coinage for third-eye perception and meets an obvious need. I don't see why the word shouldn't catch on. The vocabulary of enlightenment is in permanent need of a leg-up. Consider it my contribution to the mystical word-hoard.

Don't thank me! Invoice follows.

For a few moments I thought that maybe I was seeing my family afresh, with the rind of habit stripped away, but the whole rind-of-habit routine is part of Maya's *Greatest Hits* package, a way of making you think you have escaped illusion when she has described things in a new way, no more truthfully. This of course is part of the insidious appeal of drugs, persuading you that you've woken up when all you've done is changed the drift of the dream.

Herons and pelicans can come a cropper

I hesitate to talk in terms of normality and abnormality, and not only because those categories were so important to the lady who had just ordered me out of the house. Yet we Cromers marked ourselves out as unusual with the way we accepted this rupture as definitive.

In the past an ultimatum like the one just issued would have been treated as the beginning of a fresh round of negotiation at a higher emotional pitch, with Audrey pleading on my behalf, for instance, or Dad obliquely intervening by putting some music on the record player – whether it was a piece that she loved or one she hated was of secondary importance. The important thing was to nudge her mood in one direction or another, towards the serenity that so stubbornly eluded her or a discharge of exasperation that might leave her less absolute in her rejecting. This time, though, we seemed to have reached, if not the end of the road, then certainly the end of the rut.

The only outside agent who might have had an effect on our impasse was Joy, but she with her usual tact was leaving us alone on Christmas Day itself, though she had invited us for lunch on the 26th. Almost without a word Audrey pushed me to the Mini, already pointing in the right direction although a quick getaway had not in the end been required of it. Dad followed, carrying Phyllis in her cage.

He said, 'Perhaps I should go back with you. To make sure everything is all right . . .' This moment of concern was so out of character that it made me quite tense. Of course it would be more restful for him to be away from Bourne End for a little while, but did I really want him to play a part in my Cambridge life when he had kept his distance so far? Then he made it clear that his concern was for Phyllis. I could relax.

'Don't you think I should take a proper look at her?' he said. 'Just to make sure she hasn't got a scrap of fabric lodged in her beak? It wouldn't be easy living with yourself if she choked to death on your way home.' At least he recognised Cambridge as my home. Mum wouldn't willingly have made that concession.

To his credit Dad didn't say 'I told you so' about Phyllis's episode of panicked damage. On second thoughts it's not even to his credit, since he was too fascinated by the behaviour itself to think of assigning blame.

'Dad, parrots can't choke on their food – it's only human beings who can do that.' It was when our throats evolved to make speech possible that choking on food became a possibility.

Reluctantly he took my word for it. I wasn't consciously misleading him, I was misinformed myself, but I don't think I need to lose too much sleep over the fact that I got it wrong. Humans are the only mammals that can choke on their food, but birds can too. Lacking teeth and chewing muscles, many species swallow their food whole. In particular herons and pelicans can come a cropper, with their tendency to tip their heads back and swallow whole. Phyllis was in relatively small danger of having scraps of Mum's best curtain fabric obstruct her breathing, but it was wrong of me to dismiss the possibility outright. If she had in fact choked I wouldn't have had a leg to stand on.

I was packed off into the Mini in a charged silence. Audrey ran back into the house to get me a scarf and looped it round my neck. Then she ran back again to retrieve my drawing of Judi Dench from its hiding place, stowing it in the glove compartment. After that she just stood there wringing her hands. Hand-wringing seems to be an instinct deeply installed in the human nervous system. It's not just a piece of ham acting meant to signal helpless distress.

Finally I had to ask for my set of Downing cutlery to be returned to me. Dad examined them before he passed them through the window of the Mini to me.

'I say, John,' he said. 'You haven't half-inched these eating irons from your college mess, have you?'

I gave the aggrieved sigh appropriate to one who seemed to be being blamed for half the wrongs in the world. 'Yes, Dad, as a matter of fact that's exactly what I did.'

'Good for you, lad.'

I should have remembered – at a less exhausting moment I certainly would have remembered – that Dad had been as outraged as I was when Downing installed a hoist in the bathroom so that I could bathe more easily, and then billed Dad for it. And so despite all the kerfuffle the last words my father spoke to me that Christmas were of praise, praise for a feat of criminal initiative.

Even before I had put the Mini in gear, with Audrey still wringing her hands, I realised I would need to signal some distress of my own. I needed to phone the Major to warn him that my plans had changed, or had been changed for me. I would appreciate some help in conveying Phyllis the parrot from the Mini, registration OHM 962F, to 005 Mayflower House. Appreciate it? I couldn't see how I would manage

704

without, but 'I'd appreciate some help' was the note I would set out to strike. I would need someone to bring Phyllis in out of the cold. Who better suited for the job than the person who harboured the eccentric notion that she belonged to him?

I could have tried making the call from Trees, but then there would have been the risk of it being seen by Mum as a plea for another chance or, worse, as an opportunity for the goodwill towards men alleged to be the hallmark of the festival. I left Bourne End with quite a few regrets, one of the biggest being that nobody had asked me straight out why I had brought a parrot along. 'Because I thought there should be at least one bird on the premises without sage and onion stuffing wedged up its bum.' This line had got a laugh out of Joy Payne on the phone, and I was looking forward to giving it a proper outing. Joy wouldn't spoil my thunder by passing the remark on, I could be sure of that.

I've mentioned my feeling that cars should keep their distance from the pavement, but when I came across a telephone box on the way out of Bourne End there was no chance that I would abide by the stipulations of the Highway Code. I parked as close to the box as was possible without an actual collision, for which I'm sure exemplary penalties are laid down.

Who decided that telephone boxes needed to have such heavy doors? The doors of bank vaults are heavier, admittedly, but it's possible to follow the logic of that decision. What is it that needs to be kept out of a phone box by so implacable a mechanism? Other than me, I mean. I've never had any particular impulse to blow the doors off a bank vault but I would have been happy to visit that violence on these ones, simply because they were so unwilling to do their job of admitting the public, or else defining the public so narrowly as to exclude me.

Just as likely to have been Brut for Men

To have any chance of opening the door I needed to balance myself so as to give a little tug on the handle, a sort of semi-circular indentation unlike any other door handle I know, silver against the red of the phone box, offering purchase to a strong right hand though not to mine. After a couple of failed attempts I was able to pull it open just enough to wedge it with my crutch. This was a precarious business, since I must use the crutch as a lever while continuing to depend on it for support. In Cambridge when I was rash enough to use a public box my difficulties were so apparent that sooner or later someone would lend me a hand, but that was a lot to hope for on the outskirts of Bourne End, a town that hardly had skirts let alone outskirts, in the evening of Christmas Day.

I had been able to see my breath outside the phone box. The inside was hardly warmer. I was grateful for Audrey's scarf around my neck, and almost persuaded myself that pink might be my colour. There were still phone boxes around with the button-A-and-button-B system, in which you had to insert the coins before you dialled, but this one was more modern, though I have to say not much more Johnable for all that. I realise that 'Johnable' isn't the most elegant coinage, which may be part of the reason it has been so slow to catch on. But perhaps it's been misunderstood, if it seems to adumbrate (isn't *that* a lovely word, though?) a high standard that must be universally applied. I don't quite mean that. I don't resent arrangements that exclude me, except when they make out they're for everyone. Then I feel a little bit sour and let down, nothing that I won't get over by teatime. Not everything needs to be symmetrical to be fair. People are free to live at the top of a staircase with a thousand steps by all means, coming down to my level only when they feel like it. That's fine. But they shouldn't act surprised when I don't drop in.

The A and B system had the advantage that it let you divide the process of making a phone call into two halves. You could have a little breather between putting the coins in and dialling the number. For most purposes a table knife is the handiest extension of my reach (though I haven't looked back since I discovered the usefulness of small branches of the neem tree, so plentifully supplied with little crookèd elbows), but for effective dialling there was no substitute for a pencil. Yes, there was rather a rush to press Button A when someone answered, but that wasn't too much of a challenge. The relevant button was reasonably low down, and the pushing motion was on the level. Though I couldn't manage the receiver with one hand, I could sometimes balance it on my shoulder while I pushed the button.

With the new model of mechanism the coins had to be pushed awkwardly downwards from a higher position in the few seconds after the call had been answered, with impatient beeps telling me to hurry up or be cut off. It made sense to let go of the receiver so as to concentrate on the coins, and hope I could winch it back up to rough proximity with my mouth – 'Hello? Hang on! It's John here' – before the person I was hoping to speak to decided there was no one there. I'm no practical joker, I'm just hauling on a wire against the clock. Naturally I may be out of breath by the time I'm close enough to the apparatus to speak.

The interior smelled of stale urine, though of course it's just as likely to have been Brut for Men. Either way, and before I embarked on the call to Major Spinks, I needed to absorb the fact that I wasn't alone in the phone box. The space was filled with a sound of animal contentment – to wit, purring. The sound was amazingly loud. Could a single cat produce such a volume of audible satisfaction? Lacking the ability to look down I could only work from indirect evidence. It hardly seems likely that two cats had slipped into the phone box with me, taking advantage of my stately though agonised entrance, though I suppose it's possible. The purring was wonderfully loud, certainly, seeming to make the whole booth throb with satisfaction, though of course experiments would have to be carried out in order to rule out the possibility of a single source. Cats vary in their expressiveness like every other creature. I've seen some very lyrical slugs in the garden, paying an eloquent undulating homage to their creator, though I know perfectly well that a lot of squishing goes on the moment my back is turned, no matter how explicitly I have forbidden it.

More than once I've imagined my guru Ramana Maharshi as the spiritual equivalent of a Cheshire Cat, a disembodied smile, and I don't rule out the possibility that this was an equivalent phenomenon in the acoustic realm, a purr not accompanied by a cat. Even if I seemed to feel a strange soft lashing at the level of my ankles the presence of a tail isn't something I would want to swear to in court. Ankylosed joints make unsatisfactory witnesses to sensation.

What would Ramana Maharshi have said to me in the curious chilly acoustic of that phone box? 'Because you think that so-and-so is your wife and so-and-so are your children you also think that you are

bound to them. These thoughts are yours. They owe their very existence to you. You can entertain these thoughts or relinquish them.
The former is bondage and the latter is release. You may think these
thoughts or other thoughts. The thoughts change but not you. Let
go of the passing thoughts and hold on to the unchanging Self. The
thoughts form your bondage. If they are given up, there is release.' He
was very consistent in his teaching. 'The bondage is not external. So
no external remedy need be sought for release. It is within your competence to think and thus to become and remain bound or to cease
thinking and thus be free.'

For the moment, though, I still needed to think. I managed to
get a coin balanced in the slot, ready for the effort of forcing it down
against spring-loaded pressure the moment the Major answered – the
machinery didn't give you a lot of time. Then I realised that it was
the wrong coin, not a Two New Pence piece but an old halfpenny.
Now I'd have to retrieve it and start all over again with the legally
mandated coin.

It wasn't that it wouldn't work. That was the whole point. I knew
it would work. The pre-decimal halfpenny had the same weight and
size of the Two New Pence (I was still making the effort to say 'pence'
rather than 'pee'), perhaps not from the perspective of a laboratory
technician, but the rudimentary apparatus of the phone box certainly
couldn't tell the difference.

I certainly wasn't going to waste my halfpenny without any witnesses to the effectiveness of the ruse. Perhaps I mean wheeze, that
telltale word of Bunter-era schoolboy joy, rather than ruse. 'Did you
know you can use an old halfpenny in a phone box instead of a new
Two Pence piece?' It wouldn't be a thrilling conversation. The point
was that you needed to show people that it worked to get the slightest
mileage out of your knowledge.

I suppose we were being offered a brisk lesson in the economics of
supply and demand. In theory you were making a substantial gain
in terms of value by using the obsolete coin, an old halfpenny being
one four-hundred-and-eightieth of a pound, while two new pence
amounted to a whopping fiftieth, though the real dividend was the
gratification of one's peers. When decimal currency came in the halfpenny had only recently been withdrawn as legal tender, and most

people had some of them hanging around. But as time went by there were fewer halfpennies available, so that their low denomination threatened to be outranked by their scarcity value. Meanwhile people were no longer so familiar with the old halfpenny bit, which became an object of interest in its own right rather than a cunning substitute for something else. Before long the whole exercise would fizzle out in a diffuse pointlessness, but we weren't quite there yet. There were now two shortages ganging up on me: of the halfpennies themselves and of people in the dark about the little trick that could be played with them. I still had one last halfpenny piece, and I meant to get full value out of it with a demonstration while there was still someone around who wasn't in the know.

The Russian roulette of ethanol detection

I tried to retrieve the coin from the slot and fumbled it, though even my most adroit digital manœuvre probably counts as fumbling by the standards of pianists, safecrackers and pickpockets, so perhaps it would be fairer to say I misfumbled. Whatever the appropriate verb, the halfpenny coin fell to the floor of the phone box. There was a brief interruption in the supply of purring and then it resumed and even increased in volume. I try not to use expletives, but I have to admit that I gave a little yelp of 'Ruddy Maya!' How could you, Maya? Couldn't you take the day off in honour of Christmas? I was tired and frustrated, washed back and forth by old emotions and new difficulties. Or was it new emotions and old difficulties? I couldn't even tell.

The dropped pre-decimal halfpenny on the floor might as well have been on the dark side of the moon, but there were other, more up-to-date coins a little nearer in the bottom of the trusty tapestry bag. Then, after all my effort, the Major didn't have the good manners to be in.

Almost the moment I was back on the road surface a police car passed by, moving slowly. I was disappointed to have missed the chance of being accosted, reprimanded and arrested (if I could manage to be cheeky enough). I would like to have spent a night in the cells just once in this life. The police would certainly have taken responsibility for Phyllis off my shoulders, and her presence might have made incarceration positively jolly.

I did my best to attract official attention with a few wild zigzags of the Mini, though wrenching the steering wheel cost me a fair amount of pain. I had never even been breathalysed, which hardly seemed fair. Joy's husband Guy had once been breathalysed late one night when he could hardly stand up with all the drink he had taken. His whole career had flashed before him in the minute or so it took for his reading to register on the infernal device. How would it look for a senior executive at Vauxhall Motors to be in charge of a vehicle when there was so little blood in his alcohol stream? But then the reading had come back clear. He was too relieved to wonder how this was possible. It was some time afterwards that he realised that this had happened on a night when there had been a gala event to benefit police charities, and on such nights, as had long been rumoured, dummy breathalysers were issued to duty policemen as a matter of course, to avoid the possibility of embarrassing benefactors. (By now I'd abandoned the struggle to keep the correct *breath-analyser* in circulation rather than give respectability to the contraction – and brand name – *breathalyser*. Another triumph for the invasive grey squirrels of language over the red.) But irrespective of the validity of the result, why should Guy have his go at the Russian roulette of ethanol detection by machine when I was denied my turn, though I took every chance of delinquency that was offered me?

On to the next phone box. I tried to give the Major time to return from whatever festive expedition he was making, though he had told me he had nothing planned. I know I passed Stevenage and even Royston before I tried again. Not everything was repeated, but the difficulty of entering the box was no different and the weight of the door unchanged. More remarkably, the disembodied purring resumed the moment I entered the box. It seemed unlikely that the cat (if any) from the previous phone box had slipped into the Mini and hitched a ride with me, though the possibility can't be ruled out. I should emphasise that at no point on the journey home did I actually see a cat, but that proves nothing. Melting in and out of the visible spectrum is something cats are known to enjoy.

I don't remember consciously choosing to head for Four Lamps first rather than Mayflower House, taking my chances with a particular section of the general public rather than hoping against hope that there was someone staying in on Christmas evening who would help a pilgrim with a parrot. The Mini seemed to take the decision all by itself. It had enabled me (once I had acquired replacement hips and a driving licence) to leave behind the pitted road of family life, but since then perhaps it had developed some sly little *vasanas* of its own.

If I had gone to Mayflower House I could have got myself inside, if no one came when I sounded the horn. I might have been tempted to go to bed myself and leave Phyllis in the car. Leaving a parrot in a car overnight doesn't amount to active cruelty but it's certainly uncivil, given how much the creatures depend on company. Company was what I had undertaken to provide her, and I wouldn't fall short.

The Mini chose a place where there was likely to be some available humanity, potentially strong young men though the load proposed was light, hollow bones and feathers in a cage of wire. I wasn't too disappointed that there was nobody at Four Lamps, nobody visible at any rate, since naturally the premises were shut and locked at that hour and that time of year. Those bright lamps still sent out their message to human moths in the seasonal absence of insects. Moths don't call off their siege of the house just because the windows are closed, and I was banking on a similar helpless fidelity among frequenters of notorious public lavatories.

I did my best to send a message that would encourage anyone lurking to disclose himself. The expressive language of a car is not great, but sounding the horn, as I had done at Mayflower House, is unmistakeably a summons. I needed something more subtle, and so I decided to flash the headlights. The horn makes a demand. Headlight-flicking proposes a seduction. A car can't wiggle its bottom, but then neither can I – still, perhaps between us we could bat the Mini's equivalents of eyelashes. Should I turn the engine off before flashing my headlights or leave it running? The messages might be different. Engine on: *Let's go! – come on, I've not got all night. Orgasms are just around the corner.* Engine off: *Don't be shy. We've got all the time in the world. Let's get to know each other like civilised people.* Maybe that was how it worked. Given that there was a strong element of deception in both messages it seemed better to leave the engine running. I really didn't feel I had all the time in the world. I was dropping from fatigue and strain after my exposure to curdled mother love.

There was no response. I flashed my lights again. Nothing, again. I turned the engine off and repeated my non-mating call. If it was received then it wasn't acknowledged. I could see myself sending out isolated letters in Morse code – C-O-M-E H-I-T-H-E-R – until the battery went flat early on Boxing Day and I died of inanition not long afterwards, unless Phyllis summoned help, possibly shrieking 'Over here!' with an irreproachable use of positional language, and making more of an impression on a generally indifferent world than I had been able to do.

After a few seconds a shadowy figure loomed at the edge of the light cast by the street lights, those Four Lamps – as sure a symbol of exchange in this context as the three balls hanging outside a pawnbroker's shop. This person must have been lurking in deep cover behind the toilet block, ready to pounce or at least to sidle. As he edged forward and the top of his head caught the light I realised that I knew him. I'd have known that hairstyle anywhere. It was Mr Gerling. He stopped dead.

I would rather it had been anyone else, and there was no doubt that the horror was mutual. I would even rather it had been Dad following me from Bourne End, although his motivation would certainly have been concern for the welfare of a bird he'd only just met rather than his first-born son.

'What luck running into you, Mr Gerling!' I said with a brightness that was a crime against high spirits of any genuine kind. 'I say, do you mind helping me with Phyllis? You've met Phyllis, haven't you?' I added, knowing he had not. 'Phyllis is the parrot on the back seat. It won't take long. Why not get in the back and keep her company?' I couldn't quite face having him sit next to me, and it's not as if he was eager to be close to me, for once. There are people who have mounted the scaffold with more enthusiasm than Mr Gerling showed as he entered the Mini.

'While you're there, Mr Gerling, would you please help me off with my scarf?'

Not my scarf but Audrey's. It had not loosened itself and gone sliding down, as Newtonian physics would strongly have advised it to do, but had somehow ridden up on my face without loosening its grip, so as almost to block my view of the road. I didn't mind being seen as an outcast from my tribe, but I drew the line at presenting myself to the world unambiguously as a *bandido*.

'Okay,' he said. 'But please do call me Tony.'

No. Phyllis would call him Tony before I did.

'I've just been to see my mother,' he said when he had worked the scarf free.

As I had avoided seeking or giving any personal information I had no idea whether this might possibly be true, though it didn't seem likely. For all I knew she might live in a hut behind Four Lamps, growing mangel-wurzels and smoking a pipe. By reflex I asked, 'How is she?' but the tradition of non-communication was so well established between us that there was no real danger he would break it.

Nevertheless silence was an unbearable prospect. 'What did you get her for Christmas?'

'What did I get who?'

'What did you get your mother for Christmas?' He can hardly have thought I meant Phyllis, that I was expecting him to produce a little parcel and to post it through the bars.

'I got her a poinsettia.' I thanked the multiform Lord for this entirely conventional choice of gift, capable of expressing every shade of relationship from passionate devotion to barely veiled disgust. I could discourse on *Euphorbia pulcherrima*, not indefinitely perhaps, but certainly long enough to occupy the journey time to Mayflower House. There's a radio programme, isn't there, where you have to talk on a given subject for a minute without deviation, hesitation or repetition. The rules by which we were playing in the Mini were more forgiving, in that I could wander off the point, lose my thread and repeat myself just as much as I pleased, but there was a lot more than a minute to fill. Really the only rule was that there should be no speech from him nor silence from me. In fact I'd barely finished dealing with the vital questions of light, warmth and moisture and started on the possible shades of the plant, many of them more beguiling than the statutory Christmas scarlet, by the time we had arrived. What I'd have done if he had given the old girl a toothpick I really don't know.

713

And then after all there was a figure with a torch visible inside the lobby of the building. It was the Major, looking rather haunted in dressing gown and slippers.

'Is that you, John? You're back a day early . . .' Then, in an uneasy tone, '. . . or have I lost track of time?'

'No danger of that, Major. Your timekeeping is an example to us all.'

I felt a white lie coming on, though I wasn't sure of the details until it emerged fully formed from my mouth.

'Phyllis couldn't seem to settle. I think she missed you.'

'Really?'

'Parrots form very strong attachments.' I hoped that by saying so I would reinforce the Major's side of the bond.

'She's a dear, and I'm very pleased to see her back. Who's your friend?'

Mr Gerling was skulking behind me, unsure how wholeheartedly to enter into the rôle of parrot porter so capriciously assigned to him. 'That's Mr Gerling, the district nurse. You must have seen him before.' How was I going to account for his presence at this unsocial hour? 'I had a funny turn on the way into town and he was kind enough to help.' How this was supposed to have worked without telepathy or teleportation I had no idea, and could only pray for a lack of curiosity on the Major's part. It was usually a safe enough bet.

'Splendid. What a wonderful service you fellows provide.'

Mr Gerling was beginning to show a little exasperation at the hijacking of his evening. 'So now I'll just walk all the way home, shall I?'

The Major's manner frosted over a little. 'Well, I can't offer you a bed here, I'm afraid — it's not exactly a hotel.'

'Then I'll just walk all the way home. Good night, John.'

'Happy New Year, Mr Gerling. I'll see you next week.' I was unable to wriggle out of expressing gratitude of some muted sort. With anyone else I would have been effusive, but nothing was more crucial in my routine than that the electric fence which kept me safe from Mr Gerling's approaches was fully charged at all times and ticking with the shocks to come.

The Major seemed more interested in Mr Gerling than I had expected, asking, 'Who was that fellow? He seemed rather a bad hat to me.'

'I told you, he's the district nurse. I'm on his rota – he comes every week. But Major, don't you think it's time you paid some attention to Phyllis? She must be thirsty.' The Major was always dutiful in filling Phyllis's water bowl, I'll say that for him. And I don't mean to suggest that he was always topping himself up with less health-giving liquids.

I can't account for Boxing Day. I have no record of it, and have to draw a blank until such time as the librarian of the Akashic Records distributes request forms for particular dates. I may not even have taken Boxing Day out of its box. Granted I was recovering from chronic overexposure to family tension. That day is like the page left blank in *Tristram Shandy*, except that it is inviting the reader to supply a portrait not of the Widow Wadman but of Lady Illusion herself. What did I eat? I must have eaten, surely. I have a sinking feeling that I lived off Phyllis's leftovers, the remnants of what the Major had provided for her on her holiday, topped up by Dad with unsalted nuts. I have a disconnected memory, almost hallucinatory in its clarity, of the taste of Fru-Grains eaten without milk, above all their fibrous adherence to the roof of the mouth. When else could that have been laid down?

At some point in the day I had a phone call from the Major, inviting me to pay him, and presumably Phyllis, a social visit. 'I thought you might like to come to my flat for a glass of something tomorrow, John.'

'Well . . . certainly, Major. Is Phyllis in good order?'

'She's tip-top. Tip-top. By the way, John . . . do you by any chance have a sixpence handy? Or even two? That would be very useful.'

'Do you mean a silver sixpence, the sort you put in a Christmas pudding? You're getting rather an early start for next year, aren't you, Major? No harm in planning ahead, of course.'

'Ugh, no.' 'Ugh' doesn't pretend to transcribe the phonemes voiced, seeking merely to represent the feeling behind them. 'Just an ordinary sixpence.'

'Major, remind me – how long have we had decimal currency?'

'I'm not sure. A year perhaps?'

'It's been more than two . . . perhaps you can get used to saying 2½ pence?'

'Mm. Am I still allowed to say "a tanner"?'

'I can't stop you, Major.'

'Well, if you've got a spare tanner or two I'd be grateful.'

If he'd asked for a pre-decimal halfpenny I would have been stumped. 'I think I can oblige you, Major. I'll have a rummage round.'

'Till tomorrow, then.'

His goodnight kiss scented with blood

I remembered Klaus Eckstein of Burnham Grammar School saying that no well-brought-up German child, when invited even to tea, would dream of turning up without a hanky in the breast pocket of his jacket, a bunch of flowers and a box of chocolates for his hostess. I couldn't produce the full repertoire of gracious gestures but would undertake not to disgrace myself.

'I've brought you a bottle, Major,' I announced as I arrived.

'No need,' he said, though he glanced more than casually at my person, in search of the place such an offering might be lurking.

'If you just reach into my shoulder bag . . .' I slept in that shoulder bag for days at a time, since its general handiness when worn was considerably reduced by the particular bother of putting it on or taking it off.

The Major groped without confidence, since the bag lay almost flat, then retrieved a miniature of Gordon's gin, which he greeted with an uncertain little grin. You can't expect full measure from a guest with small body habitus. It's always likely to be a symbolic offering, a foreshortened bouquet, in this case widow's gill rather than widow's mite.

Major Spinks was turned out neatly, with a tie and a hanky in his breast pocket, but his efforts at grooming had been a little wayward. He had not abandoned the habit of shaving his earlobes as well as attending to the more usual places a razor may go, nor acquired greater skill. Little crusts of dried blood remained to bear witness. I didn't remember any particularly sturdy growth on those lobes before the morning's scraping, but what there was had certainly put up a fight, making the Major's efforts at smartness have elements in common with self-mutilation carried out on a small domestic scale.

Phyllis was in her cage, though the wire door was open. She seemed

716

to feel more comfortable inside, and I'd emphasised, exercising all my specious authority, that she shouldn't be coerced or cajoled. If a single salted peanut had the potential to overwhelm her kidneys then it stood to reason that even a short exposure to the atmosphere at Trees, undoubtedly toxic to humans, would leave her lungs severely compromised. On the other hand there were lit candles in the Major's flat. Free-flying birds and candles don't mix. I prevailed on the Major to shut the wire door of Phyllis's cage while they were alight.

The rôle of host did nothing for the Major's conversational flair. Nor did he offer me anything to drink, and though I wasn't particularly thirsty I felt I deserved better than a shared session of staring into space. I set out to bring Major Spinks out of himself. You can't ask a retired military man, not in so many words, if it was always his ambition to be the manager of a rather out-of-the-way block of flats. Nor can you quite ask someone who has wrapped himself in a shawl, if not a shroud, of melancholy if he's looking forward to what the New Year will bring.

'So, Major, how did you end up at Mayflower House? What's your history?'

'Oh Lord . . . I'm not sure I have a history. Don't things just happen? And I certainly hope I haven't "ended up" just yet! This job was not something I planned. This flat is not at all where I expected to end up – not that I'm complaining. There's nothing wrong with it. But if you had asked me ten years ago where I'd be at this moment . . . well, I wouldn't have had a clue.' Apparently that was all the hard information I was going to get. At least it established that he hadn't been a resident all that long.

I felt a qualm about asking him outright if his marriage had collapsed, though he so clearly seemed to be a casualty of divorce. There was still shame clinging to the breakdown of a marriage – in those days people would put up with extensive dilapidation, would even shore up a ruin, rather than move out of that respectable address. Children whose parents had separated were still said to come from *a broken home*, a remarkably violent phrase coming from a generation that had seen at first hand what bombs can do to masonry.

I had failed to introduce a lively conversational topic, but at least had reminded him he had a guest. 'John, around this time of day

I sometimes make up a jug of Bovril. Does that appeal? It's very warming.'

I could imagine nothing more appalling. 'Not at all, Major.' This was one of the most disgusting things I'd heard of in my whole life. Lick an abattoir floor if you must, but do it on your own time. No wonder his family had left a man who didn't know the difference between tamasic sludge and Ovaltine, the drinks mug and the gravy boat, his goodnight kiss scented with blood. If they had left, of course, as in my reflexive disgust I felt sure they had. My revulsion, though, was a very unstable thing, balanced as it was – as I was – atop a rampart of pork chops.

'Then perhaps I can suggest a glass of port?'

That was more like it. He earned my esteem by understanding my limitations in terms of drinking vessels, not in a single flash of intuition but by way of a series of dogged empirical discoveries. Good enough. First he brought me the port in a miniature wine glass, not impossible to lodge between my knuckles but impossible to bring all the way to my mouth, then took it away and poured it into a tumbler, which was still not tall enough to make lip access practicable. He left it with me and came back, after some rattling of kitchen drawers, with a straw. Thank you, Major, and Cheers! Not 'bottoms up', exactly, but Cheers, hearty Cheers.

The details, technical or gory or both

While he was in the kitchen rifling through those drawers among the toothpicks and cocktail napkins he was perhaps doing something similar in the mental realm, ransacking his memory for something to say to a guest whom he had invited for reasons yet to be revealed, and clutching at straws here also.

'Girls seem to like it when I take my shirt off. Shall I show you why? Bit of a party trick.' The offer didn't attract me, exactly, but I'm pretty much the definition of a captive audience and it was refreshing to have my interest fished for rather than simply being shown some grim anomaly.

'It helps to get the lighting right.' The room was lit by candles, and he seemed to want something both stronger and more directional. He took a torch and laid it on the table, wedging it with a book so that the beam was at the appropriate angle, whatever that might be. Then as promised he took off his jacket, tie and shirt, though his upper body was saved from nakedness by the retention of his vest.

'This all happened in Aden. Before the Emergency, though. I was well out of it by then. Though it could be adequately hairy even before.' I remembered some sort of crisis in Aden. It rang a vague bell. One year you read in the papers that our brave boys have been attacked, the next that our brave boys were on the wrong side of history. Later yet you read that history has more than one side, and what happened after they left was worse than what they did when they were there. I might have been able to find Aden on a map, as long as I was allowed to have more than one go.

'I was in charge of an exam, and things got out of hand, I have to say. There were lots of guns about, and one of them went off. Not sure the fellow was aiming at me. No reason to.'

'*You were shot while you were invigilating an exam?*' I couldn't have played down my surprise if I had been paid to. Sooner or later the blasé mask must slip.

'That's the long and the short of it. Bullet nicked the long thoracic nerve of Bell, innervates one of the shoulder muscles.' The *serratus anterior*, to be precise – I'd have loved to hear all the details, technical or gory or both, but the Major wasn't to know that. There's no fighting against the beauty of medical language. I take pleasure in anyone having a long thoracic nerve of Bell, even one that has been damaged by gunfire, even though I dare say I have a long thoracic nerve of Bell myself tucked away somewhere in the woodwork. 'Result is a "winged scapula". One winged scapula coming up. This is the test for it.' As the torchlight played on him he stood facing the wall and pressed the palms of his hands against it, as if he was making a feeble attempt to push it over and bring Mayflower House crashing down. The right shoulder blade lay flush with the flesh of his back, but the left one opened up like a strange door. His silhouette took on a fleeting hunchbacked aspect.

I didn't know what sort of response he expected to this remarkable sight. Applause seemed wrong – not that I can do it, though I can certainly convey an equivalent enthusiasm by other means. He

719

certainly didn't seem to be angling for pity. It really was a party trick, a card that can really only be played once for any individual acquaintance. Something you're pleased to have seen but have no need to see again. The girls alleged to want him to take his shirt off wouldn't exactly have gone into mourning when he put it on again. The thing I wanted to say, but would have sounded entirely wrong, was that to be injured in an invigilation incident combined the lurid and the humdrum in a way I couldn't imagine ever being bettered.

Better to stick to the personal history. 'And did you ever find out why the shot was fired?'

'Well, it seemed pretty obvious once I thought about it. Chap had bought answers to the wrong exam questions, knew he was going to fail, couldn't exactly ask for his money back and so he got shirty.' As if the word 'shirty' had reminded him obliquely of his relatively uncovered state, he started putting his clothes back on.

'The reason I asked you to bring along that sixpence—'

'—that 2½ pence coin—'

'You're quite right, John, that 2½ pence coin. We can't live in the past.' He paused for a moment, as if this was a new idea and might take some getting used to. 'When I moved here in May I wasn't sure how long I'd be staying. And you could hire a television from Miller's, you know, on the corner of Sidney Street, they have a scheme . . .'

'Millerental.' I had seen the advertisements in the *Cambridge Evening News*.

'Yes, that's what they call it.'

'Excuse me, Major, but did you say you moved here in May? Only a few months before I did?'

'Yes, that's right. Why?'

I could hardly say, because I assumed you had been installed in the building at the same time as electricity and running water.

'When I moved here I didn't think it would be for long. That was early in the summer – not long before you turned up, in fact.' This was certainly a surprise. Major Spinks was one of those people who bring a sort of rootedness with them willy-nilly. It was as if he was incapable of doing things for the first time but was constantly caught in some helpless repetition. What a *vasana*-merchant! His road was all ruts. Ten minutes after he had entered a pub for the first time you would expect to see a photo of him as captain of its dominoes team, shyly holding up the trophy after a recent round-robin tournament. He was an iron bar that rusted before your eyes. 'Never mind. You were explaining about Millerental.'

'Yes indeed. You could hire a television for a minimum of six months or you could pay a deposit then put coins in the meter on the side of the set and just pay for what you actually watched. I didn't think I'd be here for six months, and there aren't a lot of programmes I'm interested in, so I decided to do things that way. Possibly a bad bargain, as it turns out. For one thing you have to make sure you have enough change.'

'And you've run out.'

'Yes . . . and it so happens there's a programme I've rather got into the habit of watching, so I thought I'd invite you along. A little bird told me you might enjoy it. And don't worry, you'll get your money back.'

'That's perfectly all right, Major.' I could stand a loss of 2½ pence. I wondered, though, who the 'little bird' might be who had claimed knowledge of my preferences in entertainment. Exclude Phyllis and Mrs Baine seemed by far the most likely candidate.

Ode to a red cabbage

I had a thought. 'But Major, what happens if there's a power cut while your money is in the works? Won't you lose it?'

He winced. 'I hope to heaven I don't. I rang them up and asked them, in fact. It's a sort of clockwork, yes, but it may be arrested in some way if the power fails. Let's hope I never have to find out.'

'And if it starts up again you'll have to watch whatever happens to be on.'

'Oh Lord. You're right. Oh God, it might be *This Is Your Life*. I'd have something to say about that, I can tell you.' Perhaps the theme of not being able to live in the past was quietly gaining ground.

'I suppose you could always change channels.' Major Spinks admitted this as a theoretical possibility. I wondered if he would ever have the bravado to turn off the set while there was still money in the bank of the machine, still fuel in its tank of images. I imagined him

721

roused in the middle of a cold night by the hum of static from the reawakened television. Sitting there in his dressing gown shivering, to watch the shifting flux until his money ran out.

The Major downed half his port, shot his cuff to bring his watch into view and said, 'I've just got time to do my rounds, John, so I'll leave you for a few minutes, if you don't mind. I find I don't sleep if I haven't made sure that everything is secure . . . and at this time of year I'm closer to being a night watchman than a building manager.'

I graciously gave my permission. It's not often that I'm left alone in someone's room, even for a few minutes, and it would be rude not to profit from the opportunity by doing a little investigation. There was a framed photograph face down on the desk whose format suggested some sort of a family portrait, the little propping leg, the buttress on the back that would normally support it, sticking up rather than folded away. Had it been tenderly laid down or sternly flipped out of sight? There was no way of knowing. It was just that little bit too far away for me to reach, or I might have violated the Major's privacy by lifting it up, though it's always a bit of a shame to taint the imagination with facts. There was something a bit suspicious, too, about so personal an object being withheld so tantalisingly. If I didn't know better I might think it was a trap.

Still, sticking out from under the photograph frame was part of a press cutting. I could see a bit that had been outlined in red biro, which certainly piqued my curiosity since from font and layout the newspaper looked like the *Cambridge Evening News*, and what could possibly deserve added emphasis on those pages? There was a paper knife on the edge of the desk, within my reach, and after the shortest possible interval of moral self-scrutiny (Does this make me a bad person? Oh well, never mind) I managed to winkle the press cutting out from under. It was a poem called 'Happiness' from the *Cambridge Evening News*'s recurring feature 'Poets' Corner'.

It went:

> I was happy
> today
> and yet my happiness
> caused me to weep

I was peaceful
today
and yet I
had to be
surrounded by noise
I was sleepy
today
and yet my
fear of sleep
kept me awake
I was alive
today
but tomorrow
I may be dead

Why on earth had the Major preserved this item? For once I wasn't being snooty about literary quality. Despite a slightly hollow ending the poem comfortably cleared the threshold for acceptance by the *Cambridge Evening News*, and was swimming against the tide stylistically, being pared down rather than florid. Further down the page, for instance, without biro adornment, was an ode to a red cabbage (also, I have to say, above par for inclusion in 'Poets' Corner' – this isn't Westminster Abbey) that ended 'Verdigrisgreen, magenta, white, close-packed, living mosaic'. The last word was misprinted as 'mosiac', something that must have cost the contributor at least one sleepless night if the pained perfectionism of authors is more than a myth.

So why on earth did the Major cut out this particular poem and make it stand out with red biro? I started to be haunted by the idea that he had written it himself, despite the attribution to one Sophia Monro and the address given in Adams Road. Surely it wouldn't be beyond the wit of the average adult to lay an elementary false trail sufficient to satisfy enquiries from the paper that might (let's be realistic) never come? Perhaps, for instance, Mrs Baine had been let into the secret of the Major's creative impulses, and Sophia Monro was her sister. Yes, agreed, this was all extremely unlikely, but unlikelihood lay at the root of the matter and must necessarily permeate all its fruits and flowers. The possibility that the Major might have written the poem was only slightly more surprising than the attested fact that he had read it and kept it as an object of value – an anomaly that the egotism of authorship would satisfactorily tidy away.

Underneath the press cutting was another, also outlined in red ink. I had the sense of being teased and led on. The Ibsen character who says (though I still haven't found the reference) that she only plucked at a loose thread and the whole sleeve unravelled was describing one of the ways that Maya likes to work, though she's also a great one for darning. Penelope in the *Odyssey* unpicks at night what she has woven during the day, but Maya does both at once. When I saw the headline I had the sensation of the ground dropping away beneath me, very far from a standard reaction to items in the *Cambridge Evening News*. I should point out that the item in question was of the usual exemplary dullness (the sub-headline was 'Whitehall Asked to Revoke City Legal Notices'), it just happened to get me where I lived. It acted on me like . . . well, like the impregnated strip from a Christmas cracker being held in a candle flame.

The headline proper read: 'Mayflower House Not a Hotel, Say Owners'. I was inside Mayflower House reading about Mayflower House. Now I felt that the earlier shock (manager of block of flats suspected of writing poetry in his spare time) had to some extent prepared me for this second detonation. The next thing that caught my eye was the number of flats in the building – *108!* I'd known there were about a hundred flats on the seven floors of Mayflower House, but not that I'd been living all this time inside a space reverberating with a sacred number. Without measurable benefit to my life in general, true, but with an inferior numerological alignment things could have been so much worse.

Planning permission for the building of the block had been given on the basis that it was to be let out for residential use, not as a short-stay hotel. Now Cambridge City Council was serving legal notices on the owners, 'the Wembley-based J. M. Hill Group', to stop them using it for short-stay visitors. Meanwhile the owners were asking the Department of the Environment to revoke the legal notices.

The evidence given indicated that only 2.5 per cent of the accommodation was let for three nights or fewer, and more than half of the flats were let for more than two months. Of course long-stay tenants

724

like me would tend to bring the averages down, in a way that almost seemed fishy, as if we long-termers were only a cover for the real business. At £4.84 for a single night's stay, running the building as a hotel was certainly more profitable. Perhaps we long-term residents were the meat and potatoes of the business, and short stays the gravy. (Vegetarians aren't obliged to abstain from carnivorous vocabulary and images.)

The dolorific calculus of Christmas

Mayflower House had cost £300,000 to build and yielded £3,524.51 *per annum* to the Council in rates. Now the Hill Group proposed building another, smaller block, made up of 68 flats, adjacent to Mayflower House, to be run on a similar basis. Presumably that was why the Council was taking action, with the legal notices intended as a shot across their bows to deter further infringement. (Landlubbers are not required to purge their vocabularies of nautical imagery.)

What was it the Major had said when he thought Mr Gerling was trying to cadge a bed for the night? He hadn't said that Mayflower House wasn't a hotel, he had said it wasn't *exactly* a hotel. Everything seemed to fit.

I have to say that it pleased me very much that an expert gave it as his professional opinion that the crucial distinction between hotel and block of flats was inherently nebulous in law, saying, 'There seems to be no simple definition of what constitutes a hotel. There are certain obligations on a hotel but these make it easier to say when something is not a hotel.' The absence of a restaurant or bar was contended to be proof that Mayflower House was not a hotel, as was the fact that only bottles of milk and small quantities of teabags were on sale there.

Please notice that usage: 'a hotel'. Granny said An Otel without the slightest self-consciousness, but she was one of a dying breed. As breeds go, she wouldn't have wanted to belong to any other kind. There were affinities between her and the Russian Grand Duchess who protested, when the Revolution came, that executions were not being carried out in the proper order of precedence.

Was it significant that this particular issue of the *Cambridge Evening*

News hadn't reached me, given that I had a personal stake in the matter being reported? Perhaps the relevant page or pages had been subtracted from a copy that I did see, and I hadn't noticed the omission. Still, it was hard to claim that Mrs Baine was less directly affected than I was. She had her own legitimate reasons for hanging on to it.

The Major returned from his rounds, looking rather anxiously at his wristwatch. It was nearly time for his programme, or (by default) our programme. There was obviously a fine line between missing its beginning and wasting money paying for precious seconds of advertisements – to my surprise, we would be watching the commercial channel – but he seemed to be well organised in that respect. He said, 'I suppose we may as well turn the infernal thing on,' though his indifference was hardly persuasive given that he was firmly thrusting 2½p into the slider on the side of the television. I was beginning to think he knew exactly what was being broadcast and wouldn't have missed it for worlds – to use an oddly mystical phrase embedded in the plain speech of our mother tongue.

The sound came on before the picture, so we heard the enlivening slogan *'Eveninks and morninks / I drink Warninks'* before the image of a tray bearing glasses of advocaat arrived to join our little post-Christmas party. The Major said 'Filthy stuff' just as I was opening my mouth to say how appetising it looked. I do love a snowball. Then the theme music of the programme started, played on brass instruments. It was like a 'sennet' in a Shakespeare play, a distinctive ceremonial summons.

The programme seemed to be called *Crown Court*. This confirmed the notion that the 'little bird' who had informed the Major of my possible interest was Mrs Baine, since she knew all about my jury service. It was no secret that I didn't have a television, so it was a fair bet that I would have no knowledge of the programme. But I could only assume he was expecting to get a kick out of my reactions. I duly goggled at the gogglebox.

'Have you watched this programme often, Major? Is it broadcast a lot?'

I was speaking out of turn, and the Major became rather huffy. 'Do you mind awfully if we wait for the commercial break before we talk about it? I'm trying to follow the case.'

Then the brass band started playing a different tune, and despite his insistence on silence the Major muttered, 'What on earth's going on?' It was 'The First Nowell'. Ominous objects began to encroach on the edges of the screen – little ornamental bells hung on ribbon, wrapping paper with a pattern of spiky leaves and berries. A colour set would have removed all doubt, but even in black and white a festive theme soon became impossible to ignore. It began to dawn on the Major, though his degree of upset seemed disproportionate, that his favourite programme had been 'mucked about', as he put it, in a misguided attempt to honour the season. In fact he was furious. 'If I wanted a bloody Christmas special,' he muttered, 'I'd watch Morecambe and Wise.'

This of course is the dolorific calculus of Christmas, whereby those who are reluctantly separated from others are made to feel entirely alone, while those who are reluctantly attached feel an obligation to go through the motions of connection. The Major may have felt that after he had made it more or less intact through Christmas Eve, Christmas Day and Boxing Day, it was a low blow to drag him back through the holly bush and rend his flesh all over again.

Despite the festive trappings this was still a courtroom drama of sorts. The title of the episode was 'Murder Most Foul' (from *Macbeth*, isn't it?), and it started with a strange warning to 'viewers of a nervous disposition', on the basis that it concerned a crime 'so fiendish as to strike at the very foundations of life as we know it'.

As the drama unfolded it began to cast a strange dull spell. The fortified wine I sucked up at intervals through a paper cylinder no doubt abetted the torpid enchantment. To his credit the Major seemed to rally.

After a while he cleared his throat and said, 'Good old Arthur English. You can't go wrong with Arthur English.' Which accounted for the identity of the elderly gentleman on the screen, but not for the fact that the Major's voice was thick with emotion. When the advertising break arrived at last he couldn't wait to assure me that it wasn't always like this. 'It's gone haywire. This is completely potty. They're . . . they're *spoofing* it.'

He explained in a pained sort of voice that the series had been designed to have an informative or educational element, just as *The Archers* had been intended to keep farmers up to date with developments in agriculture, with government information the medicine and family saga the syrup in which it was suspended. The system of justice based on Crown Courts had only recently been established, and showing how it worked was a service rendered to the public. Would it have helped me to see the programme before becoming embroiled in such murky matters as *R. v. Millon* and *R. v. French*? Probably not. Certainly not this particular episode.

Weedkiller in a man's curry

I might not know Arthur English from Adam, but another face seen after the first set of commercials rang a bell with me. 'Who's that other actor, Major? The one playing the butler?'

The ban on talking during the programme seemed to have been lifted, perhaps because he was so dissatisfied with it. 'Can't help you, I'm afraid,' he said gloomily. 'Not familiar with him.'

I knew I knew the face, and finally I got it. John Le Mesurier! Funny, though – I would have thought he was much better known at that time than Arthur English.

I enjoyed *Crown Court*, very possibly more than the Major, since he had the higher expectations and felt disappointed, if not personally betrayed. He continued to snipe at the programme as it went on.

'It's not normally like this, John. Please don't judge the show by this episode. Weedkiller in a man's curry! It's all nonsense. That's not how it's supposed to go in Fulchester.'

Apparently the novelty of the programme was that the jury was made up of members of the public, adults on the electoral roll. They decided the outcome, just as they would in a real case. All well and good, but they didn't do anything realistic like misquote the mottoes of universities, or read *Dune*, or distribute anti-smoking propaganda. They meekly filed in and found the defendant Guilty or Not Guilty. That was it. Presumably the actors rehearsed two different versions for the bit at the end, depending on how the 'verdict' went, but their lives as judges of the facts seemed distinctly impoverished. The foreman spoke a word, or even two, on camera, so perhaps he needed to be a professional actor – but no wonder people seized any opportunity to be excused from the real thing, if fiction made it seem so drab.

At the end of the programme the brass band struck up another carol, this time 'God Rest Ye Merry, Gentlemen'.

'Christmas spoils everything,' said the Major. 'The programme is supposed to show a case – a proper case, not some nonsense about bodies in the library with Oriental daggers in them and . . . weedkiller in the curry.' He couldn't seem to get over the paraquat vindaloo. 'It's in three half-hour bits on different days, so you have time to mull things over between times. See things from different points of view. I saw it was on today, though at a different time from the normal, and then I realised it was going to be extra long. That's why I asked you . . . if you could bring along an extra 2½ pee piece.'

He didn't quite say, 'That's why I asked you along,' though I wouldn't have minded if he had. I would have found some excuse for finding out if Phyllis was all right, and he had saved me the trouble.

The legal tussle over the status of Mayflower House was still rattling around my brain, not to mention the idea of the Major as (technically) a published poet, but something I'd heard in the last few minutes brought me up short. 'Tell me, Major, what did you say the name of the place is where *Crown Court* happens?'

'Oh, it's not a real place. You can't find it on the map. I've tried! It's just a made-up name. They set it in a sort of Anytown.'

'Yes, yes, but what is this Anytown called?'

'I told you. Fulchester.'

Fulchester! The veils fell from my eyes, the wax fell from my ears. So that's what the stupid woman with the Knitting Nancy had been raving about all the time. She was comparing the administration of the Queen's justice unfavourably to a programme on ITV! Trollope had Barchester to serve as the everytown of his imagination, and Granada TV had Fulchester. I had a good mind to turn up at the grand opening of the new Cambridge branch of Dorothy Perkins just to tell everyone what a goose the new manageress was, if she had really got the job she boasted about to our jury bailiff. To me she seemed unemployable, though that seemed to be my status too.

I couldn't resist asking the Major if he had watched the Queen's Christmas message. 'Not this year,' he said. 'She's a lovely lady and she talks a lot of sense. I just wasn't in the mood.' It's only logical that when you pay for your viewing in hard currency you become more particular about your choices, though I could also imagine him squandering a sentimental coin so as not to miss the Queen addressing her loyal subjects, the way people put money in a jukebox to hear 'their tune', however well they know it – then finding he was short when his favoured programme rolled around. Subtly divided loyalties, as between the Crown and *Crown Court*.

'Did you know, Major, that the Quakers don't celebrate Christmas?'

'H'm . . . how very sensible. They've got the right idea there.'

'I'm not sure you'll like their reason, though. The idea is that you should live every day as if it was the day of Christ's birth. So really the tally isn't no Christmases but 365 of them. 366 in a leap year.'

'Oh *God*.' He made it sound as if it was the worst thing that could possibly be thought of.

'So there's really nothing Christmassy you like, Major? Not carols or mince pies?' In a way I was playing devil's advocate, arguing against my own aversion, seeking to rouse in the Major the slumbering wonderstruck child who sometimes, in spite of everything, awoke in me. I was also concerned that Phyllis should not spend her life in an environment starved of joy. What a prospect for a long-lived creature!

'I don't hate either of them. It's the whole thing I don't like. What the French call the *toot ensemble*.'

'How about candles and Christmas crackers?' I had no qualms about mentioning the instruments of my disgrace. 'You certainly seem to like candles! You've lit enough of them. And don't say it's in case there's a power cut . . . you only need to leave a night light burning. You can take it from there if you find you're suddenly in the dark.'

'That's rather good advice, John.' I should think it was! I'd come up with it as a desperate manoeuvre to stop everyone nagging me about being ready for power cuts. Thanks to Paula I could hardly move for candles in 005, and she was forever wanting me to demonstrate that I could light them in the dark. 'As it happens, there was a candle thingy I was looking at the other day, tucked away in a drawer, and I thought of getting it out and setting it alight just for the hell of it. Only cheap metal, of course, but it did look nice. The candles turn a wheel, hot air rising you know, and the little bells go ting ting ting. Do you know the sort of thing I mean?'

'Major, I'm completely in the dark.' I had no idea. It sounded a very ramshackle sort of contraption. 'Feel free to show me.'

'It's in a drawer somewhere down here.' He started rummaging. In a film there would also be empty whisky bottles in the drawer, and I'm not saying there weren't.

A turbine cranking out increments of joy

He took out a compact box and began to pull out pieces of pressed brass, wrapped in cotton wool and tissue paper. On the box it said Swedish Angel Chimes. He assembled it out of my line of sight, as if unable to deny himself the pleasure of my surprise. He struck a match and then showed me the finished article.

How to describe it? Here was a metal saucer fitted with a vertical spindle, on which was mounted a wheel, free to rotate, with angled vanes. This wheel bore cut-out metal angels, each trailing a little pivoted rod calculated to make contact with a bell mounted further down – not bells like church bells but like the ones in old-fashioned shops, to be rung by customers needing attention, the bells in this case resting loosely on their own short spindles so that the chiming they made might go on sounding without being prematurely damped. The motive energy was supplied by four candles disposed around the saucer. The angels were blowing pressed-metal trumpets, and there was a supernumerary non-rotating angel, possibly even an archangel given his physical eminence and near-upright posture, mounted on top of the central spindle. Perhaps they were playing a carol, though the Major would certainly have preferred the theme music for *Crown Court*, so as to restore the defective balance between sacred and secular music on that particular day.

The Major's chimes were powered by three candles rather than four. It wasn't that he had run out of candles – somewhere along the line one of the little holders had broken. So I suppose the vaned wheel was on the receiving end of a small amount of turbulence, rather than the evenly flowing updraught envisaged by the designers. Over time the bearing might suffer from fatigue, though the forces involved were modest enough. It was no more than a tiny turbine cranking out increments of joy and wonder, and it seemed up to the task even without its full complement of thermal engines. It was the most Christmassy thing I had seen in my life. It went ting ting ting. It went ting ting ting, in fact, like anything.

All in all, I enjoyed my time with the Major on the 27th. My twenty-fourth birthday was the best ever, precisely because it wasn't celebrated. The Major had no idea that this was a 'special' day for me, which it wasn't, or only became so by being treated with no particular attention. This corpse was unadorned. And a present offered on a birthday – I'm thinking of the news item about Mayflower House – can't be dismissed as being a birthday present. Not as an object, since I had slipped it relatively uncrumpled under the 'Happiness' poem, but as a mental possession.

I remembered the pleasure I got, when I was living in CRX, from the knowledge that I lived in two counties simultaneously, since I could be legitimately reached at either of two addresses: 'Ward 1, Canadian Red Cross Memorial Hospital, Taplow, Bucks' or 'Ward 1, Canadian Red Cross Memorial Hospital, Taplow nr Maidenhead, Berks'. Despite my ankylosed gait I straddled a historic boundary. Now it turned out that I was living in a block of residential flats that was at least in part (for who was I to argue with the Council that housed me?) An Otel. It began to look very much as if I exercised a benignly destabilising effect on my surroundings. I gave them that crucial little nudge towards indeterminacy, making everything moot. My residence in Mayflower House created a metaphysical doubt in the building that housed me about whether it was a block of flats or a hotel. Beat that, Uri! Mr Geller might be able to bend spoons, but he couldn't make them wonder whether they weren't really forks, could he? Not likely.

Reality is thixotropic, its viscosity liable to non-Newtonian thinning of shear in the presence of certain stresses. Perhaps I'm one of them. My presence in Mayflower House, light as it was, seemed to act as a lawn roller that left behind flat, unrutted surfaces where events could roll without deflection, like ideal croquet balls. Better yet, an ideal ice rink on which pucks could glide without the slightest frictional interference. I seemed to have the power of mootification – or let's call it mootation, a tidier word altogether.

If the Cromer family Christmas had played out over the full three days and two nights I would have had the pleasure and the relief of a reunion with Joy Payne. That opportunity had fallen forfeit to the explosions, literal and metaphorical, of Christmas Day at Trees, so I wasn't surprised when she phoned me, on (at a guess) the Thursday. It seemed very likely that she had heard a version, Mum's version, of what had happened on the day, but I wasn't planning to go into all that. We could laugh about it all later. I was surprised, though, and alarmed, by the lack of cordiality and the anything-goes, all-around-the-houses style of chat that was customary between us.

'John,' she asked after the bare minimum of greeting, 'have you been telling Audrey she's adopted?'

I was completely taken aback. 'No, of course I haven't. Why would I do such a thing?'

'I have no idea. But she's got it into her head that you and she are both adopted. That Dennis and Laura are not your real parents. I'm not sure how Peter fits into all this, but I'm not sure that's at the top of anyone's agenda one way or the other. You promise me you've not put the adoption idea into her head?'

'Well, let me see. I'm not sure that I can absolutely swear to that.'

'Whyever not? If I'd ever told someone she was adopted I think I'd remember.' I hadn't heard this sharp note from Joy before.

'I'm not sure it's that clear-cut.' A horrible possibility was growing in my mind. 'What I might have said . . .'

'Yes, John. Don't keep me hanging – spit it out, for heaven's sake!'

'Well, I might have said something about wombs.'

'Wombs?'

'Well, I didn't want to say . . . vaginas. Audrey's only thirteen, you know.' Indian cosmology places all the emphasis on passage through vaginas rather than residence in wombs, the event of birth rather than the process of pregnancy, and I can only apologise to anyone who finds that unseemly.

'Yes, John, I know she's thirteen, that's why I'm phoning in fact – since Audrey at thirteen is now convinced she's adopted because of something you said. What was it that you said?'

'I think I said that wombs weren't important. That we had a choice. We'd chosen the womb in the first place . . . but we never belonged there. Parents aren't really parents, children aren't really their children.'

'H'm. Sounds like posh tosh to me. Is that an Indian thing? I know you set a lot of store by Indian things.' She was referring to a millennial tradition of wisdom and self-enquiry, but I let that pass. 'And I don't think it was fair of you to confuse her like that. You're so much older, she's very susceptible, and you sound as if you know what you're talking about even when you don't. Though . . . now I think of it . . .' said Joy, with grudging fairness. A grudging Joy was a painful thing for me to hear and contemplate. '. . . my Stuart put something not too different up on his bedroom wall once, when he was a teenager. "*Your children are not your children . . .*" Something like that. I can't remember how it went on.'

'"*. . . they are the sons and daughters of life's longing for itself.*"' Ruddy Kahlil Gibran! Sometimes in those years it felt as if he was dogging my footsteps with his rubbishy mysticism, and making my devotion to my guru seem both fashionable and flimsy in the process.

'That's it. So she just got the wrong end of the stick? A rather funny sort of stick for you to be pointing in her direction, I must say. I don't know that there was a right end of it for her to get hold of. So you were trying to tell her . . . what, exactly?'

'That we must all take responsibility for our lives. That we can't blame other people for our difficulties.' This was such a crude boiling-down of things I had gleaned from any number of scriptures, not least *The Tibetan Book of the Dead*, that I felt quite ashamed of it, but even so it wasn't enough to get me out of trouble.

'Don't you think thirteen is a little young for that particular pep talk, John? And it's only fair to say that Laura is blaming you for the difficulties she's currently having with Audrey. I'd say you had blotted your copybook, except . . .'

'Except that my copybook is all blots.' The relaxed rhythm of our exchanges was beginning to re-establish itself, but the sweetness was not there, and much missed. 'Or mostly.'

'You know I've always tried to stick up for you, John, but sometimes the game doesn't seem worth the candle.' She didn't put any

734

particular emphasis on 'candle', I don't imagine she was consciously referring to the events of Christmas Day, but it seemed fair to assume she knew all about that too.

'The truth is, Joy, that I'm not very good at talking to Audrey, or thirteen-year-old girls in general.' I surprised myself by starting a sentence with the words 'The truth is', the traditional introduction to a fib, and then telling the truth, though (in my defence) I didn't know it was the truth until I heard myself say it.

'I don't exactly blame you, John. Teenagers are no picnic. But we're not exactly talking about that, are we? How are you going to untangle what you've tangled up?'

'I don't see how I can.'

'Nor do I. And I'll do what I can myself, but I don't expect it will amount to much. In the meantime, until things sort themselves out one way or the other, perhaps you shouldn't expect to hear from me for a while.'

I hadn't begged Mum not to throw me out, when the prodigal son had returned for Christmas only to have his passport impounded and revoked. The idea of estrangement from Joy grieved me far more than full rupture with family. I would have begged her not to call a halt to our telephone chats about everything and nothing, but it didn't seem fair to divide her loyalties any further. I've always had the knack of making friendships across the generations, but they don't always stand up to wear and tear as well as ones that are closer chronologically. Joy had every right to pull away – though when the subject is friendship 'rights' seem just the wrong idea.

What I had wanted to inculcate was a little healthy suspicion of the claims of motherhood, and the physical apparatus that has so much unexamined prestige, but while I was going on tiptoe to avoid vaginas I seemed to have fallen headlong into the confusion of the womb. Mind you, I wondered if this adoption idea might not simply be a stunt of Audrey's, a way of holding Mum at bay – and who could blame her if it was? I didn't fancy her chances of keeping the charade going indefinitely, even so, and then things would return to that grim state known as normality. In the meantime, if it constitutes freedom to have alienated every member of my alleged family (excepting, I suppose, Peter), a generalised achievement with the particular highlight of making my little sister think she wasn't my sister at all, while also making Bourne End's most evolved soul despair of me, then I was free.

When a flat square package arrived for me a day or two after my birthday I didn't immediately recognise it as being from Joy. I must have seen her handwriting before, but there was no return address given. Nobody put such things on envelopes in those days, unless the information was required for a special delivery, and not from laziness but a sort of politeness. After the men and women of the Post Office had shown so much initiative when faced with an envelope reading only 'The Scouts Who Love Pandas, Cornwall' it seemed insulting to doubt their ability to deliver a package to John Cromer at Mayflower House, Cambridge. Why would they need the safety net of a return address? They were skilled professionals.

Paula helped me unwrap the package. Inside two layers of corrugated cardboard, secured with white Sellotape bearing a design of holly leaves and festive bells, was a smooth though blistered sheath made from a strange transparent plastic material. Inside it was a seven-inch record, a single, and a book token, though even after we had seen them we were still hypnotised by the luxurious packing material. What peasants we were! Neither of us had seen bubble wrap before. Joy Payne must be *really* rich – or maybe Vauxhall cars were delivered from the showroom swathed in this miraculous stuff.

The title of the recording ('Jenny's Song') rang no bells. The artist responsible for this record, Trane, was also unfamiliar, though 'artist' may be an exaggerated claim, as it so often is. Even the label was new to me – admittedly there were only two record labels I could recognise with my eyes shut, Vertigo and Deutsche Grammophon Gesellschaft, both so strongly associated with MarkO that my retinæ retained them as ghostly after-images on an indefinite basis. This was something on the BBC's own label.

My generation, after many flirtatious entanglements with singles, saw itself as wedded to the serious commitment of the long-playing album, the long haul of a grown-up medium. When had I last owned a record that needed to rotate at the dizzying speed of 45 rpm? The Hacker could certainly handle this vinyl anomaly, but the knob governing its turntable speed had been untouched for so long I was surprised it still remembered what to do.

When I saw Joy's name at the end of the letter I was elated. That was a short estrangement, one of the shortest on record! But then I realised this was something that had been put in the post when Joy knew about the relatively simple bust-up (wax bomb and curtain chewing) but not the more florid ramifications, namely Audrey's new idea that she was adopted. It followed that the note inside the book token was genial in its tone. 'Dear John, this book token is for Christmas and the record is a birthday present – in fact I bought it for your last birthday except you didn't come home. I thought I'd be seeing you on Boxing Day and could hand it over then, but of course you were long gone! Next time try to stay a little longer, will you, John? With love from Joy.'

More along the lines of a *quiche lorraine*

Paula put the record on and we settled back to listen, not knowing at all what to expect. Dutifully she tapped her feet as the music started, with a piano to the fore at first, then said, 'It's not got much of a beat, has it? It's a bit of a plod. At least your aunt's not trying to turn you into a teenybopper . . . that's something!'

'She's not my aunt – wish she was. But you're right.' The lyrics were melancholy in the extreme, about how hard it is to be alone when the long day ends. Joy wasn't going to any great lengths to cheer me up! The music felt faintly familiar but I couldn't place it. The singer had to hammer home the chorus a couple of times, about the welcome that was waiting for him after all his travels, the friendly faces that he missed, before I finally understood. Friendly faces that he missed until he returned to . . .

'*Waggoners' Walk*!' I cried out. 'But this can't be the theme tune – I'd have recognised that.'

This music was as downbeat as *The Archers'* theme tune was buoyant, its opening phrase seeming to urge 'Girls and boys come out to play!', a summons irresistibly rousing whether or not you were in a position to act on it. To the best of my remembering the actual theme tune of *Waggoners' Walk* was jauntier than this dirge, though even so it was hardly likely to displace *The Archers'* in the national brain. Do they play the theme tune of *The Archers* to wake long-term coma patients or alternatively to confirm assessments of brain death? If not, they should try it. They're missing a trick.

'What's *Waggoners' Walk* anyway?'

How could I explain? 'You know *The Archers*?'

'Of course I know *The Archers*. I don't listen to it, mind, but I know about it.'

'Well, all you need to know is that *Waggoners' Walk* is like *The Archers*. Except that it's trying hard not to be like *The Archers* at all.'

'You've lost me, John.'

'We can listen to it sometime. Then you'll see what I mean.'

That had to satisfy her curiosity for the time being, though I imagine her curiosity was very mild indeed. *Waggoners' Walk* had been started by the BBC as a sort of complement to, or substitute for, *The Archers*. Perhaps the audience for the Ambridge saga was dying away, even literally dying off, and creating fears for the future in the corridors of Broadcasting House. The new serial was on Radio 2 and was aiming at a younger, more sophisticated audience. It was cod-urban rather than cod-rural. If *The Archers* was meat and two veg then I suppose *Waggoners' Walk* was more along the lines of a *quiche lorraine*. Accordingly it tackled subjects that *The Archers* ignored, previously no-go areas like abortion and homosexuality. It wasn't just infestations of warble fly and the right time to plant and harvest crops.

On the phone Joy would ask serious questions about the characters in *Waggoners' Walk* and their doings, the Nashes and the Tysons, whether the fictional department store Abercrombies was based on Harrods or Swan & Edgar, as if I had a single other reason for listening to that stupid programme other than the fact that Mum was listening to another one, on another BBC station, that was equally stupid. Joy's good nature had led her astray, making her back me up when I should really have been taken to task. I mean, we shouldn't fool each other every instant of our lives. Every now and then we should tell the truth. Whatever reason Mum had for listening to *The Archers*, my reason for listening to *Waggoners' Walk* was feebler and less defensible. I should have said it long ago: 'Face facts, Joy! We're backing a loser. There is no reason on earth why we should pretend to be bothered about the fates of these tissue-thin, altogether ridiculous fictions, these shadows of shadows of shadows.'

738

The time slots for *Waggoners' Walk*, coinciding with elevenses and teatime, must have been meant to steal listeners away from *The Archers*, but then who except Joy Payne would be loving or mad enough to follow both? I don't imagine she had friends at the BBC who could supply her with tapes (though you never know) or that she used a tape recorder so that she could catch up later. *The Archers* had an omnibus edition broadcast once a week, *Waggoners' Walk* lacking the prestige and the audience to match it in that department. Perhaps she listened to that. It was still quite an outlay of time on a trivial preoccupation for a woman with plenty of other things to do.

To me Joy Payne was a monumental presence, Colossus if not of Rhodes then of the Upper Thames, one huge foot planted on each side of the river, straining by the sheer effort of her thigh muscles, quadriceps and the three sets of hamstrings working together, *biceps femoralis* seconded by *semitendinosus* and *semimembranosus*, all of them superbly toned by years of regular swimming, to prevent the riven Cromer land-masses from drifting permanently apart, inclining her bronze head in its gigantic bathing cap, while the duckweed snagged on its appliquéd rubber sprigs was browsed by an adventurous moorhen, so as to listen to both sides of the quarrel, paying equal attention to the struggles of the city-dwellers in Waggoners' Walk somewhere near Hampstead and the country folk of Ambridge, supremely œcumenical and even syncretist in her open-mindedness. She seemed determined to keep the Cromers together, or she had been until now, submitting if need be to their collective hobbies and fixations, filtering out (with any luck) only their delusions.

To squeeze the fig with a finger

I don't have the same objection to New Year's Day that I do to personal birthdays. If people want to engage in a reckoning with past and future, as they should, it's as good a day as any other. Resolutions I'm not so fond of, since they so rarely outlast January, but there again I'm not profoundly opposed. If I had a New Year's resolution of my own then it was to help find Paula a better job. I appreciated her very much, but only a fool would say she was using her full potential, or anything like it.

739

If I did my own reckoning of the year, how would it add up? If I found myself mirrored anywhere it was in the experience of Mahādēviyakka, yes, a twelfth-century female Tamil poet—saint, but known as the archetypal sister of all souls, so why not? Her problems as explained in *Speaking of Śiva* were (1) the body, and this problem I shared, the illusion of corporeal rooting, though in a heightened form thanks to Still's Disease. I had the advantage of never taking the body for granted, its invulnerability, its autonomy and all that guff. Mine was a jalopy in a world of purring limousines, and I had less than the usual veneration for the internal combustion engine. Then she had (2) womanhood, where I had manhood, except that my manhood was really only a form of womanhood. I did not stand tall or loom large. No one expected me to impose myself on any given situation physically, least of all me. I had to rely on a softer arsenal, one not usually called on by my gender, using charm and a willingness to manipulate people, unobtrusively if possible. I could also make an appeal to pity while seeming to despise it.

Mahādēviyakka's third struggle was as a social being tyrannised by prescribed roles, and here I was with her every step of the way. Every day I was shoehorned into a set of assumptions that did not fit. Mahādēviyakka had the illusory possession that is youth – or at least her *floruit* is recorded as brief – and so did I, though I was generally relegated to an honorary old age, honorary yet somehow bringing with it all the dishonour of the real thing. I lacked her spiritual poise, her willingness to squeeze the fig with a finger (as she puts it in one *vacana*) without feeling the need to eat it.

How would Mahādēviyakka, confined like me to these scant five dimensions, these scant ten senses (as Hinduism counts them), have breasted such a deluge of the quotidian, the avalanche of trivial rubble, Green Shield Stamps, 'Jenny's Song' from *Waggoners' Walk*, the use of positional markers by *Psittacus erithacus*? Cats with markings worth hundreds of pounds or fatally addicted to confectionery, goings-on in Fulchester on *Crown Court* or in Cambridge Crown Court, the long thoracic nerve of Bell, television sets that you hire by the half-hour, the precise legal status of Mayflower House – every one of these details could be changed and make no difference to the whole. They were like the playing cards that fly up around Alice, interchangeable pasteboard, when she understands (without the benefit of being able to read *Ramana Maharshi and the Path of Self-Knowledge*) the unreality of everything she has been taking for granted – 'Why, you're nothing but a pack of cards!' The distinction between the important and the irrelevant refused to hold. Perhaps this only revealed that the distinction was itself unimportant, and that the refusal to be distracted by triviality was only another form of distraction masquerading.

'Where is the taste in the fruit? Where is the oil in the seed?' Traditional analogies for immanence, questions that suggest the answer *everywhere and nowhere*. The desired essences if they are omnipresent must also be in some sense omni-absent.

What would Mahādēviyakka have done, faced with the stimuli that surrounded me so bewilderingly? She would have swathed herself in her floor-length hair and wandered the welcoming wilderness. Lucky for some! It seemed to be a particular mortification, to cast it in appallingly personal terms, that independence for me could never be a solo project. I would always need sherpas of some description, even on the flat.

Imagining her wanderings, I had a sudden mental picture of Mahādēviyakka as Cousin Itt, the creature apparently made entirely of hair who featured in a long-ago tamely ghoulish American television series for children. I say tamely ghoulish, but Audrey would run from the room the moment she heard the first notes (a harpsichord, was it?) of the *Addams Family* theme music. Just when I wanted to stop my mind from rolling in gross quotidian clutter it retrieved more of the stuff and laid it at my feet. Yet in its way this was a hopeful sign, just the sort of thing that Maya resorts to as a distraction tactic when she knows she's cornered. Even the choice of Cousin Itt was revealing of her machinations, since the German word for the id, the one Freud actually used in his writings, was *das Es* – the It – just as he wrote *das Ich*, the I, rather than the ego.

Freud's English translators the Stracheys chose to make his vocabulary more academically respectable, less everyday. Disciples are always monkeying with the gospel! It was no different from Aldous Huxley clothing himself in what he should have been wearing for his mescaline trip rather than what he actually had on his legs. Mind-altering drugs? By all means. Blue jeans? Not on your nelly.

This was the more tempting avenue of distraction, being intellectual-historical, and my instinct was to resist it all the more sternly. But instinct may only be a *vasana* sunk so deeply in the road that it's impossible to see out from it.

Perhaps this was only a final burst of inconsequential imagery, analogous to the drowning man's supposed remembering of his entire life, before 'I' was submerged in the bliss of self-realisation, tottering forward without the crutch of a guru or the walking-stick of a mantra.

I don't remember what I did on New Year's Eve, but I was keeping tabs on a couple of other people. There was continued coverage of Uri Geller in the *Cambridge Evening News*, most of it pathetic and avoiding the really important questions.

Are These the Eyes of a Fork-Bender?

Why did Uri Geller need to be there for the spoon he was holding to realise its molecular potential? In the same way, why did Ramanujan (the other Ramanujan) need to be there for his local goddess Mahalakshmi of Namakkal to work out her theorems through him? Why did the ceremonial chariots described by Ramanujan (we're back to the first Ramanujan) in *Speaking of Śiva* need people to take the strain when the gods already wanted them to move? It's essentially the same question, whether we're positing divine traction and human agency or the other way round.

I suppose it's even the same question we discussed in the supervisions that were supposed to prepare us for the Tragedy paper in the English Tripos, the question of dual determination. How can the tragic hero make a free choice if his actions have been divinely ordained? Do fate and the tragic actor perhaps reach the same point by different routes? Though Uri Geller hardly seemed to qualify as a tragic actor.

The *Cambridge Evening News* was less lofty in its coverage. 'Are These the Eyes of a Fork-Bender?' asked one headline, next to a picture of young Brendan Tow (10) of Royston, who was inspired by Uri Geller's demonstration of his power on television and bent a large dessert spoon, into an elegant swan-necked shape no less, simply by stroking it. Then he took on a fork and finally an 'auger-type wood drill'. Of course they aren't – they're the eyes of an attention-seeking little schemer. He 'cannot explain the secret of his Geller-like powers' but thinks that they might have something to do with concentration. He can concentrate really hard when the occasion demands.

I had to concentrate really hard not to explode with exasperation at such piffle. Can he repeat the feat under test conditions? Well, he stroked a spoon intermittently over a couple of hours while the *News*'s correspondent watched, and what happened? Sweet Felicity Awkwright – Sweet Fanny Adams (as she was before she married). 'Perhaps the presence of two strangers, one of them armed with an electronic flashgun, can have an effect on Geller-like powers.' Yes, that must be it. After all, he's bent a spoon at his Gran's since then, so his powers haven't disappeared altogether – she'll swear to it. Begorrah! How can people be so gullible? That's why it's important to get reputable authorities involved, as a way of eliminating all the nonsense with which anomalous phenomena inevitably become encrusted. *Anomalous Phenomena* was the title of a Jules Verne novel I borrowed as a teenager from Bourne End Library, and if I remember nothing about it beyond the marvellous title then that is entirely as it should be. I love an anomaly.

Finally there were indications in the *Cambridge Evening News* that the questions were being asked at a more ambitious level, all the more surprisingly in an organ dedicated in the normal run of things to snuffing out any possible interest in its readers. The first article concerned a theoretical physicist from the University, Dr Edward Bastin, who had taken six tempered steel screwdrivers with him to attend a demonstration by Uri Geller in America. Is it normal to bring screwdrivers to a scientific demonstration, as if you were bringing a bottle of wine to a dinner party? Oh I see – by bringing his own tools he could be sure they hadn't been tampered with. In any case, during the demonstration the screwdrivers disappeared from their case, only to re-enter the visible world on a staircase some distance away. Four of them were returned to the case, but were found all to be broken off in the same way, near the tip.

What sloppy journalism, not to spell out whether the four screwdrivers returned to the case by natural or telekinetic means, nor to say what happened to the other two. One of the broken tips subsequently

743

vanished from the locked briefcase of Dr John Chilton, university lecturer in metallurgy, to whom they had been entrusted, though only four people knew they were there. He commented, 'Either I have been very careless or I have been very close to a most remarkable telekinetic phenomenon.' Perhaps not as compelling a statement as he would like to think . . . there must surely be a third alternative. And wouldn't it be a fine test of Dr Chilton's commitment to scientific principle if he found the missing screwdriver tip in his jacket pocket or trouser turn-up, and had to decide whether to come clean about it?

Spoons under scrutiny at Cambridge

The next article ('New Riddle in the Saga of Uri Geller') raised even more doubts in my mind about the suitability of Dr Chilton to be in charge of any investigation. 'Dr Chilton, who is a University Lecturer in Metallurgy, would not be drawn into speculation as to how the screwdrivers were broken. "I am not prepared to say anything about that at the moment. To hypothesise at this stage would be wrong. The screwdrivers were certainly not broken in a man's hands and it would seem at this stage that the break was definitely paranormal. But I must have time to think this whole thing out before I offer any kind of opinion."' Too late, mate! That's not an open mind. If it's an open anything it's an open dustbin.

It was only with the third article, under the heading of 'Science Today' ('Geller Spoons Under Scrutiny at Cambridge' by Rodney Tibbs), that I began to regain a little confidence. For one thing it was rather a dull read, innocent of any sensationalising, any doting grannies or academics playing along with the publicity machine. Dr Chilton's nerves seemed to have been steadied by the participation of a colleague, Dr Trevor Page. The two of them would be carrying out the investigations over the New Year vacation. A low-powered lens would be used to examine the areas of fracture on the utensils, checking for signs of abrasion or cutting. Was this area bright and shiny, perhaps many-faceted? Or, rather, dull and fibrous? This would suggest plastic deformation, consistent with what seemed to happen when Geller publicly broke or deformed spoons. The surface of the break would be scrutinised using a scanning electron microscope of the StereoScan type. An area of metal distant from the fracture would be polished flat and chemically etched before examination, to get the clearest possible idea of its performance under conditions short of deformation or fracture. In all this I was relying on Dr Page to rein in Dr Chilton's rather flighty side. Galileo, Copernicus, neither of them flighty. About Newton I have my doubts.

Nothing in the article mentioned the groundswell of public interest, and perhaps that is fair enough in a scientific report, however untechnical. Surely, though, acknowledgement was due from the metallurgy department to those members of the public who had been clamouring for just such scrutiny for some time, and even producing rough data to the extent that they were able. Still, it was a comfort to know that some people were showing the proper commitment to knowledge, which proceeds just as surely by refutation as by proof, and were sacrificing time with their families (which so many people value) to resolve the issue over the holiday.

On the laboratory bench in front of them, next to the low-powered lens, awaiting their turn with the electron microscope, lie screwdriver, fork, spoon, these three.

And the greatest of these

And the greatest of these is spoon.